Sasi Retnakaran
18.2.95

THE ANTHOLOGY OF GHOST STORIES

THE ANTHOLOGY OF GHOST STORIES

Edited by
Richard Dalby

TIGER BOOKS INTERNATIONAL
LONDON

This edition published in 1994 by Tiger Books International PLC, Twickenham

This collection first published by Robinson Publishing 1990

ISBN 1 85501 503 X

A copy of the British Library Cataloguing in Publication Data is available from the British Library.

Printed in Finland by Werner Söderström Oy.

Richard Dalby *is a professional author, editor, bibliographer, and rare bookdealer, specialising in fantasy and supernatural fiction. His anthologies include*
The Sorceress in Stained Glass, Dracula's Brood, Ghosts and Scholars *(with Rosemary Pardoe)*, The Virago Book of Ghost Stories *(20th Century)*, The Virago Book of Victorian Ghost Stories, Ghosts for Christmas, *and* Chillers for Christmas.

Somewhere in desolate, wind-swept space
In Shadow-land, in No-Man's-land
Two wandering souls met face to face,
And bade each other stand.

'And who art thou?' quoth one agape,
All in the grey and misty light;
'I hardly know,' the other said,
'I only died last night'.

To my parents,
two of the nicest people I know,
in gratitude for their
encouragement and shared enthusiasm
for classic ghost stories

CONTENTS

Preface xi
ROBERT AICKMAN *The Unsettled Dust* 1
LOUISA BALDWIN *How He Left The Hotel* 40
NUGENT BARKER *Whessoe* 45
E.F. BENSON *The Shuttered Room* 55
AMBROSE BIERCE *An Inhabitant of Carcosa* 68
CHARLES BIRKIN *Is There Anybody There?* 72
ALGERNON BLACKWOOD *The Whisperers* 88
L.M. BOSTON *Curfew* 94
A.M. BURRAGE *I'm Sure It Was No.31* 103
RAMSEY CAMPBELL *The Guide* 108
R. CHETWYND-HAYES *The Limping Ghost* 120
WILKIE COLLINS *Mrs. Zant and the Ghost* 136
BASIL COPPER *The House by the Tarn* 169
RALPH A. CRAM *In Kropfsberg Keep* 182
DANIEL DEFOE *The Ghost in all the Rooms* 191
CHARLES DICKENS *The Bagman's Uncle* 200
ARTHUR CONAN DOYLE *The Bully of Brocas Court* 217
AMELIA B. EDWARDS *In the Confessional* 229
SHAMUS FRAZER *The Tune in Dan's Café* 244
JOHN S. GLASBY *Beyond the Bourne* 254
WILLIAM HOPE HODGSON *The Valley of Lost Children* 267
FERGUS HUME *The Sand-Walker* 278
HENRY JAMES *The Real Right Thing* 293
M.R. JAMES *The Haunted Dolls' House* 306
ROGER JOHNSON *The Wall-Painting* 317
RUDYARD KIPLING *"They"* 331
D.H. LAWRENCE *The Last Laugh* 352
MARGERY LAWRENCE *Robin's Rath* 369
J. SHERIDAN LE FANU *The Dream* 387

R.H. MALDEN *The Sundial* 399
RICHARD MARSH *The Fifteenth Man* 409
JOHN METCALFE *Brenner's Boy* 420
EDITH NESBIT *Uncle Abraham's Romance* 436
FITZ-JAMES O'BRIEN *What Was It?* 440
VINCENT O'SULLIVAN *The Next Room* 452
ROGER PATER *The Footstep of the Aventine* 461
EDGAR ALLAN POE *William Wilson* 472
FORREST REID *Courage* 491
MRS J.H. RIDDELL *The Last of Squire Ennismore* 498
L.T.C. ROLT *The Garside Fell Disaster* 505
DAVID G. ROWLANDS *The Tears of Saint Agathé* 513
'SAKI' *The Soul of Laploshka* 524

ACKNOWLEDGEMENTS

For permission to print copyright material in this anthology, grateful acknowledgements are made to the following:

Artellus Limited, Leslie Gardner Literary Agency, for "The Unsettled Dust" © 1968, Estate of Robert Aickman
Messrs. A.P. Watt Ltd. and Mrs. Sheila Reeves for "The Whisperers" by Algernon Blackwood
Mrs. Amanda Toyne for "Is There Anybody There. . .?" by Charles Birkin
Mrs. Lucy M. Boston for her story "Curfew" © 1967 L.M. Boston
Mr. J.S.F. Burrage for "I'm Sure It Was No. 31" by A.M. Burrage
Mr. Ramsey Campbell for his story "The Guide", © 1989 by Ramsey Campbell
Mr. R. Chetwynd-Hayes for his story "The Ghost that Limped" © 1975
Mr. Basil Copper for his story "The House by the Tarn" © 1971
Mrs. Joan Frazer for "The Tune in Dan's Café" by Shamus Frazer
Mr. John S. Glasby for his story "Beyond the Bourne" © 1989
Mr. Roger Johnson for his story "The Wall-Painting" © 1983
Messrs. Hutchinson & Co. for "Robin's Rath" by Margery Lawrence
Messrs. Edward Arnold Ltd. for "The Sundial" by R.H. Malden
Mr. Stephen Gilbert for "Courage" by Forrest Reid
Mrs. Sonia Rolt for "The Garside Fell Disaster" by L.T.C. Rolt
Mr. David G. Rowlands for his story "The Tears of Saint Agathé" © 1983

Every effort has been made to trace copyright holders, but the publishers would be interested to hear from anyone not here acknowledged.

ROBERT AICKMAN
The Unsettled Dust

Robert Aickman *(1914–81) wrote some of the most highly praised ghost stories of the century, and was widely regarded as the greatest practitioner of the form during his lifetime. Gahan Wilson wrote: "Robert Aickman is the most terrifyingly intrepid explorer of the classical ghost story . . . and his tales are vital reading for anyone fond of the form."*

'The Unsettled Dust' (from Sub Rosa, *1968) is among his stories never collected or reprinted in the United States.*

During the period of my work as Special Duties Officer for the Historic Structures Fund, I have inevitably come upon many strange and unexpected things in all fields; but only three times that I can recollect have I so far encountered anything that might be thought to involve an element of the paranormal.

Since interest in paranormal phenomena appears to be growing steadily, partly no doubt as an escape from a way of life that seems every day to grow more uniform, regulated, and unambitious, I have thought for some time that it might be worth while to set out at least one of these cases, the most striking, I think, of the three, in an orderly though completely frank narrative; separated from the many other documents connected with my employment. It is not a matter of struggling for half-lost memories, since for the most part the task consists in adapting extracts from my Diary for the period of time concerned. I have now been Special Duties Officer for just over ten years, and I think the moment has come to set about the task.

It so happens that it has been during those ten years that the Fund has set up a Psychic and Occult Research Committee. As is well known, the Council hesitated for many years before taking this step, having in mind the extreme undesirability of the Fund involving itself in controversy of any kind, and also the constant danger of its being charged with crankiness or reaction; but in the end the pressure became so great that a response could no longer be avoided. I think it was inevitable. The link between an interest in old buildings (often ruinous and sometimes ecclesiastical), and an interest in what are popularly called "ghosts", is obvious. Also the Fund, like most established voluntary societies, is supported mainly by the elderly. A Psychic Committee was and is as inescapable as the Animals Committee that has been with us almost from the start.

The P. and O. Research Committee has undoubtedly done much good work, but I have hesitated to deliver to them a report of my own, despite the fact that I am possibly in a position to deliver three. The Fund is a very conservative organization (not in the party sense, of course), and my dilemma is that of the civil servant. If a civil servant takes an initiative and things go right with it, he cannot, in the nature of his employment, look for much in the way of reward; whereas if his initiative goes wrong, he can expect all kinds of trouble, everything from a reprimand to blocked promotion, and a permanent black mark against his name in the files. It is accepted, therefore, that the way to advance in the civil service, or in any field where civil service conditions prevail, is never to take an initiative and never to support anyone else's. It is inevitable that this should be so, as long as we base all our administration on the bureaucratic model. The Fund is not as hard a master as the civil service, of course, if only because no one had to answer to Parliament for its actions; but caution is compelled upon it by its sheer size, and by its obligation to offend no one, if this can possibly be avoided, not even its direct critics. A report, even if carefully edited, delivered by me to the P. and O. people on any one of my three cases could, in my judgement, lead to contention, to unpopularity in various quarters for the author, and conceivably even to a libel action in which the Fund would be involved. There are few subjects on which people are more touchy than the "supernatural", as they call it. It is the measure of the importance they attach to it, even if few of them care to admit it. The delivery of such a report would hardly be construed by the Council as lying within my duties, if trouble resulted. One can but speculate upon the mass of important information which never sees the light of day for similar reasons. I have thought it best to confine the circulation of my narrative to a few selected people, binding them in advance to the strictest confidence; and to place a copy for posterity in my small archives.

The position of Special Duties Officer, of which I have so far been the only incumbent, was created when the growth of the

Fund, and the number and variety of its properties, conjured up a miscellany of tasks, often urgent, but all outside the scope of any member of a staff which had been recruited almost solely for duties connected with preservation in the strictest sense—and which, as was freely admitted at the time, was often by then advanced in service. My ploys have varied from setting up a large bequest of sculpture in a once ducal park, to organizing a sailing-boat harbour on an island off the Welsh coast; from a frustrating six months devoted to relaying an ornamental paving, to an even longer period spent in promoting an open-air season of fertility plays with singing and dancing. Most of my work has been done in the open air, trying to dodge the British climate, the local authority philistines, and the Fund's own members, so many of whom have ideas of their own and think they have bought the entire staff with their own small subscriptions. Well, not *all* perhaps. Some of the members are very nice people, and eager to offer their hospitality. I have had my moments of cynicism, when I have felt that all that has mattered of the Fund's work has rested on my single shoulders, but that was mere self-pity and I really know quite well that I have done much better as a Fund officer than I could expect to do in any other job. I fell right on my feet when the Fund engaged me.

The events I am about to describe took place at Clamber Court in Bedfordshire, a seat of the Brakespear family, the family of which one branch is said to have provided the only Englishman ever to be Pope; who was also the Pope with the greatest physical strength of all the Popes. The Clamber Court branch was represented by two unmarried sisters. Their father, the last Lord St. Adrian, had died years before, and their mother was said to have been a little queer ever since. At least that was the gossip around the Fund office. In the end, the girls had settled Clamber on the Fund, but remained there themselves as Fund tenants. The same office gossip said that the girls had lived very wildly at one time, having no one to control them, and had got through a lot of money. Explanations like that might have been true in former times, but there is seldom much in them nowadays. It is far more likely that the Brakespears were orphans of the social storm like most of the Fund's clients.

My sojourn in the house had nothing to do with the building itself or the surrounding property, as I shall explain in a moment, but it so happens that I had paid Clamber one previous visit. It had not been in the course of my duties, which do not include any kind of regular round. I went there as an ordinary Fund member, without disclosing anything more. In those early days, I often found it instructive to do this and to note how my colleagues were faring in their endless struggle with the different buildings, often near to collapse even when offered to the Fund; and with the odd and recalcitrant people who lived in them. In those days, the Fund's aged President frequently described the staff as an extra-large family, and it was by no means only a cliché: one felt the presence of the Fund wherever one went, watching how one behaved, and difficult to get away from. Of course I felt much more at home in a year or two, much more sure of my ground. When it came to my going to places like Clamber Court, it should also be remembered that I had worked at one time in architecture, though I never qualified; and so had an interest in buildings for their own sake. Naturally that is true of many of the Fund's staff.

Clamber Court proved to be a square, four-storeyed, brick pile, with, on each side, a square, two-storeyed, smaller brick pavilion. The pavilions had slate roofs coming to points, and pilasters on three sides. They were linked to the main block by lengthy one-storey passages, with big, circular-topped windows. This branch of the large Brakespear family had become rich at the time of the Hanoverian succession, and had then entered upon a new period of importance, drifting so far from the other branches that ultimately no heir could be found to the title. A conspicuous feature of the property was two very long drives. The first one led from the front of the house, dead straight down a two-mile avenue of fine old trees to a noble, ornamental gateway on the main road. The other ran, less straight, but at no less length, from a pretty lodge at the east to a related lodge at the west (also on the main road). The drives crossed at about a quarter of a mile from the house-front. At the point of intersection was a baroque fountain, with an heroic male figure about to drive a spear into a fat boar. I found it an uncomfortable group, but redeemed by the all too unusual excellence of its condition and maintenance. In modern Europe, most estate fountains are broken, sordid, and regarded with indifference even by their owners. This one shimmered, and, supreme marvel, actually spouted water, quite probably at the proper force. I had already noted that the drive down which I had driven my Mini (the transverse drive) was clean and weeded; the gate painted; the gateman respectful. I now observed that every pane of glass in the two long corridors from the main house to the pavilions appeared to be in place, and gleaming in the spring sun. The Fund cannot always afford perfections of that kind. Almost certainly, the Brakespears must have had something left in the kitty.

The interior of the house confirmed this. Not only did it contain many objects of real excellence, but it was painted, tended, and polished. There were no sagging wallpaper and no holes in the ceiling. On the other hand, I could not say that the house was dusted. This was curious. One might have written names in the deposit on the gleaming surfaces, as Rembrandt did in Korda's film. Indeed, I did write "Historic Structures Fund" on the top of a dining-room table, and the words stood out quite clearly in the light of a sunbeam. The odd thing was that one of the house employees, a tall, grey woman in a grey nylon wrapper, just watched me do it from the other side of the room, and said nothing at all, though she was presumably stationed to keep an eye on the behaviour of the public. I particularly noticed that she didn't even smile at what I had done. I was so surprised by the dust in the house and by the indifference shown to it that the next day I sent a memo to the Fund's Regional Representative. I suggested that there might be a cement works in the district, an idea that had occurred to my during the night; and that the Fund should possibly require all the house windows to be kept shut.

That was nine years ago. Two years later, I was required to stay in the house for (as my Diary confirms) eighteen days. The reason was the need to superintend one of the maddest schemes in which the Fund ever entangled itself—indeed, the maddest of all, as I said at the time, when anyone asked me, and as events have since confirmed, to me very sincere regret: the so-called recovery of the River Bovil. For years, there had been complaints in various quarters (none of them, of course, in full possession of the facts) that the Fund was too conservationist and backward-looking; too little prepared to enter the field and do battle. The worst consequence of this uninformed agitation was that the Fund found itself saddled with the project for cleaning out the weeds and mud from this small, local river that no one had ever heard of (not even the people who lived in the district, as I soon found), and patching up the broken-down locks. The view that I (and others) expressed was the obvious one that if there was any real demand for the river, then the proper public authorities could be depended upon to attend to it. The matter was simply nothing to do with the objectives of the Fund. But there was the usual group of hot-heads, with not enough work to do in the world, as one could not but feel; and they had interested one of the local land-owners in putting up a little money, though only one landowner and nothing like *enough* money. They said that most of the work could be done by volunteers, and that the public would find the rest of the finance. Needless to say, neither claim proved to be true, and the whole business committed the Fund to endless travail, by no means ended yet, nor likely to be. The Fund is simply not equipped for struggle, argument, and publicity. Nor has my own experience disposed me in favour of what are called "voluntary workers". In practice much more is always achieved by regular, salaried staff, keeping themselves out of the limelight. And so it has proved in the case of the Bovil project. But if I say more on that topic, I shall be suspected of disloyalty to the Fund Council, which would be quite wrong. It is more a case of loyalty being often best shown by preventing mistakes being made.

After (in my view) insufficient discussion, the Bovil project was agreed to and the hottest and most thrusting of the hot-heads put in charge of the actual works, a man named Hand. I myself didn't think he was altogether an Englishman, but it was obvious that he was very young for the degree of responsibility in which he had involved himself, so I was asked to look after him during the first stages of the work, as I was twenty or more years older and had gained experience from a wide variety of different jobs. Hamish Haythorn, the National Secretary of the Fund, wrote to Miss Agnes Brakespear, reputedly the more businesslike sister, to ask if I could stay at Clamber Court while I was launching the scheme. The Fund expects people whose properties have been accepted, to help in this way, as the need may arise; though sometimes Fund employees find themselves offered only an attic and very simple fare. This had by then happened to me several times, and I was quite prepared for it at Clamber Court. (Nowadays, of course, in my case it hardly ever happens, because I have learned to enter into the different foibles of the Fund's tenants.) I remember that Miss Brakespear took a long time to answer at all, and all the while the Bovil scheme was held up; but we heard from her in the end, and off I went that very afternoon. I arrived in good time for dinner, though that, as I have just said, might not have meant very much.

There was a long tradition that the great gates on the main road were opened only for family weddings, family funerals, and visits of the Sovereign, and the smaller gate further up the same road, had been padlocked by the Fund's Regional Representative, because it had proved impossible to find a tenant for the adjoining lodge, owing to the noise of the traffic; so that I wound my way in my Mini through the lanes leading to the eastern entry, as I had done two years before. It had perhaps been not quite as much as that, because now it was earlier in the spring, with not yet a leaf on any of the big, old trees: in fact, not yet officially spring at all. This time, the man at the gate was wearing a hat, which he touched when opening for me.

My spirits rose as I saw that the long, winding drive was as spruce as before. All the hedges within view had been properly laid and many of the farm gates had been renewed. The hero huntsman when at length I reached him, was enshrined among complex traceries of water, and the doomed quarry adrip with it. The house, I thought, as I completed the finishing stretch up to the wide parterre of rectangular stones before the double staircase, looked immaculate but unfunctional, like a vast Staffordshire model. When I stopped my engine and stepped out, the complete silence contributed to the illusion. I stood for a moment looking down the slow descent to the great gates, and watching big, black rooks wheel like sheets of burnt newspaper between the bare trees, the only life there was.

"Hullo," said a casual voice from above. "Come in."

Standing with her hands on the balustrade at the top of the two flights of steps was a woman; plainly one of my two hostesses, though I had never then knowingly seen either. I wavered, as one does, between ascending the right-hand steps or the left, but she said nothing and just watched me.

"I'm Olive Brakespear," she said as I arrived, and held out her hand. I should have expected the hand to be cold, as it was one of those fine March days, which often seem the chilliest of the year. But it was not. "You're my landlord." In my experience, the tenants always either said something like that or, alternatively, did everything to pretend that the relationship was the other way round.

Miss Brakespear, however, was an unusual figure. She was well above average height for a woman (and six or eight inches above mine), and remarkably slender and well-shaped, though tough and wiry looking. The last impression was reinforced by the fact that she was wearing worn brown riding breeches, worn brown riding boots, and a dark-blue shirt, open at the neck and with the sleeves rolled up. Her face, neck, and forearms were all tanned and brown, even though it was the end of the winter. Her face was striking because she had strong, prominent bones, large, melancholy eyes, and a big, rectangular mouth, but some might have said that her head was too long, her cheeks too sunken. She had straight reddish-brown hair, starting rather far back on the brow. It was glossy and well-kept, like the mane of a racehorse, but worn shoulder-length and curled outwards at the ends, after the fashion which prevailed during the Second World War. It was very difficult to guess how old she was. Her physical style was one which is eminently durable.

"I was watching the rooks," she said. "Sometimes when the trees are bare and the light beginning to go, I do it for an hour at a time." Looking at her in her blue shirt, I am sure I must have shivered. "Come on in, or you'll get cold," said Miss Brakespear.

The big, oblong, pillared hall contained only formal furniture, though I was pleased to observe a heap of the Fund's official, blue-covered, guidebook to the house. The wide door had lain open while Miss Brakespear stood outside, so that the cavernous room was cold and echoey, especially as there was no fire. It was also dim, as evening was descending, and Miss Brakespear had not turned on the light.

She went before me up the dark main staircase, taking two steps at a time with her swinging stride. Impeded by my bundle, I followed her much less gracefully.

We turned leftwards along a high, wide passage which traversed the first floor of the house, with big white doors opening into silent rooms on either side. I had not previously been upstairs, because the rooms open to the public were all below. Miss Brakespear's step in her riding boots was sharp and swift, whereas I am sure that I merely shuffled. At the eastern end of the passage, Miss Brakespear opened the door of my room. At least I had not been relegated to one of those designed for occupation by the servants.

It was a big, square, dark red room, with a heavy dado, two windows looking down the long avenue, a modern double bed, and a general look of having been furnished by a good contractor in, perhaps, 1910.

"Turn on the light, if you like," said Miss Brakespear, "unless you prefer the dusk, as I do. There's a bathroom opposite. It's all for you, because nowadays there's never anyone else on this side of the house. My sister and I sleep at the other end. Elizabeth

Craw, our housekeeper, sleeps upstairs, and the two girls in the village. You'll find the whole house quiet for your work until the open season begins at Easter. Come down for a drink when you're ready. In the music room to the left of the hall."

She strode away down the dark passage, leaving my bedroom door open. She had a rich and liquid voice, really rather beautiful; and a casual inflection which one felt never varied, no matter what she was saying or to whom. I noticed that she had not mentioned her mother, who was supposed to live somewhere in the house also.

I shut the door and stood in the middle of the room waiting. I might well have been waiting for the twilight to become more like darkness, so that, even by Miss Brakespear's standard, I could turn on the light with a good conscience. Then I realized how absurd this was, and pressed the switch. The result was disappointing. The only light in the room came from three rather faint bulbs attached to a brass frame which the 1910 contractor had suspended from the plaster rose in the center of the coffered ceiling. They would effectively illumine neither a reader in bed nor a maker-up or report-writer at the heavy dressing table. I felt that from the park my room must look little more luminous than in the year the house was built.

I unpacked a few things and stowed them away. I set my book hopefully by the side of the bed (Christopher Hussey's *The Picturesque*, I see in my Diary that it was). I cased the room for heat of any kind. There was none. I wondered if I should change into something darker, but decided that I could decide while taking my drink, as it was still early enough to change after it, if that seemed appropriate. I crossed the passage to the bathroom.

Here the electric light seemed a little stronger. I looked at my hands as one does after a journey, to see how travel-stained they are. They were filthy. I was astonished, and as I turned the tap of the washbasin (of course, there was nothing like that in my bedroom), I worried about having shaken hands with Miss Brakespear. Then I realized that the grime had spread from darker patches at the tips of my fingers, and that I had probably picked it up in my bedroom. And only then did I remember about the dust I had noticed on my previous visit to the house. The matter had not lately been in my mind. I remembered also about the memo on the subject which I had sent to old Blantyre, the impoverished country gentleman who acted as the Fund's Regional Representative in that area. Thinking about it now, I was almost sure that Blantyre had never even sent an acknowledgement; so that, almost certainly, he had taken no action whatever. I let the water run and run, but it never ran hot.

I remembered the beautiful music room quite well. As I stood in the dark hall outside the thick, closed door, I could just hear the sound of a piano within. Real music in the music room of a British mansion is today so rare that at first I took it for granted that the wireless had been turned on, but when I opened the door and entered, I saw that Miss Brakespear was herself playing. She did not stop when I walked in, but merely indicated with a movement of her head that I should sit down. The gesture seemed quite friendly but she did not smile. I suspected that Miss Brakespear smiled seldom. In here a big log fire burnt: the supply of logs, rough and knotty, being piled high in a vast, circular bin of chased brass, itself gleaming like a yellow furnace. I know nothing about music but it seemed to me that Miss Brakespear played the piano much as she talked; beautifully, but with a casualness that was not so much indifference as the reflection of melancholy and resignation. There was no music before her, and no light by which she could have read it: quite possibly she was improvising, though she seemed to my ignorance to be doing it with depth and fluency. I daresay this was nonsense on my part, but as she played on and on, I found that I was pleased to warm myself right through at rather long last, and to listen to her and watch her dim shape by the light of the fire. I could see that she was still wearing her riding clothes, with the tips of her boots on the pedals.

I am not sure how much time passed in this way; but certainly it was quite dark outside the uncurtained windows, when the door opened and a third person stood there. It was another woman. I could not see her at all clearly, but I could see the shape of her dress and the outline of her hair. She stood for a while with the door still open behind her. Miss Brakespear went on playing, as if in a trance with herself. Then the newcomer shut the door and turned on the light: more effective lighting than in the rooms above. At once, Miss Brakespear broke off.

"Dreaming?" asked the newcomer; none too agreeably, I thought.

Miss Brakespear made no direct reply. "Agnes," she said, "this is Mr. Oxenhope, at once our landlord and our guest. Mr. Oxenhope, let me introduce my sister, Agnes."

The other Miss Brakespear (hereafter I must call them Olive and Agnes, though I do not find it comes very naturally) seemed little interested. "How do you do?" she said in an offhand way from the door.

"How do you do?" I replied.

Now that the lights were on, I glanced about for dust.

"You really are a fool," said Agnes to her sister, and walked over to the fire. One could have said she spoke in affectionate derision, as is the way within a family (the alternative commonly being silence); but I might rather have called it habitual derision, accepted derision.

Olive closed the piano and got up. At that exact distance from me, and by fairly strong artificial light, her neck, inside the open collar of her dark shirt, looked more withered and less shapely than I had thought. "How did the meeting go?" she asked quietly.

"Exactly as expected," replied Agnes, standing before the blaze, her feet slightly apart, her hands behind her back. She was of an entirely different physical type from her sister: a squarish, fattish woman of about my height, with a thickening face and neck, dark eyes and abundant dark hair in a style more fashionable than her sister's. She wore a plain dress in thick, purple wool, and black, high-heeled shoes. She might have been described by an enemy as too heavily made up, but that is a difficult problem for a woman of her build and period of life: even though I should not have cared to assess her exact age within a range of perhaps twenty years. As will be gathered, she seemed very much more the customary Englishwoman than her sister; and she had something of the frustration and suppressed, long-lost feeling that goes with the customary Englishwoman, however banal the customary manifestation of it. When one spends one's time going round the different properties of the Historic Structures Fund, one grows to learn the essential characteristics of the customary Englishwoman.

Olive had unlocked an ebony and ivory cabinet and was getting us drinks. There was no further reference to the meeting that had been mentioned. Indeed, there was silence. I knew that it was for me to help things along, but I could think of nothing to say. Agnes saved me the trouble.

"What are you feeling for?" she asked.

It seemed appallingly observant of her.

"I thought I'd dropped my handkerchief," I improvised, perhaps more readily than convincingly.

"Mr. Oxenhope's visit has nothing to do with the house," said Olive conciliatingly. It was excellently intended, no doubt, but the form of words suggested that she too had cottoned on. Because I had, of course, been feeling (as Agnes had put it) for dust. And, what was more, I had been doing it without being aware of it. Needless to say, it was very discourteous of me, socially speaking.

"And his gropings have nothing to do with his handkerchief," said Agnes drily. "With *either* of his handkerchiefs: the one in his sleeve or the pretty one in his breast pocket. Do you carry three handkerchiefs, Mr. Oxenhope?"

"No," I replied calmly. "We were sitting here in the dark and I thought the handkerchief had fallen out of my sleeve."

"I believe you, Mr. Oxenhope. Sitting in the dark is the only thing my sister really likes doing."

"Not altogether," said Olive. "As you might guess, I like riding too. Do you ride?"

"I'm afraid I don't." As a matter of fact, I had thought of trying to take it up when I began to realize what my work with the Fund would be like, but Hamish Haythorn had strongly advised me against it, saying that it was a mistake to meet the tenants on their own ground. I have since wondered whether Haythorn's view was not affected by the fact that he could neither ride himself nor be conceived as capable of it. But no doubt this was mere malice on my part.

"Just as well for you," said Agnes. "Going riding with my sister is an act of desperation."

"I'm sorry all the same," I said, looking at Olive as I spoke, and trying to meet her eyes, because, self-sufficient though she seemed, I was growing sorry for her, as well as for myself.

"Sherry?" asked Olive, either avoiding my glance or being unaware of my intention. "Or gin? Or pascado? Pascado is an aperitif that Agnes brings back from one of her committees. It is Elizabethan and based on quince juice. Or would you prefer a whisky?"

I thought that I had better make some effort to appease Agnes, so volunteered for the pascado.

"Very few people like it," said Agnes.

The evening continued to be uneasy.

The sisters were, at the least, utterly bored with one another. Such communication as they attempted was confined to jibing and belittlement. As at the start, most of the attacking seemed to come from Agnes; but I thought this might have been partly because Olive gave the impression of having years ago said all she had to say, and of by now preferring to sit in silence. Later that evening it seemed to me, however, that Olive on several occasions struck home on her own; though Agnes each time behaved as if she were too stupid to understand. It might have been the fact of the matter, but I doubted it. The sisters had obviously been committed to this form of exercise for years, and every sentence and every small action had overtones and undertones soaring and sinking beyond the apprehension of any outsider. I, of course, attempted intermittently to make "general conversation", but Agnes was antagonistic, and Olive, though perfectly polite, was indifferent and world-weary. One might have said that Olive knew it all already, but I doubted whether she really did. I suspected that she fought off knowing, and that it was really Agnes who knew much more. One often finds this with women of Agnes's type. I perhaps make it all sound as if I was having a dreadful time, and it is certainly true that I was not enjoying myself; but by then I was surprisingly accustomed to such family sessions in the houses I visited. I had found them to be common: perhaps as patrician standards merge with plebeian ones, and there is less opportunity for the graces of entertainment as distinct from the utilities. The new conditions take different people in different ways, but are seldom to the advantage of guests.

There seemed to be no question of any clothes being changed for dinner. When we entered the dining-room, the big, polished table was as dusty, beneath the shaded candles, as it had been when I saw it two years earlier in the sunlight; and the tall, grey woman who stood there waiting for us, was recognizably she who had watched my writing on it with my finger. Supposing that Agnes would be observing me, I tried to avoid all reaction.

Dinner was good and the wine excellent, but conversation there was almost none. The presence of the grey servant (still, by the way, in a grey nylon wrapper) seemed to prevent the sisters even from bickering. I felt that very little ever went into the house: not even ordinary news, let alone what are called ideas. It would be very difficult for the Brakespear sisters to have many friends. Apart from foodstuffs and practicalities, I felt that almost nothing and nobody entered but the public visitors in summer: by definition aloof and alien; merely staring in through the bars, and, even then, uncomprehending of everything that mattered, even when (occasionally) qualified to discriminate between Meissen and Nymphenburg.

And, as I had seen for myself, the visitors to Clamber Court, though, according to Haythorn, increasing slightly in number, were powerless to dispel the dust. On the dining-room table it was so thick it marked my cuffs. I observed circles left in it by platters or glasses that had been removed, became inconspicuous within minutes, and by the time the meal was finished, had almost vanished, though not quite, when one carried the exact spot in one's mind and looked keenly. But the fare was fine. In very few of the Fund houses, if any, had I been offered such wine (let alone anywhere else). I knew this even though I was by no means a connoisseur; little more than of music.

Back in the music room after dinner, a wry discussion started about the ethics of coursing. I could contribute little. The sisters disagreed about reafforestation, and later about the flowers that were being planted for the benefit of the summer visitors. My views were hardly sought. I imagine that Agnes would have despised them and Olive pitied them. Ultimately, Agnes said she must get on with the accounts, and sat by the fire making entries in a black book, with a pile of bills and receipts on the floor at her feet. "You won't mind being treated as one of the family," she had said to me before starting this labour.

Olive suggested that I might care to look for a book in the library. It was well known to be a very fine library, largely assembled by a Lord St. Adrian of the early eighteenth century and hardly disturbed since. But I said that I was in the middle of a book I had brought with me, and that I might fetch it down from my bedroom in a moment. I made no further move, because I always have difficulty in reading when in the company of others, let alone the company of strangers. Instead, I turned over the pages of *Country Life* and *Field*, dusty back numbers of which lay about the room, looking almost unopened. They would have to be burnt or stacked before the public season opened.

Olive merely sat in front of the fire, with her long legs stretched towards it. Her eyes remained open, but almost expressionless; too resigned, I thought, even to look sad. I was sure that she would have returned to the piano, if Agnes had not been there. Olive was by no means in her first youth, but there was something appealing about her, and, though it may not be a suitable comment for even this confidential record, I thought, by no means for the first time in such surroundings, what an odd way it was for people of opposite sexes to spend the evening, when, after all, there was nothing ahead that any of us could be sure of but infirmity, illness, and death. It is strange that people train themselves so carefully to go to waste so prematurely.

Every now and then, Agnes wondered sharply whether I would mind adding something up or working something out for her; and surprisingly bristly some of these small tasks of hers proved to be. Olive never even sighed. In the end, the grey servant appeared (the sisters addressed her as "Elizabeth") and brought in a large bowl of fruit.

"What time would you like breakfast?" Agnes asked me.

"What time would suit you best?" I responded politely.

"Elizabeth will bring it to your room," said Agnes. "We go our own ways."

I suggested a time and the grey servant departed.

"I understand that you'll be fully occupied throughout the day?" asked Agnes.

"Very fully," I replied, remembering what I was there for and in for.

"Then we shall see you as tonight?"

I expressed assent and gratification.

Over oranges and apples, the evening ended. Agnes ate nothing, but, as well as an apple, I accepted from Olive a whisky, and she herself consumed a noticeably stronger one. Already, on our first evening together, we were running out of generalities.

"More whisky?" asked Olive after a munching silence.

I accepted, though it was unlike me. She refilled my glass to the same strength as her own. The curious dust lay all around me in the warm light.

There was some clattering with bolts and chains, some checking of locks and hasps: all Agnes's work.

"Don't wait," she said, but we did, and all ascended the stairs together.

The sisters turned to the right, where I turned to the left, but I had not even shut the door of my imperfectly lighted room when I heard familiar steps approaching along the passage, and Olive stood in the doorway.

"I just came to say I'm sorry we're so dull." She spoke in her usual non-committal voice, but softly; perhaps so that Agnes could have no chance of overhearing.

"I'm sorry I don't ride," I said; and I still think it was clever of me to think of it so quickly.

"Yes," said Olive. "It's a pity. Especially when we can do so little to entertain you. The company of two middle-aged sisters who don't get on, isn't much fun."

"I don't see you as middle-aged at all," I replied. Whether I did or not, I saw Olive as most attractive, especially at that moment, when she stood slender and poetical in my doorway, and both of us were about to go to bed.

But she made no response. She did not even smile. There was merely a moment's silence between us.

Then she said "I apologize for us. Goodnight," and walked quickly away.

I found myself thinking of her for a long time, and being kept from sleep by the thought.

My breakfast arrived at the exact moment I had named. The grey factotum woke me when she knocked. Having fallen asleep belatedly, I had then slept deeply. It seemed very cold. Without thinking about it, I swept the dust off the polished bedside table with my pyjama sleeve. Then I realized that the grey Elizabeth, who was putting down my tray on the table, might take my action as a slight.

"The dust seems to blow in again as soon as it's swept away," I said, shivering in my unheated bedroom, and in the tone of one making an excuse for another. "There must be some dusty new industry near the house."

"It blows in off the drives," said Elizabeth. "The drives are always dusty."

"If that's what it is, I think something might be done. I'll have a word with Mr. Blantyre about it. He might arrange to have the drives tarmacked—anyway, near the house. The dust is really rather terrible." After all, I was one who had some indirect responsibility in the matter.

"Terrible, as you say," said Elizabeth non-committally. "But please don't bother. There's nothing to be done about it." She spoke with surprising authoritativeness; as if she, and not the Brakespear sisters, were the Fund's tenant—or, rather, perhaps, still the landowner.

To argue would naturally have been a mistake, so, continuing to shiver in the cold of the morning, I asserted that the coffee on the tray would suit me well and that there was no need to change it, as she had suggested, for tea.

I found it hard to accept Elizabeth's explanation of the omnipresent dust. It was true that the drives were dusty, noticeably so, quite like what I imagine country roads to have been in the early days of motoring, when veils and goggles had to be worn, and the back of the neck thickly muffled; but there was *so much* dust in the house, and with so many of the windows shut, at least during the winter. For example, I had not opened mine on going to bed the previous evening, though this was contrary to a rule of health from which I seldom depart. I drew on, over my pyjamas, the heavy sweater I had brought against the river winds; poured out excellent hot coffee with a shaking hand; chewed scrambled egg and toast; and resolved to pay Blantyre a visit, even though it meant driving more than forty miles each way, to discover why still no action seemed to have been taken on my memo of two years before.

I put on all my thickest garments, descended, looked in the cold state rooms for the sisters, failed to find them, and decided simply to depart as had been agreed the previous night. As I drove away in my Mini, I observed my wake of dust with more conscious care. There certainly was a cloud of it, a rare sight nowadays in Britain, but I still found it hard to believe that all the self-renewing, perennial dust of Clamber Court came from the two drives, long though they were.

I noticed that the water in the bowl of the huntsman fountain was patched with ice, though the jets still spurted frigidly upwards and sideways. The immaculate fountain was a symbol of the whole property: cold but kempt, as one might say. And one could only suppose that the responsibility and burden lay upon Miss Agnes Brakespear. Nobody who lacks direct knowledge of such a task can know how heavy it is in the conditions of today. I, with my increasing professional experience in such concerns, thought I could understand how irritating Olive Brakespear's attitude might be to Agnes Brakespear. Olive still behaved, however diminished her force, as if Clamber Court maintained itself; still took the house, in however reduced a degree, at its own valuation when built. The struggle lay with Agnes; and no doubt the better part of the nation owed her a debt, and others like her. All the same, I knew which of the sisters was the one to whom my greatest debt was owed. I thought sophistically that there would be little purpose in keeping up Clamber Court unless someone had at least an inkling of the style associated with dwelling there. It was a sentiment of a kind often to be discovered in the Fund's own literature. Olive Brakespear also served. Still, it seemed hard that dedicated Agnes should be additionally encumbered with so much dust. The cold wind blew it around me. It penetrated cracks in the bodywork, however shut the windows.

I drove towards the little house which young Hand had leased beside one of the broken-down locks. It had been unoccupied for years, having neither gas nor electricity, neither water, except from the river, nor a road; so that Hand did not have to pay very much for it, which was just as well, as the Fund was all too heavily committed in other directions on his behalf. I had to leave my car by the roadside and cross two freezing fields by a muddy path. Hand and a group of six or eight other youthful enthusiasts were frying bacon on a primus stove while the wind whistled through the broken windows. A row of Hounsfield beds, all unmade after having been slept in, was almost the only approach to furniture. The party seemed to be dressed entirely in garments from those places known as "surplus stores". In every way, it was an odd background for a project under the auspices of the Historic Structures Fund, though no doubt it had a certain pioneering value in its own way.

Unfortunately, I arrived considerably later than the hour we had agreed; though this did not surprise me, as I had always said that the time insisted on by Hand was far too early, especially as it was still winter—officially and in every other way. They were sarcastic about my lateness, and they were hardly of the type to appreciate my concern with the worrying problem of the dust; which, therefore, I did not even mention.

I shall say little more of the Bovil Restoration Project: partly because most of the details are already well known (at least among those likely to be interested in them), and have been the subject of an exhaustive Report, edited by Hand himself (though I myself think an independent editor would have been better); and more because it is my sojourn at Clamber Court that I am describing, upon which the Project impinged hardly at all. The two parts of my life at that time were almost in watertight compartments, to use the obvious but apt metaphor.

After that rather terrible first day on the river, freezing cold (and, later, raining as well), muddy everywhere, and spent mainly (as it now seems) in pushing through endless thickets of dead bramble and dogrose, with insufficiently defined authority over Hand's rough-mannered group, I returned to Clamber Court and a first-class dinner with much relief. The second evening with the Brakespear sisters, a replica of the first, presented the oddest contrast to my day with Hand and his noisy friends, as can easily be imagined. A really bitter wind was getting up, as it often does towards the end of March; but though it made the house creak a little, it did nothing to disturb the dust. At one point, I had proposed to mention the dust to Olive Brakespear, if I could find myself long enough alone with her; having at least made a start with the grey Elizabeth. But no possible moment seemed to arise that evening. Perhaps I was too exhausted with the river, to embark gratuitously upon new uncertainties. Probably I thought that I should wait until I knew the Brakespears better: if one ever could.

Only when back in my room for the night did it clearly strike me that Agnes might deliberately have prevented my being alone for more than a minute or two with Olive. Thinking back over the evening that had just passed, I could recall more than one moment when Agnes had obviously been about to fetch something or do something, and when, instead, she had remained. The reasons for leaving us had been tiny, and many people might have been dissuaded by mere inertia; but hardly, I felt, Agnes. She had sat on, though she had been fretful and under-occupied from the start; and was then all the more fretful, no doubt, if she felt tied by the task of never taking her eyes from two people she did not trust. Could it relate to her immediate suspicion of me concerning the dust, when first she saw me? Did she imagine that Olive and I were becoming affectionate? Was it merely that she did not believe in allowing Olive any unnecessary peace? Or had I altogether deceived myself?

One of the moments which I found to be oddest in this generally odd way of life, was the moment when I returned to the house after my day on the river. It was always evening and always I seemed quite alone in the world, or at least in the big park. There was not even a light in the house, because Olive never turned one on unless compelled, and Agnes came back an hour or so later from undertakings which were apparently demanding, apparently unsatisfying, but never quite defined (and one could hardly enquire). Everything was silent. I had to mount the curving stone steps, and disturb the silence by pressing the little bellpush at the centre of the long facade, stretching through the evening from pavilion to pavilion. The illusion of the house being a vast, empty model always returned to me at this time. That there should be any living person in the huge, dark, noiseless interior seemed either absurd or sinister.

But I never had to ring more than once. The grey Elizabeth

always appeared after the same short interval and let me in. She never put on a light for me, and I never did it for myself. I suppose we both held back out of regard for Olive. I myself found Olive's day-after-day passivity as unfathomable as Agnes's day-after-day agitation. Three or four of these days passed, and I never saw Olive on a horse, though all the time she wore the same worn riding breeches and boots. It was true that I had always left fairly early and returned fairly late, and that Olive might have tended to these clothes because she looked her best in them, as many women do. All the same, I might by now have been invited to visit the stables, at least in principle. Elsewhere, it had usually happened during my first luncheon; with the time unchallengeably fixed for immediately after it: at houses where the stables still functioned, of course, and had not been let off as a mushroom farm or school of art.

Up the dark staircase I went on my fourth evening (as I see it was from my Diary), while Elizabeth trailed back across the almost empty hall to the kitchen at the rear. I walked leftwards from the landing along the dark passage to my room.

Then something absolutely unexpected took place. I opened the door and I saw the back of a man standing before one of the two windows; the window not fronted by the big dressing table. He was looking out into the dark park: dark, but not yet completely dark, and, of course, less dark than the interior of the house. I could see perhaps a little more than just his black silhouette.

I know exactly what happened next, because I wrote it down the next morning. First, I stood there for a quite perceptible time, in plain shock and uncertainty. The man must have heard me approaching and opening the door, but he made no move. I then switched on the three poor lights, though far from sure what I ought to do next. The man did then turn and I got a quite good view of him. He was taller than I was, young and handsome, with a prominent nose and a quantity of dark hair which curled effectively on his brow. This description makes his aspect sound like that of an artist, but, in fact, it was more like that of an athlete, and perhaps most of all like that of a soldier. I cite these misleading popular types only to give some idea of the impression he left upon me during the seconds I looked at him. Undoubtedly, he was very well dressed in a conventional, unostentatious way. He might have been a visitor to the house, who, in the dusk, had strayed into the wrong room. What he next did, however, made an idea of that kind unlikely (though not impossible): he simply walked with a quick step towards me as I stood by the door, looked straight into my eyes (of that, naturally, I am certain), and then, without a word, strode past me into the passage outside. I do not think I was more than normally upset (I noted down the next morning that I was not), but, none the less, I could find nothing to say, even though silence made me look a fool. He departed down the passage and vanished in the darkness. I made no note of how far I could hear his steps if at all. I imagine that waiting for him to speak took all my attention. And now, of course, I have no recollection.

From every point of view, I should, I suppose, have followed him, but, instead, I shut the door, and walked over to the window where he had been standing. The floor boards were thick with dust, but there was no mark of his feet. It was when I saw this that real fear began to rise in me: the explanation that the dust had already covered the marks, though not, in its own way, impossible, to judge by what I had noticed elsewhere in the house, was by now hardly less unsettling than the notion of there being something queer about the man himself.

I went through my drawers and I accounted for all objects that I could remember to have left lying about. Nothing seemed missing, I was almost sorry.

I returned to the window and looked out on the darkening park. And then something really frightening took place. It was now dark enough for my ill-lighted room to reflect itself in the glass and appear in even more ill-lighted reproduction outside; but not dark enough for the room to be *all* I could see beyond the window. Through the reflection of the back wall of the room, the wall behind me as I stood, I could still see the shadows of trees and the whiteness of the intersecting drives. The outline of the huntsman fountain was clear enough quite to catch my attention. As I stared at it, I saw, or thought I saw, the figure of the man I had seen, standing on the drive a short distance to my left of it. There really was *not* enough light to distinguish one person from another, and certainly not at anything like that distance; but I had no doubt that this figure was he. Moreover, I had never before looked from my window and see anyone on the drive. It was a very isolated and, one would have thought, undermanned establishment. The moment I set eyes on the figure standing on the drive, I was carried away by terror, so that I may not be completely reliable about what happened next. I did not seem to see the figure move, but within moments, instead of being on the drive, it was somehow within the four walls of the room that was reflected immediately before me. The reflection of the room was mis-shaped, as such reflections always are, and the walls were still transparent, but it was impossible to doubt where the figure now stood. Staring out petrified, I made absolutely certain, as a child might; checking in the reflected room the different objects which I knew were in the real room behind me: and among them the figure stood.

I know, as will be seen, that at this point, I cried out. Those who deem this either weak of me or incredible, are invited to find themselves in a like situation. But I did manage to turn myself round, to confront the intruder: perhaps because it was even worse to suppose he was standing out of my sight.

I found I was alone in the room. I stared at its emptiness to make quite sure; and then looked back at the reflected room. That was now empty also, apart from my own vaguely reflected shape in the foreground. I fell into an armchair.

There was a knock at my door; and I thought that the manner of it was familiar.

"Come in."

It was the grey Elizabeth, who had knocked as when she brought my breakfasts.

I rose to my feet. I don't quite know why.

"Miss Brakespear says she heard something and asked me to find out whether anything was wrong."

On the instant, I decided to plunge.

"When I came in here a few minutes ago, a man was standing by the window looking out."

"Yes, sir," was all the grey Elizabeth said.

"What do you mean by that? Who was he?"

"Other people have supposed they saw him."

Annoyance rose in me to drive out fear.

"Are you saying that I've been given some kind of haunted room?"

"Certainly not, sir. People have seen him in many different rooms. But you won't see him again. No one has ever seen him more than once."

"Have *you* seen him?"

"No, sir."

"Who is he?"

"That's not for me to know." She looked and spoke as if I had asked her something improper.

"Then I shall ask one of the Miss Brakespears."

"Please don't do that, sir. The tale upsets the Miss Brakespears very much. Let's just keep it to ourselves, sir. I'll tell Miss Brakespear that you cried out because you'd cut yourself."

It sounded utterly absurd. It reminded me of the suggestion that the dust in the house came from the drives.

"But I haven't cut myself."

"Yes you have, sir. Look."

It was not the least astonishing thing. There was a quite bad gash on the soft part of my left hand, the area between the little finger and the wrist. Half my hand was greasily wet with blood. I did not know how I had done it, and I never learned. Possibly it had happened while I was blundering about the room a few minutes earlier.

"Let me get the first-aid box," said the grey Elizabeth. It was scarcely practicable to object. She departed and soon came back with it. The Fund's rules require that at least one box of this kind be kept at every property, because the public visitors manage to do the most extraordinary things to themselves.

The grey Elizabeth bound me up quite skilfully; so skilfully that I had to congratulate her.

"Miss Brakespear taught me," she said. "She's a qualified, trained nurse."

It was obvious that the grey Elizabeth admired Agnes. I had noticed it before.

"And now, sir," said Elizabeth, finishing me off, "if I promise that you'll see nothing ever again, will you please promise me that you'll not speak about what you've seen to the Miss Brakespears?"

It seemed to me an excessive request.

"They shouldn't have people to stay in a haunted house without warning them."

"They seldom do, sir. With respect, sir, you'll recall that you were not invited by either Miss Brakespear."

It could hardly be denied.

"And therefore, sir, I'm sure you'll agree that it would be better to leave private things unspoken."

This exceedingly plain hint brought back to me that at other properties of the Fund I had sometimes stumbled upon privacies that I should have preferred to be ignorant of; and that occasionally, small difficulties had ensued.

"You'll know better than I do, sir, that in houses where things such as we're talking about are supposed to happen, the owners often don't care for them to be spoken of."

That too I did know; and the Fund's Psychic and Occult Committee has since been much impeded by it.

But I was still doubtful, as was only natural.

"How can I be sure that nothing more will happen?"

"Those to whom anything happens, find that it happens only once. In this house, anyway," replied the grey Elizabeth, with the most convincing confidence.

"I might be an exception."

"Even if you are, sir, you wouldn't wish to do a hurt to the two ladies."

The truth was that by now I knew in my bones that it was not a thing to talk about with the sisters. I could not even imagine how I could possibly begin.

"All right," I said to the grey Elizabeth. "All right, if nothing more happens."

Suddenly Agnes Brakespear appeared in the doorway, wearing one of her dark dresses.

"Whatever is going on? Elizabeth, why didn't you come back to tell me? Mr. Oxenhope, are you hurt?"

"I foolishly managed to cut myself, and Elizabeth has been binding me up."

So that evening passed like the three previous ones.

When the time came for bed, I certainly cannot say that I was easy in my mind, but I thought that I could rely upon the grey Elizabeth. I had gone through an exhausting day in the open with Hand and his intolerable gang, and I soon fell asleep.

When Elizabeth brought me breakfast, I felt that we were parties to a bargain, and took advantage of this to make some new, exploratory remark about the dust.

"Old houses are always full of dust," she replied, calmly avoiding my eye; "do what you will. A gentleman in your position must know that better than I do." And she went without asking me a question, as she usually did, about the contents of the tray being to my liking.

That day was Saturday, but Hand had pointed out that so far from the weekend being a holiday, it was the time when we could expect the number of volunteers to be doubled. This was obvious enough, but I must have looked put out, because Hand had gone on to say that he was sure they could manage on their own if I cared to miss the Saturday and Sunday. But I was certain that something appalling would happen in my absence, so did not avail myself of his suggestion.

For example, friction had already begun with the riverside farmers, as anyone could have foreseen, and Hand was only waiting his chance to deal with them forcefully, so that the name of the Fund would quite probably have been dragged into the national press. For weeks the local paper had contained little but correspondence about the scheme, and "statements" concerning it from Mayors, Chairmen of Councils, and business men: the great majority adverse, as could well be understood. The editor had also published two long letters from Hand himself, but both so aggressive and so clever in the wrong way that they could only have done more harm than good. Hand was never able to understand the kind of objections that normal, reasonable people feel to operations that directly forward none of their interests. The majority like to confine any idealism they may have to approved outlets, and not let it enter their immediate environments and working lives. This may or may not be sensible and admirable, but it is a fact of life. Hand could never really grasp it.

At weekends on the river, there were even girl volunteers, or, more probably, girls who followed boys who had volunteered; so the chaos and confusion were worse than ever. Some of the volunteers showed qualities that were, doubtless, in many ways excellent, even though ill-adapted to the world of today, when everything at all serious is settled by agreement, manifestly or behind the scenes. I should not necessarily have been opposed even to the scheme itself, provided that the Fund had not been required to assist with it, let alone I personally. The central mistake was in the commitment of the Fund to anything so harebrained and explosive . . . All the same, I ploughed on through a welter of mud and a continuous bitter wind; doing my best among people with whom I had little in common, if only because I was older and had seen so much more of the world than they had.

And every evening I returned to the vast, dusky, silent house; ascended to the room where I had made that strange encounter; hung my clothes out to dry; scraped the worst of the mud off my boots on to a sheet of local newspaper; lay on my bed for half an hour; and then went down to Olive playing out her endless dreams on the music room piano. She sometimes spoke, but never stopped playing or offered me a drink until Agnes's step could be heard in the stone-paved hall. Where I left my car at the front of the house, Agnes left hers at the back, and entered through the kitchen quarters. When she came into the music room, she was always the first to speak, and seldom much more agreeably than on my first evening. It was plain that Olive's habitual silence irritated her in itself, and one could understand how this might be, when Agnes had to live with Olive year after year. Nor could I doubt that there were other things than silence about Olive that irritated Agnes. Agnes always wore one of the woollen dresses I have mentioned. I saw three or four of them in all. I imagine that, unlike Olive, she, to this extent, changed for dinner. I had not so far set eyes on her at any other time of the day. Agnes usually made some formal enquiry about the progress of the river project, to which I made a formal reply; and nothing more was ever said on the subject, somewhat to my relief. We talked about Agnes's local preoccupations, with Olive sometimes breaking her silence to be sarcastic, though only mildly and gently so. We discussed topics in which no one of us succeeded in interesting any of the others for a moment. Agnes produced a large embroidery frame and decussated away the hours, without, to my mind, producing anything very beautiful. The work was for presentation at Christmas to the meeting place of a women's organization in a nearby town.

One evening, I remember, we talked about the Fund itself. Agnes was not very cordial.

"Since the property was settled on the Fund," she asserted, "we haven't been able to call our souls our own."

I had heard something of the kind from other tenants, so cannot say that I was exactly shocked.

"The Fund has the ungrateful task of having to meet the requirements of the State," I replied. "It does all it can to soften the wind to the shorn lamb."

"By this time it could do more to stop the wind blowing," said Agnes.

This, for me, was too much after the style of Hand. I had been listening to such tiresome talk all day.

"The Fund has to keep out of all controversy," I said, with such deliberate firmness as I could achieve. "If it didn't, it wouldn't be permitted to hold property, and your house might have been pulled down by now, or become an institution."

"*Our* house!" exclaimed Agnes, with bitterness. The tenants all feel the same, and I suppose one cannot blame them.

"Since the Fund took over, we've been living here on sufferance, almost on charity. Our lives have ceased to be our own. We are unpaid curators. The nobility in Poland who have had their estates stolen, are sometimes permitted to go on curating a few rooms in their former houses. Though in England it is dressed up, that is our position, and nothing more. At least it is my position. I can't speak for Olive."

Olive was lying back in her usual chair before the fire, her legs stretched out, her hands beneath her head.

"Oh, I agree," she said. "We are simply waiting. Soon it will all be gone."

"The Fund," I pointed out, "likes to keep members of the family living in the house. The public doesn't take to museums, and very few of them know or care anything about architecture or pictures. What appeals to them is getting into someone else's home, and having the right to poke about inside it. It is only on that basis that the Fund keeps going. It may or may not be sensible and admirable, but it's a fact of life, and we all have to do our best to accept it, even though I quite see it's often not easy."

"You can't *live* in a house you no longer own," said Agnes. "The choices, the decisions, the responsibilities are no longer yours. You are at the best a housekeeper; at the worst, a dummy. Not that people in any way cease to hate and envy you. Often they hate and envy you more, because they've seen more. The difference is that you're tied down, and deprived of any redress against them. I hope you'll agree from what you've seen that I'm an efficient housekeeper, but I spend as little time in the house as possible. I get away as much as I can, even if what goes on outside the walls is often frustrating too."

"It won't last," said Olive. "It can't last. Not even in Poland."

"My job is to see that it does last," I said, smiling. "Or at least it is the job of my colleagues."

"We should have fought harder for ourselves," said Agnes. "We should have put up more of a struggle." She spoke as one merely placing an opinion on record; not even attempting to convince, not expecting in the least to be agreed with. Here she differed from Hand, who would have begun to make immediate plans, however impracticable.

An irritation of our age is the collapse of the rules concerning names. My hostesses had still not begun to address me as "Nugent", no doubt owing to my invidious position, of which, like many of the other tenants, they were so excessively conscious. And, in that same position, it was hardly for me to begin calling them "Agnes" and "Olive". On the other hand, the old fashioned formalities would have seemed strained; would have caused the very embarrassments they were designed to eliminate. We never altogether reached a settlement of this problem. No doubt that was symbolical. It was a house in which the rules lingered, because a house in which it was otherwise impossible to live with decency; but the rules, like Olive Brakespear, now lacked force, let alone fire.

Often I thought about Olive; about her square mouth, her slenderness, her lovely hands, her air of poetical mystery: but though there had seemed to be a certain understanding between us from the start, she took care to add not one twig to the tiny flame, one brick to the rudimentary fabric. Probably she no longer had twigs or bricks in her store.

I found that Agnes was beginning to talk much more to me, even though it was most of the time *at* me. "This whole thing about us and the Fund is grotesque," she would exclaim. "Don't you think so?" Or she would suddenly make a wide and difficult enquiry: "What do you think of Dutch barns? The Fund must have more experience of them than I have"; or "Are there any *really good people* working for the Fund? Is there even one?" Once she suddenly asked: "What is your own candid view of my sister Olive?", and this with Olive sitting there as usual, silent and indifferent unless directly addressed.

At least it all tended to ward off sheer dullness. And the food and drink continued as good as the general maintenance. And the dust remained. By then, snatching thirty minutes here and thirty minutes there, I had prowled half across five parishes looking for a cement works, but had failed to find one.

And next came the incident of the dust-cloud at dawn.

Each night, worn with the burden of communication, we went to bed rather early. I was usually quite ready for it; so hard was my life on the river—in a way, I suppose, so healthy, albeit unenjoyable. I used to fall asleep immediately, and every night thought less of the intruder I had seen; but I found that on most mornings, I awoke early. The truth was that, as in many country houses, far too long was officially set aside for slumber. I would awake, and in the cold, grey light see by the ticking French clock that it was only six, or even earlier; whereas Elizabeth could not be expected to arrive with my breakfast until half past seven. Sometimes I climbed out of bed and walked several times up and down the room in my pyjamas, deliberately chilling myself; having learned from experience elsewhere that the change from cold air to warm sheets and blankets often sends one more quickly back to sleep than anything else.

At that hour, the fountain huntsman looked both more alive and more mythological than when he stood transfixed and obsolete in the rushing world. One felt that he was the single living man in square miles of farm-haunted landscape. As I stumped about looking for new sleep, I glanced out at him, even when I had to scrub the frost off the panes to see him.

On one of these early mornings, I saw something else. The park was greyly lit, lightly frosted, and, as far as I could see and hear, perfectly unpopulated and still: an excellent world, in fact, for a stone man to hunt in. As I looked out, excited, I admit, by the cold, quiet beauty of the scene, I saw a cloud of dust bowling along the white drive from among the trees on the left; a *globe* of dust might better describe it. It was possibly ten or twelve feet high, and quite dense; and though more or less spherical, dragged a dusty train behind it, like a messy comet. The dust looked almost black in the faint dawn light, but I was sure it was really grey—the perfectly ordinary grey one would expect. It rolled along quite steadily towards the fountain; and, in the apparent absence of any wind, I thought at once that it must be raised by some small, heavy vehicle—or, anyway, moving object—at the invisible centre of it. The invisibility was especially odd, however: one would expect to have seen something of such a vehicle, probably the front of it, butting out from the cloud that followed it. I was so carried away that I actually opened one of the heavy sash windows with their thick glazing bars, and listened for the noise of an engine. I could hear nothing at all: not even awakening rooks and hedgehoppers.

Leaning further out, I saw the dust-cloud roll on until it reached the intersection of drives at the fountain; and then the episode ended in total anticlimax: somehow the cloud was not there at all. It could not really have blown away, because there was no wind; and that quite apart from the question of there having presumably been some solid object to cause it, though still none was visible. I could not even say that I had seen the cloud disperse. It was more as if I had been so concentrated on the movement and character of the cloud that I had been half-asleep to the particulars of its dissolution, to a development so unanticipated. Anyway, there was now neither cloud nor cause for cloud: nothing but the cold, still morning with the stone huntsman perched half-iced at the centre of it.

I shut the window, shivered a little, and returned to bed, though not to sleep. In fact, it was this seeming freak of nature that I have described, which really propelled me to Blantyre. That same morning, I drove round to Hand's lock cottage; told the assembled volunteers that other Fund business, coming unexpectedly, would compel me to be missing from the river that day; made no reference to the rather obvious looks of relief which followed my words; and drove off to Bagglesham, where Blantyre, the Fund's Regional Representative, operated from his crumbling, half-timbered house in a side street. It had once belonged to a family of pargeters, and legend said one could still smell the dung that went into their special kind of plaster; but that was a paranormal manifestation that never came my way.

Basil Blantyre, who has since, unfortunately, died (still in harness), was already nearer to eighty than to seventy, and sensibly reluctant to leave the warm fire in March weather; but he welcomed me in most cordially, though I had not been able to tell him I was coming. There was a telephone at Clamber Court, but I had never heard it in use, and I thought that a call to the Fund's local luminary could, if overheard, cause only trouble. Blantyre most kindly made me a cup of instant coffee with his own hands. He lived quite alone, his wife having never fully recovered (as I had been given by Hamish Haythorn to understand) from the shock of the bankruptcy and the compulsion to leave the house where the Blantyre family had lived, reputedly, since the Middle Ages. To Blantyre, as to me (and others), the Fund had proved a welcome haven from life's storm.

"I want the lowdown on Clamber Court and the Brakespear sisters," I said, pushing back the scum on the hot coffee.

"There was a lot of sadness in the family. I speak of the time before Clamber was settled on the Fund."

"There hasn't been much happiness since, judging by what I've seen and heard."

"What can you expect, Oxenhope? People don't like losing their houses and still living on in them. That at least Millicent and I were spared."

Quite possibly this was a form of sour grapes, as the Blantyre house had been much too far gone for any decision but demolition.

"There may be more to it than that," I said. "What splendid coffee! There seem to me some very odd goings-on at Clamber Court."

"So I have heard," said Blantyre, looking away from me and into the blazing logs.

"To start with, the Brakespear girls appear to have no visitors.

Apart, of course, from the public."

"Poor old dears!" exclaimed Blantyre vaguely.

"They're not as old as that. I acknowledge that I myself find one of them quite attractive."

"So-ho!" exclaimed Blantyre in the same vague way. It was manifest that he had long ago lost all touch with the Clamber situation.

"And then," I said, "the house is full of dust."

"Yes," said Blantyre. "I know. That's just it."

"That's just what?" I asked, putting down my cup. The second half of the contents was thick and muddy.

Blantyre did not answer. After a pause, he answered with another question.

"Did you see anything else? Or hear?"

"See," I said, lowering my voice, as one does; even though it was still the middle of the morning. "Not hear."

"You saw *him*?" asked Blantyre.

"I think so," I said. "I suppose so."

"And *it*? You perhaps saw *it* as well?"

"Yes," I said. "This very morning, as a matter of fact."

"You don't say so." Blantyre turned back towards me.

"If what I saw was the same it."

"I have no doubt of it," replied Blantyre.

"I first saw the dust, the ordinary dust, when I visited the house two years ago. I went incognito, you know."

"You should never do that," said Blantyre very seriously.

Coming from a man almost twice my age, I let the reproof go.

"At the time I sent you a memo on the dust," I said.

"I don't wonder. Many people do."

"You mean that there's nothing to be done about it?"

"What do *you* think about that?" asked Blantyre. "Now that you've had more experience."

"The servant says it blows in off the long drives."

"So it does," said Blantyre: "In a way." Here he started coughing rather alarmingly, as if the dust had entered his own lungs.

"Can't I get you something?" I asked.

"No, thank you," Blantyre wheezed. "Just give me a minute or two. You haven't finished your coffee."

I swallowed a little more, and then sat looking into the fire, as Blantyre had done. Before long, his breath seemed to be coming more easily.

"Will you please tell me the story?" I asked, still staring at the logs. "All within the four walls of the Fund, of course."

"You mean that I shan't last long? That I ought to pass it on before I go?"

"Of course not. I never thought of such a thing. After all, the Brakespear girls must know, and almost certainly, Elizabeth, and doubtless others."

"Not many others," said Blantyre. "Or only village tales. If the Fund has to have official knowledge of the story, it is my successor I should tell, but I don't know who he'll be and I daresay I shall never meet him, so I'm prepared to tell you. You've been *staying* in the house, I believe? Spending nights there?"

"Yes," I said. "And still am. All thanks to young Mr. Hand."

"There's a good lad," said Blantyre unexpectedly. "It's a bad thing for England that they're not more like him."

"Who knows if you're not right, but you can be glad you don't have to work with him."

"Men of the best type are seldom easy to work with. Being easy to work with is a talent that often doesn't call for any other talents in support of it."

I said nothing: again remembering Blantyre's age. This time the gulf between the generations positively yawned at my feet.

"If you're called upon to live in the house," said Blantyre, "you've possibly a claim to the story. Not that I've heard of actual harm coming to anyone. Not physical harm, anyway. Only to Tony Tilbury, who was killed. But he was just run over."

"I don't follow," I said.

"The one certain fact is that Tony Tilbury was run down and killed early one morning by a car which Agnes Brakespear was driving."

"Oh," I said, feeling a little sick.

"Olive Brakespear saw it happen from one of the windows. That's another fact: at least, I suppose so. There is considerable doubt as to how far her account of the details can be relied on."

"I shouldn't have thought it was an easy place to have an accident of that kind; especially with nothing else about."

"You're not the only person to have thought that, and, in fact, if it hadn't been for Olive's evidence, Agnes would have been in serious trouble. A manslaughter charge, at least. Even murder, perhaps."

"Who *was* Tony Tilbury?"

"He was a fine-looking young chap; descended from one of Queen Elizabeth's admirals. I met him myself several times, when we were still in the old place. But then I think you may have seen for yourself what he looked like. If we understood one another just now. The thing was that Tilbury and Olive Brakespear were in love—very much in love, people say—and Agnes objected."

"You mean she was in love with him herself?"

"Perhaps," said Blantyre. "That's one of the many things that no one knows, or can be expected to know, unless one of the sisters speaks up, and I should say that's pretty unlikely by this time. But there's no doubt at all about the rows it all caused between them. There were plenty of people who were quite prepared, or said they were, to swear to having seen Agnes setting about Olive, and even threatening to kill her."

"That seems an unlikely thing to threaten before witnesses."

"It's what people said. Whether they would really have taken an oath on it when it came to the point, is, needless to say, another matter. It never did come to a point of that kind, because Olive swore at the inquest that she had seen the whole thing from one of the windows and that the car had quite obviously got out of control. She swore that she saw Agnes struggling with it and doing all she could be expected to do. Even so, there were a lot of unanswered questions, when it had come to running down a solitary man in all that open space. And, apparently, Olive at one point half-admitted that she couldn't *really* see, because of all the dust which the car had stirred up. Agnes made a big thing of the dust too, in her own evidence. She put a lot of the blame on it. In the end the Coroner gave Agnes the benefit of the doubt, and the jury brought in Accidental Death. I daresay the dust was pretty decisive, however you look at it. It can get into people's eyes, like smoke. That's not the only dusty verdict I've known to come from a coroner's jury. Inquests often take place in rather a rush, oddly enough; though I didn't attend the one on Tony Tilbury."

"Why did people suppose he was standing about all by himself at that hour of a winter morning?"

"It wasn't winter," said Blantyre. "It was pretty near midsummer. Hence all the dust."

"Oh," I said. "I hadn't realized." Blantyre waited for me to go on. "At Clamber there seems dust enough at any time. Even so, what was Tilbury doing?"

"Agnes and Olive told a story about Tilbury sleeping badly and often going out in the early hours to walk about the park. I daresay it was more or less true. But what people said was something different. They said that on the morning in question, Tilbury was about to elope with Olive. A far-fetched thing to do, in all the circumstances, but the two of them were said to have been driven to it by Agnes's behaviour. The idea seems to me to leave a lot of unanswered questions also. And I don't know that there's any real evidence for it at all. Tilbury's own car—a racing sort of thing—was found in the background along the drive, but there was nothing very remarkable about that. As a matter of fact, I'm not sure that the whole business, queer though it was, would have started so many tales, or at least kept the tales going for so long, had it not been for one or two other things."

"What were they?" I asked.

"In the first place, Olive had a complete breakdown after the inquest—or so, once again, it was said: I suppose one can't be certain even of that. All that is certain is that she was missing for more than a year. And when she came back, she had changed. She had intended to be a professional pianist, as you possibly know: perhaps before she met Tony Tilbury. Even that was odd: the effect that Tilbury appears to have had on her. Tilbury was an agreeable young chap, and good-looking, of course, but perfectly ordinary, as far as I could ever see; and it was hard to imagine why a sensitive, artistic creature like Olive should be so gone on *him* in particular. Because I think she really was gone on him. I don't think there's much doubt about that. I'm told they behaved quite absurdly together, even in public. Anyway, when she came back, after more than a year, from wherever it had been, she'd given up music and gone nuts on riding; and not the usual sort of riding either, but endless treks all by herself. She still does it, or did, the last I heard. But you'll probably know more about that than I do."

"Olive still plays the piano as well," I said. "Whenever Agnes lets her."

"I see," said Blantyre, looking me in the eye. "Well, there you are. I mean as to the relationship between them. You've summed it up from your own observation."

"I'd believe almost anything about their relationship. But what's the next reason why people still talk?"

"Do you have to ask? You're not the only one to have seen things and heard things—or to have *said* they'd seen and heard them. Not that I wish to reflect any doubt upon you personally, you understand."

"Elizabeth told me that no one sees anything more than once. At least, she said that no one sees what I now take to have been Tilbury's figure more than once?"

"Did she now? That's a new superstition to me. But it follows a familiar line, of course, and when things like that are alive at all, they always grow. Also I haven't been to Clamber for some time, though that's probably something I shouldn't admit. I just don't like the place, and, between ourselves, I don't go out much more than I can help in any case, unless it happens to be set fair weather."

"Elizabeth implied that people have seen him in many different rooms in the house."

"I suspect," replied Blantyre, "that he's just *in* the whole place, and that the people who see him, do so when they happen to be in the right mood. What exactly that means, I have no idea, but none of the theories that are supposed to explain these things, goes very far, as you may have noticed. 'All telepathy', people say, for example. What does it mean? Whether it's true or not? It gets one almost no distance at all, though it may perhaps just be worth saying. I claim no more for what I have just suggested about Tony Tilbury at Clamber."

"And, from what you say, we know no more about what those three people were doing all up and about so early in the morning?"

"Not a thing. Nor ever shall, in all probability. Of course the father had died years before. As a matter of fact, he killed himself: so much seems certain, though they succeeded in hushing it up, and I've never come upon so much as a rumour as to his reasons. The older people who knew him, just say he always seemed depressed or always seemed aloof, or some such word. All in all, they're not a lucky family. The mother went queer after her husband's death, though she's still alive."

"I was told in the Fund offices that she lived in the house."

"I don't think so," said Blantyre, smiling a little. "It's the sort of thing that I should be notified about officially, wouldn't you say? I suspect it's another example of the growth that takes place in the absence of facts. Or have you heard the old thing screaming in the night above your head?"

"Never," I replied.

"Well, I hope you don't. It's not a pleasant sound, I assure you."

Blantyre spoke as if it were one with which he was thoroughly familiar.

"And that reminds me," he went on. "I shouldn't be frightened of Clamber, if I were you, or let it get me down. I mention this because that might be the tendency of some of the things I've said. I think it is quite unnecessary. It's true that I don't like the place, but it's far more true that no one was ever hurt by a ghost yet, unless he made use of the ghost to hurt himself. Ghosts don't hit you over the head: you do it yourself when you're not thinking about it, and blame them for it because you can't understand yourself. A homely illustration, but all the records confirm the truth of it. It's only in fiction that there's anything *really* dangerous. And of course old houses do tend to dust up when their families no longer own them: though that's not a line of thought we are permitted to pursue. So now let me make you another cup of coffee."

Despite Blantyre's reassurances, I was thereafter really afraid not only of Clamber Court, but of the two sisters as well. Fortunately, I had only four more nights to stay there; because my nights had become as forbidding as my days.

Driving back from seeing Blantyre, I actually came upon Olive on her horse, visibly now a rather elderly animal, though once, I had no doubt, a nice roan. Despite all the references to riding, I had never seen her mounted before, probably because I had always before driven about the countryside either too early or too late. The horse was stepping out slowly towards me, along a very minor road. The reins were quite loose in Olive's hand. There seemed little chance of the desperate galloping and charging that Agnes had implied was Olive's manner of equitation; though I could well believe that Olive was entirely capable of such things, perhaps even longed for them. Possibly it was what once she did, but did no more. The weather was as bleak as ever, with a bitter wind getting up under a cold sky, but Olive wore a sand-coloured shirt, open at the neck, and so old that, when I came up with her, I saw little tears in it. When first I saw her, she was looking up at the grey, almost white, heavens, while the horse found his own way. There was no reason why she should have taken any notice of my car, nowadays one of so many in the lanes, had I not slowed almost to a stop, because of the horse and because it was Olive.

She met my eyes through the windscreen, even smiled a little, and raised her left hand in greeting, like a female centaur. She made no sign of stopping or speaking, but rode slowly on. I watched her for a few seconds through my rear window: noticing the small tears in her shirt, noticing and admiring the straightness of her back, the sleekness of her hair, the perfection of her posture.

Although I had stayed for a simple lunch with Blantyre, because he seemed lonely and pressed it upon me, and because it hardly seemed worth visiting the river for a short spell of failing light, I arrived back at Clamber Court much earlier than usual. Naturally, the grey Elizabeth looked surprised.

"I've been visiting Mr. Blantyre, our local Representative," I said.

It was an explanation that was unlikely to be well received, and Elizabeth's surprise duly changed to hostility and suspicion.

"Aren't we doing what they want?" she asked.

"Of course you are. I was only passing the time of day with him."

But I cannot deny that, going along the familiar passage to my room, I felt very quavery. I even hesitated before opening my door. The room, however, was merely much lighter than it usually was when I came back to it.

An indefensible thought struck me. For the first time, I was more or less alone in the house and it was still daylight. I resolved to look about, starting with the room next to my own. Or at least to try the door. It was better, I thought, to know than not to know.

Still in my overcoat, I tiptoed back into the passage. There were little cold draughts, and I pushed back my own door as far as it would go. I did not want it to slam and bring upstairs the grey Elizabeth. I did not want it to make a noise of any kind or to shut me out.

The door of the next room was locked. It was only to be expected. I did something even more indefensible. I removed the key from the lock of my own door and tried it in the lock of the next door. My thought was that when the house had been built, an operation of this kind would have had small chance of success, but that the 1910 contractor who had plainly made big changes, might well have installed new locks that were not merely standard but identical. I was right. The lock stuck a bit, but I made the key turn. I did not just peek in, but threw the door wide open, though, at the same time, I did it as quietly as I could.

The room was entirely empty of furniture, but the air was charged with moving dust. It was almost as thick as the snow in those snowstorm glasses one used to buy from pedlars in Oxford Street. Moreover, it seemed to move in the same, slow, dreary swirl as moves the toy snow when the glass is reversed and the fall begins. There was a bitter wind outside the house, as I have said, and draughts inside it, but the room was fusty and stuffy, and I could not see how the March wind could explain everything.

Not that it mattered: at least to begin with; for through the wheeling dust I could see that at the window of the empty room a figure stood with its back to me, looking out towards the park.

It was Agnes, dressed in her day clothes; and I could see another key of the room lying on the window sill. She had locked herself in. I had been wrong in taking it for granted that at that hour she would every day be occupied with her committees and public works.

So much time passed while I just gazed through the terrifying dust at Agnes's motionless back that I really thought I might succeed in shutting the door and getting away. But exactly as I was nerving myself to move, and to move quietly, Agnes turned and looked at me.

"I know it's no longer our house, my sister's and mine," she said, "but still you are our guest, Mr. Oxenhope, even if only in a sense."

"I apologize," I said. "I had no idea the room was not empty. I have been seeing Mr. Blantyre today. Unfortunately, he's not very well, and there are one or two things I thought I should check on his behalf, before the house opens to the public."

"Of course it is what we expect and have become accustomed to. I am not complaining. What else would you like to see? The key of your room doesn't open every door."

"I don't think any of the other little items will involve keys," I replied, "though thank you very much. As for this room, I only wanted to make sure it was empty, because we should like to store a few things in it."

"There are other empty rooms in the house," said Agnes, "and I am sure we can spare this one."

"All the same, I do apologize again for not speaking to you first. It was simply that I had a little time on my hands, as today I haven't visited the river."

"It is no longer our house," said Agnes, "so that, strictly speaking, there is no obligation on you to ask us about anything. Has Mr. Blantyre any criticisms of my housekeeping?"

"None," I assured her. "We agreed that it is one of the best maintained of all the Fund's many properties."

And, interestingly enough, the dust had by then ceased to swirl, though I am sure it still lay thick on the room floor, the floors of the other rooms, the passages, the stairs, the furniture, and all our hearts.

LOUISA BALDWIN
How He Left the Hotel

Louisa Baldwin *(1845–1925), a prolific writer of fiction and children's tales at the turn of the century, lived long enough to see her only son (Stanley) become Prime Minister. This story is taken from* The Shadow on the Blind *(1895), a collection of ghost stories dedicated to her nephew Rudyard Kipling.*

I used to work the passenger lift in the Empire Hotel, that big block of building in lines of red and white brick like streaky bacon, that stands at the corner of Bath Street. I'd served my time in the army and got my discharge with good conduct stripes, and how I got the job was in this way. The hotel was a big company affair, with a managing committee of retired officers and such like, gentlemen with a bit o' money in the concern and nothing to do but fidget about it, and my late Colonel was one of 'em. He was as good tempered a man as ever stepped when his will wasn't crossed, and when I asked him for a job, "Mole," says he, "you're the very man to work the lift at our big hotel. Soldiers are civil and business-like, and the public like 'em only second best to sailors. We've had to give our last man the sack, and you can take his place."

I liked my work well enough and my pay, and kept my place a year, and I should have been there still if it hadn't been for a circumstance—but more about that just now. Ours was a hydraulic lift. None o' them ricketty things swung up like a poll-parrot's cage in a well staircase, that I shouldn't care to trust my neck to. It ran as smooth as oil, a child might have worked it, and safe as standing on the ground. Instead of being stuck full of advertisements like a' omnibus, we'd mirrors in it, and the ladies would look at themselves, and pat their hair, and set their mouths when I was taking 'em downstairs dressed of an evening. It was a little sitting room with red velvet cushions to sit down on, and you'd nothing to do but get into it, and it 'ud float you up, or float you down, as light as a bird.

All the visitors used the lift one time or another, going up or coming down. Some of them was French, and they called the lift the "assenser," and good enough for them in their language no doubt, but why the Americans, that can speak English when they choose, and are always finding out ways o' doing things quicker than other folks, should waste time and breath calling a lift an "elevator," I can't make out.

I was in charge of the lift from noon till midnight. By that time the theatre and dining-out folks had come in, and any one returning later walked upstairs, for my day's work was done. One of the porters worked the lift till I came on duty in the morning, but before twelve there was nothing particular going on, and not much till after two o'clock. Then it was pretty hot work with visitors going up and down constant, and the electric bell ringing you from one floor to another like a house on fire. Then came a quiet spell while dinner was on, and I'd sit down comfortable in the lift and read my paper, only I mightn't smoke. But nobody else might neither, and I had to ask furren gentlemen to please not to smoke in it, it was against the rule. I hadn't so often to tell English gentlemen. They're not like furreners, that seem as if their cigars was glued to their lips.

I always noticed faces as folks got into the lift, for I've sharp sight and a good memory, and none of the visitors needed to tell me twice where to take them. I knew them, and I knew their floor as well as they did themselves.

It was in November that Colonel Saxby came to the Empire Hotel. I noticed him particularly because you could see at once that he was a soldier. He was a tall, thin man about fifty, with a hawk nose, keen eyes, and a grey moustache, and walked stiff from a gunshot wound in the knee. But what I noticed most was the scar of a sabre cut across the right side of the face. As he got in the lift to go to his room on the fourth floor, I thought what a difference there is among officers. Colonel Saxby put me in mind of a telegraph post for height and thinness, and my old Colonel was like a barrel in uniform, but a brave soldier and a gentleman all the same. Colonel Saxby's room was number 210, just opposite the glass door leading to the lift, and every time I stopped on the fourth floor Number 210 stared me in the face.

The Colonel used to go up in the lift every day regular, though he never came down in it, till—but I'm coming to that presently. Sometimes, when we was alone in the lift, he'd speak to me. He asked me in what regiment I'd served, and said he knew the officers in it. But I can't say he was comfortable to talk to. There was something stand off about him, and he always seemed deep in his own thoughts. He never sat down in the lift. Whether it was empty or full he stood bolt upright, under the lamp, where the light fell on his pale face and scarred cheek.

One day in February I didn't take the Colonel up in the lift, and as he was regular as clockwork, I noticed it, but I supposed he'd gone away for a few days, and I thought no more about it. Whenever I stopped on the fourth floor the door of Number 210 was shut, and as he often left it open, I made sure the Colonel was away. At the end of a week I heard a chambermaid say that Colonel Saxby was ill, so thinks I that's why he hadn't been in the lift lately.

It was a Tuesday night, and I'd had an uncommonly busy time of it. It was one stream of traffic up and down, and so it went on the whole evening. It was on the stroke of midnight, and I was about to put out the light in the lift, lock the door, and leave the key in the office for the man in the morning, when the electric bell rang out sharp. I looked at the dial, and saw I was wanted on the fourth floor. It struck twelve as I stept into the lift. As I past the second and third floors I wondered who it was that had rung so late, and thought it must be a stranger that didn't know the rule of the house. But when I stopped at the fourth floor and flung open the door of the lift, Colonel Saxby was standing there wrapped in his military cloak. His room door was shut behind him, for I read the number on it. I thought he was ill in his bed, and ill enough he looked, but he had his hat on, and what could a man that had been in bed ten days want with going out on a winter midnight? I don't think he saw me, but when I'd set the lift in motion, I looked at him standing under the lamp, with the shadow of his hat hiding his eyes, and the light full on the lower part of his face that was deadly pale, the scar on his cheek showing still paler.

"Glad to see you're better, sir," but he said nothing, and I didn't like to look at him again. He stood like a statue with his cloak about him, and I was downright glad when I opened the door for him to step out in the hall. I saluted as he got out, and he went past me towards the door.

"The Colonel wants to go out," I said to the porter who stood staring. He opened the front door and Colonel Saxby walked out into the snow.

"That's a queer go," said the porter.

"It is," said I. "I don't like the Colonel's looks; he doesn't seem himself at all. He's ill enough to be in his bed, and there he is, gone out on a night like this."

"Anyhow he's got a famous cloak to keep him warm. I say, supposing he's gone to a fancy ball and got that cloak on to hide his dress," said the porter, laughing uneasily. For we both felt queerer than we cared to say, and as we spoke there came a loud ring at the door bell.

"No more passengers for me," I said, and I was really putting the light out this time, when Joe opened the door and two gentlemen entered that I knew at a glance were doctors. One was tall and the other short and stout, and they both came to the lift.

"Sorry, gentlemen, but it's against the rule for the lift to go up after midnight."

"Nonsense!" said the stout gentleman, "it's only just past twelve, and it's a matter of life and death. Take us up at once to the fourth floor," and they were in the lift like a shot.

When I opened the door, they went straight to Number 210. A nurse came out to meet them, and the stout doctor said, "No change for the worse, I hope." And I heard her reply, "The patient died five minutes ago, sir."

Though I'd no business to speak, that was more than I could stand. I followed the doctors to the door and said, "There's some mistake here, gentlemen; I took the Colonel down in the lift since the clock struck twelve, and he went out."

The stout doctor said sharply, "A case of mistaken identity. It was someone else you took for the Colonel."

"Begging your pardon, gentlemen, it was the Colonel himself, and the night porter that opened the door for him knew him as well as me. He was dressed for a night like this, with his military cloak wrapped round him."

"Step in and see for yourself," said the nurse. I followed the doctors into the room, and there lay Colonel Saxby looking just as I'd seen him a few minutes before. There he lay, dead as his forefathers, and the great cloak spread over the bed to keep him warm that would feel heat and cold no more. I never slept that night. I sat up with Joe, expecting every minute to hear the Colonel ring the front door bell. Next day every time the bell for the lift rang sharp and sudden, the sweat broke out on me and I shook again. I felt as bad as I did the first time I was in action. Me and Joe told the manager all about it, and he said we'd been dreaming, but, said he, "Mind you, don't you talk about it, or the house'll be empty in a week."

The Colonel's coffin was smuggled into the house the next night. Me and the manager, and the undertaker's men, took it up in the lift, and it lay right across it, and not an inch to spare. They carried it into Number 210, and while I waited for them to come out again, a queer feeling came over me. Then the door opened softly, and six men carried out the long coffin straight across the passage, and set it down with its foot towards the door of the lift, and the manager looked round for me.

"I can't do it, sir," I said. "I can't take the Colonel down *again*, I took him down at midnight yesterday, and that was enough for me."

"Push it in!" said the manager, speaking short and sharp, and they ran the coffin into the lift without a sound. The manager got in last, and before he closed the door he said, "Mole, you've worked this lift for the last time, it strikes me." And I had, for I wouldn't have stayed on at the Empire Hotel after what had happened, not if they'd doubled my wages, and me and the night porter left together.

NUGENT BARKER
Whessoe

Nugent Barker *(1888–1955) was educated at Cheltenham College, where one of his contemporaries was Herman Cyril McNeile, later to become world-famous as 'Sapper'. Barker followed a writing career, and wrote many excellent short stories, but never approached McNeile's fame. His work enjoyed a vogue between the wars, and 'Whessoe' was voted the Best Short Story of 1928. Barker wrote it while living in Oscar Wilde's old house in Tite Street, Chelsea. Soon after completing it he claimed he had the pleasure of meeting Whistler's ghost at midnight in the garden. Twenty-one of Nugent Barker's best stories were collected in a now very scarce volume entitled* Written with My Left Hand, *published in 1951.*

Those who had seen him, those who had endeavoured to speak with him, face to face, until suddenly they had realised that it would be ridiculous to carry the conversation further—these people searched diligently among the proper sources, and called him Whessoe. It may be that there was more than the merest ghost of a reason for such a name. Yet he was so secret, so illusive, they could not be sure.

His habitation was a great, silent, early Victorian house, and it stood on a semi-circle of drive behind two gates that swung rheumatically on their creaky hinges, off the leafiest avenue of that old watering town. There are many such houses, sunk in sleep, on the verdured, lazy borders of Chelsover. Their emptiness of all sound save the frequent mutter of rain-drops from the eaves; the filmy stare of their windows; their endless, aimless hours—these things give them the air of old, querulous people who have found no benefit in the health-giving waters of Chelsover, but have sat themselves down within sight of that hope-shattering spa, to watch others pass by them on the same misguided errand, beneath the whispering trees. Especially the two gates were two old snuffy gentlemen, who wheezed, and croaked, and told doubtful stories, whenever anyone took them for a moment by the latches, and walked, with silent footsteps, up the lichened drive, to the old house where the old man lived.

They say that he wore knee-breeches, and that, whenever he took his walks abroad, a threadbare, plum-coloured surtout, with the tightest of waists, and a whole battalion of buttons, glowed like a dying smithy amidst the leaf-shadows. But Whessoe of Two Gates walked so rarely in the day-time, and seldom beyond the confines of his house: the night was his, and the very early morning, when the moon, shining into an open upper window, brightened the gleam in his eye, and darkened the lines on his face.

Then would certain belated residents of Chelsover, lifting their heads, gaze fearfully at the old man lurking there.

Those of them that knew his story. . . . Yet they never ceased to wonder, when that strange figure met their eyes. They wondered at the truth of many tales concerning him; they wondered at the relentless spirit that would not let him sleep. There were occasions when he was not to be seen at his accustomed vigil: times when these same residents peered anxiously over the lower windows, to catch the fleeting glimpses of his ghostly figure as it wandered from room to room. It was so white, so frail, it shone so queerly in the dark passages and the half-light of the hall. Sometimes, when he caught sight of himself in the dusky, all but invisible, depths and boundaries of a mirror, Whessoe, too, would start and shudder at the spectral shape that had confronted him there. His face was as white and crumpled as a ball of paper; his shrunken legs appeared as though they might drop at any moment from the loosely buckled ends of his knee-breeches; his knuckles were as big as buttons—as big as the buttons on his plum-coloured surtout. But the contemplation of this disturbing figure seldom held him for long; soon he would be through with the ghost-gazing, would be off again upon his nocturnal rambles, drifting and gliding, watching at the window, caring for no man, a shadow of fled glories passing through the house.

And as silently as Whessoe, the years passed too; time was long in bringing change to the sombre mansion; and the dread invasion, when it *did* come, came neither very suddenly nor very gradually: it seemed to slip into his life like a visitor who had hailed him before opening the door: it seemed, perhaps, even more vividly, to have slipped out from a world that had nothing whatever to do with his own . . . a world with a dry mouth, and a grisly tongue in its cheek, that caused him rather frantically to think of ghosts.

Ghosts in the old house! Ghosts within the gates! Impossible, thought the old man restlessly—yet in the same moment realised that the signs had come, and he had not heeded them. For a week, a month, the visitor had hailed, and Whessoe had not attempted to open the door. Surely they were incontestable, those once unmeaning events that suddenly he remembered one very early April morning in the shuttered drawing-room, where his eyes were opened by a sign which in its own turn was a prelude to a greater sign in store!

An odour had reached him, a sweet, ineffable odour that seemed to wrap his frail body in kindly, pleading voices of the Past; he fancied that a window must be open, and a shutter unlatched; but he knew that no flowers grew now in the unwalked wilderness of a garden, nor was there any scent in the sycamore tree whose topmost branches fell barely short of his bedroom window-sill. The incident had disturbed him, without giving cause for any particular fear in his awakening mind; but sometime later, when he had left the drawing-room, and was moving noiselessly across the black spaces of the hall, a sound had started at his elbow, a tiny catch of the breath, as though—ah, yes—a ghost had sighed . . . and he had fled in a high frenzy up the staircase, to fashion the moonbeams of his bedroom into the forms and murmurs of ghosts. The moon left his window, and went her way; but still he sat on, round-eyed, probing shadows of the immediate past.

A week, a month ago, the signs had come, and he had not heeded them! A vague hint of *preparation*—he could not define it exactly—in rooms, and hall, and passages; a brighter, cleaner atmosphere, even at midnight, that seemed to envelope him at every turn of the stair—these were the little things, scarcely felt in the hour of their happening, that jumped to his memory now, and kept him vigilant for many weeks to come. Sleeping by day, and walking by night, his long-established mode of living was highly favourable to a proper study of ghosts. He would sit in the great, lofty bedroom whose windows looked over the sycamore tree: he would sit there very silently, with the door a little open, hoping for the arrival of those invading spirits whose voices he dreaded to hear.

It was a faded, murky room, that in which the crowning

evidence of a supernatural world had come to him at last. The bed stood out like a draped coffin on a bier; heavy curtains hid the two tall windows that might have been the black mouths of tombs. One of these windows had been open, and the curtains parted, on the night when he heard the spectral cry. The sound had awakened him; and for many moments afterwards he fancied that he could hear the whistle of the wind. But the cord of the window-blind hung motionless in the still, night air; nothing stirred in that vast tomb behind two parted curtains; and suddenly he knew that the sound was coming from within the house—that in some distant room a ghostly company was dancing to a quiver of spectral music, and a riot of fitful, elfin laughter.

Trembling in every limb, old Whessoe flung off the bed clothes, and hurried to the door; but the lock was rusty, and the key refused to turn in his nerveless fingers. He went to the window, peeped down into the garden and up into the sky; he was scared, he was shaking, he wanted to hide the tempestuous music that danced in his ears. A sickle moon was rising above the avenue that led into Chelsover: already, through the mesh of distant leaves, she had begun to sprinkle her dust onto the sleepy head of the sycamore tree. And now a cool wind blew into the old man's face, and the far-distant shunting of a train told him that his usual hour for rising was near. But this time he did not rise. Instead, he lay again beneath the bed-clothes, with fingers pressed into his ears, and the sheets pulled over his thin, grey hair; and at intervals throughout the night, in his waking moments, and in his troubled dreams, he heard the company of ghosts, and the flying music, and the distant room, and the whole house, dancing and dancing. . . .

So the ghosts came, and Whessoe knew now that the manifestations were something more real than the vague voices of house and garden. He did not hear them on the following night. A week went by, and the heart of the house was wrapped in silence. His first thought was to locate the room of the riotous dancing; he fancied it must be the drawing-room; but when at last he ventured within it, no sign of the dancing was there. His heart thumped as he glided, silent as a shadow, across the moonlit floor. But again the odour assailed him, subtle and frightening, speaking to him in voices of the Past. Old Whessoe caught his breath. So they were here always, now. In every crack and corner, watching him, watching him, never to go. He was able no longer to think of the house as his own.

When they came again, he was ready for them. He was sitting in his room with the door open, ready and waiting, dressed in the plum-coloured surtout and loose knee-breeches of a bygone year; and they began their display by creaking the stairs, and uttering little outbursts of laughter, until presently all individual sounds were swallowed in the dance. The music swirled, the voices rose and fell, the house rocked as before; and Whessoe stood in his doorway, round-eyed and with his mouth pursed as for whistling, trying to summon up courage to obey the almost articulate voices that he fancied he could hear, at odd moments, calling to him to join them.

Thenceforth, the wild, elfin music of the ghosts became an established custom in that house. Whessoe would await it in fear; but the fear was changed into a momentary wonder when the first gay notes arrived. He did not hear it every night. Often a whole week would go by, and the long, early hours of the morning brought no sign. He would sit in the great, lofty bedroom whose windows looked over the sycamore tree; he would sit there very silently, with the door a little open, hoping for the return of those invading spirits whose voices he dreaded to hear. And when they came, and the wrinkled cheeks of the house were smoothed out with the great burst of music, always the first fear would creep back into Whessoe; and it was many weeks before he ventured beyond the doorway while the ghosts danced.

But as time brought less restraint to the ghostly visitors, so also it brought a sense of boldness to Whessoe. The anxiety of waiting for their return was lessened by these shortening intervals of silence, his first horror began to depart; and he found himself looking forward with increasing pleasure to those nights when music tossed above the whistle of the wind, and the wind tossed over the trees, calling his name:

"Whes-s-s-oe! Whes-s-s-oe!"

At first he was scared, sitting there, unable to tell the fancied voice from the real; then from the wild elements of nature, he began to separate the wild elements of the house—the one became a stepping stone to the other—and when at last he realised that a spirit world was taking possession of the old building, superimposing itself upon everything within it, creeping into every crack and cranny, usurping the house's soul, Whessoe was not afraid. He felt soothed, and strangely gratified at so much ghostly attention. He became quietly interested, and began to think.

"What are these phantoms like?" he thought, and strove to picture them. He wondered whether they walked in the day-time, and whether they could be seen outside the realms of darkness; from his scanty knowledge of the ways of ghosts, he decided these two questions in the negative. And sometimes, in his cunning way, he tried to catch the tunes that were filling his nights with pleasure, that bid him leave their singers unmolested because they were as lovely as the shy songs of birds. And although there were moments when his curiosity urged him to put the phantoms to the proof in the broad light of day, yet always he remained loyal to the songs' bidding; but as the weeks passed, there came a more daring note to his nightly vigils.

There was a cracked, spare piano which in old days had been relegated to some dim room on the drawing-room floor; and one early morning, when the singing and the dancing were over, and the house was quiet, Whessoe stole down, and seated himself in front of the instrument; and there, in the darkness, with notes that came softly at first and finally filled the whole house with song, he, as though to pay back the ghosts in their own ghostly coin, played many bars of his favourite *Lucia*.

When August came, and the thick trees of Chelsover lay like a dust-sheet over the town, the spirits kept away; and the old house slept dreamlessly with its head upon its arm. Whessoe was puzzled. He who once had known and welcomed solitude, fretted when he found it again. The round mouth of the night drew near him and pressed its soundless, thick lips to his ear; the empty corners stared at him with tightly lidded eyes. But such a state did not exist for long; the ghostly period had been of too short a duration to have become a necessity for his soul. On the approach of September, his feelings suffered a certain change. Whenever the wind sang, he did not hesitate any longer to attribute the singing to the wind; and it sang to him in warning tones that told him that the ghosts' music had been rather monstrously evil. He was not ignorant of such a popular opinion in regard to ghostly phenomena, and his grey head nodded sagely as he wandered from room to room. That strange air of preparation—that freshness in the rooms and passages—a sense of wings flying down the well of the staircase, and beating the whole cubical atmosphere of the hall—these facts that had disturbed his solitude as far back as the previous December spoke to him now of the evil nature of ghosts. To minds far less fanciful than his, the creatures might have seemed the more terrible because they had arisen from renovation and progress, and not from decay. He visualised a kind of perverted fungus, growing more readily in sweet and dry places of the earth. And when he saw it like this, he shivered in the surtout, and rattled at the knees.

He wanted very earnestly to stamp out the evil. Therefore one morning, when the moon was still shining, and the whole world of Chelsover lay asleep, Whessoe crept down to the vast, shutterless library, and began to write. . . . He wrote long and laboriously, and without a pause; he wrote until the room grew cold and a breeze sighed, and shadows stretched sleepily in the garden just before dawn. It was late, very late in the day for Whessoe, with his crumpled face losing all its lines in the soft half-light, his shrunken body merging into the dark pit of the chair; and the old man put away the pen. But on the next evening he rose before midnight, and finished his letter; and his buckled shoes went noiselessly up the lichened drive.

The gate coughed and wheezed on its rusty hinges; the arched avenue beyond rained countless spears of moonlight and shadow. Screwing up his eyes, he saw that this road into Chelsover was not deserted. A figure stood by the far-distant pillar-box, a postman, collecting letters in the light of a lamp.

Whessoe halloed at him, and began to run.

"Hi-yi-yi!" But his rather thin, high voice trailed off dismally into the silence. "Hi-yi-yi!" he called. Perhaps it was difficult for people to see his spare figure amid the spears of moonlight and shadow.

"Ahoy-y-y!" shouted Whessoe again, but the postman did not hear. The fellow shouldered his bag, and bustled away; and the plum-coloured surtout and faded knee-breeches moved slowly in the direction of the pillar-box. There was no need to hurry now, there was no need at all . . . But there had been no need to hurry at any time during the whole hard business of the letter-writing. Although he waited many days, Whessoe received no answer; nobody answered the letter that he had written to the Society for Psychical Research, at immense pains, on two sheets of note-paper, craving help.

Near the end of September the equinoctial gales set in, and the dark, cavernous avenue rocked its high head, and buried its feet in a spatter of autumn leaves. And the passing residents of Chelsover stopped in their walk with a renewed wonder, lifted their eyes towards an open upper window into which the moon was shining, and muttered in their hearts: "There's that Whessoe again."

There's that strange Whessoe, as white as a sheet, crouching at the window while the winds cry *Whessoe*! The spirit is gone from the old man now. A terrible weariness is within him, left by long weeks of waiting for a letter that has not come; and anger, too deep to raise a murmur in the shrunken body, is there; and hope is near dying, and will be quite dead soon, a dead thing drifting in the wake of the Past when a few more nights have run, and Whessoe has spent his final hours of sitting in the library until the day has broken, peering over long shelves, poring over old books in the still moonshine, hunting for some record of a riddle that he is unable to solve. And always the weariness and the anger are nourished by a return of that tremendous solitude whose embracing arms seem stronger now because he can hear the ghosts' music again. Soaring, whirling, thumping, flying, the phantom tunes are crowding his nights with a fresh fury, while Whessoe sits in his room, ignored. Hell is summoning its powers to drive him away, yet all its energies are concentrated on the house. The entity of the whole place is being usurped, its blood is being sapped, the spirits of evil are taking possession, there will be no house of his in Chelsover soon. . . .

The leaves of the sycamore shiver against the moon. But the shadow in the old man's mind is deeper than the shadows of the leaves that twist, and twirl, and mould a myriad jests, the whole night long, upon the staring face.

Near the dawn of a day in late October, Whessoe found the book for which he had been searching. It was big, and heavy, and time had steeped it in a musty odour; and on its front and side, in golden lettering, these words were seen: *The Chelsover Chronicles*.

He opened it thoughtfully; peered into its pages; then, with an impish action, weighed it in his hand. A bulky book; a book that required much time for reading. Ho, ho! Utterly foolish to read it here, where at any moment the ghostly crowd might break in upon his studies! So he glided noiselessly up the staircase, with the great book tucked beneath his arm.

As soon as he had entered his bedroom, he pulled up a chair, and began to read. But the windows were closed, and the thick curtains were drawn; and the wind soothed him with its subdued thunders, so that after a time he could not keep from nodding. And because he had not found the information that he wanted, he crept into bed, and there fell asleep.

He awoke some hours later, tired and uneasy; all through his slumbers he had been haunted by the persistent knowledge that he must continue to read. He listened; and thought that he could hear shrill voices out on the old road to Chelsover—boys' whistling voices—and sometimes the clatter of cart wheels, beyond the heavy curtains. It occurred to him mildly that daylight was come. But the great book lay on a table at his bedside; he stretched out an arm, and took up the heavy volume, resting it against his propped knees.

An hour passed, and Whessoe discovered the secret of Two Gates. The print was small, on a leaf stained yellow with age; nevertheless, he was able to read it easily with his tiny, staring eyes:

". . . Let us conclude this chapter in the Chronicles of Chelsover, in the history of the Environments and of the Approaches, with the name of one Sylvester Whessoe, Colonel of Artillery, who, on his retirement from the Thunders of the Battlefield, spent the remainder of his years in the seclusion of his Ancestral Home. Doubtless the event would have been of little interest to my readers——"

He looked up suddenly, straining his ears. Voices were coming up the stairs—*their* voices, talking and laughing—

Sylvester Whessoe read on:

"—had not the aged Colonel died rather suddenly, though not very violently, by means of his own hand. A gentle dose of Chloroform, taken in the Silence of the Night——"

They were coming now. The ghosts—the ghosts—they were nearing the door. . . . He took the book under the bedclothes, pulled the sheets over his head, and still he read on—". . . taken in the Silence of the Night. . . ."

The door opened, and a girl's voice leaped into the room.

"Oh, dear!" it cried, "how dark it is! As dark as pitch!"

Footsteps hurried across the floor. Then the curtains swished back, the blinds tore up, and the vast old room was flooded with the afternoon light. Her eyes glistened as she turned to the young man at her side.

"How brave of you to want to sleep here! Yes! This is our haunted room—the room where our poor ghost lives. I've never seen him, but so I am told." She filled the place with laughter. "The bed's too terribly comfy, they say."

She shuddered a little comically as she approached it. "Behold our famous bed!" She flung back the bedclothes, piling them up.

On the cold sheet lay a heavy book, thickly coated with dust that was disturbed but lightly where the sheets had brushed it; and when she saw it lying there, her laugh went, and her heart stopped, and she stood as white as a ghost.

E.F. BENSON
The Shuttered Room

Edward Frederic Benson *(1867–1940), now best known for his "Mapp and Lucia" novels, was a long-time friend of M.R. James, and the author of four classic ghost story collections:* The Room in the Tower *(1912),* Visible and Invisible *(1923),* Spook Stories *(1928), and* More Spook Stories *(1934). Benson's home, Lamb House in Rye, appears (thinly disguised) in several of his best ghost stories, notably 'Machaon', 'Naboth's Vineyard', 'The Flint Knife', and 'The Shuttered Room'. This story originally appeared in* Weird Tales, *December 1929.*

Hugh Lister and his wife had come down from London to attend the funeral of his uncle, that strange old hermit of a man who had lived for the last year utterly recluse and indeed practically unseen in the charming Georgian house and high-walled garden, which, at his death, had now come into possession of his nephew. Two bachelor brothers, so Hugh remembered, had originally bought the place, and for some years had lived together there. But he knew almost nothing of their history, though he could recollect seeing them both, as a boy, when they spent the night at his mother's house in town on their way abroad for some piece of holiday-travel in which they annually indulged: grim, odd-looking, men, much alike, who quarrelled about the price of the tickets, and seemed considerably to dislike each other. They lived together, it appeared, because a joint establishment was cheaper than two separate houses, and they had a strong community of tastes in their love of money, and their dislike of other people. . . .

Hugh's fugitive recollection had now, after the funeral, been reinforced and amplified by a talk with Mr. Hodgkin, his uncle's solicitor, and he had learned more of these queer brothers. They had lived entirely withdrawn from the local life of this little town of Trenthorpe: no guest ever crossed their threshold, nor did they set foot at all in the houses of their neighbours. Seldom were they ever seen outside their house and garden, and, indeed, not often within, for their domestic requirements were provided by a woman who went in for a few hours every morning to make their beds and lay their breakfasts, and cook some food for their dinner, but she would be busy in the kitchen when they came downstairs, and sometimes for days together she never set eyes on either of them. Except for her, the only human being who for the last four or five years had had access to any portion of the premises was the man who had charge of the furnace in the back yard behind the house which heated the radiators through its rooms and passages. Every day throughout the year he must come in the morning and consult the thermometer which hung in a shaded nook on a wall there, and should it register below 60° Fahrenheit, the furnace must be lit, and stoked twice during the day, before he paid his final visit at ten o'clock at night, and made up a fire that would keep the house warm till morning again.

No window ever appeared to be opened in that hermitage, and seldom cleaned; the meals were of the most frugal; an overheated house and complete solitude were all that the brothers asked of life. The man and the woman who looked after their needs went for their wages every week to Mr. Hodgkin, who also discharged for the brothers their bills and paid for them the rates and taxes of the freehold house. But this dismal frugality and joylessness was not the consequence of insufficient means, for they each had an income of five or six hundred a year, of which they spent not half. The rest merely accumulated at the bank, for they made no investments. One or other of them was occasionally seen in the early morning walking by the bank of the tidal river that swept under the hill on which Trenthorpe stood, and debouched into the sea a mile or two away, but he would have returned to the house before nine in the morning, and thereafter appeared no more.

Most of this was news to Hugh and Violet: then Mr. Hodgkin went on to speak of an event which they knew had occurred, though the details had not reached them.

"That was the manner of life of your two uncles, Mr. Lister," he said, "until a year ago when the mysterious disappearance of the younger, Mr. Henry, took place. I had just come downstairs one morning, and was beginning my breakfast when Mr. Robert, whose funeral we have just attended, was announced. He had found the front door of his house, which, as you will presently see when we visit it, is secured by a multitude of bolts and locks and chains, standing wide open. It had not been forced from outside, for the bolts had been withdrawn from within. He called to his brother, but got no answer, and ascending to his room, found that it was empty. His bed had been slept in, his instruments of toilet had been used, but there was no trace of him anywhere either in the house or the garden. It seemed most likely, therefore, that it was he who had gone out, leaving the door wide, but this was so extraordinary a thing for him to have done that Mr. Robert instantly came round to tell me about it. It struck me also as so odd that I rang up the police office, search and enquiries were made, and within an hour a cloth cap, which Mr. Robert identified as belonging to his brother, was found on the bank of the river, where sometimes he walked, and next day his walking-stick was found at low tide on a sand-shoal a mile farther down. The tide—it was one of the big spring-tides—had been at the flood about five o'clock in the morning on which he disappeared, and assuming that he left the house soon after that, it must have been running very strong to the sea, and the river was dragged without result. Then came further evidence, for a labourer in the town who had gone out to work at day-break, said that he had seen a man, answering to the description which was circulated, crossing the bridge above the bank where the cap was found."

"Was it supposed to have been an accident?" asked Hugh.

"There was not sufficient evidence to make that clear. It is possible that Mr. Henry might have slipped while walking along the bank, for the ground was very miry: on the other hand, Mr. Robert, in the statement he made to the police, said that for several days his brother had been very queer in his behaviour, and possibly it was suicide, but there could, of course, be no inquest, since the body was never found. Death was presumed after the due legal period, and by the will which both your uncles had made, which was in my keeping, and by which the survivor of the two was named as the heir of the deceased, Mr. Henry's property passed to his brother. That was completed only a few days ago. Previously to that, Mr. Robert, as you know, had made a further will under which you inherit."

Mr. Hodgkin paused a moment, but Hugh had no question to put to him, and he continued in the same even voice.

"After Mr. Henry's disappearance," he said, "your surviving uncle became more recluse than ever, and once only, as far as I am aware, he left his house and garden, and that was when he came to see me to make his will. The charwoman continued to go in every morning, but now she hardly ever saw him. He moved from the bedroom upstairs next to Mr. Henry's, both of which looked out on to the garden, and occupied a small room on the ground floor looking out on to the street, and the two bedrooms upstairs were locked and the keys were in his keeping. He similarly locked the two corresponding rooms on the ground floor which look on to the garden, though he used them himself, and the charwoman left his food on a small table in the hall outside, and he took it in after she had gone, putting the plates and utensils he had used in the same place for her to wash up next day. Her range, in fact, was entirely confined to the kitchen and your uncle's bedroom, from which he had always gone into one of the locked rooms on the ground floor before she arrived. If he wanted anything ordered for him, there would be a note for her on the table by his bed stating his requirements. So it went on till last Thursday, the day of his death."

Again the lawyer paused.

"It is a painful and terrible account I have to give you, Mr. Lister," he said. "She went to his bedroom as usual, and found him crouching in a corner of the room, and he screamed out with fright, she said, when he saw her, and kept crying out: 'No, no! have mercy on me, Henry!' Like a sensible woman she ran straight for the doctor, and as she went past his window, she heard him still screaming. Dr. Soleham was in, and came at once: your uncle was still in some wild access of terror, and he slipped by them, and ran out into the street. Then quite suddenly he spun round and collapsed. They brought him back into the house, and in a few minutes it was all over."

Such was the grim manner in which Hugh Lister entered into his inheritance: it was all horrible and mysterious enough, but no question of personal grief or loss came into it, since he was practically a stranger to these queer relations of his. Mr. Hodgkin went into other business matters with him; there was a considerable sum of money which was his, also this house and garden, of which the house, so the lawyer told him, was in a state of the most hideous dilapidation and disrepair. Of the garden he knew nothing, for though it stood in the middle of the little town, its high brick walls screened it from all scrutiny of the houses round, and the rooms which looked on to it from the house had long been kept locked. Hugh and his wife slept that night at an inn, and next morning Mr. Hodgkin called to take them over the property.

Pitiable indeed was the neglect into which this charming and dignified little mansion had fallen. The roof leaked in a dozen places, the mildewed paper was peeling off the walls, the carpets were rotted by damp and drip: here they were faded by the sun, here they were mere rags and ribands. The casement bars of the windows were perished, the panes so crusted with dust and spiders' webs that scarce a glimpse of the street outside could be seen; doors sagged on their hinges; a litter of sticks and straws from the nests of starlings that had built in the chimneys littered the hearths; pictures had fallen from the walls and lay in fragments of splintered glass and broken frames on the floor. Then there were the four locked rooms which looked on to the garden, two upstairs and two below, to be explored. A bunch of keys was found in the bedroom below, which Robert Lister had used, and they began their investigations upstairs, starting with the first door on the landing: this was the room, the charwoman told them, which Mr. Henry had occupied, and which had been locked ever since his disappearance.

The key grated rustily in the boards, but soon the door stood open, and they saw that the room was quite dark, for the windows were shuttered. A little fumbling revealed the fastenings, and Hugh, throwing them open, gave an exclamation of surprise. For the room, though long closed and neglected, with sagging ceiling and damp-stained walls, bore all signs of use: the bed-clothes, coverlet and blankets and moldy sheets were still on the bed, half-turned back, as if its occupant had only just left it. On the washstand were sponge and tooth-brush, and beside it on the floor stood a brass hot-water can, green with verdigris: in the window was a dressing-table with a looking-glass, blurred and foggy, and by it a pair of hair-brushes and a shaving-brush, and a rusty razor with the dried stain of soap on the blade. There were a couple of pairs of boots, efflorescent with grey mildew below it; the chest of drawers was full of clothes. Nothing had been touched since the morning when Henry Lister left it, not to return.

Violet felt a sudden qualm of misgiving, coming from she knew not what secret cell in her brain. The room, with its dead air and vanished occupant, was still horribly alive. She moved across to the window, with the notion of throwing it open, so that the wholesome morning breeze could enter. The windows from having been shuttered were less opaquely coated with dust than those below, and she saw what lay outside.

"Hugh, look at the garden," she called. "It's a perfect jungle: paths, lawn, flower-beds all covered with the wild."

He peered out.

"There's a job in front of us then," he said. "But we'll take that after we've been through the house. It's a queer room, this, Vi."

The chamber next door was as queer: this was the bedroom, said the charwoman, which Mr. Robert had occupied when the two brothers were living together in the house. At Mr. Henry's disappearance he had moved on to the ground floor into the room which he used until the day of his death. This upper room had been locked up since then: she had not seen it since the day when Mr. Robert had slept downstairs. His bed had been moved down, his wardrobe and his washing-stand: a couple of crazy chairs alone now stood there, and as in the room next door, the shutters were closed when they entered. Mr. Robert, she told them, had forbidden her to go upstairs any more when Mr. Henry left them. Three more bedrooms, all absolutely empty of furniture, and a bathroom with brown stains down the side of the bath below the taps, completed this floor: the bedrooms had never been furnished at all, as far as she knew, and yet, for all the emptiness of this story of the house, it seemed to Violet as if something followed them as they went downstairs again.

There remained for exploration the two rooms on the ground-floor which looked out on to the garden, and which for the last year had always been kept locked: these were scarcely more fit for human habitation than the rest. The dust lay thick everywhere, the carpet was in rags, the windows bleared with dirt. One must have been Robert Lister's dining-room, for there were pieces of crockery and cutlery on the table, a glass, and a half-empty bottle of whisky, a jug of water and a salt-cellar, and a few tattered books were scattered on the floor beside it. One window looked out on to the street, and on the wall at right angles to that a glass-paned door led out into the garden. This was bolted at top and bottom; evidently it had long been in disuse for entrance and egress, and it was with difficulty that Hugh managed to push the bolts back into their rusty grooves. When that was done, he wrenched the door open, and it was good to let a breath of the sweet untainted air of outside penetrate into that sick and deadened atmosphere.

"My uncle never went out into the town, you tell me," he said to Mr. Hodgkin, "and we can see that he never went into the garden. He must have lived indoors altogether, and indoors he never set foot upstairs. Good God! it's ghastly: just these three rooms with no presence there except his own. Enough to drive a man mad. And yet he chose to do it. . . . What's that?"

He turned round as he spoke, wheeling quickly, and went out into the hall outside. But there was nothing there; a stair perhaps had creaked, or perhaps it was the yellow-underwing moth that flapped against the pane that made him think that there was something astir.

The garden into which they now stepped was, as Violet had said, a mere jungle of wild and riotous growth, but it was easy to see how delectable a plot it must have been, and to feel what overgrown charms still lingered there. It was spacious for an enclosed space like this, with streets and houses all round it, a liberal acre in extent, and defended by its high brick walls from any intrusive eye. From no quarter could it be overlooked, so tall was its mellowed fencing, and only the peaks of house-roofs and their chimneys and the vane on the church-tower peered above the copings. A broad strip of flower-bed had once sunned itself along the house-front, bordered by box-hedging; a paved walk led by it, and beyond had been a stretch of lawn up to the farther wall. To the left the plot had once been divided by a trellis that now leaned tipsily askew this way and that, with great gaps in it, through which could be seen fruit-trees, now in flower, on this spring afternoon: there no doubt had been the kitchen-garden. But now rank weeds and grasses had triumphed over everything on lawn and border; the paved walk was plumed with them and thickly overlaid with mosses; creepers that must once have been trained up the walls sprawled fallen across the ground-growths, and tendrils of degenerated rose-trees threaded their thorns through the shrubby clumps of the box-edgings.

The two men pushed across the lawn through briers and thick grasses and entanglements, but Violet said she had had enough and sat down to wait for them on a stone bench, crumbled and mossy, which stood on the edge of the paved walk. The charm of the place struggled with the melancholy disorder of it, and she could imagine it cultivated and cared for, with its beds glowing again with ordered jewels, its lawn smooth-napped, its paved walks free of the tangle of growth, but there was something more than this tangle of weeds that had to be cleared away before peace could return to it. Something beyond mere neglect was amiss with it; something dead but horribly alive was watching her even as in the shuttered room at the head of the stairs. . . .

The stone seat faced the sun, and a little dazzled by its brightness, though delighting in the genial warmth of it after the airless seclusion of the house, Violet closed her eyes, wondering what it could be that wrought this strange perturbation within her. Hugh and Mr. Hodgkin had vanished now behind the crazy trellis; their voices no longer came to her, and she felt extraordinarily sundered from the touch of human intercourse. And yet she was not alone: there was some presence, not theirs, moving up closer to her and watching her. Once she opened her eyes to reassure herself that it was only her imagination thus playing tricks with her, but of course there was nothing there, and again she closed them. An odd drowsiness invaded her, and she saw a shadow come across the red field of her closed eyelids. She thought to herself that the two men were approaching her, and that it was they who had come between her and the sun, and she waited for the sound of their voices or their steps. Perhaps Hugh thought she was asleep, and meant to give her forty winks or so: if that was in his mind, she wished he would stand aside, for with him cutting off the sunlight from her, the air had become very cold. She gave a little shiver, and opened her eyes. There was no one there.

It was startling: she had felt quite sure there had been someone standing close in front of her, but it certainly was not Hugh, nor indeed was there any sign of a living presence. But there he was, stepping over the fallen trellis, and coming quickly toward her.

"Violet, dear," he said, "isn't the place utterly enchanting? I'm going to have all the rags and rubbish turned out of the house at once, and get it washed and cleaned and renewed. I shall furnish it, too, and put a caretaker in, and then we'll bring the garden into order again. Then when it's all habitable we can settle what we shall do with it, let it, or sell it, or keep it. What extraordinary odd fellows they must have been, living in squalor and discomfort and letting everything go to ruin! But I shall restore it all with the money they saved over it. And frankly, I've fallen in love with the place: I want to keep it terribly."

Hugh set to work with his usual volcanic energy to put the place in order again: he and Violet took rooms at the inn near, and spent hot and laborious days in turning out the dirty raffle that filled the house, reserving for later examination any papers that might possibly be of interest. All the upholstery was perished;

carpets, curtains and rugs were only fit for the fire: there were cupboards, and presses full of threadbare stuffs, moth-eaten blankets and moldy linen, and a clean sweep had to be made of all these before the cleaning and redecoration of the house could begin. Day after day a bonfire in the kitchen-garden smoldered and burst into flames and smoldered again, for little even of the solider furniture was serviceable: rickety tables and broken-seated chairs seemed to have been sufficient for the uncles. After that the walls must be stripped of their torn and flapping papers, and scraped of their discoloured paint, the roof must be repaired, ceilings and fittings of doors and windows renovated. To Violet all this holocaust of moldy raffles signified something more than the mere material cleaning-up, even as the opening of windows long-closed and the admission into the house of the air and the sun and the wholesome winds did more than refresh the staleness of its actual atmosphere: both were symbolical outward signs of some interior purging. And yet, even when all was clean and empty, ready for its new furnishing, the very essence of what they had been turning out still lingered. All was not well with the house: in some strange manner the shadow that had come between her closed eyes and the sun as she sat on the garden-bench had entered, and was establishing itself more firmly day by day.

She knew how fantastic such a notion was, and so, though it persisted, she could not bring herself to speak to Hugh about it. It haunted the rooms and the passages, and though she got no direct vision of its presence it was there, like some shy creature wary in hiding itself, but yet wishing to make itself manifest: sometimes it seemed malignant, sometimes sad and pitiful. Most of all it was perceptible in that pleasant square room at the top of the stairs which they had found shuttered, where the bedclothes were turned back as if he who had slept there had just quitted it, and where the apparatus of a man's toilet still lay on the dressing-table: the room, so the charwoman had told them, occupied by Henry Lister. Had this presence something to do with him, she wondered? She felt it also in the room downstairs occupied after his disappearance by Robert: there she felt it as something fierce or revengeful. Finally she began to wonder whether Hugh was conscious that there was something queer in that room at the head of the stairs, for at first he had intended to make his private den there, but he had abandoned that, and though the furnishing of the house was proceeding apace he had left it empty.

It was early in May that the house was ready to be occupied in a tentative picnicking fashion: vans had been unloading all day, a couple of servants had come down, and tonight Hugh and Violet were to sleep here, for to be on the premises, said Hugh, was the surest way of speeding such tasks as picture-hanging and carpet-laying. The dusk of the evening was warm, and he and Violet were sitting on the stone bench in the garden with a box of papers between them which must be looked through before they could be consigned to the bonfire. The garden was rapidly being tamed, the lawn had been scythed in preparation for the mowing-machine, the paved walk had been cleared of moss, and weeding was going on in the beds.

"But the soil is wretched and sour," said Hugh, as he untied a bundle of papers. "That bed by the house must be dug over deep and a cartload of rich stuff put in before it's fit for planting. Hullo, a photograph . . . Why, it's of the two uncles, and was taken here in the garden. They're sitting on the stone bench where we are now. Before they became hermits, I suppose."

Violet looked over his shoulder.

"Which is Uncle Robert?" she said.

"That one on the left, the older of the two, the bald one."

"And the other the one who disappeared?" asked Violet.

"Yes."

He looked up quickly as he spoke, and Violet, following his eye, thought she saw for a moment in the dusk some figure standing on the paved walk twenty yards away. But it resolved itself into a pale stain on the wall and a bush immediately below, and she took another glance at the faded photograph. There was a strong family resemblance between them; she would have guessed that the two faces, rather long-nosed, with eyes very wide apart, were those of brothers, but they were quite distinguishable.

Presently Hugh came to the end of the packet, and he took the bulk of it to toss on to the smoldering bonfire. The evening was now beginning to get chilly, and when he had gone she rose and took a turn down the paved walk. The light from the west glowed dusky-red on the brick front of the house, and glancing idly up at the window of the room at the head of the stairs, she saw a man standing there within, looking down on her. The glimpse she got of his face was but brief, for almost immediately he turned away, but she had seen enough to know that it was the face of the younger of the two brothers at whose photograph she had just been looking.

For one moment sheer terror clutched at her: the next, as if by some subtle recognition her mind told her that here was the visible manifestation of the presence of which she had for days been conscious. It was he who had shadowed her closed eyelids, it was he who, as yet unseen, had haunted the house, and in especial the room at the window of which she now beheld him. Though the flesh of her still quaked at the thought that she had looked on one who had passed beyond the dread dim gate, it was terribly interesting, and she continued looking up, half dreading, half hoping that she would see him again. Then she heard Hugh's step returning from his errand.

"What's the matter, Violet?" he said. "You're white: your hands are trembling."

She pulled herself together.

"It's nothing," she said. "Something startled me just now."

Looking at him, she guessed with a sense of certainty what was in his mind when he asked her what was the matter.

"Hughie, have you seen something too that—that comes from beyond?" she asked.

He shook his head.

"No, but I know it's there," he said, "and it's chiefly in that room at the top of the stairs. That's why I've done nothing with it. Have you seen it? Was it that which startled you just now? What was it?"

She pointed to the window.

"There," she said. "A man looked out on me from the window. It was Henry Lister. His room, you know."

They were both looking up now, and even as she spoke the figure appeared there again. Once more it turned away, and vanished.

For a long moment they met each other's eyes.

"Violet, are you frightened?" he said.

"I'm not going to be," she said. "Whatever it is, whatever it's here for, it can't hurt us. I think it wants us to do something for it . . . But, Hughie, why did Robert scream out 'Have mercy?' Why did he run from the house?"

Hugh had no answer for this.

"I shall go in," he said at length, "and open the door of that room, and see what is there. I left it locked, I know. Don't come with me, Violet."

"But I wish to," she said; "I want to know all that there is to be known. What we have seen means something."

They went upstairs together, and paused for a second outside the door. The key was in the lock, and Hugh turned it and threw the door wide.

The room was lit by the fading evening light, but clearly visible. It was completely furnished as on the day when they had first looked into it. On the bed there lay the figure of a man faintly twitching. His face was turned away, but with a final movement his head fell back on the pillows, and they saw who it was. The mouth drooped open, the cheeks and forehead were of a mottled purple in colour, and round the neck was tied a cord . . . And then they saw that they were looking into a perfectly empty room, unfurnished, but newly papered and painted.

The deep digging-over of the flower-bed along the house front began next morning, and an hour later the gardener came in to tell Hugh what he had found. The digging was resumed under the supervision of the police-inspector, and the body when disinterred was removed to the mortuary. The identity was established at the inquest; it was established also that death had been due to strangulation, for a piece of rope was still tied round the neck. Though there could be no absolute certainty as to the history of the murder, only one reconstruction of it would fit the facts which were known; namely, that Henry Lister had been strangled by his brother during the night preceding his disappearance, and buried in the garden. Very early next morning Robert Lister, who in height and general appearance strongly resembled his brother, must have gone down to the river-bank (having been seen on his way there by the laborer from the town) and left his cap on the path, and thrown the stick into the river. He must also with a diabolical cunning have arranged his brother's room to look as if he had got up and dressed himself as usual. He then returned, and an hour or two later went to Mr. Hodgkin's house, saying that he had found the front door open, and that his brother was missing. No search was made in the house or garden, for the evidence all pointed to his having dressed and gone out and met his death in the river. Why Robert Lister in that seizure of panic which gripped him just before he died called on his brother to have mercy on him was no affair for police investigation, but it seems likely that he saw, or thought he saw, some very terrible thing, some strange spectre such as was certainly seen by Hugh and

Violet in the room at the top of the stairs. But that is conjecture only.

The two brothers now lie side by side in the cemetery on the hill outside Trenthorpe: it may be added that in all England there is no more wholesome or tranquil house than that which was once the scene of so tragic a history and of so grim and ghostly a manifestation.

AMBROSE BIERCE
An Inhabitant of Carcosa

Ambrose Bierce *(1842–1914?), the brilliant American journalist, was portrayed on screen by Gregory Peck in* The Old Gringo. *'An Inhabitant of Carcosa' is one of the most influential stories in nineteenth century supernatural fiction, alongside other Bierce classics 'An Occurrence at Owl Creek Bridge' and 'The Middle Toe of the Right Foot.'*

For there be divers sort of death – some wherein the body remaineth; and in some it vanisheth quite away with the spirit. This commonly occurreth only in solitude (such is God's will) and, none seeing the end, we say the man is lost, or gone on a long journey – which indeed he hath; but sometimes it hath happened in sight of many, as abundant testimony showeth. In one kind of death the spirit also dieth, and this it hath been known to do while yet the body was in vigour for many years. Sometimes, as is veritably attested, it dieth with the body, but after a season is raised up again in that place where the body did decay.

Pondering these words of Hali (whom God rest) and questioning their full meaning, as one who, having an intimation, yet doubts if there be not something behind, other than that which he has discerned, I noted not whither I had strayed until a sudden chill wind striking my face revived in me a sense of my surroundings. I observed with astonishment that everything seemed unfamiliar. On every side of me stretched a bleak and desolate expanse of plain, covered with a tall overgrowth of sere grass, which rustled and whistled in the autumn wind with Heaven knows what mysterious and disquieting suggestion. Protruded at long intervals above it, stood strangely shaped and sombre-coloured rocks, which seemed to have an understanding with one another and to exchange looks of uncomfortable significance, as if they had reared their heads to watch the issue of some foreseen event. A few blasted trees here and there appeared as leaders in this malevolent conspiracy of silent expectation.

The day, I thought, must be far advanced, though the sun was invisible; and although sensible that the air was raw and chill my consciousness of that fact was rather mental than physical – I had no feeling of discomfort. Over all the dismal landscape a canopy of low, lead-coloured clouds hung like a visible curse. In all this there was a menace and a portent – a hint of evil, an intimation of doom. Bird, beast, or insect there was none. The wind sighed in the bare branches of the dead trees and the grey grass bent to whisper its dread secret to the earth; but no other sound nor motion broke the awful repose of that dismal place.

I observed in the herbage a number of weather-worn stones, evidently shaped with tools. They were broken, covered with moss and half sunken in the earth. Some lay prostrate, some leaned at various angles, none was vertical. They were obviously headstones of graves, though the graves themselves no longer existed as either mounds or depressions; the years had levelled all. Scattered here and there, more massive blocks showed where some pompous tomb or ambitious monument had once flung its feeble defiance at oblivion. So old seemed these relics, these vestiges of vanity and memorials of affection and piety, so battered and worn and stained – so neglected, deserted, forgotten the place, that I could not help thinking myself the discoverer of the burial-ground of a prehistoric race of men whose very name was long extinct.

Filled with these reflections, I was for some time heedless of the sequence of my own experiences, but soon I thought, "How came I hither?" A moment's reflection seemed to make this all clear and explain at the same time, though in a disquieting way, the singular character with which my fancy had invested all that I saw or heard. I was ill. I remembered now that I had been prostrated by a sudden fever, and that my family had told me that in my periods of delirium I had constantly cried out for liberty and air, and had been held in bed to prevent my escape out-of-doors. Now I had eluded the vigilance of my attendants and had wandered hither to – to where? I could not conjecture. Clearly I was at a considerable distance from the city where I dwelt – the ancient and famous city of Carcosa.

No signs of human life were anywhere visible nor audible; no rising smoke, no watch-dog's bark, no lowing of cattle, no shouts of children at play – nothing but that dismal burial-place, with its air of mystery and dread, due to my own disordered brain. Was I not becoming again delirious, there beyond human aid? Was it not indeed *all* an illusion of my madness? I called aloud the names of my wives and sons, reached out my hands in search of theirs, even as I walked among the crumbling stones and in the withered grass.

A noise behind me caused me to turn about. A wild animal – a lynx – was approaching. The thought came to me: if I break down here in the desert – if the fever return and I fail, this beast will be at my throat. I sprang toward it, shouting. It trotted tranquilly by within a hand's-breadth of me and disappeared behind a rock.

A moment later a man's head appeared to rise out of the ground a short distance away. He was ascending the farther slope of a low hill whose crest was hardly to be distinguished from the general level. His whole figure soon came into view against the background of grey cloud. He was half naked, half clad in skins. His hair was unkempt, his beard long and ragged. In one hand he carried a bow and arrow; the other held a blazing torch with a long trail of black smoke. He walked slowly and with caution, as if he feared falling into some open grave concealed by the tall grass. This strange apparition surprised but did not alarm, and taking such a course as to intercept him I met him almost face to face, accosting him with the familiar salutation, "God keep you."

He gave no heed, nor did he arrest his pace.

"Good stranger," I continued, "I am ill and lost. Direct me, I beseech you, to Carcosa."

The man broke into a barbarous chant in an unknown tongue, passing on and away.

An owl on the branch of a decayed tree hooted dismally and was answered by another in the distance. Looking upward, I saw through a sudden rift in the clouds Alderbaran and the Hyades! In all this there was a hint of night – the lynx, the man with the torch, the owl. Yet I saw – I saw even the stars in absence of the darkness. I saw, but was apparently not seen nor heard. Under what awful spell did I exist?

I seated myself at the root of a great tree, seriously to consider what it were best to go. That I was mad I could no longer doubt, yet recognized a ground of doubt in the conviction. Of fever I had no trace. I had, withal, a sense of exhilaration and vigour altogether unknown to me – a feeling of mental and physical exaltation. My senses seemed all alert; I could feel the air as a ponderous substance; I could hear the silence.

A great root of the giant tree against whose trunk I leaned as I sat held enclosed in its grasp a slab of stone, a part of which protruded into a recess formed by another root. The stone was thus partly protected from the weather, though greatly decomposed. Its edges were worn round, its corners eaten away, its surface deeply furrowed and scaled. Glittering particles of mica were visible in the earth about it – vestiges of its decomposition. This stone had apparently marked the grave out of which the tree had sprung ages ago. The tree's exacting roots had robbed the grave and made the stone a prisoner.

A sudden wind pushed some dry leaves and twigs from the uppermost face of the stone; I saw the low-relief letters of an inscription and bent to read it. God in heaven! *my* name in full – the date of *my* birth! – the date of *my* death!

A level shaft of light illuminated the whole side of the tree as I sprang to my feet in terror. The sun was rising in the rosy east. I stood between the tree and his broad red disk – no shadow darkened the trunk!

A chorus of howling wolves saluted the dawn. I saw them sitting on their haunches, singly and in groups, on the summits of irregular mounds and tumuli filling a half of my desert prospect and extending to the horizon. And then I knew that these were ruins of the ancient and famous city of Carcosa.

Such are the facts imparted to the medium Bayrolles by the spirit Hoseib Alar Robardin.

CHARLES BIRKIN

"Is There Anybody There?"

Sir Charles Birkin *(1907–85) contributed several horror stories to the* Creeps *series (1932–36) as 'Charles Lloyd', and made a comeback to the genre after retirement thirty years later with seven paperback original collections comprising over 80 tales. Nearly all these concentrate on* grand guignol *physical, non-supernatural horror, but among them can be found a small number of excellent ghost stories. "Is There Anybody There?" is taken from* The Smell of Evil *(1965).*

"Is there anybody there?"

Millie Ackland knew that she was all alone in the cottage. It had been stupid of her to call out, but she could not help feeling nervous. She had pretended to Ida that she had not minded her going off to London for two nights. She had told her that she did not mind in the very least, and that of course she would be all right, perfectly all right she had repeated with emphasis. What could possibly happen to her? She appreciated her solicitude, but honestly there was no need for it.

She had said what Ida had wished her to say, and had felt a little heroic. It was unfortunate that Ida was ignorant of the extent of her heroism. No doubt she had reassured herself about Millie's safety with the fact that their neighbours, the Kearnons, lived only a few yards away, to the left of the blue gate at the bottom of the path. Blue had been Ida's choice—everyone else had their gates painted green or white, so why should they not show some originality? Then there was Monica Findhorn, whose house was on the other side, and who could actually look into their garden from her bathroom window. There was no reason for apprehension, how could there be? Ida must go off to her cousin and enjoy herself as she had arranged, and there was no more to be said.

Millie Ackland and Ida Rankin had shared Rosemary Cottage for the past two years, and they had done a great deal to improve it, more, in fact, than they had been able to afford. They had installed a bathroom and an up-to-date kitchen and had built on a lean-to glasshouse on the south side, and they had hermasealed the warped windows, which nobody could deny had been essential for health as well as for comfort, and which could not be regarded as having been an extravagance.

Millie had known Ida since they had been at Hatchdean together more than fifty years ago. It sounded so antediluvian when she said it aloud, which she did sometimes, to hear the gratifying astonishment that was her listeners' reaction. "Ida and I," she would boast, "have known one another for more than half a century, since we first met in the Lower Fourth at Hatchdean in nineteen hundred and six!" And it was true. They had always "kept up", and when the time had come for their respective retirements from the scholastic careers which each had chosen what could have been more natural than for them to decide to enjoy the closing years of their lives in one another's company. "Ida may have her shortcomings," Millie often said with a twinkle, "but then so have I, and we have no unpleasant shocks in store for one another as sometimes happens to newlyweds!" She meant nothing peculiar by this announcement.

Ida had been headmistress at Moatlands, an expensive and rather snobbish school which had grown even more militantly exclusive after the arrival there of several of the European princesses. Millie herself had never been officially a headmistress, but on occasion had acted as such at Charleville House when there had been illness among the staff. Charleville House had been intended originally for the daughters of the clergy and professional classes and Millie considered it to be, both in education and in games, far in advance of Moatlands. She did not of course say this to dear Ida. The majority of the Charleville girls had had to work in later life and had been trained to become useful, self reliant and cultured citizens.

Rosemary Cottage had, to begin with, been a labourer's dwelling with, in house agents' parlance, 'two up and two down'. That was before they had added the improvements. The 'down' which had been the former kitchen, was now the dining-room, and the new kitchen, with a communicating hatch, had been built on at the back underneath the bathroom. It was all most convenient.

They had bought the cottage for fifteen hundred pounds which, in view of its deplorable condition and lack of amenities, they had considered to be daylight robbery, but they had been assured that it had in point of fact been a bargain. Millie gravely doubted if her father, the Reverend Maurice Ackland, had he been alive, would have regarded it as such, but then values had changed and everything had become so terribly dear.

Monica Findhorn had had the nerve to tell them that they had managed to get it so 'cheaply' owing to its 'reputation'. Ida had looked at her with quizzically raised eyebrows waiting for her to explain herself, and when she had failed to do so she had said humorously: "Are you implying, dear Miss Findhorn, that our sweet cottage used to be the local house of ill fame?"

Miss Findhorn had smiled and shaken her head, sharing in the joke. "No, Miss Rankin, I am not! It is supposed to be haunted. A young ploughman is said to have murdered his wife soon after the end of the first war. It was before my day. There was a lot of speculation, and although some people declared that he was innocent and that it was a case of *cherchez la femme* he was executed for the crime, and is said to be 'earthbound'! Since then Rosemary Cottage has changed hands no less than three times. You know how superstitious villagers can be about such matters, especially in East Anglia." She had busied herself with the teapot. "For you ladies," she went on playfully, "the idiotic tale has proved most beneficial for, as you know, the price of property around here has risen scandalously! He worked for the Fillingham family," she finished inconsequently.

"I am not likely to lose any sleep over your revelations," Ida had said. "There is not a house in the country that has not been the scene of a death, and the older the building the more of them it must have witnessed."

"But not deaths by violence," Millie had put in. "When did it happen, Miss Findhorn?"

"In twenty-one . . . twenty-two? I'm afraid I can't tell you the precise date. But it was on Midsummer Eve. And please will you call me Monica, both of you. I hope that we may be good friends as well as near neighbours."

Ida had laughed about it on their way home. "We are apparently indebted to Piers Plowman for getting us a real bargain!" she had said. "It's an ill wind . . . not that it was not bad luck on the wretched victim." She had no patience with the psychic world. She had once misguidedly attended a séance and it had been perfectly obvious to her that the medium, a woman, had been an outrageous fraud. Tommy-rot!

She was not certain that Millie altogether shared her views, for, although the dear thing had known better than to express openly any such beliefs, she had been known to drop hints. Ida suspected that Millie thought herself receptive to vibrations from the Other World and that she was rather proud of it, as it made her feel superior, like claims of being 'old souls' always heartened reincarnationists and made them quite insufferable. Millie naturally refrained from parading her fanciful theories for she knew that if she did so they would inevitably receive short shrift.

Millicent Ackland had, with difficulty, kept her accomplishment to herself. She was devoted to Ida and would do nothing which might annoy or vex her, or which could endanger the harmony of their lives together, and it was for this reason that she had resolved to hold her tongue.

She had begun to hear things the very evening after they had been to tea with Monica Findhorn. Perhaps, she thought, it had been Miss Findhorn's disclosures that had opened the door of her awareness, had tuned her in to the right wavelength. She would have known in any case that the house was haunted, but the knowledge might not have come to her so soon.

At first she had caught only a few disjointed and whispered words, and weeks and sometimes months had gone by before she had heard more; but with the passing of time the voices had grown gradually more distinct and had come to her with more regularity, and recently she had begun to think that if she were to turn her head quickly enough she would be able to catch sight of the speakers.

She tried to do so now. "Is there anybody there?" she called. She knew that with the supernatural one must never show fear.

There were four of them; she had discovered that very early on. A man, two women and a child. When they spoke to one another Millie was usually alone in a room, but of late they had started to do so even when Ida had been seated opposite to her, reading or knitting or engaged in solving a crossword puzzle, but invariably Ida had appeared sublimely unconscious of anything untoward and Millie had hesitated to alarm her or to draw down upon herself the pungent dryness of her tolerant rebuke.

Beyond Miss Findhorn's somewhat vague statement that a murder had taken place in their cottage Millie had had no very clear picture of the personalities concerned, but by now the characters were familiar to her to the extent that she was sometimes tempted to take part in the dialogue.

There was Adam Loft, the dominant figure who, from what she had heard and subsequently observed, had been a handsome, conceited and hard-drinking man with a controlled but bullying nature. There was his wife, Nancy, a young woman of dull mind who subconsciously rejoiced in being downtrodden, and who gave every evidence of being a mental and physical slattern. Then there was their child, Lucy, a tiresome little girl who was alternately spoiled and punished by her father and nagged at by her mother.

Millie found Judith Cromer the most interesting. She was having an affair with Adam. She lived in the village, was unmarried, and was obviously terrified that her family would discover the liaison in which she was engaged. She was quite intelligent, but her judgement had been clouded by her overwhelming sexual desire. She had been trying to persuade Adam to emigrate with her to Australia. Millie knew that he had no intention of doing so, and she knew also that he was a man of considerable obstinacy. All that he wanted to do was to continue his cohabitation with Judith in his own house and on his own terms, and to prevent his wife and Judith's parents from finding out about their relationship.

Millie acknowledged that, in spite of herself, despite her natural alarm, she was growing more and more interested and involved in the lives of these people, just as some viewers are inextricably netted by the enthralling dramas of television serials. She knew that she should switch off, but was incapable of closing her mind. She had been jockeyed into being an unwilling eavesdropper and it had not been of her own choosing, and she began to fear that she might easily find herself slipping into the role of *voyeur* of scenes and also of actions that were for the eyes of the participants alone.

She remembered the first snatch of talk which she had overheard. There had been the slam of a door and the man had said to his wife: "*I don't know what you do with yourself all day, Nance, honest I don't. Lucy looks like a gypsy, and the house is no better than a slum. There's not even a hot meal on the table, and nought in the oven, I'll bet. Search me why I married you. Must have been off my rocker.*" He had spoken with unconcealed bitterness.

And Nancy had answered him: "*I'm out of sorts, Adam. Really I am. It's the headache. Somehow it don't seem to lift, no matter what. Lucy's been that trying, you've no idea. If it's not one thing it's another. I'll be glad when she gets off to school."* She had paused and there had been the sound of sniffing. *"And I'll be gladder still when she's old enough to go into service, 'tho that won't be for a long while yet, not for another nine years. I try to do my best, Lord knows."*

There had been a silence, then the man had said roughly: *"Just look at you! Like something the cat brought in. You might be fifty, not thirty. You can't be bothered with cooking or cleaning, and you're always tired out."*

The voices had grown indistinct, and Ida had come in and stripped off her gardening gloves and had said: "We must order some more coal so as to be ready for the winter. Do remind me, Millie. Oh, and Miss Findhorn—Monica, I should say—telephoned while you were at the chemist's this morning. I forgot to tell you. She wondered if we would take charge of the tombola at the church fete in July. I told her that we would be delighted to do so. Did I do right, Millie?" She had smiled kindly, aware that her friend enjoyed the companionship of such social activities.

Adam Loft's voice had been very different when he had been talking to Judith Cromer. It was slower and softer and took on a caressing and deeper slur. Not that he was in the habit of speaking a great deal when they were together. It seemed to Millie that it was the girl who did most of the talking. On each occasion when Judith called there were just the two of them. Nancy and Lucy were always out.

After they had made love, and Millie was perfectly aware that this was the sole object of Judith's visits, the girl would keep on pestering Adam about his leaving Nancy and going away with her to start a new life. *"Nobody would know us,"* she used to say, *"if we went overseas, we could make a fresh start. Nancy's no good to you, Adam, and you know it. She'll only drag you down to her own level. You don't love her, and she loves nobody but herself. She's not got it in her. She'll ruin you, mark my words. Don't I mean anything to you, darling? We could be someone if we went to Canada or Australia. Achieve something. There's wonderful openings in the Colonies for people like us. I had a letter from John only yesterday. He and Doris are doing ever so well in Vancouver."*

Adam had avoided replying directly to these urgings. Instead there had been sounds of kissing and half-hearted protests and the creaking of leather which, Millie thought, must have come from the old hide sofa which she and Ida had found abandoned in an outhouse, and which, the cost of repair having proved exorbitant, they had subsequently sold at an auction on the Green for ten shillings.

And so the story had unfolded. There were no twists, no unexpected developments. Adam's affair with Judith gathered momentum; his irritation with, and dislike of, his wife increased, as did the mounting tediousness of his child's behaviour, which maddened him and frayed his nerves. Then, a few days before Ida's proposed visit to London, Judith had come to Adam and told him that she was pregnant. Millie had not heard this scene before. She did not think that the girl was unduly distressed by this occurrence, no doubt largely because the circumstance might enable her to force Adam's hand, and rather to her surprise the young man, after a brief outburst of impatient disgruntlement, had taken the news quite well and had made no effort to dispute her claim of his paternity.

The events which she overheard were not, to Millie's annoyance, always in continuity. She was anxious to know the outcome, but, on the next occasion when she was able to tune in, it was to a conversation that she had already listened to several times and thus she knew exactly what would happen. Adam had come in from work and had sat down to unbuckle his leggings, which he would throw over to Nancy to clean and polish for him while he went out to wash at the pump. Her protest at his request would be followed by the thud of his heavy boots as they too were tossed in her direction, and then would come her whining voice: "*It seems so silly and such a waste of time. They'll only get muddy again in the morning, and I've been on the go all day. Hardly been off my feet since you left the house.*"

"*So you want me to go down to the village all mucky, is that it?*"

"*I don't want you to go down to the village at all, Adam, and well you know it. Wasting your money in the Pelican with that Bill Haskins and all the rest, and then stumbling back home with a skinful and a face as black as thunder, so that I'm afraid to open my mouth.*"

"*Well, I earn the bloody money, don't I?*"

"*I'm not denying that it's your money, and I do wish you wouldn't swear in front of Lucy. It's how you spend your wages that riles me. Lucy's not had a new frock this year, and come to that nor more have I, not for a twelve-month. After all, we are your wife and child . . . your own flesh and blood."*

"*Why can't I have a new dress?*" It was the little girl. "*Why must you drink so much beer, Daddy?*"

"*For Christ's sake, shut up, can't you?*"

It was by now the second week of June, and it had been during March that Millie had just seen the hazy outlines of the speakers, outlines which had grown increasingly detailed until she had been able to discern their features.

Adam Loft was about thirty, clean-shaven and broad-shouldered, dark and sullenly handsome, with the strength of one of the shire horses with which he worked. Nancy had once been pretty, but discontent and fatigue had left their mark, sapping away the good looks which she had formerly possessed. Her reddish hair was streaked with grey and hung in wisps which she was forever pushing away from her forehead with the back of her hand. Lucy was a miniature replica of her mother at the same age.

Judith Cromer could not have been more than eighteen or nineteen. Millie had imagined from her voice that she would have been older, a bold and probably buxom hussy, but she was nothing of the sort. On the contrary, she was tall and slim with beautiful hands and feet, and had an exotic charm which was almost oriental and which was unexpected to come across in the wind-swept plains of the Norfolk countryside.

The next happening of which Millie had not been previously aware had taken place after tea on the day following the one on which she had learned of Judith's pregnancy. She had no means of knowing if it had occurred before or after that event.

Adam had been shrugging on his jacket preparatory to departing for the Pelican, when Nancy had said: "*Lucy, run along, dear. I want to have a word with your father alone.*"

Adam had paused with his fingers on the door latch. "*Can't it wait?*" he had asked tersely.

"*No,*" Nancy had been unaccustomedly firm. "*Do as I tell you, Lucy.*" The small girl had left the room.

"*Well, what is it?*" Adam had demanded, and he was holding his watch in his hand to underline his impatience.

"*I met Lily Rickett this afternoon,*" Nancy had said quietly, "*and she told me.*"

"*Told you what?*" Adam had asked brusquely.

"About you and that Judith Cromer."

"What about me and Judith Cromer? What did she say? Are you daft? You ought to know better than to gossip with an old faggot like Lily Rickett." Even to Millie's ears, let alone Nancy's, it was obvious that he was put out and was stalling.

"She told me that every time I took Lucy over to Watton to see Mother, Judith Cromer creeps in here to whore with you. That's what she told me. She says it's common talk."

Adam swung arrogantly round towards her. He slipped the watch back in his pocket and stood with his thumbs tucked behind the long links of its silver chain, rocking slowly on his heels. *"And did you believe her?"* he had asked expressionlessly. *"And if you did, what do you think you can do about it?"*

"If she comes here again," Nancy had said, *"I'm going straight to her parents. That's what I'm going to do about it. She's a dirty lustful little tart, that's all she is, coming into my house as soon as my back is turned, and carrying on like a bitch on heat."*

There had been a silence before Adam had said in a voice thick with anger: *"I shouldn't act foolish, Nancy, if I were you. I really shouldn't."* He had turned abruptly on his heel and the door had banged behind him, and Nancy had stood staring after him until the picture had faded.

Ida had gone to the station. There had been no flurry, no last minute checking of what she might have forgotten. She was too well organized and experienced to indulge in such behaviour. Millie had received a peck on the cheek and had been told that Ida would be back in good time for supper on Monday, and would Millie please plant out the zinnias and dahlias, and she was not to forget to cut down on the milk-man's delivery for, as Millie well knew, she abhorred waste.

Millie had arranged to have luncheon with Miss Findhorn, but otherwise she had made no social engagements for the week-end. The afternoon was hot, with a hint of thunder, and the flower beds were dry, which had necessitated a lot of watering in case the storm did not break, which was questionable as the clouds were slowly drifting in the direction of the coast and would most likely spill themselves into the sea.

It was when she had finished the task of bedding out, and had washed her hands and taken the tea tray into the neat drawing-room with its chintzes and lime green walls studded with gilt framed water colours that she heard Nancy Loft's voice.

She had stationed herself not more than three feet away from where Millie was sitting with the tray on her lap, and she was as clear and as real as if she had been there in the flesh. Millie had the odd feeling that it was she herself, and not Nancy Loft, who was in fact the ghost. She glanced quickly from the stiff figure of the woman to the doorway which framed Judith Cromer.

"*Won't you come in, Miss Cromer?*" Nancy said. "*Adam's not home yet. Perhaps you would like to wait?*" she suggested with heavy sarcasm. "*I expect you're taken aback to find me here. When you have called before I've never been in, have I?*" She spoke with venom.

Judith did not seem at all put out by this reception. "*It was you I came to see today, Mrs. Loft,*" she said with composure. "*Adam told me that he would be working late.*"

Nancy was by the side of the table which had been laid with half a loaf of bread and a slab of margarine, together with an opened tin of sardines and three slices of cold pork that had been arranged on a chipped willow pattern plate. She waited for the girl to continue. "*He did?*" she said at last.

"*Yes. I wanted to tell you that I am going to have a baby, and that it is Adam's.*"

"*Does he know?*"

"*Yes.*" Judith stepped forward into the room. "*He is going to ask you to give him a divorce.*"

Nancy laughed. "*There's no harm in asking, is there?*" The hatred between the two women was palpable. "*Does he admit responsibility? A bun in the oven might be the work of more than one baker!*"

"*If you don't divorce him,*" said Judith evenly, "*he will come away with me just the same. He hates you. You are repulsive to him. He's told me so frequently.*"

"*So you've decided not to face the music,*" said Nancy. "*You're going elsewhere to have your bastard. I can't say that I blame you. It's your parents that I'm sorry for.*" Her face was pinched and white. "*But I may as well tell you, Judith Cromer, that I will never divorce Adam, not for you or any other slant-eyed slut from the village whom he may have seen fit to pleasure. He's no better than a randy bull. And now get out of my house,*" she said, her voice rising. "*Get out before I do you and your disgusting brat an injury.*" She snatched up the bread knife from the table and stepped forward.

The two women grappled desperately with each other for possession of the weapon. Their struggle seemed to Millie to last for an interminable time. Their feet scarcely moved, but their breathing grew loud and stertorous. Then Judith Cromer took a sudden pace backward holding the knife which had become steeped in blood up to its bone handle.

Nancy Loft sank to her knees, her mouth open as if in astonishment. As she fell she clutched at the tablecloth, bringing the cups and plates crashing around her to the floor. Judith stood over her, gazing down in horror.

There was a step on the oilcloth in the narrow hall and Adam came in. He stood stock still, taking in the tableau. "*Good God, Judith!*" he said. "*Good God!*" The girl let the knife fall as she turned to him.

Millie's hands were clenched. Over Judith's head the young man was looking straight at her, and when he spoke his words were slow and distinct and his dark eyes held hers. "*So now you know, Miss Ackland,*" he said. "*You have been watching us, and now you know the truth of what happened although I took the blame. You're on to us, Miss Ackland, aren't you? And you will be the next, if you talk. And talk you will! We'll get you one of these days, just you see if we don't.*"

Millie closed her eyes to shut out his livid mocking face, and she was tense with terror, and when at last she dared to open them again the room was empty and exactly as it had been, and she was once more alone.

Upon her return from London Ida was most distressed to find Millie in what she could only describe as a state of near collapse. After considerable pressure as to the cause Millie was at length persuaded to talk, and Ida listened patiently and anxiously as her friend poured out the whole story.

It was pure imagination of course, but poor Millie appeared to believe every word of what she said. She must take her away for a holiday and then she would realize what nonsense it had all been. Otherwise, unless she was able to put her groundless fears into proper perspective, in all probability she would want to sell Rosemary Cottage, which would be sheer foolishness.

It was decided finally that they should book on a two weeks cruise to the northern capitals at the end of the month. Millie had proposed that they should go to Greece, with all its beauty and ancient culture, but Ida had objected that it would be intolerably hot at this time of year, and besides which they would not be able to afford to stay away for so long. Millie quite understood and was pleased with, and grateful for, the Scandinavian compromise. When they had been quite young women they had gone together on a vacation to Rome and Venice, and Ida had proved herself a most entertaining and well informed travelling companion.

The next morning, however, brought an unexpected complication, for Ida received a letter from her brother, Francis. She was in the habit of saying that she was more like his aunt than his sister, since he was twenty years her junior. He ran an art gallery in Manchester, and somewhat to Ida's surprise, a few years after his wife's death he had married *en deuxième-noce* a girl not long out of her teens, a competent sensible and nice looking girl whose father had been his friend. Now it transpired she had met with an accident and was laid up with a slipped disc, leaving him to cope not only with the running of his business but with the management of the house and also of their two-year-old son. Could Ida conceivably come and stay for ten days to help him out? They were expecting an *au pair* girl from Madrid, but she could not be arriving for at least another week.

Ida read through this *cri de coeur* twice. She was very fond of Francis and knew how utterly helpless he would be in such a dilemma. She could not go for the whole of the ten days, but she would have to put in an appearance and try to find someone to tide him over. Men were so unenterprising, they accepted defeat so readily in any domestic crisis. She wondered how she herself would make out with a male two-year-old. It would be so different from her girls!

But what was to be done about Millie? If she were to leave her by herself she wouldn't know a moment's peace. She could consult Monica Findhorn, who was a tower of strength. Perhaps she might know of some woman locally who might be bribed or persuaded to come in and oblige. It was both extraordinary and inconvenient that Francis's request should have arrived so soon after her London trip. It had been months since she had stirred from Rosemary Cottage. And now twice within a week!

When Ida broached the matter to Miss Findhorn that lady looked dubious. There was really no one in Swaffam, no one at all. Any available daily help was so quickly snapped up. She realized the urgency and would certainly make inquiries and she would telephone Ida at lunchtime. She was sorry to hear that Millie had been unwell. It had been rather naughty of her not to have let her know. She would pop round and see her as often as she could, but that was by no means the same thing as having somebody living in, was it? She would have been delighted to ask her to stay, but at the moment the spare room was being redecorated. Wasn't life difficult?

Ida walked back to Rosemary Cottage torn by conflicting loyalties. She would say nothing to Millie until the afternoon, but if she was to be of help to Francis she could not long delay the answer to his S.O.S.

At five minutes to one Monica Findhorn telephoned saying that she had heard of someone who might be willing to move in for a short while. She was not acquainted with her personally. She was a Mrs. Tarriman; and she was by no means young. As it happened, she was here on a visit from Tasmania and was a great aunt of Mabel Smith's, who lived in one of the new Council houses in Ramsden Road, and Mabel had told her that the old lady was becoming rather bored with nothing to do. She was nearing the end of a month's visit, for which she had practically invited herself. Mabel had not previously known her, but she had loyally decided that blood was thicker than water, and Mrs. Tarriman had written that she had saved up for a long time to pay a visit to the Old Country.

Ida went for an interview as soon as Millie had been settled down for her *siesta*, as she liked to call it. Mrs. Tarriman was not young, but she was not as ancient as Miss Findhorn had implied. She must, thought Ida, be roughly her own contemporary, maybe a little younger, a woman in her middle sixties. Still, she seemed pleasant and was prepared to be of assistance. She could start tomorrow if Miss Rankin wished that she should do so, and could remain until Saturday or even Sunday. She must be in Southampton by Tuesday to catch her boat. As to remuneration she would leave that to Miss Rankin. It was agreed that she should come to Rosemary Cottage on the following morning.

Ida telephoned Francis to announce that she would be in Manchester the next evening. Millie accepted this arrangement cheerfully. She was aware that Ida did not want to let Francis down and declared that as she would have a companion her friend must not give the matter a second thought. There was no problem. She would look forward to Ida coming back as soon as she had made the necessary arrangements for her brother. Mrs. Tarriman sounded excellent, and it would only be for a few days.

"She has good bone structure," Ida had added. "When she was young she must have been quite beautiful. You'll get on together like a house on fire. Don't worry, Millie." But when the taxi had come and had driven Ida to the station Millie felt some of her old fear return. She hated Ida going away and wished that the time would come for the beginning of their cruise.

Doctor Cripps had been insistent that she take things quietly, so Millie stayed in bed until noon and retired again directly after the news at a quarter past nine. She hoped that she was not giving too much trouble—but Ida had been adamant that she should carry out the doctor's orders. Millie comforted herself that by Sunday or Monday, when her friend would be back, such self indulgence would be no longer necessary.

At half past seven on the evening of Mrs. Tarriman's second day at the cottage Millie could hear her preparing supper. The doors which gave from the drawing-room and kitchen on to the passage were both ajar. Millie was lying on the sofa, an unopened copy of the *Spectator* beside her. She was scrutinizing the *Queen*, which she pretended to despise. It was Ida who was the subscriber, as she liked to be *au fait* with the activities of her 'old girls', although Millie maintained that the publication was a frivolous extravagance.

She put the magazine to one side and began a polite, if rather loud, conversation with Mrs. Tarriman. Nowadays you had to treat domestic help as human beings, try to make them feel a part of the family. It was no use being aloof. The supper would be simple; a cup of hot *consommé*, some cold beef and pickles left over from luncheon, and perhaps an apple. The beef had been far too rare for Millie's taste, almost blue, but she had not liked to comment adversely on it.

Had Mrs. Tarriman, she inquired, ever regretted having emigrated? Life in Tasmania must be very different from that in England. It had a marvellous climate, or so she had heard. Had she many relatives living there?

Mrs. Tarriman replied that on the whole she liked it very much. She had one son and two grand-daughters in Hobart. When their mother had died the girls had been nearly grown up, and they had married early, so after she had lost her own husband she had moved in to housekeep for their father. It was a fine country for the young, what with the sunshine and the space and all and, if Miss Ackland would pardon her for saying so, there were no class barriers, which was nice. Her visit 'home' had been enjoyable, but she was getting to be an old woman these days and it would be unlikely that she would be making another one. Of course, Tasmania had its snags, like all places, but there was plenty of scope out there and people could get on in the world.

Millie continued to talk. She had realized, ever since Ida's departure, that tonight would be Midsummer Eve, and she had no desire to participate again as an eye-witness of the long ago murder. If she went on chatting to Mrs. Tarriman there would be less likelihood that she would be swept in, and when she went up to bed she would take a sleeping pill.

"And did you know this part of the country when you were a girl?" asked Millie. "Or did you come to Norfolk just to visit your great niece?"

"I was Norfolk born," said Mrs. Tarriman, "'tho they've all gone from hereabouts, that is . . . all of my immediate relations. I lost touch with them these many years back. Mabel is the only one that's left. The two wars took a heavy toll of the menfolk, and Mabel's brothers went off in their turn, same as I did, one to New Zealand and the other to South Africa. She tells me they've done very well for themselves." She hesitated and then added: "You might say I used to know this village well."

"All the same it must be sad," said Millie, "to see all the old places passing into new ownership." She paused, and asked: "What was your maiden name?"

Mrs. Tarriman came to the doorway and Millie saw that the big carving knife in her hand was red with blood. "My name?" she asked. "Why do you ask me that, Miss Ackland? It would mean nothing to you. As a matter of fact it was Cromer . . . Judy Cromer."

A chill breeze seemed to play over Millie and she shivered. Judith Cromer had come back. She was here in this room beside her, and on Midsummer Eve. Millie studied her nails. She must not allow herself to look up. Was that the sound of the front door opening? Who was it that was coming in? She knew with a sudden ghastly certainty who it would be that she would see. Against her will she raised her head. "Is there anybody there?" she called.

Framed in the door behind Mrs. Tarriman stood the burly figure of Adam Loft and his expression as he watched Millie was one of triumph, and she heard once more his whispered words: "*You're on to us, Miss Ackland, aren't you? And you will be the next. We'll get you one of these days*." And she had talked. She had told Ida.

Millie was gripped by a searing pain, as if a mailed hand was squeezing relentlessly at her heart. She found it impossible to get her breath. This was death that had come to claim her—and she recognized it as such. She gave a strangled cry and her head fell forward on to her chest.

Mrs. Tarriman had moved away, her thoughts in the past. Judy Cromer had been her maiden name. It had been curious how drawn her mother had been to the letter 'Jay', James . . . John . . . her elder sister Judith, who had drowned herself on the day of Adam Loft's execution . . . poor tragic Judith . . . it had been in this very cottage that the young man had lived . . . and Julia. Why, instead of Judith, had it been herself, Julia, who had been the one who had always been known as 'Judy'? It had been a family quirk which had had no explanation.

Hearing a sound of distress from the sofa Mrs. Tarriman hurried back into the room, the carving knife with which she had been slicing the beef still held in her hand. She knelt down by Millie. "Miss Ackland," she said with concern. "Miss Ackland, dear . . . what is it?" She felt for her pulse. "Miss Ackland, dear," she said once more. Then with her face starched with worry, she went across to the telephone to call Doctor Cripps.

ALGERNON BLACKWOOD
The Whisperers

Algernon Blackwood *(1869–1951) was one of the finest and most prolific British writers in the realm of supernatural literature. Several different collections of his short stories—of which the best known (and most reprinted) are 'The Willows' and 'The Wendigo'—have appeared since his death with consistent regularity. One of his less familiar tales is 'The Whisperers' (from* Ten-Minute Stories, *1914).*

To be too impressionable is as much a source of weakness as to be hyper-sensitive: so many messages come flooding in upon one another that confusion is the result; the mind chokes, imagination grows congested.

Jones, as an imaginative writing man, was well aware of this, yet could not always prevent it; for if he dulled his mind to one impression, he ran the risk of blunting it to all. To guard his main idea, and picket its safe conduct through the seethe of additions that instantly flocked to join it, was a psychological puzzle that sometimes overtaxed his powers of critical selection. He prepared for it, however. An editor would ask him for a story—"about five thousand words, you know"; and Jones would answer, "I'll send it you with pleasure—when it comes." He knew his difficulty too well to promise more. Ideas were never lacking, but their length of treatment belonged to machinery he could not coerce. They were alive; they refused to come to heel to suit mere editors. Midway in a tale that stared crystal clear and definite in its original germ, would pour a flood of new impressions that either smothered the first conception, or developed it beyond recognition. Often a short story exfoliated in this bursting way beyond his power to stop it. He began one, never knowing where it would lead him. It was ever an adventure. Like Jack the Giant Killer's beanstalk it grew secretly in the night, fed by everything he read, saw, felt, or heard. Jones was too impressionable; he received too many impressions, and too easily.

For this reason, when working at a definite, short idea, he preferred an empty room, without pictures, furniture, books, or anything suggestive, and with a skylight that shut out scenery—just ink, blank paper, and the clear picture in his mind. His own interior, unstimulated by the geysers of external life, he made some pretence of regulating; though even under these favourable conditions the matter was not too easy, so prolifically does a sensitive mind engender.

His experience in the empty room of the carpenter's house was a curious case in point—in the little Jura village where his cousin lived to educate his children. "We're all in a pension above the Post Office here," the cousin wrote, "but just now the house is full, and besides is rather noisy. I've taken an attic room for you at the carpenter's near the forest. Some things of mine have been stored there all the winter, but I moved the cases out this morning. There's a bed, writing-table, wash-handstand, sofa, and a skylight window—otherwise empty, as I know you prefer it. You can have your meals with us," etc. And this just suited Jones, who had six weeks' work on hand for which he needed empty solitude. His "idea" was slight and very tender; accretions would easily smother clear presentment; its treatment must be delicate, simple, unconfused.

The room really was an attic, but large, wide, high. He heard the wind rush past the skylight when he went to bed. When the cupboard was open he heard the wind there too, washing the outer walls and tiles. From his pillow he saw a patch of stars peep down upon him. Jones knew the mountains and the woods were close, but he could not see them. Better still, he could not smell them. And he went to bed dead tired, full of his theme for work next morning. He saw it to the end. He could almost have promised five thousand words. With the dawn he would be up and "at it," for he usually woke very early, his mind surcharged, as though subconsciousness had matured the material in sleep. Cold bath, a cup of tea, and then—his writing-table; and the quicker he could reach the writing-table the richer was the content of imaginative thought. What had puzzled him the night before was invariably cleared up in the morning. Only illness could interfere with the process and routine of it.

But this time it was otherwise. He woke, and instantly realised, with a shock of surprise and disappointment, that his mind was—groping. It was groping for his little lost idea. There was nothing physically wrong with him; he felt rested, fresh, clear-headed; but his brain was searching, searching, moreover, in a crowd. Trying to seize hold of the train it had relinquished several hours ago, it caught at an evasive, empty shell. The idea had utterly changed; or rather it seemed smothered by a host of new impressions that came pouring in upon it—new modes of treatment, points of view, in fact development. In the light of these extensions and novel aspects, his original idea had altered beyond recognition. The germ had marvellously exfoliated, so that a whole volume could alone express it. An army of fresh suggestions clamoured for expression. His subconsciousness had grown thick with life; it surged—active, crowded, tumultuous.

And the darkness puzzled him. He remembered the absence of accustomed windows, but it was only when the candle-light brought close the face of his watch, with two o'clock upon it, that he heard the sound of confused whispering in the corners of the room, and realised with a little twinge of fear that those who whispered had just been standing beside his very bed. The room was full.

Though the candle-light proclaimed it empty—bare walls, bare floor, five pieces of unimaginative furniture, and fifty stars peeping through the skylight—it was undeniably thronged with living people whose minds had called him out of heavy sleep. The whispers, of course, died off into the wind that swept the roof and skylight; but the Whisperers remained. They had been trying to get at him; waking suddenly, he had caught them in the very act. . . . And all had brought new interpretations with them; his thought had fundamentally altered; the original idea was snowed under; new images brimmed his mind, and his brain was working as it worked under the high pressure of creative moments.

Jones sat up, trembling a little, and stared about him into the empty room that yet was densely packed with these invisible Whisperers. And he realised this astonishing thing—that he was the object of their deliberate assault, and that scores of other minds, deep, powerful, very active minds, were thundering and beating upon the doors of his imagination. The onset of them was terrific and bewildering, the attack of aggressive ideas obliterating his original story beneath a flood of new suggestions. Inspiration had become suddenly torrential, yet so vast as to be unwieldy, incoherent, useless. It was like the tempest of images that fever brings. His first conception seemed no longer "delicate," but petty. It had turned unreal and tiny, compared with this enormous choice of treatment, extension, development, that now overwhelmed his throbbing brain.

Fear caught vividly at him, as he searched the empty attic-room in vain for explanation. There was absolutely nothing to produce this tempest of new impressions. People seemed to be talking to him all together, jumbled somewhat, but insistently. It was obsession, rather than inspiration; and so bitingly, dreadfully real.

"Who are you all?" his mind whispered to blank walls and vacant corners.

Back from the shouting floor and ceiling came the chorus of images that stormed and clamoured for expression. Jones lay still and listened; he let them come. There was nothing else to do. He lay fearful, negative, receptive. It was all too big for him to manage, set to some scale of high achievement that submerged his own small powers. It came, too, in a series of impressions, all separate, yet all somehow interwoven.

In vain he tried to sort them out and sift them. As well sort out waves upon an agitated sea. They were too self-assertive for direction or control. Like wild animals, hungry, thirsty, ravening, they rushed from every side and fastened on his mind.

Yet he perceived them in a certain sequence.

For, first, the unfurnished attic-chamber was full of human passion, of love and hate, revenge and wicked cunning, of jealousy, courage, cowardice, of every vital human emotion ever longed for, enjoyed, or frustrated, all clamouring for —expression.

Flaming across and through these, incongruously threaded in and out, ran next a yearning softness of incredible beauty that sighed in the empty spaces of his heart, pleading for impossible fulfilment. . . .

And, after these, carrying both one and other upon their surface, huge questions flashed and dived and thundered in a patterned, wild entanglement, calling to be unravelled and made straight. Moreover, with every set came a new suggested treatment of the little clear idea he had taken to bed with him five hours before.

Jones adopted each in turn. Imagination writhed and twisted beneath the stress of all these potential modes of expression he must choose between. His small idea exfoliated into many volumes, work enough to fill a dozen lives. It was most gorgeously exhilarating, though so hopelessly unmanageable. He felt like many minds in one. . . .

Then came another chain of impressions, violent, yet steady owing to their depth; the voices, questions, pleadings turned to pictures; and he saw, struggling through the deeps of him, enormous quantities of people, passing along like rivers, massed, herded, swayed here and there by some outstanding figure of command who directed them like flowing water. They shrieked, and fought, and battled, then sank out of sight, huddled and destroyed in—blood. . . .

And their places were taken instantly by white crowds with shining eyes, and yearning in their faces, who climbed precipitous heights towards some Radiance that kept ever out of sight, like sunrise behind mountains that clouds then swallow. . . . The pelt and thunder of images was destructive in its torrent; his little, first idea was drowned and wrecked. . . . Jones sank back exhausted, utterly dismayed. He gave up all attempt to make selection.

The driving storm swept through him, on and on, now waxing, now waning, but never growing less, and apparently endless as the sky. It rushed in circles, like the turning of a giant wheel. All the activities that human minds have ever battled with since thought began came booming, crashing, straining for expression against the imaginative stuff whereof his mind was built. The walls began to yield and settle. It was like the chaos that madness brings. He did not struggle against it; he let it come, lying open and receptive, pliant and plastic to every detail of the vast invasion. And the only time he attempted a complete obedience, reaching out for the pencil and notebook that lay beside his bed, he desisted instantly again, sinking back upon his pillows with a kind of frightened laughter. For the tempest seemed then to knock him down and bruise his very brain. Inextricable confusion caught him. He might as well have tried to make notes of the entire Alexandrian Library in half an hour. . . .

Then, most singular of all, as he felt the sleep of exhaustion fall upon his tired nerves, he heard that deep, prodigious sound. All that had preceded, it gathered marvellously in, mothering it with a sweetness that seemed to his imagination like some harmonious, geometrical skein including all the activities men's minds have ever known. Faintly he realised it only, discerned from infinitely far away. Into the streams of apparent contradiction that warred so strenuously about him, it seemed to bring some hint of unifying, harmonious explanation. . . . And, here and there, as sleep buried him, he imagined that chords lay threaded along strings of cadences, breaking sometimes even into melody—music that rose everywhere from life and wove Thought into a homogeneous Whole. . . .

"Sleep well?" his cousin inquired, when he appeared very late next day for *déjeuner*. "Think you'll be able to work in that room all right?"

"I slept, yes, thanks," said Jones. "No doubt I shall work there right enough—when I'm rested. By the bye," he asked presently, "what has the attic been used for lately? What's been in it, I mean?"

"Books, only books," was the reply. "I've stored my 'library' there for months, without a chance of using it. I move about so much you see. Five hundred books were taken out just before you came. I often think," he added lightly, "that when books are unopened like that for long, the minds that wrote them must get restless and——"

"What sort of books were they?" Jones interrupted.

"Fiction, poetry, philosophy, history, religion, music. I've got two hundred books on music alone."

L.M. BOSTON
Curfew

Mrs. Lucy Maria Boston *(b. 1892) launched her writing career at the age of 62, and is still active in her 98th year. She is best known for the Green Knowe series of books, featuring a strange haunted house near Cambridge. 'Curfew' originally appeared in the anthology* The House of the Nightmare and other Eerie Tales *(1967).*

While my two brothers and I were at a preparatory school our parents were living abroad, so that we had to spend our holidays with relatives.

Our favourite uncle and aunt had bought a farmhouse on the outlying land of an old manor, of which the estate was being broken up. The big house, Abbey Manor, was being allowed to fall down in its own good time, the owner living in a small dower house in the park.

The cottage which Uncle Tom and Aunt Catherine bought had also been empty for a long time. Nettles grew up to the front door and even between the flagstones in the larder. The cottage however had been well built, with stone mullions, leaded windows and tiled floors. It had escaped the wanton smashing up that is the fate of most empty houses, perhaps because of its isolation. A profound silence brooded over it and the acres that went with it.

My Aunt had a passion for gardening, and there was much to be done before this weed-infested land should be disciplined to her intentions, but the wildness was a paradise for children.

Walks in the adjacent park were among the excitements of our visits. There was the empty Manor with its staring windows and lost melancholy garden, its weedy paths leading to locked gates. We had Sir Roger's permission to wander there, but never climbed the gate without a thrill, or chill, of expectation. One wing of the fifteenth century Manor had, with sacrilegious defiance, been built over the former Abbey graveyard. Here and there in the grounds, lying open among the rhododendrons were the empty stone coffins of forgotten Abbots, left there perhaps as being too heavy to carry away, or out of boastfulness. They were grand things, hand-hewn from solid blocks of local stone hollowed to the austerest outline of the human body with a round resting place for the head. We passed them with great awe and even with a kind of affection, as noble things treated with contempt and now part of our private landscape.

There was also a lake, reflecting the house and the stables, which were dusty, echoing and forlorn. Uncle Tom, who liked everything ship-shape, used to sigh over all this decay, but his wife had an eye open for everything that could be moved, bought, or made use of, such as a small wrought-iron gate, a sundial, or even, in an ambitious moment, as we all stood looking up at it, the little bell tower on the stables. Its four open arches and lead dome had the beauty of extreme simplicity against the pale green sky. "Why should it rot here?" she said. "It would suit our yard just as well;" but the yard, surrounded by fine old barns, was Uncle's special domain and he resented intrusion. "Rubbish," he said, "it's sure to be rotten. Besides I hate pretentiousness."

On our first visit to their farmhouse Aunt Catherine had been busy making a wild garden out of an acre or two of heather and stone. It was boggy in places and we helped to make water courses for her, while she laid stepping stones and contrived rough slab bridges. There was a high mound in the middle of this patch, apparently artificial, though of some age, judging by the hawthorn tree that grew on it, and it was crowned by a large boulder. In the course of her construction Aunt Catherine needed soil to raise her beds above the level of the surrounding damp, and, resourceful woman, looking at this hillock, decided to shift the top. With what delight we responded to her invitations to see if we could roll the boulder off; but our efforts were in vain. In the end it took a team of all hands, with levers, under the personal command of Uncle in his most arbitrary mood, to dislodge it. But at last the slope took possession of it and away it rolled on a clumsy and fortuitous course and came to rest at the edge of one of our little boggy streams. "Perfect," said Aunt Catherine by way of thanks and dismissal.

When next we came to stay, already her heather garden was taking shape. She had perfectly preserved the wild atmosphere, and the hillock was down almost to the level of the rest.

"Look, boys," she said, "we struck on this yesterday." She showed us the top of a trough or coffer of stone which her digging had half uncovered. The slab over it that had served as a lid had been prized up and now rested sideways, leaving a gaping hole through which the loose earth on top had poured in.

Aunt Catherine stopped with a gasp.

"When did you open it?" she asked Uncle.

"I haven't touched it, my dear."

"Then who has been here, and why?"

Was it a burglar? Was it treasure? We were all agog.

Aunt Catherine laughed uneasily and said she would guess that whatever was once in was now out, unless it was just old bones, and if so she was not going to disturb them.

"Old bones?" said Robert. "It's not the right shape for a coffin. Not like the Abbots'. There's no place for a head. Perhaps it was a criminal who had been beheaded. Or perhaps it was a case of 'Double him up, double him up' like Punch's victims."

"Or perhaps an animal Thing," suggested John hesitantly. He was young and imaginative.

Robert had been rather gingerly shovelling off the clay that still clung to the lid. "There are words on it," he said.

We all got busy with penknives, trowel and sticks to clean the letters.

Libera nos quaesimus Domine ab Malo

Uncle Tom translated it for us. "Deliver us O Lord from the Evil One."

"I don't like it," said Aunt Catherine. Then she shrugged and became practical again. "I'm short of a slab for my stepping stones," she said. "This will do very well. Come on, boys. All together, lift."

The slab took its useful place face downward in one of the paths, and the coffin itself was skilfully planted with bushes of rosemary and Spanish gorse and trailing rock-roses. By the time this story really begins it had a natural and undisturbed appearance, and around the wild garden that it dominated the lapwings and wagtails made themselves at home.

It was at the beginning of the long summer holidays. Aunt Catherine having completed one plan, was now looking for something new, and the suggestion of moving the bell tower from the Manor stables was raised again. We set off with Uncle Tom one afternoon to examine it. The Manor stables surrounded three sides of a courtyard and were in atrocious condition. The once beautiful and elaborate coach house let in the rain through a hole in the roof. The loose boxes were crumbling with dry rot. Our footsteps and voices rang intrusively as we did a tour of inspection before mounting the ladder to the lofts, and we explored such of these as had floors that would bear us. Spiders and rats were all that moved there now. Uncle Tom was the first to go up the second ladder and thrust his body as far as the knees into the little cupola, while Robert and John were jostling on the lower rungs, their heads level with the opening. I was alone on a little square landing; on one side of me was the ladder, on three were doors opening into dark lofts. We had already explored them and knew them to be empty, and therefore I was very scared to hear a hoarse burst of laughter rather like a horse's cough that seemed to come from one of them. I tugged at my brothers, and they came down, including Uncle who had finished his measuring and tapping. I told them there was someone there, and we all went round again, and I am afraid I took care neither to be first nor last, in or out, of any of the rooms. But we saw nothing and I was mercilessly teased for my fear as we returned home.

At supper that night my Aunt heard all about it. The measurements were very suitable, the condition not bad—"Though the bell's missing," said Uncle Tom; "You get a splendid view of our place from the roof, Catherine; I could see your Bad Man's coffin quite plainly. There's the chap that heard him too," he added, pointing his fork at me. "Made us all feel quite queer. I'll go and see Sir Roger tomorrow. They say he'd sell the hat off his head if he could. I like the idea of having a bit of the old house here. Anything new looks new."

"Don't you bring anything too old over from the Manor," said Aunt Catherine; "leave the ghosts behind anyway."

"It's too late to warn me about that," he retorted. "It was you who took the lid off the Bad Man's coffin."

"It was open already."

"Well, who rolled the boulder away that was supposed to keep him down?" and again he pointed at us with his fork, and we grinned, though shudders ran down our spines.

The next day Sir Roger himself happened to pass our gate. He stopped to speak to us all, even Robert, John and me, grimy and barefoot as we were.

"You are digging yourselves in very nicely here, I must say," he said to Uncle. "It all looks very jolly. I like the way you do it, too. Of course I have no choice but to sell what I can, but these gimcrack buildings do gall me."

This was a good opening, and before long bargaining for the bell tower had begun. It ended in Uncle's favour, because at the last moment he brought out his trump card—there was no bell.

"But there being no bell is one of its greatest attractions," said Sir Roger. "There's a legend, you know. It was called the Judas bell, but where it originally came from and who betrayed what I don't know. It was the old curfew, and of course if people are out when they ought to be in, things are likely to happen to them. The old people round here say the bell had a 'familiar'. The last person who rang it was my great grandfather, who did it for a wager. And it is a fact that he was found dead. Rather horribly dead. After that the bell was taken down and destroyed."

"Well, you can't expect me to buy a legend about a bell that is missing," said Uncle Tom, and the bargain was settled at a very small figure.

Before the end of the holidays the graceful little bell tower was set up on the middle building in our stableyard. Both Uncle and Aunt were pleased. It was repainted to match its new position and looked well there.

Wet weather had set in. We had grown tired of all the games that can be played in the house. Then Robert said he would go and fish in the Manor brook and we followed with jam jars of worms. We had to cross the wild garden, which had, since Uncle's jokes, begun to stir sinister feelings in us. The lapwings cried and veered and flung themselves along the wind, the thin rain pattered in the little brown streams, and the wagtails looked sharply at us, and ran hither and thither as though disguising their real activities. We began to run, and shooed them away as if they were unwanted thoughts, but as we paused half-way across the stile into the park and looked back, there they all were as before, and the curlews sounded derisive as if we had no business there. The little stream through the park had invaded the grass at its edge beyond the cast of Thomas's 10/6d fishing rod, and the lake into which it flowed had swollen into damaging proportions. The cinder road that led to the Manor farm was under water, and the farmer was there with Sir Roger, bitterly complaining that it was all because the outlet sluice was blocked and had never been mended, and that the lake itself was silting up and so full of weeds you couldn't tell where it began and where it ended. Sir Roger was listening with a pained expression. He promised to have it seen to as soon as the flood subsided enough to allow work to begin. As for us, we spent the afternoon happily testing the depth of every overflow and returned home wet to the skin.

A week later dredging operations began on the lake. The sluice was opened and the water sank to mud level. The weeds were cut down, and a band of old men in waders were wheeling the smelly fibrous mud in barrows along planks. We were there of course to watch. Much came to light that would never have been expected. A sunken boat, a scythe blade, a weather vane, a skull, and most surprising of all, a bell. It was of unusual shape, but covered thickly with sharp flakes of rust. The pivot of its tongue was rusted up solid so that it could not swing.

"It's the old Judas bell like enough," said one old man. "Didn't I hear tell that your Uncle had bought the bell tower? That's an odd thing for anyone to buy. I'd like to hear what my old woman would say if I came back one day and said I'd bought her a bell tower."

We ran back to announce the find at home, and Uncle Tom called for Sir Roger and took him along to look at it. Uncle had a flair for antiques, and he thought that the bell might prove to be incised in some pattern which might be curious or of interest. But Sir Roger was interested in nothing but "Sherry and whippets", as we knew from Uncle's indiscreet conversation. "Look at the rust on it," he said, "I can't take any money for a thing like that. Certainly, do what you like with it. I'm not superstitious, but I wouldn't touch it."

Uncle shook his head at me and said we must expect the worst.

The bell was sent away to be cleaned and repaired, but even in its absence we now had a prickly feeling of foreboding. I remember the golden September weather, the scent of southern wood and lavender, and the yellow leaves spotted with black that were beginning to fall. But for us the garden had become haunted. We no longer basked in it quite at our ease, or felt as heretofore that earth and fields, trees and sky were all our own. There were darker corners where we definitely did not go, where in a game of "I spy," for instance, nobody thought of hiding or looking.

It was on the last morning of the holidays that the bell came back. It was delivered by van, wrapped in sacking, with its now mobile tongue thickly wedged and muffled in felt. We all hung around while Uncle unwrapped it. Seeing us so deeply interested, he made quite a ritual of it, marching off to the barn with us in procession behind him. The clapper he had kept muffled till the last. It was to be "unveiled". When at last he pulled the first toll the sound that it gave out was so unexpected as to be quite shocking. It was a high wide-carrying note, and though it had a certain churchiness, there was in it something wild and almost screamlike. The afternote that vibrated long after within the bell sent a creeping chill up my spine. When the last sinister tingle had faded out of the shaken air, Aunt Catherine said, "I'm certainly not going to have *that* rung for dinner. It would take away my appetite." Uncle seemed not disposed to dispute it. He said, "If they rang that at curfew, they gave you fair warning."

We were to go back to school the next day, and this was a thought that blotted out all others. It was important to get the most out of the last afternoon. Towards sunset when we were playing "I spy", I was crouching in a deep clump of red dog-wood, not far from the house, holding my panting breath and listening for the approach of Robert and John. I heard their voices drawing off in the wrong direction, and was beginning to feel I had time to straighten my stiff knees before they could possibly return, and then to hope they wouldn't be too long, when with no other warning a feeling of utter isolation and panic took me. I felt I was deserted, exposed to unknown dangers, perhaps trapped. I turned involuntarily to look behind me, and saw two long-nailed soily hands begin to part the leaves, and an evil face looked in. His hair and cheeks were clotted with earth, through which his yellow teeth showed more on one side than the other, his eye sockets were appallingly hollow, and he lifted his chin as the blind do when they seek.

I shot out of the bushes like a rabbit when the ferret looks in, and ran as hard as my legs would carry me to the house. My clamour soon brought Robert and John and Aunt Catherine, to whom I could give no better explanation than that I had seen a horrible face. She calmed me as best she could, saying it was probably a tramp coming in to pick up apples, and Uncle Tom should go round and send him off. Confidently she and Uncle exchanged that word as if it met the case perfectly—some tramps, a tramp, the tramp—as if a casual word like that could cover such lurking horror. Uncle Tom went striding off looking very fierce, but he came back having seen nobody.

Dusk had come. It was cold and the wind was rising, and we, as may be imagined, had no heart to play outside. So after tea Aunt Catherine let us light the fire, and we persuaded her and Uncle to stay with us and tell us ghost tales—the others I think out of pure love of sensation, and I because it was the only way that I could get company for my thoughts and persuade the grown-ups to talk, however insincerely, on the same subject. The session opened of course with a little lecture from Aunt Catherine about the folly of the whole thing. Then the curtains were drawn and Uncle Tom began. His personality and prestige added to the effect, for he was tall and bony and we held him in awe. He told the old stories about midnight coaches, about grinning lift-men who had been seen in a dream the night before, about grey monks who had passed people on the stairs and figures standing at midnight by one's bed; and they all to me had the same face.

The wind rose rapidly in accompaniment to his tales, and our feelings of horror were already far outstripping the merits of his invention, when a really terrible thing happened. A gust of wind tore open the casement and at the same time the bell in the tower gave a jerky ring. There was no need to tell us any more stories. Our hearts were tight with presentiment. Its variable sound came and went with the gusts even after the window was tightly closed again. It was not like a bell rung on purpose, but a bell evilly twitching on its own.

"This is quite intolerable," said Aunt Catherine. "No one will sleep a wink tonight if that goes on."

"Don't get in a fuss," said Uncle; "I'll go and take out the clapper. Nothing could be simpler. Now, boys, off to bed."

Up we went perforce, keeping close together, and clustered at our bedroom window to see him do this act of bravery. He seemed to waste hours talking to Aunt in the hall while we waited upstairs and listened to that vibrating shudder from the bell, the irregularity of which made it even more fraying to the nerves. The shadows under the yard walls were peopled for me with precise terror, and so was the room at my back. The key-hole howled too, and the wind in the chimney buffeted hollowly. At last we saw Uncle Tom come out into the light from the back door, and go down the yard where we could only by straining keep him in sight. Shadows swallowed him up and we heard the barn door slam behind him. We fixed our eyes on the outline of the bell tower, and again it seemed an age before we thought we could distinguish his head, shoulders and arms waving against the sky.

"There he is," said John, in a whisper. Uncle had seized the bell and the clanging stopped; but a moment later we heard him yell with the whole force of his great lungs, and his body disappeared down the man-hole. The bell had stopped, but the wind still blew and it was hard to tell where sounds came from. Robert thought he heard a dog-fight going on somewhere. But Uncle Tom didn't come back. Time seemed too short now. We imagined how long it would be before he would appear, then doubled it, trebled it, and began again.

At last Aunt Catherine came out and shouted for him, ran half-way down the yard and shouted again. The maid came out too, and presently the yard was full of people with lamps and flash-lights. They went into the barn after Aunt Catherine, and came staggering out carrying someone towards the house. We were seized with shame and undressed as quickly as we could, jumping into our beds. But Robert went on to the landing and called down the stairs to ask what had happened.

"Go to bed, boys, and for the Lord's sake keep quiet and keep out of the way," said a woman neighbour. "Your uncle has had a nasty accident."

And then we heard the horrible mad banshee sound of the maid having hysterics in the kitchen.

A.M. BURRAGE
"I'm Sure it was No.31"

Alfred McLelland Burrage *(1889–1956) had his greatest success in 1930 with his novel* War is War *(under the pseudonym 'Ex-Private X'), but he is now remembered mainly as one of the finest English ghost story writers, alongside Benson, Wakefield and James. His half-century career as a prolific writer for the popular magazines began at the age of seventeen, and this fascinating autobiographical tale recalling these early days was the very last piece he wrote (published in the London* Evening Standard *10 May 1955).*

It happened many years ago when I was a boy of 18, out house-hunting for my mother in a London suburb within a mile and a half of where we were then living. There were many houses to be let in those happy Edwardian days, and, having a bicycle and knowing my mother's requirements, I could thus save her fruitless journeys to some which I knew she would not consider. I had in my pocket several "orders to view" from local agents, and was on my way to an address when the strangest incident of my life befell me. It was on a sunny October afternoon, and, apart from feeling lethargic and depressed, I believe I was in a normal state of health.

My way took me along a tram-route, and all the side-roads on my left were culs-de-sacs, ending at the boundary wall of a great park. I looked down all these side-roads as I passed, and suddenly I stopped at a corner and got off my machine—for I had seen a "to let" board slanting over some railings about half-way down on the right.

It was a road of small villas, just suitable for our purpose, and the board belonged to agents with whom we were already in touch. Then—although I could find no house in that road on my list—I decided to go and investigate. So I rode up, balanced my machine against the kerb, and rang the bell.

I was quite unprepared for the sight of the lady who came to the door. She seemed old to my young eyes, although I daresay she was under forty, and I forget how she was dressed, but instinct told me at a glance that she was out of her proper setting in that shabby little house.

I quickly explained my errand, and apologised for having no order to view. At the same time I offered to show her other "orders" from the same agent.

"Oh," she said, "I'm sorry. The men ought to have taken the board away. I've decided to stay on."

I think she recognised me—as already I had recognised her—as someone who had seen better days. I was a shabby, untidy, lank-haired, sallow boy, not at all of the type to interest a heart-hungry widow. Probably I looked very tired and jaded.

Whatever the reason, she said: "Won't you come in and have a cup of tea?"

She was just like some other fellow's mater in the days before poverty had changed my environment, and all my shyness went from me on the instant. I followed her into the front room, where two surprises awaited me. The lesser of these was the furniture (much too massive for its setting) and the oil-paintings of Army and Navy officers of past generations. The greater surprise was the girl of about sixteen who rose to greet me as her mother said: "This is my daughter, Mumps, darling, I don't yet know this gentleman's name—"

I daresay I was still staring as I supplied it. She was about the most vivid and striking young person I had ever seen, with long black hair hanging loose over her shoulders and a wonderful warm complexion which seemed to light the room for me. Chocolate-box prettiness? Well, perhaps it was, but it reduced me for a time to bashful nervousness.

We sat talking for a while and my hostess succeeded in overcoming my shyness by talking about herself. Her name was Ellis, and I gathered that she was a widow. Invariably she addressed her daughter as "Mumps", and I never knew the girl's real Christian name.

Presently I noticed on one of the walls an oil painting of "Mumps" done apparently a year or two before. It looked a little amateurish beside the others, and I was not surprised to hear that it was Mrs. Ellis's own work.

"Oh, Mumps is a much better artist than I am," she laughed. "Show him some of your drawings, dear, while I get the tea."

"Mumps" had little to say for herself and seemed as shy as her new acquaintance. But she unearthed a portfolio and increased my embarrassment by showing some figure-drawings which struck me as being extremely well done but rather startling. However, she displayed them in the same manner in which she might have shown me views of a cathedral.

Had I been older and more experienced I might have jumped to a certain conclusion about that mother and daughter, and I am sure that I should have been wrong. Whatever the mother may have done—and I suspect nothing worse than unpaid bills—there was nothing coarse about her. Besides, a shabby boy with only coppers in his pocket was hardly fair game for harpies.

Over tea I told them about myself. I wonder if they really believed that I had been—and probably still was—the youngest professional writer in the country, and that I had had a story accepted a year before I left school.

But even if Mrs. Ellis took me for a young liar I was well aware that she liked me. She had told me little about herself save that she was a widow, but mentioned one of her relatives when I told her about my father's terrible illness—which had left me a schoolboy of 17 with a penniless mother to support.

"What a pity," she said, "that he didn't see my uncle." And she named a knighted physician in Harley Street.

Well, I could not stay for ever and the time came for me to go. "Mumps" and her mother preceded me into the little hall, and I took leave first of the girl. Mrs. Ellis opened the door and I said goodbye to her on the step.

Of course, I had been hoping that she would ask me to come again, but she did not. Her manner, despite her self-possession, was in the circumstances extraordinary. She seemed almost tearful, and might have been parting for ever from an old and dear friend. For I knew that she liked me, just as I knew that she knew I had fallen in love with "Mumps". Had I done the incredible in bending over and kissing her, I know she would have given me a little hug. And a moment later she would have closed the door softly upon me for ever.

Why? I do not know. It all seemed very strange. But I was yet to realise how extraordinary had been the events of that afternoon.

Of course I remembered Mrs. Ellis's address. The road was marked by a corner shop—I bought cigarettes there on my way home—and the number 31 was easily memorised as the reverse of the unlucky 13.

During the following day—and indeed for many days—I could not get the girl out of my head. She baulked my efforts to write cheap fiction. I felt that I must see her again or go mad.

It did not seem so difficult, for a short cycle ride brought me to the corner of her road. Even if she still went to school—and my impression was that she did not—there was always the chance of meeting her mother out shopping and getting a casual invitation to tea.

For hours at a time, mornings and afternoons, I haunted the main street of that other suburb during the next fortnight and haunted it in vain. Passing and repassing the top of the road I could catch no glimpse of either lady, but saw, as I had expected, that the estate-agent's board was gone.

At the end of the fortnight I decided in desperation to make an uninvited call, timing myself to arrive at tea-time. My excuse? Oh, I could tell Mrs. Ellis that we had not yet found a suitable house and ask if she had heard of one. She would see through me, of course, but I could not help it. I knew I ought to keep away, but I went—to desolation and bewilderment.

I thought at first it was a charwoman who came to the door, although I could see that the furniture in the hall had changed—and not for the better—since my other visit.

"Mrs. Ellis?" said the woman, shaking her head. "No, I don't know the name around here, and we've been here nearly two years."

I apologised and bolted. After all, I must have made a mistake in the number. But I was sure of the road, because it was marked by the corner shop, and the man there would know. I went in and bought a packet of cigarettes and it was the same man who served me again. He gave me a strange look.

"Mrs. Ellis? Well, she used to live at No. 31, but she's been gone about two years now."

Then, probably mistaking the look on my face, he added: "A lot of people would like to know what became of *her*."

The innuendo was obvious. A moonlight flit and money owed all round. Yes, but I'd had tea with her in that house a fortnight before. There was a stupid mistake somewhere.

But the man described her and "Mumps", even mentioning the silly nickname. Further, he knew about the Harley Street doctor.

"Yes," he said, "she was a well-connected lady. I wonder where she went. It's a long time now. Your guv'nor's going to have a job to find her."

I was too shocked and dazed to resent being taken for a debt-collector's spy. All I realised was that a fortnight before I had had tea with two ladies in the house from which they had vanished two years earlier—while at the same time it was occupied by others! Further, that I had been strongly attracted to a girl who might be a ghost or a dream.

Of course she could be neither! But on the other hand what had become of her and her mother? I could not possibly have "dreamed" of real people of whom I had never heard.

And never since have I heard of them nor met any who knew them. I could, of course, have written to the Harley Street doctor, but such a letter would be difficult enough for me even today. It was beyond the troubled lad of 18 who was afraid of being taken for a liar or of plunging into troubled waters where he had no business.

So I never solved the mystery and now—but for some very strange chance indeed—I know that I never shall.

RAMSEY CAMPBELL
The Guide

In the quarter-century since the publication of his first collection The Inhabitant of the Lake *(1964),* Ramsey Campbell *(b.1946) has become one of the pillars of modern British horror fiction. He has received the World Fantasy Award twice, and the British Fantasy Award a record four times. His acclaimed novels and short story collections include* Dark Companions, The Parasite, The Hungry Moon, Ancient Images, *and* Dark Feasts: the World of Ramsey Campbell. 'The Guide' *first appeared in* Post Mortem *(edited by P.F. Olsen & D.B. Silva, 1989). The lullaby verse has been revised by the author for the present anthology.*

The used bookshops seemed to be just as useless. In the first, Kew felt as if he had committed a gaffe by asking for the wrong James or even by asking for a book. The woman who was minding the next bookshop, her lap draped in black knitting so voluminous that she appeared to be mending a skirt she had on, assured him that the bookseller would find him something in the storeroom. "He's got lots of books in the back," she confided to Kew, and as he leaned on his stick and leafed through an annual he'd read seventy years ago, she kept up a commentary: "Fond of books, are you? I've read some books, books I'd *call* books. Make you sneeze, though, some of these old books. Break your toes, some of these books, if you're not careful. I don't know what people want with such big books. It's like having a stone slab on top of you, reading one of those books . . ." As Kew sidled toward the door, she said ominously, "He wouldn't want you going before he found you your books."

"My family will be wondering what's become of me," Kew offered, and fled.

Holidaymakers were driving away from the beach, along the narrow street of shops and small houses encrusted with pebbles and seashells. Some of the shops were already closing. He made for the newsagent's, in the hope that though all the horror books had looked too disgusting to touch, something more like literature might have found its way unnoticed onto one of the shelves, and then he realized that what he'd taken for a booklover's front room, unusually full of books, was in fact a shop. The sill inside the window was crowded with potted plants and cacti. Beyond them an antique till gleamed on a desk, and closer to the window, poking out of the end of a shelf, was a book by M. R. James.

The door admitted him readily and tunefully. He limped quickly to the shelf, and sighed. The book was indeed by James: Montague Rhodes James, O. M., Litt. D., F. B. A., F. S. A., Provost of Eton. It was a guide to Suffolk and Norfolk.

The shopkeeper appeared through the bead curtain of the doorway behind the desk. "That's a lovely book, my dear," she croaked smokily, pointing with her cigarette, "and cheap."

Kew glanced at the price penciled on the flyleaf. Not bad for a fiver, he had to admit, and only today he'd been complaining that although this was James country there wasn't a single book of his to be seen. He leafed through the guide, and the first page he came to bore a drawing of a bench end, carved with a doglike figure from whose grin a severed head dangled by the hair. "I'll chance it," he murmured, and dug his wallet out of the pocket of his purple cardigan.

The shopkeeper must have been too polite or too eager for a sale to mention that it was closing time, for as soon as Kew was on the pavement he heard her bolt the door. As he made his way to the path down to the beach, a wind from the sea fluttered the brightly striped paper in which she'd wrapped the volume. Laura and her husband, Frank, were shaking towels and rolling them up while their eight-year-olds kicked sand at each other. "Stop that, you two, or else," Laura cried.

"I did say you should drop me and go on somewhere," Kew said as he reached them.

"We wouldn't dream of leaving you by yourself, Teddy," Frank said, brushing sand from his bristling gingery torso.

"He means we'd rather stay with you," Laura said, yanking at her swimsuit top, which Kew could see she hadn't been wearing.

"Of course that's what I meant, old feller," Frank shouted as if Kew were deaf.

They were trying to do their best for him, insisting that he come with them on this holiday—the first he'd taken since Laura's mother had died—but why couldn't they accept that he wanted to be by himself? "Granddad's bought a present," Bruno shouted.

"Is it for us?" Virginia demanded.

"I'm afraid it isn't the kind of book you would like."

"We would if it's horrible," she assured him. "Mum and Dad don't mind."

"It's a book about this part of the country. I rather think you'd be bored."

She shook back her hair, making her earrings jangle, and screwed up her face. "I already am."

"If you make faces like that no boys will be wanting you tonight at the disco," Frank said, and gathered up the towels and the beach toys, trotted to the car, which he'd parked six inches short of a garden fence near the top of the path, hoisted his armful with one hand while he unlocked the hatchback with the other, dumped his burden in, and pushed the family one by one into the car. "Your granddad's got his leg," he rumbled when the children complained about having to sit in the backseat, and Kew felt more of a nuisance than ever.

They drove along the tortuous coast road to Cromer, and Kew went up to his room. Soon Laura knocked on his door to ask whether he was coming down for an apéritif. He would have invited her to sit with him so that they could reminisce about her mother, but Frank shouted, "Come on, old feller, give yourself an appetite. We don't want you fading away on us."

Kew would have had more of an appetite if the children hadn't swapped horrific jokes throughout the meal. "That's enough, now," Laura kept saying. Afterward coffee was served in the lounge, and Kew tried to take refuge in his book.

It was more the M. R. James he remembered nostalgically than he would have dared hope. Comic and macabre images lay low amid the graceful sentences. Here was "that mysterious being Sir John Shorne," Rector of North Marston, who "was invoked against ague; but his only known act was to conjure the devil into a boot, the occasion and sequelae of this being alike unknown." Here were the St. Albans monks, who bought two of St. Margaret's fingers; but who, Kew wondered, were the Crouched Friars, who had "one little house, at Great Whelnetham"? Then there were "the three kings or young knights who are out hunting and pass a churchyard, where they meet three terrible corpses, hideous with the ravages of death, who say to them, 'As we are, so will you be'"—a popular subject for decorating churches, apparently. Other references were factual, or at least were presented as such: not only a rector named Blastus Godly, but a merman caught at Orford in the thirteenth century, who "could not be induced to take an interest in the services of the church, nor indeed to speak." Kew's grunt of amusement at this attracted the children, who had finished reading the horror comics they'd persuaded their father to buy them. "Can we see?" Virginia said.

Kew showed them the sketch of the bench-end with the severed head, and thought of ingratiating himself further with them by pointing out a passage referring to the tradition that St. Erasmus had had his entrails wound out of him on a windlass, the kind of thing the children's parents tried halfheartedly to prevent them from watching on videocassettes. Rebuking himself silently, he leafed in search of more acceptably macabre anecdotes, and then he stared. "Granddad," Bruno said as if Kew needed to be told, "someone's been writing in your book."

A sentence at the end of the penultimate chapter—"It is almost always worth while to halt and look into a Norfolk church"—had been ringed in greyish ink, and a line as shaky as the circumscription led to a scribbled paragraph that filled the lower half of the page. "I hope they knocked a few quid off the price for that, old feller," Frank said. "If they didn't I'd take it back."

"Remember when you smacked me," Laura said to Kew, "for drawing in one of Mummy's books?"

Frank gave him a conspiratorial look which Kew found so disturbing that he could feel himself losing control, unable to restrain himself from telling Laura that Virginia shouldn't be dressed so provocatively, that the children should be inbed instead of staying up for the disco, that he was glad Laura's mother wasn't here to see how they were developing. . . . He made his excuses and rushed himself up to his room.

He should sleep before the dull sounds of the disco made that impossible, but he couldn't resist poring over the scribbled paragraph. After a few minutes he succeeded in deciphering the first phrase, which was underlined. "Best left out," it said.

If the annotation described something better than the book included, Kew would like to know what it was. Studying the phrase had given him a headache, which the disco was liable to worsen. He got ready for bed and lay in the dark, improvising a kind of silent lullaby out of the names of places he'd read in the guidebook:

Great Snoring and Creeting St Mary,
Bradfield Combust and Breckles and Snape;
Herringfleet, Rattlesden,
Chipley and Weeting;
Bungay and Blickling and Diss. . .

Almost asleep, too much so to be troubled by the draft that he could hear rustling paper near his bed, he wondered if the scribbled phrase could mean that the omission had been advisable. In that case, why note it at such length?

He slept, and dreamed of walking from church to church, the length and breadth of East Anglia, no longer needing his stick. He found the church he was looking for, though he couldn't have said what his criteria were, and lay down beneath the ribbed vault that somehow reminded him of himself. Laura and the children came to visit him, and he sat up. "As I am, so will you be," he said in a voice whose unfamiliarity dismayed him. They hadn't come to visit but to view him, he thought, terrified of doing so himself. It seemed he had no choice, for his body was audibly withering, a process which dragged his head down to show him what had become of him. Barely in time, his cry wakened him.

If the dream meant anything, it confirmed that he needed time by himself. He lay willing his heartbeat to slacken its pace; his eardrums felt close to bursting. He slept uneasily and woke at dawn. When he limped to the toilet, his leg almost let him down. He hawked, splashed cold water on his face, massaged his hands for several minutes before opening the book. If he couldn't read James's ghost stories, then viewing a location that had suggested one of them might be as much of an experience.

The book fell open at the scribbled page, and he saw that the line beneath the phrase he'd read last night wasn't underlining after all. It led from the next word, which was "map," across the page and onto the fore edge. Rubbing together his fingers and thumb, which felt dusty, he opened the book where the line ended, at a map of Norfolk.

The line led like the first thread of a cobweb to a blotch on the Norfolk coast, where the map identified nothing in particular, showing only beach and fields for miles. The next scribbled phrase, however, was easily read: "churchyard on the cliff—my old parish." It sounded irresistibly Jamesian, and not to his family's taste at all.

In the hotel lounge before breakfast he read on: "There was a man so versed in the black arts that he was able to bide his time until the elements should open his grave . . ." Either Kew was becoming used to the scrawl or it grew increasingly legible as it progressed. He might have read more if the family hadn't come looking for him. "We're going to give Granddad a good day out today, aren't we?" Frank declared.

"We said so," Bruno muttered.

Virginia frowned reprovingly at him. "You have to say where we're going," she told her grandfather with a faintly martyred air.

"How about to breakfast?"

At the table Kew said to the children, "I expect you'd like to go to Hunstanton, wouldn't you? I understand there are dodgems and roller coasters and all sorts of other things to make you sick."

"Yes, yes, yes," the children began to chant, until Laura shushed them.

"That doesn't sound like you, Daddy," she said.

"You can drop me off on your way. I've found somewhere I want to walk to, that wouldn't have anything to offer you youngsters."

"I used to like walking with you and Mummy," Laura said, and turned on her son. "That's disgusting, Bruno. Stop doing that with your egg."

Kew thought of inviting her to walk to the church with him, but he'd seen how intent Frank and the children had become when she'd hinted at accompanying him. "Maybe we'll have time for a stroll another day," he said.

He sat obediently in the front seat of the car, and clutched his book and his stick while Frank drove eastward along the coast road. Whenever he spoke, Frank and Laura answered him so competitively that before long he shut up. As the road swung away from the coast, the towns and villages grew fewer. A steam train paced the car for a few hundred yards as if it were ushering them into James's era. A sea wind rustled across the flat land, under a sky from which gulls sailed down like flakes of the unbroken cloud. On the side of the road toward the coast, the stooped grass looked pale with salt and sand.

Apart from the occasional fishmonger's stall at the roadside, the miles between the dwindling villages were deserted. By the time the car arrived at the stretch of road that bordered the unnamed area that the blotch of grayish ink marked on the map, Bruno and Virginia had begun to yawn at the monotonousness of the landscape. Where a signpost pointed inland along a road, an inn stood by itself, and beyond it Kew saw an unmarked footpath that led toward the sea. "This'll do me. Let me out here," he said.

"Thirsty, old feller? This one's on me."

Kew felt both dismayed by the idea of being distracted from the loneliness of the setting and ashamed of his feelings. "They'll be open in a few minutes," Laura said.

"Boring, boring," the children started chanting, and Kew took the opportunity to climb out and close the door firmly. "Don't spoil the children's day on my account," he said, "or mine will be spoiled as well."

Now he'd made it sound as if they were ruining his holiday. He patted Laura's cheek awkwardly, and then Virginia's, and leaned back from the open window. "Five o'clock here suit you?" Frank said. "If we're late, there's always the pub."

Kew agreed, and watched the car race away. The children waved without turning their heads, but Laura kept him in sight as long as she could. Just as the car reached the first bend, Kew wanted to wave his stick urgently, to call out to Frank that he'd changed his mind. Six hours out here seemed a more generous helping of solitude than even he needed. Then the car was gone, and he told himself that the family deserved a break from him.

He sat on a rustic bench outside the building striped with timber, and turned to the scribbled page while he waited for the door to be unlocked. He found he was able to read straight on to the end, not least because the ink appeared darker.

> *There was a man so versed in the black arts that he was able to bide his time until the elements should open his grave; only the passage of so many years, and the stresses to which the falling away of the land subjected the grave, twisted not only the coffin almost beyond recognition but also what laired within. Imagine, if you will, a spider in human form with only four limbs, a spider both enraged and made ungainly by the loss, especially since the remaining limbs are by no means evenly distributed. If anything other than simple malevolence let him walk, it was the knowledge that whoever died of the sight of him would be bound to him.*

Kew shivered and grinned at himself. So he could still derive a frisson from that kind of writing, all the more pleasurable when he remembered that James had never believed in his ghosts. Was it really possible that Kew was holding in his hands an unpublished episode by James? He didn't know what else to think. He gazed along the path through the swaying grass and wondered what it led to that had produced the description he'd just read, until the sound of bolts being slid back made him jump.

The landlord, a hairy bespectacled man whose ruddiness and girth suggested that he enjoyed his beer, looked out at Kew and then at the book. "Bit out of your way if you're walking, aren't you?" he said, so heartily that it served as a welcome. "Come in and wet your whistle, my lad."

A bar bristling with decorated handles and thick as a castle parapet marked off a quarter of the L-shaped room, beyond which were a few small tables draped with cloths, and a staircase guarded by a visitors' book. The landlord hauled on the nearest handle and gave Kew a pint of murky beer. "I was driven here," Kew explained. "I'm just about to start walking."

"Are you not using that book?"

"Why, do you know it?"

"I know all of that man's work that's set around this countryside. He had the touch, and no mistake." The landlord pulled himself a pint and drank half of it in one gulp. "But he didn't find anything round here that he wanted to write about."

Kew thought of showing the landlord the annotation but wasn't quite sure of himself. "Do you know if he ever came this way?"

"I should say so. He signed the book."

Excitement made Kew grip the handle of his tankard. "Could I see?"

"Certainly, if I can dig it out. Were you thinking of eating?" When Kew said that he better had, the landlord served him bread and cheese before unlocking a cupboard beside the stairs. Kew glanced at the handwritten paragraph to remind himself what the writing looked like, and then watched the landlord pull out visitors' book after visitors' book and scan the dates. Eventually he brought a volume to Kew's table. "Here he is."

Kew saw the date first: 1890. "He hadn't written any of his stories then, had he?"

"Not one."

Kew ran his gaze down the column of faded signatures and almost didn't see the name he was searching for. As he came back to it, he saw why he had passed over it: the signature bore no resemblance to the handwriting in the guidebook. He sighed and then sucked in a breath. The signature directly beneath James's was in that handwriting.

Was the signature "A. Fellows"? He touched it with his fingertip and tried to rub the cobwebby feel of it off his finger with his thumb. "Who was this, do you know?"

"Whoever came after Monty James."

The landlord seemed to be trying not to grin, and Kew gazed at him until he went on. "You'd think these East Anglians would be proud to have James write about their countryside," the landlord said, "but they don't like to talk about his kind of stories. Maybe they believe in that kind of thing more than he did. The chap who ran this place was on his deathbed when he told my father about that signature. It seems nobody saw who made it. It's like one of Monty's own yarns."

"Have you any idea where James had been that day?"

"Some old ruin on the cliff," the landlord said, and seemed to wish he had been less specific.

"Along the path outside?"

"If it was, there's even less there now, and you'll have noticed that he didn't think it had any place in his book."

The annotator had believed otherwise, and Kew thought that was a mystery worth investigating. He finished his lunch and drained his tankard, and was at the door when the landlord said, "I wouldn't stray too far from the road if I were you. Remember we're open till three."

This felt so like the protectiveness Kew had escaped earlier that he made straight for the path. Didn't anyone think he was capable of taking care of himself? He'd fought in the war against Hitler, he'd been a partner in an accountancy firm, he'd run every year in the London marathon until his leg had crippled him, he'd tended Laura's mother during her last years and had confined himself to places where he could wheel her in her chair, and after all that, he wasn't to be trusted to go off the road by himself? James had followed the path, and it didn't seem to have done him any harm. Kew stuffed the book under one arm and tramped toward the sea, cutting at the ragged grassy edges of the path with his stick.

The fields of pale grass stretched into the distance on both sides of him. The low cloud, featureless except for the infrequent swerving gull, glared dully above him. After twenty minutes' walking he felt he had scarcely moved, until he glanced back and found that the inn was out of sight. He was alone, as far as he could see, though the grass of the fields came up to his shoulder now. A chilly wind rustled through the fields, and he limped fast to keep warm, faster when he saw a building ahead.

At least, he thought it was a building until he was able to see through its broken windows. It was the front wall of a cottage, all that remained of the house. As he came abreast of it he saw other cottages farther on, and a backward look showed him foundations under the grass. He'd been walking through a ruined village without realizing it. One building, however, appeared still to be intact: the church, ahead at the edge of the ruins.

The church was squat and blackened, with narrow windows and a rudimentary tower. Kew had to admit that it didn't look very distinguished—hardly worth singling out for the guidebook—though wasn't there a large gargoyle above one of the windows that overlooked the wide grey sea? In any case, the sight of the church, alone on the cliff top amid the fringe of nodding grass, seemed worth the walk. He threw his shoulders back and breathed deep of the sea air, and strode toward the church.

He needn't have been quite so vigorous; there was nobody to show off for. He had to laugh at himself, for in his haste he dug his stick into a hole in the overgrown pavement and almost overbalanced. Rather than risk tearing the paper jacket by trying to hold onto the guidebook, he let the book fall on the grass, where it fell open at the scribbled page.

He frowned at the handwriting as he stooped carefully, gripping the stick, and wondered if exposure to sunlight had affected the ink. The first lines appeared blurred, so much so that he couldn't read the words "best left out" at all. Perhaps the dead light was affecting his eyes, because now as he peered toward the church he saw that there was no gargoyle. He could only assume that the wind had pushed forward the withered shrub which he glimpsed swaying out of sight around the corner closest to the sea, and a trick of perspective had made it look as if it were protruding from high up on the wall.

The church door was ajar. As Kew limped in the direction of the cliff edge, to see how stable the foundations of the building were, he discerned pews and an altar in the gloomy interior, and a figure in black moving back and forth in front of the glimmering altar. Could the church still be in use? Perhaps the priest was another sightseer.

Kew picked his way alongside the building, over illegibly weathered gravestones whose cracks looked cemented with moss, to the jagged brink, and then he shoved the book under the arm that held the stick and grabbed the cold church wall to support himself. Apart from the slabs he'd walked on, the graveyard had vanished; it must have fallen to the beach as the centuries passed. The church itself stood at the very edge of the sheer cliff now, its exposed foundations sprouting weeds that rustled in the sandy wind. But it wasn't the precariousness of the building that had made Kew feel suddenly shaky, in need of support; it was that there was no shrub beside the church, nothing like the distorted shrunken brownish shape he'd glimpsed as it withdrew from sight. Beside that corner of the church, the cliff fell steeply to the beach.

He clutched the wall, bruising his fingertips, while he tried to persuade himself that the shrub and the portion of ground on which it stood had just lost their hold on the cliff, and then he shoved himself away from the wall, away from the crumbling edge. As he did so, he heard a scrabbling above him, on the roof. A chunk of moss, too large to have been dislodged by a bird, dropped on the grass in front of him. He clapped his free hand to his chest, which felt as if his heart were beating its way to the surface, and fled to the entrance to the church.

The priest was still by the altar. Kew could see the blotch of darkness that was his robe, and the whitish glint of his collar. Thoughts were falling over one another in Kew's head: the guidebook was a late edition, and so the scribbled annotation must have been made decades later than the signature at the inn, yet the handwriting hadn't aged at all, and couldn't the words in the visitors' book which Kew had taken for a signature have been "A Follower"? The only thought he was able to grasp was how far he would have to run across the deserted land from the church to the inn—too far for him to be able to keep up the pace for more than a few minutes. He dodged into the gloomy church, his stick knocking against a pew, and heard a larger movement overhead. "Please," he gasped, stumbling down the aisle into the dimness.

He hardly knew what he was saying or doing, but where else could he go for help except to the priest? He wished he could see the man's face, though rather less fervently once the priest spoke. "It brought you," he said.

It wasn't just his words but also his voice that disturbed Kew. Perhaps it was an echo that made it sound so hollow, but why was its tone so eager? "You mean the book," Kew stammered.

"We mean what you read."

Kew was almost at the altar now. As his eyes adjusted, he saw that what he'd taken to be dimness draping the pews and the altar was a mass of dust and cobwebs. More than the tone and timbre of the voice, its forced quality was beginning to unnerve him. "Your friend James thought it, but he didn't write it," the voice said. "We inspired him, and then I had to write it for him."

If James had used the handwritten paragraph in one of his tales and identified the setting as he tended to, Kew thought with the clarity of utter panic, more people would have visited this church. He was backing toward the door when he heard something clamber down from the roof and land just outside the doorway with a sound like the fall of a bundle of sticks and leather. "James nearly saw, but he didn't believe," said the figure by the altar, and stepped into the light that seeped through a pinched grimy window. "But you will," it said out of the hole that was most of its face.

Kew closed his eyes tight. His panic had isolated a single thought at the centre of him: that those who died of seeing would be bound to what they saw. He felt the guidebook slip out of his hands, he heard its echoes clatter back and forth between the walls, and then it gave way to another sound, of something that scuttled lopsidedly into the church and halted to wait for him. He heard the priest's feet, bare of more than clothing, begin to drag across the floor toward him. He turned, frantically tapping the pews with his stick, and shuffled in the direction of the door. Beyond it was the path, the inn, his family at five o'clock, further than his mind could grasp. If he had to die, please let it not be here! What terrified him most, as he swung the stick in front of him and prayed that it would ward off any contact, was what might be done to him to try and make him look.

R. CHETWYND-HAYES
The Limping Ghost

Ronald Chetwynd-Hayes *(b. 1919), 'Britain's Prince of Chill', is one of Britain's most prolific writers of horror and ghost stories, with paperback sales alone in excess of one million copies. Two horror films,* From Beyond the Grave *(1973) and* The Monster Club *(1980), have been based on his collections. In the latter, he was portrayed on screen by John Carradine. 'The Limping Ghost' is taken from* The Night Ghouls *(1975).*

Mother said Brian was not to play with matches and of course he did, setting light to the old summerhouse, so that Father had to put the fire out with the garden hose.

Father maintained that Brian should be spanked but Mother would not let him, stating with cool simplicity, that words were more powerful than blows.

"That's all very well," Father grumbled, "but one day . . ."

"He's only seven," Mother pointed out, "and we must reason with him. It's not as though any real damage was done."

Julia went out to look at the summerhouse, and truly the damage was negligible. The doorsteps were slightly scorched, but this added to the old-world, time-beaten appearance of the ancient building.

When she came back to the house, Mother was explaining to Brian the virtues and evils of fire.

"The fire keeps us warm; it cooks our food and is nice to look at."

"Makes pretty pictures," Brian stated, "lots of mountains and valleys."

"Yes," Mother agreed, "and therefore fire is a good friend, but when you set light to the summerhouse, then it was a bad enemy. You—all of us could have been burnt to death."

"Death . . . death," Brian repeated the words with some satisfaction. "What is death?"

Mother frowned, then proceeded to choose her words with care.

"The body . . . your arms and legs become still, and you can't use your body any more. You . . . become like Mr Miss-One."

Brian grinned with impish delight.

"I'd like to be Mr Miss-One."

Mother took the small boy into her arms and shook her beautiful head, so that the fair curls danced like corn in sunlight.

"No, my darling. No. You wouldn't like being Mr Miss-One."

Julia came down late for dinner for she had fallen asleep in her room, and dreamt a strange dream. It seemed that she had been in the drawing-room when Mr Miss-One entered. He had limped across the room and sank down beside her on the sofa; and for the first time, he seemed to know she was present. He stared straight at her and looked so very, very sad, that when she awoke, tears were rolling down her cheeks.

"You look pale," Mother remarked, "and your eyes are red. I hope you aren't sickening for something."

Julia said: "No," then seated herself opposite Brian, who made a face and poked his tongue out.

"Behave yourself," Father warned, "and, Julia, you're not to tease him."

"I didn't . . ." Julia began to protest but Mother said: "You're not to answer your father back."

She hung her head and fought back the scalding tears. The terrible injustice was a burning pain and she felt shut out—unwanted. Brian was a child, a doll for her parents to pet; she was sixteen, tall, awkward, not particularly pretty, which meant being unloved, isolated, scolded; who knows, perhaps hated.

"Julia, sit up," Mother continued with a sharp voice, "don't slouch. Heavens above, when I was your age, I was as straight as a larch. Really, I can't imagine who you take after."

"Listen to your mother," Father ordered, smiling at Brian whose mouth was smeared with custard. "She is talking for your own good."

They might have been talking to a stranger or casting words at a statue. Her very presence, every action, provoked a series of stock phrases. She moved in her chair.

"Don't fidget," Mother snapped.

"For heaven's sake, sit still," said Father.

Julia got up and ran from the room.

"Oh, no," Mother exclaimed, "not another fit of the sulks!"

"She'll get over it," Father pronounced.

The garden dozed under the afternoon sun, while bees and blue-bottles hummed with contentment in the heat. Julia lay back in a deck-chair and basked in a lake of misery, wallowing in the melancholy stream of her self-pity.

"I wish I could die. Death is like a beautiful woman in a grey robe who closes our eyes with gentle fingers, then wipes the slate of memory clean."

She decided this was a noble thought, and really she was quite definitely a genius, which explained why everyone was so unkind.

"I am different," she told herself and at once felt much more cheerful. "I think on a much higher plane. Mother is so stupid, afraid to smile in case she makes a line on her face, and as for Father . . . he's an echo, a nothing. Brian is a horrible, spoilt little beast. But I'm—I'm a genius."

Having reached this satisfactory conclusion, she was about to rise when Mr Miss-One entered the garden. He was carrying a hoe and walking over to one of the flower-beds he began to turn the soil, or rather gave the appearance of doing so, for Julia knew that not even a single stone would be disturbed. She crept up to him like a puppy approaching its master, uncertain of its reception. She stopped some three feet from him and sank down on the grass, gazing up into his face.

He was so beautiful. There was no other word to describe that kind, sensitive face. Mother was always a little frightened of Mr Miss-One, saying that though he appeared harmless, nevertheless, he wasn't natural. Father regarded him in much the same way, as if he were a stray cat that refused to be dislodged.

"We must be mad to live in a house with a bally ghost," he had once protested. "Never know when the damned thing is going to pop up."

This attitude of course, only confirmed their mundane, unimaginative outlook, and showed up Julia's exceptional powers of perception. Mr Miss-One was beautiful, kind, and must have been, long ago, a remarkable person. Julia had no evidence to support this theory for Mr Miss-One never spoke, was apparently oblivious of their presence, and only performed little, non-productive chores, strolling aimlessly through the house or garden. Furthermore, Mr Miss-One was not young, possibly as old as Julia's father, for his black hair was flecked with grey and there were tired lines around his eyes and mouth. But these signs of age enhanced his beauty, making him a strange, exciting figure, combining the attributes of father and lover. Now he stood upright, leaning upon the hoe and stared thoughtfully back at the house.

"Mr Miss-One," Julia whispered, "who are you? I want to know so much. How long ago did you live? When did you die? And why do you haunt the house and garden? Haunt! That's a funny word. It sounds frightening, and you don't frighten me at all."

Mr Miss-One returned to his work and continued to turn soil that never moved.

"Father says you don't exist, but are only a time image of someone who lived here years and years ago. That's nonsense. I could not fall in love with a shadow or dream about a patch of coloured air."

"Julia." Mother was standing in the doorway and her voice held an angry, fearful tone. "Julia, come here at once."

Reluctantly she rose and left Mr Miss-One to his ghostly gardening, willing herself not to look back. Mother slapped her bare arm, a punishment that had been applied in childhood.

"I've told you once, I've told you a thousand times, you're not to go near that—that thing. It's not healthy. It ought to be exercised or something."

"Exorcised," Julia corrected.

"And don't answer me back. I think sometimes, you're a little mad. Go to your room and don't come down until I say so."

From her bedroom window, Julia watched Mr Miss-One. He was pushing a ghostly lawnmower over the lawn, limping laboriously in its wake, seemingly oblivious that no grass leapt into the box, that the whirling blades made no sound.

"I expect he was killed in a war," Julia though as he disappeared behind a rhododendron bush. She waited for him to reappear but the garden remained empty, and when, presently, the setting sun sent long tree-shadows across the grass, she knew, for the time being at least, the play was over.

"I thought we might run down to the coast today," Father announced over the breakfast table.

"Good idea." Mother nodded her agreement. "Julia, sit up, child, don't slouch."

"Listen to your mother," Father advised. "Yes, a breath of sea air will do us all good. Brian will enjoy it, won't you old fellow?"

"Yes," Brian nodded vigorously. "Throw stones at seagulls."

Both fond parents laughed softly and Mother admonished gently: "You mustn't throw stones at dicky-birds."

"Why?"

"Because . . ." For once Mother seemed lost for an explanation and it was left to Father to express an opinion.

"Because it's not nice."

"We won't go," Julia thought. "We never go. Something will happen to stop us."

But preparations went on after breakfast. Mother packed a hamper and Brian produced a coloured bucket and wooden spade from the attic, while Julia was instructed to brighten up and look cheerful for a change.

"Maybe we will go this time," she whispered, putting on her best summer dress with polka-dots. "Perhaps nothing will happen to stop us."

The feeling of optimism grew as the entire family walked round the house to the garage, Father carrying the hamper, Mother fanning herself with a silk handkerchief, and Brian kicking the loose gravel. Father opened the garage door, took one step forward, then stopped.

"Damnation hell," he swore. "This really is too much."

Mr Miss-One was cleaning the car.

A bright yellow duster whisked over the dust that remained undisturbed. White liquid from a green tin was sprayed on to the bonnet but somehow never reached its surface. Mr Miss-One rubbed the chromework vigorously but there was no sign that his labour was to be rewarded. The dull bloom persisted, and at times he appeared to be polishing the empty space on either side of the bonnet, thereby suggesting to Julia's watchful eye, that another and much larger car was the object of his ministrations.

"What the hell do we do?" asked Father.

'Well," Mother backed away. "I, for one, am staying at home. Nothing on earth will get me in that car. Heavens above, he might come with us."

"We shouldn't allow it to dominate our lives," Father protested but without much conviction. "I mean to say, it's only a damn time image. Doesn't really exist, you know."

"Thank you very much, but it's got too much life for me." Mother began to walk back towards the house. "Honestly, if you were any sort of man, you would get rid of it."

"What am I supposed to do?" Father was almost running to keep up with her. "I can't kick it; there's nothing solid for me to get to grips with. I do think, my dear, you're being a little unreasonable."

Mother grunted, fanning herself vigorously, then she turned on Julia.

"It's all your fault. You encourage it."

"I . . ." Julia tried to defend herself but a sense of guilt paralysed her tongue.

"You ought to be ashamed." Father glared, wiping his forehead with his top pocket, never-to-be-used handkerchief. "You've no right to encourage it. Spoiling our day out, upsetting your mother and depriving your little brother of good sea-air."

Mother flopped down into a deck-chair, where she continued to wave her handkerchief back and forth.

"Yesterday evening I caught her at it. Talking to it, she was. Lying there on the grass, and talking to it. She's mad. Heavens above knows who she takes after. Certainly my family were sane enough. I don't know what's to become of us."

"We could move," Father suggested.

"And to where?" Mother sat up and put away her handkerchief. "Who would buy a house with a ghost—an active ghost? And where would we get another house that's so secluded and off the beaten track? You know I must have solitude, peace and quiet."

"Perhaps it will go away," Father said after a short silence. "They do, you know. The atmosphere sort of dispels after a bit."

"Not while that girl encourages it," Mother stated. "Not while she moons around it, like a lovesick puppy."

"Keep away from it," warned Father.

Brian punched her thigh with his small fist.

"Keep away from it."

Days passed without an appearance from Mr Miss-One. Julia wondered if her Mother's anger had built a wall through which he could not pass, and mourned for him, as though for a loved friend who had recently died. Sometimes, when she escaped from the vigilance of her parents, she went looking for him; roamed the garden, or suddenly opened a door, hoping to see him leaning against the mantelpiece, or lounging in a chair. But he had become a shadow that flees before sunlight. Even Father commented on his non-appearance.

"Six days now, and we haven't seen hair or hide of it. What did I tell you? The atmosphere has dispelled."

"Stuff and nonsense," Mother snapped. "Atmosphere indeed. Lack of encouragement, more likely. I've been keeping an eye on someone I could touch with a very small stick."

Three pairs of eyes were turned in Julia's direction and she blushed. Brian kicked her ankle under the table.

"Keep away from it."

"I am of the opinion," Mother went on, "that he must have been a bad character. I mean to say, respectable people don't go haunting places after they're dead. They go to wherever they're supposed to go, and don't keep traipsing about, making a nuisance of themselves. He probably murdered someone and can't rest."

"No."

All Julia's reticence, her lifelong submission to her parents' opinions, disappeared in a flood of righteous anger. A part of her looked on and listened with profound astonishment to the torrent of words that poured out of her mouth.

"He was not bad. I know it. He was sad, and that's why he walks . . . I know . . . I know . . . Perhaps once he was happy here, or maybe it is sadness that chains him to this house, but he's not evil . . . he's not . . . You're bad, small, stupid . . . and you've driven him away . . . I'll never forgive you . . . ever . . ."

Mother was so shocked that for a while she was incapable of speech, Father stared at the rebel with dilated eyes. Finally Mother's tongue resumed its natural function.

"I always said the girl was mad and at last I have proof. I feel quite faint. Heavens, did you see her eyes? Really, Henry, are you just going to sit there while she insults us? Do something."

"What? Yes." Father rose as though he were about to deliver a speech. "That's no way to talk to your parents, particularly your mother . . ."

"Oh, for heaven's sake." Mother pointed with dramatic emphasis towards the door. "Get out . . . go on . . . go to your room, and I don't care if I never see your face again."

But the earthquake was still erupting, and Julia shouted back, her brain a red cavern of pain.

"I hate you . . . hate . . . hate . . ."

Mother screamed and fell back in her chair, while Father so far forgot himself as to stamp his foot.

"How dare you speak to your mother like that? Go to your room."

Remorse flooded her being and she craved forgiveness like a soul in torment.

"I didn't mean it. Please . . ."

But Father had eyes and ears only for Mother, who was gasping and writhing in a most alarming fashion. Brian watched the ingrate with joyous excitement.

Julia ran to her room. She flung herself face down on the bed and sobbed soundlessly, her slender shoulders shaking, her long fingers clutching the bedclothes. Presently the storm abated and she became still. Her eyes opened and her sixth sense sent out invisible fingers. All at once—she knew.

She sat up and spun round. Mr Miss-One was standing in the recess by the side of the fireplace. As usual he was busy, but it took some minutes for her to understand what he was doing. A hand-drill! He appeared to be making holes in the wall, although of course the pink flower-patterned wallpaper remained unmarked. Julia got up and walked cautiously towards him, joy blended with curiosity. He slipped little cylinders of fibre into the wall then drove screws into the invisible holes. Light illuminated the darkness of Julia's ignorance.

"He's fitting a bookshelf. How sweet."

She moved a little nearer so as to observe his actions with more clarity. His face was a study in concentration. The teeth were clenched, the muscles round the mouth taut, and once, when the screwdriver slipped, the lips parted as though mouthing a silent curse. She spoke her thoughts aloud, even as a penitent unburdens his soul to an invisible priest.

"Mother is right. I shouldn't be thinking of you all the time. Look at you, fixing a shelf that probably mouldered away years ago. If only I could talk to you, hear your voice most of all, make you realize I exist."

Mr Miss-One lifted the Formica-covered shelf and fitted it into position. It immediately disappeared but he continued to work, seemingly content that all was well.

"You are more real to me than Mother or Father and I feel I ought to tell you all manner of things. But there's no point when you ignore me. Is there no way I can reach you?"

Mr Miss-One took up a hammer and began to tap the wall. Julia moved one step nearer. She could see a small cut on his chin.

"You cut yourself shaving. How long ago did that happen? Ten . . . twenty . . . thirty years ago? Oh, you must know I am here. Can't you feel something? A coldness—an awareness? Surely there must be something; a certainty that you are not alone; the urge to look back over one shoulder . . . Look at me . . . look . . . turn your head . . . you must . . . must . . ."

The hammer struck Mr Miss-One's thumb and he swore.

"Blast!"

The solitary word exploded across the room and shattered the silence, making Julia shrink back. She retreated to the opposite wall, pressed her shoulders against its unrelenting surface and watched him. He dropped the hammer which fell to the floor with a resounding crash, sucked the afflicted thumb, then stared in Julia's direction. For a period of five seconds, he was a statue; a frozen effigy of a man; then his mouth popped open, the hand dropped away and his eyes were blue mirrors reflecting astonishment—disbelief—fear.

"You can see me!" Julia's joyous cry rang out, and she took two steps forward to find he had vanished. Man, hammer, plus the assortment of tools, disappeared and Julia was left banging her fist against the recess wall. Her voice rang out in a shriek of despair.

"Why . . . why . . .?"

Mother, Father, even the carefully tutored Brian, treated her to the silence reserved for the outcast. Some speech was unavoidable but this was delivered in ice-coated voices with impeccable politeness.

"Will you kindly pass the salt," Mother requested on one occasion, "if it is not too much trouble."

Father appeared to be applying the sanctions with some reluctance but he was forced to obey a higher authority.

"More tea . . .?" His hand was on the teapot, then he remembered his ordained line of conduct and pushed it towards her. "Help yourself."

Brian was more direct.

"I mustn't talk to you."

This isolationist treatment created comfort when it was designed to produce misery. She was no longer the target for admonishing barbs, corrective slaps or stinging words. She could fidget, sulk, slouch, or spend hours in her room without a single rebuke, although on occasion Mother was clearly sorely provoked, and once or twice her silence policy almost collapsed.

Free from supervision she was able to continue her pursuit of Mr Miss-One, but once again he seemed to have gone into hiding.

The hum and roar of speeding cars drifted across the sleeping meadows. The roar of an overhead jet could be heard above the wind in the trees. Yet the living had no place in Julia's heart, or for that matter, in any place in the house or garden.

Of late a dream had taken root in her imagination. Now it dominated her waking and sleeping life. The seed had first been sown when she saw Mr Miss-One cleaning his car.

"Suppose," whispered her imagination, "you were to get into the car and let Mr Miss-One drive you out into the world. Let him rescue you, carry you off, and never—never come back."

The voice of reason, a nasty, insinuating whisper, interrupted with: "But he is dead. A ghost."

Reason was hoist by its own petard.

"If he is dead—if he is a ghost, then there is only one way in which I can join him."

The twin daggers of shock and horror became blunt as the dream grew. It was the solution to all problems, the key to open the door to Mr Miss-One. She began to consider ways and means.

Poison! She had no means of obtaining any. Cut her throat? Slash her wrists? She shied from such grim prospects like a horse from a snake. Rope—hanging? That would be easy and should not be too painful. There was a length of plastic clothesline in the garage and a convenient beam. If she jumped from the car roof, the leap would be completed in the space of a single heartbeat. It was all so very simple and Julia wondered why she had not thought of it before.

She began to make plans.

From two to four o'clock in the afternoon would be best, for it was then that the family took their after-lunch nap. Mother undressed and went to bed; Father, weather permitting, stretched himself out on a garden hammock, or if wind or rain confined him to the house, he lay prostrate on the sitting-room sofa. Brian slept anywhere. Like an animal, he shut off his consciousness whenever his elders set the example. Without doubt the time to die was between two and four in the afternoon.

The situation was somewhat complicated by Mother suddenly relaxing her rule of silence and making overtures for peace. She actually smiled and said sweetly: "Good morning, dear," before cracking her breakfast egg. "You're looking quite pretty this morning," she went on to remark, an obvious untruth, that suggested a desire to please. Julia was near despair. How could one die with an easy conscience when the enemy spiked their own guns and flew the white flag? Fortunately Mother had a relapse with the cutting remark: "Prettiness without grace is like a wreath without flowers," and instantly Julia's resolve became a determination. She would die when the sun was high, take the fatal step in full daylight, and refuse to be diverted by smile or insult.

However, she made one last effort to contact Mr Miss-One, creeping from room to room and searching the garden, praying that he might appear and acknowledge her existence with a smile. For she could not deny the unpalatable fact, that on the one occasion when Mr Miss-One had seen her in the bedroom, his reaction had been one of fear. At least this established him as an intelligent personality, instead of the mindless time image Father so glibly dismissed, but it was, to say the least, a little disconcerting to know one's appearance inspired fear in a ghost. Of course, once she had assumed the same status, there would be no reason for him to fear her at all. Like would appeal to like. She waited with burning impatience for the hour of two.

At the lunch table, all signs indicated that normality had returned.

"Don't slouch," ordered Mother.

"Sit upright," Father chimed in. "Try to be more like your mother."

Brian displayed signs of budding brilliance.

"You're not pretty, you're not ugly. You're pretty ugly."

The fond parents smiled.

"He takes after me," pronounced Mother, "I could always turn a phrase."

Julia's impatience to be gone grew and destroyed her last lingering doubts.

Father had intended to take his nap in the garden, but just before two o'clock the first cold needles of rain began to fall, so he retreated to the sitting-room and was soon prostrate on the sofa. Mother climbed the stairs; the bedroom door slammed, and Julia murmured an inaudible goodbye. Brian lay down on the dining-room hearthrug and appeared to fall asleep but Julia wondered if this was not a pretence put on for her benefit. Fortunately the door had a key in the lock, so she turned it before leaving the house.

A rising wind drove a curtain of rain across the lawn. It forced proud trees to bend their heads in submission, and turned Julia's dress into a wet shroud. She ran for the garage, water splashing up her legs, dripping down her nose and chin, but it did not feel cold or even wet and she marvelled at the sense of well-being.

The garage doors were open and there was no time to consider why this was so, for there, standing in the gloomy interior, was a large, red car. Julia stood within the entrance and stared at this stranger with wide-eyed astonishment. There should have been an ancient, black family Austin; instead a sleek, rather vicious-looking, red monster occupied the entire floor. A creation of highly polished red enamel, gleaming chromework, black tyres and bulging mudguards, it seemed to be a thing of latent power, just waiting for the right finger to touch a switch, to send it hurling along straight roads, across the barriers of time and space into a million tomorrows.

The off-side door was open and Julia, her plans for self-destruction forgotten, slid on to the red, plastic covered seat and feasted her eyes on the complicated switchboard, the black steering wheel, the gleaming gear levers. Curiosity turned to wonderment, then ripened into pure joy.

"A ghost car!"

It must be, of course. This was the vehicle Mr Miss-One had been cleaning, only then it was invisible, due undoubtedly to the base thoughts of Mother, Father and that little beast, Brian. Now she could see it, feel it, and heavens be praised, actually smell it. This must be the result of suffering, loving him with all her being. She giggled, clasped her hands, and waited with joyous anticipation.

Mr Miss-One entered the garage limping, carrying a small, overnight bag. He was plainly prepared for a journey. A terrible fear struck Julia: "Please don't make it all disappear. Let me go with him—wherever he goes. Anywhere at all."

He opened the right-hand door, slung his bag on to the back seat, then climbed in. He closed the door, turned a key on the switchboard, and the engine roared with instant, pulsating life.

"Don't let it all disappear. Let me go with him."

The car slid out of the garage. The garden and house swept by the windows and Julia spared a thought for Mother, Father and Brian, blissfully asleep, unaware that the despised one was passing out of their lives forever.

"It's happening. I'm going out. At last . . . Oh, merciful God—going out."

The main gates, new, glossy with black paint, were open, and Mr Miss-One swung the car out on to a country road.

They were away at last, speeding along under an arcade of trees, flashing by meadows, snarling past lovely red-bricked houses, while windscreen wipers made neat half-moons in the driving rain.

Mr Miss-One suddenly reached over and opened a narrow flap in the switchboard. His hand was a bare inch from Julia's breast, and she wanted to touch it, clasp the strong fingers, but was afraid that this wonderful dream might dispel. He took out a packet of cigarettes, adroitly popped one into his mouth, then replaced the carton and shut the flap. He lit the cigarette with a strange contraption from the switchboard, then inhaled, letting the smoke trickle down through his nose.

By the time they had reached the main by-pass, the novelty was wearing off, and Julia permitted herself a measure of confidence. The dream, if such it was, displayed no signs of breaking down. The car was solid. She could feel the seat beneath her, hear the muted roar of the engine, smell the smoke from Mr Miss-One's cigarette, see the road sliding away under the car wheels.

The by-pass was straight, a grey ribbon that stretched out into infinity as their speed built up. Sixty, seventy, eighty miles an hour. Julia watched the needle climb on the speedometer. Then she turned her head and looked at Mr Miss-One.

Poor ghost, entirely oblivious in his ghost car, he did not know she was there. How was she to declare her presence and break through the wall that still separated them? She began to talk, spilling out her thoughts in a jumble of low spoken words.

"Mr Miss-One—I'm sorry I don't know your real name, but Brian, the horrible little beast, first called you Mr Miss-One because of your limp. You sort of miss a step. Please, don't think it's meant unkindly, at least by me. In fact, the limp adds to your appearance; makes you more romantic. I guess that sounds silly, but I am silly—I can't help it. I've been in love with you ever since that day when you first walked across the dining-room and Mother went screaming under the table. She did look funny. I remember you took something we couldn't see from the sideboard, then disappeared by the kitchen door. Can't you see, or at least hear me?"

It might have been imagination, but Mr Miss-One did appear to be a little uneasy. He slid down the window to throw away his half-consumed cigarette. Julia sighed.

"I wonder where we are going? Is this your world? Are the people out there wandering shadows left over from yesteryear, or are we racing, invisible, through today? Please try to see me."

She could see his left wrist. His jacket sleeve had slid down and the wrist was bare. Sun-tanned, muscular, covered with fine hair. It was also covered with goose pimples. She gasped, then gave a little cry.

"Oh, you're cold. My poor darling, you're cold."

She had not meant to touch him—not yet—but there was no controlling the automatic impulse. Her hand flew to his wrist. For a brief moment she touched warm flesh, actually felt the fast beating pulse, then the car swerved, and Mr Miss-One jerked his head round and stared straight at her.

His face was a mask of pure, blood-chilling terror, and his mouth opened as he screamed. His hands clawed at the steering wheel, as though some part of his brain were trying to right the skid, and the scream erupted into isolated words, like black rocks crashing through a sheet of ice.

"Dead . . . family . . . burnt . . . dead . . . fifty . . . years . . . dead . . . dead . . . dead . . ."

The screech of tortured rubber mingled with the screaming words. Outside the grey road was spinning round and round. A black shape came hurtling through the rain. There was a mighty, soul-uprooting crash, then for a brief second—nothing. A heartbeat of total oblivion.

Julia was standing by the roadside watching the car burn. Like a giant red beetle it lay on its back, while beautiful scarlet flames rose from its corpse, like poppies from a long-filled grave. The red enamel bubbled and drooled down the seething metal, as blood tears from the eyes of a dying man, and somewhere in the heart of the shrieking inferno, something moved.

Sound flickered, then ceased. Cars drew up, and the occupants climbed out; mouths opened, faces assumed expressions of horror, shock, or morbid excitement. But they were so many, silent, pathetic ghosts.

Julia turned and walked away.

Home was but a few steps away.

Over the grass verge, through a hedge, under some trees, and there were the gates—broken, rusty, one had lost a hinge and was reeling like a drunken man. Once back in the garden, sound returned. Birds sang, bees hummed, and the sun peeped through a broken cloud bank, making the raincoated flowers glisten like coloured fragments. Julia opened the front door and made her way to the dining-room. The family was seated round the table which was laid for tea.

"At last," exclaimed Mother. "I called until my voice was hoarse. Honestly, I don't know who you think you are."

"It's really too bad," Father echoed. "Your mother was nearly out of her mind. Where have you been?"

Julia did not answer, but sank down, staring blankly at the tablecloth. Brian kicked her ankle.

"You locked me in."

"I ask you," Mother addressed the ceiling, "is that the action of a rational person? Locking your little brother in the dining-room? Heavens above knows what might have happened. Well, don't just sit there, we are waiting for an explanation."

"Answer your mother," Father instructed.

Julia took a deep breath.

"We're dead. All of us—dead."

The first shadows of night crept in through the long French window and the silence was coated with the dust of long-dead time. Julia looked up. They were watching her with blank, pale faces.

"Don't you understand? We're dead. We died fifty years ago in a fire. Brian did it. He set light to the bedroom curtains. The whole place went up in fire and smoke."

The ticking of the mantelpiece clock seemed to grow louder; Brian stirred in his chair with a frantic denial.

"I didn't."

"You did." Julia turned on him savagely. "You were told not to play with matches. It was you. You burnt us all to death."

"I didn't. I didn't."

He hammered the table with his mall, clenched fists, while tears ran down his cheeks, then rose and ran to Father, who put his arms round the shaking body.

"Make her stop. I didn't. I didn't play with matches."

"It's all right," Father whispered. "It's all right. Your sister isn't well."

Mother could not speak, could only stare at Julia with wide open eyes. Occasionally she shook her head as though in disbelief.

"Please," Julia pleaded, "try to understand. We are all dead. Mr Miss-One was the living. We were—we are—ghosts."

"Go to your room, dear." Father's voice was unexpectedly gentle. "Go to bed, like a good girl. We'll look after you. Don't worry."

"Yes." Mother spoke at last. "Please forgive me. I never knew. I'll never say a cross word again—ever."

Julia rose very slowly, and as she did so, understanding exploded in her brain.

"You think I'm mad."

Mother shuddered and Father shook his head firmly.

"No—no, of course not, dear. Just tired, ill maybe. But not mad. Dear God, not mad."

Julia fled before their naked terror, and as always, took refuge in her room. She lay upon the bed and stared up at the ceiling, gradually allowing the veil to fall from the awful face of truth. She could never be happy again. She knew. Knowledge was brutal, knowledge destroyed the comforting curtain of doubt.

Father, clearly ill at ease, brought her some food on a tray, talked much too quickly of the healing virtues of sleep, plenty of good food, peace of mind, then departed. Julia heard the key turn in the lock.

Presently she sat by the window and watched the sun put the garden to bed. Shadows lengthened, flowers folded their petals, trees hung their heads, and the evening breeze went dancing across the lawn. For a while there was a great, healing peace.

Then a dark shape limped up the drive. At first Julia thought it might be Father, but as it drew nearer, she saw the black, charred face. The hands were shrivelled, twisted; patches of white bone gleamed through the gaping, roasted flesh. Eyes still glittered in the naked skull, and they stared up at Julia's window.

Julia tried to scream, but her vocal cords refused to function. The most she could make was a hoarse, croaking sound. But out of the heart of her all-demanding terror, a single rational thought ran across her brain like a ribbon of fire.

"Is this how I appear to him?"

All that remained of Mr Miss-One limped up the front steps and disappeared from view. Julia knew her prayer had been answered. She would never be parted from him again.

WILKIE COLLINS
Mrs. Zant and the Ghost

Wilkie Collins *(1824–89), friend and associate of Charles Dickens, is best known today for his novels* The Woman in White, The Moonstone *and* No Name. *G.K. Chesterton once wrote of Dickens and Collins: "There were no two men who could be exceeded at telling a ghost story". 'Mrs.Zant and the Ghost' appeared in Collins's last collection* Little Novels *(1887).*

I

The course of this narrative describes the return of a disembodied spirit to earth, and leads the reader on new and strange ground.

Not in the obscurity of midnight, but in the searching light of day, did the supernatural influence assert itself. Neither revealed by a vision, nor announced by a voice, it reached mortal knowledge through the sense which is least easily self-deceived: the sense that feels.

The record of this event will of necessity produce conflicting impressions. It will raise, in some minds, the doubt which reason asserts; it will invigorate, in other minds, the hope which faith justifies; and it will leave the terrible question of the destinies of man, where centuries of vain investigation have left it—in the dark.

Having only undertaken in the present narrative to lead the way along a succession of events, the writer declines to follow modern examples by thrusting himself and his opinions on the public view. He returns to the shadow from which he has emerged, and leaves the opposing forces of incredulity and belief to fight the old battle over again, on the old ground.

2

The events happened soon after the first thirty years of the present century had come to an end.

On a fine morning, early in the month of April, a gentleman of middle age (named Rayburn) took his little daughter Lucy out for a walk, in the woodland pleasure-ground of Western London, called Kensington Gardens.

The few friends whom he possessed reported of Mr. Rayburn (not unkindly) that he was a reserved and solitary man. He might have been more accurately described as a widower devoted to his only surviving child. Although he was not more than forty years of age, the one pleasure which made life enjoyable to Lucy's father was offered by Lucy herself.

Playing with her ball, the child ran on to the southern limit of the Gardens, at that part of it which still remains nearest to the old Palace of Kensington. Observing close at hand one of those spacious covered seats, called in England "alcoves," Mr. Rayburn was reminded that he had the morning's newspaper in his pocket, and that he might do well to rest and read. At that early hour, the place was a solitude.

"Go on playing, my dear," he said; "but take care to keep where I can see you."

Lucy tossed up her ball; and Lucy's father opened his newspaper. He had not been reading for more than ten minutes, when he felt a familiar little hand laid on his knee.

"Tired of playing?" he inquired—with his eyes still on the newspaper.

"I'm frightened, papa."

He looked up directly. The child's pale face startled him. He took her on his knee and kissed her.

"You oughtn't to be frightened, Lucy, when I am with you," he said gently. "What is it?" He looked out of the alcove as he spoke, and saw a little dog among the trees. "Is it the dog?" he asked.

Lucy answered:

"It's not the dog—it's the lady."

The lady was not visible from the alcove.

"Has she said anything to you?" Mr. Rayburn inquired.

"No."

"What has she done to frighten you?"

The child put her arms round her father's neck.

"Whisper, papa," she said; "I'm afraid of her hearing us. I think she's mad."

"Why do you think so, Lucy?"

"She came near to me. I thought she was going to say something.

She seemed to be ill."

"Well? And what then?"

"She looked at me."

There, Lucy found herself at a loss how to express what she had to say next—and took refuge in silence.

"Nothing very wonderful, so far," her father suggested.

"Yes, papa—but she didn't seem to see me when she looked."

"Well, and what happened then?"

"The lady was frightened—and that frightened me. I think," the child repeated positively, "she's mad."

It occurred to Mr. Rayburn that the lady might be blind. He rose at once to set the doubt at rest.

"Wait here," he said, "and I'll come back to you."

But Lucy clung to him with both hands; Lucy declared that she was afraid to be by herself. They left the alcove together.

The new point of view at once revealed the stranger, leaning against the trunk of a tree. She was dressed in the deep mourning of a widow. The pallor of her face, the glassy stare in her eyes, more than accounted for the child's terror—it excused the alarming conclusion at which she had arrived.

"Go nearer to her," Lucy whispered.

They advanced a few steps. It was now easy to see that the lady was young, and wasted by illness—but (arriving at a doubtful conclusion perhaps under present circumstances) apparently possessed of rare personal attractions in happier days. As the father and daughter advanced a little, she discovered them. After some hesitation, she left the tree; approached with an evident intention of speaking; and suddenly paused. A change to astonishment and fear animated her vacant eyes. If it had not been plain before, it was now beyond all doubt that she was not a poor blind creature, deserted and helpless. At the same time, the expression of her face was not easy to understand. She could hardly have looked more amazed and bewildered, if the two strangers who were observing her had suddenly vanished from the place in which they stood.

Mr. Rayburn spoke to her with the utmost kindness of voice and manner.

"I am afraid you are not well," he said. "Is there anything that I can do——"

The next words were suspended on his lips. It was impossible to realize such a state of things; but the strange impression that she had already produced on him was now confirmed. If he could believe his senses, her face did certainly tell him that he was invisible and inaudible to the woman whom he had just addressed! She moved slowly away with a heavy sigh, like a person disappointed and distressed. Following her with his eyes, he saw the dog once more—a little smooth-coated terrier of the ordinary English breed. The dog showed none of the restless activity of his race. With his head down and his tail depressed, he crouched like a creature paralysed by fear. His mistress roused him by a call. He followed her listlessly as she turned away.

After walking a few paces only, she suddenly stood still.

Mr. Rayburn heard her talking to herself.

"Did I feel it again?" she said, as if perplexed by some doubt that awed or grieved her. After a while, her arms rose slowly, and opened with a gentle caressing action—an embrace strangely offered to the empty air! "No," she said to herself sadly, after waiting a moment. "More perhaps when to-morrow comes—no more to-day." She looked up at the clear blue sky. "The beautiful sunlight! the merciful sunlight!"she murmured. "I should have died if it had happened in the dark."

Once more she called to the dog; and once more she walked slowly away.

"Is she going home, papa?" the child asked.

"We will try and find out," the father answered.

He was by this time convinced that the poor creature was in no condition to be permitted to go out without someone to take care of her. From motives of humanity, he was resolved on making the attempt to communicate with her friends.

3

The lady left the Gardens by the nearest gate; stopping to lower her veil before she turned into the busy thoroughfare which leads to Kensington. Advancing a little way along the High Street, she entered a house of respectable appearance, with a card in one of the windows which announced that apartments were to let.

Mr. Rayburn waited a minute—then knocked at the door, and asked if he could see the mistress of the house. The servant showed him into a room on the ground floor, neatly but scantily furnished. One little white object varied the grim brown monotony of the empty table. It was a visiting-card.

With a child's unceremonious curiosity Lucy pounced on the card, and spelt the name, letter by letter:

"Z.A.N.T" she repeated. "What does that mean?"

Her father looked at the card, as he took it away from her, and put it back on the table. The name was printed, and the address was added in pencil: "Mr. John Zant, Purley's Hotel."

The mistress made her appearance. Mr. Rayburn heartily wished himself out of the house again, the moment he saw her. The ways in which it is possible to cultivate the social virtues are more numerous and more varied than is generally supposed. This lady's way had apparently accustomed her to meet her fellow-creatures on the hard ground of justice without mercy. Something in her eyes, when she looked at Lucy, said:

"I wonder whether that child gets punished when she deserves it?"

"Do you wish to see the rooms which I have to let?" she began.

Mr. Rayburn at once stated the object of his visit—as clearly, as civilly, and as concisely as a man could do it. He was conscious (he added) that he had been guilty perhaps of an act of intrusion.

The manner of the mistress of the house showed that she entirely agreed with him. He suggested, however, that his motive might excuse him. The mistress's manner changed, and asserted a difference of opinion.

"I only know the lady whom you mention," she said, "as a person of the highest respectability, in delicate health. She has taken my first-floor apartments, with excellent references; and she gives remarkably little trouble. I have no claim to interfere with her proceedings, and no reason to doubt that she is capable of taking care of herself."

Mr. Rayburn unwisely attempted to say a word in his own defence.

"Allow me to remind you——" he began.

"Of what, sir?"

"Of what I observed, when I happened to see the lady in Kensington Gardens."

"I am not responsible for what you observed in Kensington Gardens. If your time is of any value, pray don't let me detain you."

Dismissed in those terms, Mr. Rayburn took Lucy's hand and withdrew. He had just reached the door, when it was opened from the outer side. The Lady of Kensington Gardens stood before him. In the position which he and his daughter now occupied, their backs were towards the window. Would she remember having seen them for a moment in the Gardens?

"Excuse me for intruding on you," she said to the landlady. "Your servant tells me my brother-in-law called while I was out. He sometimes leaves a message on his card."

She looked for the message, and appeared to be disappointed: there was no writing on the card.

Mr. Rayburn lingered a little in the doorway, on the chance of hearing something more. The landlady's vigilant eyes discovered him.

"Do you know this gentleman?" she said maliciously to her lodger.

"Not that I remember."

Replying in those words, the lady looked at Mr. Rayburn for the first time; and suddenly drew back from him.

"Yes," she said, correcting herself; "I think we met——"

Her embarrassment overpowered her; she could say no more.

Mr. Rayburn compassionately finished the sentence for her.

"We met accidentally in Kensington Gardens," he said.

She seemed to be incapable of appreciating the kindness of his motive. After hesitating a little she addressed a proposal to him, which seemed to show distrust of the landlady.

"Will you let me speak to you upstairs in my own rooms?" she asked.

Without waiting for a reply, she led the way to the stairs. Mr. Rayburn and Lucy followed. They were just beginning the ascent to the first floor, when the spiteful landlady left the lower room, and called to her lodger over their heads:

"Take care what you say to this man, Mrs. Zant! He thinks you're mad."

Mrs. Zant turned round on the landing, and looked at him. Not a word fell from her lips. She suffered, she feared, in silence. Something in the sad submission of her face touched the springs of innocent pity in Lucy's heart. The child burst out crying.

That artless expression of sympathy drew Mrs. Zant down the few stairs which separated her from Lucy.

"May I kiss your dear little girl?" she said to Mr. Rayburn. The landlady, standing on the mat below, expressed her opinion of the value of caresses, as compared with a sounder method of treating young persons in tears: "If that child was mine," she remarked, "I would give her something to cry for."

In the meantime, Mrs. Zant led the way to her rooms.

The first words she spoke showed that the landlady had succeeded but too well in prejudicing her against Mr. Rayburn.

"Will you let me ask your child," she said to him, "why you think me mad?"

He met this strange request with a firm answer.

"You don't know yet what I really do think. Will you give me a minute's attention?"

"No," she said positively. "The child pities me, I want to speak to the child. What did you see me do in the Gardens, my dear, that surprised you?" Lucy turned uneasily to her father; Mrs. Zant persisted. "I first saw you by yourself, and then I saw you with your father," she went on. "When I came nearer to you, did I look very oddly—as if I didn't see you at all?"

Lucy hesitated again; and Mr. Rayburn interfered.

"You are confusing my little girl," he said. "Allow me to answer your questions—or excuse me if I leave you."

There was something in his look, or in his tone, that mastered her. She put her hand to her head.

"I don't think I'm fit for it," she answered vacantly. "My courage has been sorely tried already. If I can get a little rest and sleep, you may find me a different person. I am left a great deal by myself; and I have reasons for trying to compose my mind. Can I see you to-morrow? Or write to you? Where do you live?"

Mr. Rayburn laid his card on the table in silence. She had strongly excited his interest. He honestly desired to be of some service to this forlorn creature—abandoned so cruelly, as it seemed to her own guidance. But he had no authority to exercise, no sort of claim to direct her actions, even if she consented to accept his advice. As a last resource he ventured on an allusion to the relative of whom she had spoken downstairs.

"When do you expect to see your brother-in-law again?" he said.

"I don't know," she answered. "I should like to see him—he is so kind to me."

She turned aside to take leave of Lucy.

"Good-bye, my little friend. If you live to grow up, I hope you will never be such a miserable woman as I am." She suddenly looked round at Mr. Rayburn. "Have you got a wife at home?" she asked.

"My wife is dead."

"And *you* have a child to comfort you! Please leave me; you harden my heart. Oh, sir, don't you understand? You make me envy you!"

Mr. Rayburn was silent when he and his daughter were out in the street again. Lucy, as became a dutiful child, was silent, too. But there are limits to human endurance—and Lucy's capacity for self-control gave way at last.

"Are you thinking of the lady, papa?" she said.

He only answered by nodding his head. His daughter had interrupted him at that critical moment in a man's reflections, when he is on the point of making up his mind. Before they were at home again Mr Rayburn had arrived at a decision. Mrs. Zant's brother-in-law was evidently ignorant of any serious necessity for his interference—or he would have made arrangements for immediately repeating his visit. In this state of things, if any evil happened to Mrs. Zant, silence on Mr. Rayburn's part might be indirectly to blame for a serious misfortune. Arriving at that conclusion, he decided upon running the risk of being rudely received, for the second time, by another stranger.

Leaving Lucy under the care of her governess, he went at once to the address that had been written on the visiting-card left at the lodging-house, and sent in his name. A courteous message was returned. Mr. John Zant was at home, and would be happy to see him.

4

Mr. Rayburn was shown into one of the private sitting-rooms of the hotel.

He observed that the customary position of the furniture in a room had been, in some respects altered. An armchair, a side-table, and a footstool had all been removed to one of the windows, and had been placed as close as possible to the light. On the table lay a large open roll of morocco leather, containing rows of elegant little instruments in steel and ivory. Waiting by the table, stood Mr. John Zant. He said "Good-morning" in a bass voice, so profound and so melodious that those two commonplace words assumed a new importance, coming from his lips. His personal appearance was in harmony with his magnificent voice—he was a tall finely-made man of dark complexion; with big brilliant black eyes, and a noble curling beard, which hid the whole lower part of his face. Having bowed with a happy mingling of dignity and politeness, the conventional side of this gentleman's character suddenly vanished; and a crazy side, to all appearance, took its place. He dropped on his knees in front of the footstool. Had he forgotten to say his prayers that morning, and was he in such a hurry to remedy the fault that he had no time to spare for consulting appearances? The doubt had hardly suggested itself, before it was set at rest in a most unexpected manner. Mr. Zant looked at his visitor with a bland smile, and said:

"Please let me see your feet."

For the moment, Mr. Rayburn lost his presence of mind. He looked at the instruments on the side-table.

"Are you a corn-cutter?" was all he could say.

"Excuse me, sir," returned the polite operator, "the term you use is quite obsolete in our profession." He rose from his knees, and added modestly: "I am a Chiropodist."

"I beg your pardon."

"Don't mention it! You are not, I imagine, in want of my professional services. To what motive may I attribute the honour of your visit?"

By this time Mr. Rayburn had recovered himself.

"I have come here," he answered, "under circumstances which require apology as well as explanation."

Mr. Zant's highly polished manner betrayed signs of alarm; his suspicions pointed to a formidable conclusion—a conclusion that shook him to the innermost recesses of the pocket in which he kept his money.

"The numerous demands on me——" he began.

Mr. Rayburn smiled.

"Make your mind easy," he replied. "I don't want money. My object is to speak with you on the subject of a lady who is a relation of yours."

"My sister-in-law!" Mr. Zant exclaimed. "Pray, take a seat."

Doubting if he had chosen a convenient time for his visit, Mr. Rayburn hesitated.

"Am I likely to be in the way of persons who wish to consult you?" he asked.

"Certainly not. My morning hours of attendance on my clients are from eleven to one." The clock on the mantelpiece struck the quarter-past one as he spoke. "I hope you don't bring me bad news?" he said, very earnestly. "When I called on Mrs. Zant this morning, I heard that she had gone out for a walk. Is it indiscreet to ask how you became acquainted with her?"

Mr. Rayburn at once mentioned what he had seen and heard in Kensington Gardens; not forgetting to add a few words, which described his interview afterwards with Mrs. Zant.

The lady's brother-in-law listened with an interest and sympathy, which offered the strongest possible contrast to the unprovoked rudeness of the mistress of the lodging-house. He declared that he could only do justice to his sense of obligation by following Mr. Rayburn's example, and expressing himself as frankly as if he had been speaking to an old friend.

"The sad story of my sister-in-law's life," he said, "will I think, explain certain things which must have naturally perplexed you. My brother was introduced to her at the house of an Australian gentleman, on a visit to England. She was then employed as governess to his daughters. So sincere was the regard felt for her by the family that the parents had, at the entreaty of their children, asked her to accompany them when they returned to the Colony. The governess thankfully accepted the proposal."

"Had she no relations in England?" Mr. Rayburn asked.

"She was literally alone in the world, sir. When I tell you that she had been brought up in the Foundling Hospital, you will understand what I mean. Oh, there is no romance in my sister-in-law's story! She never has known, or will know, who her parents were or why they deserted her. The happiest moment in her life was the moment when she and my brother first met. It was an instance, on both sides, of love at first sight. Though not a rich man, my brother had earned a sufficient income in mercantile pursuits. His character spoke for itself. In a word, he altered all the poor girl's prospects, as we then hoped and believed, for the better. Her employers deferred their return to Australia, so that she might be married from their house. After a happy life of a few weeks only——"

His voice failed him; he paused, and turned his face from the light.

"Pardon me," he said; "I am not able, even yet, to speak composedly of my brother's death. Let me only say that the poor young wife was a widow, before the happy days of the honeymoon were over. That dreadful calamity struck her down. Before my brother had been committed to the grave, her life was in danger from brain-fever."

Those words placed in a new light Mr. Rayburn's first fear that her intellect might be deranged. Looking at him attentively, Mr. Zant seemed to understand what was passing in the mind of his guest.

"No!" he said. "If the opinions of the medical men are to be trusted, the result of the illness is injury to her physical strength—not injury to her mind. I have observed in her, no doubt, a certain waywardness of temper since her illness; but that is a trifle. As an example of what I mean, I may tell you that I invited her, on her recovery, to pay me a visit. My house is not in London—the air doesn't agree with me—my place of residence is at St. Sallins-on-Sea. I am not myself a married man; but my excellent housekeeper would have received Mrs. Zant with the utmost kindness. She was resolved—obstinately resolved, poor thing—to remain in London. It is needless to say that, in her melancholy position, I am attentive to her slightest wishes. I took a lodging for her; and, at her special request, I chose a house which was near Kensington Gardens."

"Is there any association with the Gardens which led Mrs. Zant to make that request?"

"Some association, I believe, with the memory of her husband. By the way, I wish to be sure of finding her at home, when I call to-morrow. Did you say (in the course of your interesting statement) that she intended—as you supposed—to return to Kensington Gardens to-morrow? Or has my memory deceived me?"

"Your memory is perfectly accurate."

"Thank you. I confess I am not only distressed by what you have told me of Mrs. Zant—I am at a loss to know how to act for the best. My only idea, at present, is to try change of air and scene. What do you think yourself?"

"I think you are right."

Mr. Zant still hesitated.

"It would not be easy for me, just now, he said, "to leave my patients and take her abroad."

The obvious reply to this occurred to Mr. Rayburn. A man of larger worldly experience might have felt certain suspicions, and might have remained silent. Mr. Rayburn spoke.

"Why not renew your invitation and take her to your house at the seaside?" he said.

In the perplexed state of Mr. Zant's mind, this plain course of action had apparently failed to present itself. His gloomy face brightened directly.

"The very thing!" he said. "I will certainly take your advice. If the air of St. Sallins does nothing else, it will improve her health, and help her to recover her good looks. Did she strike you as having been (in happier days) a pretty woman?"

This was a strangely familiar question to ask—almost an indelicate question, under the circumstances. A certain furtive expression in Mr. Zant's fine dark eyes seemed to imply that it had been put with a purpose. Was it possible that he suspected Mr. Rayburn's interest in his sister-in-law to be inspired by any motive which was not perfectly unselfish and perfectly pure? To arrive at such a conclusion as this, might be to judge hastily and cruelly of a man who was perhaps only guilty of a want of delicacy of feeling. Mr. Rayburn honestly did his best to assume the charitable point of view. At the same time, it is not to be denied that his words, when he answered, were carefully guarded, and that he rose to take his leave.

Mr. John Zant hospitably protested.

"Why are you in such a hurry? Must you really go? I shall have the honour of returning your visit to-morrow, when I have made arrangements to profit by that excellent suggestion of yours. Good-bye. God bless you."

He held out his hand: a hand with a smooth surface and a tawny colour, that fervently squeezed the fingers of a departing friend.

"Is that man a scoundrel?" was Mr. Rayburn's first thought, after he had left the hotel. His moral sense set all hesitation at rest—and answered: "You're a fool if you doubt it."

5

Disturbed by presentiments, Mr. Rayburn returned to his house on foot, by way of trying what exercise would do towards composing his mind.

The experiment failed. He went upstairs and played with Lucy; he drank an extra glass of wine at dinner; he took the child and her governess to a circus in the evening; he ate a little supper, fortified by another glass of wine, before he went to bed—and still those vague forebodings of evil persisted in torturing him. Looking back through his past life, he asked himself if any woman (his late wife of course excepted!) had ever taken the predominant place in his thoughts which Mrs. Zant had assumed—without any discernible reason to account for it? If he had ventured to answer his own question, the reply would have been: Never!

All the next day he waited at home, in expectation of Mr. John Zant's promised visit, and waited in vain.

Towards evening the parlour-maid appeared at the family tea-table, and presented to her master an unusually large envelope sealed with black wax, and addressed in a strange handwriting. The absence of stamp and postmark showed that it had been left at the house by a messenger.

"Who brought this?" Mr. Rayburn asked.

"A lady, sir—in deep mourning."

"Did she leave any message?"

"No, sir."

Having drawn the inevitable conclusion, Mr. Rayburn shut himself up in his library. He was afraid of Lucy's curiosity and Lucy's questions, if he read Mrs. Zant's letter in his daughter's presence.

Looking at the open envelope after he had taken out the leaves of writing which it contained, he noticed these lines traced inside the cover:

> *My one excuse for troubling you, when I might have consulted my brother-in-law, will be found in the pages which I enclose. To speak plainly, you have been led to fear that I am not in my right senses. For this very reason, I now appeal to you. Your dreadful doubt of me, sir, is my doubt too. Read what I have written about myself—and then tell me, I entreat you, which I am: A person who has been the object of a supernatural revelation? or an unfortunate creature who is only fit for imprisonment in a mad-house?*

Mr. Rayburn opened the manuscript. With steady attention, which soon quickened to breathless interest, he read what follows:

6

THE LADY'S MANUSCRIPT

Yesterday morning, the sun shone in a clear blue sky—after a succession of cloudy days, counting from the first of the month.

The radiant light had its animating effect on my poor spirits. I had passed the night more peacefully than usual; undisturbed by the dream, so cruelly familiar to me, that my lost husband is still living—the dream from which I always wake in tears. Never, since the dark days of my sorrow, have I been so little troubled by the self-tormenting fancies and fears which beset miserable women, as when I left the house, and turned my steps towards Kensington Gardens—for the first time since my husband's death.

Attended by my only companion, the little dog who had been his favourite as well as mine, I went to the quiet corner of the Gardens which is nearest to Kensington.

On that soft grass, under the shade of those grand trees, we had loitered together in the days of our betrothal. It was his favourite walk; and he had taken me to see it in the early days of our acquaintance. There, he had first asked me to be his wife. There, we had felt the rapture of our first kiss. It was surely natural that I should wish to see once more a place sacred to such memories as these? I am only twenty-three years old; I have no child to comfort me, no companion of my own age, nothing to love but the dumb creature who is so faithfully fond of me.

I went to the tree under which we stood, when my dear one's eyes told his love before he could utter it in words. The sun of that vanished day shone on me again; it was the same noontide hour; the same solitude was round me. I had feared the first effect of the dreadful contrast between past and present. No! I was quiet and resigned. My thoughts, rising higher than earth, dwelt on the better life beyond the grave. Some tears came into my eyes. But I was not unhappy. My memory of all that happened may be trusted, even in trifles which relate only to myself—I was not unhappy.

The first object that I saw, when my eyes were clear again, was the dog. He crouched a few paces away from me, trembling pitiably, but uttering no cry. What had caused the fear that overpowered him?

I was soon to know.

I called to the dog; he remained immovable—conscious of some mysterious coming thing that held him spellbound. I tried to go to the poor creature, and fondle and comfort him.

At the first step forward that I took, something stopped me.

It was not to be seen, and not to be heard. It stopped me.

The still figure of the dog disappeared from my view: the lonely scene round me disappeared—excepting the light from heaven, the tree that sheltered me, and the grass in front of me. A sense of unutterable expectation kept my eyes riveted on the grass. Suddenly, I saw its myriad blades rise erect and shivering. The fear came to me of something passing over them with the invisible swiftness of the wind. The shivering advanced. It was all round me. It crept into the leaves of the tree over my head; they shuddered, without a sound to tell of their agitation: their pleasant natural rustling was struck dumb. The songs of the birds had ceased. The cries of the water-fowl on the pond were heard no more. There was a dreadful silence.

But the lovely sunshine poured down on me, as brightly as ever.

In that dazzling light, in that fearful silence, I felt an Invisible Presence near me.

It touched me gently.

At the touch, my heart throbbed with an overwhelming joy. Exquisite pleasure thrilled through every nerve in my body. I knew him! From the unseen world—himself unseen—he had returned to me. Oh, I knew him!

And yet, my helpless mortality longed for a sign that might give me assurance of the truth. The yearning in me shaped itself into words. I tried to utter the words. I would have said, if I could have spoken: "Oh, my angel, give me a token that it is You!" But I was like a person struck dumb—I could only think it.

The Invisible Presence read my thought. I felt my lips touched, as my husband's lips used to touch them when he kissed me. And that was my answer. A thought came to me again. I would have said, if I could have spoken: "Are you here to take me to the better world?"

I waited. Nothing that I could feel touched me.

I was conscious of thinking once more. I would have said, if I could have spoken: "Are you here to protect me?"

I felt myself held in a gentle embrace, as my husband's arms used to hold me when he pressed me to his breast. And that was my answer.

The touch that was like the touch of his lips, lingered and was lost; the clasp that was like the clasp of his arms, pressed me and fell away. The garden-scene resumed its natural aspect. I saw a human creature near, a lovely little girl looking at me.

At that moment, when I was my own lonely self again,

the sight of the child soothed and attracted me. I advanced, intending to speak to her. To my horror I suddenly ceased to see her. She disappeared as if I had been stricken blind.

And yet I could see the landscape round me; I could see the heaven above me. A time passed—only a few minutes, as I thought—and the child became visible to me again; walking hand-in-hand with her father. I approached them; I was close enough to see that they were looking at me with pity and surprise. My impulse was to ask if they saw anything strange in my face or my manner. Before I could speak, the horrible wonder happened again. They vanished from my view.

Was the Invisible Presence still near? Was it passing between me and my fellow-mortals; forbidding communication, in that place and at that time?

It must have been so. When I turned away in my ignorance, with a heavy heart, the dreadful blankness which had twice shut out from me the beings of my own race, was not between me and my dog. The poor little creature filled me with pity; I called him to me. He moved at the sound of my voice, and followed me languidly; not quite awakened yet from the trance of terror that had possessed him.

Before I had retired by more than a few steps, I thought I was conscious of the Presence again. I held out my longing arms to it. I waited in the hope of a touch to tell me that I might return. Perhaps I was answered by indirect means? I only know that a resolution to return to the same place, at the same hour, came to me, and quieted my mind.

The morning of the next day was dull and cloudy; but the rain held off. I set forth again to the Gardens.

My dog ran on before me into the street—and stopped: waiting to see in which direction I might lead the way. When I turned towards the Gardens, he dropped behind me. In a little while I looked back. He was following me no longer; he stood irresolute. I called to him. He advanced a few steps—hesitated—and ran back to the house.

I went on by myself. Shall I confess my superstition? I thought the dog's desertion of me a bad omen.

Arrived at the tree, I placed myself under it. The minutes followed each other uneventfully. The cloudy sky darkened. The dull surface of the grass showed no shuddering consciousness of an unearthly creature passing over it.

I still waited, with an obstinacy which was fast becoming

the obstinacy of despair. How long an interval elapsed, while I kept watch on the ground before me, I am not able to say. I only know that a change came.

Under the dull gray light I saw the grass move—but not as it had moved, on the day before. It shrivelled as if a flame had scorched it. No flame appeared. The brown underlying earth showed itself winding onward in a thin strip—which might have been a footpath traced in fire. It frightened me. I longed for the protection of the Invisible Presence; I prayed for a warning of it, if danger was near.

A touch answered me. It was as if a hand unseen had taken my hand—had raised it, little by little—had left it, pointing to the thin brown path that wound towards me under the shrivelled blades of grass.

I looked to the far end of the path.

The unseen hand closed on my hand with a warning pressure: the revelation of the coming danger was near me—I waited for it; I saw it.

The figure of a man appeared, advancing towards me along the thin brown path. I looked in his face as he came nearer. It showed me dimly the face of my husband's brother—John Zant.

The consciousness of myself as a living creature left me. I knew nothing; I felt nothing; I was dead.

When the torture of revival made me open my eyes, I found myself on the grass. Gentle hands raised my head, at the moment when I recovered my senses. Who had brought me to life again? Who was taking care of me?

I looked upward, and saw—bending over me—John Zant.

THERE the manuscript ended.

Some lines had been added on the last page; but they had been so carefully erased as to be illegible. These words of explanation appeared below the cancelled sentences:

"I had begun to write the little that remains to be told, when it struck me that I might, unintentionally, be exercising an unfair influence on your opinion. Let me only remind you that I believe absolutely in the supernatural revelation which I have endeavoured to describe. Remember this—and decide for me what I dare not decide for myself."

There was no serious obstacle in the way of compliance with this request.

Judged from the point of view of the materialist, Mrs. Zant might no doubt be the victim of illusions (produced by a diseased state of the nervous system), which have been known to exist—as in the celebrated case of the bookseller, Nicolai, of Berlin—without being accompanied by derangement of the intellectual powers. But Mr. Rayburn was not asked to solve any such intricate problem as this. He had been merely instructed to read the manuscript, and to say what impression it had left on him of the mental condition of the writer; whose doubt of herself had been, in all probability, first suggested by remembrance of the illness from which she had suffered—brain-fever.

Under these circumstances, there could be little difficulty in forming an opinion. The memory which had recalled, and the judgment which had arranged, the succession of events related in the narrative revealed a mind in full possession of its resources.

Having satisfied himself so far, Mr. Rayburn abstained from considering the more serious question suggested by what he had read.

At any time, his habits of life and his ways of thinking would have rendered him unfit to weigh the arguments, which assert or deny supernatural revelation among the creatures of earth. But his mind was now so disturbed by the startling record of experience which he had just read, that he was only conscious of feeling certain impressions—without possessing the capacity to reflect on them. That his anxiety on Mrs. Zant's account had been increased, and that his doubts of Mr. John Zant had been encouraged, were the only practical results of the confidence placed in him of which he was thus far aware. In the ordinary exigencies of life a man of hesitating disposition, his interest in Mrs. Zant's welfare, and his desire to discover what had passed between her brother-in-law and herself, after their meeting in the Gardens, urged him into instant action. In half an hour more, he had arrived at her lodgings. He was at once admitted.

8

Mrs. Zant was alone, in an imperfectly lit room. "I hope you will excuse the bad light," she said; "my head has been burning as if the fever had come back again. Oh, don't go away! After what I have suffered, you don't know how dreadful it is to be alone."

The tone of her voice told him that she had been crying. He at once tried the best means of setting the poor lady at ease, by telling her of the conclusion at which he had arrived, after reading her manuscript. The happy result showed itself instantly: her face brightened, her manner changed; she was eager to hear more.

"Have I produced any other impression on you?" she asked.

He understood the allusion. Expressing sincere respect for her own convictions, he told her honestly that he was not prepared to enter on the obscure and terrible question of supernatural interposition. Grateful for the tone in which he had answered her, she wisely and delicately changed the subject.

"I must speak to you of my brother-in-law," she said. "He has told me of your visit; and I am anxious to know what you think of him. Do you like Mr. John Zant?"

Mr. Rayburn hesitated.

The care-worn look appeared again in her face. "If you had felt as kindly towards him as he feels towards you," she said, "I might have gone to St. Sallins with a lighter heart."

Mr. Rayburn thought of the supernatural appearances, described at the close of her narrative. "You believe in that terrible warning," he remonstrated; "and yet, you go to your brother-in-law's house!"

"I believe," she answered, "in the spirit of the man who loved me in the days of his earthly bondage. I am under *his* protection. What have I to do but to cast away my fears, and to wait in faith and hope? It might have helped my resolution if a friend had been near to encourage me." She paused and smiled sadly. "I must remember," she resumed, "that your way of understanding my position is not my way. I ought to have told you that Mr. John Zant feels needless anxiety about my health. He declares that he will not lose sight of me until his mind is at ease. It is useless to attempt to alter his opinion. He says my nerves are shattered—and who that sees me can doubt it? He tells me that my only chance of getting better is to try change of air and perfect repose—how can I contradict him? He reminds me that I have no relation but himself, and no house open to me but his own—and God knows he is right!"

She said those last words in accents of melancholy resignation, which grieved the good man whose one merciful purpose was to serve and console her. He spoke impulsively with the freedom of an old friend.

"I want to know more of you and Mr. John Zant, than I know

now," he said. "My motive is a better one than mere curiosity. Do you believe that I feel a sincere interest in you?"

"With my whole heart."

That reply encouraged him to proceed with what he had to say. "When you recovered from your fainting-fit," he began, "Mr. John Zant asked questions, of course?"

"He asked what could possibly have happened, in such a quiet place as Kensington Gardens, to make me faint."

"And how did you answer?"

"Answer? I couldn't even look at him!"

"You said nothing?"

"Nothing. I don't know what he thought of me; he might have been surprised, or he might have been offended."

"Is he easily offended?" Mr. Rayburn asked.

"Not in my experience of him."

"Do you mean your experience of him before your illness?"

"Yes. Since my recovery, his engagements with country patients have kept him away from London. I have not seen him since he took these lodgings for me. But he is always considerate. He has written more than once to beg that I will not think him neglectful, and to tell me (what I knew already through my poor husband) that he has no money of his own, and must live by his profession."

"In your husband's lifetime, were the two brothers on good terms?"

"Always. The one complaint I ever heard my husband make of John Zant was that he didn't come to see us often enough, after our marriage. Is there some wickedness in him which we have never suspected? It may be—but *how* can it be? I have every reason to be grateful to the man against whom I have been supernaturally warned! His conduct to me has been always perfect. I can't tell you what I owe to his influence in quieting my mind, when a dreadful doubt arose about my husband's death."

"Do you mean doubt if he died a natural death?"

"Oh, no! no! He was dying of rapid consumption—but his sudden death took the doctors by surprise. One of them thought that he might have taken an overdose of his sleeping drops, by mistake. The other disputed this conclusion, or there might have been an inquest in the house. Oh, don't speak of it any more! Let us talk of something else. Tell me when I shall see you again."

"I hardly know. When do you and your brother-in-law leave London?"

"To-morrow." She looked at Mr. Rayburn with a piteous entreaty in her eyes; she said timidly: "Do you ever go to the seaside, and take your dear little girl with you?"

The request, at which she had only dared to hint, touched on the idea which was at that moment in Mr. Rayburn's mind.

Interpreted by his strong prejudice against John Zant, what she had said of her brother-in-law filled him with forebodings of peril to herself; all the more powerful in their influence, for this reason—that he shrank from distinctly realising them. If another person had been present at the interview, and had said to him afterwards: "That man's reluctance to visit his sister-in-law, while her husband was living, is associated with a secret sense of guilt which her innocence cannot even imagine: he, and he alone, knows the cause of her husband's sudden death: his feigned anxiety about her health is adopted as the safest means of enticing her into his house"—if those formidable conclusions had been urged on Mr. Rayburn, he would have felt it his duty to reject them, as unjustifiable aspersions on an absent man. And yet, when he took leave that evening of Mrs. Zant, he had pledged himself to give Lucy a holiday at the seaside; and he had said, without blushing, that the child really deserved it, as a reward for general good conduct and attention to her lessons!

9

Three days later, the father and daughter arrived towards evening at St. Sallins-on-Sea. They found Mrs. Zant at the station.

The poor woman's joy, on seeing them, expressed itself like the joy of a child. "Oh, I am so glad! so glad!" was all she could say when they met. Lucy was half-smothered with kisses, and was made supremely happy by a present of the finest doll she had ever possessed. Mrs. Zant accompanied her friends to the rooms which had been secured at the hotel. She was able to speak confidentially to Mr. Rayburn, while Lucy was in the balcony hugging her doll, and looking at the sea.

The one event that had happened during Mrs. Zant's short residence at St. Sallins, was the departure of her brother-in-law that morning, for London. He had been called away to operate on the feet of a wealthy patient who knew the value of his time: his housekeeper expected that he would return to dinner.

As to his conduct towards Mrs. Zant, he was not only as attentive as ever—he was almost oppressively affectionate in his language and manner. There was no service that a man could render which he had not eagerly offered to her. He declared that he already perceived an improvement in her health; he congratulated her on having decided to stay in his house; and (as a proof, perhaps, of his sincerity) he had repeatedly pressed her hand. "Have you any idea what all this means?" she said simply.

Mr. Rayburn kept his idea to himself. He professed ignorance; and asked next what sort of person the housekeeper was.

Mrs. Zant shook her head ominously.

"Such a strange creature," she said, "and in the habit of taking such liberties, that I begin to be afraid she is a little crazy."

"Is she an old woman?"

"No—only middle-aged. This morning, after her master had left the house, she actually asked me what I thought of my brother-in-law! I told her, as coldly as possible, that I thought he was very kind. She was quite insensible to the tone in which I had spoken; she went on from bad to worse. 'Do you call him the sort of man who would take the fancy of a young woman?' was her next question. She actually looked at me (I might have been wrong; and I hope I was) as if the 'young woman' she had in her mind was myself! I said, 'I don't think of such things, and I don't talk about them.' Still, she was not in the least discouraged; she made a personal remark next: 'Excuse me—but you do look wretchedly pale.' I thought she seemed to enjoy the defect in my complexion; I really believe it raised me in her estimation. 'We shall get on better in time,' she said; 'I'm beginning to like you.' She walked out humming a tune. Don't you agree with me? Don't you think she's crazy?"

'I can hardly give an opinion until I have seen her. Does she look as if she might have been a pretty woman at one time of her life?"

"Not the sort of pretty woman whom I admire!"

Mr. Rayburn smiled. "I was thinking," he resumed, "that this person's odd conduct may perhaps be accounted for. She is probably jealous of any young lady who is invited to her master's house—and (till she noticed your complexion) she began by being jealous of you."

Innocently at a loss to understand how *she* could become an object of the housekeeper's jealousy, Mrs. Zant looked at Mr. Rayburn in astonishment. Before she could give expression to her feeling of surprise, there was an interruption—a welcome interruption. A waiter entered the room, and announced a visitor; described as "a gentleman."

Mrs. Zant at once rose to retire.

"Who is the gentleman?" Mr. Rayburn asked—detaining Mrs. Zant as he spoke.

A voice which they both recognised answered gaily, from the outer side of the door:

"A friend from London."

10

"Welcome to St. Sallins!" cried Mr. John Zant. "I knew that you were expected, my dear sir, and I took my chance of finding you at the hotel." He turned to his sister-in-law, and kissed her hand with an elaborate gallantry worthy of Sir Charles Grandison himself. "When I reached home, my dear, and heard that you had gone out, I guessed that your object was to receive our excellent friend. You have not felt lonely while I have been away? That's right! that's right!" He looked towards the balcony, and discovered Lucy at the open window, staring at the magnificent stranger. "Your little daughter, Mr. Rayburn? Dear child! Come, and kiss me."

Lucy answered in one positive word: "No."

Mr. John Zant was not easily discouraged. "Show me your doll, darling," he said. "Sit on my knee."

Lucy answered in two positive words—"I won't."

Her father approached the window to administer the necessary reproof. Mr. John Zant interfered in the cause of mercy with his best grace. He held up his hands in cordial entreaty. "Dear Mr. Rayburn! The fairies are sometimes shy; and *this* little fairy doesn't take to strangers at first sight. Dear child! All in good time. And what stay do you make at St. Sallins? May we hope that our poor attractions will tempt you to prolong your visit?"

He put his flattering little question with an ease of manner which was rather too plainly assumed; and he looked at Mr. Rayburn with a watchfulness which appeared to attach undue importance to the reply. When he said: "What stay do you make at St. Sallins?" did he really mean: "How soon do you leave us?" Inclining to adopt this conclusion, Mr. Rayburn answered cautiously, that his stay at the seaside would depend on circumstances. Mr. John Zant looked at his sister-in-law, sitting silent in a corner with Lucy on her lap. "Exert your attractions," he said; "make the circumstances agreeable to our good friend. Will you dine with us to-day, my dear sir, and bring your little fairy with you?"

Lucy was far from receiving this complimentary allusion in the spirit in which it had been offered. "I'm not a fairy," she declared. "I'm a child."

"And a naughty child," her father added, with all the severity that he could assume.

"I can't help it, papa; the man with the big beard puts me out."

The man with the big beard was amused—amiably, paternally amused—by Lucy's plain speaking. He repeated his invitation to dinner; and he did his best to look disappointed when Mr. Rayburn made the necessary excuses.

"Another day," he said (without, however, fixing the day). "I think you will find my house comfortable. My housekeeper may perhaps be eccentric—but in all essentials a woman in a thousand. Do you feel the change from London already? Our air at St. Sallins is really worthy of its reputation. Invalids who come here are cured as if by magic. What do you think of Mrs. Zant? How does she look?"

Mr. Rayburn was evidently expected to say that she looked better. He said it. Mr. John Zant seemed to have anticipated a stronger expression of opinion.

"Surprisingly better!" he pronounced. "Infinitely better! We ought both to be grateful. Pray believe that we *are* grateful."

"If you mean grateful to me," Mr. Rayburn remarked, "I don't quite understand——"

"You don't quite understand? Is it possible that you have forgotten our conversation when I first had the honour of receiving you? Look at Mrs. Zant again."

Mr. Rayburn looked; and Mrs. Zant's brother-in-law explained himself.

"You notice the return of her colour, the healthy brightness of her eyes. (No, my dear, I am not paying you idle compliments; I am stating plain facts.) For that happy result, Mr. Rayburn, we are indebted to you."

"Surely not?"

"Surely yes! It was at your valuable suggestion that I thought of inviting my sister-in-law to visit me at St. Sallins. Ah, you remember it now. Forgive me if I look at my watch; the dinner hour is on my mind. Not, as your dear little daughter there seems to think, because I am greedy, but because I am always punctual, in justice to the cook. Shall we see you to-morrow? Call early, and you will find us at home."

He gave Mrs. Zant his arm, and bowed and smiled, and kissed his hand to Lucy, and left the room. Recalling their interview at the hotel in London, Mr. Rayburn now understood John Zant's object (on that occasion) in assuming the character of a helpless man in need of a sensible suggestion. If Mrs. Zant's residence under his roof became associated with evil consequences, he could declare that she would never have entered the house but for Mr. Rayburn's advice.

With the next day came the hateful necessity of returning this man's visit.

Mr. Rayburn was placed between two alternatives. In Mrs. Zant's interests he must remain, no matter at what sacrifice of his own inclinations, on good terms with her brother-in-law—or he must return to London, and leave the poor woman to her fate. His choice, it is needless to say, was never a matter of doubt. He called at the house, and did his innocent best—without in the least deceiving Mr. John Zant—to make himself agreeable during the short duration of his visit. Descending the stairs on his way out, accompanied by Mrs. Zant, he was surprised to see a middle-aged woman in the hall, who looked as if she was waiting there expressly to attract notice.

"The housekeeper," Mrs. Zant whispered. "She is impudent enough to try to make acquaintance with you."

This was exactly what the housekeeper was waiting in the hall to do.

"I hope you like our watering-place, sir," she began. "If I can be of service to you, pray command me. Any friend of this lady's has a claim on me—and you are an old friend, no doubt. I am only the housekeeper; but I presume to take a sincere interest in Mrs. Zant; and I am indeed glad to see you here. We none of us know—do we?—how soon we may want a friend. No offence, I hope? Thank you, sir. Good morning."

There was nothing in the woman's eyes which indicated an unsettled mind; nothing in the appearance of her lips which suggested habits of intoxication. That her strange outburst of familiarity proceeded from some strong motive seemed to be more than probable. Putting together what Mrs. Zant had already told him, and what he had himself observed, Mr. Rayburn suspected that the motive might be found in the housekeeper's jealousy of her master.

11

Reflecting in the solitude of his own room, Mr. Rayburn felt that the one prudent course to take would be to persuade Mrs. Zant to leave St. Sallins. He tried to prepare her for this strong proceeding, when she came the next day to take Lucy out for a walk.

"If you still regret having forced yourself to accept your brother-in-law's invitation," was all he ventured to say, "don't forget that you are perfect mistress of your own actions. You have only to come to me at the hotel, and I will take you back to London by the next train."

She positively refused to entertain the idea.

"I should be a thankless creature indeed," she said, "if I accepted your proposal. Do you think I am ungrateful enough to involve you in a personal quarrel with John Zant? No! If I find myself forced to leave the house, I will go away alone."

There was no moving her from this resolution. When she and Lucy had gone out together, Mr. Rayburn remained at the hotel, with a mind ill at ease. A man of readier mental resources might have felt at a loss how to act for the best, in the emergency that now confronted him. While he was still as far as ever from arriving at a decision, some person knocked at the door.

Had Mrs. Zant returned? He looked up as the door was opened, and saw to his astonishment—Mr. John Zant's housekeeper.

"Don't let me alarm you, sir," the woman said. "Mrs. Zant has been taken a little faint, at the door of our house. My master is attending to her."

"Where is the child?" Mr. Rayburn asked.

"I was bringing her back to you, sir, when we met a lady and her little girl at the door of the hotel. They were on their way to the beach—and Miss Lucy begged hard to be allowed to go with them. The lady said the two children were playfellows, and she was sure you would not object."

"The lady is quite right. Mrs. Zant's illness is not serious, I hope?"

"I think not, sir. But I should like to say something in her interests. May I? Thank you." She advanced a step nearer to him, and spoke her next words in a whisper. "Take Mrs. Zant away from this place, and lose no time in doing it."

Mr. Rayburn was on his guard. He merely asked:

"Why?"

The housekeeper answered in a curiously indirect manner—partly in jest, as it seemed, and partly in earnest.

"When a man has lost his wife," she said, "there's some difference of opinion in Parliament, as I hear, whether he does right or wrong, if he marries his wife's sister. Wait a bit! I'm coming to the point. My master is one who has a long head on his shoulders; he sees consequences which escape the notice of people like me. In his way of thinking, if one man may marry his wife's sister, and no harm done, where's the objection if another man pays a compliment to the family, and marries his brother's widow? My master, if you please, is that other man. Take the widow away before she marries him."

This was beyond endurance.

"You insult Mrs. Zant," Mr. Rayburn answered, "if you suppose that such a thing is possible!"

"Oh! I insult her, do I? Listen to me. One of three things will happen. She will be entrapped into consenting to it—or frightened into consenting to it—or drugged into consenting to it——"

Mr. Rayburn was too indignant to let her go on.

"You are talking nonsense," he said. "There can be no marriage; the law forbids it."

"Are you one of the people who see no farther than their noses?" she asked insolently. "Won't the law take his money? Is he obliged to mention that he is related to her by marriage, when he buys the licence?" She paused; her humour changed; she stamped furiously on the floor. The true motive that animated her showed itself in her next words, and warned Mr. Rayburn to grant a more favourable hearing than he had accorded to her yet. "If you won't stop it," she burst out, "I will! If he marries anybody, he is bound to marry ME. Will you take her away? I ask you, for the last time—*will* you take her away?"

The tone in which she made that final appeal to him had its effect.

"I will go back with you to John Zant's house," he said, "and judge for myself."

She laid her hand on his arm:

"I must go first—or you may not be let in. Follow me in five minutes; and don't knock at the street door."

On the point of leaving him, she abruptly returned.

"We have forgotten something," she said. "Suppose my master refuses to see you. His temper might get the better of him; he might make it so unpleasant for you that you would be obliged to go."

"*My* temper might get the better of *me*," Mr. Rayburn replied; "and—if I thought it was in Mrs. Zant's interests—I might refuse to leave the house unless she accompanied me."

"That will never do, sir."

"Why not?"

"Because I should be the person to suffer."

"In what way?"

"In this way. If you picked a quarrel with my master, I should be blamed for it because I showed you upstairs. Besides, think of the lady. You might frighten her out of her senses, if it came to a struggle between you two men."

The language was exaggerated; but there was a force in this last objection which Mr. Rayburn was obliged to acknowledge.

"And, after all," the housekeeper continued, "he has more right over her than you have. He is related to her, and you are only her friend."

Mr. Rayburn declined to let himself be influenced by this consideration.

"Mr. John Zant is only related to her by marriage," he said. "If she prefers trusting in me—come what may of it, I will be worthy of her confidence."

The housekeeper shook her head.

"That only means another quarrel," she answered. "The wise way, with a man like my master, is the peaceable way. We must manage to deceive him."

"I don't like deceit."

"In that case, sir, I'll wish you good-bye. We will leave Mrs. Zant to do the best she can for herself."

Mr. Rayburn was unreasonable. He positively refused to adopt this alternative.

"Will you hear what I have got to say?" the housekeeper asked.

"There can be no harm in that," he admitted. "Go on."

She took him at his word.

"When you called at our house," she began, "did you notice the doors in the passage, on the first floor? Very well. One of them is the door of the drawing-room, and the other is the door of the library. Do you remember the drawing-room, sir?"

"I thought it a large well-lit room," Mr. Rayburn answered. "And I noticed a doorway in the wall, with a handsome curtain hanging over it."

"That's enough for our purpose," the housekeeper resumed. "On the other side of the curtain, if you had looked in, you would have found the library. Suppose my master is as polite as usual, and begs to be excused for not receiving you, because it is an inconvenient time. And suppose you are polite on your side, and take yourself off by the drawing-room door. You will find me waiting downstairs, on the first landing. Do you see it now?"

"I can't say I do."

"You surprise me, sir. What is to prevent us from getting back softly into the library, by the door in the passage? And why shouldn't we use that second way into the library as a means of discovering what may be going on in the drawing-room? Safe behind the curtain, you will see him if he behaves uncivilly to Mrs. Zant, or you will hear her if she calls for help. In either case, you may be as rough and ready with my master as you find needful; it will be he who has frightened her, and not you. And who can blame the poor housekeeper because Mr. Rayburn did his duty, and protected a helpless woman? There is my plan, sir. Is it worth trying?"

He answered, sharply enough: "I don't like it."

The housekeeper opened the door again, and wished him good-bye.

If Mr. Rayburn had felt no more than an ordinary interest in Mrs. Zant, he would have let the woman go. As it was, he stopped her; and, after some further protest (which proved to be useless), he ended in giving way.

"You promise to follow my directions?" she stipulated.

He gave the promise. She smiled, nodded, and left him. True to his instructions, Mr. Rayburn reckoned five minutes by his watch, before he followed her.

12

The housekeeper was waiting for him, with the street-door ajar.

"They are both in the drawing-room," she whispered, leading the way upstairs. "Step softly, and take him by surprise."

A table of oblong shape stood midway between the drawing-room walls. At the end of it which was nearest to the window, Mrs. Zant was pacing to and fro across the breadth of the room.

At the opposite end of the table, John Zant was seated. Taken completely by surprise, he showed himself in his true character. He started to his feet, and protested with an oath against the intrusion which had been committed on him.

Heedless of his action and his language, Mr. Rayburn could look at nothing; could think of nothing, but Mrs. Zant. She was still walking slowly to and fro, unconscious of the words of sympathy which he addressed to her, insensible even as it seemed to the presence of other persons in the room.

John Zant's voice broke the silence. His temper was under control again: he had his reasons for still remaining on friendly terms with Mr. Rayburn.

"I am sorry I forgot myself just now," he said.

Mr. Rayburn's interest was concentrated on Mrs. Zant: he took no notice of the apology.

"When did this happen?" he asked.

"About a quarter of an hour ago. I was fortunately at home. Without speaking to me, without noticing me, she walked upstairs like a person in a dream."

Mr. Rayburn suddenly pointed to Mrs. Zant.

"Look at her!" he said. "There's a change!"

All restlessness in her movements had come to an end. She was standing at the farther end of the table which was nearest to the window, in the full flow of sunlight pouring at that moment over her face. Her eyes looked out straight before her—void of all expression. Her lips were a little parted; her head drooped slightly towards her shoulder, in an attitude which suggested listening for something or waiting for something. In the warm brilliant light, she stood before the two men, a living creature self-isolated in a stillness like the stillness of death.

John Zant was ready with the expression of his opinion.

"A nervous seizure," he said. "Something resembling catalepsy, as you see."

"Have you sent for a doctor?"

"A doctor is not wanted."

"I beg your pardon. It seems to me that medical help is absolutely necessary."

"Be so good as to remember," Mr. John Zant answered, "that the decision rests with me, as the lady's relative. I am sensible of the honour which your visit confers on me. But the time has been unhappily chosen. Forgive me if I suggest that you will do well to retire."

Mr. Rayburn had not forgotten the housekeeper's advice, or the promise which she had exacted from him. But the expression in John Zant's face was a serious trial to his self-control. He hesitated, and looked back at Mrs. Zant.

If he provoked a quarrel by remaining in the room, the one alternative would be the removal of her by force. Fear of the consequences to herself, if she was suddenly and roughly roused from her trance, was the one consideration which reconciled him to submission. He withdrew.

The housekeeper was waiting for him below, on the first landing. When the door of the drawing-room had been closed again, she signed to him to follow her, and returned up the stairs. After another struggle with himself, he obeyed. They entered the library from the corridor—and placed themselves behind the closed curtain which hung over the doorway. It was easy so to arrange the edge of the drapery as to observe, without exciting suspicion, whatever was going on in the next room.

Mrs. Zant's brother-in-law was approaching her, at the time when Mr. Rayburn saw him again.

In the instant afterwards, she moved—before he had completely passed over the space between them. Her still figure began to tremble. She lifted her drooping head. For a moment, there was a shrinking in her—as if she had been touched by something. She seemed to recognise the touch: she was still again.

John Zant watched the change. It suggested to him that she was beginning to recover her senses. He tried the experiment of speaking to her.

"My love, my sweet angel, come to the heart that adores you!"

He advanced again; he passed into the flood of sunlight pouring over her.

"Rouse yourself!" he said.

She still remained in the same position; apparently at his mercy, neither hearing him nor seeing him.

"Rouse yourself!" he repeated. "My darling, come to me!"

At the instant when he attempted to embrace her—at the instant when Mr. Rayburn rushed into the room—John Zant's arms, suddenly turning rigid, remained outstretched. With a shriek of horror, he struggled to draw them back—struggled, in the empty brightness of the sunshine, as if some invisible grip had seized him.

"What has got me?" the wretch screamed. "Who is holding my hands? Oh, the cold of it! the cold of it!"

His features became convulsed; his eyes turned upwards until only the white eye-balls were visible. He fell prostrate with a crash that shook the room.

The housekeeper ran in. She knelt by her master's body. With one hand she loosened his cravat. With the other she pointed to the end of the table.

Mrs. Zant still kept her place; but there was another change. Little by little, her eyes recovered their natural living expression—then slowly closed. She tottered backwards from the table, and lifted her hands wildly, as if to grasp at something which might support her. Mr. Rayburn hurried to her before she fell—lifted her in his arms—and carried her out of the room.

One of the servants met them in the hall. He sent her for a carriage. In a quarter of an hour more, Mrs. Zant was safe under his care at the hotel.

13

That night a note, written by the housekeeper, was delivered to Mrs. Zant.

The doctors give little hope. The paralytic stroke is spreading upwards to his face. If death spares him, he will live a helpless man. I shall take care of him to the last. As for you—forget him.

Mrs. Zant gave the note to Mr. Rayburn.

"Read it, and destroy it," she said. "It is written in ignorance of the terrible truth."

He obeyed—and looked at her in silence, waiting to hear more. She hid her face. The few words that she addressed to him, after a struggle with herself, fell slowly and reluctantly from her lips.

She said, "No mortal hand held the hands of John Zant. The guardian spirit was with me. The promised protection was with me. I know it. I wish to know no more."

Having spoken, she rose to retire. He opened the door for her, seeing that she needed rest in her own room.

Left by himself, he began to consider the prospect that was before him in the future. How was he to regard the woman who had just left him? As a poor creature weakened by disease, the victim of her own nervous delusion? or as the chosen object of a supernatural revelation—unparalleled by any similar revelation that he had heard of, or had found recorded in books? His first discovery of the place that she really held in his estimation dawned on his mind, when he felt himself recoiling from the conclusion which presented her to his pity, and yielding to the nobler conviction which felt with her faith, and raised her to a place apart among other women.

14

They left St. Sallins the next day.

Arrived at the end of the journey, Lucy held fast by Mrs. Zant's hand. Tears were rising in the child's eyes. "Are we to bid her good-bye?" she said sadly to her father.

He seemed to be unwilling to trust himself to speak; he only said, "My dear, ask her yourself."

But the result justified him. Lucy was happy again.

BASIL COPPER
The House by the Tarn

Basil Copper *(b.1926), described as "unquestionably one of the greatest living macabre writers" has had his best horror stories from the 1960s and 70s collected in* Not After Nightfall *(1967),* From Evil's Pillow *(1973),* When Footsteps Echo *(1975),* And Afterwards The Dark *(1977),* Here Be Daemons *(1978) and* Voices of Doom *(1980). Taken from the latter volume, the author considers 'The House by the Tarn' his best 'pure' ghost story to date.*

Kemp kept on walking. The high, shadowed spines of the hills which reared about him emphasised and reinforced the coldness of the winter's day. Hoar-frost silvered the blades of grass which fringed the road. The road itself, its gravel coagulated and bonded by the iron-cold of the air, led up between the blunt mounds of the hills and Kemp followed it, walking easily, his hands thrust deep into the pockets of his thick overcoat, his breath smoking from his nostrils as he ascended.

There was a profound silence apart from the faint scraping of his feet in the gravel. There was no traffic on the road and no birds were in the air. The sky was overcast and unfriendly. The intense melancholy of the scene made Kemp realise why most travellers preferred to avoid the turnpike, which had long been superseded by a modern motor road which looped to the north, avoiding the clasping arms of the remote hills.

Once he stopped as if overcome by the silence and alien starkness of the terrain; on another occasion the road descended briefly, then rose again, more gently this time, between dark thickets of thorn and scrub, bare and shivering now in the keening wind. A harsh cry from the interior of the bushes startled the man and seemed to constrict his heart with momentary foreboding; he stood irresolute for a moment, peering nervously about him. Then the sound came again; Kemp's shoulders relaxed. A raven, perhaps? A crow? More fancifully still, a vulture? Kemp's lips curved in a sardonic smile; he turned away and took in the barren curve of the hills. It was not beyond the bounds of possibility with such a mise-en-scène. He resumed his walk, his powerful neck hunched deeper into the warm raglan overcoat, his back turned to protect him from the full force of the wind.

It blew in insidious, fitful gusts, that had a habit of getting through his guard; the main force was directed across the bald crests of the hills and set up a low, hushed moan. The skirts of the wind, descending into the hollows, rasped unpleasantly among the dried stems of ossified undergrowth and scratched at the grass blades and the frozen masses of soil which held them undulate like a miniature sea.

Kemp consulted his watch; he had been walking for an hour. He should reach his destination in a little more than half that now. Which would leave ample time for him to retrace his steps in daylight and regain the main road. A long calvary on such a day to visit the shell of a house. Curious enough to cause Tregorran to put his car at Kemp's disposal; it was typical of Kemp to refuse the offer in a somewhat peremptory manner. That would have spoiled the game for him; cheating was perhaps too strong a word but at the very least it would have dissipated the ambiance of the occasion, have robbed it of all flavour. And flavour was the essential ingredient of such small adventures.

Kemp had left his bag at the inn; he would stay the night on his return and continue on his lecture tour the following day. His schedule would allow him two clear days before the next date on the programme. And in the meantime there was the house. His friend Tregorran had set him on to it. Tregorran was his host at the university where he had last lectured; an old friend, gruff, reliable and dedicated entirely to the higher learning, though not in any narrow way. Their talk, over pipes and punch the previous evening had turned, as conversation often will of a winter's night, on the darker things; of the legends of this gnarled and strangely fashioned countryside; of arcane secrets long handed down by the country folk; and of matters whispered by old people behind closed shutters in the small hours of the winter nights. Kemp was fascinated by the more subtle manifestations of legend and mythology; particularly when it impinged on modern life and Tregorran's halting references to the house had intrigued him from the start. The host knew that his visitor was the author of several small but best-selling volumes on such matters and he was sure of his ground when he came to broach the subject long after the clock in his study had chimed away midnight.

Hence Kemp's sudden resolve; the motor journey with Tregorran the next morning and his refusal of the use of the car. He had been right, he reflected, as he set his face upward again, into the bleaker fastnesses of the hill road. The clouds came louring down as though to intimidate the earth; overhead, the bare branches made a heavy lattice which penned in the dark and sullen sky. Kemp was content; this was his métier, the material from which he could fashion the stuff of scholarly, fastidiously worked volumes which would sell steadily over the years. And the house had all the aspects of a classic doom which had seized upon his imagination from the beginning; the fact that it was a bare fifty miles from the direct route of his lecture tour and so easy of access during his only two-day stopover could only be regarded as providential. Poe himself could not have improved upon the circumstances.

So thought Kemp as he continued to climb, his musings blending with the steady beat of his feet, the story Tregorran had told him backgrounded by the inhuman cry of the wind which continued to rise as his measured paces brought him to the higher plateau. The hills were now harsher in outline, their flanks black, like volcanic ash and completely denuded of vegetation by the scouring gales of the uplands.

Despite his ascent towards the source of light the sky seemed, if anything, to become darker, even though it was the brightest time of day and twice Kemp paused, fearing somehow that his watch might have stopped. But the homely tick reassured him and he walked on, a diminutive and lonely figure among the austere irregularities of that lunar landscape.

He could not forget the thin form of Tregorran, his white eyebrows and tired face lit by the flickering firelight in the study the night before; and the even stranger story he had to tell. The house had been empty for some time, Tregorran said. In fact more than three decades had passed over its scarred mass; the granite walls still standing but the slate roof long since fallen; the floors rotted; the windows glassless; and the doors demolished by the constant battering of the wind.

Four Winds was its name; grimly appropriate Kemp had felt from Tregorran's description but he was only now beginning to appreciate the reality. The slamming and buffeting from these wide skies would, in time, reduce even granite to ground level, he believed.

The house had once belonged to a retired silk merchant, who had built it on a scale and in a style he felt to be commensurate with his wealth and dignity, said Tregorran. But long years in the East had inured him to more temperate climates; the winters unnerved him, he grew melancholy and introspective and his temper withered in face of the gales which howled at the house through long days and nights and months of the dark season.

His wife and three children, all girls, were equally fixed in their dislike of the place, though within all was elegance and warmth; everything that money could buy had been lavished on furnishing and interior. There was crystal and silver and pewter; fine old English furniture ransacked from antique shops the length and breadth of the land; and the collection of eighteenth century French pictures in the gallery was one of the most envied in private hands.

All this, said Tregorran, quoting Poe, was in the olden time, long ago. Yet despite the outpouring of effort and money, the family did not flourish in their new home. The fabric of the house was subject to mildew and there was much shaking of heads among the experts hurriedly summoned from long distances. A type of mould; a strange spore which left purple and scarlet lichen, infected the walls in some rooms; yet there was no perceptible trace of damp.

The drainage system was painstakingly reviewed and improved by builders but still the trouble continued, though the cellars had been filled in. The servants complained of the nauseating stench in their quarters and indeed they had just cause for comment; the owners of the house, descending on one of their rare expeditions, were forced to regain the upper floors with handkerchiefs clapped to their faces. The old kitchen quarters were thereafter boarded up and new rooms assigned for this purpose on the main floor occupied by the family.

As if this were not inconvenience enough, there was much illness in the household, though reputable physicians affirmed that they could trace no connection between the malady complained of and the mysterious lichen which spread silently and inexorably like a plague through the lower region of the house. A more enlightened young doctor with a scientific turn of mind informally advised the owner of Four Winds to drain the lake which adjoined the main building.

But the old man was reluctant to do that; it was one of the glories of the place. For the lake was immensely old, according to ancient deeds and maps; it was its superb location on a crest of the hills which had decided the owner on the site of the house.

To confess defeat on a mere point of dampness was an absurdity to one who had once held sway over hundreds of estate workers and body servants in the East.

This was the impasse which had been reached when one of the daughters died suddenly and shockingly, said Tregorran; curiously, it was not the result of the wasting fever which had attacked her father and mother. She had gone out one darkling winter afternoon on a walk round the foreshore of the lake. This had long been Estelle's practice and as she sometimes spent hours in such pursuits the family felt no unease at her continued absence.

Her father had passed the afternoon reading in a small turret chamber he had constructed out into the lake; the structure projected from the main house and was approached by a passage and the unfortunate old man often sat there in clear weather, reading and occasionally surveying the dark surface of the tarn with a telescope. And, as Tregorran proceeded with his tale, Kemp had felt as though the silk-merchant were responsible for creating a latter-day House of Usher in that remote spot.

But in reality the prosaic man had never heard of Poe and his fancy had run to the wild romanticism of Chillon, which he had once visited on a Grand Tour of Europe. Hence his penchant for the pseudo-Gothic tower in which he passed so much of his time. On this particular afternoon he had read until he was conscious that the light was beginning to fail.

Looking up from his book and training his eyes across the lake he was arrested by something moving in the water; he became aware of a slowly writhing mass of weed floating on the dank surface of the tarn. It came gradually across the field of his vision, though there was no visible current in the lake, and the merchant presently made out a broken mass of white at the centre of the weed.

The occasion was so curious as to be a cause for some comment in that placid place and the old man first called his wife before seeking his telescope from its leather case. So it fell that the wife was the first to put the glass to her eye with some pardonable wonder in the strange phenomena that floated before her.

Her horrified shriek and subsequent faint caused a minor crisis in the household; when the servants had carried their mistress from the room the old man, much agitated, had himself seized the telescope before following the small party down the corridor. What he saw was the drowned face of his daughter; the long hair of Estelle spreading out on the surface of the lake the old man's poor eyesight had mistaken for weed. The staring eyes, open mouth and mud plastering the dead features had accounted for the broken aspect of the white mass.

Kemp had remained cynically aloof as Tregorran had continued his narrative; the former's attitude resembled a mental rubbing of the hands. The blood raced through his veins at a slightly heightened rate; this was distinctly promising he told himself. But Tregorran's narrative bore all the stamps of a Gothic novella and Kemp himself suspected the tale to be half legend, half embroidery which the locals had handed down over the intervening years.

But he merely stretched himself in his corner by the fire, reached out his hand for the re-filled glass of punch his host proffered and observed, "There is more to come, I take it?"

Tregorran gazed at him grimly, perhaps conscious of the slight cynicism in Kemp's eyes.

"Assuredly," he said crisply.

2

The ever-steepening road wound about in sharp, corkscrew curves; deep groves of pine and birchwood hemmed in the lane, the edges of which were becoming blurred with growths of moss and lichen. The ragged spears of the branches were like sentinels blocking Kemp's escape to right and left and their darkness emphasised the brooding solitude of the day.

His ear was presently caught by the thin, high tinkle of falling water and turning another shallow curve he saw the white freshet of a small waterfall, like a scar across the blackness of the landscape; falling freely beyond the trees, then torn by rocks, descending again to view and finally being engulfed by the dense thickets farther down. Curiously enough his heart was not lightened by the sight; the whiteness of the water was like the pale flabbiness of something long dead and only emphasised the surrounding desolation.

The faint roar of the water strengthened the overpowering sense of loneliness in these far hills and Kemp was glad when the final fret of the fall at last died away and his footsteps rang out clear and strong on the gritty surface of the road. He pushed his chin down into the warm collar of his coat and set to musing on Tregorran's story of the unfortunate silk merchant and his family.

The drowned daughter had begun a long chapter of dark incidents, ranging from the sickness of the servants to the madness and eventual deaths of other members of the household. Tregorran had certain theories, which he had hinted to Kemp, but out of respect for what he called his visitor's professional ethics he had refused to clarify his suspicions. The most he would say, heavily enigmatic in the firelight, was that the two men would compare notes—after the visit.

The silk merchant had died of a wasting fever a short while after the incident described by Tregorran, and his wife had followed him within a year; a mass exodus of servants began and the household was eventually reduced to the two surviving daughters, a body servant and housekeeper. They lived a miserable existence on an upper storey and a priest who visited the family and had befriended them greatly in their troubles described the situation as being like a siege.

This old man himself died a violent and unexplainable death when he fell down an iron staircase after one of his nocturnal visits; the authorities hushed up the exact circumstances but one of the remaining servants told the sisters that spores of lichen were clustered about his mouth and eyes; his frenzied efforts to clear his throat and vision were the probable causes of his fall.

Within a very few days of this latest tragedy the survivors and their staff had decamped and the great house was left to decay on through the years, a prey to the buffeting winds of the uplands, the dark ruffled waters of the lake reflecting the sombre edifice which had been the scene of so much sorrow. So far as was known, said Tregorran, who had adopted a consciously Gothic tone when recounting the story to Kemp, only three visitors had since set foot inside the building.

The first had been found dead at the edge of the lake; a prospective purchaser, who had walked up like Kemp, to absorb atmosphere, as Tregorran put it, his body was huddled in a curious position, with strange markings in the mud at the fringe of the lake, which suggested that someone—or something—had attempted to pull him into the water.

The second visitor, also a prospective purchaser, was a middle-aged lady. She had driven up one afternoon on a tour of inspection only to collapse an hour or so later. She had been the victim of a heart attack; or at least that was the conclusion reached by a judicial inquiry. The third intruder, for so Kemp had come to describe them in his own mind, was a surveyor sent on behalf of the family estate to assess the condition of the structure. He too had died at the foot of the iron staircase.

Since that time Four Winds had been a shunned house; legend had it that the three who died had been the only people to set foot inside the house proper though Kemp found that difficult to believe. There must have been policemen, officials, and others concerned in the investigations; but he found the stories intriguing. Nowadays, Tregorran said, local people would view the house only from a distance, across the valley from the nearest road, and then they would hurry on, leaving the broken shell to its solitary vigil.

It stood up, like a jagged tooth, against a great promontory of woodland, with the lake hidden beneath the mass of trees. A secondary road, looping round from the old turnpike, would take the visitor to its door. And so it was that at last Kemp came out from the fringe of the far woods and saw the side road below him.

He descended a spiral path that debouched from the main turnpike and found himself on a rutted, unmade road which he knew led eventually to Four Winds. The sky was strangely dark and to his surprise he had not yet seen the house; but as he set foot on the moss-strewn pathway he came suddenly to a break in the trees and there was the great mass of granite, barely distinguishable against the far slopes, its frameless, glassless windows like blank sockets in the structure. He barely paused in his pacing, the glimpse he had obtained had been so much of an anti-climax.

The boughs pressed in on him like a long tunnel and his feet in the moss made furtive, sucking noises; Kemp guessed that some freshet debouching into the lake passed underground at this point, making the ground spongy and swamplike. Sure enough, as he turned on his tracks, his solitary shoe-marks in the lichen were silently filling with water. The silvery sheen looked like metal in the dim light which filtered through the branches.

After another three or four minutes the trees dropped away and he found himself on a wild and desolate shore; it was sheltered here and only an occasional swirl of wind touched the calm and limpid water of the tarn, so that it looked to him as though subterranean disturbances were causing the surface to erupt. The place smelt bad. Kemp, with his long experience of such things, knew that he was looking at a landscape filled with infinite evil;

nearer the lake-edge foul, scummy bubbles burst in the thickets of sedge which caked the shore like the poison round an abscess. The shadows of the trees wrote themselves again in the sullen waters of the lake. Yet, despite himself, Kemp was secretly exalted.

"Melancholy House of Usher," he said aloud. The words seemed to hang motionless on the freezing air before slowly dying away in tiny vibrations. Kemp looked down. In the black water at his feet weeds swirled and twined quietly where there was no current. A pale sphere broke the surface. He found himself looking at a girl's drowned face.

His smothered cry was followed by a cracking sound; as he involuntarily started back his heel had caught a dead branch, snapping it. White-faced, Kemp forced himself to look down at the water; of course, there was nothing there. What he had mistaken for hair was indeed weed; and where the pale oval of face had been was nothing but the reflection of a portion of sky, framed between entwining branches in the thicket at his back.

Kemp passed on, his ragged nerves fretting; Tregorran had done his work too well, he felt ruefully. The legends and stories with which he had kept his guest entertained the previous night had penetrated deep; even now he could not disentangle fact from embellishment. And yet he could not really imagine that his host would depart from the strict letter of the truth; he had known him far too long to be mistaken in such an important aspect.

Incredible to suppose for one moment that Tregorran had been playing an elaborate joke on him; if it were so a friendship of many years would be in the balance.

Kemp dismissed the supposition from his mind without a tremor; the atmosphere of Four Winds and particularly the lake foreshore should have been enough to satisfy him that here was no imaginative day-dreaming on the part of a fanciful savant. On the contrary, any normal person would have re-traced his passage without a moment's hesitation, thought Kemp, with the suspicion of a wry smile.

His mind was alert now, its receptivity attuned to any manifestations that the place might be giving off; the professional attitude of the experienced investigator was taking over the primal fears of his unconscious. From now on and throughout the visit he would be on guard; a scientific observer merely, weighing dispassionately and putting all data on the scales of logic. Easy enough to say, thought Kemp, looking round him; hard enough to achieve under these conditions.

He skirted the lake and came closer to the house; its granite mass crouched under the dark sky and the darker trees like something waiting to engulf him. He walked towards it reluctantly, with heavy steps, as though wary of the first contact. His way took him past a great old tree with withered limbs that framed Four Winds like a Cranach engraving. A path wound here and passed round and beneath the massive spread of branches. The faint echo of the wind plucked at the skirts of the thicket and Kemp paused, as though a chill engendered not only of the physical conditions of the day had entered into him.

Then, he knew not why, he turned and circled the gnarled trunk of the tree, on the landward side. As he did so the wind blew again out of the freezing sky; there was a crack and an impact that shuddered the soft earth on which Kemp stood. He continued his walk around the tree and looked behind him; a branch that overhung the path, its mass larger than a man's body and its weight enough to dash the life from anything beneath had fallen; the force of the shock had shattered the immense bough to fragments, its impact burying the main shaft several inches into the ground.

Kemp stood very still; he smiled at the house, baring his teeth under the dark sky. He knew he must look foolish but it was essential to show it that he was not afraid. Backwards he could not go; the house was watching him and it was essential at all times to see what it was doing; he felt no fear now, only that he must go on. It had become a personal thing, something between him and the house; a contest that could only be resolved in one of two ways. And to bring it to a successful conclusion Kemp knew that he must not reveal, even by so much as a fraction, that he was conscious of the force of the naked fear that gibbered in that freezing air, beneath that low sky.

He studied Four Winds for a moment, under half-closed lids; the great Palladian porch, only one pillar upright now; the roof quite gone; the floors as Tregorran had said, completely fallen in. All that was left was the jagged shell, open to the wide, inhuman sky. Kemp marvelled at the stubbornness which had kept the silk merchant and his family here; perhaps kept them still.

He skirted the frontage of the house cautiously; there was not a door remaining, not a window to be seen; the wind keened uneasily through the structure, probing with expert fingers for any hidden flaws, the air ruffling the long fronds of fern and weeds that grew in dirt-grimed cracks, like the hands of a lover passing through the beloved's hair. Kemp knew he had to be careful now; he had been given two warnings. Traditionally, the third might be the last; he did not intend to be taken by surprise.

He passed the end of the building, stopped abruptly; a turret jutted out into the lake, its glassless windows showing vistas of the waters beyond. He remembered Tregorran's story of the old man's vigil and wondered again about that tragic scene of long ago. The house was challenging him; to beat it and to break the spell the dark stories had woven for the country people, he had to venture within and emerge unscathed.

He remained irresolute for a moment or two longer; then he retraced his steps and found himself again on what had once been a wide gravel forecourt facing the lake. He passed up a shallow flight of grass-grown steps and into the ruin of the porch; within the floorless walls, Four Winds stared rooflessly to the pitiless sky; the wind soughed about the shattered pediments and through the glassless window sockets. Not a bird sang, no scutter of any living creature broke the deadness of the scene.

Then Kemp saw the steps; they were a jagged ruin, little more than a thin line of slabs let into the wall at one side of the main structure but they led upwards and unmistakably towards the turret room. Kemp knew that the house was daring him; knew equally well that if he hesitated he could not face it. He pushed up the steps, his feet uncertain on the slimy paving, gained what had once been the first storey; the view downwards was like looking into an awful pit; through the gaping window-holes in front the darkness of the lake sat and watched him.

There was a curious stench as he ascended to the second floor. The steps were firm and solid; there was no danger here, but he now saw that the wall at his left hand was pitted and scarred. Looking closer he noticed minute spores; striated lichens and strangely coloured polyps which clung limpet-like to the old granite. The stench came from these; Kemp grasped involuntarily at the wall as he stumbled.

Something broke away in his hand and he nearly fell; he held a flabby object, shaped like a human finger and of pallid and unhealthy hue. The fungus seemed to pulse in his hand as he stared at it; little spores emanated from it and flew in clouds round Kemp's head. The smell was really awful; Kemp's head was reeling and his eyes smarted. He gave a muffled cry and slipped again. He hurled the fungi-thing from him with a hoarse shout of terror.

His vision cleared and he scrambled and lurched up the last remaining flights to the turret room, his heart thumping uncontrollably, his nerves screaming; there was no floor in the turret chamber, only a continuation of the rough-slabbed stone which formed the staircase. Kemp stood at an open revetment in the wall and wiped his face with his handkerchief; there was a palsied tremor in his limbs. A few grey spores flew about his head as though they had volition of their own, as he passed the handkerchief across his forehead.

He stayed crouched there for several minutes until his racing heart had steadied and his nerves were back to normal; he coughed, as though the commonplace sound confirmed his triumph. For it had been a definite victory, Kemp felt, in his confrontation with what he considered to be the evil spirit of the house. And the third sign had been overcome without anything more unpleasant happening to him than a nasty fright. He gazed down into the floorless well of the house and willed his nerves into normality.

After all, there had to be an occasion when the power of the house was confronted with the equally remorseless will of a professional occultist. Though he knew the house was not done with him, Kemp felt he was several points to the good. Four Winds squatted there and waited; it had him in its maw but the third warning had been given and overcome and still Kemp survived, like Jonah in the belly of the whale.

He put back the handkerchief in his pocket, straightened his tie and reached for his notebook. It was only then that he noticed the gap in the staircase; about ten feet farther down, over the stone across which Kemp had just advanced, there was now a space of about fifteen feet which barred him from the lower part of the house. Kemp stared for a moment; it was a nasty shock. The house's trump card, so to speak. Paradoxically, Kemp felt his spirits rising; he was equal to the challenge.

Kemp laughed. The sound rang round the old shell with the impact of a bell pealing in the airless confines of a vault. Let the house do its worst, the gesture seemed to say; the human spirit was unbreakable. As the last echo died away Kemp stood poised, his hands braced against the damp stone, his ears straining for a sign. Would the house accept defeat.

Aeons seemed to pass. Kemp stood by the wall, drained of all emotion; he had an unshakable conviction that he had won. At last the house had been defeated. It was growing dark but even with the gap in the staircase Kemp knew he could regain the ground floor safely.

Still he lingered, his mind filled with age-old dreams; the lake lapped below, the wind murmured coldly through the granite cage of the ruined building and his triumph soared, reflected in the smile in his eyes.

And the sign came.

Down below a door slammed where there was no door and heavy footsteps, echoing where there was no floor, advanced towards him.

RALPH A. CRAM
In Kropfsberg Keep

Ralph Adams Cram *(1863-1942) was one of America's leading architects. He began a revival of mediaeval Gothic forms, particularly in the design of churches. Among his many books are* The Ruined Abbeys of Great Britain, The Gothic Quest, *and* My life in Architecture. *His first book was a collection of weird and supernatural tales,* Black Spirits and White, *from which the following story is taken.*

To the traveller from Innsbrück to Munich, up the lovely valley of the silver Inn, many castles appear, one after another, each on its beetling cliff or gentle hill—appear and disappear, melting into the dark fir trees that grow so thickly on every side—Laneck, Lichtwer, Ratholtz, Tratzberg, Matzen, Kropfsberg, gathering close around the entrance to the dark and wonderful Zillerthal.

But to us—Tom Rendel and myself—there are two castles only: not the gorgeous and princely Ambras, nor the noble old Tratzberg, with its crowded treasures of solemn and splendid mediaevalism; but little Matzen, where eager hospitality forms the new life of a never-dead chivalry, and Kropfsberg, ruined, tottering, blasted by fire and smitten with grievous years—a dead thing, and haunted—full of strange legends, and eloquent of mystery and tragedy.

We were visiting the von C—s at Matzen, and gaining our first wondering knowledge of the courtly, cordial castle life in the Tyrol—of the gentle and delicate hospitality of noble Austrians. Brixleg had ceased to be but a mark on a map, and had become a place of rest and delight, a home for homeless wanderers on the face of Europe, while Schloss Matzen was a synonym for all that was gracious and kindly and beautiful in life. The days moved on in a golden round of riding and driving and shooting: down to Landl and Thiersee for chamois, across the river to the magic Achensee, up the Zillerthal, across the Schmerner Joch, even to the railway station at Steinach. And in the evenings after the late dinners in the upper hall where the sleepy hounds leaned against our chairs looking at us with suppliant eyes, in the evenings when the fire was dying away in the hooded fireplace in the library, stories. Stories, and legends, and fairy tales, while the stiff old portraits changed countenance constantly under the flickering firelight, and the sound of the drifting Inn came softly across the meadows far below.

If ever I tell the story of Schloss Matzen, then will be the time to paint the too inadequate picture of this fair oasis in the desert of travel and tourists and hotels; but just now it is Kropfsberg the Silent that is of greater importance, for it was only in Matzen that the story was told by Fräulein E——, the gold-haired niece of Frau von C——, one hot evening in July, when we were sitting in the great west window of the drawing-room after a long ride up the Stallenthal. All the windows were open to catch the faint wind, and we had sat for a long time watching the Otzethaler Alps turn rose-colour over distant Innsbrück, then deepen to violet as the sun went down and the white mists rose slowly until Lichtwer and Laneck and Kropfsberg rose like craggy islands in a silver sea.

And this is the story as Fräulein E— told it to us—the Story of Kropfsberg Keep.

A great many years ago, soon after my grandfather died, and Matzen came to us, when I was a little girl, and so young that I remember nothing of the affair except as something dreadful that frightened me very much, two young men who had studied painting with my grandfather came down to Brixleg from Munich, partly to paint, and partly to amuse themselves—"ghost-hunting" as they said, for they were very sensible young men and prided themselves on it, laughing at all kinds of "superstition," and particularly at that form which believed in ghosts and feared them. They had never seen a real ghost, you know, and they belonged to a certain set of people who believed nothing they had not seen themselves—which always seemed to me *very* conceited. Well, they knew that we had lots of beautiful castles here in the "lower valley", and they assumed, and rightly, that every castle has at least *one* ghost story connected with it, so they chose this as their hunting ground, only the game they sought was ghosts, not chamois. Their plan was to visit every place that was supposed to be haunted, and to meet every reputed ghost, and prove that it really was no ghost at all.

There was a little inn down in the village then, kept by an old man named Peter Rosskopf, and the two young men made this their headquarters. The very first night they began to draw from the old innkeeper all that he knew of legends and ghost stories connected with Brixleg and its castles, and as he was a most garrulous old gentleman he filled them with the wildest delight by his stories of the ghosts of the castles about the mouth of the Zillerthal. Of course the old man believed every word he said, and you can imagine his horror and amazement when, after telling his guests the particularly blood-curdling story of Kropfsberg and its haunted keep, the elder of the two boys, whose surname I have forgotten, but whose Christian name was Rupert, calmly said "Your story is most satisfactory: we will sleep in Kropfsberg Keep tomorrow night, and you must provide us with all that we may need to make ourselves comfortable."

The old man nearly fell into the fire. "What for a blockhead are you?" he cried, with big eyes. "The keep is haunted by Count Albert's ghost, I tell you!"

"That is why we are going there tomorrow night; we wish to make the acquaintance of Count Albert."

"But there was a man stayed there once, and in the morning he was dead."

"Very silly of him; there are two of us, and we carry revolvers."

"But it's a *ghost*, I tell you," almost screamed the innkeeper; "are ghosts afraid of firearms?"

"Whether they are or not, we are *not* afraid of *them*."

Here the younger boy broke in—he was named Otto von Kleist. I remember the name, for I had a music teacher once by that name. He abused the poor old man shamefully; told him that they were going to spend the night in Kropfsberg in spite of Count Albert and Peter Rosskopf, and that he might as well make the most of it and earn his money with cheerfulness.

In a word, they finally bullied the old fellow into submission, and when the morning came he set about preparing for the suicide, as he considered it, with sighs and mutterings and ominous shakings of the head.

You know the condition of the castle now—nothing but scorched walls and crumbling piles of fallen masonry. Well, at the time I tell you of, the keep was still partially preserved. It was finally burned out only a few years ago by some wicked boys who came over from Jenbach to have a good time. But when the ghost hunters came, though the two lower floors had fallen into the crypt, the third floor remained. The peasants said it *could* not fall, but that it would stay until the Day of Judgment, because it was in the room above that the wicked Count Albert sat watching the flames destroy the great castle and his imprisoned guests, and where he finally hung himself in a suit of armour that had belonged to his mediaeval ancestor, the first Count Kropfsberg.

No one dared touch him, and so he hung there for twelve years, and all the time venturesome boys and daring men used to creep up the turret steps and stare awfully through the chinks in the door at that ghostly mass of steel that held within itself the body of a murderer and suicide, slowly returning to the dust from which it was made. Finally it disappeared, none knew whither, and for another dozen years the room stood empty but for the old furniture and the rotting hangings.

So, when the two men climbed the stairway to the haunted room, they found a very different state of things from what exists now. The room was absolutely as it was left the night Count Albert burned the castle, except that all trace of the suspended suit of armour and its ghastly contents had vanished.

No one had dared to cross the threshold, and I suppose that for forty years no living thing had entered that dreadful room.

On one side stood a vast canopied bed of black wood, the damask hangings of which were covered with mould and mildew. All the clothing of the bed was in perfect order, and on it lay a book, open, and face downward. The only other furniture in the room consisted of several old chairs, a carved oak chest, and a big inlaid table covered with books and papers, and on one corner two or three bottles with dark solid sediment at the bottom, and a glass, also dark with the dregs of wine that that been poured out almost half a century before. The tapestry on the walls was green with mould, but hardly torn or otherwise defaced, for although the heavy dust of forty years lay on everything the room had been preserved from further harm. No spider web was to be seen, no trace of nibbling mice, not even a dead moth or fly on the sills of the diamond-paned windows; life seemed to have shunned the room utterly and finally.

The men looked at the room curiously, and, I am sure, not without some feelings of awe and unacknowledged fear; but, whatever they may have felt of instinctive shrinking, they said nothing, and quickly set to work to make the room passably inhabitable. They decided to touch nothing that had not absolutely to be changed, and therefore they made for themselves a bed in one corner with the mattress and linen from the inn. In the great fireplace they piled a lot of wood on the caked ashes of a fire dead for forty years, turned the old chest into a table, and laid out on it all their arrangements for the evening's amusement: food, two or three bottles of wine, pipes and tobacco, and the chess-board that was their inseparable travelling companion.

All this they did themselves: the innkeeper would not even come within the walls of the outer court; he insisted that he had washed his hands of the whole affair, the silly dunderheads might go to their death their own way. *He* would not aid and abet them. One of the stable boys brought the basket of food and the wood and the bed up the winding stone stairs, to be sure, but neither money nor prayers nor threats would bring him within the walls of the accursed place, and he stared fearfully at the hare-brained boys as they worked around the dead old room preparing for the night that was coming so fast.

At length everything was in readiness, and after a final visit to the inn for dinner Rupert and Otto started at sunset for the Keep. Half the village went with them, for Peter Rosskopf had babbled the whole story to an open-mouthed crowd of wondering men and women, and as to an execution the awestruck crowd followed the two boys dumbly, curious to see if they surely would put their plan into execution. But none went farther than the outer doorway of the stairs, for it was already growing twilight. In absolute silence they watched the two foolhardy youths with their lives in their hands enter the terrible Keep, standing like a tower in the midst of the piles of stones that had once formed walls joining it with the mass of the castle beyond. When a moment later a light showed itself in the high windows above, they sighed resignedly and went their ways, to wait stolidly until morning should come and prove the truth of their fears and warnings.

In the meantime the ghost hunters built a huge fire, lighted their many candles, and sat down to await developments. Rupert afterwards told my uncle that they really felt no fear whatever, only a contemptuous curiosity, and they ate their supper with good appetite and an unusual relish. It was a long evening. They played many games of chess, waiting for midnight. Hour passed after hour, and nothing occurred to interrupt the monotony of the evening. Ten, eleven, came and went—it was almost midnight. They piled more wood in the fireplace, lighted new candles, looked to their pistols—and waited. The clocks in the village struck twelve; the sound coming muffled through the high, deep-embrasured windows. Nothing happened, nothing to break the heavy silence; and with a feeling of disappointed relief they looked at each other and acknowledged that they had met another rebuff.

Finally they decided that there was no use in sitting up and boring themselves any longer, they had much better rest; so Otto threw himself down on the mattress, falling almost immediately asleep. Rupert sat a little longer, smoking, and watching the stars creep along behind the shattered glass and the bent leads of the lofty windows; watching the fire fall together, and the strange shadows move mysteriously on the mouldering walls. The iron hook in the oak beam, that crossed the ceiling midway, fascinated him, not with fear, but morbidly. So, it was from that hook that for twelve years, twelve long years of changing summer and winter, the body of Count Albert, murderer and suicide, hung in its strange casing of mediaeval steel; moving a little at first, and turning gently while the fire died out on the hearth, while the ruins of the castle grew cold, and horrified peasants sought for the bodies of the score of gay, reckless, wicked guests whom Count Albert had gathered in Kropfsberg for a last debauch, gathered to their terrible and untimely death. What a strange and fiendish idea it was, the young, handsome noble who had ruined himself and his family in the society of the splendid debauchees, gathering them all together, men and women who had known only love and pleasure, for a glorious and awful riot of luxury, and then, when they were all dancing in the great ballroom, locking the doors and burning the whole castle about them, the while he sat in the great keep listening to their screams of agonized fear, watching the fire sweep from wing to wing until the whole mighty mass was one enormous and awful pyre, and then, clothing himself in his great-great-grandfather's armour, hanging himself in the midst of the ruins of what had been a proud and noble castle. So ended a great family, a great house.

But that was forty years ago.

He was growing drowsy; the light flickered and flared in the fireplace; one by one the candles went out; the shadows grew thick in the room. Why did that great iron hook stand out so plainly? why did that dark shadow dance and quiver so mockingly behind it?—why—But he ceased to wonder at anything. He was asleep.

It seemed to him that he woke almost immediately; the fire still burned, though low and fitfully on the hearth. Otto was sleeping, breathing quietly and regularly; the shadows had gathered close around him, thick and murky; with every passing moment the light died in the fireplace; he felt stiff with cold. In the utter silence he heard the clock in the village strike two. He shivered with a sudden and irresistible feeling of fear, and abruptly turned and looked towards the hook in the ceiling.

Yes, It was there. He knew that It would be. It seemed quite natural, he would have been disappointed had he seen nothing; but now he knew that the story was true, knew that he was wrong, and that the dead *do* sometimes return to earth, for there, in the fast-deepening shadow, hung the black mass of wrought steel, turning a little now and then, with the light flickering on the tarnished and rusty metal. He watched it quietly; he hardly felt afraid; it was rather a sentiment of sadness and fatality that filled him, of gloomy forebodings of something unknown, unimaginable. He sat and watched the thing disappear in the gathering dark, his hand on his pistol as it lay by him on the great chest. There was no sound but the regular breathing of the sleeping boy on the mattress.

It had grown absolutely dark; a bat fluttered against the broken glass of the window. He wondered if he was growing mad, for—he hesitated to acknowledge it to himself—he heard music; far, curious music, a strange and luxurious dance, very faint, very vague, but unmistakable.

Like a flash of lightning came a jagged line of fire down the blank wall opposite him, a line that remained, that grew wider, that let a pale cold light into the room, showing him now all its details—the empty fireplace, where a thin smoke rose in a spiral from a bit of charred wood, the mass of the great bed, and, in the very middle, black against the curious brightness, the armoured man, or ghost, or devil, standing, not suspended, beneath the rusty hook. And with the rending of the wall the music grew more distinct, though sounding still very, very far away.

Count Albert raised his mailed hand and beckoned to him; then turned, and stood in the riven wall.

Without a word, Rupert rose and followed him, his pistol in hand. Count Albert passed through the mighty wall and disappeared in the unearthly light. Rupert followed mechanically. He felt the crushing of the mortar beneath his feet, the roughness of the jagged wall where he rested his hand to steady himself.

The keep rose absolutely isolated among the ruins, yet on passing through the wall Rupert found himself in a long, uneven corridor, the floor of which was warped and sagging, while the walls were covered on one side with big faded portraits of an inferior quality, like those in the corridor that connects the Pitti and Uffizzi in Florence. Before him moved the figure of Count Albert—a black silhouette in the ever-increasing light. And always the music grew stronger and stranger, a mad, evil, seductive dance that bewitched even while it disgusted.

In a final blaze of vivid, intolerable light, in a burst of hellish music that might have come from Bedlam, Rupert stepped from the corridor into a vast and curious room where at first he saw nothing, distinguished nothing but a mad, seething whirl of sweeping figures, white, in a white room, under white light, Count Albert standing before him, the only dark object to be seen. As his eyes grew accustomed to the fearful brightness, he knew that he was looking on a dance such as the damned might see in hell, but such as no living man had ever seen before.

Around the long, narrow hall, under the fearful light that came from nowhere, but was omnipresent, swept a rushing stream of unspeakable horrors, dancing insanely, laughing, gibbering hideously; the dead of forty years. White, polished skeletons, bare of flesh and vesture, skeletons clothed in the dreadful rags of dried and rattling sinews, the tags of tattering graveclothes flaunting behind them. These were the dead of many years ago. Then the dead of more recent times, with yellow bones showing only here and there, the long and insecure hair of their hideous heads writhing in the beating air. Then green and grey horrors, bloated and shapeless, stained with earth or dripping with spattering water; and here and there white, beautiful things, like chiselled ivory, the dead of yesterday, locked it may be, in the mummy arms of rattling skeletons.

Round and round the cursed room, a swaying, swirling maelstrom of death, while the air grew thick with miasma, the floor foul with shreds of shrouds, and yellow parchment, clattering bones, and wisps of tangled hair.

And in the very midst of this ring of death, a sight not for words nor for thought, a sight to blast forever the mind of the man who looked upon it: a leaping, writhing dance of Count Albert's victims, the score of beautiful women and reckless men who danced to their awful death while the castle burned around them, charred and shapeless now, a living charnel-house of nameless horror.

Count Albert, who had stood silent and gloomy, watching the dance of the damned, turned to Rupert, and for the first time spoke.

"We are ready for you now; dance!"

A prancing horror, dead some dozen years, perhaps, flaunted from the rushing river of the dead, and leered at Rupert with eyeless skull.

"Dance!"

Rupert stood frozen, motionless.

"Dance!"

His hard lips moved. "Not if the devil came from hell to make me."

Count Albert swept his vast two-handled sword into the foetid air while the tide of corruption paused in its swirling, and swept down on Rupert with gibbering grins.

The room, and the howling dead, and the black portent before him circled dizzily around, as with a last effort of departing consciousness he drew his pistol and fired full in the face of Count Albert.

Perfect silence, perfect darkness; not a breath, not a sound: the dead stillness of a long-sealed tomb. Rupert lay on his back, stunned, helpless, his pistol clenched in his frozen hand, a smell of powder in the black air. Where was he? Dead? In hell? He reached his hand out cautiously; it fell on dusty boards. Outside, far away, a clock struck three. Had he dreamed? Of course; but how ghastly a dream! With chattering teeth he called softly—

"Otto!"

There was no reply, and none when he called again and again. He staggered weakly to his feet, groping for matches and candles. A panic of abject terror came on him; the matches were gone! He turned towards the fireplace: a single coal glowed in the white ashes. He swept a mass of papers and dusty books from the table, and with trembling hands cowered over the embers, until he succeeded in lighting the dry tinder. Then he piled the old books on the blaze, and looked fearfully around.

No: It was gone—thank God for that; the hook was empty.

But why did Otto sleep so soundly; why did he not awake?

He stepped unsteadily across the room in the flaring light of the burning books, and knelt by the mattress.

So they found him in the morning, when no one came to the inn from Kropfsberg Keep, and the quaking Peter Rosskopf arranged a relief party—found him kneeling beside the mattress where Otto lay, shot in the throat and quite dead.

DANIEL DEFOE

The Ghost in All the Rooms

Daniel Defoe *(1660–1731), author of* Robinson Crusoe *and* Moll Flanders, *made a study of ghosts for over forty years, culminating in his* Essay on the Reality of Apparitions *(1727).*

His most reprinted narrative in this vein is "The True Relation of the Apparition of one Mrs Veal" (1706), and among his other tales are 'The Spectre and the Highwayman', 'The Friendly Demon', and 'The Ghost in All the Rooms', all reputed to be based on true occurrences.

A certain person of quality, being with his family at his country seat for the summer season, according to his ordinary custom, was obliged, upon a particular occasion of health, to leave his said seat and go to Aix-la-Chapelle, to use the baths there. This was, it seems, in the month of August, being two months sooner than the usual time of his returning to court for the winter.

Upon thus removing sooner than ordinary he did not then disfurnish the house, as was the ordinary usage of the family, or carry away his plate and other valuable goods, but left his steward and three servants to look after the house. And the padre or parish priest was desired to keep his eye upon them too and to succor them from the village adjoining, if there was occasion.

The steward had no public notice of any harm approaching, but for three or four days successively he had secret strange impulses of dread and terror upon his mind that the house was beset, and was to be assaulted by a troop of banditti, or as we call them here housebreakers, who would murder them all, and after they had robbed the house would set it on fire. And this followed him so fast and made such impression upon his mind that he could think of nothing else.

Upon this, the third day he went to the padre or parish priest and made his complaint. Upon which the priest and the steward had the following discourse, the steward beginning thus:

"Father," said he, "you know what a charge I have in my custody and how my lord has entrusted me with the whole house, and all the rich furniture is standing. I am in great perplexity about it and come to you for your advice."

Priest: Why, what's the matter? You have not heard of any mischief threatened, have you?

Steward: No, I have heard nothing. But I have such apprehensions and it has made such impression upon me for these three days that—

Here he told him the particulars of the uneasiness he had been in and added, besides what is said above, that one of the servants had the same and had told him of it, though he had communicated nothing to that servant in the least.

Priest: It may be you dreamed of these things?

Steward: No, indeed, padre! I am sure I could not dream of them, for I could never sleep.

Priest: What can I do for you? What would you have me do?

Steward: I would have you first of all tell me what you think of these things, and whether there is any notice to be taken of them.

Here the padre examined him more strictly about the particulars, and sent for the servant and examined him apart and being a very judicious honest man, he answered him thus:

Priest: Look you, Mr. Steward, I do not lay a very great stress upon such things, but yet I don't think they are to be wholly slighted. And therefore I would have you be upon your guard, and if you have the least alarm, let me know.

Steward: That is poor satisfaction to me to be upon my guard, if I am overpowered. I suppose if any villains have a design to attack me they know my strength.

Priest: Shall I reinforce your garrison?

Steward: I wish you would.

Priest: Well, I'll send you some men with firearms to lie there this night.

Accordingly the priest sent him five stout fellows with fusees, and a dozen of hand grenadoes with them, and while they continued in the house nothing appeared. But the padre, finding nothing come of it and being loath to put his patron to so continued a charge, sent for the steward and in a chiding angry tone told him his mind.

Priest: I know not how you will answer it to my lord, but you have put him to a prodigious expense here, in keeping a garrison in the house all this while.

Steward: I am sorry for it, padre, but what can I do?

Priest: Do! Why, compose your mind, and keep up your heart, and don't let my lord spend two or three hundred livres here to cure you of the vapours.

Steward: Why, you said yourself, padre, that it was not to be wholly slighted.

Priest: That's true; but I said also I would not lay too great a stress upon it.

Steward: What must I do then?

Priest: Do! Why, dismiss the men again and take what care you can. And if you have any notice of mischief that may be depended upon, let me have notice too, and I will assist you.

Steward: Well, then, the good angel must protect my lord's house, I see, for nobody else will.

"Amen," says the padre, "I trust the good spirits will keep you all." So he blessed the steward (in his way) and the steward went away grumbling very much that he took away his garrison and left him to the good spirits.

It seems, for all this, that the steward's notices, however secret and from he knew not who, were not of so light an import as the padre thought they were. For as he had this impulse upon his mind that such mischief was brewing, so it really was, as you will see presently.

A set of robbers, who had intelligence that the nobleman with his family was gone to Aix-la-Chapelle, but that the house was left furnished and all the plate and the things of value were left in it, had formed a design to plunder the house and afterwards to burn it, just as the steward had said.

They were two and twenty strong, in the whole, and thoroughly armed for mischief. Yet while the additional force which the padre had placed to reinforce the steward were in the house, of whom, including the other four, three sat up every night, they did not dare attempt it.

But as soon as they heard that the guard was dismissed, they formed their design anew, and to make the story short they attacked the house about midnight. Having, I suppose, proper instruments about them, they soon broke open a window and twelve of them got into the house, the rest standing sentinel at such places as they thought proper, to prevent any succours from the town.

The poor steward and his three men were in great distress. They were indeed above stairs, and had barricaded the staircases as well as they could, hearing the fellows were breaking in. But when they found they were got in, they expected nothing but to be kept above stairs till the house was plundered, and then to be burnt alive.

But it seems the good spirits the priest spoke of, or somebody else, made better provision for them, as you will see presently.

When the first of the fellows got into the house, and had opened the door and let in as many of their gang as they thought fit, which, as above, was twelve in number, they shut the door again and shut themselves in; leaving two without the door, who had a watchword, to go and call more help if they wanted it.

The twelve ranging over the great hall found little there to gratify their greedy hopes. But breaking next into a fine well-furnished parlour where the family usually sat, behold! in a great easy chair sat a grave ancient man with a long full-bottomed black wig, a rich brocaded gown, and a lawyer's laced band, but looking as if in great surprise, seemed to make signs to them for mercy; but said not a word, nor they much to him, except that one of them, starting, cried, "Ha! who's here?"

Immediately the rogues fell to pulling down the fine damask curtains in the windows, and other rich things; but one said to another with an oath, "Make the old dog tell us where the plate is hid." And another said, "If he won't tell you, cut his throat immediately."

The ancient gentleman, with signs of entreaty, as if begging for his life, and in a great fright, points to a door which being opened would let them into another parlour, which was the gaming room, and served as a drawing room to the first parlour, and by another door opened into the great saloon which looked into the gardens. They were some time forcing their way into that room, but when they came in, they were surprised to see the same old man, in the same dress and the same chair, sitting at the upper end of the room, making the same gestures and silent entreaties as before.

They were not much concerned at first, but thought he had come in by another door, and began to swear at him for putting them to the trouble of breaking open the door when there was another way into the room. But another, wickeder than the first, said with a heavy curse: the old dog was got in by another door on purpose to convey away the plate and money; and bade knock his brains out. Upon which the first swore at him that if he did not immediately show them where it was he was a dead dog that moment.

Upon this furious usage he points to the doors which opened into the saloon, which, being a thin pair of folding doors, opened presently, and in they run into the great saloon; when looking at the further end of the room, there sat the ancient man again, in the same dress and posture as before.

Upon this sight, those that were foremost among them cried out aloud, "Why this old fellow deals with the Devil, sure! He's here afore us again."

But the case differed a little now, for when they came out of the first parlour, being eager for the plate and money and willing to find it all, the whole body of them run into the second parlour. But now, the ancient man pointing to the third room, they did not all immediately rush out into the saloon, but four of them were left behind in the parlour or gaming room mentioned just now, not by order or design, but accidentally.

By this means they fell into the following confusion: for while some of them called out from the saloon that the old rogue was there before them again, others answered out of the parlour, "How the devil can that be? Why, he is here still in his chair, and all his rubbish."

With that, two of them run back into the first parlour, and there they saw him again sitting as before. Notwithsanding all this, far from guessing what the occasion should be, they fancied they were gamed, or suggested that they were but jested with, and that there were three several old men all dressed up in the same habits for the very same occasion, and to mock them, as if to let them know that the men above in the house were not afraid of them.

"Well," says one of the gang, "I'll despatch one of the old rogues. I'll teach one of them how to make game at us." Upon which, raising his fusee as high as his arm would let him, he struck at the ancient man, as he thought it was, with all his force. But behold! there was nothing in the chair, and his fusee flew into a thousand pieces, wounding his hand most grievously. And a piece of the barrel, striking him on the head, broke his face and knocked him down backward.

At the same time, one of those in the saloon running at the ancient man that sat there, swore he would tear his fine brocaded gown off, and then he would cut his throat. But when he went to take hold of him, there was nothing in the chair.

This happening in both rooms, they were all in most horrible confusion, and cried out in both rooms at the same moment, in a terrible manner.

As they were in the utmost amazement at the thing, so after the first clamor they stood looking upon one another for some time, without speaking a word more. But at length one said, "Let's go back into the first parlour and see if that's gone too."

And with that word, two or three that were on that side run into the room, and there sat the ancient figure as at first. Upon which they called to the company and told them they believed they were all bewitched, and it was certain they only fancied they saw a man in the other rooms, for there was the real old man sitting where he was at first.

Upon this they all run thither, saying they would see whether it was the devil or no. And one of them said, "Let me come. I'll speak to him. 'Tis not the first time I have talked with the devil."

"Nay," says another, "so will I." And then added with an oath: gentlemen that were upon such business as they were ought not to be afraid to speak to the devil.

A third (for now their courage began to rise again) calls aloud, "Let it be the devil, or the devil's grandmother, I'll parley with it. I am resolved I'll know what it is."

And with that he runs forward before the rest, and, crossing himself, says to the ancient man in the chair, "In the name of St. Francis, and St.—(and so reckoned up two or three saints' names that he depended were enough to fright the devil), what art thou?"

The figure never moved or spoke. But looking at its face, they presently found that instead of his pitiful looks and seeming to beg for his life, as he did before, he was changed into the most horrible monster that ever was seen, and such as I cannot describe. And that instead of his hands held up to them to cry for mercy, there were two large fiery daggers, not flaming, but redhot and pointed with a livid bluish flame, and, in a word, the devil or something else in the most frightful shape that can be imagined. And it was my opinion, when I first read the story, the rogues were so frighted that their imagination afterwards formed a thing in their thoughts more terrible than the devil himself could appear in.

But be that as it will, his figure was such that when they came up to him not a man of them had courage to look in his face, much less talk to him. And he that was so bold, and thus came armed with half a regiment of saints in his mouth, fell down flat on the ground, having fainted away, as they call it, with fright.

The steward and his three men were all this while above stairs, in the utmost concern at the danger they were in and expecting every moment the rogues would strive to force their way up, and cut their throats. They heard the confused noise that the fellows made below but could not imagine what it was, and much less the meaning of it. But while it lasted it came into the mind of one of the servants, that as it was certain the fellows were all in the parlour, and very busy there, whatever it was about, he might go up to the top of the house and throw one of their hand grenades down the chimney, and perhaps it might do some execution among them.

The steward approved of this design, only with his addition. "If we throw down but into one parlour, they will all fly into the gaming room, and so it will do no execution. But," says he, "take three, and put down one into each chimney, for the funnels go up all together, and then they will not know which way to run."

With these orders, two of the men who very well knew the place went up, and firing the fuses of the grenades, they put one shell into each of the funnels; and down they went roaring in the chimney with a terrible noise, and (which was more than all the rest) they came down into the parlour where almost all the rogues were, just at the moment that the fellow that spoke to the spectre was frighted into a swooning fit and fallen on the floor.

The whole gang was frighted beyond expression. Some run back into to the gaming parlour whence they came, and some run to the other door which they came in at from the hall, but all at the same instant heard the devil, as they thought it was, coming down the chimney.

Had it been possible that the fusees of the grenades could have continued burning in the funnel of the chimneys, where the sound was a thousand times doubled by the hollow of the place, and where the soot burning fell down in flakes of fire, the rogues had been frighted out of their understandings; imagining, that as they had one dreadful devil just among them in the chair, so there were ten thousand more coming down the chimney to destroy them all, and perhaps to carry them all away.

But that could not be. So after they had been sufficiently scared with the noise, down came the shells into the rooms, all three together. It happened as luckily as if it had been contrived on purpose, that the shell which came down into the parlour where they all were, burst as soon as ever it came to the bottom, so that it did not give them time so much as to think what it might be, much less to know that it was really a hand grenade. But as it did great execution among them, so they as certainly believed it was the devil as they believed the spectre in the chair was the devil.

The noise of the bursting of the shell was so sudden and so unexpected that it confounded them, and the mischief was also terrible. The man that fainted and who lay on the ground was killed outright, and two more that stood just before the chimney. Five of them were desperately wounded, whereof one had both his legs broken, and was so desperate that when the people from the country came in, he shot himself through the head with his own pistol to prevent his being taken.

Had the rest of them fled out of the parlour into the two other rooms, it is probable they had been wounded by the other shells. But as they heard the noise in both the outer rooms, and besides were under the surprise of its being not a hand grenade, but the devil, they had no power to stir. Nor if they had could they know which way to go to be safe. So they stood still till both the shells in the other rooms burst also. At which, being confounded, as well with the noise as with the smoke, and expecting more devils down the chimney where they stood, they run out all that way, and made to the door, helping their wounded men along as well as they could. Whereof one died in the fields after they were got away.

It must be observed, when they were thus alarmed with they knew not what coming down the chimney, they cried out that the devil in the chair had sent for more devils to destroy them. And it was supposed that had the shells never come down, they would all have run away. But certain it was that the artificial devil joining so critically as to time with the visionary devils, or whatever they were, completed their disorder and forced them to fly.

When they came to the door to the two men, they made signals for their comrades who were posted in the avenues to the house to come to their relief; who accordingly came up, and assisted to carry off their wounded men. But after hearing the relation of those that had been in the house and calling a short council a little way from the door (which, though dark as it was, the steward and his men could perceive from the window), they all resolved to make off.

There was another concurring accident which, though it does not relate to my subject, I must set down to complete the story: that two of these grenades by the fire of their fuses set the chimneys on fire. The third, being in a funnel that had no soot in it, the room having not been so much used, did not. This fire flaming out at the top, as is usual, was seen by somebody in the village, who run immediately and alarmed the priest or padre, and he again raised the whole town, believing there was some mischief fallen out and that the house was set on fire.

Had the rest of the gang not resolved to make off as is said above, they had certainly fallen into the hands of the townsmen, who ran immediately with what arms came next to hand, to the house. But the rogues were fled, leaving, as above, three of their company dead in the house, and one in the field.

CHARLES DICKENS
The Bagman's Uncle

The Victorian era witnessed an enormous rise in public demand for the traditional ghost story, following the more antiquated Gothic horrors of Horace Walpole, Ann Radcliffe, and the 'penny dreadfuls'. In 1836, the year before Victoria's accession, Charles Dickens *(1812–70) – the most important popularizer of the genre – introduced several ghost stories in his* Pickwick Papers, *all destined to be classics: 'The Story of the Goblins who Stole a Sexton' (precursor of* A Christmas Carol*), 'The Bagman's Story', and 'The Bagman's Uncle'.*

"My uncle, gentlemen," said the bagman, "was one of the merriest, pleasantest, cleverest fellows that ever lived. I wish you had known him, gentlemen. On second thoughts, gentlemen, I *don't* wish you had known him; for if you had, you would have been all by this time, in the ordinary course of nature, if not dead, at all events so near it as to have taken to stopping at home and giving up company, which would have deprived me of the inestimable pleasure of addressing you at this moment. Gentlemen, I wish your fathers and mothers had known my uncle. They would have been amazingly fond of him, especially your respectable mothers; I know they would. If any two of his numerous virtues predominated over the many that adorned his character, I should say they were his mixed punch and his after-supper song. Excuse my dwelling on these melancholy recollections of departed worth; you won't see a man like my uncle every day in the week.

"I have always considered it a great point in my uncle's character, gentlemen, that he was the intimate friend and companion of Tom Smart, of the great house of Bilson and Slum, Cateaton Street, City. My uncle collected for Tiggin and Welps, but for a long time he went pretty near the same journey as Tom; and the very first night they met, my uncle took a fancy for Tom, and Tom took a fancy for my uncle. They made a bet of a new hat, before they had known each other half an hour, who should brew the best quart of punch and drink it the quickest. My uncle was judged to have won the making, but Tom Smart beat him in the drinking by about half a salt-spoonful. They took another quart apiece to drink each other's health in, and were staunch friends ever afterwards. There's a destiny in these things, gentlemen; we can't help it.

"In personal appearance my uncle was a trifle stouter than the middle size; he was a thought stouter, too, than the ordinary run of people, and perhaps his face might be a shade redder. He had the jolliest face you ever saw, gentlemen—something like Punch, with a handsomer nose and chin; his eyes were always twinkling and sparkling with good-humour; and a smile—not one of your unmeaning wooden grins, but a real, merry, hearty, good-tempered smile—was perpetually on his countenance. He was pitched out of his gig once, and knocked, head first, against a milestone. There he lay, stunned, and so cut about the face with some gravel which had been heaped up alongside it, that, to use my uncle's own strong expression, if his mother could have revisited the earth, she wouldn't have known him. Indeed, when I come to think of the matter, gentlemen, I feel pretty sure she wouldn't; for she died when my uncle was two years and seven months old, and I think it's very likely that, even without the gravel, his top-boots would have puzzled the good lady not a little, to say nothing of his jolly red face. However, there he lay, and I have heard my uncle say, many a time, that the man said who picked him up that he was smiling as merrily as if he had tumbled out for a treat, and that after they had bled him, the first faint glimmerings of returning animation were his jumping up in bed, bursting out into a loud laugh, kissing the young woman who held the basin, and demanding a mutton chop and a pickled walnut instantly. He was very fond of pickled walnuts, gentlemen. He said he always found that, taken without vinegar, they relished the beer.

"My uncle's great journey was in the fall of the leaf, at which time he collected debts and took orders in the north, going from London to Edinburgh, from Edinburgh to Glasgow, from Glasgow back to Edinburgh, and thence to London by the smack. You are to understand that his second visit to Edinburgh was for his own pleasure. He used to go back for a week, just to look up his old friends; and what with breakfasting with this one, lunching with that, dining with a third, and supping with another, a pretty tight week he used to make of it. I don't know whether any of you, gentlemen, ever partook of a real substantial hospitable Scotch breakfast, and then went out to a slight lunch of a bushel of oysters, a dozen or so of bottled ale, and a noggin or two of whisky to close up with. If you ever did, you will agree with me that it requires a pretty strong head to go out to dinner and supper afterwards.

"But bless your hearts and eyebrows, all this sort of thing was nothing to my uncle! He was so well seasoned that it was mere child's play. I have heard him say that he could see the Dundee people out any day, and walk home afterwards without staggering; and yet the Dundee people have as strong heads and as strong punch, gentlemen, as you are likely to meet with between the poles. I have heard of a Glasgow man and a Dundee man drinking against each other for fifteen hours at a sitting. They were both suffocated, as nearly as could be ascertained, at the same moment, but with this trifling exception, gentlemen, they were not a bit the worse for it.

"One night, within four-and-twenty hours of the time when he had settled to take shipping for London, my uncle supped at the house of a very old friend of his, a Bailie Mac-something and four syllables after it, who lived in the old town of Edinburgh. There were the Bailie's wife, and the Bailie's three daughters, and the Bailie's grown-up son, and three or four stout, bushy-eyebrowed, canty old Scotch fellows, that the Bailie had got together to do honour to my uncle, and help to make merry. It was a glorious supper. There were kippered salmon, and Finnan Haddocks, and a lamb's head, and a haggis—a celebrated Scotch dish, gentlemen, which my uncle used to say always looked to him, when it came to table, very much like a Cupid's stomach—and a great many other things besides that I forget the names of, but very good things notwithstanding. The lassies were pretty and agreeable, the Bailie's wife one of the best creatures that ever lived, and my uncle in thoroughly good cue. The consequence of which was that the young ladies tittered and giggled, and the old lady laughed out loud, and the Bailie and the other old fellows roared till they were red in the face the whole mortal time. I don't quite recollect how many tumblers of whisky toddy each man drank after supper, but this I know, that about one o'clock in the morning the Bailie's grown-up son became insensible while attempting the first verse of 'Willie brewed a peck of maut'; and he having been, for half an hour before, the only other man visible above the mahogany, it occurred to my uncle that it was almost time to think about going, especially as drinking had set in at seven o'clock, in order that he might get home at a decent hour. But thinking it might not be quite polite to go just then, my uncle voted himself into the chair, mixed another glass, rose to propose his own health, addressed himself in a neat and complimentary speech, and drank the toast with great enthusiasm. Still nobody woke; so my uncle took a little drop more—neat this time, to prevent the toddy disagreeing with him—and laying violent hands on his hat, sallied forth into the street.

"It was a wild, gusty night when my uncle closed the Bailie's door, and settling his hat firmly on his head to prevent the wind from taking it, thrust his hands into his pockets, and looking upwards, took a short survey of the state of the weather. The clouds were drifting over the moon at their giddiest speed—at one time wholly obscuring her; at another suffering her to burst forth in full splendour and shed her light on all the objects around; anon driving over her again with increased velocity, and shrouding everything in darkness. 'Really, this won't do,' said my uncle, addressing himself to the weather, as if he felt himself personally offended. 'This is not at all the kind of thing for my voyage. It will not do at any price,' said my uncle, very impressively. Having repeated this several times, he recovered his balance with some difficulty—for he was rather giddy with looking up into the sky so long—and walked merrily on.

"The Bailie's house was in the Canongate, and my uncle was going to the other end of Leith Walk, rather better than a mile's journey. On either side of him there shot up against the dark sky tall, gaunt, straggling houses, with time-stained fronts, and windows that seemed to have shared the lot of eyes in mortals, and to have grown dim and sunken with age. Six, seven, eight stories high were the houses—story piled above story, as children build with cards—throwing their dark shadows over the roughly-paved road, and making the dark night darker. A few oil lamps were scattered at long distances, but they only served to mark the dirty entrance to some narrow close, or to show where a common stair communicated, by steep and intricate windings, with the various flats above. Glancing at all these things with the air of a man who had seen them too often before to think them worthy of much notice now, my uncle walked up the middle of the street, with a thumb in each waistcoat pocket, indulging from time to time in various snatches of song, chanted forth with such goodwill and spirit that the quiet, honest folk started from their first sleep, and lay trembling in bed till the sound died away in the distance; when, satisfying themselves that it was only some drunken ne'er-do-weel finding his way home, they covered themselves up warm and fell asleep again.

"I am particular in describing how my uncle walked up the middle of the street with his thumbs in his waistcoat pockets, gentlemen, because, as he often used to say (and with great reason too), there is nothing at all extraordinary in this story, unless you distinctly understand at the beginning that he was not by any means of a marvellous or romantic turn.

"Gentlemen, my uncle walked on with his thumbs in his waistcoat pockets, taking the middle of the street to himself, and singing, now a verse of a love song, and then a verse of a drinking one; and when he was tired of both, whistling melodiously until he reached the North Bridge, which at this point connects the old and new towns of Edinburgh. Here he stopped for a minute to look at the strange, irregular clusters of lights, piled one above the other, and twinkling afar off so high in the air that they looked like stars, gleaming from the castle walls on the one side, and the Calton Hill on the other, as if they illuminated veritable castles in the air; while the old, picturesque town slept heavily on, in gloom and darkness below, its palace and chapel of Holyrood, guarded day and night, as a friend of my uncle's used to say, by old Arthur's Seat, towering, surly and dark, like some gruff genius, over the ancient city he has watched so long. I say, gentlemen, my uncle stopped here for a minute to look about him, and then, paying a compliment to the weather, which had a little cleared up, though the moon was sinking, walked on again as royally as before, keeping the middle of the road with great dignity, and looking as if he should very much like to meet with somebody who would dispute possession of it with him. There was nobody at all disposed to contest the point, as it happened, and so on he went, with his thumbs in his waistcoat pockets, like a lamb.

"When my uncle reached the end of Leith Walk, he had to cross a pretty large piece of waste ground, which separated him from a short street which he had to turn down to go direct to his lodging. Now, in this piece of waste ground there was at that time an enclosure belonging to some wheel-wright, who contracted with the Post-office for the purchase of old, worn-out mail-coaches; and my uncle, being very fond of coaches, old, young, or middle-aged, all at once took it into his head to step out of his road for no other purpose than to peep between the palings at these mails—about a dozen of which he remembered to have been seen crowded together in a very forlorn and dismantled state inside. My uncle was a very enthusiastic, emphatic sort of person, gentlemen; so, finding that he could not obtain a good peep between the palings, he got over them, and sitting himself quietly down on an old axle-tree, began to contemplate the mail-coaches with a deal of gravity.

"There might be a dozen of them, or there might be more—my uncle was never quite certain on this point, and being a man of very scrupulous veracity about numbers, didn't like to say—but there they stood, all huddled together in the most desolate condition imaginable. The doors had been torn from their hinges, and removed; the linings had been stripped off, only a shred hanging here and there by a rusty nail; the lamps were gone, the poles had long since vanished, the ironwork was rusty, the paint worn away; the wind whistled through the chinks in the bare woodwork and the rain, which had collected on the roofs, fell, drop by drop, into the insides with a hollow and melancholy sound. They were the decaying skeletons of departed mails, and in that lonely place, at that time of night, they looked chill and dismal.

"My uncle rested his head upon his hands, and thought of the busy, bustling people who had rattled about years before in the old coaches, and were now as silent and changed; he thought of the numbers of people to whom one of those crazy, mouldering vehicles had borne, night after night, for many years and through all weathers, the anxiously-expected intelligence, the eagerly looked-for remittance, the promised assurance of health and safety, the sudden announcement of sickness and death. The merchant, the lover, the wife, the widow, the mother, the school-boy, the very child who tottered to the door at the postman's knock—how had they all looked forward to the arrival of the old coach. And where were they all now?

"Gentlemen, my uncle used to *say* that he thought all this at the time, but I rather suspect he learned it out of some book afterwards; for he distinctly stated that he fell into a kind of doze as he sat on the old axle-tree, looking at the decayed mail-coaches, and that he was suddenly awakened by some deep church bell striking two. Now, my uncle was never a fast thinker; and if he had thought all these things, I am quite certain it would have taken him till full half-past two o'clock, at the very least. I am, therefore, decidedly of opinion, gentlemen, that my uncle fell into the kind of doze without having thought about anything at all.

"Be this as it may, a church bell struck two. My uncle woke, rubbed his eyes, and jumped up in astonishment.

"In one instant after the clock struck two the whole of this deserted and quiet spot had become a scene of most extraordinary life and animation. The mail-coach doors were on their hinges, the lining was replaced, the ironwork was as good as new, the paint was restored, the lamps were alight, cushions and greatcoats were on every coach-box, porters were thrusting parcels into every boot, guards were stowing away letter-bags, hostlers were dashing pails of water against the renovated wheels, numbers of men were rushing about, fixing poles into every coach; passengers arrived, portmanteaus were handed up, horses were put to; and, in short, it was perfectly clear that every mail there was to be off directly. Gentlemen, my uncle opened his eyes so wide at all this that to the very last moment of his life he used to wonder how it fell out that he had ever been able to shut 'em again.

" 'Now, then!' said a voice, as my uncle felt a hand on his shoulder, 'you're booked for one inside. You'd better get in.'

" '*I* booked!' said my uncle, turning round.

" 'Yes, certainly.'

"My uncle, gentlemen, could say nothing, he was so very much astonished. The queerest thing of all was, that although there was such a crowd of persons, and although fresh faces were pouring in every moment, there was no telling where they came from. They seemed to start up, in some strange manner, from the ground or the air, and disappear in the same way. When a porter had put his luggage in the coach and received his fare, he turned round and was gone; and before my uncle had well begun to wonder what had become of him, half a dozen fresh ones started up, and staggered along under the weight of parcels which seemed big enough to crush them. The Passengers were all dressed so oddly too: large, broad-skirted laced coats, with great cuffs and no collars; and wigs, gentlemen—great formal wigs, with a tie behind. My uncle could make nothing of it.

" 'Now, *are* you going to get in?' said the person who had addressed my uncle before. He was dressed as a mail guard, with a wig on his head and most enormous cuffs to his coat, and had a lantern in one hand and a huge blunderbuss in the other, which he was going to stow away in his little arm-chest. '*Are* you going to get in, Jack Martin?' said the guard, holding the lantern to my uncle's face.

" 'Hallo!' said my uncle, falling back a step or two. 'That's familiar!'

" 'It's so on the way-bill,' replied the guard.

" 'Isn't there a "Mister" before it?' said my uncle. For he felt, gentlemen, that for a guard he didn't know to call him Jack Martin was a liberty which the Post-office wouldn't have sanctioned if they had known it.

" 'No, there is not,' rejoined the guard, coolly.

" 'Is the fair paid?' inquired my uncle.

" 'Of course it is,' rejoined my uncle.

" 'It is, is it?' said my uncle. 'Then here goes! Which coach?'

" 'This,' said the guard, pointing to an old-fashioned Edinburgh and London Mail, which had the steps down and the door open. 'Stop! Here are the other passengers; let them get in first.'

"As the guard spoke, there all at once appeared, right in front of my uncle, a young gentleman in a powdered wig, and a sky-blue coat trimmed with silver, made very full and broad in the skirts, which were lined with buckram. Tiggin and Welps were in the printed calico and waistcoat-piece line, gentlemen, so my uncle knew all the materials at once. He wore knee breeches, and a kind of leggings rolled up over his silk stockings, and shoes with buckles; he had ruffles at his wrists, a three-cornered hat on his head, and a long taper sword by his side. The flaps of his waistcoat came half-way down his thighs, and the ends of his cravat reached to his waist. He stalked gravely to the coach door, pulled off his hat and held it above his head at arm's length, cocking his little finger in the air at the same time, as some affected people do when they take a cup of tea. Then he drew his feet together, and made a low, grave bow, and then put out his left hand. My uncle was just going to step forward and shake it heartily, when he perceived that these attentions were directed, not towards him, but to a young lady who just then appeared at the foot of the steps, attired in an old-fashioned green velvet dress with a long waist and stomacher. She had no bonnet on her head, gentlemen, which was muffled in a black silk hood; but she looked round for an instant as she prepared to get into the coach, and such a beautiful face as she discovered my uncle had never seen—not even in a picture. She got into the coach, holding up her dress with one hand; and, as my uncle always said with a round oath when he told the story, he wouldn't have believed it possible that legs and feet could have been brought to such a state of perfection unless he had seen them with his own eyes.

"But in this one glimpse of the beautiful face my uncle saw that the young lady had cast an imploring look upon him and that she appeared terrified and distressed. He noticed, too, that the young fellow in the powdered wig, notwithstanding his show of gallantry, which was all very fine and grand, clasped her tight by the wrist when she got in, and followed himself immediately afterwards. An uncommonly ill-looking fellow, in a close brown wig and a plum-coloured suit, wearing a very large sword, and boots up to his hips, belonged to the party; and when he sat himself down next to the young lady who shrunk into a corner at his approach, my uncle was confirmed in his original impression that something dark and mysterious was going forward, or, as he always said to himself, that 'there was a screw loose somewhere.' It's quite surprising how quickly he made up his mind to help the lady at any peril, if she needed help.

" 'Death and lightning!' exclaimed the young gentleman, laying his hand upon his sword as my uncle entered the coach.

" 'Blood and thunder!' roared the other gentleman. With this he whipped his sword out, and made a lunge at my uncle without further ceremony. My uncle had no weapon about him, but with great dexterity he snatched the ill-looking gentleman's three-cornered hat from his head, and receiving the point of his sword right through the crown, squeezed the sides together, and held it tight.

" 'Pink him behind!' cried the ill-looking gentleman to his companion, as he struggled to regain his sword.

" 'He had better not,' cried my uncle, displaying the heel of one of his shoes in a threatening manner. 'I'll kick his brains out, if he has any, or fracture his skull if he hasn't.' Exerting all his strength at this moment, my uncle wrenched the ill-looking man's sword from his grasp, and flung it clean out of the coach window, upon which the younger gentleman vociferated 'Death and lightning!' again, and laid his hand upon the hilt of his sword in a very fierce manner, but didn't draw it. Perhaps, gentlemen, as my uncle used to say with a smile—perhaps he was afraid of alarming the lady.

" 'Now, gentlemen,' said my uncle, taking his seat deliberately, 'I don't want to have any death, with or without lightning, in a lady's presence, and we have had quite blood and thundering enough for one journey; so, if you please, we'll sit in our places like quiet insides. —Here, guard, pick up that gentleman's carving-knife.'

"As quickly as my uncle said the words, the guard appeared at the coach window with the gentleman's sword in his hand. He held up his lantern, and looked earnestly in my uncle's face as he handed it in; when by its light my uncle saw, to his great surprise, that an immense crowd of mail-coach guards swarmed round the window, every one of whom had his eyes earnestly fixed upon him too. He had never seen such a sea of white faces, and red bodies, and earnest eyes, in all his born days.

" 'This is the strangest sort of thing I ever had anything to do with,' thought my uncle. 'Allow me to return you your hat, sir.'

"The ill-looking gentleman received his three-cornered hat in silence, looked at the hole in the middle with an inquiring air, and finally stuck it on the top of his wig with a solemnity the effect of which was a trifle impaired by his sneezing violently at the moment and jerking it off again.

" 'All right!' cried the guard with the lantern, mounting into his little seat behind. Away they went. My uncle peeped out of the coach window as they emerged from the yard, and observed that the other mails, with coachmen, guards, horses, and passengers complete, were driving round and round in circles, at a slow trot of about five miles an hour. My uncle burnt with indignation, gentlemen. As a commercial man, he felt that the mail bags were not to be trifled with, and he resolved to memorialize the Post-office on the subject the very instant he reached London.

"At present, however, his thoughts were occupied with the young lady who sat in the farthest corner of the coach, with her face muffled closely in her hood—the gentleman with the sky-blue coat sitting opposite to her, and the other man in the plum-coloured suit by her side, and both watching her intently. If she so much as rustled the folds of her hood, he could hear the ill-looking man clap his hand upon his sword, and could tell by the other's breathing (it was so dark he couldn't see his face) that he was looking as big as if he were going to devour her at a mouthful. This roused my uncle more and more, and he resolved, come what might, to see the end of it. He had a great admiration for bright eyes, and sweet faces, and pretty legs and feet; in short, he was fond of the whole sex. It runs in our family, gentlemen. So am I.

"Many were the devices which my uncle practised to attract the lady's attention, or at all events to engage the mysterious gentlemen in conversation. They were all in vain; the gentlemen wouldn't talk, and the lady didn't dare. He thrust his head out of the coach window at intervals, and bawled out to know why they didn't go faster? But he called till he was hoarse; nobody paid the least attention to him. He leaned back in the coach, and thought of the beautiful face and the feet and legs. This answered better; it whiled away the time, and kept him from wondering where he was going, and how it was that he found himself in such an odd situation. Not that this would have worried him much, anyway; he was a mighty free-and-easy, roving, devil-may-care sort of person, was my uncle, gentlemen.

"All of a sudden the coach stopped. 'Hallo!' said my uncle, 'what's in the wind now?'

" 'Alight here,' said the guard, letting down the steps.

" 'Here!' cried my uncle.

" 'Here,' rejoined the guard.

" 'I'll do nothing of the sort,' said my uncle.

" 'Very well, then, stop where you are,' said the guard.

" 'I will,' said my uncle.

" 'Do,' said the guard.

"The other passengers had regarded this colloquy with great attention, and finding that my uncle was determined not to alight, the younger man squeezed past him, to hand the lady out. At this moment the ill-looking man was inspecting the hole in the crown of his three-cornered hat. As the young lady brushed past, she dropped one of her gloves into my uncle's hand, and softly whispered, with her lips so close to his face that he felt her warm breath on his nose, the single word, 'Help!' Gentlemen, my uncle leaped out of the coach at once, with such violence that it rocked on the springs again.

" 'Oh! you've thought better of it, have you?' said the guard when he saw my uncle standing on the ground.

"My uncle looked at the guard for a few seconds, in some doubt whether it wouldn't be better to wrench his blunderbuss from him, fire it in the face of the man with the big sword, knock the rest of the company over the head with the stock, snatch up the young lady, and go off in the smoke. On second thoughts, however, he abandoned this plan, as being a shade too melodramatic in the execution, and followed the two mysterious men, who, keeping the lady between them, were now entering an old house in front of which the coach had stopped. They turned into the passage, and my uncle followed.

"Of all the ruinous and desolate places my uncle had ever beheld, this was the most so. It looked as if it had once been a large house of entertainment; but the roof had fallen in in many places, and the stairs were steep, rugged, and broken. There was a huge fireplace in the room into which they walked, and the chimney was blackened with smoke; but no warm blaze lighted it up now. The white feathery dust of burn wood was still strewed over the hearth, but the stove was cold and all was dark and gloomy.

" 'Well,' said my uncle, as he looked about him, 'a mail travelling at the rate of six miles and a half an hour, and stopping for an indefinite time at such a hole as this, is rather an irregular sort of proceeding, I fancy. This shall be made known. I'll write to the papers.'

"My uncle said this in a pretty loud voice, and in an open unreserved sort of manner, with the view of engaging the two strangers in conversation if he could. But neither of them took any more notice of him than whispering to each other, and scowling at him as they did so. The lady was at the farther end of the room, and once she ventured to wave her hand, as if beseeching my uncle's assistance.

"At length the two strangers advanced a little, and the conversation began in earnest.

" 'You don't know this is a private room, I suppose, fellow?" said the gentleman in sky-blue.

" 'No, I do not, fellow,' rejoined my uncle. 'Only, if this is a private room specially ordered for the occasion, I should think the public room must be a *very* comfortable one.' With this my uncle sat himself down in a high-backed chair, and took such an accurate measure of the gentlemen with his eyes, that Tiggin and Welps could have supplied him with printed calico for a suit, and not an inch too much or too little, from that estimate alone.

" 'Quit this room,' said both the men together, grasping their swords.

" 'Eh?' said my uncle, not at all appearing to comprehend their meaning.

" 'Quit the room, or you are a dead man,' said the ill-looking fellow with the large sword, drawing it at the same time and flourishing it in the air.

" 'Down with him!' cried the gentleman in sky-blue, drawing his sword also, and falling back two or three yards—'down with him!' The lady gave a loud scream.

"Now my uncle was always remarkable for great boldness and great presence of mind. All the time that he had appeared so indifferent to what was going on, he had been looking slyly about for some missile or weapon of defence, and at the very instant when the swords were drawn, he espied, standing in the chimney corner, an old basket-hilted rapier in a rusty scabbard. At one bound my uncle caught it in his hand, drew it, flourished it gallantly above his head, called aloud to the lady to keep out of the way, hurled the chair at the man in sky-blue, and the scabbard at the man in plum-colour, and taking advantage of the confusion, fell upon them both, pell-mell.

"Gentleman, there is an old story—none the worse for being true—regarding a fine young Irish gentleman, who being asked if he could play the fiddle, replied he had no doubt he could, but he couldn't exactly say for certain, because he had never tried. This is not inapplicable to my uncle and his fencing. He had never had a sword in his hand before except once, when he played Richard the Third at a private theatre; upon which occasion it was arranged with Richmond that he was to be run through from behind, without showing fight at all. But here he was, cutting and slashing with two experienced swordsmen—thrusting and guarding and poking and slicing, and acquitting himself in the most manful and dexterous manner possible, although up to that time he had never been aware that he had the least notion of the science. It only shows how true the old saying is, that a man never knows what he can do till he tries, gentlemen.

"The noise of the combat was terrific—each of the three combatants swearing like troopers, and their swords clashing with as much noise as if all the knives and steels in Newport market were rattling together at the same time. When it was at its very height, the lady (to encourage my uncle, most probably) withdrew her hood entirely from her face, and disclosed a countenance of such dazzling beauty that he would have fought against fifty men, to win one smile from it, and die. He had done wonders before, but now he began to powder away like a raving mad giant.

"At this very moment the gentleman in sky-blue, turning round and seeing the young lady with her face uncovered, vented an exclamation of rage and jealousy, and turning his weapon against her beautiful bosom, pointed a thrust at her heart, which caused my uncle to utter a cry of apprehension that made the building ring. The lady stepped lightly aside and snatching the young man's sword from his hand before he had recovered his balance, drove him to the wall, and running it through him and the panelling, up to the very hilt pinned him there, hard and fast. It was a splendid example. My uncle, with a loud shout of triumph and a strength that was irresistible, made his adversary retreat in the same direction, and plunging the old rapier into the very centre of a large red flower in the pattern of his waistcoat, nailed him beside his friend. There they both stood, gentlemen, jerking their arms and legs about in agony, like the toy-shop figures that are moved by a piece of pack-thread. My uncle always said afterwards that this was one of the surest means he knew of for disposing of an enemy; but it was liable to one objection on the ground of expense, inasmuch as it involved the less of a sword for every man disabled.

" 'The mail, the mail!' cried the lady, running up to my uncle and throwing her beautiful arms round his neck; 'we may yet escape.'

" '*May*!' cried my uncle; 'why, my dear, there's nobody else to kill, is there?' My uncle was rather disappointed, gentlemen; for he thought a little quiet bit of love-making would be agreeable after the slaughtering, if it were only to change the subject.

" 'We have not an instant to lose here,' said the young lady. 'He' (pointing to the young gentleman in sky-blue) 'is the only son of the powerful Marquess of Filletoville.'

" 'Well, then my dear, I'm afraid he'll never come to the title,' said my uncle, looking coolly at the young gentleman as he stood fixed up against the wall, in the cockchafer fashion I have described. 'You have cut off the entail, my love.'

" 'I have been torn from my home and friends by these villains,' her features glowing with indignation. 'That wretch would have married me by violence in another hour.'

" 'Confound his impudence!' said my uncle, bestowing a very contemptuous look on the dying heir of Filletoville.

" 'As you may guess from what you have seen,' said the young lady, 'the party were prepared to murder me if I appealed to anyone for assistance. If their accomplices find us here, we are lost. Two minutes hence may be too late. The mail!' With these words, overpowered by her feelings, and the exertion of sticking the young Marquess of Filletoville, she sunk into my uncle's arms. My uncle caught her up, and bore her to the house-door. There stood the mail, with four long-tailed, flowing-maned, black horses, ready harnessed; but no coachman, no guard, no hostler even, at the horses' heads.

"Gentlemen, I hope I do no injustice to my uncle's memory when I express my opinion, that although he was a bachelor, he *had* held some ladies in his arms before this time; I believe, indeed, that he had rather a habit of kissing barmaids; and I know that in one or two instances he had been seen by credible witnesses to hug a landlady in a very perceptible manner. I mention the circumstance to show what a very uncommon sort of person this beautiful young lady must have been to have affected my uncle in the way she did; he used to say that as her long, dark hair trailed over his arm, and her beautiful dark eyes fixed themselves upon his face when she recovered, he felt so strange and nervous that his legs trembled beneath him. But who can look in a sweet, soft pair of dark eyes without feeling queer? *I* can't, gentlemen. I am afraid to look at some eyes I know, and that's the truth of it.

" 'You will never leave me,' murmured the young lady.

" 'Never,' said my uncle. And he meant it too.

" 'My dear preserver!' exclaimed the young lady—'my dear, kind, brave preserver!'

" 'Don't,' said my uncle, interrupting her.

" 'Why?' inquired the young lady.

" 'Because your mouth looks so beautiful when you speak,' rejoined my uncle, 'that I am afraid I shall be rude enough to kiss it.'

"The young lady put up her hand as if to caution my uncle not to do so, and said—no, she didn't say anything—she smiled. When you are looking at a pair of the most delicious lips in the world, and see them gently break into a roguish smile—if you are very near them, and nobody else by—you cannot better testify your admiration of their beautiful form and colour than by kissing them at once. My uncle did so, and I honour him for it.

" 'Hark!' cried the young lady, starting: 'the noise of wheels and horses!'

" 'So it is,' said my uncle, listening. He had a good ear for wheels and tramping of hoofs; but there appeared to be so many horses and carriages rattling towards them from a distance, that it was impossible to form a guess at their number. The sound was like that of fifty brakes, with six blood cattle in each.

" 'We are pursued!' cried the young lady, crisping her hands. 'We are pursued. I have no hope but in you!'

"There was such an expression of terror in her beautiful face that my uncle made up his mind at once. He lifted her into the coach, told her not to be frightened, pressed his lips to hers once more, and then advising her to draw up the window to keep the cold air out, mounted the box.

" 'Stay, love,' cried the young lady.

" 'What's the matter?' said my uncle, from the coach-box.

" 'I want to speak to you,' said the young lady, 'only a word—only one word, dearest.'

" 'Must I get down?' inquired my uncle. The lady made no answer, but she smiled again. Such a smile, gentlemen! it beat the other one all to nothing. My uncle descended from his perch in a twinkling.

" 'What is it, my dear?' said my uncle, looking in at the coach window. The lady happened to bend forward at the same time, and my uncle thought she looked more beautiful than she had done yet. He was very close to her just then, gentlemen, so he really ought to know.

" 'What is it, my dear?' said my uncle.

" 'Will you never love any one but me—never marry any one beside?' said the young lady.

"My uncle swore a great oath that he never would marry anybody else, and the young lady drew in her head and pulled up the window. He jumped upon the box, squared his elbows, adjusted the ribbons, seized the whip which lay on the roof, gave one flick to the off leader, and away went the four long-tailed, flowing-maned black horses, at fifteen good English miles an hour, with the old mail-coach behind them. Whew! how they tore along!

"The noise behind grew louder. The faster the old mail went, the faster came the pursuers—men, horses, dogs were leagued in the pursuit. The noise was frightful, but above all rose the voice of the young lady, urging my uncle on, and shrieking: 'Faster! faster!'

"They whirled past the dark trees as feathers would be swept before a hurricane. Houses, gates, churches, haystacks, objects of every kind they shot by, with a velocity and noise like roaring waters suddenly let loose. Still the noise of pursuit grew louder, and still my uncle could hear the young lady wildly screaming: 'Faster! faster!'

"My uncle plied whip and rein, and the horses flew onward till they were white with foam; and yet the noise behind increased, and yet the young lady cried: 'Faster! faster!' My uncle gave a loud stamp on the foot in the energy of the moment, and—found that it was grey morning, and he was sitting in the wheelwright's yard, on the box of an old Edinburgh mail, shivering with the cold and wet, and stamping his feet to warm them! He got down, and looked eagerly inside for the beautiful young lady. Alas! there was neither door nor seat to the coach; it was a mere shell.

"Of course my uncle knew very well that there was some mystery in the matter, and that everything had passed exactly as he used to relate it. He remained staunch to the great oath he had sworn to the beautiful young lady—refusing several eligible landladies on her account, and dying a bachelor at last. He always said what a curious thing it was that he should have found out, by such a mere accident as his clambering over the palings, that the ghosts of mail-coaches and horses, guards, coachmen, and passengers were in the habit of making journeys every night. He used to add that he believed he was the only living person who had ever been taken as a passenger on one of these excursions. And I think he was right, gentlemen—at least I never heard of any other."

ARTHUR CONAN DOYLE
The Bully of Brocas Court

The overwhelming popularity of Sherlock Holmes has always overshadowed Arthur Conan Doyle's *other stories, especially those dealing with the occult and the supernatural, for which the author held a strong passion in real life, and he eventually devoted himself full-time to the study of spiritualism.*

One of his more conventional, and less familiar, ghost stories (with a strong sporting connection) is 'The Bully of Brocas Court', which first appeared in the Strand *magazine, November 1921.*

That year—it was in 1878—the South Midland Yeomanry were out near Luton, and the real question which appealed to every man in the great camp was not how to prepare for a possible European war, but the far more vital one how to get a man who could stand up for ten rounds to Farrier-Sergeant Burton. Slogger Burton was a fine upstanding fourteen stone of bone and brawn, with a smack in either hand which would leave any ordinary mortal senseless. A match must be found for him somewhere or his head would outgrow his dragoon helmet. Therefore Sir Fred Milburn, better known as Mumbles, was dispatched to London to find if among the fancy there was no one who would make a journey in order to take down the number of the bold dragoon.

They were bad days, those, in the prize-ring. The old knuckle-fighting had died out in scandal and disgrace, smothered by the pestilent crowd of betting men and ruffians of all sorts who hung upon the edge of the movement and brought disgrace and ruin upon the decent fighting men, who were often humble heroes whose gallantry has never been surpassed. An honest sportsman who desired to see a fight was usually set upon by villains, against whom he had no redress, since he was himself engaged on what was technically an illegal action. He was stripped in the open street, his purse taken, and his head split open if he ventured to resist. The ring-side could only be reached by men who were prepared to fight their way there with cudgels and hunting-crops. No wonder that the classic sport was attended now by those only who had nothing to lose.

On the other hand, the era of the reserved building and the legal glove-fight had not yet arisen, and the cult was in a strange intermediate condition. It was impossible to regulate it, and equally impossible to abolish it, since nothing appeals more directly and powerfully to the average Briton. Therefore there were scrambling contests in stableyards and barns, hurried visits to France, secret meetings at dawn in wild parts of the country, and all manner of evasions and experiments. The men themselves became as unsatisfactory as their surroundings. There could be no honest open contest, and the loudest bragger talked his way to the top of the list. Only across the Atlantic had the huge figure of John Lawrence Sullivan appeared, who was destined to be the last of the earlier system and the first of the later one.

Things being in this condition, the sporting Yeomanry Captain found it no easy matter among the boxing saloons and sporting pubs of London to find a man who could be relied upon to give a good account of the huge Farrier-Sergeant. Heavy-weights were at a premium. Finally his choice fell upon Alf Stevens of Kentish Town, an excellent rising middle-weight who had never yet known defeat and had indeed some claims to the championship. His professional experience and craft would surely make up for the three stone of weight which separated him from the formidable dragoon. It was in this hope that Sir Fred Milburn engaged him, and proceeded to convey him in his dog-cart behind a pair of spanking greys to the camp of the Yeomen. They were to start one evening, drive up the Great North Road, sleep at St. Albans, and finish their journey next day.

The prize-fighter met the sporting Baronet at the Golden Cross, where Bates, the little groom, was standing at the head of the spirited horses. Stevens, a pale-faced, clean-cut young fellow, mounted beside his employer and waved his hand to a little knot of fighting men, rough, collarless, reefer-coated fellows who had gathered to bid their comrade good-bye. "Good luck, Alf!" came in a hoarse chorus as the boy released the horses' heads and sprang in behind, while the high dog-cart swung swiftly round the curve into Trafalgar Square.

Sir Frederick was so busy steering among the traffic in Oxford Street and the Edgware Road that he had little thought for anything else, but when he got into the edges of the country near Hendon, and the hedges had at last taken the place of that endless panorama of brick dwellings, he let his horses go easy with a loose rein while he turned his attention to the young man at his side. He had found him by correspondence and recommendation, so that he had some curiosity now in looking him over. Twilight was already falling and the light dim, but what the Baronet saw pleased him well. The man was a fighter every inch, clean-cut, deep-chested, with the long straight cheek and deep-set eye which goes with an obstinate courage. Above all, he was a man who had never yet met his master and was still upheld by the deep sustaining confidence which is never quite the same after a single defeat. The Baronet chuckled as he realized what a surprise packet was being carried north for the Farrier-Sergeant.

"I suppose you are in some sort of training, Stevens?" he remarked, turning to his companion.

"Yes, sir; I am fit to fight for my life."

"So I should judge by the look of you."

"I live regular all the time, sir, but I was matched against Mike Connor for this last week-end and scaled down to eleven four. Then he paid forfeit, and here I am at the top of my form."

"That's lucky. You'll need it all against a man who has a pull of three stone and four inches."

The young man smiled.

"I have given greater odds than that, sir."

"I dare say. But he's a game man as well."

"Well, sir, one can but do one's best."

The Baronet liked the modest but assured tone of the young pugilist. Suddenly an amusing thought struck him, and he burst out laughing.

"By Jove!" he cried. "What a lark if the Bully is out to-night!"

Alf Stevens pricked up his ears.

"Who might he be, sir?"

"Well, that's what the folk are asking. Some say they've seen him, and some say he's a fairy-tale, but there's good evidence that he is a real man with a pair of rare good fists that leave their marks behind him."

"And where might he live?"

"On this very road. It's between Finchley and Elstree, as I've heard. There are two chaps, and they come out on nights when the moon is at full and challenge the passers-by to fight in the old style. One fights and the other picks up. By George! the fellow *can* fight, too, by all accounts. Chaps have been found in the morning with their faces all cut to ribbons to show that the Bully had been at work upon them."

Alf Stevens was full of interest.

"I've always wanted to try an old-style battle, sir, but it never chanced to come my way. I believe it would suit me better than the gloves."

"Then you won't refuse the Bully?"

"Refuse him! I'd go ten miles to meet him."

"By George! it would be great!" cried the Baronet. "Well, the moon is at the full, and the place should be about here."

"If he's as good as you say," Stevens remarked, "he should be known in the ring, unless he is just an amateur who amuses himself like that."

"Some think he's an ostler, or maybe a racing man from the training stables over yonder. Where there are horses there is boxing. If you can believe the accounts, there is something a bit queer and outlandish about the fellow. Hi! Look out, damn you, look out!"

The Baronet's voice had risen to a sudden screech of surprise and of anger. At this point the road dips down into a hollow, heavily shaded by trees, so that at night it arches across like the mouth of a tunnel. At the foot of the slope there stand two great stone pillars, which, as viewed by daylight, are lichen-stained and weathered, with heraldic devices on each which are so mutilated by time that they are mere protuberances of stone. An iron gate of elegant design, hanging loosely upon rusted hinges, proclaims both the past glories and the present decay of Brocas Old Hall, which lies at the end of the weed-encumbered avenue. It was from the shadow of this ancient gateway that an active figure had sprung suddenly into the centre of the road and had, with great dexterity, held up the horses, who ramped and pawed as they forced back upon their haunches.

"Here, Rowe, you 'old the tits, will ye?" cried a high strident voice. "I've a little word to say to this 'ere slap-up Corinthian before 'e goes any farther."

A second man had emerged from the shadows and without a word took hold of the horses' heads. He was a short, thick fellow, dressed in a curious brown many-caped overcoat, which came to his knees, with gaiters and boots beneath it. He wore no hat, and those in the dog-cart had a view, as he came in front of the side-lamps, of a surly red face with an ill-fitting lower lip clean shaven, and a high black cravat swathed tightly under the chin. As he gripped the leathers his more active comrade sprang forward and rested a bony hand upon the side of the splashboard while he looked keenly up with a pair of fierce blue eyes at the faces of the two travellers, the light beating full upon his own features. He wore a hat low upon his brow, but in spite of its shadow both the Baronet and the pugilist could see enough to shrink from him, for it was an evil face, evil but very formidable, stern, craggy, high-nosed, and fierce, with an inexorable mouth which bespoke a nature which would neither ask for mercy nor grant it. As to his age, one could only say for certain that a man with such a face was young enough to have all his virility and old enough to have experienced all the wickedness of life. The cold, savage eyes took a deliberate survey, first of the Baronet and then of the young man beside him.

"Aye, Rowe, it's a slap-up Corinthian, same as I said," he remarked over his shoulder to his companion. "But this other is a likely chap. If 'e isn't a millin' cove 'e ought to be. Any'ow, we'll try 'im out."

"Look here," said the Baronet, "I don't know who you are, except that you are a damned impertinent fellow. I'd put the lash of my whip across your face for two pins!"

"Stow that gammon, gov'nor! It ain't safe to speak to me like that."

"I've heard of you and your ways!" cried the angry soldier. "I'll teach you to stop my horses on the Queen's high road! You've got the wrong men this time, my fine fellow, as you will soon learn."

"That's as it may be," said the stranger. "May'ap, master, we may all learn something before we part. One or other of you 'as got to get down and put up your 'ands before you get any farther."

Stevens had instantly sprung down into the road.

"If you want a fight you've come to the right shop," said he; "it's my trade, so don't say I took you unawares."

The stranger gave a cry of satisfaction.

"Blow my dickey!" he shouted. "It *is* a millin' cove, Joe, same as I said. No more chaw-bacons for us, but the real thing. Well, young man, you've met your master to-night. Happen you never 'eard what Lord Longmore said o' me? 'A man must be made special to beat you,' says 'e. That's wot Lord Longmore said."

"That was before the Bull came along," growled the man in front, speaking for the first time.

"Stow your chaffing, Joe! A little more about the Bull and you and me will quarrel. 'E bested me once, but it's all betters and no takers that I glut 'im if ever we meet again. Well, young man, what d'ye think of me?"

"I think you've got your share of cheek."

"Cheek. Wot's that?"

"Impudence, bluff—gas, if you like."

The last word had a surprising effect upon the stranger. He smote his leg with his hand and broke out into a high neighing laugh, in which he was joined by his gruff companion.

"You've said the right word, my beauty," cried the latter, " 'Gas' is the word and no error. Well, there's a good moon, but the clouds are comin' up. We had best use the light while we can."

Whilst this conversation had been going on the Baronet had been looking with an ever-growing amazement at the attire of the stranger. A good deal of it confirmed his belief that he was connected with some stables, though making every allowance for this his appearance was very eccentric and old-fashioned. Upon his head he wore a yellowish-white top-hat of long-haired beaver, such as is still affected by some drivers of four-in-hands, with a bell crown and a curling brim. His dress consisted of a short-waisted swallow-tail coat, snuff-coloured, with steel buttons. It opened in front to show a vest of striped silk, while his legs were encased in buff knee-breeches with blue stockings and low shoes. The figure was angular and hard, with a great suggestion of wiry activity. This Bully of Brocas was clearly a very great character, and the young dragoon officer chuckled as he thought what a glorious story he would carry back to the mess of this queer old-world figure and the thrashing which he was about to receive from the famous London boxer.

Billy, the little groom, had taken charge of the horses, who were shivering and sweating.

"This way!" said the stout man, turning towards the gate. It was a sinister place, black and weird, with the crumbling pillars and the heavy arching trees. Neither the Baronet nor the pugilist liked the look of it.

"Where are you going, then?"

"This is no place for a fight," said the stout man. "We've got as pretty a place as ever you saw inside the gate here. You couldn't beat it on Molesey Hurst."

"The road is good enough for me," said Stevens.

"The road is good enough for two Johnny Raws," said the man with the beaver hat. "It ain't good enough for two slap-up millin' coves like you an' me. You ain't afeard, are you?"

"Not of you or ten like you," said Stevens, stoutly.

"Well, then, come with me and do it as it ought to be done."

Sir Frederick and Stevens exchanged glances.

"I'm game," said the pugilist.

"Come on, then."

The little party of four passed through the gateway. Behind them in the darkness the horses stamped and reared, while the voice of the boy could be heard as he vainly tried to soothe them. After walking fifty yards up the grass-grown drive the guide turned to the right through a thick belt of trees, and they came out upon a circular plot of grass, white and clear in the moonlight. It had a raised bank, and on the farther side was one of those little pillared stone summer-houses beloved by the early Georgians.

"What did I tell you?" cried the stout man, triumphantly. "Could you do better than this within twenty mile of town? It was made for it. Now, Tom, get to work upon him, and show us what you can do."

It had all become like an extraordinary dream. The strange men, their odd dress, their queer speech, the moonlit circle of grass, and the pillared summer-house all wove themselves into one fantastic whole. It was only the sight of Alf Stevens's ill-fitting tweed suit, and his homely English face surmounting it, which brought the Baronet back to the workaday world. The thin stranger had taken off his beaver hat, his swallow-tailed coat, his silk waistcoat, and finally his shirt had been drawn over his head by his second. Stevens in a cool and leisurely fashion kept pace with the preparations of his antagonist. Then the two fighting men turned upon each other.

But as they did so Stevens gave an exclamation of surprise and horror. The removal of the beaver hat had disclosed a horrible mutilation of the head of his antagonist. The whole upper forehead had fallen in, and there seemed to be a broad red weal between his close-cropped hair and his heavy brows.

"Good Lord," cried the young pugilist. "What's amiss with the man?"

The question seemed to rouse a cold fury in his antagonist.

"You look out for your own head, master," said he. "You'll find enough to do, I'm thinkin', without talkin' about mine."

This retort drew a shout of hoarse laughter from his second. "Well said, my Tommy!" he cried. "It's Lombard Street to a China orange on the one and only."

The man whom he called Tom was standing with his hands up in the centre of the natural ring. He looked a big man in his clothes, but he seemed bigger in the buff, and his barrel chest, sloping shoulders, and loosely-slung muscular arms were all ideal for the game. His grim eyes gleamed fiercely beneath his misshapen brows, and his lips were set in a fixed hard smile, more menacing than a scowl. The pugilist confessed, as he approached him, that he had never seen a more formidable figure. But his bold heart rose to the fact that he had never yet found the man who could master him, and that it was hardly credible that he would appear as an old-fashioned stranger on a country road. Therefore, with an answering smile, he took up his position and raised his hands.

But what followed was entirely beyond his experience. The stranger feinted quickly with his left, and sent in a swinging hit with his right, so quick and hard that Stevens had barely time to avoid it and to counter with a short jab as his opponent rushed in upon him. Next instant the man's bony arms were round him, and the pugilist was hurled into the air in a whirling cross-buttock, coming down with a heavy thud upon the grass. The stranger stood back and folded his arms while Stevens scrambled to his feet with a red flush of anger upon his cheeks.

"Look here," he cried. "What sort of game is this?"

"We claim foul!" the Baronet shouted.

"Foul be damned! As clean a throw as ever I saw!" said the stout man. "What rules do you fight under?"

"Queensberry, of course."

"I never heard of it. It's London prize-ring with us."

"Come on, then!" cried Stevens, furiously. "I can wrestle as well as another. You won't get me napping again."

Nor did he. The next time that the stranger rushed in Stevens caught him in as strong a grip, and after swinging and swaying they came down together in a dog-fall. Three times this occurred, and each time the stranger walked across to his friend and seated himself upon the grassy bank before he recommenced.

"What d'ye make of him?" the Baronet asked, in one of these pauses.

Stevens was bleeding from the ear, but otherwise showed no sign of damage.

"He knows a lot," said the pugilist. "I don't know where he learned it, but he's had a deal of practice somewhere. He's as strong as a lion and as hard as a board, for all his queer face."

"Keep him at out-fighting. I think you are his master there."

"I'm not so sure that I'm his master anywhere, but I'll try my best."

It was a desperate fight, and as round followed round it became clear, even to the amazed Baronet, that the middle-weight champion had met his match. The stranger had a clever draw and a rush which, with his springing hits, made him a most dangerous foe. His head and body seemed insensible to blows, and the horribly malignant smile never for one instant flickered from his lips. He hit very hard with fists like flints, and his blows whizzed up from every angle. He had one particularly deadly lead, an uppercut at the jaw, which again and again nearly came home, until at last it did actually fly past the guard and brought Stevens to the ground. The stout man gave a whoop of triumph.

"The whisker hit, by George! It's a horse to a hen on my Tommy! Another like that, lad, and you have him beat."

"I say, Stevens, this is going too far," said the Baronet, as he supported his weary man. "What will the regiment say if I bring you up all knocked to pieces in a bye-battle! Shake hands with this fellow and give him best, or you'll not be fit for your job."

"Give him best? Not I!" cried Stevens, angrily. "I'll knock that damned smile off his ugly mug before I've done."

"What about the Sergeant?"

"I'd rather go back to London and never see the Sergeant than have my number taken down by this chap."

"Well, 'ad enough?" his opponent asked, in a sneering voice, as he moved from his seat on the bank.

For answer young Stevens sprang forward and rushed at his man with all the strength that was left to him. By the fury of his onset he drove him back, and for a long minute had all the better of the exchanges. But this iron fighter seemed never to tire. His step was as quick and his blow as hard as ever when this long rally had ended. Stevens had eased up from pure exhaustion. But his opponent did not ease up. He came back on him with a shower of furious blows which beat down the weary guard of the pugilist. Alf Stevens was at the end of his strength and would in another instant have sunk to the ground but for a singular intervention.

It has been said that in their approach to the ring the party had passed through a grove of trees. Out of these there came a peculiar shrill cry, a cry of agony, which might be from a child or from some small woodland creature in distress. It was inarticulate, high-pitched, and inexpressibly melancholy. At the sound the stranger, who had knocked Stevens on to his knees, staggered back and looked round him with an expression of helpless horror upon his face. The smile had left his lips and there only remained the loose-lipped weakness of a man in the last extremity of terror.

"It's after me again, mate!" he cried.

"Stick it out, Tom! You have him nearly beat! It can't hurt you."

"It can 'urt me! It will 'urt me!" screamed the fighting man. "My God! I can't face it! Ah, I see it! I see it!"

With a scream of fear he turned and bounded off into the brushwood. His companion, swearing loudly, picked up the pile of clothes and darted after him, the dark shadows swallowing up their flying figures.

Stevens, half-senselessly, had staggered back and lay upon the grassy bank, his head pillowed upon the chest of the young Baronet, who was holding his flask of brandy to his lips. As they sat there they were both aware that the cries had become louder and shriller. Then from among the bushes there ran a small white terrier, nosing about as if following a trail and yelping most piteously. It squattered across the grassy sward, taking no notice of the two young men. Then it also vanished into the shadows. As it did so the two spectators sprang to their feet and ran as hard as they could tear for the gateway and the trap. Terror had seized them—a panic terror far above reason or control. Shivering and shaking, they threw themselves into the dog-cart, and it was not until the willing horses had put two good miles between that ill-omened hollow and themselves that they at last ventured to speak.

"Did you ever see such a dog?" asked the Baronet.

"No," cried Stevens. "And, please God, I never may again."

Late that night the two travellers broke their journey at the Swan Inn, near Harpenden Common. The landlord was an old acquaintance of the Baronet's, and gladly joined him in a glass of port after supper. A famous old sport was Mr. Joe Horner, of the Swan, and he would talk by the hour of the legends of the ring, whether new or old. The name of Alf Stevens was well known to him, and he looked at him with the deepest interest.

"Why, sir, you have surely been fighting," said he. "I hadn't read of any engagement in the papers."

"Enough said of that," Stevens answered, in a surly voice.

"Well, no offence! I suppose"—his smiling face became suddenly very serious— "I suppose you didn't, by chance, see anything of him they call the Bully of Brocas as you came north?"

"Well, what if we did?"

The landlord was tense with excitement.

"It was him that nearly killed Bob Meadows. It was at the very gate of Brocas Old Hall that he stopped him. Another man was with him. Bob was game to the marrow, but he was found hit to pieces on the lawn inside the gate where the summer-house stands."

The Baronet nodded.

"Ah, you've been there!" cried the landlord.

"Well, we may as well make a clean breast of it," said the Baronet, looking at Stevens. "We have been there, and we met the man you speak of—an ugly customer he is, too!"

"Tell me!" said the landlord, in a voice that sank to a whisper. "Is it true what Bob Meadows says, that the men are dressed like our grandfathers, and that the fighting man has his head all caved in?"

"Well, he was old-fashioned, certainly, and his head was the queerest ever I saw."

"God in Heaven!" cried the landlord. "Do you know, sir, that Tom Hickman, the famous prize-fighter, together with his pal, Joe Rowe, a silversmith of the City, met his death at that very point in the year 1822, when he was drunk, and tried to drive on the wrong side of a wagon? Both were killed and the wheel of the wagon crushed in Hickman's forehead."

"Hickman! Hickman!" said the Baronet. "Not the gasman?"

"Yes, sir, they called him Gas. He won his fights with what they called the 'whisker hit,' and no one could stand against him until Neate—him that they called the Bristol Bull—brought him down."

Stevens had risen from the table as white as cheese.

"Let's get out of this, sir. I want fresh air. Let us get on our way."

The landlord clapped him on the back.

"Cheer up, lad! You've held him off, anyhow, and that's more than anyone else has ever done. Sit down and have another glass of wine, for if a man in England has earned it this night it is you. There's many a debt you would pay if you gave the Gasman a welting, whether dead or alive. Do you know what he did in this very room?"

The two travellers looked round with startled eyes at the lofty room, stone-flagged and oak-panelled, with great open grate at the farther end.

"Yes, in this very room. I had it from old Squire Scotter, who was here that very night. It was the day when Shelton beat Josh Hudson out St. Albans way, and Gas had won a pocketful of money on the fight. He and his pal Rowe came in here upon their way, and he was mad-raging drunk. The folk fairly shrunk into the corners and under the tables, for he was stalkin' round with the great kitchen poker in his hand, and there was murder behind the smile upon his face. He was like that when the drink was in him—cruel, reckless, and a terror to the world. Well, what think you that he did at last with the poker? There was a little dog, a terrier as I've heard, coiled up before the fire, for it was a bitter December night. The Gasman broke its back with one blow of the poker. Then he burst out laughin', flung a curse or two at the folk that shrunk away from him, and so out to his high gig that was waiting outside. The next we heard was that he was carried down to Finchley with his head ground to a jelly by the wagon wheel. Yes, they do say the little dog with its bleeding skin and its broken back has been seen since then, crawlin' and yelpin' about Brocas Corner, as if it were lookin' for the swine that killed it. So you see, Mr. Stevens, you were fightin' for more than yourself when you put it across the Gasman."

"Maybe so," said the young prize-fighter, "but I want no more fights like that. The Farrier-Sergeant is good enough for me, sir, and if it is the same to you, we'll take a railway train back to town."

AMELIA B. EDWARDS
In the Confessional

Amelia B.Edwards *was one of the celebrated and select band of writers who collaborated with Charles Dickens in supplying ghost stories for the Christmas Numbers of* All the Year Round *in the 1860s, destined to become classics of the genre. Several of these were included in* The Supernatural Omnibus *(edited by Montague Summers, 1931). The best of her later tales, 'In the Confessional', first appeared in* All the Year Round, *December 1871.*

The things of which I write befell—let me see, some fifteen or eighteen years ago. I was not young then; I am not old now. Perhaps I was about thirty-two; but I do not know my age very exactly, and I cannot be certain to a year or two one way or the other.

My manner of life at that time was desultory and unsettled. I had a sorrow—no matter of what kind—and I took to rambling about Europe; not certainly in the hope of forgetting it, for I had no wish to forget, but because of the restlessness that made one place after another *triste* and intolerable to me.

It was change of place, however, and not excitement, that I sought. I kept almost entirely aloof from great cities, Spas, and beaten tracks, and preferred for the most part to explore districts where travellers and foreigners rarely penetrated.

Such a district at that time was the Upper Rhine. I was traversing it that particular Summer for the first time, and on foot; and I had set myself to trace the course of the river from its source in the great Rhine glacier to its fall at Schaffhausen. Having done this, however, I was unwilling to part company with the noble river; so I decided to follow it yet a few miles farther—perhaps as far as Mayence, but at all events as far as Basle.

And now began, if not the finest, certainly not the least charming part of my journey. Here, it is true, were neither Alps, nor glaciers, nor ruined castles perched on inaccessible crags; but my way lay through a smiling country, studded with picturesque hamlets, and beside a bright river, hurrying along over swirling rapids, and under the dark arches of antique covered bridges, and between hill-sides garlanded with vines.

It was towards the middle of a long day's walk among such scenes as these that I came to Rheinfelden, a small place on the left bank of the river, about fourteen miles above Basle.

As I came down the white road in the blinding sunshine, with the vines on either hand, I saw the town lying low on the opposite bank of the Rhine. It was an old walled town, enclosed on the land side and open to the river, the houses going sheer down to the water's edge, with flights of slimy steps worn smooth by the wash of the current, and overhanging eaves, and little built-out rooms with pent-house roofs, supported from below by jutting piles black with age and tapestried with water-weeds. The stunted towers of a couple of churches stood up from amid the brown and tawny roofs within the walls.

Beyond the town, height above height, stretched a distance of wooded hills. The old covered bridge, divided by a bit of rocky island in the middle of the stream, led from bank to bank—from Germany to Switzerland. The town was in Switzerland; I, looking towards it from the road, stood on Baden territory; the river ran sparkling and foaming between.

I crossed, and found the place all alive in anticipation of a Kermess, or fair, that was to be held there the next day but one. The townsfolk were all out in the streets or standing about their doors; and there were carpenters hard at work knocking up rows of wooden stands and stalls the whole length of the principal thoroughfare. Shop-signs in open-work of wrought iron hung over the doors. A runlet of sparkling water babbled down a stone channel in the middle of the street. At almost every other house (to judge by the rows of tarnished watches hanging in the dingy parlour windows), there lived a watchmaker; and presently I came to a fountain—a regular Swiss fountain, spouting water from four ornamental pipes, and surmounted by the usual armed knight in old grey stone.

As I rambled on thus (looking for an inn, but seeing none), I suddenly found that I had reached the end of the street, and with it the limit of the town on this side. Before me rose a lofty, picturesque old gate-tower, with a tiled roof and a little window over the archway; and there was a peep of green grass and golden sunshine beyond. The town walls (sixty or seventy feet in height, and curiously roofed with a sort of projecting shed on the inner side) curved away to right and left, unchanged since the Middle Ages. A rude wain, laden with clover and drawn by mild-eyed, cream-coloured oxen, stood close by in the shade.

I passed out through the gloom of the archway into the sunny space beyond. The moat outside the walls was bridged over and filled in—a green ravine of grasses and wild-flowers. A stork had built its nest on the roof of the gate-tower. The cicalas shrilled in the grass. The shadows lay sleeping under the trees, and a family of cocks and hens went plodding inquisitively to and fro among the cabbages in the adjacent field. Just beyond the moat, with only this field between, stood a little solitary church—a church with a wooden porch, and a quaint, bright-red steeple, and a churchyard like a rose-garden, full of colour and perfume, and scattered over with iron crosses wreathed with immortelles.

The churchyard gate and the church door stood open. I went in. All was clean, and simple, and very poor. The walls were whitewashed; the floor was laid with red bricks; the roof raftered. A tiny confessional like a sentry-box stood in one corner; the font was covered with a lid like a wooden steeple; and over the altar, upon which stood a pair of battered brass candlesticks and two vases of artificial flowers, hung a daub of the Holy Family, in oils.

All here was so cool, so quiet, that I sat down for a few moments and rested. Presently an old peasant woman trudged up the church-path with a basket of vegetables on her head. Having set this down in the porch, she came in, knelt before the altar, said her simple prayers, and went her way.

Was it not time for me also to go my way? I looked at my watch. It was past four o'clock, and I had not yet found a lodging for the night.

I got up, somewhat unwillingly; but, attracted by a tablet near the altar, crossed over to look at it before leaving the church. It was a very small slab, and bore a very brief German inscription to this effect:—

TO THE SACRED MEMORY
OF
THE REVEREND PÈRE CHESSEZ,
For twenty years the beloved Pastor of this Parish.
Died April 16th, 1825. Aged 44.
HE LIVED A SAINT; HE DIED A MARTYR.

I read it over twice, wondering idly what story was wrapped up in the concluding line. Then, prompted by a childish curiosity, I went up to examine the confessional.

It was, as I have said, about the size of a sentry-box, and was painted to imitate old dark oak. On the one side was a narrow door with a black handle, on the other a little opening like a ticket-taker's window, closed on the inside by a faded green curtain.

I know not what foolish fancy possessed me, but, almost without considering what I was doing, I turned the handle and opened the door. Opened it—peeped in—found the priest sitting in his place—started back as if I had been shot—and stammered an unintelligible apology.

"I—I beg a thousand pardons," I exclaimed. "I had no idea—seeing the church empty——"

He was sitting with averted face, and clasped hands lying idly in his lap—a tall, gaunt man, dressed in a black soutane. When I paused, and not till then, he slowly, very slowly, turned his head, and looked me in the face.

The light inside the confessional was so dim that I could not see his features very plainly. I only observed that his eyes were large, and bright, and wild-looking, like the eyes of some fierce animal, and that his face, with the reflection of the green curtain upon it, looked lividly pale.

For a moment we remained thus, gazing at each other, as if fascinated. Then, finding that he made no reply, but only stared at me with those strange eyes, I stepped hastily back, shut the door without another word, and hurried out of the church.

I was very much disturbed by this little incident; more disturbed, in truth, than seemed reasonable, for my nerves for the moment were shaken. Never, I told myself, never while I lived could I forget that fixed attitude and stony face, or the glare of those terrible eyes. What was the man's history? Of what secret despair, of what life-long remorse, of what wild unsatisfied longings was he the victim? I felt I could not rest till I had learned something of his past life.

Full of these thoughts, I went on quickly into the town, half running across the field, and never looking back. Once past the gateway and inside the walls, I breathed more freely. The wain was still standing in the shade, but the oxen were gone now, and two men were busy forking out the clover into a little yard close by. Having inquired of one of these regarding an inn, and being directed to the Krone, "over against the Frauenkirche," I made my way to the upper part of the town, and there, at one corner of a forlorn, weed-grown market-place, I found my hostelry.

The landlord, a sedate, bald man in spectacles, who, as I presently discovered, was not only an inn-keeper but a clock-maker, came out from an inner room to receive me. His wife, a plump, pleasant body, took my orders for dinner. His pretty daughter showed me to my room. It was a large, low, whitewashed room, with two lattice windows overlooking the market-place, two little beds, covered with puffy red eiderdowns at the farther end, and an army of clocks and ornamental timepieces arranged along every shelf, table, and chest of drawers in the room. Being left here to my meditations, I sat down and counted these companions of my solitude.

Taking little and big together, Dutch clocks, cuckoo clocks, *châlet* clocks, skeleton clocks, and *pendules* in ormolu, bronze, marble, ebony, and alabaster cases, there were exactly thirty-two. Twenty-eight were going merrily. As no two among them were of the same opinion as regarded the time, and as several struck the quarters as well as the hours, the consequence was that one or other gave tongue about every five minutes. Now, for a light and nervous sleeper such as I was at that time, here was a lively prospect for the night!

Going downstairs presently with the hope of getting my landlady to assign me a quieter room, I passed two eight-day clocks on the landing, and a third at the foot of the stairs. The public room was equally well-stocked. It literally bristled with clocks, one of which played a spasmodic version of Gentle Zitella with variations every quarter of an hour. Here I found a little table prepared by the open window, and a dish of trout and a flask of country wine awaiting me. The pretty daughter waited upon me; her mother bustled to and fro with the dishes; the landlord stood by, and beamed upon me through his spectacles.

"The trout were caught this morning, about two miles from here," he said, complacently.

"They are excellent," I replied, filling him out a glass of wine, and helping myself to another. "Your health, Herr Wirth."

"Thanks, mein Herr—yours."

Just at this moment two clocks struck at opposite ends of the room—one twelve, and the other seven. I ventured to suggest that mine host was tolerably well reminded of the flight of time; whereupon he explained that his work lay chiefly in the repairing and regulating line, and that at that present moment he had no less than one hundred and eighteen clocks of various sorts and sizes on the premises.

"Perhaps the Herr Engländer is a light sleeper," said his quick-witted wife, detecting my dismay. "If so, we can get him a bedroom elsewhere. Not, perhaps, in the town, for I know no place where he would be as comfortable as with ourselves; but just outside the Friedrich's Thor, not five minutes' walk from our door."

I accepted the offer gratefully.

"So long," I said, "as I ensure cleanliness and quiet, I do not care how homely my lodgings may be."

"Ah, you'll have both, mein Herr, if you go where my wife is thinking of," said the landlord. "It is at the house of our pastor—the Père Chessez."

"The Père Chessez!" I exclaimed. "What, the pastor of the little church out yonder?"

"The same, mein Herr."

"But—but surely the Père Chessez is dead! I saw a tablet to his memory in the chancel."

"Nay, that was our pastor's elder brother," replied the landlord, looking grave. "He has been gone these thirty years and more. His was a tragical ending."

But I was thinking too much of the younger brother just then to feel any curiosity about the elder; and I told myself that I would put up with the companionship of any number of clocks, rather than sleep under the same roof with that terrible face and those unearthly eyes.

"I saw your pastor just now in the church," I said, with apparent indifference. "He is a singular-looking man."

"He is too good for this world," said the landlady.

"He is a saint upon earth!" added the pretty Fräulein.

"He is one of the best of men," said, more soberly, the husband and father. "I only wish he was less of a saint. He fasts, and prays, and works beyond his strength. A little more beef and a little less devotion would be all the better for him."

"I should like to hear something more about the life of so good a man," said I, having by this time come to the end of my simple dinner. "Come, Herr Wirth, let us have a bottle of your best, and then sit down and tell me your pastor's history!"

The landlord sent his daughter for a bottle of the "green seal," and, taking a chair, said:—

"Ach Himmel! mein Herr, there is no history to tell. The good father has lived here all his life. He is one of us. His father, Johann

Chessez, was a native of Rheinfelden and kept this very inn. He was a wealthy farmer and vine-grower. He had only those two sons—Nicholas, who took to the church and became pastor of Feldkirche; and this one, Matthias, who was intended to inherit the business; but who also entered religion after the death of his elder brother, and is now pastor of the same parish."

"But why did he 'enter religion?'" I asked. "Was he in any way to blame for the accident (if it was an accident) that caused the death of his elder brother?"

"Ah Heavens! no!" exclaimed the landlady, leaning on the back of her husband's chair. "It was the shock—the shock that told so terribly upon his poor nerves! He was but a lad at that time, and as sensitive as a girl—but the Herr Engländer does not know the story. Go on, my husband."

So the landlord, after a sip of the "green seal," continued:—

"At the time my wife alludes to, mein Herr, Johann Chessez was still living. Nicholas, the elder son, was in holy orders and established in the parish of Feldkirche, outside the walls; and Matthias, the younger, was a lad of about fourteen years old, and lived with his father. He was an amiable good boy—pious and thoughtful—fonder of his books than of the business. The neighbour-folk used to say even then that Matthias was cut out for a priest, like his elder brother. As for Nicholas, he was neither more nor less than a saint. Well, mein Herr, at this time there lived on the other side of Rheinfelden, about a mile beyond the Basel Thor, a farmer named Caspar Rufenacht and his wife Margaret. Now Caspar Rufenacht was a jealous, quarrelsome fellow; and the Frau Margaret was pretty; and he led her a devil of a life. It was said that he used to beat her when he had been drinking, and that sometimes, when he went to fair or market, he would lock her up for the whole day in a room at the top of the house. Well, this poor, ill-used Frau Margaret—"

"Tut, tut, my man," interrupted the landlady. "The Frau Margaret was a light one!"

"Peace, wife! Shall we speak hard words of the dead? The Frau Margaret was young and pretty, and a flirt; and she had a bad husband, who left her too much alone."

The landlady pursed up her lips and shook her head, as the best of women will do when the character of another woman is under discussion. The inn-keeper went on.

"Well, mein Herr, to cut a long story short, after having been jealous first of one and then of another, Caspar Rufenacht became furious about a certain German, a Badener named Schmidt, living on the opposite bank of the Rhine. I remember the man quite well—a handsome, merry fellow, and no saint; just the sort to make mischief between man and wife. Well, Caspar Rufenacht swore a great oath that, cost what it might, he would come at the truth about his wife and Schmidt; so he laid all manner of plots to surprise them—waylaid the Frau Margaret in her walks; followed her at a distance when she went to church; came home at unexpected hours; and played the spy as if he had been brought up to the trade. But his spying was all in vain. Either the Frau Margaret was too clever for him, or there was really nothing to discover; but still he was not satisfied. So he cast about for some way to attain his end, and, by the help of the Evil One, he found it."

Here the innkeeper's wife and daughter, who had doubtless heard the story a hundred times over, drew near and listened breathlessly.

"What, think you," continued the landlord, "does this black-souled Caspar do? Does he punish the poor woman within an inch of her life, till she confesses? No. Does he charge Schmidt with having tempted her from her duty, and fight it out with him like a man? No. What else then? I will tell you. He waits till the vigil of St. Margaret—her saint's day—when he knows the poor sinful soul is going to confession; and he marches straight to the house of the Père Chessez—the very house where our own Père Chessez is now living—and he finds the good priest at his devotions in his little study, and he says to him:

" 'Father Chessez, my wife is coming to the church this afternoon to make her confession to you.'

" 'She is,' replies the priest.

" 'I want you to tell me all she tells you,' says Caspar; and I will wait here till you come back from the church, that I may hear it. Will you do so?'

" 'Certainly not,' replies the Père Chessez. 'You must surely know, Caspar, that we priests are forbidden to reveal the secrets of the confessional.'

" 'That is nothing to me,' says Caspar, with an oath. 'I am resolved to know whether my wife is guilty or innocent; and know it I will, by fair means or foul.'

" 'You shall never know it from me, Caspar,' says the Père Chessez, very quietly.

" 'Then, by Heavens!' says Caspar, 'I'll learn it for myself.' And with that he pulls out a heavy horse-pistol from his pocket, and with the butt end of it deals the Père Chessez a tremendous blow upon the head, and then another, and another, till the poor young man lay senseless at his feet. Then Caspar, thinking he had quite killed him, dressed himself in the priest's own soutane and hat; locked the door; put the key in his pocket; and stealing round the back way into the church, shut himself up in the confessional."

"Then the priest died!" I exclaimed, remembering the epitaph upon the tablet.

"Ay, mein Herr—the Père Chessez died; but not before he had told the story of his assassination, and identified his murderer."

"And Caspar Rufenacht, I hope, was hanged?"

"Wait a bit, mein Herr, we have not come to that yet. We left Caspar in the confessional, waiting for his wife."

"And she came?"

"Yes, poor soul! she came."

"And made her confession?"

"And made her confession, mein Herr."

"What did she confess?"

The innkeeper shook his head.

"That no one ever knew, save the good God and her murderer."

"Her murderer!" I exclaimed.

"Ay, just that. Whatever it was that she confessed, she paid for it with her life. He heard her out, at all events, without discovering himself, and let her go home believing that she had received absolution for her sins. Those who met her that afternoon said she seemed unusually bright and happy. As she passed through the town, she went into the shop in the Mongarten Strasse, and bought some ribbons. About half an hour later, my own father met her outside the Basel Thor, walking briskly homewards. He was the last who saw her alive.

"That evening (it was in October, and the days were short), some travellers coming that way into the town heard shrill cries, as of a woman screaming, in the direction of Caspar's farm. But the night was very dark, and the house lay back a little way from the road; so they told themselves it was only some drunken peasant quarrelling with his wife, and passed on. Next morning Caspar Rufenacht came to Rheinfelden, walked very quietly into the Polizei, and gave himself up to justice.

" 'I have killed my wife,' said he. 'I, have killed the Père Chessez. And I have committed sacrilege.'

"And so, indeed, it was. As for the Frau Margaret, they found her body in an upper chamber, well-nigh hacked to pieces, and the hatchet with which the murder was committed lying beside her on the floor. He had pursued her, apparently, from room to room; for there were pools of blood and handfuls of long light hair, and marks of bloody hands along the walls, all the way from the kitchen to the spot where she lay dead."

"And so he was hanged?" said I, coming back to my original question.

"Yes, yes," replied the innkeeper and his womankind in chorus. "He was hanged—of course he was hanged."

"And it was the shock of this double tragedy that drove the younger Chessez into the church?"

"Just so, mein Herr."

"Well, he carries it in his face. He looks like a most unhappy man."

"Nay, he is not that, mein Herr!" exclaimed the landlady. "He is melancholy, but not unhappy."

"Well, then, austere."

"Nor is he austere, except towards himself."

"True, wife," said the innkeeper; "but, as I said, he carries that sort of thing too far. You understand, mein Herr," he added, touching his forehead with his forefinger, "the good pastor has let his mind dwell too much upon the past. He is nervous—too nervous, and too low."

I saw it all now. That terrible light in his eyes was the light of insanity. That stony look in his face was the fixed, hopeless melancholy of a mind diseased.

"Does he know that he is mad?" I asked, as the landlord rose to go.

He shrugged his shoulders and looked doubtful.

"I have not said that the Père Chessez is *mad*, mein Herr," he replied. "He has strange fancies sometimes, and takes his fancies for facts—that is all. But I am quite sure that he does not believe himself to be less sane than his neighbours."

So the innkeeper left me, and I (my head full of the story I had just heard) put on my hat, went out into the marketplace, asked my way to the Basel Thor, and set off to explore the scene of the Frau Margaret's murder.

I found it without difficulty—a long, low-fronted, beetle-browed farm-house, lying back a meadow's length from the road. There were children playing upon the threshold, a flock of turkeys gobbling about the barn-door, and a big dog sleeping outside his kennel close by. The chimneys, too, were smoking merrily. Seeing these signs of life and cheerfulness, I abandoned all idea of asking to go over the house. I felt that I had no right to carry my morbid curiosity into this peaceful home; so I turned away, and retraced my steps towards Rheinfelden.

It was not yet seven, and the sun had still an hour's course to run. I re-entered the town, strolled back through the street, and presently came again to the Friedrich's Thor and the path leading to the church. An irresistible impulse seemed to drag me back to the place.

Shudderingly, and with a sort of dread that was half longing, I pushed open the churchyard gate and went in. The doors were closed; a goat was browsing among the graves; and the rushing of the Rhine, some three hundred yards away, was distinctly audible in the silence. I looked round for the priest's house—the scene of the first murder; but from this side, at all events, no house was visible. Going round, however, to the back of the church, I saw a gate, a box-bordered path, and, peeping through some trees, a chimney and the roof of a little brown-tiled house.

This, then, was the path along which Caspar Rufenacht, with the priest's blood upon his hands and the priest's gown upon his shoulders, had taken his guilty way to the confessional! How quiet it all looked in the golden evening light! How like the church-path of an English parsonage!

I wished I could have seen something more of the house than that bit of roof and that one chimney. There must, I told myself, be some other entrance—some way round by the road! Musing and lingering thus, I was startled by a quiet voice close against my shoulder, saying:—

"A pleasant evening, mein Herr!"

I turned, and found the priest at my elbow. He had come noiselessly across the grass, and was standing between me and the sunset, like a shadow.

"I—I beg your pardon," I stammered, moving away from the gate. "I was looking—"

I stopped in some surprise, and indeed with some sense of relief, for it was not the same priest that I had seen in the morning. No two, indeed, could well be more unlike, for this man was small, white-haired, gentle-looking, with a soft, sad smile inexpressibly sweet and winning.

"You were looking at my arbutus?" he said.

I had scarcely observed the arbutus till now, but I bowed and said something to the effect that it was an unusually fine tree.

"Yes," he replied; "but I have a rhododendron round at the front that is still finer. Will you come in and see it?"

I said I should be pleased to do so. He led the way, and I followed.

"I hope you like this part of our Rhine-country?" he said, as we took the path through the shrubbery.

"I like it so well," I replied, "that if I were to live anywhere on the banks of the Rhine, I should certainly choose some spot on the Upper Rhine between Schaffhausen and Basle."

"And you would be right," he said.

"Nowhere is the river so beautiful. Nearer the glaciers it is milky and turbid—beyond Basle it soon becomes muddy. Here we have it blue as the sky—sparkling as champagne. Here is my rhododendron. It stands twelve feet high, and measures as many in diameter. I had more than two hundred blooms upon it last Spring."

When I had duly admired this giant shrub, he took me to a little arbour on a bit of steep green bank overlooking the river, where he invited me to sit down and rest. From hence I could see the porch and part of the front of his little house; but it was all so closely planted round with trees and shrubs that no clear view of it seemed obtainable in any direction. Here we sat for some time chatting about the weather, the approaching vintage, and so forth, and watching the sunset. Then I rose to take my leave.

"I heard of you this evening at the Krone, mein Herr," he said. "You were out, or I should have called upon you. I am glad that chance has made us acquainted. Do you remain over tomorrow?"

"No; I must go on tomorrow to Basle," I answered. And then, hesitating a little, I added:—"you heard of me, also, I fear, in the church."

"In the church?" he repeated.

"Seeing the door open, I went in—from curiosity—as a traveller; just to look round for a moment and rest."

"Naturally."

"I—I had no idea, however, that I was not alone there. I would not for the world have intruded—"

"I do not understand," he said, seeing me hesitate. "The church stands open all day long. It is free to every one."

"Ah! I see he has not told you!"

The priest smiled but looked puzzled.

"He? Whom do you mean?"

"The other priest, mon père—your colleague. I regret to have broken in upon his meditations; but I had been so long in the church, and it was all so still and quiet, that it never occurred to me that there might be some one in the confessional."

The priest looked at me in a strange, startled way.

"In the confessional!" he repeated, with a catching of his breath. "You saw some one—in the confessional?"

"I am ashamed to say that, having thoughtlessly opened the door—"

"You saw—what did you see?"

"A priest, mon père."

"A priest! Can you describe him? Should you know him again? Was he pale, and tall, and gaunt, with long black hair?"

"The same, undoubtedly."

"And his eyes—did you observe anything particular about his eyes?"

"Yes; they were large, wild-looking, dark eyes, with a look in them—a look I cannot describe."

"A look of terror!" cried the pastor, now greatly agitated. "A look of terror—of remorse—of despair!"

"Yes, it was a look that might mean all that," I replied, my astonishment increasing at every word. "You seem troubled. Who is he?"

"But instead of answering my question, the pastor took off his hat, looked up with a radiant, awe-struck face, and said:—

"All-merciful God, I thank Thee! I thank Thee that I am not mad, and that Thou hast sent this stranger to be my assurance and my comfort!"

Having said these words, he bowed his head, and his lips moved in silent prayer. When he looked up again, his eyes were full of tears.

"My son," he said, laying his trembling hand upon my arm, "I owe you an explanation; but I cannot give it to you now. It must wait till I can speak more calmly—till to-morrow, when I must see you again. It involves a terrible story—a story peculiarly painful to myself—enough now if I tell you that I have seen the Thing you describe—seen It many times; and yet, because It has been visible to my eyes alone, I have doubted the evidence of my senses. The good people here believe that much sorrow and meditation have touched my brain. I have half believed it myself till now. But you—you have proved to me that I am the victim of no illusion."

"But in Heaven's name," I exclaimed, "what do you suppose I saw in the confessional?"

"You saw the likeness of one who, guilty also of a double murder, committed the deadly sin of sacrilege in that very spot, more than thirty years ago," replied the Père Chessez, solemnly.

"Caspar Rufenacht!"

"Ah! you have heard the story? Then I am spared the pain of telling it to you. That is well."

I bent my head in silence. We walked together without another word to the wicket, and thence round to the church-yard gate. It was now twilight, and the first stars were out.

"Good-night, my son," said the pastor, giving me his hand. "Peace be with you."

As he spoke the words, his grasp tightened—his eyes dilated—his whole countenance became rigid.

"Look!" he whispered. "Look where it goes!"

I followed the direction of his eyes, and there, with a freezing horror which I have no words to describe, I saw—distinctly saw through the deepening gloom—a tall, dark figure in a priest's soutane and broad-brimmed hat, moving slowly across the path leading from the parsonage to the church. For a moment it seemed to pause—then passed on to the deeper shade, and disappeared.

"You saw it?" said the pastor.

"Yes—plainly."

He drew a deep breath; crossed himself devoutly; and leaned upon the gate, as if exhausted.

"This is the third time I have seen it this year," he said. "Again I thank God for the certainty that I see a visible thing, and that His great gift of reason is mine unimpaired. But I would that He were graciously pleased to release me from the sight—the horror of it is sometimes more than I know how to bear. Good night."

With this he again touched my hand; and so, seeing that he wished to be alone, I silently left him. At the Friedrich's Thor I turned and looked back. He was still standing by the churchyard gate, just visible through the gloom of the fast deepening twilight.

I never saw the Père Chessez again. Save his own old servant, I was the last who spoke with him in this world. He died that night—died in his bed, where he was found next morning with his hands crossed upon his breast, and with a placid smile upon his lips, as if he had fallen asleep in the act of prayer.

As the news spread from house to house, the whole town rang with lamentations. The church-bells tolled; the carpenters left their work in the streets; the children, dismissed from school, went home weeping.

"'Twill be the saddest Kermess in Rheinfelden tomorrow, mein Herr!" said my good host of the Krone, as I shook hands with him at parting. "We have lost the best of pastors and of friends. He was a saint. If you had come but one day later, you would not have seen him!"

And with this he brushed his sleeve across his eyes, and turned away.

Every shutter was up, every blind down, every door closed, as I passed along the Friedrich's Strasse about midday on my way to Basle; and the few townsfolk I met looked grave and downcast. Then I crossed the bridge and, having shown my passport to the German sentry on the Baden side, I took one long, last farewell look at the little walled town as it lay sleeping in the sunshine by the river—knowing that I should see it no more.

SHAMUS FRAZER
The Tune in Dan's Café

Shamus Frazer *(1912–66) wrote several novels including* Acorned Hog *(1933) and* Blow Blow Your Trumpets *(1945). During the 1950s he produced a series of excellent "tales of the Dead and the Undead" entitled* Where Human Pathways End. *Although this collection has never been published in its entirety, some of the best tales (notably 'Florinda' and 'The Fifth Mask') have appeared in magazines and anthologies, and 'The Tune in Dan's Cafe' was televised in the* Night Gallery *series in 1971.*

At that hour it was the only place open in the little town. A gap-lettered red neon sign above the door spelt out DAN CAFE, giving off Californian overtones that the drizzle on that greasy sub-suburban road made at once pert and woebegone, like a fiery painted nose on a consumptive clown. The mechanic at the all-night garage had told us it would be a long job before our car was ready: all of ninety minutes. Yes, we might fill up on coffee and bangers at Dan's place, the next corner beyond the lights.

There was no one in the place when we entered, but the juke box was wailing sadly in its alcove: a dying moan—

There's only this thing you gotta learn
Like two times two
That I'll return to you
Oh baby, I'll re . . . re . . . TURN

The mechanism whirred: metal claws picked up the record, twisted and slipped it into the trough among the others: cogs whirred again and clicked into immobility and silence.

We chose a table by the window where the neon sign dabbled our hands and the plastic cloth with little pools of blood, and spread over one side of Helen's face a crimson glow. I thought a bell had rung faintly as we pushed open the door, but this might have been imagination for no one appeared at its summons. We stared out on the emptying street: the drizzle had become a downpour and wind-tugged umbrellas tapped and scratched now and then like great bats on the glass, shadowing for the instant our table. I don't know why we had chosen this table with its view of the rain-filled street to one further down the warm interior of the cafe: but somehow it seemed more cheerful than those ranged nearer the little bar with its polished espresso machine and its bubbling cylinders of orange and lemon drink, or by the shallow alcove where the juke box gleamed. We had chosen this table as if by instinct, and now we looked out on the rain and waited, but no one came.

There was a hand-bell one end of the bar, and a notice RING TWICE FOR PROMPT SERVICE propped against the coffee machine; but neither of us seemed to wish to walk down between the rows of tables, pick up the bell and shake it. We preferred to wait for someone to appear from the rear quarters; and we looked through that rain-beaded window and made comment on the few passers-by and the weather in unnatural voices that grew purposefully louder as the minutes ticked by, as though we felt someone would be sure to hear us before long and so make unnecessary the journey between the empty tables to the bell.

"A perambulator at this hour, Charles." Helen's lipstick was a purplish black in the neon glow. "Two hoods too. Twins?"

"She can only bring it out at twenty to midnight, Helen—and in the rain. Two hoods so that no one can look inside."

"But why shouldn't they look inside?"

"Because they'd die of shock if they did—and she loves it so."

"I think you're being *revolting*, Charles."

"It wasn't her fault. She'd been reading Space Fiction in the Labour Ward, and . . ."

"No," said Helen, "you're NOT to tell me."

"But whatever it is it died six months ago."

"It's probably her afternoon's shopping—huge packets of cereals and detergents . . . and a second hand television set."

"At this hour? . . . Now she's turning off by the Baptist Chapel, look."

"Oh Charles, d'you think she's going to blackmail the minister?"

"I know," I said, "I know for a certainty that minister has anthropopophagous tastes. He was once a missionary in darkest, oh *darkest* Africa."

"I thought I was hungry," said Helen in a wail 'but you're putting me off."

"It's as well. I suspect Dan's forgotten to hang the 'Closed' sign on the door."

"Darling you look diabolic in this light . . . Charles, did you see *that*?"

"What?"

"That umbrella tilted, and it was a *negress* under it."

"She too is turning down by the Baptist Chapel, you'll notice."

"What a dismal place to have a *break-down*!"

"Have psycho-analysts ever attempted to analyse *places*, Helen?"

The forced-smart conversation might have gone on interminably if the juke box had not interrupted it. Surprisingly, for no one had come in from the street, it had started to play—and the same wailing dirge as before: the rhymes seemed to be hammered into the cheap varnished lyric like coffin nails—"*learn*" and "*burn*", "*spurn*" with the inevitable "*yearn*"—and like a rattle of earth the refrain "*that I'll return to you . . . Oh baby, I'll return*".

"He must have come in," said Helen "and just not seen us."

"Dan?" I said. "He couldn't have helped seeing us. But oh baby he'll return. I'll toll that bell on the bar until he does."

"No," said Helen quickly, "don't leave me." And as if to disguise the intensity of that plea, "He's probably nipped back to fetch his false teeth. He'll be back in a minute."

"He might have said something while he was here."

"Some people are touchy about being caught without their teeth."

The song keened into crescendo.

"If he hasn't got them in by now," I said, "I hope he swallows them. It's we who want to eat."

I walked to the bar—resolutely I hoped, or at least not showing the discomfort I felt. The song was working itself out, and I wanted to get past that juke box and back to our table before the whirring began. I seized the bell—tourist's Benares work—and jangled it twice. There was no prompt service. I shook it again and went on shaking it, and a voice which sounded as if it came from the basement cried: "All right . . . all right. I *heard* . . . Is it you, Bob?"

"No," I said, "it's not. Is that Dan? We want something to eat."

"All right. I'm on my way."

I went back to Helen. The juke box was silent now.

"He's on his way," I said.

I don't know who we expected to see, but certainly not this big cheerful fellow in the blue jeans and bright cowboy shirt.

"Sorry," he said. "I was putting up the Zeds in there."

"Putting up the *what*?" asked Helen. "Do you mean you're closing?"

"Not a bit of it. Just taking a Sizz . . . z . . . z. Zeds, see? A spot of shut-eye to you, sister. We keep open all night. They come here off of night-shift—and there's always the lorries . . . What can I do you?"

"What *can* you do us?"

"Fried eggs, beans, chips, pork bangers—fresh today—a nice rasher of bacon . . ."

"Everything," said Helen, "except the baked beans. But pints of black coffee."

He began laying the table, rattling the sauce bottles into formation in the centre.

"You didn't see us," I said, "when you came in first."

"See you?" he exclaimed. "I heard you on the bell, as if you wanted to wake the dead."

"Earlier," I said. "Ten minutes ago, at least."

"You're not telling me you rang that bell for ten blinking minutes."

"We waited, and when you didn't come back I tried the bell."

"That's right. Told you I'd been kipping. Sorry. There's that notice by the bell, but the regulars usually shout 'Dan! Hi there!'—see. Not that there's many just at this time, after I've cleared the cinema couples. Got my head down and my feet up at eleven tonight. Must have fallen off."

He had moved behind Helen and was setting out the cutlery, ostentatiously wiping the forks on a crumpled paper napkin he had picked up from the next table.

"Then you weren't the disc-jockey?" I said.

"Disc-jockey? Come again."

"Someone was plugging a record on the juke box," I said, "but he couldn't have seen us."

A fork and knives clattered among the sauce bottles.

"*You didn't see him*?" said Dan. "What I mean is you didn't see no one at the juke box?"

"We saw no one. We thought it odd," said Helen. "We were looking out of the window, but as soon as the tune started up again we looked round of course—and there was nobody there."

"Again?" said Dan. "You mean you heard it before?"

"As we came in," I said, "and then after a bit someone started up the same tune."

"One of the girls that does my washing up, I expect," said Dan, and the lie was as shaky as the hands that groped for the dropped cutlery and set it uncertainly in place. "They knock off about then. She started it up, then seeing you nipped behind the bar—that's about it . . . There, I knew I'd forgotten something. You'll want mustard."

It was an excuse to turn away, an attempt to break the tension that held him or to forestall a question that might increase it. He brought over a tube of mustard from a nearby table and placed it in a pool of red light beside our sauce bottles. "How's that, eh?" he had recovered some of his old breeziness of manner, but now it blew too gustily. "That's real hot stuff, that is . . . I'll be back with your order soon as it takes, and if that's too long ring the bell like you done before: I'll come riding in on the fire engine."

"Like twice times two," I said, "we prefer to wait for you. Till you return."

His features sagged: he looked at me a moment with sick, hopeless eyes. He tried to speak but no sound came. He turned and moved off in the cheerless gaudy light, walking the gauntlet between the vacant tables; and I noticed how he quickened his pace and dropped his shoulders in almost a cringing gesture as he passed the alcove where the juke box stood.

"That man's terrified," Helen whispered, when he had disappeared, "and I think I am too."

"He's got guts," I said, "to-ing and fro-ing all night in this abysmal den. There and back was enough for me."

"You noticed how relieved he was we hadn't seen *him*, whoever he is?"

"You mean one of the girls that do his washing up?"

"Eye wash! But why should he want to lie?"

"Because he's scared," I said, "and doesn't want to scare us."

"But we *are* scared, Charles. Who's he trying to shield? Whoever it is he's the end, the unutterable end—like the tune he plays."

"Oh for Heaven's sake, darling, let sleeping skeletons lie in the cupboards provided for them. I'm hungry."

"I've an awful feeling," said Helen, after a minute, "that he's crawling about on hands and knees under the tables."

"Dead to the world, you mean, and pressing the juke box buttons in a kind of drunken stupor?"

"You're like the cowboy, now. You're trying to pretend there's nothing. You're trying to persuade yourself you aren't scared."

"I'm hungry," I said, "I'll feel better after sausages and chips."

"But you know that he's somewhere about the place—and that he's a horror, don't you Charles?"

"Look here, darling—it's the place, it's the whole place," I said. "It's not a question of any individual. I told you the place needed analysis."

"It's what I'm trying to do. You know as well as I—and Dan—there's someone about the place, who's . . . *wrong*."

"Perhaps I do—but I don't want to make the autopsy, please Helen, until I've had some coffee at least."

But Helen persisted.

"Dan wants to keep him out of our way. Why? I think it may be because he's his brother, and he knows he's a criminal lunatic. What do you think, Charles?"

"I think of sausages, Helen, grilled sausages—bronzed but pink in parts like sunbathers: and a fried egg like the noonday sun, and—" I broke off, and I suppose that like Dan's my features sagged.

"Oh, my God!" said Helen in a tone that was not quite a sob, not exactly a protest and not wholly a prayer but seemed to comprehend in a breath the emotions of all three. "I knew he was still here."

That abandoned tune had started moaning again out of the juke box. We looked at one another, at the raucous, empty alcove and again at one another: we tried to speak, but the tune was spinning round us like a whirlpool and we were drowning in it.

At last I struggled free to gasp: "Shall we cut and run?"

Helen slipped a hand like Lady Macbeth's across the table and clutched my own.

"We can't!" she seemed to be shouting, but her words were the merest croak. "We couldn't move."

"When it stops. We'll bolt—when it stops."

"And Dan? We'd seem like the proverbial rats."

"This ship isn't sinking," I got out, "it's submerged."

But the thought of that pathetic cowboy bringing our supper past the rows of empty tables only to find our table empty too, was so intolerable that it made what we had to bear seem suddenly endurable.

"If you can take it, darling, we'll stay."

"Oh, it'll be over soon."

So we sat the tune out, clutching hands over the dabbled plastic cloth, and leering at one another like honeymooners.

When it ended I said: "After all it *may* be a mechanical fault, Helen."

Helen said nothing at all, just squeezed my hand more tightly. We were still holding hands when Dan came in with the supper. Obviously he had not heard the tune in his basement, for he was whistling: he did not give the alcove a glance this time—but the whistling stopped and he moved more quickly as he passed it.

"You'd like your coffee now or after?" he asked, as he set the heaped plates before us.

"Now, please," said Helen.

He went back to the bar and busied himself there with the machine. Thence he called to us occasionally for companionship—and we returned his hails.

"Sugar?"

"Yes, please."

"Like cream?"

"Black for me . . . It's a good grill you've done us."

"Glad you like it."

"It's what we wanted."

"Got far to drive?"

"Highgate."

"Should do it in under the hour."

"We'd be home by now," said Helen. "We had a breakdown."

"Where've you left it? Awcock's?"

"Two blocks up the street."

"That's Awcock's. They'll fix it, Awcock's will."

Spurts of small talk echoing down the long empty room, they seemed to belong there as little as the human cries that fall from space out of the television screen; and yet in their very triviality they were significant—a glimpse of order in the heart of chaos.

He brought us the coffee and stood watching us finish the meal.

"Good, eh?"

"Good! Been here long?"

"Couple of years. I could do with a change."

"It must be a strain," I said, "keeping open all night. You're single handed?"

"I get help most nights."

Helen lit a cigarette and said: "You're not alone tonight? What about the girls who do the washing up?"

"They've knocked off. I told you."

"Someone came back just now and started the juke box going."

"*What*? Since I been away cooking?"

"It stopped just before you came in."

"There's some fault with that box. I mean to have it seen to."

"Does it always play the same tune?"

He looked haggard and deflated; "When it starts by itself it's usually the one tune," he admitted. "It plays normal when customers select a record, perfectly normal."

"Why," said Helen, "there's someone bending over it now."

"It can't be!" said Dan. "I've only *seen* him twice myself."

"No—there's nobody." Helen blinked. "I could have sworn, but there's nobody . . . But look, *look*," she added on a more shrill note, "it's moving, it's beginning to work!"

There was a scratching noise, and then the cafe was engulfed in the opening bars of that hideous, forlorn song. Dan stumbled into a chair, edged it up to our table; and there the three of us sat, frozen and motionless until it ended.

"Why don't you destroy the record?" I asked out of the breathing silence.

"Of course I destroyed it. What do you think?" said Dan, wildly. "I smashed it up the week after. It's a new juke box I had in too. But it makes no difference. He comes back about eleven to play it, and keeps right on to the end. It's all right after one in the morning. It's all over with, see. You hear the bang—and it's done with till the following night. It's like one of these West End plays that goes on night after night after night—only there's no matinee performances to this one. Not everyone hears it plain as you, but enough's heard it; and I say like I done to you it's one of the girls or it's something gone wrong with the juke box. My regulars know it's Dave of course, and they don't visit here except those hours they know he won't be about—before he comes and after it's done with . . ."

"Who is Dave?" I asked, and corrected myself. "Who *was* Dave?"

"He wasn't no regular," said Dan, "at least not while he was alive. But he came in some weekends with his girl. He was a London Ted, duck-arsed hair dyed red, shoestring tie, pale blue eyes that bulged so you saw the bloodshot rims, slack mouth sucking a cigarette, or a bit of gum, or his teeth. But his girl? Oh, she was *really* something to look at. Dark and pale, tight black sweater and slacks, and great eyes painted with blue shadow, and pouted lips pale as a corpse's with that kind of off-beat lipstick: she had her hair wound up like a beeskep, and she sat there as quiet as a statue drinking her coffee and smoking while Dave worked the juke box. Moira he called her: some kind of model, I suppose. They kept themselves close: never talked with the others, and took themselves off about midnight till the next weekend or the one after that when they'd be back, sitting at that table by the juke box there."

"They were regulars then—of a sort?" said Helen.

"Not my sort. Well one night—mid-week it was—this Dave came in. Seemed excited about something. Asked if his girl had been in. It was about eleven—not many customers. He'd wait, he said: she'd be along. He sat slopped at his table in the alcove, smoking, and calling for more coffee, and getting up to set the juke box off again. Always the same record he picked what we've . . . what we just been listening to. Restless he seemed—kind of smouldering. Asked me questions. Did his girl ever come here other times—in company or alone? Had she come in during the day? And he smiled when I gave him a 'no' to all and said ssshe'd be looking in soon, and he wanted another packet of fags quick. And all the time, off and on, that refrain blaring out of the juke box to tell her he'd returned." Dan paused to light the cigarette I'd offered him. "Thanks . . . She never came, but it was just before one when the cops arrived. He flattened himself quick as a rat in the alcove and he shot the first to enter—a big fellow in a grey hat. They pulled their man out into the roadway and got him safe round the corner while Dave shot at them three times from the alcove through the window glass and missed. Then a voice started up on a loudspeaker—from a police car somewhere out of harm's way—telling him the place was surrounded and to throw down his gun and come out. I was behind the bar and Dave yelled: 'If any of you bastards tries anything I'll plug Dan.' He'd hardly time to whip his gun round in my direction when arms pulled me down under the bar and I tumbled among a bunch of crouching coppers. They'd guns too: must have crawled in from the back while Dave was watching the street. The loudspeaker was gone persuasive now, mingling in with that song out of the juke box. 'It's no use, Dave. You'll never get out. Be sensible. Moira here wants you to be sensible. We've enough tear gas here for a Top Red's funeral.' A plain clothes cop warned in my ear: 'Keep still.

He may make a run for the back, and we can collar him then.' The loudspeaker broke off: no one showed in the street but you could tell they'd be using the windows of the house over the way by now. Dave must have known he'd had it. That song sobbed on for a bit, and then there was the noise of the claws on the record—the recovery mechanism, see—and that click. The bang followed like a door slammed, and the cops were scrambling in a bunch for the alcove. I saw him flattened against the wall and toppling: his gun clattered and someone kicked it away. He'd blown the top of his head off and scattered what brains he had over my alcove wallpaper. It's all cleaned up and re-papered of course but sometimes I've fancied it shows like it was when I saw it then, and it gets me cold-sick in the heart."

"What had he done—*before*?" asked Helen with a shiver.

"Robbed a bank that morning and killed one of the cashiers. His girl tipped the police he'd be coming here to wait for her. Got her picture spread all over the front page next morning: she was something to look at too—*photogenic* . . ."

"She never came back. You never saw her again?"

"Never . . . That swine Dave's waiting for her still, you know. About a year he's been waiting—and I expect he'll be waiting till doomsday. But I can tell you I've had enough of him. I'm selling up. Got my hooks on a little place in Kent, out beyond Swanley on the Maidstone Road: lorries mostly. The new bloke will have Dave with the fittings—and good luck to him, I say."

It was twenty to one. We did not wait for the end of the performance. Dan seemed to be in a hurry too to clear our table and get back to his basement. As we let ourselves out into the street I glanced back: Dan was hustling with his tray down to the bar: I thought I made out a restless shadow moving in the alcove but this may have been imagination. As the door swung to behind me, it sounded as if the juke box had started wailing again: I did not stay to make sure. Helen was waiting for me on the corner: "Oh Charles," she said, "I pity that girl if ever she comes back," and as she took my arm she added, "men don't like being kept waiting. Even you if you had to wait till doomsday might be rather sore . . ." Her arm trembled against mine, and the joke faltered. "If Dave was the end—without end—what is she? Does she carry a broken gramophone record in her head? What thoughts are swarming under that beeskep of dark hair?"

"About some man or other," I said. "Some other man."

JOHN S. GLASBY
Beyond the Bourne

John Stephen Glasby *(b. 1928), research chemist and astronomer, was elected a Fellow of the Royal Astronomical Society in 1960. Among his books are* The Dwarf Novae *(1970) and* The Variable Star Observer's Handbook *(1971). He has written over 500 stories in various genres, mainly war and westerns, science fiction, crime and supernatural horror, most appearing under pseudonyms in the 1950s and 1960s.*

Sheila Kirby heard the footsteps the second day in the cottage. She was seated at her typewriter with the spring sunlight streaming through the open windows behind her.

Sheila had rented the cottage on the outskirts of Redforde, a small Cornish village, in a frantic attempt to complete her novel. The deadline set by the publishers was now only five short weeks away and it had proved impossible to work in her London flat; too many distractions, the phone ringing incessantly, the noise of the traffic which went on well into the early hours of the morning, friends dropping in at the most inconvenient times.

In the end she had had to get away from it all. Total seclusion in amenable surroundings was what she needed and here, she felt sure, she had found it.

Redforde was a picturesque little village on the coast and Rose Cottage was situated a little over a mile away, set well back from the narrow country lane with a well-stocked rock garden leading up to the low latticed windows.

She had already arranged for one of the women in the village to come in for four hours every day, just to keep the place tidy while she got to grips with her writing.

The small front room was ideal as a work study. The large oak table held her papers, electric typewriter and books and the room itself was light and airy with the scent of early spring flowers wafting through the windows. Yet, curiously, she was finding it difficult to put her thoughts into a coherent order and set them down on paper.

She had been feeling strange ever since moving in; a sensation of vague unease as if there was some presence in the cottage, an unspoken threat hanging in the air.

And now the unmistakable sound of footsteps just outside the door.

She pushed back her chair and walked hesitantly towards the door, checking her watch. It was too early for Mrs Manley. She would not arrive for another quarter of an hour. Besides, the footsteps were light and furtive like those of a child.

Trembling a little, she flung the door open. The hallway was empty but the front door stood ajar. Stepping outside, she glanced quickly around the garden, half-expecting to see a small form scampering away down the lane. Indeed, just for an instant she *did* think she saw a slight movement among the bushes at the edge of the rock garden.

But she had caught it with averted vision and the instant she swung her head round to stare at it directly, it disappeared and she could not be certain there had been anyone there at all.

Puzzled, she went back to her typewriter and sat staring at the words on the page. Had it been one of the village children? she wondered. It seemed unlikely they would venture this far from the village. But perhaps they had been in the habit of coming out here when the cottage had lain empty, playing in the garden where their parents couldn't see them. Maybe one, more adventurous than the rest, had sneaked into the house and had fled precipitously on hearing her get up and go to the door.

She tried to settle down to her work, forcing herself to concentrate, but it was no use. The ideas simply refused to come. Her thoughts persisted in flying off at a tangent. Lighting a cigarette, she leaned back, staring abstractly at the ceiling.

"Would you like a cup of tea, Miss?"

The voice from the doorway made her jump nervously.

Mrs Manley stood there, her broad, good-natured face creased in a smile.

"I was just going to put the kettle on before starting work."

"Thank you, Mrs Manley. I'd love one."

"Sorry if I startled you but the door was open and this hall carpet is so thick you wouldn't hear me come in."

"That's all right. I guess I was miles away."

Mrs Manley took off her hat and coat. "It won't be a minute," she called as she went through into the kitchen.

Sheila stubbed out her cigarette and realized her hand was trembling. What Mrs Manley had said was true. That carpet was thick enough to deaden the sound so that she would not have heard her come in.

But she had heard those other light footsteps clearly, even through the closed door!

In spite of the warmth in the room, Sheila felt momentarily cold as if a blast of chill air had suddenly blown in through the window.

Mrs Manley came in with two cups of tea and some biscuits on a tray. She set them down on the table.

As casually as she could, Sheila said, "Did you notice anyone running down the lane on your way here, Mrs Manley?"

"Why no. Don't tell me you've had someone prowling around."

"I'm not sure. Maybe it was just my imagination but a little while ago I was certain I heard someone in the hall. When I went, there was no one there but the front door was open and—"

She stopped. Mrs Manley had turned a shade pale and was staring oddly at her across the table.

"Is something wrong?" Sheila asked.

"Why no, Miss. It's just that—" she broke off sharply, looking away.

"Please tell me," Sheila said. "After all, I have rented the cottage now, so I have a right to know."

Mrs Manley glanced nervously towards the door. "Really, it's nothing. I don't set any store by these old superstitions anyway."

"So there is something odd about this cottage." Sheila drew in a deep breath. For a moment, her heart thumped rapidly, hammering away against her ribs. "Somehow, I sensed it the moment I moved in." She paused, then went on a trifle unsteadily, "You're trying to tell me the place is haunted, aren't you?"

Mrs Manley looked uncomfortable, eyes downcast, studying the teacup in her hand.

"There are some folk in the village who say that, Miss. But like I said, I don't believe in such things myself. I'm a God-fearing woman and I believe the dead stay dead until the Judgement Day."

Sheila drained her cup and set it down on the tray. Inwardly, she was surprised at how calm she now felt.

"Tell me about it," she urged finally, lighting another cigarette.

"Very well, Miss, if you're sure you want to know. It was all a very long time ago. I was only a child then but I can still remember it as clearly as if it were only yesterday. A young couple had Rose Cottage then. They only had one child, Timothy. He was a pale-faced little chap, I recall. Never mixed with the rest of us in the village. In fact, I don't think I ever saw him outside the garden."

"You mean his parents never allowed him to leave the place?" Sheila asked, astonished.

"That's the long and the short of it, Miss. Virtual prisoner he was. Probably they thought he was too delicate to play with other children."

Sheila took one of the biscuits and nibbled at it. "And what happened to him?"

"Pneumonia, I heard my mother say. He was playing alone in the garden when there was a sudden storm. He got soaked to the skin afraid to run into the cottage. Within a week, he was dead. Only seven, he was."

"Poor little mite," Sheila said softly. "He didn't have much of a life."

"Not much of a death either if you listen to the villagers," Mrs Manley retorted.

"I don't understand."

"You wanted to know the whole story, Miss. They say that Timothy haunts the cottage and garden. They buried his body in the churchyard down the hill yonder. But his spirit can't pass beyond the garden perimeter any more than he could when he was alive."

"And you think it may have been him I heard outside the door?" Sheila pushed the plate of biscuits away. Oddly, she didn't feel as frightened by Mrs Manley's tale as she had thought.

"If you heard anything at all, Miss."

Mrs Manley got up briskly and collected the cups on the tray. "I'd better be getting on with my work now."

And I'd better try to get on with mine, Sheila thought determinedly. The publishers would not wait beyond the deadline and she had never before been late in delivering a manuscript.

Strangely, she found it easier to concentrate now than it had been before Mrs Manley had told her that strange story. The words seemed to flow from her brain, into her hands and onto the paper.

By noon, she had already completed a further two chapters and after lunch she decided to go for a brief walk, leaving Mrs Manley to lock up the cottage with her own key.

There was a pleasant warmth in the air as she walked down the garden path and only a few lacy clouds to spoil the blue mirror of the sky.

At the gate, she reached out to lift the metal latch, then paused uncertainly as an odd compulsion came over her not to open the gate and go through into the lane. It lasted for only a brief second but it made her breath catch in her throat as she fought instinctively against it.

Once in the lane she began walking quickly and tried to drive out the weirdly oppressive feeling that was threatening to overwhelm her. Back at the gate there had been the inescapable sensation that something had been deliberately trying to hold her back, to prevent her from leaving the garden.

She had intended walking into the village for she had seen very little of it when she had arrived. But near the bottom of the hill she came upon a small lane on her right and once more she experienced that strange urge, not so strong as earlier, but definitely present, telling her to turn down through the trees. Almost of their own volition, her legs took her between the low hedgerows now coming into full leaf.

In front of her was a small wooden gate and among the trees, a small Norman church with its square stone tower and a clock face which stood eternally at a quarter past four. The churchyard looked very old with ragged rows of headstones, some just visible above the mossy grass. Many were so overgrown that she could not read the names carved into the stone.

Acting on a sudden impulse, Sheila left the path and advanced towards the far corner of the graveyard between the mossy mounds where a small, solitary grave stood out on the edge of a black shadow thrown by a massive oak. She had to go down on one knee in the grass to remove some of the tangled weeds before she could read the inscription.

There was only the name and the dates. "Timothy Wynall. 1932–1939."

There was no doubt in her mind that this was the grave of the boy who had died at Rose Cottage fifty years before. Yet what strange instinct had led her directly to it? What had made her turn off the lane instead of going on into the village as she had intended?

Sheila rose quickly to her feet as a sudden chill seized her. The sun had gone behind a cloud and strange shadows seemed to move around the churchyard. With an effort, Sheila straightened her back and sucked in a deep breath. Now she really was letting her imagination run away with her. There was nothing here of which to be afraid, she told herself fiercely, nor at the cottage. She made her way a little unsteadily back to the lane, debated inwardly for a moment whether to go into the village, then turned and went back to the cottage.

Closing the door behind her, she stood with her back pressed against it, listening intently to the silence, waiting for some sound to break the stillness.

Nothing.

Letting her breath go in a long sigh, she went into the front room where Mrs Manley had lit a fire in the wide stone grate. Standing in front of it, she held out her hands, feeling the warm glow spread into her body. She put more coal onto the fire before making herself something to eat, sitting in the chair next the fireplace with the plate balanced on her knees.

Afterwards, she tried to write but the inspiration had left her. Realizing the futility of trying to work, she took a book from the small bookcase and tried to read for a while. The walk in the country air had made her tired and after skimming through a couple of pages she found her eyelids closing, her head drooping towards her chest.

Then, abruptly, she snapped upright, eyes darting towards the window. Something tapped the glass from the outside!

Her hand fluttered to her mouth as she started from the chair. A little germ of panic set her heart palpitating in her chest and her flesh twitched with a strange blend of terror and anticipation.

The tapping came again and as she edged forward, past the large oak table, she thought she glimpsed a white hand—just a hand, nothing more—visible through the window pane, the small fingers rapping lightly against the glass. Her whole system had been prodded into alertness by the sound, her tiredness forgotten. With a wild, inarticulate cry, she dashed to the window and threw it open.

There was nothing there.

She shook herself mentally and tried to control the trembling in her limbs. What in God's name was wrong with her? Maybe it was because, subconsciously, she was dwelling on the past, on what Mrs Manley had told her and that visit to the small grave in the churchyard.

For a few seconds, she remained there, peering out into the deepening dusk striving to find some other external cause of the sound. But there were no trees or bushes close at hand whereby the breeze might have set a branch rattling against the pane. Perhaps she had fallen into a doze and the sound had been in a dream from which she had abruptly woken, carrying the noise over into a bemused half-awake state and her fertile imagination had added the rest.

She made to pull the window shut, glancing down as she did so. What she saw then made her recoil instinctively into the room, pressing her back hard against the table for support. In the soft earth immediately below the window were the imprints of shoes, small shoes belonging to a child!

Her thoughts stopped suddenly, retreating into a darkness which seemed to envelop her mind. Then reality jerked into place around her. She forced herself to consider the situation rationally, recalling the sense of sadness she had felt when Mrs Manley had first told her of Timothy's short life. If he *was* doomed to haunt the cottage, there had, so far, been no malevolence in his actions. Perhaps, all he had been doing was trying to attract her attention to his presence. After all, what harm could there be in the earthbound spirit of a lonely seven-year-old boy?

She suddenly found herself able to move. Closing the window, she drew the curtains and returned to the fire. The feel of a presence in the cottage was strong now yet strangely, in contrast to her earlier fear, there was something oddly comforting about it as if it were glad there was now someone else living there.

An hour later, she undressed and slipped between the cool sheets, falling almost at once into a deep and dreamless sleep from which she woke feeling calm and refreshed.

For the next three weeks, the pattern remained the same. Sheila slept like a log every night, something she had never been able to do before when engaged on a novel. During the day, she hammered out page after page with scarcely a correction or revision necessary. Timothy's ghost—if such it was—left her undisturbed. It was as if, having made his presence known to her, he was content to remain in the background, unseen and unheard.

Once or twice, thinking about him, Sheila wondered if, her acceptance of him and her actions had somehow allowed his shackled spirit to leave the confines of the cottage and garden enabling him to pass on to some other realm of existence.

Mrs Manley also noticed the change in her. One morning, shortly after she arrived at the cottage, she broached the subject of Timothy, a topic they had both avoided for almost a fortnight.

"I hope you don't mind me saying so, Miss, but somehow I thought you might have left the cottage before now."

"Why should I?" She looked up from the typewriter to where Mrs Manley stood just inside the doorway, wiping her hands on her apron.

Mrs Manley seemed unsure how to respond. She continued to twist her hands in the apron even though they were completely dry.

"I thought you might have heard other things in the cottage which would interfere with your writing."

"No. I've heard nothing since that first day. Besides, there's something about this place which seems to help me with my work. I've almost finished, three weeks ahead of the deadline."

"And will you be leaving once the novel is finished?"

Sheila tapped her teeth with her pen. "I'm not sure. I did rent the cottage for six weeks. It would be a pity to cut my stay short. It's so peaceful here compared with London."

"Peaceful it may seem but things are not always what they appear."

"Surely you're not beginning to believe in what they say about the cottage being haunted, Mrs Manley?"

"It's not a question of what I believe, Miss. It's what you believe. There've been others who've rented Rose Cottage in the past. None of them stayed here as long as you have." She added the last sentence in an ominous tone.

"Perhaps they were afraid of the ghost." Sheila could not help the touch of malicious humour in her voice.

Mrs Manley busied herself arranging the flowers in the vase on the mantlepiece and Sheila noticed she was evidently trying to keep her emotions in check.

"You really do believe that Timothy's spirit is here, don't you?" Sheila said insistently when Mrs Manley made no move to reply.

"I believe there are certain things in this world which are best not tampered with, Miss."

"But surely you're not suggesting that Timothy would do anything evil?"

"If there are such things as ghosts, it can only mean they're earthbound for a purpose." Mrs Manley declared stubbornly. She stepped back awkwardly to look at her handiwork. "I had a talk with my husband only a week ago. He asked me how you were getting on in the cottage. And he said I ought to warn you about staying here."

"Warn me?" Sheila opened the box of a new ribbon for her typewriter and slotted the spools into place. "About what?"

"Andrew's a native of these parts," Mrs Manley said by way of explanation, "his family have lived here for generations. So, maybe, he's much closer to nature and these things than I am. But he reckons Timothy desperately wants to leave this place where he's been bound for fifty years."

Glancing up at Mrs Manley, Sheila saw there was an expression of deadly seriousness on her face. "And how do you think he'll be able to do that?"

"I don't know, I'm sure. But Andrew said that the noises here aren't of much account. Just so long as you don't see him."

Sheila recalled the small disembodied hand she was sure she had seen tapping at the window. She got up from her chair a little more quickly than she had intended. This was ridiculous, she told herself. She had already convinced herself that if Timothy's ghost did haunt this cottage and the garden outside, he meant her no harm. Indeed, she had the feeling that his mere presence had somehow helped her to complete the novel well inside the deadline she had set herself.

"I can't see what difference seeing him will make," Sheila said a trifle sharply. She placed the cover over the typewriter.

"I think I'll go for a walk while the sun's out."

She put on her coat, leaving Mrs Manley to finish her work, and went out into the garden. Bringing up the subject of the ghost had disturbed her and she found herself peering into the bushes, half expecting to see a small white face watching her. For some reason she felt tired and irritable. Had Mrs Manley deliberately set out to frighten her? Maybe those other tenants who had left here so hurriedly had received the same kind of warning.

It was quite possible that the folk here resented strangers coming into their midst. Looking back on the curious events of the first two or three days of her stay, she couldn't be absolutely certain they had not been anything more than products of her own imagination. Even those tiny footprints she thought she had seen in the earth beneath the windows had vanished the following morning and there had been no rain that night to have washed them away.

Well, she told herself firmly, if they were trying to get her to leave before the end of her tenancy, they had another think coming. The thought of returning to London with its traffic roar and the constant ringing of the telephone, appalled her. With a little luck, she would have the novel finished by that evening and then she would spend a few more weeks just relaxing. There would be time enough to plan further work once she got back.

Mrs Manley had on her hat and coat when Sheila went back inside. "I've left your tea on the tray, Miss," she said, pausing at the door. "Don't let it get cold. And don't forget what I told you. Be careful if you mean to stay here much longer."

"I'll bear what you said in mind," Sheila said. She waited until Mrs Manley had disappeared down the lane, then closed the door and locked it. The cottage was very quiet.

That evening, her fingers seemed to fly over the typewriter keys as if every part of her being was anxious to complete the novel. Never had her thoughts flowed so easily. By ten o'clock it was finished, the last neatly-typed page stapled into place.

Heaving a sigh of relief, Sheila leaned back and lit a cigarette, smoking it slowly, savouring the feeling of contentment and final fulfilment. In the morning, she would pack it carefully and post it away in the small post office in Redforde.

Finishing her cigarette, she cleared away the tea things, switched off the lights and went to bed.

Sheila woke with a start. Her forehead was damp with sweat and her heart was thumping fiercely. She lay absolutely still for several minutes, struggling to calm herself. She had had a vivid nightmare, the first since arriving there and the dregs of it were still strong in her mind. There had been a face in her dream, the features startlingly clear; a child's face framed by jet-black curly hair and wide eyes that had stared at her pleadingly, imploring her mutely to do something, but she hadn't known what it was he wanted her to do.

Then she had been standing at the foot of an open grave, looking down at the small coffin. But the coffin had been empty and glancing over her shoulder she had seen, far in the distance, Rose Cottage on top of the hill and a small figure standing just inside the gate, looking at her over the intervening distance with that same beseeching expression on its face.

Dressing quickly, she swallowed a couple of aspirins in an attempt to ease the throbbing inside her skull. The best way to get rid of these nightmarish memories was to busy hereself packing up the manuscript and get out into the fresh air, she told herself.

The nightmare seemed not quite so menacing as she let herself out of the door into the warm sunlight, carrying the heavy parcel under her arm. Her headache was quite gone by the time she reached the village and discovered the post office crushed between the 'Red Lion' Inn and a small butchers shop.

The loud jangling of the bell above the door brought a young woman hurrying from the back. Taking Sheila's parcel, she weighed it, took the proferred five-pound note and stuck the stamps on the right-hand corner, hitting them hard with the cancellation stamp.

Sliding the change beneath the grille, she said quietly, "You're the writer who's up at Rose Cottage, aren't you."

"That's right." Sheila gave a brief nod as she slipped the coins into her purse.

"I suppose you know it's supposed to be—" The woman broke off hastily as if realizing she had said something she had not intended.

"Haunted?" Sheila finished for her. "Yes, I've heard all the grisly details from Mrs Manley."

"Aren't you the least bit scared?"

Sheila's lips tightened. "No. There's nothing there to be afraid of, believe me. People tend to exaggerate such things whether they believe them or not."

She was suddenly aware of rain slashing at the small leaded window accompanied by a low rumble of thunder. There had been no sign of clouds in the sky during her walk but here, near the coast, she knew these storms could sweep in from the sea within minutes.

"You're not thinking of walking back in that?" said the post mistress as Sheila made for the door. "You'll be drenched to the skin before you leave the village."

Sheila opened the door and looked out. The rain came sweeping along the street in gusts, blown by the wind. Overhead, the dark, lowering clouds scudded swiftly across the heavens. Lightning flashed briefly to the west. There was no sign of any clearance towards the horizon.

The young woman came around the counter and stood beside her.

"If it's important you should get back, you can borrow my bicycle," she said, pointing to the cycle propped against the wall beside the bow window. "I won't need it until tomorrow and you can return it as soon as the storm passes."

Sheila hesitated, then muttered her thanks. It was several years since she had ridden a bicycle but after a few minutes she was pedalling furiously along the narrow road, head down against the wind and slashing rain.

By the time she reached the bottom of the hill, the storm was at its height and she was regretting she had not decided to remain in the comparative comfort of the post office until it had passed over. Her leg muscles were beginning to protest as she began the uphill climb.

Then, just as she neared the brow of the hill there came a glaring streak of blue as the vicious lightning bolt speared across her vision. It struck the bare, stunted oak by the side of the lane. The glare momentarily blinded her and the cacophanous roar of the thunder hammered at her ears as she jammed on the brakes.

Through her stultified vision she saw the oak sway, realized in an instant of sheer terror that it would crash across the lane in front of her. The front wheel slewed round on the wet, treacherous surface. Wildly, she threw out her right leg in the hope of saving herself from falling.

She felt the front tyre bump against the fallen trunk, buckling the wheel, hurling her forward. Somehow, she managed to remain upright, blinking the rain from her still dazzled eyes. It was obvious the bicycle would take her no further and her only thought was to leave it there and get into the cottage out of the rain.

Violent tremors were coursing through her body as the closeness of her lucky escape penetrated her numbed mind. Somehow, she succeeded in clambering over the bare trunk. There was the sharp smell of ozone in her nostrils as she began to run blindly towards the gate a few yards away. She grasped it and thrust it open in her frenzied haste, staggering along the path to the front door. Fumbling in her bag, she found the key and inserted it in the lock, turning it jerkily.

Inside the hall, she shrugged off her sodden coat and switched on the light. Then her mouth gaped, her throat constricted until she thought she was going to choke. The small figure stood in the entrance to the front room, regarding her with solemn eyes. There was a faint smile on the curved lips.

Somehow, she found her voice. "Timothy?" She got the word out with an effort.

The boy nodded, still smiling. Sheila felt herself grow tense and shuddery as the figure advanced slowly, not hesitantly, she noticed, but with a strange singleness of purpose. Cold fingers closed around her hand. She felt herself being pulled towards the front door.

But you're a ghost, she wanted to say, *even though I can see you, it's impossible for you to touch me like this*.

Unable to help herself, she stepped outside and all the while the small figure beside her was urging her towards the gate. Rain still swept across the grey world in sheets but she was scarcely aware of it.

For a moment, she felt a sense of surprise as Timothy passed through the gate and into the lane. She wanted to ask him how he was able to leave the garden after being doomed to wander there for fifty years but already, he was tugging at her more urgently, drawing her closer to where the great trunk of the oak lay across the lane.

She wanted to drag herself away, back to the cottage. But already his free hand was pointing downward and she saw the twisted remains of the bicycle pinned beneath the tree—and the crumpled, familiar figure lying beside it, eyes staring sightlessly in the rain-washed face!

WILLIAM HOPE HODGSON
The Valley of Lost Children

The works of William Hope Hodgson *(1877–1918) have enjoyed a well-deserved revival in recent years, notably* The Night Land, The House on the Borderland *and* Carnacki the Ghost-Finder. *'The Valley of Lost Children' originally appeared in the* Cornhill, *February 1906.*

The two of them stood together and watched the boy, and he, a brave little fellow near upon his fourth birthday, having no knowledge that he was watched, hammered a big tom-cat with right lusty strokes, scolding it the while for having killed a "mices." Presently the cat made its escape, followed by the boy, whose chubby little legs twinkled in the sunlight, and whose tossed head of golden tangle was as a star of hope to the watchers. As he vanished among the nearer bushes the woman pulled at the man's sleeve.

"Our b'y," she said, in a low voice.

"Aye, Sus'n, thet's so," he replied, and laid a great arm about her neck in a manner which was not displeasing to her.

They were neither of them young, and marriage had come late in life; for fortune had dealt hardly with the man, so that he had been unable to take her to wife in the earlier days. Yet she had waited, and at last a sufficiency had been attained, so that in the end they had come together in the calm happiness of middle life. Then had come the boy, and with his coming a touch of something like passionate joy had crept into their lives.

It is true that there was a mortgage upon the farm, and the interest had to be paid before Abra'm could touch his profits; but what of that! He was strong, uncommonly so, and then there was the boy. Later he would be old enough to lend a hand; though Abra'm had a secret hope that before that time he would have the mortgage cleared off and be free of all his profits.

For a while longer they stood together, and so, in a little, the boy came running back out of the bushes. It was evident that he must have had a tumble, for the knees of his wee knickers were stained with clay-marks. He ran up to them and held out his left hand, into which a thorn was sticking; yet he made no movement to ask for sympathy, for was he not a man?—ay, every inch of his little four-year body! His intense manliness will be the better understood when I explain that upon that day he had been "breeked," and four years old in breeks has a mighty savour of manliness.

His father plucked the thorn from his hand, while his mother made shift to remove some of the clay; but it was wet, and she decided to leave it until it had dried somewhat.

"Hev ter put ye back inter shorts," threatened his mother; whereat the little man's face showed a comprehension of the direness of the threat.

"No! no! no!" he pleaded, and lifted up to her an ensnaring glance from dangerous baby eyes.

Then his mother, being like other women, took him into her arms, and all her regret was that she could take him no closer.

And Abra'm, his father, looked down upon the two of them, and felt that God had dealt not unkindly with him.

Three days later the boy lay dead. A swelling had come around the place which the thorn had pricked, and the child had complained of pains in the hand and arm. His mother, thinking little of the matter in a country where rude health is the rule, had applied a poultice, but without producing relief. Towards the close of the second day it became apparent to her that the child ailed something beyond her knowledge or supposition, and she had hurried Abra'm off to the doctor, a matter of forty miles distant; but she was childless or ever she saw her husband's face again.

2

Abra'm had digged the tiny grave at the foot of a small hill at the back of the shanty, and now he stood leaning upon his spade and waiting for that which his wife had gone to bring. He looked neither to the right nor to the left; but stood there a very effigy of stony grief, and in this wise he chanced not to see the figure of a little man in a rusty-black suit, who had come over the brow of the hill some five minutes earlier.

Presently Sus'n came out from the back of the shanty, and walked swiftly towards the grave. At the sight of that which she carried, the little man upon the hill stood up quickly and bared his head, bald and shiny, to the sun. The woman reached the grave, stood one instant irresolute, then stooped and laid the burden gently into the place prepared. Then, after one long look at the little shape, she went aside a few paces and turned her face away. At that, Abra'm bent and took a shovelful of earth, intending to fill in the grave; but in that moment the voice of the stranger came to him, and he looked up. The little bald-headed man had approached to within a few feet of the grave, and in one hand he carried his hat, while in the other he held a small, much-worn book.

"Nay, me friend," he said, speaking slowly, "gev not ther child's body ter ther arth wi'out commendin' ther sperret ter ther Almighty. Hev I permisshun ter read ther sarvice fer them as's dead in ther Lord?"

Abra'm looked at the little old stranger for a short space, and said no word; then he glanced over to where his wife stood, after which he nodded a dumb assent.

At that the old man kneeled down beside the grave, and, rustling over the leaves of his book, found the place. He began to read in a steady voice. At the first word, Abra'm uncovered, and stood there leaning upon his spade; but his wife ran forward and fell upon her knees near the old man.

And so for a solemn while no sound but the aged voice. Presently he stretched out his hand to the earth beside the grave, and, taking a few grains, loosed them upon the dead, commending the spirit of the child into the Everlasting Arms. And so, in a little, he had made an end.

When all was over, the old man spread out his hands above the tiny grave as though invoking a blessing. After a moment he spoke; but so low that they who were near scarce heard him:

"Leetle One," he said, in a half whisper, "mebbe ye'll meet wi' thet gell o' mine in yon valley o' ther lost childe'. Ye'll telt hur's I'm prayin' ter ther Father's 'E'll purmit thess ole sinner ter come nigh 'er agin."

And after that he knelt awhile, as though in prayer. In a little he got upon his feet, and, stretching out his hands, lifted the woman from her knees. Then, for the first time, she spoke:

"Reckon I'll never see 'im no mor'," she said, in a quiet, toneless voice, and without tears.

The old man looked into her face, and, having seen much sorrow, knew somewhat of that which she suffered. He took one of her cold hands between his old, withered ones, with a strange gesture of reverence.

"Hev no bitterness, Ma'am," he said. "I know ye lack ther pow'r jest now ter say: "Ther Lord gev, an' ther Lord 'ath teken away; blessed be ther Name o'ther Lord;" but I reckon 'E don't 'spect mor'n ye can gev. 'E's mighty tender wi' them's is stricken."

As he spoke, unconsciously he was stroking her hand, as though to comfort her. Yet the woman remained dry-eyed and set-featured; so that the old man, seeing her need of stirring, bade her "set" down while he told her a "bit o' a tale."

"Ye'll know," he began, when she was seated, " 's I unnerstan' hoo mighty sore ye feel, w'en I tell ye I lost a wee gell o'mine way back."

He stopped a moment, and the woman's eyes turned upon him with the first dawning of interest.

"I wus suthin' like yew," he continued. "I didn't seem able nohow ter get goin' agin in ther affairs o' thess 'arth. I cudn't eat, 'n I cudn't sleep. Then one night, 's I wus tryin' ter get a bit o' rest 'fore ther morn come in, I heerd a Voice sayin' in me ear 's 'twer:

" ''Cept ye become 's leetle childer, ye shall not enter inter ther Kingdom o' 'Eaven." But I hedn't got shet o' ther bitterness o' me grief, 'n I tarned a deaf ear. Then agin ther Voice kem, 'n agin I shet ther soul o' me ter et's callin'; but 'twer' no manner uv use; for it kem agin an' agin, 'n I grew tur'ble feared 'n humble.

" 'Lord,' I cried out, 'guess ther oldest o' us 's on'y childer in ther sight o' God.'

"But agin ther Voice kem, an' ther sperret thet wer in me quaked, 'n I set up in ther bed, cryin' upon ther Lord:

" 'Lord, shet me not oot o' ther Kingdom!' Fer I wus feared 's I mightn't get ter see ther wee gell 's 'ad gone on befor'. But agin kem ther Voice, an' ther sperret in me became broke, 'n I wus 's er lonesome child, 'n all ther bitterness wer gone from me. Then I said ther words thet had not passed me lips by reason o' ther bitterness o' me stubborn 'art:

" 'Ther Lord gev, an' ther Lord 'ath teken away; blessed be ther Name o' ther Lord.'

"An' ther Voice kem agin; but 'twer' softer like, 'n I no longer wus feared.

" 'Lo!' et said, 'thy 'art is become like unter ther 'art o' one o' ther leetle ones whose sperrets dew always behold ther face o' ther Father. Look now wi' ther eyes o' a child, 'n thou shalt behold ther

Place o' ther Leetle Ones—ther valley wher' maybe be found ther lost childer o' ther 'arth. Know thou thet ther leetle folk whom ther Lord teketh pass not inter ther Valley o' ther Shadder, but inter ther Valley o' Light."

"An' immediate I looked, an' saw right thro' ther logs o' ther back o' ther shanty. I cud see 's plain 's plain. I wus lookin' out onter a mighty wilderness o' country, 'n et seemed 's tho' ther sperret o' me went forrard a space inter ther night, an' then, mighty suddin et wer', I wus lookin' down inter a tur'ble big valley. 'Twer' all lit up 'n shinin'; tho' 'twer' midnight, 'n everywher' wer' mighty flowers 's seemed ter shine o' ther own accord, an thar wer' leetle brooks runnin' among 'em 'n singin' like canary birds, 'n grass 's fresh 's ther 'art o' a maid. An' ther valley wer' all shet in by mortial great cliffs 's seemed ter be made o' nothin' but mighty walls o' moonstone; fer they sent out light 's tho' moons wer' sleepin' ahind 'em.

"After awhile I tuk a look way up inter ther sky 'bove ther valley, an' 'twer' 's tho' I looked up a mighty great funnel—hunder 'n hunder o' miles o' night on each side o' et; but ther sky 'bove ther valley wer' most wonnerful o' all; fer thar wer' seven suns in et, 'n each one o' a diff'rent colour, an' soft tinted, like 's tho'a mist wer' round 'em.

"An' presently, I tarned an' looked agin inter ther valley; fer I hedn't seen ther half o'et, 'n now I made out sumthin' s' I'd missed befor'—a wee bit o' a child sleepin' under a great flower, 'n now I saw more—Eh! but I made out a mighty multitoode o' em. They 'adn't no wings, now I come ter think o 'et, an' no closes; but I guess closes wer'n't needed; fer 't must hev bin like a 'tarnal summer down thar; no I guess——"

The old man stopped a moment, as though to meditate upon this point. He was still stroking the woman's hand, and she, perhaps because of the magnetism of his sympathy, was crying silently.

In a moment he resumed:

"Et wer' jest after discoverin' ther childer 's I made out 's thar wer' no cliff ter ther end o' ther valley upon me left. Inste'd o' cliff, et seemed ter me 's a mighty wall o' shadder went acrost from one side ter ther other. I wus starin' an' wonderin', w'en a voice whispered low in me ear: 'Ther Valley o' ther Shadder o' Death,' 'n I knew 's I'd come ter ther valley o' ther lost childer—which wer' named ther Valley o' Light. Fer ther Valley o' ther Shadder, 'n ther Valley o' ther Lost Childer come end ter end.

"Fer a while I stared, 'n presently et seemed ter me 's I could see ther shadders o' grown men 'n wimmin within ther darkness o' ther Valley o' Death, an' they seemed ter be gropin' 'n gropin'; but down in ther Valley o' Light some o' ther childer hed waked, 'n wer' playin' 'bout, an' ther light o' ther seven suns covered 'em, 'n made 'em j'yful.

"Et wer' a bit later 's I saw a bit o' a gell sleepin' in ther shade o' a leetle tree all covered wi' flowers. Et seemed ter me 's she hed er look o' mine; but I cudn't be sure, cause 'er face wer' hid by a branch. Presently, 'owever, she roused up 'n started playin' round wi' some o' ther others, 'n I seed then 's 'twer' my gell right enuff, 'n I lifted up me voice 'n shouted; but 'twern't no good. Seemed 's ef thar wer' sumthin' thet come betwixt us, 'n I cudn't 'ear 'er, 'n she cudn't 'ear me. Guess I felt powerful like sheddin' tears!

"An' then, suddin, ther hull thing faded 'n wer' gone, an' I wer' thar alone in ther midst o' ther night. I felt purty 'mazed 'n sore, an' me 'art seemed like ter harden wi' ther grief o' ther thing, 'n then, 'fore I'd time ter make a fool o' meself, et seemed 's I 'eard ther Voice saying:

" 'Ef ye, bein' eevil, know how ter gev good gifts unter yer childer, how much more shall yer Father w'ich es in 'eaven gev good things ter them thet asks 'Im.'

"An' ther next moment I wus settin' up 'n me bed, 'n et wer' broad daylight."

"Must hev bin a dream," said Abra'm.

The old man shook his head, and in the succeeding silence the woman spoke:

"Hev ye seen et sence?"

"Nay, Ma'am," he replied; "but"—with a quiet, assuring nod—"I tuk ther hint 's ther Voice gev me, 'n I've bin askin' ther Father ever sence 's I might come acrost thet valley o' ther lost childer."

The woman stood up.

"Guess I'll pray thet way 's well," she said simply.

The old man nodded, and, turning, waved a shrivelled hand towards the West, where the sun was sinking.

"Thet minds one o' death," he said slowly; then, with sudden energy, "I tell ye thar's no sunset ever 'curs 's don't tell ye o' life hereafter. Yon blood-coloured sky es ter us ther banner o' night 'n Death; but 'tes ther unwrapping o' ther flag o' dawn 'n Life in some other part o' ther 'arth."

And with that he got him to his feet, his old face aglow with the dying light.

"Must be goin'," he said. And though they pressed him to remain the night, he refused all their entreaties.

"Nay," he said quietly. "Ther Voice hev called, 'n I must jest go."

He turned and took off his old hat to the woman. For a moment he stood thus, looking into her tear-stained face. Then, abruptly, he stretched out an arm and pointed to the vanishing day.

"Night 'n sorrow 'n death come upon ther 'arth; but in ther Valley o' ther Lost Childer es light 'n joy 'n life etarnal."

And the woman, weary with grief, looked back at him with very little hope in her eyes.

"Guess tho' we'm too old fer ther valley o' ther childer," she said slowly.

The old man caught her by the arm. His voice rang with conviction:

"'Cept ye become 's leetle childer, ye shall not enter inter ther Kingdom o' 'Eaven."

He shook her slightly, as though to impress some meaning upon her. A sudden light came into her dull eyes.

"Ye mean——" she cried out, and stopped, unable to formulate her thought.

"Aye," he said, in a loud, triumphant voice. "I guess we'm on'y childer 'n ther sight o' God. But we hev ter be mighty 'umble o' 'art 'fore 'E 'lows us in wi' ther leetle ones, mighty 'umble."

He moved from her and knelt by the grave.

"Lord," he muttered, "some o' us, thro' bitter stubbornness o' 'art, hev ter wander in ther Valley o' ther Shadder; but them as 's 'umble 'n childlike 'n faith find no shadder in ther valley; but light, 'n ther lost j'yfulness o' child'ood, w'ich es ther nat'ral state o' ther soul. I guess, Lord, 's Thou'lt shew thess woman all ther marcifulness o' Thy 'art, 'n bring 'er et last ter ther Valley o' ther Lost Childer. 'N while I'm et it, Lord, I puts up a word fer meself, 's Thou'lt bring thess ole sinner et last ter the same place."

Then, still kneeling, he cried out: "Hark!" And they all listened; but the farmer and his wife heard only a far distant moan, like the cry of the night wind rising.

The old man hasted to his feet.

"I must be goin'," he said. "Ther Voice 's callin'."

He placed his hat upon his head.

"Till we meet in ther valley 'o ther 'arth's lost childer," he cried, and went from them into the surrounding dusk.

3

Twenty years had added their count to Eternity, and Abra'm and his wife Sus'n had come upon old age. The years had dealt hardly with the twain of them, and disaster overshadowed them in the shape of foreclosure; for Abra'm had been unable to pay off the mortgage, and latterly the interest had fallen in arrears.

There came a bitter time of saving and scraping, and of low diet; but all to no purpose. The foreclosure was effected, and a certain morning ushered in the day when Abra'm and Sus'n were made homeless.

He found her, a little after dawn, kneeling before the ancient press. She had the lowest drawer open, and a little heap of clothing filled her lap. There was a tiny guernsey, a small shoe, a wee, wee pair of baby boy's trousers, and the knees were stained with clay. Then, with about it a most tearful air of manfulness, a "made" shirt, with "real" buttoning wristbands; but it was not at any of these that the woman looked. Her gaze, passing through half-shed tears, was fixed upon something which she held out at arm's length. It was a diminutive pair of braces, so terribly small, so unmistakably the pride of some manly minded baby-boy—and so little worn!

For the half of a minute Abra'm said no word. His face had grown very stern and rugged during the stress of those twenty years' fight with poverty; yet a certain steely look faded out of his eyes as he noted that which his wife held.

The woman had not seen him, nor heard his steps; so that, unconscious of his presence, she continued to hold up the little suspenders. The man caught the reflection of her face in a little tinsel-framed mirror opposite, and saw her tears, and abruptly his hard features gave a quiver that made them almost grotesque: it was such an upheaval of *set* grimness. The quivering died away, and his face resumed its old, iron look. Probably it would have retained it, had not the woman, with a sudden, extraordinary gesture of hopelessness, crumpled up the tiny braces and clasped them in her hands above her hair. She bowed forward almost on to her face, and her old knuckles grew tense with the stress she put upon that which she held. A few seconds of silence came and went; then a sob burst from her, and she commenced to rock to and fro upon her knees.

Across the man's face there came again that quivering upheaval, as unaccustomed emotions betrayed their existence; he stretched forth a hand, that shook with half-conscious longing, towards an end of the braces which hung down behind the woman's neck and swayed as she rocked.

Abruptly, he seemed to come into possession of himself and drew back silently. He calmed his face and, making a noise with his feet, stepped over to where his wife kneeled desolate. He put a great, crinkled hand upon her shoulder.

"Et wer' a powerful purty thought o' yon valley o' ther lost childer," he said quietly, meaning to waken her memory to it.

"Aye! Aye!" she gasped between her sobs. "But——" and she broke off, holding out to him the little suspenders.

For answer the man patted her heavily on the shoulder, and thus a space of time went by until presently she calmed.

A little later he went out upon a matter to which he had to attend. While he was gone she gathered the wee garments hastily into a shawl, and when he returned the press was closed, and all that he saw was a small bundle which she held jealously in one hand.

They left shortly before noon, having singly and together visited a little mound at the foot of the hill. The evening saw them upon the verge of a great wood. They slept that night upon its outskirts, and the next day entered into its shades.

Through all that day they walked steadily. They had many a mile to go before they reached their destination—the shanty of a distant relative with whom they hoped to find temporary shelter.

Twice as they went forward Sus'n had spoken to her husband to stop and listen; but he declared he heard nothing.

"Kind o' singin' et sounded like," she explained.

That night they camped within the heart of the wood, and Abra'm made a great fire, partly for warmth, but more to scare away any evil thing which might be lurking amid the shadows.

They made a frugal supper off the poor things which they had brought with them, though Sus'n declared she had no mind for eating, and, indeed, she seemed woefully tired and worn.

Then it was just as she was about to lie down for the night, she cried out to Abra'm to hark.

"Singin'," she declared. "Milluns o' childer's voices."

Yet still her husband heard nothing beyond the whispering of the trees one to another, as the night wind shook them.

For the better part of an hour after that she listened; but heard no further sounds, and so, her weariness returning upon her, she fell asleep; the which Abra'm had done a while since.

Some time later she woke with a start. She sat up and looked about her, with a feeling that there had been a sound where now all was silent. She noticed that the fire had burned down to a dull mound of glowing red. Then, in the following instant, there came to her once more a sound of children singing—the voices of a nation of little ones. She turned and looked to her left, and became aware that all the wood on that side was full of a gentle light. She rose and went forward a few steps, and as she went the singing grew louder and sweeter. Abruptly, she came to a pause; for there right beneath her was a vast valley. She knew it on the instant. It was the Valley of the Lost Children. Unlike the old man, she noted less of its beauties than the fact that she looked upon the most enormous concourse of Little Ones that can be conceived.

"My b'y! My b'y!" she murmured to herself, and her gaze ran hungrily over that inconceivable army.

"Ef on'y I cud get down," she cried, and in the same instant it seemed to her that the side upon which she stood was less steep. She stepped forward and commenced to clamber down. Presently she walked. She had gotten half-way to the bottom of the valley when a little naked boy ran from out of the shadow of a bush just ahead of her.

"Possy," she cried out. "Possy."

He turned and raced towards her, laughing gleefully. He leapt into her arms, and so a little while of extraordinary contentment passed.

Presently, she loosed him, and bade him stand back from her.

"Eh!" she said, "yew've not growed one bit!"

She laid her bundle on the ground, and commenced to undo it.

"Guess they'll fet ye same 's ever," she murmured, and held up the little trousers for him to see; but the boy showed no eagerness to take them.

She put out her hand to him, but he ran from her. Then she ran after him, carrying the little trousers with her. Yet she could not catch him, for he eluded her with an elf-like agility and ease.

"No, no, no," he screamed out in a very passion of glee.

She ceased to chase him, and came to a stand, hands upon her hips.

"Come yew 'ere, Possy, immediate!" she called in a tone of command. "Come yew 'ere!"

But the baby elf was in a strange mood, and disobeyed her in a manner which made her rejoice that she was his mother.

"Oo tarnt ketch me," he cried, and at that she dropped the little knickers and went a-chase of him. He raced down the remaining half of the slope into the valley, and she followed, and so came to a country where there are no trousers—where youth is, and age is not.

4

When Abra'm waked in the early morn he was chill and stiff; for during the night he had taken off his jacket and spread it over the form of his sleeping wife.

He rose with quietness, being minded to let her sleep until he had got the fire going again. Presently he had a pannikin of steaming tea ready for her, and he went across to wake her; but she waked not, being at that time chased by a chubby baby-boy in the Valley of Lost Children.

FERGUS HUME
The Sand-Walker

Before Sherlock Holmes achieved immortality in the pages of the Strand *magazine, the bestselling detective story of the period was* The Mystery of a Hansom Cab *(1886), with estimated sales in excess of half a million copies. Its author* Fergus Hume *(1859–1932) never duplicated this success, but went on to write over a hundred further mystery and detective novels, and several excellent ghost stories which have rarely been reprinted.*

I make no endeavour to explain this experience. Explanation of it is impossible. I can conceive no theory upon which to base even the most slender attempt. It baffles me, it has always baffled me and it will continue to baffle me. Yet the impress of the thing loses nothing of its vividness with time. It is as clear before me now, as it was within a few hours of its event. I believe I heard a ghost knocking; I am certain I saw a ghost moving. "Indigestion, fancy, an overwrought and distorted brain," you will say, no doubt.

I wish I could think it was. But it wasn't. The sequel to that glimpse of the dead was too terrible, the cause too pertinent to the effect, to permit for one moment of any attribution to disorder, mental or alimentary. No—What I saw was actual self-existent. I will set down the facts for you as they occurred, and you shall explain them away—if you can. Then, if you remain unconvinced—go to Gartholm, by the German Ocean, and hear what the folk there have to say. They are a stodgy people, incapable utterly of the most insignificant hyperbole. They will tell you this tale plainly as I tell it to you. They believe as I believe.

It was in the summer of '96. I was travelling in "woollens" for the great Huddersfield firm of Carbury and Crank. Furnished with a gig and a fast-trotting mare, it was my duty to exploit the more scattered parts of the country, where the railroad was still unknown and civilisation, as we use the term, tarried a while.

Gartholm is the name given to a certain wide, low-lying plain, shut in from the North Sea by mile upon mile of sandhills. They are heaped up like hummocks along the coast. It was along a kind of causeway running straight through many miles of grain that I drove that hot July. I had never been in these parts, and I rejoiced at such ample evidence of fertility. It argued prosperity for those around; hence good business for myself and my employers. I made up my mind to remain there for at least a month. I left in less than half that time.

As if the plain itself were not sufficiently damp and low-lying, the village of Gartholm had been built in a kind of central depression, immediately beside the river. In other respects it differed but slightly from the ordinary English village, save that there was no inn. Close by the tower of the rubble-built church there was a pot-house, licensed for the sale of liquor "to be drunk on the premises," but I failed there to get sleeping room either for myself or Tilly, my weary mare.

Darkness was close upon us and I was worn out with my day's drive. There seemed little prospect of comfort, even had I gained admittance to this miserable hovel. But that was denied me. The landlord, a bulky monumental lump of indolence, stood in the doorway and effectually blocked all entrance. A dozen or so of idlers collected to admire Tilly and amuse themselves at my expense. And I realised that there were worse fates than that of being cast upon an uninhabited island, even in this England of ours at the close of the nineteenth century.

While I was in this plight, arguing with the landlord and endeavouring to arrive approximately at the sense of his dialect, a being, human by contrast to those around, made his appearance from out of the crowd, and approached my gig. He turned out to be the village schoolmaster, and those around called him "Muster Abram."

"You are looking for a lodging?" he said, in a smooth and (by comparison) strangely civilised voice.

"I am," I replied, soothing Tilly, who, small blame to her, in no wise appreciated her immediate surroundings. I'm Dick Trossall, C.T. to Carbury and Crank, if you've ever heard of 'em in this forsaken hole."

"C.T.?" repeated Master Abraham interrogatively, cocking his one eye (he had lost the other) which was as bright as any robin's.

"Commercial Traveller," said I in explanation; "or bagman if you like it better. You don't comprehend Queen's English I see in these parts."

"Hardly; when so abbreviated. But if it really be board and lodging you seek, you can get that only from Mrs. Jarzil at the Beach Farm."

There was a murmur from those at hand, as he said the name, and, I thought, a somewhat dubious expression upon the faces of one or two. I did not on the whole, feel drawn towards Mrs. Jarzil and her farm, and I looked at the schoolmaster enquiringly. Utterly ignoring this, and vouchsafing me no reply, he proceeded straightway to climb into my gig, without so much as "by your leave." There was neither modesty nor undue hesitancy about Master Abraham.

"We will get on, then to Mrs. Jarzil's farm," said I. A touch from the whip and Tilly was off at a good spanking trot in the direction Master Abraham had indicated. In a few moments we were out of sight of the hangers-on and driving through the street—into another causeway similar to the first. In the distance we could see the house lying under the lee of the sandhills. A dismal sort of place it seemed, and wholly solitary.

"Yes, yonder is the Beach Farm," said the schoolmaster, "and Mrs. Jarzil—" He stopped suddenly, so that I turned to look at him.

"What on earth is the matter with Mrs. Jarzil?"

"Nothing, nothing—I was merely wondering, not so much if she could, as whether she would, accommodate you. You see Mrs. Jarzil had some trouble with her last lodger. He was a botanist. He called himself Amber—Samuel Amber. Some two years ago it was; he boarded at the Beach Farm, then suddenly he disappeared."

"Disappeared? Good Lord! what do you mean?"

"Exactly what I say. He walked out of yonder house one night, and never returned."

We were close to the house now. It loomed up suddenly in the mist, which lay thick and heavy over the sandhills. I felt horribly depressed. Apart from the intense gloominess of the surroundings, the damp and darkness and desolation, all of which had perhaps more than their due effect upon my jaded nerves, I was conscious of an indefinite sense of uneasiness. This one-eyed creature at my elbow made me decidedly uncomfortable. I have not a robust nervous system at the best of times, and he with his sinister innuendoes was fast gaining a hold upon me.

"There was a daughter, you see," he went on, before I could speak.

"Oh, there was a daughter, was there?" I repeated, somewhat relieved. It might be, after all, that he was nothing more than a mere scandal-monger. I fervently hoped so.

"Yes; and Mr. Amber made love to her—at least so it is supposed. At all events she disappeared, too."

"At the same time as the man?"

"Lottie was her name," continued Master Abraham, utterly heedless of my query, "and a pretty pink and white creature she was, with the loveliest golden hair. I used to call her Venus of the Fen. She was at the Farm when Amber first arrived. After a while he left, and she with him. He did not return for a twelvemonth, and then only to—to disappear."

"What on earth are you telling me all this rigmarole for? I don't care twopence for any of your Ambers and Lotties or Venuses either, for that matter. If the girl was as pretty as you say, I don't blame the man for going off with her. I presume she was a willing party to the arrangement."

"Mrs. Jarzil will have it that Amber forced her daughter to elope with him. You see he returned a year later—alone."

"Well, what explanation did he make?"

"None—none whatever."

"And what did the lady have to say to that?"

"Nothing. Amber took up his residence at the Farm as before, and remained there until—until he disappeared."

Upon my soul I was beginning to feel thoroughly scared.

"Do you mean to tell me that Mrs. Jarzil got rid of him by foul play?"

"Oh, dear me, no; nothing of the kind. Mrs. Jarzil is a most religious woman."

"Then what the—; perhaps you will kindly make yourself clear. For what reason do you retail to me this parcel of rubbish?"

"Only this——" He laid his skinny hand upon my arm. We were turning into the drive which led up to the house. He pointed with the other hand towards the sand-ridge.

"Only what?"

The man nodded. Then he whispered to me. "The Sand-Walker, you know."

An elderly woman had come to the door and was standing there. The chief thing I noticed about her was her determinedly masculine appearance. For the rest she was a veritable study in half tone. Her hair, her dress, her complexion, in fact everything about her, was of various shades of grey. Her mouth denoted a vile if not a violent temper.

My reception was anything but cordial; in fact at the outset she refused altogether to take me in, but under the persuasive eloquence of Master Abraham she relented so far as to agree to board me by the week at what to me seemed an exorbitant charge. She was evidently grasping as well as religious—a highly unpleasant combination I thought. But in the circumstances I had no option but to accept the inevitable. It was a case of any port in a storm.

As I proceeded to drive round to the stable to put up Tilly—a thing which I invariably attended to myself—Master Abraham accompanied me. And somehow I was glad of even his company. There was not a living soul about. I asked him why this was.

"Mrs. Jarzil keeps no servants," he replied. "She has not kept any since Lottie and Mr. Amber went away; or rather, to be precise, since Mr. Amber disappeared."

"How is that?"

"She can get none to come here—or to remain if they do come. They are afraid of the Sand-Walker."

I asked him point blank what he meant. But I could get nothing out of him.

"Whatever you do, don't go on to the beaches at dusk," was all he said. Then he vanished. I say vanished advisedly, for though I ran after him to the door for the moment I could see no sign of him; I rushed on round the corner of the house, and came plump on to Mrs. Jarzil.

"Master Abraham!" I gasped.

Then Mrs. Jarzil pointed down the road, and I saw a flying figure disappearing into the darkness.

"Why does he run off like that?" I asked. I began to think I was losing my senses.

"Everyone runs from Beach Farm," replied the woman in the coolest manner possible, and with that she left me staring in amazement.

I don't think anyone could dub me a coward, but this place unnerved me. Both within and without the house all was mysterious, weird, and uncanny. My spirits sank to zero and my nerves were strung up to a tension positively unendurable. Even the bright light from the kitchen fire filled me with apprehension. I could not touch food or drink.

Mrs. Jarzil, gliding about the room, in no wise reassured me. Masculine and ponderous as she was, the deftness and stealthiness of her movements were uncomfortably incongruous. She spoke not a word. She totally ignored my presence. I began to loathe the woman. But I determined that anything was better than the horrible suspense I was enduring. So I went straight for the thing which was making havoc of me.

"What is the Sand-Walker, Mrs. Jarzil?"

At the moment she was polishing a dish cover. As I spoke it crashed on the floor. I never saw a woman turn quite so pale as she did then.

"Who has been talking to you about the Sand-Walker?"

"Master Abraham," was my answer. By this time she was visibly shaking.

"Fool!" she exclaimed. "A triple fool, and dangerous, too. See here, you Mr. Trossall. I am willing to board you, but not to answer your silly questions. And if you don't like my house and my ways, you can leave them both. I can do without you. God knows I have had enough of boarders."

Though it was rash, and for all I knew dangerous, willy-nilly the name Amber slipped my tongue. But she had regained her self-possession now, and laughed contemptuously as she picked up the dish cover.

"I see Abraham's been telling you my story. It is not a very pretty story, is it? Yes, Mr. Amber was a scoundrel. He carried off my daughter Lottie to London. Ay, and he had the boldness, too, to return here after his wickedness. I said nothing. It was my duty to forgive him, like a Christian, and I did. Although a mother, I am a Christian first. Poor Lottie! Poor child! I wonder where she is now."

"Do you know where Mr. Amber is?"

"Yes, Abraham told you no doubt that he disappeared. One would think he had been caught up into the moon; the way the fools round here talk. Yet the explanation is perfectly simple. The man was accustomed to walk on the Beaches at night. There are quicksands there, and he fell into one."

"How do you know that?"

"I found his hat by one of the worst of them. He had sunk. I am glad he did. He ruined my life and Lottie's. But 'Vengeance is Mine; I will repay saith the Lord.' "

"And this Sand-Walker; who, what is it?"

"That does not concern you. I have told you enough. I am not going to answer all your silly questions," she reiterated.

Not another word would she say. Still I felt somewhat relieved. Abraham had contrived to surround with an atmosphere of mystery what after all was purely an accident. I saw that now; and I was able to go to bed in a much more tranquil state of mind than I would otherwise have done.

My room was just off the kitchen. I hadn't been in it more than half an hour when I heard Mrs. Jarzil at her devotional exercises. I could hear her reading aloud certain Biblical extracts of a uniformly comminatory character. Her voice was peculiarly resonant and booming. Her choice seemed to me to range from Deuteronomy to Ezekiel and back again. "And Thine eye shall not pity; but life shall go for life, eye for eye, tooth for tooth, hand for hand, foot for foot."

"And the earth opened her mouth and swallowed them up; they and all that appertained to them went down alive into the pit, and the earth closed upon them."

"The wicked are overthrown and are not."

So for half an hour or more she went on, until I was in a cold perspiration. Then she knelt down and prayed, I was in hopes she had unbosomed herself for the night at all events. But then followed such a prayer as I have never heard. The ban of Jeremiah was a blessing to it. She cursed Amber, dead though he was. She cursed her daughter and called down upon her unfortunate head such visitations that I confess I shuddered. The woman was raving; yet all the time I could hear her sobbing, sobbing bitterly. The whole thing was ghastly, revolting. I would have given anything to get away.

At last she ceased, and, I presume, went to bed; though how she could sleep after such an indulgence was a marvel to me. But perhaps now that she had so assuaged her wrath, exhaustion if not relief would follow. I hoped so. At all events she was quiet. After a while I got up, to make sure that my door was securely fastened. Then I scrambled back to bed, and fell into an uneasy fitful doze. So I got through the long night. I never once slept soundly, and when I awoke in the morning I felt but little refreshed.

With the light came the sense of shame. I was inclined to deal severely with myself for my—as they now appeared to me—absurd apprehensions of the previous night. I made up my mind then and there that I should be a downright coward if I carried out my determination to leave the place. My room was comfortable, and the food was good. And I rated myself roundly for being such an impressionable booby. Besides, I knew enough to make me curious to know more.

Albeit as silent as ever, I found Mrs. Jarzil civil and composed enough at breakfast. So although I had not succeeded in getting rid wholly of my aversion to the place, I started off in quest of business, saying that I would return about five o'clock.

I soon found out that so far as business went, at all events, I had fallen on my feet. The very excellent woollen goods of Messrs. Carbury and Crank appealed to these fen dwellers. They were a rheumatic lot. But that was more the fault of the locality than of themselves. At any rate the local dealers seized upon my samples with avidity, and I booked more orders in the day than I was accustomed to do in a week in some places. I returned therefore that evening to the Beach Farm in the best of spirits, but at the gate I encountered Master Abraham. He soon reduced them to a normal level.

"Well, how did you sleep?" he said, I thought with a twinkle in his eye.

"Like a top, of course; I always do."

"You heard nothing at your window?"

"Of course not. What should I hear?"

"Then you didn't go on to the Beaches?"

"Certainly not. I was only too glad to get to bed. Besides, were you not at particular pains to advise me against going there?"

"Yes, perhaps I was; and I repeat my advice. If you do, it will come to you at the window."

"What in heaven's name do you mean, man?"

"I mean the Sand-Walker."

At that moment Tilly made a bound forward—she hates standing—and there was nothing for it but to let her go. The schoolmaster took himself off, and I drove up to the door.

But I silently swore at that skinny Abraham for bringing back to me the uneasy feelings of the previous night. His warning still rang in my ears. I could not get rid of it. I was determined I would not pass the night in ignorance. I resolved to take the bull by the horns and face whatever there was to face then and there.

After a "high tea" (that was between six and seven o'clock) I mentioned casually to Mrs. Jarzil that I was going for a stroll. She neither bade me go nor stay; so over the sandhills at the back of the house I scrambled until I found myself on the sea shore.

The beach was very dreary. All was still, save for the gentle swash of the wavelets breaking in upon the ribbed sand. There was but little wind To right and left of me there stretched an interminable vista of sand, vanishing only to blend itself in the distance with the heavy mists, which even at that season of the year hung around. The little land-locked pools were blood-red with reflection of the sun. Through the off-shore of the sea and sun were ablaze with crimson light. I felt an awful sense of desolation as I sat there in the dip of a sand-hill watching the departing sun ring its changes on the spectrum. The crimson merged to amethyst, the amethyst to pearl, until in sombre greyness the light shut down upon the lonely shore.

A mad purposeless impulse seized me. With a whoop I ran down the firm sand to the brink of the water. I stood there for some moments looking out to sea. When I turned, the mists were thick even between me and the sand-hills. Darkness came down fold over fold. Every moment the fog became more damp and clammy, the sense of desolation more intense. I was isolated from all that was human; from God for aught I knew.

Then I thought of the quicksands—of Mr. Amber—of Mr. Amber's hat found lying there; and I ran back, as I thought, to the sandhills. But I must have moved circuitously, for I could not reach even their friendly shelter. I lost my bearings hopelessly. Where the sea or where the hills I knew not. I rushed first this way, and then that, heedless and without design, intent only on escaping from the enshrouding mists, from the awesome desolation.

Suddenly the sands quaked under me. I stopped. The fate of Korah and his brethren flashed through my mind. My heart drummed loudly in the stillness. The mists grew thicker, the night darker. Then it was I saw It beside me.

At first I thought it was mortal—human—for its shape was that of a man. With an exclamation of thankfulness I endeavoured to approach it. But try as I might, I could not get near it. It did not walk, it did not glide, it did not fly. It simply melted in the mist, yet always visible, always retreating. That was the horror of the Thing.

My flesh creeped. I felt an icy cold through every pore of my skin. With awful insistence it was borne in upon me I was in the presence of the dead. Yet I was powerless. I could utter no cry. I could not even stop myself. On, on I went following that melting receding thing, until suddenly my foot stumbled on a sand-hill. Then It became mist with the mist, and I saw It no more. I scrambled up the hill and wept like a child.

How I reached the Beach Farm I cannot tell. I stumbled, blind with terror into the lamplight of the kitchen. I almost fell into Mrs. Jarzil's arms. She uttered no word of surprise, but sat there staring at my terror-stricken face and quivering limbs, silent and unsympathetic. At last she spoke.

"You have seen the Sand-Walker?"

"In God's name what is it?"

"God has nothing to do with the Sand-Walker," she replied. "It is wholly of hell."

I could speak no more that night. By help of some raw spirit I managed to pull myself together sufficiently to scramble into bed. The very sheets were a comfort to me; at all events they were between me and It.

I was utterly exhausted, and for a few hours I slept. I awoke suddenly with every nerve on the stretch, every sense acute almost beyond bearing. Mrs. Jarzil was vociferating in the kitchen, and sobbing between whiles. Then, as surely as I am a man and a Christian, I heard three loud knocks upon the window-pane. Mrs. Jarzil turned her imprecations into prayer. In her deep voice she boomed out verses from the Psalms: "Hear my cry, O God; attend unto my prayer."

I could stand it no longer. I flung myself out of bed, wrapped the coverlet around me, and rushed into the kitchen. Mrs. Jarzil was kneeling. Her face poured with perspiration. She paused as I appeared. There were three loud knocks at the door.

"What—O God, what is it?" I cried.

"The Sand-Walker."

Then she prayed again: "I will abide in Thy tabernacle for ever. I will trust in the cover of Thy wings."

I made for the door, but Mrs. Jarzil seized me by the arm.

"Don't let him in, don't let him in. He wants me. It is Amber, I tell you. It is Amber."

"Amber! The Sand-Walker!"

"Yes, yes. He is the Sand-Walker. He wants me—down on the Beaches. If you open the door I am bound to go. He draws me; he compels me. But the Lord is my strength, and shall prevail against the powers of hell."

I had to prevent her from unbarring the door. She flung herself upon it and fumbled with the lock in frenzy. I dragged her back fearful lest she should admit the thing outside. Gradually she grew more calm, until at last she stood before me with a composure almost as terrible to behold as had been her frenzy.

"I have resisted the Devil, and he is fled!" she said. "You can go to bed now, Mr. Trossall. You will be disturbed no more. There will be no more knocking, no—more—knocking." She caught up the candle to go. I detained her till I took a light from it. Then I went to bed. I kept the light burning all night, but there was no more knocking.

Next morning not a word passed between us about what had occurred. I ate my breakfast and drove off to my business. In the main street I met Abraham. I hailed him.

"Is there no other place where I can find a lodging?" I asked him.

"Ah! so you have been on the Beaches?"

"Yes. I was there yesterday evening."

"You have seen the Sand-Walker?"

"For God's sake don't speak of it," I said. For it terrified me even in the open day—here with the sunshine hot upon me.

"And you have heard the knocking?"

"Yes, I have heard everything—seen everything; let that suffice. Can I find another lodging, I ask you?"

"No; there is none other in the district. But why need you fear? It is she—not you, the Sand-Walker wants, ay, and he'll get her one night."

"You know this Sand-Walker, as you call him, is Amber."

"All Gartholm knows that. He has been walking for a year past now on the Beaches. No one would go there now for any money you could offer them—at least not after sun-down. I warned you, you remember."

"I know you did. But nevertheless I went, you see. And this Sand-Walker saved my life. For he led me back to the sand hills when I had lost myself hopelessly in the fog."

"It's not you he wants, I tell you, it's she."

"Why does he want her?" I asked.

The man's tone was very strange.

"Ask of the quicksands!" he replied; and with that disappeared in a hurry. I was getting quite accustomed to this, and would have been surprised had he taken his leave in anything approaching a rational manner.

Now, you may perhaps hardly credit it, but I tossed a shilling then and there to decide my action in the immediate future. "Heads I go, tails I stay."

The coin spun up in the sunlight. Tails it was. So I was to remain, and in that devil-haunted house. Well, at all events I was doing a brisk trade. There was some comfort in that.

During the next ten days I drove for miles over the district, and did uncommonly well everywhere. I found that the legend of the Beach Farm was universally familiar, and they all shook their heads very gravely indeed when they learned that I lodged there. In fact, I am not at all sure that this was not of assistance to me rather than otherwise. I became an object of intense interest, and, no doubt, of sympathy had I known it.

After that terrible night, there was a lull in the torment of the Sand-Walker. Occasionally it rapped at the door or the window, but that was all. As for me I walked no more on the Beaches.

But the time was near at hand when the Devil would have his own. It came one evening about six o'clock. There had been heavy rain, and the marshy lands were flooded and the mists were thick around. Overhead all was opaque and grey, and the ground was sodden under foot. I was anxious to get home, and Tilly was doing all she knew.

"On arrival I looked after her as was my wont, first and foremost. When I had made her comfortable for the night I returned to the kitchen. To my surprise I found Mrs. Jarzil in conversation with a girl, in whom from Abraham's description, meagre though it had been, I had no difficulty in recognising his Venus of the Fen. She was certainly pretty. I agreed with Abraham there. She was crying bitterly, whilst her mother raged at her. They both stopped short as I entered—a sense of delicacy, no doubt.

"Whatever is the matter?" I asked, surveying the pair of them.

"Oh, sir, you are mother's new lodger, aren't you?" said the girl. "Master Abraham told me as she had one. Do please ask her to hear reason, do, I implore you, sir."

"I will allow no one to interfere with my private affairs," said Mrs. Jarzil, stamping her foot. "If you are wise you will not seek to make public your disgrace."

"There is no disgrace. I have done nothing to be ashamed of, I tell you."

"No disgrace? No disgrace in allowing yourself to be beguiled by that man—to be fooled by his good looks and soft speeches?"

"What do you mean, mother? I have nothing to do with Mr. Amber."

"Liar, you ran away with him. What more could you have to do with him, I should like to know?"

Lottie's spirit rose, and with it the colour to her cheeks. "I ran away with him? Indeed I did nothing of the kind. It was you who made me run away. You treated me so cruelly that I determined to go into service in London. I was sick to death of your scolding, and your preaching and praying, and this dismal house, and these horrible mists, and never a soul to speak to, sick to death of it I tell you. That's why I went. Mr. Amber indeed!" (this with a toss of her head). "I have more taste than to take up with the likes of him. I met him as he was leaving here. I was walking, and he offered me a lift——"

"Abr'am saw you; Abr'am saw you both!" interrupted her mother savagly. "He told me you had eloped with the man."

"That was a lie. I parted from Mr. Amber at the London railway station. From that time to this I have never set eyes upon him. For my own sake I made him promise to hold his tongue."

"He did—he did!" cried Mrs. Jarzil, wildly. "God help him and me, he did. He returned here, but he said nothing—made no explanation. I believed he had ruined you. Now, oh now, I see it all. And you have ruined me."

"Oh, mother, what do you mean?"

"Why did you not let him speak? Oh, why did you not write and explain? I believed—I thought he had robbed me of you—and I revenged myself upon him.

"Revenged yourself?" I cried. I began to have an inkling of what was coming. But Mrs. Jarzil paid no heed to me. She shook Lottie furiously."

"Do you know what your silence has cost me?" (She was beside herself now). "It has cost me my soul—my soul, I say. Oh, why did you let me believe him guilty? I killed him. I murdered him for your sake. It was not vengeance, it was not justice, it was crime—crime and evil."

"You—killed—Mr. Amber?"

"Yes; I killed him. I swore he should pay for what he had done. His own curiosity did for him. I played upon it. I lured him to the quicksands."

"The quicksands?" I repeated, horrified.

"I placed a lantern on the brink of the most dangerous of them," the woman continued, feverishly. "He used habitually to walk on the Beaches at dark. His curiosity did the rest. He had to see what that light was. I knew he would. It was the last light he ever saw in this world. Yes, you call it murder. It was murder. But it was your fault—your fault. And now he walks, and taps at the door for me. He wants me; he wants me. I thought I had justice on my side—that I was avenging your disgrace; and I fought with my soul; oh, how I fought! But now—I see he is right. It is I who must now be punished. I must go. I must go. Oh, God be merciful to me, a sinner."

Lottie lay stretched on the floor. She had fainted. I placed myself between her mother and the door. I dared not let her out.

"Where would you go?" I cried, seizing her by the arm and frustrating a desperate effort to get away. She was fairly demented, and seemed possessed of strength almost demoniacal.

"To the Beaches—to my death. Let me go—let me go. An eye for an eye, I say—a tooth for a tooth. That is the law of God. Hark! Listen! He calls—he calls me." (I could hear nothing but the howling of the wind.) "I must go, I must go, I must——"

She was too quick for me. Before I had time to stop her she was away into the desolate night. I rushed after her. In her present condition there was no knowing what she might do. Clearly her mind was unhinged. I could hardly see for the rain. It was nearly dark too. But on through the mire and the mist I went. I jostled up against a man. It was Abraham. I remembered it was he who had caused all this, and with the thought I lost control of myself. I gripped him by the throat.

"You dog—you liar! Lottie the girl has come back!"

"I—I—I know!" he gasped. "I was coming up to see her. Leave me alone. What do you mean by this?"

"You deserve it, and more, you villain. You know well the girl did not go with Amber. You lied to her mother; you made her think so. You were in love with her yourself. The man's death lies at your door more than at hers. She has gone to the Beaches—to her death, I tell you—unless she is stopped."

Then I realised that I was wasting time. I hastened on, regretting deeply that my feelings had so got the better of me just then.

It was blowing half a gale, though it was not till I had crossed the sandhills that I realised it. Then the full blast of the wind struck me. It was as much as I could do to keep my feet. I could not see the woman anywhere, though I peered into the gloom until my head swam. Not a sign of her or any living creature could I see. There was nothing but the roar of the wind and the sea, and the swish of the driving rain.

Then I thought I heard a cry—a faint cry. I ploughed my way down in the direction whence I fancied it came. I became aware that Abraham had followed me. He was close behind me. Together we groped blindly on.

"He'll get her this time!" shouted the man.

"Come on! Come on!" I roared at him. "Yonder she is."

"And yonder the Sand-Walker."

The wretch hung back. Then a gust of wind, more concentrated and more fierce than before, seemed to rend an opening in the fog. Two shadows could be seen fluttering along—one a man of unusual height, the other a woman, reeling and swaying. She followed the Thing. As we gazed, a light appeared in the distance, radiant as a star. Its brilliance grew, and spread far and wide through the fog. The tall figure moved up to and past the light—the other following, always following.

She staggered and flung up her arms, and a wild and despairing cry rang out above the elements. And the light gradually died away, and the wind howled on, driving the mists across the sinking figure.

Slowly she sank into the sand, deeper and deeper. One last terrible moan reached us where we were, then she disappeared. For the moment the storm seemed to hush. Then all was darkness.

HENRY JAMES
The Real Right Thing

Henry James *(1843–1916) declared, early in his career, that a good ghost-story must be connected at a hundred points with the common objects of life. He wrote over a dozen ghostly tales including the classics 'Owen Wingrave', and 'The Turn of the Screw' (1898). His next story, 'The Real Right Thing' (1899) was the first he produced after moving into Lamb House, Rye, later to be the home of another master of the genre, E.F. Benson.*

When, after the death of Ashton Doyne— but three months after—George Withermore was approached, as the phrase is, on the subject of a "volume", the communication came straight from his publishers, who had been, and indeed much more, Doyne's own; but he was not surprised to learn, on the occurrence of the interview they next suggested, that a certain pressure as to the early issue of a Life had been brought to bear upon them by their late client's widow. Doyne's relations with his wife had been, to Withermore's knowledge, a very special chapter—which would present itself, by the way, as a delicate one for the biographer; but a sense of what she had lost, and even of what she had lacked, had betrayed itself, on the poor woman's part, for the first days of her bereavement, sufficiently to prepare an observer at all initiated for some attitude of reparation, some espousal even exaggerated of the interests of a distinguished name. George Withermore was, as he felt, initiated; yet what he had not expected was to hear that she had mentioned him as the person in whose hands she would most promptly place the materials for a book.

These materials—diaries, letters, memoranda, notes, documents of many sorts—were her property, and wholly in her control, no conditions at all attaching to any portion of her heritage; so that she was free at present to do as she liked—free, in particular, to do nothing. What Doyne would have arranged had he had time to arrange could be but supposition and guess. Death had taken him too soon and too suddenly, and there was all the pity that the only wishes he was known to have expressed were wishes that put it positively out of account. He had broken short off—that was the way of it; and the end was ragged and needed trimming. Withermore was conscious, abundantly, how close he had stood to him, but he was not less aware of his comparative obscurity. He was young, a journalist, a critic, a hand-to-mouth character, with little, as yet, as was vulgarly said, to show. His writings were few and small, his relations scant and vague. Doyne, on the other hand, had lived long enough—above all had had talent enough—to become great, and among his many friends gilded also with greatness were several to whom his wife would have struck those who knew her as much more likely to appeal.

The preference she had, at all events, uttered—and uttered in a roundabout, considerate way that left him a measure of freedom—made our young man feel that he must at least see her and that there would be in any case a good deal to talk about. He immediately wrote to her, she as promptly named an hour, and they had it out. But he came away with his particular idea immensely strengthened. She was a strange woman, and he had never thought her an agreeable one; only there was something that touched him now in her bustling, blundering impatience. She wanted the book to make up, and the individual whom, of her husband's set, she probably believed she might most manipulate was in every way to help it to make up. She had not taken Doyne seriously enough in life, but the biography should be a solid reply to every imputation on herself. She had scantly known how such books were constructed, but she had been looking and had learned something. It alarmed Withermore a little from the first to see that she would wish to go in for quantity. She talked of "volumes"—but he had his notion of that.

"My thought went straight to *you*, as his own would have done," she had said almost as soon as she rose before him there in her large array of mourning—with her big black eyes, her big black wig, her big black fan and gloves, her general gaunt, ugly, tragic, but striking and, as might have been thought from a certain point of view, "elegant" presence. "You're the one he liked most; oh, *much*!"—and it had been quite enough to turn Withermore's head. It little mattered that he could afterward wonder if she had known Doyne enough, when it came to that, to be sure. He would have said for himself indeed that her testimony on such a point would scarcely have counted. Still, there was no smoke without fire; she knew at least what she meant, and he was not a person she could have an interest in flattering. They went up together, without delay, to the great man's vacant study, which was at the back of the house and looked over the large green garden—a beautiful and inspiring scene, to poor Withermore's view—common to the expensive row.

"You can perfectly work here, you know," said Mrs. Doyne; "you shall have the place quite to yourself—I'll give it all up to you; so that in the evenings, in particular, don't you see? for quiet and privacy, it will be perfection."

Perfection indeed, the young man felt as he looked about—having explained that, as his actual occupation was an evening paper and his earlier hours, for a long time yet, regularly taken up, he would have to come always at night. The place was full of their lost friend; everything in it had belonged to him; everything they touched had been part of his life. It was for the moment too much for Withermore—too great an honour and even too great a care; memories still recent came back to him, and, while his heart beat faster and his eyes filled with tears, the pressure of his loyalty seemed almost more than he could carry. At the sight of his tears Mrs. Doyne's own rose to her lids, and the two, for a minute, only looked at each other. He half expected her to break out: "Oh, help me to feel as I know you know I want to feel!" And after a little one of them said, with the other's deep assent—it didn't matter which: "It's here that we're *with* him." But it was definitely the young man who put it, before they left the room, that it was there he was with *them*.

The young man began to come as soon as he could arrange it, and then it was, on the spot, in the charmed stillness, between the lamp and the fire and with the curtains drawn, that a certain intenser consciousness crept over him. He turned in out of the black London November; he passed through the large, hushed house and up the red-carpeted staircase where he only found in his path the whisk of a soundless trained maid, or the reach, out of a doorway, of Mrs. Doyne's queenly weeds and approving tragic face; and then, by a mere touch of the well-made door that gave so sharp and pleasant a click, shut himself in for three or four warm hours with the spirit—as he had always distinctly declared it—of his master. He was not a little frightened when, even the first night, it came over him that he had really been most affected, in the whole matter, by the prospect, the privilege, and the luxury, of his sensation. He had not, he could now reflect, definitely considered the question of the book—as to which there was here, even already, much to consider: he had simply let his affection and admiration—to say nothing of his gratified pride—meet, to the full, the temptation Mrs. Doyne had offered them.

How did he know, without more thought, he might begin to ask himself, that the book was, on the whole, to be desired? What warrant had he ever received from Ashton Doyne himself for so direct and, as it were, so familiar an approach? Great was the art of biography, but there were lives and lives, there were subjects and subjects. He confusedly recalled, so far as that went, old words dropped by Doyne over contemporary compilations, suggestions of how he himself discriminated as to other heroes and other panoramas. He even remembered how his friend, at moments, would have seemed to show himself as holding that the "literary" career might—save in the case of a Johnson and a Scott, with a Boswell and a Lockhart to help—best content itself to be represented. The artist was what he *did*—he was nothing else. Yet how, on the other hand, was not *he*, George Withermore, poor devil, to have jumped at the chance of spending his winter in an intimacy so rich? It had been simply dazzling—that was the fact. It hadn't been the "terms," from the publishers—though these were, as they said at the office, all right; it had been Doyne himself, his company and contact and presence—it had been just what it was turning out, the possibility of an intercourse closer than that of life. Strange that death, of the two things, should have the fewer mysteries and secrets! The first night our young man was alone in the room it seemed to him that his master and he were really for the first time together.

2

Mrs Doyne had for the most part let him expressively alone, but she had on two or three occasions looked in to see if his needs had been met, and he had had the opportunity of thanking her on the spot for the judgment and zeal with which she had smoothed his way. She had to some extent herself been looking things over and had been able already to muster several groups of letters; all the keys of drawers and cabinets she had, moreover, from the first placed in his hands, with helpful information as to the apparent whereabouts of different matters. She had put him, in a word, in the fullest possible possession, and whether or no her husband had trusted her, she at least, it was clear, trusted her husband's friend. There grew upon Withermore, nevertheless, the impression that, in spite of all these offices, she was not yet at peace, and that a certain unappeasable anxiety continued even to keep step with her confidence. Though he was full of consideration, she was at the same time perceptibly *there*: he felt her, through a supersubtle sixth sense that the whole connection had already brought into play, hover, in the still hours, at the top of landings and on the other side of the doors, gathered from the soundless brush of her skirts the hint of her watchings and waitings. One evening when, at his friend's table, he had lost himself in the depths of correspondence, he was made to start and turn by the suggestion that some one was behind him. Mrs. Doyne had come in without his hearing the door, and she gave a strained smile as he sprang to his feet. "I hope," she said, "I haven't frightened you."

"Just a little—I was so absorbed. It was as if, for the instant," the young man explained, "it had been himself."

The oddity of her face increased in her wonder. "Ashton?"

"He does seem so near," said Withermore.

"To you too?"

This naturally struck him. "He does then to you?"

She hesitated, not moving from the spot where she had first stood, but looking round the room as if to penetrate its duskier angles. She had a way of raising to the level of her nose the big black fan which she apparently never laid aside and with which she thus covered the lower half of her face, her rather hard eyes, above it, becoming the more ambiguous. "Sometimes."

"Here," Withermore went on, "it's as if he might at any moment come in. That's why I jumped just now. The time is so short since he really used to—it only *was* yesterday. I sit in his chair, I turn his books, I use his pens, I stir his fire, exactly as if, learning he would presently be back from a walk, I had come up here contentedly to wait. It's delightful—but it's strange."

Mrs. Doyne, still with her fan, listened with interest. "Does it worry you?"

"No—I like it."

She hesitated again. "Do you ever feel as if he were—a—quite—a— personally in the room?"

"Well, as I said just now," her companion laughed, "on hearing you behind me I seemed to take it so. What do we want, after all," he asked, "but that he shall be with us?"

"Yes, as you said he would be—that first time." She stared in full assent. "He *is* with us."

She was rather portentous, but Withermore took it smiling. "Then we must keep him. We must do only what he would like."

"Oh, only that, of course—only. But if he *is* here——?" And her sombre eyes seemed to throw it out, in vague distress, over her fan.

"It shows that he's pleased and wants only to help? Yes, surely; it must show that."

She gave a light gasp and looked again round the room. "Well," she said as she took leave of him, "remember that I too want only to help." On which, when she had gone, he felt sufficiently—that she had come in simply to see he was all right.

He was all right more and more, it struck him after this, for as he began to get into his work he moved, as it appeared to him, but the closer to the idea of Doyne's personal presence. When once this fancy had begun to hang about him he welcomed it, persuaded it, encouraged it, quite cherished it, looking forward all day to feeling it renew itself in the evening, and waiting for the evening very much as one of a pair of lovers might wait for the hour of their appointment. The smallest accidents humoured and confirmed it, and by the end of three or four weeks he had come quite to regard it as the consecration of his enterprise. Wasn't it what settled the question of what Doyne would have thought of what they were doing? What they were doing was what he wanted done, and they could go on, from step to step, without scruple or doubt. Withermore rejoiced indeed at moments to feel this certitude: there were times of dipping deep into some of Doyne's secrets when it was particularly pleasant to be able to hold that Doyne desired him, as it were, to know them. He was learning many things that he has not suspected, drawing many curtains, forcing many doors, reading many riddles, going, in general, as they said, behind almost everything. It was an occasional sharp turn of some of the duskier of these wanderings "behind" that he really, of a sudden, most felt himself, in the intimate, sensible way, face to face with his friend; so that he could scarcely have told, for the instant, if their meeting occurred in the narrow passage and tight squeeze of the past, or at the hour and in the place that actually held him. Was it '67, or was it but the other side of the table?

Happily, at any rate, even in the vulgarest light publicity could ever shed, there would be the great fact of the way Doyne was "coming out." He was coming out too beautifully—better yet than such a partisan as Withermore could have supposed. Yet, all the while, as well, how would this partisan have represented to any one else the special state of his own consciousness? It wasn't a thing to talk about—it was only a thing to feel. There were moments, for instance, when, as he bent over his papers, the light breath of his dead host was as distinctly in his hair as his own elbows were on the table before him. There were moments when, had he been able to look up, the other side of the table would have shown him this companion as vividly as the shaded lamplight showed him his page. That he couldn't at such a juncture look up was his own affair, for the situation was ruled—that was but natural—by deep delicacies and fine timidities, the dread of too sudden or too rude an advance. What was intensely in the air was that if Doyne *was* there it was not nearly so much for himself as for the young priest of his altar. He hovered and lingered, he came and went, he might almost have been, among the books and the papers, a hushed, discreet librarian, doing the particular things, rendering the quiet aid, liked by men of letters.

Withermore himself, meanwhile, came and went, changed his place, wandered on quests either definite or vague; and more than once, when, taking a book down from a shelf and finding in it marks of Doyne's pencil, he got drawn on and lost, he had heard documents on the table behind him gently shifted and stirred, had literally, on his return, found some letter he had mislaid pushed again into view, some wilderness cleared by the opening of an old journal at the very date he wanted. How should he have gone so, on occasion, to the special box or drawer, out of fifty receptacles, that would help him, had not his mystic assistant happened, in fine prevision, to tilt its lid, or to pull it half open, in just the manner that would catch his eye?—in spite, after all, of the fact of lapses and intervals in which, *could* one have really looked, one would have seen somebody standing before the fire a trifle detached and over-erect—somebody fixing one the least bit harder than in life.

3

That this auspicious relation had in fact existed, had continued, for two or three weeks, was sufficiently proved by the dawn of the distress with which our young man found himself aware that he had, for some reason, from a certain evening, begun to miss it. The sign of that was an abrupt, surprised sense—on the occasion of his mislaying a marvellous unpublished page which, hunt where he would, remained stupidly, irrecoverably lost—that his protected state was, after all, exposed to some confusion and even to some depression. If, for the joy of the business, Doyne and he had, from the start, been together, the situation had, within a few days of his first new suspicion of it, suffered the odd change of their ceasing to be so. That was what was the matter, he said to himself, from the moment an impression of mere mass and quantity struck him as taking, in his happy outlook at his material, the place of his pleasant assumption of a clear course and a lively pace. For five nights he struggled; then never at his table, wandering about the room, taking up his references only to lay them down, looking out of the window, poking the fire, thinking strange thoughts, and listening for signs and sounds not as he suspected or imagined, but as he vainly desired and invoked them, he made up his mind that he was, for the time at least, forsaken.

The extraordinary thing thus became that it made him not only sad not to feel Doyne's presence, but in a high degree uneasy. It was stranger, somehow, that he shouldn't be there than it had ever been that he *was*—so strange, indeed, at last that Withermore's nerves found themselves quite inconsequently affected. They had taken kindly enough to what was of an order impossible to explain, perversely reserving their sharpest state for the return to the normal, the supersession of the false. They were remarkably beyond control when, finally, one night, after resisting an hour or two, he simply edged out of the room. It had only now, for the first time, become impossible to him to remain there. Without design, but panting a little and positively as a man scared, he passed along his usual corridor and reached the top of the staircase. From this point he saw Mrs. Doyne looking up at him from the bottom quite as if she had known he would come; and the most singular thing of all was that, though he had been conscious of no notion to resort to her, had only been prompted to relieve himself by escape, the sight of her position made him recognise it as just, quickly feel it as a part of some monstrous oppression that was closing over both of them. It was wonderful how, in the mere modern London hall, between the Tottenham Court Road rugs and the electric light, it came up to him from the tall black lady, and went again from him down to her, that he knew what she meant by looking as if he would know. He descended straight, she turned into her own little lower room, and there, the next thing, with the door shut, they were, still in silence and with queer faces, confronted over confessions that had taken sudden life from these two or three movements. Withermore gasped as it came to him why he had lost his friend. "He has been with *you*?"

With this it was all out—out so far that neither had to explain and that, when "What do you suppose is the matter?" quickly passed between them, one appeared to have said it as much as the other. Withermore looked about at the small, bright room in which, night after night, she had been living her life as he had been living his own upstairs. It was pretty, cosy, rosy; but she had by turns felt in it what he had felt and heard in it what he had heard. Her effect there—fantastic black, plumed and extravagant, upon deep pink—was that of some "decadent" coloured print, some poster of the newest school. "You understood he had left me?" he asked.

She markedly wished to make it clear. "This evening—yes. I've made things out."

"You knew—before—that he was with me?"

She hesitated again. "I felt he wasn't with *me*. But on the stairs——"

"Yes?"

"Well—he passed, more than once. He was in the house. And at your door——"

"Well?" he went on as she once more faltered.

"If I stopped I could sometimes tell. And from your face," she added, "to-night, at any rate, I knew your state."

"And that was why you came out?"

"I thought you'd come to me."

He put out to her, on this, his hand, and they thus, for a minute, in silence, held each other clasped. There was no peculiar presence for either, now—nothing more peculiar than that of each for the other. But the place had suddenly become as if consecrated, and Withermore turned over it again his anxiety. "What *is* then the matter?"

"I only want to do the real right thing," she replied after a moment.

"And are we not doing it?"

"I wonder. Are *you* not?"

He wondered too. "To the best of my belief. But we must think."

"We must think," she echoed. And they did think—thought, with intensity, the rest of that evening together, and thought, independently—Withermore at least could answer for himself—during many days that followed. He intermitted for a little his visits and his work, trying, in meditation, to catch himself in the act of some mistake that might have accounted for their disturbance. Had he taken, on some important point—or looked as if he might take—some wrong line or wrong view? had he somewhere benightedly falsified or inadequately insisted? He went back at last with the idea of having guessed two or three questions he might have been on the way to muddle; after which he had, above stairs, another period of agitation, presently followed by another interview, below, with Mrs. Doyne, who was still troubled and flushed.

"He's there?"

"He's there."

"I knew it!" she returned in an odd gloom of triumph. Then as to make it clear: "He has not been again with *me*."

"Nor with me again to help," said Withermore.

She considered. "Not to help?"

"I can't make it out—I'm at sea. Do what I will, I feel I'm wrong."

She covered him a moment with her pompous pain. "How do you feel it?"

"Why, by things that happen. The strangest things. I can't describe them—and you wouldn't believe them."

"Oh yes, I would!" Mrs. Doyne murmured

"Well, he intervenes." Withermore tried to explain. "However I turn, I find him."

She earnestly followed. " 'Find' him?"

"I meet him. He seems to rise there before me."

Mrs Doyne, staring, waited a little. "Do you mean you see him?"

"I feel as if at any moment I may. I'm baffled. I'm checked." Then he added: "I'm afraid."

"Of *him*?" asked Mrs. Doyne.

He thought. "Well—of what I'm doing."

"Then what, that's so awful, *are* you doing?"

"What you proposed to me. Going into his life."

She showed, in her gravity, now a new alarm. "And don't you *like* that?"

"Doesn't *he*? That's the question. We lay him bare. We serve him up. What is it called? We give him to the world."

Poor Mrs. Doyne, as if on a menace to her hard atonement, glared at this for an instant in deeper gloom. "And why shouldn't we?"

"Because we don't know. There are natures, there are lives, that shrink. He mayn't wish it," said Withermore. "We never asked him."

"How *could* we?"

He was silent a little. "Well, we ask him now. That's after all, what our start has, so far, represented. We've put it to him."

"Then—if he has been with us—we've had his answer."

Withermore spoke now as if he knew what to believe. "He hasn't been 'with' us—he has been against us."

"Then why did you think——"

"What I *did* think, at first—that what he wishes to make us feel is his sympathy? Because, in my original simplicity, I was mistaken. I was—I don't know what to call it—so excited and charmed that I didn't understand. But I understand at last. He only wanted to communicate. He strains forward out of his darkness; he reaches toward us out of his mystery; he makes us dim signs out of his horror."

" 'Horror'?" Mrs. Doyne gasped with her fan up to her mouth.

"At what we're doing." He could by this time piece it all together. "I see now that at first——"

"Well, what?"

"One had simply to feel he was there, and therefore not indifferent. And the beauty of that misled me. But he's there as a protest."

"Against *my* Life?" Mrs. Doyne wailed.

"Against *any* Life. He's there to *save* his Life. He's there to be let alone."

"So you give up?" she almost shrieked.

He could only meet her. "He's there as a warning."

For a moment, on this, they looked at each other deep. "You *are* afraid!" she at last brought out.

It affected him, but he insisted. "He's there as a curse!"

With that they parted, but only for two or three days; her last word to him continuing to sound so in his ears that, between his need really to satisfy her and another need presently to be noted, he felt that he might not yet take up his stake. He finally went back at his usual hour and found her in her usual place. "Yes, I *am* afraid," he announced as if he had turned that well over and knew now all it meant. "But I gather that you're not."

She faltered, reserving her word. "What is it you fear?"

"Well, that if I go on I *shall* see him."

"And then——?"

"Oh, then," said George Withermore, "I *should* give up!"

She weighed it with her lofty but earnest air. "I think, you know, we must have a clear sign."

"You wish me to try again?"

She hesitated. "You see what it means—for me—to give up."

"Ah, but *you* needn't," Withermore said.

She seemed to wonder, but in a moment she went on. "It would mean that he won't take from me——" But she dropped for despair.

"Well, what?"

"Anything," said poor Mrs. Doyne.

He faced her a moment more. "I've thought myself of the clear sign. I'll try again."

As he was leaving her, however, she remembered. "I'm only afraid that to-night there's nothing ready—no lamp and no fire."

"Never mind," he said from the foot of the stairs; "I'll find things."

To which she answered that the door of the room would probably, at any rate, be open; and retired again as if to wait for him. She had not long to wait; though, with her own door wide and her attention fixed, she may not have taken the time quite as it appeared to her visitor. She heard him, after an interval, on the stair, and he presently stood at her entrance, where, if he had not been precipitate, but rather, as to step and sound, backward and vague, he showed at least as livid and blank.

"I give up."

"Then you've seen him?"

"On the threshold—guarding it."

"Guarding it?" She glowed over her fan. "Distinct?"

"Immense. But dim. Dark. Dreadful," said poor George Withermore.

She continued to wonder. "You didn't go in?"

The young man turned away. "He forbids!"

"You say *I* needn't," she went on after a moment. "Well then, need I?"

"See him?" George Withermore asked.

She waited an instant. "Give up."

"You must decide." For himself he could at last but drop upon the sofa with his bent face in his hands. He was not quite to know afterwards how long he had sat so; it was enough that what he did next know was that he was alone among her favourite objects. Just as he gained his feet, however, with this sense and that of the door standing open to the hall, he found himself afresh confronted, in the light, the warmth, the rosy space, with her big black perfumed presence. He saw at a glance, as she offered him a huger, bleaker stare over the mask of her fan, that she had been above; and so it was that, for the last time, they faced together their strange question. "You've seen him?" Withermore asked.

He was to infer later on from the extraordinary way she closed her eyes, and, as if to steady herself, held them tight and long, in silence, that beside the unutterable vision of Ashton Doyne's wife his own might rank as an escape. He knew before she spoke that all was over. "I give up."

M.R. JAMES
The Haunted Dolls' House

Montague Rhodes James *(1862–1936), regarded by many contemporaries as the greatest scholar of his generation, succeeded— more than any other writer—in reviving and restyling the fine art of the ghost story at the turn of the century. His* Ghost Stories of an Antiquary *(1904) is the single most important book in the twentieth-century literature of the supernatural.*

"I suppose you get stuff of that kind through your hands pretty often?" said Mr. Dillet, as he pointed with his stick to an object which shall be described when the time comes: and when he said it, he lied in his throat, and knew that he lied. Not once in twenty years—perhaps not once in a lifetime—could Mr. Chittenden, skilled as he was in ferreting out the forgotten treasures of half a dozen counties, expect to handle such a specimen. It was collectors' palaver, and Mr. Chittenden recognized it as such.

"Stuff of that kind, Mr. Dillet! It's a museum piece, that is."

"Well, I suppose there are museums that'll take anything."

"I've seen one, not as good as that, years back," said Mr. Chittenden thoughtfully. "But that's not likely to come into the market: and I'm told they 'ave some fine ones of the period over the water. No: I'm only telling you the truth, Mr. Dillet, when I say that if you was to place an unlimited order with me for the very best that could be got—and you know I 'ave facilities for getting to know of such things, and a reputation to maintain—well, all I can say is, I should lead you straight up to that one and say, 'can't do no better for you than that, sir.' "

"Hear, hear!" said Mr. Dillet, applauding ironically with the end of his stick on the floor of the shop. "How much are you sticking the innocent American buyer for it, eh?"

"Oh, I shan't be over hard on the buyer, American or otherwise. You see, it stands this way, Mr. Dillet—if I knew just a bit more about the pedigree——"

"Or just a bit less," Mr. Dillet put in.

"Ha, ha! you will have your joke, sir. No, but as I was saying, if I knew just a little more than what I do about the piece—though anyone can see for themselves it's a genuine thing, every last corner of it, and there's not been one of my men allowed to so much as touch it since it came into the shop—there'd be another figure in the price I'm asking."

"And what's that: five and twenty?"

"Multiply that by three and you've got it, sir. Seventy-five's my price."

"And fifty's mine," said Mr. Dillet.

The point of agreement was, of course, somewhere between the two, it does not matter exactly where—I think sixty guineas. But half an hour later the object was being packed, and within an hour Mr. Dillet had called for it in his car and driven away. Mr. Chittenden, holding the cheque in his hand, saw him off from the door with smiles, and returned, still smiling, into the parlour where his wife was making the tea. He stopped at the door.

"It's gone," he said.

"Thank God for that!" said Mrs. Chittenden, putting down the teapot. "Mr. Dillet, was it?"

"Yes, it was."

"Well, I'd sooner it was him than another."

"Oh, I don't know; he ain't a bad feller, my dear."

"Maybe not, but in my opinion he'd be none the worse for a bit of a shake up."

"Well, if that's your opinion, it's my opinion he's put himself into the way of getting one. Anyhow, *we* shan't have no more of it, and that's something to be thankful for."

And so Mr. and Mrs. Chittenden sat down to tea.

And what of Mr. Dillet and of his new acquisition? What it was, the title of this story will have told you. What it was like, I shall have to indicate as well as I can.

There was only just room enough for it in the car, and Mr. Dillet had to sit with the driver: he had also to go slow, for though the rooms of the Dolls' House had all been stuffed carefully with soft cotton-wool, jolting was to be avoided, in view of the immense number of small objects which thronged them; and the ten-mile drive was an anxious time for him, in spite of all the precautions he insisted upon. At last his front door was reached, and Collins, the butler, came out.

"Look here, Collins, you must help me with this thing—it's a delicate job. We must get it out upright, see? It's full of little things that mustn't be displaced more than we can help. Let's see, where shall we have it? (After a pause for consideration.) Really, I think I shall have to put it in my own room, to begin with at any rate. On the big table—that's it."

It was conveyed—with much talking—to Mr. Dillet's spacious room on the first floor, looking out on the drive. The sheeting was unwound from it, and the front thrown open, and for the next hour or two Mr. Dillet was fully occupied in extracting the padding and setting in order the contents of the rooms.

When this thoroughly congenial task was finished, I must say that it would have been difficult to find a more perfect and attractive specimen of a Dolls' House in Strawberry Hill Gothic than that which now stood on Mr. Dillet's large kneehole table, lighted up by the evening sun which came slanting through three tall sash-windows.

It was quite six feet long, including the Chapel or Oratory which flanked the front on the left as you faced it, and the stable on the right. The main block of the house was, as I have said, in the Gothic manner: that is to say, the windows had pointed arches and were surmounted by what are called ogival hoods, with crockets and finials such as we see on the canopies of tombs built into church walls. At the angles were absurd turrets covered with arched panels. The Chapel had pinnacles and buttresses, and a bell in the turret and coloured glass in the windows. When the front of the house was open you saw four large rooms, bedroom, dining-room, drawing-room and kitchen, each with its appropriate furniture in a very complete state.

The stable on the right was in two storeys, with its proper complement of horses, coaches and grooms, and with its clock and Gothic cupola for the clock bell.

Pages, of course, might be written on the outfit of the mansion—how many frying-pans, how many gilt chairs, what pictures, carpets, chandeliers, four-posters, table linen, glass, crockery and plate it possessed; but all this must be left to the imagination. I will only say that the base or plinth on which the house stood (for it was fitted with one of some depth which allowed of a flight of steps to the front door and a terrace, partly balustraded) contained a shallow drawer or drawers in which were neatly stored sets of embroidered curtains, changes of raiment for the inmates, and, in short, all the materials for an infinite series of variations and refittings of the most absorbing and delightful kind.

"Quintessence of Horace Walpole, that's what it is: he must have had something to do with the making of it." Such was Mr. Dillet's murmured reflection as he knelt before it in a reverent ecstasy. "Simply wonderful! this is my day and no mistake. Five hundred pound coming in this morning for that cabinet which I never cared about, and now this tumbling into my hands for a tenth, at the very most, of what it would fetch in town. Well, well! It almost makes one afraid something'll happen to counter it. Let's have a look at the population, anyhow."

Accordingly, he set them before him in a row. Again, here is an opportunity, which some would snatch at, of making an inventory of costume: I am incapable of it.

There were a gentleman and lady, in blue satin and brocade respectively. There were two children, a boy and a girl. There was a cook, a nurse, a footman, and there were the stable servants, two postilions, a coachman, two grooms.

"Anyone else? Yes, possibly."

The curtains of the four-poster in the bedroom were closely drawn round all four sides of it, and he put his finger in between them and felt in the bed. He drew the finger back hastily, for it almost seemed to him as if something had—not stirred, perhaps, but yielded—in an odd live way as he pressed it. Then he put back the curtains, which ran on rods in the proper manner, and extracted from the bed a white-haired old gentleman in a long linen night-dress and cap, and laid him down by the rest. The tale was complete.

Dinner-time was now near, so Mr. Dillet spent but five minutes in putting the lady and children into the drawing-room, the gentleman into the dining-room, the servants into the kitchen and stables, and the old man back into his bed. He retired into his dressing-room next door, and we see and hear no more of him until something like eleven o'clock at night.

His whim was to sleep surrounded by some of the gems of his collection. The big room in which we have seen him contained his bed: bath, wardrobe, and all the appliances of dressing were in a commodious room adjoining: but his four-poster, which itself was a valued treasure, stood in the large room where he sometimes wrote, and often sat, and even received visitors. To-night he repaired to it in a highly complacent frame of mind.

There was no striking clock within earshot—none on the staircase, none in the stable, none in the distant church tower. Yet it is indubitable that Mr. Dillet was startled out of a very pleasant slumber by a bell tolling One.

He was so much startled that he did not merely lie breathless with wide-open eyes, but actually sat up in his bed.

He never asked himself, till the morning hours, how it was that, though there was no light at all in the room, the Dolls' House on the kneehole table stood out with complete clearness. But it was so. The effect was that of a bright harvest moon shining full on the front of a big white stone mansion—a quarter of a mile away it might be, and yet every detail was photographically sharp. There were trees about it, too—trees rising behind the chapel and the house. He seemed to be conscious of the scent of a cool still September night. He thought he could hear an occasional stamp and clink from the stables, as of horses stirring. And with another shock he realized that, above the house, he was looking, not at the wall of his room with its pictures, but into the profound blue of a night sky.

There were lights, more than one, in the windows, and he quickly saw that this was no four-roomed house with a movable front, but one of many rooms, and staircases—a real house, but seen as if through the wrong end of a telescope. "You mean to show me something," he muttered to himself, and he gazed earnestly on the lighted windows. They would in real life have been shuttered or curtained, no doubt, he thought; but, as it was, there was nothing to intercept his view of what was being transacted inside the rooms.

Two rooms were lighted—one on the ground floor to the right of the door, one upstairs, on the left—the first brightly enough, the other rather dimly. The lower room was the dining-room: a table was laid, but the meal was over, and only wine and glasses were left on the table. The man of the blue satin and the woman of the brocade were alone in the room, and they were talking very earnestly, seated close together at the table, their elbows on it: every now and again stopping to listen, as it seemed. Once *he* rose, came to the window and opened it and put his head out and his hand to his ear. There was a lighted taper in a silver candlestick on a sideboard. When the man left the window he seemed to leave the room also; and the lady, taper in hand, remained standing and listening. The expression on her face was that of one striving her utmost to keep down a fear that threatened to master her—and succeeding. It was a hateful face, too; broad, flat and sly. Now the man came back and she took some small thing from him and hurried out of the room. He, too, disappeared, but only for a moment or two. The front door slowly opened and he stepped out and stood on the top of the *perron*, looking this way and that; then turned towards the upper window that was lighted, and shook his fist.

It was time to look at that upper window. Through it was seen a four-post bed: a nurse or other servant in an arm-chair, evidently sound asleep; in the bed an old man lying: awake, and, one would say, anxious, from the way in which he shifted about and moved his fingers, beating tunes on the coverlet. Beyond the bed a door opened. Light was seen on the ceiling, and the lady came in: she set down her candle on a table, came to the fireside and roused the nurse. In her hand she had an old-fashioned wine bottle, ready uncorked. The nurse took it, poured some of the contents into a little silver saucepan, added some spice and sugar from casters on the table, and set it to warm on the fire. Meanwhile the old man in the bed beckoned feebly to the lady, who came to him, smiling, took his wrist as if to feel his pulse, and bit her lip as if in consternation. He looked at her anxiously, and then pointed to the window, and spoke. She nodded, and did as the man below had done; opened the casement and listened—perhaps rather ostentatiously: then drew in her head and shook it, looking at the old man, who seemed to sigh.

By this time the posset on the fire was steaming, and the nurse poured it into a small two-handled silver bowl and brought it to the bedside. The old man seemed disinclined for it and was waving it away, but the lady and the nurse together bent over him and evidently pressed it upon him. He must have yielded, for they supported him into a sitting position, and put it to his lips. He drank most of it, in several draughts, and they laid him down. The lady left the room, smiling good night to him, and took the bowl, the bottle and the silver saucepan with her. The nurse returned to the chair, and there was an interval of complete quiet.

Suddenly the old man started up in his bed—and he must have uttered some cry, for the nurse started out of her chair and made but one step of it to the bedside. He was a sad and terrible sight—flushed in the face, almost to blackness, the eyes glaring whitely, both hands clutching at his heart, foam at his lips.

For a moment the nurse left him, ran to the door, flung it wide open, and, one supposes, screamed aloud for help, then darted back to the bed and seemed to try feverishly to soothe him—to lay him down—anything. But as the lady, her husband, and several servants, rushed into the room with horrified faces, the old man collapsed under the nurse's hands and lay back, and the features, contorted with agony and rage, relaxed slowly into calm.

A few moments later, lights showed out to the left of the house, and a coach with flambeaux drove up to the door. A white-wigged man in black got nimbly out and ran up the steps, carrying a small leather trunk-shaped box. He was met in the doorway by the man and his wife, she with her handkerchief clutched between her hands, he with a tragic face, but retaining his self-control. They led the new-comer into the dining-room, where he set his box of papers on the table, and, turning to them, listened with a face of consternation at what they had to tell. He nodded his head again and again, threw out his hands slightly, declined, it seemed, offers of refreshment and lodging for the night, and within a few minutes came slowly down the steps, entering the coach and driving off the way he had come. As the man in blue watched him from the top of the steps, a smile not pleasant to see stole slowly over his fat white face. Darkness fell over the whole scene as the lights of the coach disappeared.

But Mr. Dillet remained sitting up in the bed: he had rightly guessed that there would be a sequel. The house front glimmered out again before long. But now there was a difference. The lights were in other windows, one at the top of the house, the other illuminating the range of coloured windows of the chapel. How he saw through these is not quite obvious, but he did. The interior was as carefully furnished as the rest of the establishment, with its minute red cushions on the desks, its Gothic stall-canopies, and its western gallery and pinnacled organ with gold pipes. On the centre of the black and white pavement was a bier: four tall candles burned at the corners. On the bier was a coffin covered with a pall of black velvet.

As he looked the folds of the pall stirred. It seemed to rise at one end: it slid downwards: it fell away, exposing the black coffin with its silver handles and name-plate. One of the tall candlesticks swayed and toppled over. Ask no more, but turn, as Mr. Dillet hastily did, and look in at the lighted window at the top of the house, where a boy and girl lay in two truckle-beds, and a four-poster for the nurse rose above them. The nurse was not visible for the moment; but the father and mother were there, dressed now in mourning, but with very little sign of mourning in their demeanour. Indeed, they were laughing and talking with a good deal of animation, sometimes to each other, and sometimes throwing a remark to one or other of the children, and again laughing at the answers. Then the father was seen to go on tiptoe out of the room, taking with him as he went a white garment that hung on a peg near the door. He shut the door after him. A minute or two later it was slowly opened again, and a muffled head poked round it. A bent form of sinister shape stepped across to the truckle-beds, and suddenly stopped, threw up its arms and revealed, of course, the father, laughing. The children were in agonies of terror, the boy with the bedclothes over his head, the girl throwing herself out of bed into her mother's arms. Attempts at consolation followed—the parents took the children on their laps, patted them, picked up the white gown and showed there was no harm in it, and so forth; and at last putting the children back into bed, left the room with encouraging waves of the hand. As they left it, the nurse came in, and soon the light died down.

Still Mr. Dillet watched immovable.

A new sort of light—not of lamp or candle—a pale ugly light, began to dawn around the door-case at the back of the room. The door was opening again. The seer does not like to dwell upon what he saw entering the room: he says it might be described as a frog—the size of a man—but it had scanty white hair about its head. It was busy about the truckle-beds, but not for long. The sound of cries—faint, as if coming out of a vast distance—but, even so, infinitely appalling, reached the ear.

There were signs of a hideous commotion all over the house: lights moved along and up, and doors opened and shut, and running figures passed within the windows. The clock in the stable turret tolled one, and darkness fell again.

It was only dispelled once more, to show the house front. At the bottom of the steps dark figures were drawn up in two lines, holding flaming torches. More dark figures came down the steps, bearing, first one, then another small coffin. And the lines of torch-bearers with the coffins between them moved silently onward to the left.

The hours of night passed on—never so slowly, Mr. Dillet thought. Gradually he sank down from sitting to lying in his bed—but he did not close an eye: and early next morning he sent for the doctor.

The doctor found him in a disquieting state of nerves, and recommended sea-air. To a quiet place on the East Coast he accordingly repaired by easy stages in his car.

One of the first people he met on the sea front was Mr. Chittenden, who, it appeared, had likewise been advised to take his wife away for a bit of a change.

Mr. Chittenden looked somewhat askance upon him when they met: and not without cause.

"Well, I don't wonder at you being a bit upset, Mr. Dillet. What? yes, well, I might say 'orrible upset, to be sure, seeing what me and my poor wife went through ourselves. But I put it to you, Mr. Dillet, one of two things: was I going to scrap a lovely piece like that on the one 'and, or was I going to tell customers: 'I'm selling you a regular picture-palace-dramar in reel life of the olden time, billed to perform regular at one o'clock a.m.'? Why, what would you 'ave said yourself? And next thing you know, two Justices of the Peace in the back parlour, and pore Mr. and Mrs. Chittenden off in a spring cart to the County Asylum and everyone in the street saying, 'Ah, I thought it 'ud come to that. Look at the way the man drank!'—and me next door, or next door but one, to a total abstainer, as you know. Well, there was my position. What? Me 'ave it back in the shop? Well, what do *you* think? No, but I'll tell you what I will do. You shall have your money back, bar the ten pound I paid for it, and you make what you can."

Later in the day, in what is offensively called the "smoke-room" of the hotel, a murmured conversation between the two went on for some time.

"How much do you really know about that thing, and where it came from?"

"Honest, Mr. Dillet, I don't know the 'ouse. Of course, it came out of the lumber room of a country 'ouse—that anyone could guess. But I'll go as far as say this, that I believe it's not a hundred miles from this place. Which direction and how far I've no notion. I'm only judging by guess-work. The man as I actually paid the cheque to ain't one of my regular men, and I've lost sight of him; but I 'ave the idea that this part of the country was his beat, and that's every word I can tell you. But now, Mr. Dillet, there's one thing that rather physicks me. That old chap—I suppose you saw him drive up to the door—I thought so: now, would he have been the medical man, do you take it? My wife would have it so, but I stuck to it that was the lawyer, because he had papers with him, and one he took out was folded up."

"I agree," said Mr. Dillet. "Thinking it over, I came to the conclusion that was the old man's will, ready to be signed."

"Just what I thought," said Mr. Chittenden, "and I took it that will would have cut out the young people, eh? Well, well! It's been a lesson to me, I know that. I shan't buy no more dolls' houses, nor waste no more money on the pictures—and as to this business of poisonin' grandpa, well, if I know myself, I never 'ad much of a turn for that. Live and let live: that's bin my motto throughout life, and I ain't found it a bad one."

Filled with these elevated sentiments, Mr. Chittenden retired to his lodgings. Mr. Dillet next day repaired to the local Institute, where he hoped to find some clue to the riddle that absorbed him. He gazed in despair at a long file of the Canterbury and York Society's publications of the Parish Registers of the district. No print resembling the house of his nightmare was among those that hung on the staircase and in the passages. Disconsolate, he found himself at last in a derelict room, staring at a dusty model of a church in a dusty glass case: *Model of St. Stephen's Church, Coxham. Presented by J. Merewether, Esq., of Ilbridge House*, 1877. *The work of his ancestor James Merewether, d.* 1786. There was something in the fashion of it that reminded him dimly of his horror. He retraced his steps to a wall map he had noticed, and made out that Ilbridge House was in Coxham Parish. Coxham was, as it happened, one of the parishes of which he had retained the name when he glanced over the file of printed registers, and it was not long before he found in them the record of the burial of Roger Milford, aged 76, on the 11th of September, 1757, and of Roger and Elizabeth Merewether, aged 9 and 7, on the 19th of the same month. It seemed worth while to follow up this clue, frail as it was; and in the afternoon he drove out to Coxham. The east end of the north aisle of the church is a Milford chapel, and on its north wall are tablets to the same persons; Roger, the elder, it seems, was distinguished by all the qualities which adorn "the Father, the Magistrate, and the Man": the memorial was erected by his attached daughter Elizabeth, "who did not long survive the loss of a parent ever solicitous for her welfare, and of two amiable children." The last sentence was plainly an addition to the original inscription.

A yet later slab told of James Merewether, husband of Elizabeth, "who in the dawn of life practised, not without success, those arts which, had he continued their exercise, might in the opinion of the most competent judges have earned for him the name of the British Vitruvius: but who, overwhelmed by the visitation which deprived him of an affectionate partner and a blooming offspring, passed his Prime and Age in a secluded yet elegant Retirement: his grateful Nephew and Heir indulges a pious sorrow by this too brief recital of his excellences."

The children were more simply commemorated. Both died on the night of the 12th of September.

Mr. Dillet felt sure that in Ilbridge House he had found the scene of his drama. In some old sketch-book, possibly in some old print, he may yet find convincing evidence that he is right. But the Ilbridge House of to-day is not that which he sought; it is an Elizabethan erection of the forties, in red brick with stone quoins and dressings. A quarter of a mile from it, in a low part of the park, backed by ancient, stag-horned, ivy-strangled trees and thick undergrowth, are marks of a terraced platform overgrown with rough grass. A few stone balusters lie here and there, and a heap or two, covered with nettles and ivy, of wrought stones with badly-carved crockets. This, someone told Mr. Dillet, was the site of an older house.

As he drove out of the village, the hall clock struck four, and Mr. Dillet started up and clapped his hands to his ears. It was not the first time he had heard that bell.

Awaiting an offer from the other side of the Atlantic, the dolls' house still reposes, carefully sheeted, in a loft over Mr. Dillet's stables, whither Collins conveyed it on the day when Mr. Dillet started for the sea coast.

ROGER JOHNSON
The Wall-Painting

Roger Johnson *(b.1947) has written several fine ghost stories in the Jamesian tradition. Most of these are set in his native Essex. A librarian by profession, he also edits (in his spare time) an invaluable newsletter,* The District Messenger, *for the Sherlock Holmes Society. 'The Wall-Painting' first appeared in Saints and Relics (Haunted Library, 1983).*

"You must understand," said Harry Foster, "that this isn't my own story." He looked at us with some concern. "I say, I hope you don't think I'm here under false pretences!"

He was a large, tweedy, red-faced man, giving something of the impression of a corpulent and amiable fox. I had been surprised to learn that he was – as he still is – an antiquarian bookseller, with premises in the West End and a house in Upper Norwood.

"That's all right," said George Cobbett. "It's the story itself that we're interested in." He began to fill his pipe, waiting for our visitor to justify his journey into Essex.

"Good, good. Well, it came into my hands after a house-clearance. I specialise, as you know, in sporting books, but I keep a fair amount of general material on the shelves, which usually comes from auctions and clearances. This particular item was among a job-lot that came from a house in Surrey. The owner had died, and the heirs—distant relatives—simply sold up the house and the entire contents. They couldn't tell me anything about the book, and I've been quite unable to learn how it came into the old man's possession. Maybe we'll never know. At all events, here it is."

He placed on the table a large notebook or diary, rather battered, with dark blue covers that were fading to grey. It had probably come from a cheap stationer's some seventy or eighty years ago.

"The name inside the cover," said Harry, "is the Reverend Stephen Gifford, Vicar of Welford St Paul in Essex. I used to know the place fairly well—a friend of mine had a cottage nearby—and that's what persuaded me to read the thing. It's —well—unusual, you know."

He put on a pair of horn-rimmed glasses and began to read to us in a slightly hoarse, fruity voice.

This Parish of Welford St Paul is large in area and small in numbers. Visitors are often surprised to learn that the church is dedicated to St Lawrence, and I am obliged to tell them that the village, like so many in Essex, was named for the Lords of the Manor—in this case, the Dean and Chapter of St Paul's Cathedral. They owned, and still own, a good deal of land in the county. Indeed, they may well constitute the oldest landed family in England!

The church is very old. Much of the fabric is Norman work, but the chancel walls and the north wall of the sanctuary were clearly built by the Anglo-Saxons and cannot be less than one thousand years old. It is a respectable age, even for this ancient county. The building is small and plain, with no really distinctive features, and consists of sanctuary, chancel and nave, with a squat western tower. There are no aisles, and the unpretentious southern porch was erected by one of my predecessors early in the last century. Inside, the walls are coated with a solution of lime, whose whiteness gives the small building a surprisingly light and spacious appearance.

Upon my first visit, however, I noticed a number of cracks in this whitewash, and experience suggested to me that I should call in a building surveyor. The result was as I had feared: the northern walls of both nave and chancel were in a very sad state. With the subsequent arrival of the builders began a period of activity and disruption such as this little church had not known for centuries.

It was on the afternoon of the fourth day that the cautious, patient work of the repairers uncovered a small patch of startlingly bright colour beneath the whiteness of the north wall of the sanctuary. I took upon myself the responsibility of sealing off that wall and calling in a specialist. Fortunately I knew just the man. His name was Howard Faragher, and I had met him some months previously at the London Library, when I had called in to visit my friend the sub-librarian. I did not have his address, but my friend was able to put me in touch with him. He arrived at Welford St Paul two days later, a tall rangy man in his middle thirties, with untidy yellow hair and an amiably eager expression.

"Well," said he, after he had examined the little patch of green and red, "it's certainly a medieval painting, and from the colours and the way they're applied I'd say it's an early one – possibly late twelfth century."

"But it's all so fresh!" I protested. "I thought that in fresco . . ."

He interrupted me. "Not all wall-painting is fresco, you know, though all fresco is wall-painting. The technique is really only suitable in a warm dry climate, so it's hardly known in this country. No, this is what's called *secco*. The paints were mostly compounded of oxides and applied to a lime-wash surface that had been fixed with casein – simple skimmed milk. The colours do remain quite bright. Now, Gifford, I'm going to need several days to remove the rest of this covering – no doubt it was put on during the Reformation – and I daren't attempt to make up my mind about the picture until I've finished, so please leave any questions until then."

He worked for nearly a week, with meticulous care, fending off with cheerful patience my eager curiosity. Each evening he would hang a cloth over the painting and return with me to the vicarage. My impatient attempts to draw him out met with a polite but firm refusal, and our conversation over dinner turned mostly to history and music. After dinner on the fifth day, he folded his napkin and said abruptly, "Well, I've finished. No, don't go rushing out to look at it just yet. I'd rather you saw the thing by daylight, and besides, I want a word with you before you see it. I suggest that we go down the road to the *Axe and Compasses* and chat over a pint of beer. I think I deserve a drink."

He would not say any more until we were comfortably settled in the parlour of our local inn. Then, after taking a deep draught of his beer, he looked at me rather quizzically and said, "I think we've found St Tosti."

Frankly, I did not know what to make of this. The name was unfamiliar to me. "Tosti?" I said. "An Italian?"

Faragher chuckled at this. "You're thinking of the composer," he said. "No, no, the saint was as English as you or I – more so, I suppose, since he was an Anglo-Saxon, with no Norman blood in his veins. He was never, I think, very widely known, but he flourished in the early decades of the eleventh century."

I began to understand. "He lived too late, then, to be mentioned in Bede's history."

"Just so, and too early to have encountered the Norman invaders. But really, you know, you should be telling me about him." Again that sardonic smile.

"I? But . . ." I was lost for words.

"You really don't know, do you? The fact is that your church was once dedicated to St Tosti. Oh, there's no doubt about it. When we met at the London Library, I was actually researching the ecclesiastical history of Tendring Hundred for a client, and that was one of the facts that came to my attention. But as to Tosti himself, information is not plentiful: a few scraps in the Library, a little more among the London Diocesan Archives – that's all. The name is certainly Anglo-Saxon. You may recall that King Harold Godwinson had a brother called Tosti or Tostig, who treacherously allied himself with Harold Hardrada."

"But this is remarkable!" I exclaimed. "There's no mention of it in the Parish Records. I take it that Tosti was what you might call a local saint – not recognised by the Vatican." It was certainly true that the Pontiff did not reserve to himself the right of canonisation until the thirteenth century. Before then there had been all sorts of irregularities, which the new decree swiftly crushed. The cult of St Tosti, like many others, must have found itself regarded quite suddenly as an unorthodox and unacceptable excrescence upon the body of the Church. "That would explain why I had never heard of him. And yet many of these local saints were eventually accepted and granted canonisation. What was there about this man?"

Faragher shrugged his narrow shoulders. "I really don't know. He just seems to have been – well – dubious. Records are scarce, as I told you, and I didn't take any particular note of them, but I can recall nothing that suggested sanctity in the man's life. One account, written, I think, in the late twelfth century, did lay particular stress upon his celibate life, but where you would expect some suggestion that the saint was following the example of Our Lord, or was wedded to the Church, there was nothing. Just the bald statement. In fact, he doesn't seem to have had much to do with the Church at all."

"How very interesting. Then what was it that caused people to regard him as a saint?"

"There are the vaguest references to miracles. For the moment, Gifford, you will have to be satisfied with that. You see, all the records that I've come across date from long after Tosti's supposed death." Faragher's long face brightened suddenly. "Ah, yes. That is an interesting matter. A clerk who wrote in about the year 1120 says that Tosti was actually in the midst of an address or sermon to his brothers – that's the word he uses – when he simply disappeared. The statement is quite unequivocal: he did not die, he disappeared. That is the only surviving account of the end of St Tosti, and our clerk says that he had the story from an eye-witness. Curious, eh?"

"Very curious," I said. "And why do you think that the wall-painting depicts this rather dubious saint?"

My companion stifled a yawn, and I suddenly realised how tired he looked. "I think," he replied, "that I'll answer that question tomorrow, when you see the picture. Afterwards, perhaps, the two of us could make the journey into Colchester and investigate the Archdeaconry Records. Now, if you don't mind, we'll change the subject. I should like just one more drink, and then I'll be ready for a good night's sleep."

My first duty on the next day was to conduct a short Eucharist. This weekday service was rarely well-attended, and I was gratified that Faragher elected to join the congregation. Indeed, his presence actually increased the attendance by fifty per centum. The simple and moving words of the ritual, hallowed both by the Spirit of God and by the spirit of our fathers, absorbed my attention throughout, so that it was not until after I had pronounced the Benediction that my curiosity about the wall-painting returned. Howard Faragher was waiting for me outside the vestry when I had slipped off my surplice and cassock. His eagerness to show me the painting was quite as great as mine to see it. We crossed the sanctuary to where a sheet of dark cloth, some seven feet by four, covered this unexpected treasure. Faragher raised his hand and, with an almost theatrical gesture, whipped the cloth from the wall.

I am sure that I gasped. My first reaction was of astonishment at the sheer beauty of this hidden jewel of the church, but it was followed closely by another feeling – of unease, engendered by something too subtle to define. Was it the proud, ascetic expression of the man who stood, fully life-size, before us? Was it the extraordinarily bright eyes with which he regarded us? Was it the strangely uncertain figure, as it might be the shadow of a dog or a wolf, that lurked at his feet, half-hidden by the folds of his robe?

The whole painting measured about six feet high by two and a half wide. There was a border, painted in remarkably clever imitation of a romanesque arch, the pillars no more than two inches wide. Within it, against a grey background and upon a floor of green, stood the saint. I could not doubt that he was regarded as a saint – why else would his likeness have been enshrined in a Christian church? – but there was that about his calm and arrogant expression which suggested something other. The figure was tall and thin, with hairless and rather nutcracker jaws and the most remarkable eyes. At first I had taken these piercing orbs to be blue, but a closer look showed that the colour was actually a curiously indeterminate grey. I was pondering upon this when Faragher spoke.

"You've noticed the eyes? No doubt the man's eyes were actually blue, as was common among the Anglo-Saxons . . ." He paused for a moment, then resumed: "By Tosti's time, of course, the various invading races – yes, including the Scandinavians – had become melded into a truly English people, in whose veins also ran much good Celtic blood. Besides, this part of north-eastern Essex was variously claimed by the East Saxons and the East Angles, and there's no telling to which people the saint himself belonged." A longer pause, while he seemed to gather his thoughts. "Ha! Yes, blue eyes. Well, real blue is rare in medieval wall-paintings. It was usually made from azurite, and not easy to come by. Mostly the artists used, as here, a cunning mixture of black and lime white, with the slightest touch of red ochre. You would expect the result to be a sort of dull brown, but there's no doubt that this is intended to be blue. No doubt at all." His voice trailed off, and I looked away, with some reluctance, from the compelling gaze of the painted figure.

The left hand was raised, as if in blessing, but instead of the first two fingers being extended, as I had seen before, only the forefinger was lifted; it pointed directly upwards. I mentioned this, and my companion, roused from his reverie, replied, "Yes, interesting, isn't it? It gives credence to the notion that there was something unsaintly about this saint. The forefinger, extended on its own, is usually a symbol of condemnation in these murals, and as this one is pointing upwards – well, one wonders. I'm curious that it should be the left hand too, and not the right. Have you noticed, by the way, what he holds in his right hand? Uncommonly like a cat-o'-nine-tails, isn't it? That's really what decided for me that this must be St Tosti. You see, he's mentioned in more than one of the records as driving his enemies before him with a scourge. *His* enemies, notice, not the enemies of Christ."

"It was not a symbol of martyrdom, then?"

"Ah, that would naturally occur to you. You are thinking of the grid-iron associated with St Lawrence. No, there seems no doubt that it was Tosti who wielded the whip. Still, Our Lord himself flogged the moneylenders in the temple, so perhaps we should not read too much into that. But tell me what you make of this."

He indicated the curious, shadowy figure to which I have referred. It seemed to stand or squat, perhaps half the height of the saint, just by his left foot, and partly concealed by the folds of his red gown. No features could be distinguished, and indeed, the closer I looked, the less sure I was that the figure was actually there. It might have been merely a darker stain upon the grey background of the painting. Yet such was the meticulous care with which the saint had been depicted that I was inclined to doubt this.

I asked Faragher, "Is there perhaps some animal – a dog or a wolf – which is associated with the legend of St Tosti?"

His reply was negative. "And yet," he added, after a moment's thought, "something, some fact or suggestion, is nagging at my mind." He gestured, wryly. "Perhaps we'll find out when we look at the Archdeaconry Records. And that reminds me, the time is getting on. If we're to get any real work done in Colchester, we had better go now."

With some reluctance, I left the presence of that enigmatic and dubious saint, and scurried towards the vestry to collect my overcoat and hat. As I went, I observed that Howard Faragher was gazing intently at one portion of the wall-painting and murmuring, almost to himself, "What are you? I wish you would show yourself, so that I could be sure."

The journey into Colchester is not a long one, and usually, upon a morning in early spring, it is particularly pleasant. My impatience, however, made it seem rather long and tedious, and I could see that my companion found it so as well. Still, we reached the town at last, and made our way to the offices of the Archdeaconry. Our eagerness was not well rewarded: the information about St Tosti and the early history of Welford St Paul was quite as scant as Faragher had supposed. After nearly three hours, we had uncovered no more than a few very uncertain references to miraculous events, and one late version—dating from the mid-thirteenth century—of the story that St Tosti had whipped his foes before him. Here, though, there was the qualifying statement that "the Brethren of Tosti cried aloud to magnify the name of Christ", but this was probably a pious interpolation.

At two o'clock, the Archdeacon's clerk remarked rather pointedly that of course the Archives could be made available for our inspection another day, but at present his duties were pressing. Indeed, I myself had begun to feel that our quest was something of a wild goose chase. But at that moment Howard Faragher gave a sudden cry of satisfaction. "Hah! Gifford, listen to this: it's from a pamphlet issued in 1612 by the Puritan Richard Fine of Colchester. The pamphlet was called *England, Rome and Babylon*, and it cost Richard Fine both his ears in those intolerant times. All copies were destroyed except for this one page, and that is charred along one edge . . ."

"But what does it say?" I cried.

"It starts in the middle of a sentence, thus: 'to his Lord while in Converse with his Brethren'—a reference to the disappearance, I think. Then it continues, 'This Tosti was knowne to consorte with an Angell, as some say, others a Sprite of different sorte, not being a Creature of *God* but of the *Divell*.' After that there's a new paragraph, fulminating in general terms against the Popish superstition."

The clerk, uncomprehending, interrupted with a discreet cough, and Faragher hastily laid down the ancient paper. "I do beg your pardon," he said. "We mustn't keep you any longer." He glanced at his watch and added, "We should go now, in any case, if we are to find somewhere open for luncheon." Polite, but triumphant, he accompanied me from the office. He said no more for a while, but his look as we bade farewell to the harassed clerk clearly said, "What do you think of that, my friend?"

There was but one thought in my mind: that the shadowy figure who accompanied the painted saint had little about it of the angelic.

As we drove into Welford St Paul, Faragher said, "If you don't mind, I should like to stay here for a day or two longer. This matter becomes more and more curious, and I'd rather like to put off unveiling the picture until we know what there is to know about it. I suppose that the builders . . .?"

"You need not worry," I replied. "The builders know only that a painting of some kind has been uncovered, and that it is being examined by an expert."

"Splendid! Well, let's go and have another look at it, shall we, while the light lasts?"

The shade that clung to St Tosti was as disturbing and indefinable as ever. After peering at it for several minutes, Faragher said, "Please go if you want to, Gifford. I must see if I can date this thing at all accurately." He looked up at me with a smile. "Who knows, I may yet be able to tell you who the artist was."

I left him, but with slight and amorphous misgivings. Whatever the truth about St Tosti, I was sure that the painting itself was unholy. The proud face of the ascetic, the lazy and arrogant way in which he held his wicked-looking scourge, the sinister, almost shapeless figure of his unknown companion . . . The companion! I could not be certain but the suspicion would not leave my mind that that shadowy form had actually moved since we had last seen it.

The light had almost gone when Howard Faragher returned to the vicarage. He looked and sounded preoccupied, tapping his long forefinger against his lips and muttering to himself. In answer to my question, he said, "No further, I'm afraid. My original estimate of the date may even be too late; it might just be late eleventh century. Did you notice the folds of the saint's robe, how carefully they were moulded? That's a pretty sure sign of early work in this country. Later artists tended away from the continental ideal and concentrated much more on essential purity of outline. I doubt very much that we'll ever find out who painted Tosti for us—he was simply far too early."

Faragher said little more until after dinner, when he observed, "Tomorrow, I think I shall pay a visit to the Diocesan Offices in London—I don't think there's much point in going to Rochester or St Alban's—and see if their records have any more to offer. I'll bring my camera back with me, and a magnesium flare, and we'll try to get a decent photograph of our mysterious saint."

I retired early that night, leaving Faragher to his musings. I was very tired, and yet I did not sleep well, for I had a most unsettling dream. It was not a nightmare, in the sense that it did not induce fear or horror, but it was instinct with a sense of isolation and menace. I stood in the churchyard of Welford St Paul, and about me was only a dark, vague greyness. Before me was the church, its windows illuminated fitfully by the feeble glow of candles. From the building came the sound of singing or chanting, though that too was faint, almost ethereal, and I cannot recall whether the words or the music were known to me. I walked unsteadily to the porch and unlocked the door. As I entered the building, it was suddenly darkened, though the singing continued, as faint and attenuated a sound as before. I did not realise the fact until I considered the dream in the morning, but the interior of this building was not that of Welford church. I had an impression of vast, almost infinite space; huge, dark and cold—made to seem more so, perhaps, by the singularly distant quality of the incorporeal singing. And as I progressed, there came upon me the feeling that I was not wanted here, nor ever would be, though for what reason I could not tell. Something—something huge, perhaps the building itself—was, with a disturbing subtlety, hostile to me. That is all I remember, but it is enough.

At breakfast, Faragher, though still seeming abstracted, was more open. He greeted me with the question, "Did you sleep well?" Not waiting for an answer, he continued, "I didn't—I had a very disturbing dream."

Putting aside my own vision, I said, "Tell me about it."

"I was walking alone," he said, "through some sort of forest or heathland. The sky was darkening, and I knew that I must reach my destination before the light was quite gone. No, I have no idea what that destination was, nor why I was in such haste. I walked faster, and as I did so, I became aware that something was stalking me. I could not see it, nor tell precisely where it was, but I could hear it moving, with a rather horrible ease, not very far from me."

"It was something, then, and not someone?"

"I can't be certain. That's the devil of it! I could only sense the rustling and stepping of its long legs as it kept pace with me. I think that it was toying with me, as a cat does with a mouse. Yes, it had very long legs—but, Gifford, I couldn't tell *how many* long legs!"

Before Faragher set out for Colchester and the London train, we went once more to look at the wall-painting. My friend said nothing—though he glanced at me rather uneasily—but again it seemed to me that Tosti's shadowy companion had moved.

I was crossing the churchyard after Evensong when he arrived back from London. He smiled ruefully and waved to me, then began to unload two large packages from the dog-cart—a square, bulky object which contained his camera and plates and a long bag such as golfers use. This held the tripod. I went over to help him carry them into the vicarage.

"We'll have dinner first," I said, "and then you can tell me what you've learned."

"There's little to tell," he replied. "One thirteenth-century document, written by a clerk of St Paul's, which refers cryptically to a *reliqua Sancti Tostigii,* and an episcopal order from the reign of Edward VI that a monstrance be destroyed at Welford Church. That's all. There was nothing to identify the relic, and only the absence of other probabilities leads me to suppose that the monstrance was connected with it. It must have contained a relic of some sort, and it might as well have been Tosti's."

After dinner, we took the photographic equipment into the darkened church. With the magnesium flare, of course, there was no need for adequate light in the building, and half a dozen candles sufficed while we erected the tripod and set the camera upon it. Only then did we look closely at the painting. Faragher's next words made my heart sink: "When we first examined this, wasn't Tosti's companion partly hidden by his robe?"

"It was," I replied, hesitantly. "But now there is a clear gap between the two. The shadow has definitely moved towards the edge of the picture." Insanely, the thought occurred to me that it was trying to get out! But this quite impossible happening seemed only to have increased my friend's interest. With calm determination, he took three photographs of the painting—I averted my gaze each time, but the sudden flash of light seemed to sear my eyes—and then he began to pack up his equipment, saying, "I'll develop these in the morning, and we'll see whether any secrets are revealed."

I carried the tripod out of the church, while Faragher took the camera and its precious photographic plates. The moon had not yet risen, and a thick cloud obscured the stars. It seemed almost unnaturally dark in the churchyard. No lights could be seen in the vicarage, for my housekeeper had left long before. Fortunately the walk is short and straight, so that we had no difficulty in reaching the vicarage gate, but there, as chance would have it, I slipped upon the step and fell, giving my ankle a severe twist. I had dropped the heavy bag, but Faragher retrieved it unharmed. Then carrying both loads, he supported me while I hobbled, and we soon reached the door of the house.

I found my key and unlocked the door, so that he might go in and switch on the electric light before helping me. I felt, rather than saw, him enter and feel for the light-switch, which is just inside the door and to the left. There was a dull click, but no light. Faragher's voice said, "I'm sorry about this; I think the bulb must have blown. Shall I try the light in the study?"

"If you please," I replied. "The door is just a few feet along on the same side."

A moment later I heard the study door open, and again a muffled click in the darkness. Then Faragher returned to me. "This is most annoying," he said. "I think we shall have to make do with candles tonight, and tomorrow we'll see about getting the electricity restored."

I sighed, no doubt with some petulance. "Very well. The candles are kept in the kitchen, in a cupboard beneath the sink. That's the second door on the right, remember—about twenty feet along."

"All right," he said, and I heard him feeling his way along the wall. The moments seemed to pass interminably, and when I heard his voice again it seemed curiously muffled. "Gifford! You did say it was the second door on the right, didn't you? Only I must have gone twenty feet already, and I haven't come across a door yet."

Something like fear touched me then. It was true that I had not lived long at the vicarage, but long enough, surely, to know where all the rooms were. Then came the voice again, clearer this time, but fainter: "There seems to be a bend in the hallway here. I don't remember that." Neither did I; I *knew* that the hall ran quite straight from the front to the back of the house, where it gave onto the back garden. There was, I think, a note of hysteria in Faragher's voice as he continued: "I'll try down here—perhaps I'll find the door this way!"

A moment later the faint voice said, "There's no door here." Then there was a dreadful long pause, and I heard my friend's voice for the last time, seeming to reach me from an infinite distance. The words were simple and, in the circumstances, terrifying: "Dear God!" The sound seemed to ring, echoing, as though from an abyss; I heard it for long minutes after it had actually ceased.

Desperately, I stood upon the doorstep, not caring for the pain in my ankle, and fumbled hopelessly for the light-switch. I found it, pressed it—and the light went on, to reveal the hallway as I had always known it, running quite straight from the front to the back of the house. "Faragher!" I cried, and again: "Faragher!" Then the pain and the confusion overcame me. My ankle gave way, and I fell to the floor in a faint.

I awoke in the grey dawn, my body shivering with cold and my head feeling as if it would burst. Desperately, hopelessly,

I hobbled and crawled throughout the house, seeking for some sign of my friend. I found nothing. The back door was locked, and had not been unlocked. The windows, too, were all closed against the chill night, and while I could not swear that he had not returned to the front door and stepped over my unconscious body into the darkness, yet I knew that it was not so. The answer was not outside the house, nor was it within. I lay for fully two hours upon the sofa in my study, with both my head and my ankle throbbing. and at the end I could only think, as I had suspected at the beginning, that the answer lay in that damnable wall-painting, with the false saint and his infernal companion. It was an answer, I thought, which they would keep to themselves for ever.

In that I was mistaken. With the aid of a strong stick, I staggered across to the church and let myself in, not knowing, but fearing, what I might find. In the sanctuary, the sheet of dark cloth still covered the painting, but before removing it I knelt at the altar and prayed for understanding of what I should do, and resolution to do it. Strengthened, but no less uneasy, I went to the north wall and firmly pulled down the cloth. The light was quite sufficient for me to see the painting clearly, and every detail of it is impressed upon my mind. For several minutes I gazed at it, a sickness growing within my spirit, and then I did what I knew I had to. Blessing the caution that had prevented me from letting the builders see the picture, I raised my stick and hammered at the wall, blow after blow, until every scrap of painted plaster was gone from it. Then I ground the lumps of plaster beneath my feet, so that soon there was nothing but powder upon the floor. It would not be hard to devise a story that would satisfy the builders. At last, sobbing and choking, I knelt before the altar again and prayed for the soul of Howard Faragher.

The wall-painting upon that last day was just as we had first seen it, save for one small detail. The gaunt figure of St Tosti still stood, clutching his whip and pointing derisively toward heaven, and the shadowy form of his companion again lurked by his left foot, partly hidden by his robe. But now the features of the shadow could be distinguished; they were faint, but quite clear, and they were the features of Howard Faragher.

Harry Foster laid down the book and removed his glasses. "There's just one thing to add," he said. "Gifford says that when the photographs were developed he found that they showed only the figure of Tosti. There was no sign of a shadow or of any sort of companion. He burnt the prints and had the plates ground to a powder." Harry looked from one to the other of us with a sardonic smile, as if to say, "What do you make of that, my friends?"

Hesitantly, I said, "Have you made any inquiries about the story—in the parish records, for example? And what about this Tosti . . .?"

Harry lit a cigar and drew upon it before answering. "I haven't been back to Welford St Paul," he said, "and I don't intend to do so. Perhaps because I'm afraid that the story is true, perhaps because I'm afraid that it is not. All I can tell you is this—a few weeks ago I acquired a copy of Crockford's clerical directory for the year 1910, and I found that one Stephen Gifford had actually been the vicar of Welford St Paul since February 1907." He shrugged his shoulders. "Let's leave it at that, shall we?"

I glanced at George Cobbett, whose eyes were fixed upon the table in front of him. His brow was furrowed and his lips pursed. I could see that he was thinking, as I was, "Shall we?"

RUDYARD KIPLING
"They"

Rudyard Kipling *(1865–1936), like many other great names in English literature, constantly returned to the allegorical world of fantasy and the supernatural. 'They', one of his finest tales, was included in the collection* Traffics *and* Discoveries *(1904), and also was published separately in a special edition a year later.*

THE RETURN OF THE CHILDREN

Neither the harps nor the crowns amused, nor the cherubs' dove-winged races—
Holding hands forlornly the Children wandered beneath the Dome;
Plucking the radiant robes of the passers-by, and with pitiful faces
Begging what Princes and Powers refused:— "Ah, please will you let us go home?"

Over the jewelled floor, nigh weeping, ran to them Mary the Mother,
Kneeled and caressed and made promise with kisses, and drew them along to the gateway—
Yea, the all-iron unbribeable Door which Peter must guard and none other.
Straightway She took the Keys from his keeping, and opened and freed them straightway.

Then to Her Son, Who had seen and smiled, She said: "On the night that I bore Thee
What didst Thou care for a love beyond mine or a heaven that was not my arm?
Didst Thou push from the nipple, O Child, to hear the angels adore Thee?
When we two lay in the breath of the kine?" And He said:— "Thou hast done no harm."

So through the Void the Children ran homeward merrily hand in hand,

Looking neither to left nor right where the breathless Heavens stood
still;
And the Guards of the Void resheathed their swords, for they heard
the Command:
"Shall I that have suffered the children to come to me hold them
against their will?"

"THEY"

One view called me to another; one hilltop to its fellow, half across the county, and since I could answer at no more trouble than the snapping forward of a lever, I let the country flow under my wheels. The orchid-studded flats of the East gave way to the thyme, ilex, and grey grass of the Downs; these again to the rich cornland and fig-trees of the lower coast, where you carry the beat of the tide on your left hand for fifteen level miles; and when at last I turned inland through a huddle of rounded hills and woods I had run myself clean out of my known marks. Beyond that precise hamlet which stands godmother to the capital of the United States, I found hidden villages where bees, the only things awake, boomed in eighty-foot lindens that overhung grey Norman churches; miraculous brooks diving under stone bridges built for heavier traffic than would ever vex them again; tithe-barns larger than their churches, and an old smithy that cried out aloud how it had once been a hall of the Knights of the Temple. Gipsies I found on a common where the gorse, bracken, and heath fought it out together up a mile of Roman road; and a little farther on I disturbed a red fox rolling dog-fashion in the naked sunlight.

As the wooded hills closed about me I stood up in the car to take the bearings of that great Down whose ringed head is a landmark for fifty miles across the low countries. I judged that the lie of the country would bring me across some westward running road that went to his feet, but I did not allow for the confusing veils of the woods. A quick turn plunged me first into a green cutting brimful of liquid sunshine, next into a gloomy tunnel where last year's dead leaves whispered and scuffled about my tyres. The strong hazel stuff meeting overhead had not been cut for a couple of generations at least, nor had any axe helped the moss-cankered oak and beech to spring above them. Here the road changed frankly into a carpeted ride on whose brown velvet spent primrose-clumps showed like jade, and a few sickly, white-stalked blue-bells nodded together. As the slope favoured I shut off the power and slid over the whirled leaves, expecting every moment to meet a keeper; but I only heard a jay, far off, arguing against the silence under the twilight of the trees.

Still the track descended. I was on the point of reversing and working my way back on the second speed ere I ended in some swamp, when I saw sunshine through the tangle ahead and lifted the brake.

It was down again at once. As the light beat across my face my fore-wheels took the turf of a great still lawn from which sprang horsemen ten feet high with levelled lances, monstrous peacocks, and sleek round-headed maids of honour—blue, black, and glistening—all of clipped yew. Across the lawn—the marshalled woods besieged it on three sides—stood an ancient house of lichened and weather-worn stone, with mullioned windows and roofs of rose-red tile. It was flanked by semi-circular walls, also rose-red, that closed the lawn on the fourth side, and at their feet a box hedge grew man-high. There were doves on the roof about the slim brick chimneys, and I caught a glimpse of an octagonal dove-house behind the screening wall.

Here, then, I stayed; a horseman's green spear laid at my breast; held by the exceeding beauty of that jewel in that setting.

"If I am not packed off for a trespasser, or if this knight does not ride a wallop at me," thought I, "Shakespeare and Queen Elizabeth at least must come out of that half-open garden door and ask me to tea."

A child appeared at an upper window, and I thought the little thing waved a friendly hand. But it was to call a companion, for presently another bright head showed. Then I heard a laugh among the yew-peacocks, and turning to make sure (till then I had been watching the house only) I saw the silver of a fountain behind a hedge thrown up against the sun. The doves on the roof cooed to the cooing water; but between the two notes I caught the utterly happy chuckle of a child absorbed in some light mischief.

The garden door—heavy oak sunk deep in the thickness of the wall—opened farther: a woman in a big garden hat set her foot slowly on the time-hollowed stone step and as slowly walked across the turf. I was forming some apology when she lifted up her head and I saw that she was blind.

"I heard you," she said. "Isn't that a motor car?"

"I'm afraid I've made a mistake in my road. I should have turned off up above—I never dreamed"—I began.

"But I'm very glad. Fancy a motor car coming into the garden! It will be such a treat—" She turned and made as though looking about her. "You—you haven't seen anyone, have you—perhaps?"

"No one to speak to, but the children seemed interested at a distance."

"Which?"

"I saw a couple up at the window just now, and I think I heard a little chap in the grounds."

"Oh, lucky you!" she cried, and her face brightened. "I hear them, of course, but that's all. You've seen them and heard them?"

"Yes," I answered. "And if I know anything of children one of them's having a beautiful time by the fountain yonder. Escaped, I should imagine."

"You're fond of children?"

I gave her one or two reasons why I did not altogether hate them.

"Of course, of course," she said. "Then you understand. Then you won't think it foolish if I ask you to take your car through the gardens, once or twice—quite slowly. I'm sure they'd like to see it. They see so little, poor things. One tries to make their life pleasant, but—" she threw out her hands towards the woods. "We're so out of the world here."

"That will be splendid," I said. "But I can't cut up your grass."

She faced to the right. "Wait a minute," she said. "We're at the South gate, aren't we? Behind those peacocks there's a flagged path. We call it the Peacock's Walk. You can't see it from here, they tell me, but if you squeeze along by the edge of the wood you can turn at the first peacock and get on to the flags."

It was sacrilege to wake that dreaming house-front with the clatter of machinery, but I swung the car to clear the turf, brushed along the edge of the wood and turned in on the broad stone path where the fountain-basin lay like one star-sapphire.

"May I come too?" she cried. "No, please don't help me. They'll like it better if they see me."

She felt her way lightly to the front of the car, and with one foot on the step she called: "Children, oh, children! Look and see what's going to happen!"

The voice would have drawn lost souls from the Pit, for the yearning that underlay its sweetness, and I was not surprised to hear an answering shout behind the yews. It must have been the child by the fountain, but he fled at our approach, leaving a little toy boat in the water. I saw the glint of his blue blouse among the still horsemen.

Very disposedly we paraded the length of the walk, and at her request backed again. This time the child had got the better of his panic, but stood far off and doubting.

"The little fellow's watching us," I said. "I wonder if he'd like a ride."

"They're very shy still. Very shy. But, oh, lucky you to be able to see them! Let's listen."

I stopped the machine at once, and the humid stillness, heavy with the scent of box, cloaked us deep. Shears I could hear where some gardener was clipping; a mumble of bees and broken voices that might have been the doves.

"Oh, unkind!" she said weariedly.

"Perhaps they're only shy of the motor. The little maid at the window looks tremendously interested."

"Yes?" She raised her head. "It was wrong of me to say that. They are really fond of me. It's the only thing that makes life worth living—when they're fond of you, isn't it? I daren't think what the place would be without them. By the way, is it beautiful?"

"I think it is the most beautiful place I have ever seen."

"So they all tell me. I can feel it, of course, but that isn't quite the same thing."

"Then have you never—?" I began, but stopped abashed.

"Not since I can remember. It happened when I was only a few months old, they tell me. And yet I must remember something, else how could I dream about colours. I see light in my dreams, and colours, but I never see *them*. I only hear them just as I do when I'm awake."

"It is difficult to see faces in dreams. Some people can, but most of us haven't the gift," I went on, looking up at the window where the child stood all but hidden.

"I've heard that too," she said. "And they tell me that one never sees a dead person's face in a dream. Is that true?"

"I believe it is—now I come to think of it."

"But how is it with yourself—yourself?" The blind eyes turned towards me.

"I have never seen the faces of my dead in any dream," I answered.

"Then it must be as bad as being blind."

The sun had dipped behind the woods and the long shades were possessing the insolent horsemen one by one. I saw the light die from off the top of a glossy-leaved lance and all the brave hard green turn to soft black. The house, accepting another day at end, as it had accepted an hundred thousand gone, seemed to settle deeper into its nest among the shadows.

"Have you ever wanted to?" she said after the silence.

"Very much, sometimes," I replied. The child had left the window as the shadows closed upon it.

"Ah! So've I, but I don't suppose it's allowed. . . . Where d'you live?"

"Quite the other side of the county—sixty miles and more, and I must be going back. I've come without my big lamp."

"But it's not dark yet. I can feel it."

"I'm afraid it will be by the time I get home. Could you lend me someone to set me on my road at first? I've utterly lost myself."

"I'll send Madden with you to the cross-roads. We are so out of the world, I don't wonder you were lost! I'll guide you round to the front of the house; but you wili go slowly, won't you, till you're out of the grounds? It isn't foolish, do you think?"

"I promise you I'll go like this," I said, and let the car start herself down the flagged path.

We skirted the left wing of the house, whose elaborately cast lead guttering alone was worth a day's journey; passed under a great rose-grown gate in the red wall, and so round to the high front of the house which in beauty and stateliness as much excelled the back as that all others I had seen.

"Is it so very beautiful?" she said wistfully when she heard my raptures. "And you like the lead-figures too? There's the old azalea garden behind. They say that this place must have been made for children. Will you help me out, please? I should like to come with you as far as the cross-roads, but I mustn't leave them. Is that you, Madden? I want you to show this gentleman the way to the cross-roads. He has lost his way but—he has seen them."

A butler appeared noiselessly at the miracle of old oak that must be called the front door, and slipped aside to put on his hat. She stood looking at me with open blue eyes in which no sight lay, and I saw for the first time that she was beautiful.

"Remember," she said quietly, "if you are fond of them you will come again," and disappeared within the house.

The butler in the car said nothing till we were nearly at the lodge gates, where, catching a glimpse of a blue blouse in a shrubbery, I swerved amply lest the devil that leads little boys to play should drag me in to child-murder.

"Excuse me," he asked of a sudden, "but why did you do that, sir?"

"The child yonder."

"Our young gentleman in blue?"

"Of course."

"He runs about a good deal. Did you see him by the fountain, sir?"

"Oh, yes, several times. Do we turn here?"

"Yes, sir. And did you 'appen to see them upstairs too?"

"At the upper window? Yes."

"Was that before the mistress come out to speak to you, sir?"

"A little before that. Why d'you want to know?"

He paused a little. "Only to make sure that—that they had seen the car, sir, because with children running about, though I'm sure you're driving particularly careful, there might be an accident. That was all, sir. Here are the cross-roads. You can't miss your way from now on. Thank you, sir, but that isn't *our* custom, not with—"

"I beg your pardon," I said, and thrust away the British silver.

"Oh, it's quite right with the rest of 'em as a rule. Good-bye, sir."

He retired into the armour-plated conning tower of his caste and walked away. Evidently a butler solicitous for the honour of his house, and interested, probably through a maid, in the nursery.

Once beyond the signposts at the cross-roads I looked back, but the crumpled hills interlaced so jealously that I could not see where the house had lain. When I asked its name at a cottage along the road, the fat woman who sold sweetmeats there gave me to understand that people with motors cars had small right to live—much less to "go about talking like carriage folk." They were not a pleasant-mannered community.

When I retraced my route on the map that evening I was little wiser. Hawkin's Old Farm appeared to be the Survey title of the place, and the old County Gazetteer, generally so ample, did not allude to it. The big house of those parts was Hodnington Hall, Georgian with early Victorian embellishments, as an atrocious steel engraving attested. I carried my difficulty to a neighbour—a deep-rooted tree of that soil—and he gave me a name of a family which conveyed no meaning.

A month or so later—I went again, or it may have been that my car took the road of her own volition. She over-ran the fruitless Downs, threaded every turn of the maze of lanes below the hills, drew through the high-walled woods, impenetrable in their full leaf, came out at the cross-roads where the butler had left me, and a little farther on developed an internal trouble which forced me to turn her in on a grass way-waste that cut into a summer-silent hazel wood. So far as I could make sure by the sun and a six-inch Ordnance map, this should be the road flank of that wood which I had first explored from the heights above. I made a mighty serious business of my repairs and a glittering shop of my repair kit, spanners, pump, and the like, which I spread out orderly upon a rug. It was a trap to catch all childhood, for on such a day, I argued, the children would not be far off. When I paused in my work I listened, but the wood was so full of the noises of summer (though the birds had mated) that I could not at first distinguish these from the tread of small cautious feet stealing across the dead leaves. I rang my bell in an alluring manner, but the feet fled, and I repented, for to a child a sudden noise is very real terror. I must have been at work half an hour when I heard in the wood the voice of the blind woman crying: "Children, oh, children, where are you?" and the stillness made slow to close on the perfection of that cry. She came towards me, half feeling her way between the tree boles, and though a child it seemed clung to her skirt, it swerved into the leafage like a rabbit as she drew nearer.

"Is that you," she said, "from the other side of the county?"

"Yes, it's me from the other side of the county."

"Then why didn't you come through the upper woods? They were there just now."

"They were here a few minutes ago. I expect they knew my car had broken down, and came to see the fun."

"Nothing serious, I hope? How do cars break down?"

"In fifty different ways. Only mine has chosen the fifty-first."

She laughed merrily at the tiny joke, cooed with delicious laughter, and pushed her hat back.

"Let me hear," she said.

"Wait a moment," I cried, "and I'll get you a cushion."

She set her foot on the rug all covered with spare parts, and stooped above it eagerly. "What delightful things!" The hands through which she saw glanced in the chequered sunlight. "A box here—another box! Why, you've arranged them like playing shop!"

"I confess now that I put it out to attract them. I don't need half those things really."

"How nice of you! I heard your bell in the upper wood. You say they were here before that?"

"I'm sure of it. Why are they so shy? That little fellow in blue who was with you just now ought to have got over his fright. He's been watching me like a Red Indian."

"It must have been your bell," she said. "I heard one of them go past me in trouble when I was coming down. They're shy—so shy even with me." She turned her face over her shoulder and cried again: "Children! Oh, children! Look and see!"

"They must have gone off together on their own affairs," I suggested, for there was a murmur behind us of lowered voices broken by the sudden squeaking giggles of childhood. I returned to my tinkerings and she leaned forward, her chin on her hand, listening interestedly.

"How many are they?" I said at last. The work was finished, but I saw no reason to go.

Her forehead puckered a little in thought. "I don't quite know," she said simply. "Sometimes more—sometimes less. They come and stay with me because I love them, you see."

"That must be very jolly," I said, replacing a drawer, and as I spoke I heard the inanity of my answer.

"You—you aren't laughing at me," she cried. "I—I haven't any of my own. I never married. People laugh at me sometimes about them because—because——"

"Because they're savages," I returned. "It's nothing to fret for. That sort laugh at everything that isn't in their own fat lives."

"I don't know. How should I? I only don't like being laughed at about *them*. It hurts; and when one can't see. . . . I don't want to seem silly," her chin quivered like a child's as she spoke, "but we blindies have only one skin, I think. Everything outside hits straight at our souls. It's different with you. You've such good defences in your eyes—looking out—before anyone can really pain you in your soul. People forget that with us."

I was silent reviewing that inexhaustible matter—the more than inherited (since it is also carefully taught) brutality of the Christian peoples, besides which the mere heathendom of the West Coast nigger is clean and restrained. It led me a long distance into myself.

"Don't do that!" she said of a sudden, putting her hands before her eyes.

"What?"

She made a gesture with her hand.

"That! It's—it's all purple and black. Don't! That colour hurts."

"But, how in the world do you know about colours?" I exclaimed, for here was a revelation indeed.

"Colours as colours?" she asked.

"No. *Those* Colours which you saw just now."

"You know as well as I do," she laughed, "else you wouldn't have asked that question. They aren't in the world at all. They're in *you*—when you went so angry."

"D'you mean a dull purplish patch, like port-wine mixed with ink?" I said.

"I've never seen ink or port-wine, but the colours aren't mixed. They are separate—all separate."

"Do you mean black streaks and jags across the purple?"

She nodded. "Yes—if they are like this," and zigzagged her finger again, "but it's more red than purple—that bad colour."

"And what are the colours at the top of the—whatever you see?"

Slowly she leaned forward and traced on the rug the figure of the Egg itself.

"I see them so," she said, pointing with a grass stem, "white, green, yellow, red, purple, and when people are angry or bad, black across the red—as you were just now."

"Who told you anything about it—in the beginning?" I demanded.

"About the colours? No one. I used to ask what colours were when I was little—in table-covers and curtains and carpets, you see—because some colours hurt me and some made me happy. People told me; and when I got older that was how I saw people." Again she traced the outline of the Egg which it is given to very few of us to see.

"All by yourself?" I repeated.

"All by myself. There wasn't anyone else. I only found out afterwards that other people did not see the Colours."

She leaned against the tree-bole plaiting and unplaiting chance-plucked grass stems. The children in the wood had drawn nearer. I could see them with the tail of my eye frolicking like squirrels.

"Now I am sure you will never laugh at me," she went on after a long silence. "Nor at *them*."

"Goodness! No!" I cried, jolted out of my train of thought. "A man who laughs at a child—unless the child is laughing too—is a heathen!"

"I didn't mean that, of course. You'd never laugh *at* children, but I thought—I used to think—that perhaps you might laugh about *them*. So now I beg your pardon. . . . What are you going to laugh at?"

I had made no sound, but she knew.

"At the notion of your begging my pardon. If you had done your duty as a pillar of the state and a landed proprietress you ought to have summoned me for trespass when I barged through your woods the other day. It was disgraceful of me—inexcusable."

She looked at me, her head against the tree trunk—long and steadfastly—this woman who could see the naked soul.

"How curious," she half whispered. "How very curious."

"Why, what have I done?"

"You don't understand . . . and yet you understood about the Colours. Don't you understand?"

She spoke with a passion that nothing had justified, and I faced her bewilderedly as she rose. The children had gathered themselves in a roundel behind a bramble bush. One sleek head bent over something smaller, and the set of the little shoulders told me that fingers were on lips. They, too, had some child's tremendous secret. I alone was hopelessly astray there in the broad sunlight.

"No," I said, and shook my head as though the dead eyes could note. "Whatever it is, I don't understand yet. Perhaps I shall later –if you'll let me come again."

"You will come again," she answered. "You will surely come again and walk in the wood."

"Perhaps the children will know me well enough by that time to let me play with them–as a favour. You know what children are like."

"It isn't a matter of favour but of right," she replied, and while I wondered what she meant, a dishevelled woman plunged round the bend of the road, loose-haired, purple, almost lowing with agony as she ran. It was my rude, fat friend of the sweetmeat shop. The blind woman heard and stepped forward. "What is it, Mrs. Madehurst?" she asked.

The woman flung her apron over her head and literally grovelled in the dust, crying that her grandchild was sick to death, that the local doctor was away fishing, that Jenny, the mother, was at her wits' end, and so forth, with repetitions and bellowings.

"Where's the next nearest doctor?" I asked between paroxysms.

"Madden will tell you. Go round to the house and take him with you. I'll attend to this. Be quick!" She half-supported the fat woman into the shade. In two minutes I was blowing all the horns of Jericho under the front of the House Beautiful, and Madden, in the pantry, rose to the crisis like a butler and a man.

A quarter of an hour at illegal speeds caught us a doctor five miles away. Within the half-hour we had decanted him, much interested in motors, at the door of the sweetmeat shop, and drew up the road to await the verdict.

"Useful things, cars," said Madden, all man and no butler. "If I'd had one when mine took sick she wouldn't have died."

"How was it?" I asked.

"Croup. Mrs. Madden was away. No one knew what to do. I drove eight miles in a tax cart for the doctor. She was choked when we came back. This car'd ha' saved her. She'd have been close on ten now."

"I'm sorry," I said. "I thought you were rather fond of children from what you told me going to the cross-roads the other day."

"Have you seen 'em again, sir—this mornin'?"

"Yes, but they're well broke to cars. I couldn't get any of them within twenty yards of it."

He looked at me carefully as a scout considers a stranger—not as a menial should lift his eyes to his divinely appointed superior.

"I wonder why," he said just above the breath that he drew.

We waited on. A light wind from the sea wandered up and down the long lines of the woods, and the wayside grasses, whitened already with summer dust, rose and bowed in sallow waves.

A woman, wiping the suds off her arms, came out of the cottage next the sweetmeat shop.

"I've be'n listenin' in de back-yard," she said cheerily. "He says Arthur's unaccountable bad. Did ye hear him shruck just now? Unaccountable bad. I reckon 'twill come Jenny's turn to walk in de wood nex' week along, Mr. Madden."

"Excuse me, sir, but your lap-robe is slipping," said Madden deferentially. The woman started, dropped a curtsey, and hurried away.

"What does she mean by 'walking in the wood'?" I asked.

"It must be some saying they use hereabouts. I'm from Norfolk myself," said Madden. "They're an independent lot in this county. She took you for a chauffeur, sir."

I saw the Doctor come out of the cottage followed by a draggle-tailed wench who clung to his arm as though he could make treaty for her with Death. "Dat sort," she wailed—"dey're just as much to us dat has 'em as if dey was lawful born. Just as much—just as much! An' God he'd be just as pleased if you saved 'un, Doctor.

Don't take it from me. Miss Florence will tell ye de very same. Don't leave 'im, Doctor!"

"I know, I know," said the man, "but he'll be quiet for a while now. We'll get the nurse and the medicine as fast as we can." He signalled me to come forward with the car, and I strove not to be privy to what followed; but I saw the girl's face, blotched and frozen with grief, and I felt the hand without a ring clutching at my knees when we moved away.

The Doctor was a man of some humour, for I remembered he claimed my car under the Oath of Aesculapius, and used it and me without mercy. First we convoyed Mrs. Madehurst and the blind woman to wait by the sick bed till the nurse should come. Next we invaded a neat county town for prescriptions (the Doctor said the trouble was cerebro-spinal meningitis), and when the County Institute, banked and flanked with scared market cattle, reported itself out of nurses for the moment, we literally flung ourselves loose upon the county. We conferred with the owners of great houses—magnates at the ends of overarching avenues whose big-boned womenfolk strode away from their tea-tables to listen to the imperious Doctor. At last a white-haired lady sitting under a cedar of Lebanon and surrounded by a court of magnificent Borzois—all hostile to motors—gave the Doctor, who received them as from a princess, written orders which we bore many miles at top speed, through a park, to a French nunnery, where we took over in exchange a pallid-faced and trembling Sister. She knelt at the bottom of the tonneau telling her beads without pause till, by short cuts of the Doctor's invention, we had her to the sweetmeat shop once more. It was a long afternoon crowded with mad episodes that rose and dissolved like the dust of our wheels; cross-sections of remote and incomprehensible lives through which we raced at right angles; and I went home in the dusk, wearied out, to dream of the clashing horns of cattle; round-eyed nuns walking in a garden of graves; pleasant tea-parties beneath shaded trees; the carbolic-scented, grey-painted corridors of the County Institute; the steps of shy children in the wood, and the hands that clung to my knees as the motor began to move.

I had intended to return in a day or two, but it pleased Fate to hold me from that side of the county, on many pretexts, till the elder and the wild rose had fruited. There came at last a brilliant day, swept clear from the south-west, that brought the hills within hand's reach—a day of unstable airs and high filmy clouds. Through no merit of my own I was free, and set the car for the third time on that known road. As I reached the crest of the Downs I felt the soft air change, saw it glaze under the sun; and, looking down at the sea, in that instant beheld the blue of the Channel turn through polished silver and dulled steel to dingy pewter. A laden collier hugging the coast steered outward for deeper water and, across copper-coloured haze, I saw sails rise one by one on the anchored fishing-fleet. In a deep dene behind me an eddy of sudden wind drummed through sheltered oaks, and spun aloft the first dry sample of autumn leaves. When I reached the beach road the sea-fog fumed over the brickfields, and the tide was telling all the groins of the gale beyond Ushant. In less than an hour summer England vanished in chill grey. We were again the shut island of the North, all the ships of the world bellowing at our perilous gates; and between their outcries ran the piping of bewildered gulls. My cap dripped moisture, the folds of the rug held it in pools or sluiced it away in runnels, and the salt-rime stuck to my lips.

Inland the smell of autumn loaded the thickened fog among the trees, and the drip became a continuous shower. Yet the late flowers—mallow of the wayside, scabious of the field, and dahlia of the garden—showed gay in the mist, and beyond the sea's breath there was little sign of decay in the leaf. Yet in the villages the house doors were all open, and bare-legged, bare-headed children sat at ease on the damp doorsteps to shout "pip-pip" at the stranger.

I made bold to call at the sweetmeat shop, where Mrs Madehurst met me with a fat woman's hospitable tears. Jenny's child, she said, had died two days after the nun had come. It was, she felt, best out of the way, even though insurance offices, for reasons which she did not pretend to follow, would not willingly insure such stray lives. "Not but what Jenny didn't tend to Arthur as though he'd come all proper at de end of de first year—like Jenny herself." Thanks to Miss Florence, the child had been buried with a pomp which, in Mrs. Madehurst's opinion, more than covered the small irregularity of its birth. She described the coffin, within and without, the glass hearse, and the evergreen lining of the grave.

"But how's the mother?" I asked.

"Jenny? Oh, she'll get over it. I've felt dat way with one or two o' my own. She'll get over. She's walkin' in de wood now."

"In this weather?"

Mrs. Madehurst looked at me with narrowed eyes across the counter.

"I dunno but it opens de 'eart like. Yes, it opens de 'eart. Dat's where losin' and bearin' comes so alike in de long run, we do say."

Now the wisdom of the old wives is greater than that of all the Fathers, and this last oracle sent me thinking so extendedly as I went up the road, that I nearly ran over a woman and a child at the wooded corner by the lodge gates of the House Beautiful.

"Awful weather!" I cried, as I slowed dead for the turn.

"Not so bad," she answered placidly out of the fog. "Mine's used to 'un. You'll find yours indoors, I reckon."

Indoors, Madden received me with professional courtesy, and kind inquiries for the health of the motor, which he would put under cover.

I waited in a still, nut-brown hall, pleasant with late flowers and warmed with a delicious wood fire—a place of good influence and great peace. (Men and women may sometimes, after great effort, achieve a creditable lie; but the house, which is their temple, cannot say anything save the truth of those who have lived in it.) A child's cart and a doll lay on the black-and-white floor, where a rug had been kicked back. I felt that the children had only just hurried away—to hide themselves, most like—in the many turns of the great adzed staircase that climbed statelily out of the hall, or to crouch and gaze behind the lions and roses of the carven gallery above. Then I heard her voice above me, singing as the blind sing—from the soul:—

In the pleasant orchard-closes.

And all my early summer came back at the call.

In the pleasant orchard-closes,
God bless all our gains say we—
But may God bless all our losses,
Better suits with our degree.

She dropped the marring fifth line, and repeated—

Better suits with our degree!

I saw her lean over the gallery, her linked hands white as pearl against the oak.

"Is that you—from the other side of the county?" she called.

"Yes, me—from the other side of the county," I answered, laughing.

"What a long time before you had to come here again." She ran down the stairs, one hand lightly touching the broad rail. "It's two months and four days. Summer's gone!"

"I meant to come before, but Fate prevented."

"I knew it. Please do something to that fire. They won't let me play with it, but I can feel it's behaving badly. Hit it!"

I looked on either side of the deep fireplace, and found but a half-charred hedge-stake with which I punched a black log into flame.

"It never goes out, day or night," she said, as though explaining. "In case anyone comes in with cold toes, you see."

"It's even lovelier inside than it was out," I murmured. The red light poured itself along the age-polished dusky panels till the Tudor roses and lions of the gallery took colour and motion. An old eagle-topped convex mirror gathered the picture into its mysterious heart, distorting afresh the distorted shadows, and curving the gallery lines into the curves of a ship. The day was shutting down in half a gale as the fog turned to stringy scud. Through the uncurtained mullions of the broad window I could see the valiant horsemen of the lawn rear and recover against the wind that taunted them with legions of dead leaves.

"Yes, it must be beautiful," she said. "Would you like to go over it? There's still light enough upstairs."

I followed her up the unflinching, wagon-wide staircase to the gallery whence opened the thin fluted Elizabethan doors.

"Feel how they put the latch low down for the sake of the children." She swung a light door inward.

"By the way, where are they?" I asked. "I haven't even heard them to-day."

She did not answer at once. Then, "I can only hear them," she replied softly. "This is one of their rooms—everything ready, you see."

She pointed into a heavily-timbered room. There were little low gate tables and children's chairs. A doll's house, its hooked front half open, faced a great dappled rocking-horse, from whose padded saddle it was but a child's scramble to the broad window-seat over-looking the lawn. A toy gun lay in a corner beside a gilt wooden cannon.

"Surely they've only just gone," I whispered. In the failing light a door creaked cautiously. I heard the rustle of a frock and the patter of feet—quick feet through a room beyond.

"I heard that," she cried triumphantly. "Did you? Children, O children, where are you?"

The voice filled the walls that held it lovingly to the last perfect note, but there came no answering shout such as I had heard in the garden. We hurried on from room to oak-floored room; up a step here, down three steps there; among a maze of passages; always mocked by our quarry.

One might as well have tried to work an unstopped warren with a single ferret. There were bolt-holes innumerable—recesses in walls, embrasures of deep slitten windows now darkened, whence they could start up behind us; and abandoned fireplaces, six feet deep in the masonry, as well as the tangle of communicating doors. Above all, they had the twilight for their helper in our game. I had caught one or two joyous chuckles of evasion, and once or twice had seen the silhouette of a child's frock against some darkening window at the end of a passage; but we returned empty-handed to the gallery, just as a middle-aged woman was setting a lamp in its niche.

"No, I haven't seen her either this evening, Miss Florence," I heard her say, "but that Turpin he says he wants to see you about his shed."

"Oh, Mr. Turpin must want to see me very badly. Tell him to come to the hall, Mrs. Madden."

I looked down into the hall whose only light was the dulled fire, and deep in the shadow I saw them at last. They must have slipped down while we were in the passages, and now thought themselves perfectly hidden behind an old gilt leather screen. By child's law, my fruitless chase was as good as an introduction, but since I had taken so much trouble I resolved to force them to come forward later by the simple trick, which children detest, of pretending not to notice them. They lay close, in a little huddle, no more than shadows except when a quick flame betrayed an outline.

"And now we'll have some tea," she said. "I believe I ought to have offered it you at first, but one doesn't arrive at manners somehow when one lives alone and is considered—h'm—peculiar." Then with very pretty scorn, "Would you like a lamp to see to eat by?"

"The firelight's much pleasanter, I think." We descended into that delicious gloom and Madden brought tea.

I took my chair in the direction of the screen ready to surprise or be surprised as the game should go, and at her permission, since a hearth is always sacred, bent forward to play with the fire.

"Where do you get these beautiful short faggots from?" I asked idly. "Why, they are tallies!"

"Of course," she said. "As I can't read or write I'm driven back on the early English tally for my accounts. Give me one and I'll tell you what it meant."

I passed her an unburned hazel-tally, about a foot long, and she ran her thumb down the nicks.

"This is the milk-record for the home farm for the month of April last year, in gallons," said she. "I don't know what I should have done without tallies. An old forester of mine taught me the system. It's out of date now for everyone else; but my tenants respect it. One of them's coming now to see me. Oh, it doesn't matter. He has no business here out of office hours. He's a greedy, ignorant man—very greedy or—he wouldn't come here after dark."

"Have you much land, then?"

"Only a couple of hundred acres in hand, thank goodness. The other six hundred are nearly all let to folk who knew my folk before me, but this Turpin is quite a new man—and a highway robber."

"But are you sure I sha'n't be—?"

"Certainly not. You have the right. He hasn't any children."

"Ah, the children!" I said, and slid my low chair back till it nearly touched the screen that hid them. "I wonder whether they'll come out for me."

There was a murmur of voices—Madden's and a deeper note—at the low, dark side-door, and a ginger-headed, canvas-gaitered giant of the unmistakable tenant farmer type stumbled or was pushed in.

"Come to the fire, Mr. Turpin," she said.

"If—if you please, Miss, I'll—I'll be quite as well by the door." He clung to the latch as he spoke like a frightened child. Of a sudden I realized that he was in the grip of some almost overpowering fear.

"Well?"

"About that new shed for the young stock—that was all. These first autumn storms settin' in . . . but I'll come again, Miss." His teeth did not chatter much more than the door latch.

"I think not," she answered levelly. "The new shed—m'm. What did my agent write you on the 15th?"

"I—fancied p'raps that if I came to see you—ma—man to man like, Miss. But—"

His eyes rolled into every corner of the room wide with horror. He half opened the door through which he had entered, but I noticed it shut again—from without and firmly.

"He wrote what I told him," she went on. "You are overstocked already. Dunnet's Farm never carried more than fifty bullocks—even in Mr. Wright's time. And *he* used cake. You've sixty-seven and you don't cake. You've broken the lease in that respect. You're dragging the heart out of the farm."

"I'm—I'm getting some minerals—superphosphates— next week. I've as good as ordered a truck-load already. I'll go down to the station to-morrow about 'em. Then I can come and see you man to man like, Miss in the daylight. . . . That gentleman's not going away, is he?" He almost shrieked.

I had only slid the chair a little farther back, reaching behind me to tap on the leather of the screen, but he jumped like a rat.

"No. Please attend to me, Mr. Turpin." She turned in her chair and faced him with his back to the door. It was an old and sordid little piece of scheming that she forced from him—his plea for the new cowshed at his landlady's expense, that he might with the covered manure pay his next year's rent out of the valuation after, as she made clear, he had bled the enriched pastures to the bone. I could not but admire the intensity of his greed, when I saw him out-facing for its sake whatever terror it was that ran wet on his forehead.

I ceased to tap the leather—was, indeed, calculating the cost of the shed—when I felt my relaxed hand taken and turned softly between the soft hands of a child. So at last I had triumphed. In a moment I would turn and acquaint myself with those quick-footed wanderers. . . .

The little brushing kiss fell in the centre of my palm—as a gift on which the fingers were, once, expected to close: as the all-faithful half-reproachful signal of a waiting child not used to neglect even when grown-ups were busiest—a fragment of the mute code devised very long ago.

Then I knew. And it was as though I had known from the first day when I looked across the lawn at the high window.

I heard the door shut. The woman turned to me in silence, and I felt that she knew.

What time passed after this I cannot say. I was roused by the fall of a log, and mechanically rose to put it back. Then I returned to my place in the chair very close to the screen.

"Now you understand," she whispered, across the packed shadows.

"Yes, I understand—now. Thank you."

"I—I only hear them." She bowed her head in her hands. "I have no right, you know—no other right. I have neither borne nor lost—neither borne nor lost!"

"Be very glad, then," said I, for my soul was torn open within me.

"Forgive me!"

She was still, and I went back to my sorrow and my joy.

"It was because I loved them so," she said at last, brokenly. "*That* was why it was, even from the first—even before I knew that they—they were all I should ever have. And I loved them so!"

She stretched out her arms to the shadows and the shadows within the shadow.

"They came because I loved them—because I needed them. I—I must have made them come. Was that wrong, think you?"

"No—no."

"I—I grant you that the toys and—and all that sort of thing were nonsense, but—but I used to so hate empty rooms myself when I was little." She pointed to the gallery. "And the passages all empty. . . . And how could I ever bear the garden door shut? Suppose—"

"Don't! For pity's sake, don't!" I cried. The twilight had brought a cold rain with gusty squalls that plucked at the leaded windows.

"And the same thing with keeping the fire in all night. I don't think it so foolish—do you?"

I looked at the broad brick hearth, saw, through tears I believe, that there was no unpassable iron on or near it, and bowed my head.

"I did all that and lots of other things—just to make believe. Then they came. I heard them, but I didn't know that they were not mine by right till Mrs. Madden told me—"

"The butler's wife? What?"

"One of them—I heard—she saw. And knew. Hers! *Not* for me. I didn't know at first. Perhaps I was jealous. Afterwards, I began to understand that it was only because I loved them, not because— . . . Oh, you *must* bear or lose," she said piteously. "There is no other way—and yet they love me. They must! Don't they?"

There was no sound in the room except the lapping voices of the fire, but we two listened intently, and she at least took comfort from what she heard. She recovered herself and half rose. I sat still in my chair by the screen.

"Don't think me a wretch to whine about myself like this, but—but I'm all in the dark, you know, and *you* can see."

In truth I could see, and my vision confirmed me in my resolve, though that was like the very parting of spirit and flesh. Yet a little longer I would stay, since it was the last time.

"You think it is wrong, then?" she cried sharply, though I had said nothing.

"Not for you. A thousand times no. For you it is right. . . . I am grateful to you beyond words. For me it would be wrong. For me only. . . ."

"Why?" she said, but passed her hand before her face as she had done at our second meeting in the wood. "Oh, I see," she went on simply as a child. "For you it would be wrong." Then with a little indrawn laugh, "And, d'you remember, I called you lucky—once—at first. You who must never come here again!"

She left me to sit a little longer by the screen, and I heard the sound of her feet die out along the gallery above.

D.H. LAWRENCE
The Last Laugh

David Herbert Lawrence *(1885–1930), celebrated for his novels* Women in Love, Sons and Lovers, The Rainbow *and* Lady Chatterley's Lover, *was equally adept with poetry, short stories, travel books, and the fascinating studies* Psychoanalysis and the Unconscious *(1921) and* Fantasia of the Unconscious *(1922). The short stories in* The Woman Who Rode Away *(1928) and other volumes are among his best work.*

There was a little snow on the ground, and the church clock had just struck midnight. Hampstead in the night of winter for once was looking pretty, with clean white earth and lamps for moon, and dark sky above the lamps.

A confused little sound of voices, a gleam of hidden yellow light. And then the garden door of a tall, dark Georgian house suddenly opened, and three people confusedly emerged. A girl in a dark blue coat and fur turban, very erect: a fellow with a little dispatch-case, slouching: a thin man with a red beard, bareheaded, peering out of the gateway down the hill that swung in a curve downwards towards London.

"Look at it! A new world!" cried the man in the beard, ironically, as he stood on the step and peered out.

"No, Lorenzo! It's only whitewash!" cried the young man in the overcoat. His voice was handsome, resonant, plangent, with a weary sardonic touch. As he turned back his face was dark in shadow.

The girl with the erect, alert head, like a bird, turned back to the two men.

"What was that?" she asked, in her quick, quiet voice.

"Lorenzo says it's a new world. I say it's only whitewash," cried the man in the street.

She stood still and lifted her woolly, gloved finger. She was deaf and was taking it in.

Yes, she had got it. She gave a quick, chuckling laugh, glanced very quickly at the man in the bowler hat, then back at the man in the stucco gateway, who was grinning like a satyr and waving good-bye.

"Good-bye, Lorenzo!" came the resonant, weary cry of the man in the bowler hat.

"Good-bye!" came the sharp, night-bird call of the girl.

The green gate slammed, then the inner door. The two were alone in the street, save for the policeman at the corner. The road curved steeply downhill.

"You'd better mind how you *step*!" shouted the man in the bowler hat, leaning near the erect, sharp girl, and slouching in his walk. She paused a moment, to make sure what he had said.

"Don't mind me, I'm quite all right. Mind yourself!" she said quickly. At that very moment he gave a wild lurch on the slippery snow, but managed to save himself from falling. She watched him, on tiptoes of alertness. His bowler hat bounced away in the thin snow. They were under a lamp near the curve. As he ducked for his hat he showed a bald spot, just like a tonsure, among his dark, thin, rather curly hair. And when he looked up at her, with his thick black brows sardonically arched, and his rather hooked nose self-derisive, jamming his hat on again, he seemed like a satanic young priest. His face had beautiful lines, like a faun, and a doubtful martyred expression. A sort of faun on the Cross, with all the malice of the complication.

"Did you hurt yourself?" she asked, in her quick, cool, unemotional way.

"No!" he shouted derisively.

"Give me the machine, won't you?" she said, holding out her woolly hand. "I believe I'm safer."

"Do you *want* it?" he shouted.

"Yes, I'm sure I'm safer."

He handed her the little brown dispatch-case, which was really a Marconi listening machine for her deafness. She marched erect as ever. He shoved his hands deep in his overcoat pockets and slouched along beside her, as if he wouldn't make his legs firm. The road curved down in front of them, clean and pale with snow under the lamps. A motor-car came churning up. A few dark figures slipped away into the dark recesses of the houses, like fishes among rocks above a sea-bed of white sand. On the left was a tuft of trees sloping upwards into the dark.

He kept looking around, pushing out his finely shaped chin and his hooked nose as if he were listening for something. He could still hear the motor-car climbing on to the Heath. Below was the yellow, foul-smelling glare of the Hampstead Tube station. On the right the trees.

The girl, with her alert pink-and-white face looked at him sharply, inquisitively. She had an odd nymph-like inquisitiveness, sometimes like a bird, sometimes a squirrel, sometimes a rabbit: never quite like woman. At last he stood still, as if he would go no farther. There was a curious, baffled grin on his smooth, cream-coloured face.

"James," he said loudly to her, leaning towards her ear. "Do you hear somebody *laughing*?"

"Laughing?" she retorted quickly. "Who's laughing?"

"I don't know. *Somebody!*" he shouted, showing his teeth at her in a very odd way.

"No, I hear nobody," she announced.

"But it's most *extraordinary*!" he cried, his voice slurring up and down. "Put on your machine."

"Put it on?" she retorted. "What for?"

"To see if you can *hear* it," he cried.

"Hear what?"

"The *laughing*. Somebody laughing. It's most *extraordinary*."

She gave her odd little chuckle and handed him her machine. He held it while she opened the lid and attached the wires, putting the band over her head and the receivers at her ears, like a wireless operator. Crumbs of snow fell down the cold darkness. She switched on: little yellow lights in glass tubes shone in the machine. She was connected, she was listening. He stood with his head ducked, his hands shoved down in his overcoat pockets.

Suddenly he lifted his face and gave the weirdest, slightly neighing laugh, uncovering his strong, spaced teeth and arching his black brows, and watching her with queer, gleaming goat-like eyes.

She seemed a little dismayed.

"There!" he said. "Didn't you hear it?"

"I heard *you*!" she said, in a tone which conveyed that *that* was enough.

"But didn't you hear *it*?" he cried, unfurling his lips oddly again.

"No!" she said.

He looked at her vindictively, and stood again with ducked head. She remained erect, her fur hat in her hand, her fine bobbed hair banded with the machine-band and catching crumbs of snow, her odd, bright-eyed, deaf nymph's face lifted with blank listening.

"There!" he cried, suddenly jerking up his gleaming face. "You mean to tell me you can't—" He was looking at her almost diabolically. But something else was too strong for him. His face wreathed with a startling, peculiar smile, seeming to gleam, and suddenly the most extraordinary laugh came bursting out of him, like an animal laughing. It was a strange, neighing sound, amazing in her ears. She was startled, and switched her machine quieter.

A large form loomed up: a tall, clean-shaven young policeman.

"A radio?" he asked laconically.

"No, it's my machine. I'm deaf!" said Miss James quickly and distinctly. She was not the daughter of a peer for nothing.

The man in the bowler hat lifted his face and glared at the fresh-faced young policeman with a peculiar white glare in his eyes.

"Look here!" he said distinctly. "Did you hear someone laughing?"

"Laughing? I heard you, sir."

"No, *not* me." He gave an impatient jerk of his arm, and lifted his face again. His smooth, creamy face seemed to gleam, there were subtle curves of derisive triumph in all its lines. He was careful not to look directly at the young policeman. "The most extraordinary laughter I ever heard," he added, and the same touch of derisive exultation sounded in his tones.

The policeman looked down on him cogitatingly.

"It's perfectly all right," said Miss James coolly. "He's not drunk. He just hears something that we don't hear."

"Drunk!" echoed the man in the bowler hat, in profoundly amused derision. "If I were merely drunk—" And off he went again in the wild, neighing, animal laughter, while his averted face seemed to flash.

At the sound of the laughter something roused in the blood of the girl and of the policeman. They stood nearer to one another, so that their sleeves touched and they looked wonderingly across at the man in the bowler hat. He lifted his black brows at them.

"Do you mean to say you heard nothing?" he asked.

"Only you," said Miss James.

"Only you, sir!" echoed the policeman.

"What was it like?" asked Miss James.

"Ask me to *describe* it!" retorted the young man, in extreme contempt. "It's the most marvellous sound in the world."

And truly he seemed wrapped up in a new mystery.

"Where does it come from?" asked Miss James, very practical.

"*Apparently*," he answered in contempt, "from over there." And he pointed to the trees and bushes inside the railings over the road.

"Well, let's go and see!" she said. "I can carry my machine and go on listening."

The man seemed relieved to get rid of the burden. He shoved his hands in his pockets again and sloped off across the road. The policeman, a queer look flickering on his fresh young face, put his hand round the girl's arm carefully and subtly, to help her. She did not lean at all on the support of the big hand, but she was interested, so she did not resent it. Having held herself all her life intensely aloof from physical contact, and never having let any man touch her, she now, with a certain nymph-like voluptuousness, allowed the large hand of the young policeman to support her as they followed the quick wolf-like figure of the other man across the road uphill. And she could feel the presence of the young policeman, through all the thickness of his dark-blue uniform, as something young and alert and bright.

When they came up to the man in the bowler hat, he was standing with his head ducked, his ears pricked, listening beside the iron rail inside which grew big black holly trees tufted with snow, and old, ribbed, silent English elms.

The policeman and the girl stood waiting. She was peering into the bushes with the sharp eyes of a deaf nymph, deaf to the world's noises. The man in the bowler hat listened intensely. A lorry rolled downhill, making the earth tremble.

"There!" cried the girl, as the lorry rumbled darkly past. And she glanced round with flashing eyes at her policeman, her fresh soft face gleaming with startled life. She glanced straight into the puzzled, amused eyes of the young policeman. He was just enjoying himself.

"Don't you see?" she said, rather imperiously.

"What is it, miss?" answered the policeman.

"I mustn't point," she said. "Look where I look."

And she looked away with brilliant eyes, into the dark holly bushes. She must see something, for she smiled faintly, with subtle satisfaction, and she tossed her erect head in all the pride of vindication. The policeman looked at her instead of into the bushes. There was a certain brilliance of triumph and vindication in all the poise of her slim body.

"I always knew I should see him," she said triumphantly to herself.

"Whom do you see?" shouted the man in the bowler hat.

"Don't you see him, too?" she asked, turning round her soft, arch, nymph-like face anxiously. She was anxious for the little man to see.

"No, I see nothing. What do you see, James?" cried the man in the bowler hat, insisting.

"A man."

"Where?"

"There. Among the holly bushes."

"Is he there now?"

"No! He's gone."

"What sort of a man?"

"I don't know."

"What did he look like?"

"I can't tell you."

But at that instant the man in the bowler hat turned suddenly, and the arch, triumphant look flew to his face.

"Why, he must be *there*!" he cried, pointing up the grove. "Don't you hear him laughing? He must be behind those trees."

And his voice, with curious delight, broke into a laugh again, as he stood and stamped his feet on the snow, and danced to his own laughter, ducking his head. Then he turned away and ran swiftly up the avenue lined with old trees.

He slowed down as a door at the end of a garden path, white with untouched snow, suddenly opened, and a woman in a long-fringed black shawl stood in the light. She peered out into the night. Then she came down to the low garden gate. Crumbs of snow still fell. She had dark hair and a tall dark comb.

"Did you knock at my door?" she asked of the man in the bowler hat.

"I? No!"

"Somebody knocked at my door."

"Did they? Are you sure? They can't have done. There are no footmarks in the snow."

"Nor are there!" she said. "But somebody knocked and called something."

"That's very curious," said the man. "Were you expecting someone?"

"No. Not exactly expecting anyone. Except that one is always expecting. Somebody, you know." In the dimness of the snow-lit night he could see her making big, dark eyes at him.

"Was it someone laughing?" he said.

"No. It was no one laughing, exactly. Someone knocked, and I ran to open, hoping as one always hopes, you know—"

"What?"

"Oh—that something wonderful is going to happen."

He was standing close to the low gate. She stood on the opposite side. Her hair was dark, her face seemed dusky, as she looked up at him with her dark, meaningful eyes.

"Did you wish someone would come?" he asked.

"Very much," she replied, in her plangent Jewish voice. She must be a Jewess."

"No matter who?" he said, laughing.

"So long as it was a man I could like," she said in a low, meaningful, falsely shy voice.

"Really!" he said. "Perhaps, after all, it was I who knocked—without knowing."

"I think it was," she said. "It must have been."

"Shall I come in?" he asked, putting his hand on the little gate.

"Don't you think you'd better?" she replied.

He bent down, unlatching the gate. As he did so the woman in the black shawl turned, and, glancing over her shoulder, hurried back to the house, walking unevenly in the snow, on her high-heeled shoes. The man hurried after her, hastening like a hound to catch up.

Meanwhile the girl and the policeman had come up. The girl stood still when she saw the man in the bowler hat going up the garden walk after the woman in the black shawl with the fringe.

"Is he going in?" she asked quickly.

"Looks like it, doesn't it?" said the policeman.

"Does he know that woman?"

"I can't say. I should say he soon will," replied the policeman.

"But who is she?"

"I couldn't say who she is."

The two dark, confused figures entered the lighted doorway, then the door closed on them.

"He's gone," said the girl outside on the snow. She hastily began to pull off the band of her telephone-receiver, and switched off her machine. The tubes of secret light disappeared, she packed up the little leather case. Then, pulling on her soft fur cap, she stood once more ready.

The slightly martial look which her long, dark-blue, military-seeming coat gave her was intensified, while the slightly anxious, bewildered look of her face had gone. She seemed to stretch herself, to stretch her limbs free. And the inert look had left her full soft cheeks. Her cheeks were alive with the glimmer of pride and a new dangerous surety.

She looked quickly at the tall young policeman. He was clean-shaven, fresh-faced, smiling oddly under his helmet, waiting in subtle patience a few yards away. She saw that he was a decent young man, one of the waiting sort.

The second of ancient fear was followed at once in her by a blithe, unaccustomed sense of power.

"Well!" she said. "I should say it's no waiting." She spoke decisively.

"You don't have to wait for him, do you?" asked the policeman.

"Not at all. He's much better where he is." She laughed an odd, brief laugh. Then glancing over her shoulder, she set off down the hill, carrying her little case. Her feet felt light, her legs felt long and strong. She glanced over her shoulder again. The young policeman was following her, and she laughed to herself. Her limbs felt so lithe and strong, if she wished she could easily run faster than he. If she wished she could easily kill him, even with her hands.

So it seemed to her. But why kill him? He was a decent young fellow. She had in front of her eyes the dark face among the holly bushes, with the brilliant mocking eyes. Her breast felt full of power, and her legs felt long and strong and wild. She was surprised herself at the strong, bright, throbbing sensation beneath her breasts, a sensation of triumph and of rosy anger. Her hands felt keen on her wrists. She who had always declared she had not a muscle in her body! Even now, it was not muscle, it was a sort of flame.

Suddenly it began to snow heavily, with fierce frozen puffs of wind. The snow was small, in frozen grains, and hit sharp on her face. It seemed to whirl round her as if she herself were whirling in a cloud. But she did not mind. There was a flame in her, her limbs felt flamey and strong, amid the whirl.

And the whirling, snowy air seemed full of presences, full of strange unheard voices. She was used to the sensation of noises taking place which she could not hear. This sensation became very strong. She felt something was happening in the wild air.

The London air was no longer heavy and clammy, saturated with ghosts of the unwilling dead. A new, clean tempest swept down from the Pole, and there were noises.

Voices were calling. In spite of her deafness she could hear someone, several voices, calling and whistling, as if many people were hallooing through the air:

"He's come back! Aha! He's come back!"

There was a wild, whistling, jubilant sound of voices in the storm of snow. Then obscured lightning winked through the snow in the air.

"Is that thunder and lightning?" she asked of the young policeman, as she stood still, waiting for his form to emerge through the veil of whirling snow.

"Seems like it to me," he said.

And at that very moment the lightning blinked again, and the dark, laughing face was near her face, it almost touched her cheek.

She started back, but a flame of delight went over her.

"There!" she said. "Did you see that?"

"It lightened," said the policeman.

She was looking at him almost angrily. But then the clean, fresh animal look of his skin, and the tame-animal look in his frightened eyes amused her, she laughed her low, triumphant laugh. He was obviously afraid, like a frightened dog that sees something uncanny.

The storm suddenly whistled louder, more violently, and, with a strange noise like castanets, she seemed to hear voices clapping and crying:

"He is here! He's come back!"

She nodded her head gravely.

The policeman and she moved on side by side. She lived alone in a little stucco house in a side street down the hill. There was a church and a grove of trees and then the little old row of houses. The wind blew fiercely, thick with snow. Now and again a taxi went by, with its lights showing weirdly. But the world seemed empty, uninhabited save by snow and voices.

As the girl and the policeman turned past the grove of trees near the church, a great whirl of wind and snow made them stand still, and in the wild confusion they heard a whirling of sharp, delighted voices, something like seagulls, crying:

"He's here! He's here!"

"Well, I'm jolly glad he's back," said the girl calmly.

"What's that?" said the nervous policeman, hovering near the girl.

The wind let them move forward. As they passed along the railings it seemed to them the doors of the church were open, and the windows were out, and the snow and the voices were blowing in a wild career all through the church.

"How extraordinary that they left the church open!" said the girl.

The policeman stood still. He could not reply.

And as they stood they listened to the wind and the church full of whirling voices all calling confusedly.

"*Now* I hear the laughing," she said suddenly.

It came from the church: a sound of low, subtle, endless laughter, a strange, naked sound.

"Now I hear it!" she said.

But the policeman did not speak. He stood cowed, with his tail between his legs, listening to the strange noises in the church.

The wind must have blown out one of the windows, for they could see the snow whirling in volleys through the black gap, and whirling inside the church like a dim light. There came a sudden crash, followed by a burst of chuckling, naked laughter. The snow seemed to make a queer light inside the building, like ghosts moving, big and tall.

There was more laughter, and a tearing sound. On the wind, pieces of paper, leaves of books, came whirling among the snow through the dark window. Then a white thing, soaring like a crazy bird, rose up on the wind as if it had wings, and lodged on a black tree outside, struggling. It was the altar-cloth.

There came a bit of gay, trilling music. The wind was running over the organ-pipes like pan-pipes, quickly up and down. Snatches of wild, gay, trilling music, and bursts of the naked low laughter.

"Really!" said the girl. "This is most extraordinary. Do you hear the music and the laughing?"

"Yes, I hear somebody on the organ!" said the policeman.

"And do you get the puff of warm wind? Smelling of spring. Almond blossom, that's what it is! A most marvellous scent of almond blossom. *Isn't* it an extraordinary thing!"

She went on triumphantly past the church, and came to the row of little old houses. She entered her own gate in the little railed entrance.

"Here I am!" she said finally. "I'm home now. Thank you very much for coming with me."

She looked at the young policeman. His whole body was white as a wall with snow, and in the vague light of the arc-lamp from the street his face was humble and frightened.

"Can I come in and warm myself a bit?" he asked humbly. She knew it was fear rather than cold that froze him. He was in mortal fear.

"Well!" she said. "Stay down in the sitting-room if you like. But don't come upstairs, because I am alone in the house. You can make up the fire in the sitting-room, and you can go when you are warm."

She left him on the big, low couch before the fire, his face bluish and blank with fear. He rolled his blue eyes after her as she left the room. But she went up to her bedroom, and fastened her door.

In the morning she was in her studio upstairs in her little house, looking at her own paintings and laughing to herself. Her canaries were talking and shrilly whistling in the sunshine that followed the storm. The cold snow outside was still clean, and the white glare in the air gave the effect of much stronger sunshine than actually existed.

She was looking at her own paintings, and chuckling to herself over their comicalness. Suddenly they struck her as absolutely absurd. She quite enjoyed looking at them, they seemed to her so grotesque. Especially her self-portrait, with its nice brown hair and its slightly opened rabbit-mouth and its baffled, uncertain rabbit eyes. She looked at the painted face and laughed in a long, rippling laugh, till the yellow canaries like faded daffodils almost went mad in an effort to sing louder. The girl's long, rippling laugh sounded through the house uncannily.

The housekeeper, a rather sad-faced young woman of a superior sort—nearly all people in England are of the superior sort, superiority being an English ailment—came in with an inquiring and rather disapproving look.

"Did you call, Miss James?" she asked loudly.

"No. No, I didn't call. Don't shout, I can hear quite well," replied the girl.

The housekeeper looked at her again.

"You knew there was a young man in the sitting-room?" she said.

"No. Really!" cried the girl. "What, the young policeman? I'd forgotten all about him. He came in in the storm to warm himself. Hasn't he gone?"

"No, Miss James."

"How extraordinary of him! What time is it? Quarter to nine! Why didn't he go when he was warm? I must go and see him, I suppose."

"He says he's lame," said the housekeeper censoriously and loudly.

"Lame! That's extraordinary. He certainly wasn't last night. But don't shout. I can hear quite well."

"Is Mr. Marchbanks coming in to breakfast, Miss James?" said the housekeeper, more and more censorious.

"I couldn't say. But I'll come down as soon as mine is ready. I'll be down in a minute, anyhow, to see the policeman. Extraordinary that he is still here."

She sat down before her window, in the sun, to think a while. She could see the snow outside, the bare, purplish trees. The air all seemed rare and different: as if some skin or integument had broken, as if the old, mouldering London sky had crackled and rolled back, like an old skin, shrivelled, leaving an absolutely new blue heaven.

"It really is extraordinary!" she said to herself. "I certainly saw that man's face. What a wonderful face it was! I shall never forget it. Such laughter! He laughs longest who laughs last. He certainly will have the last laugh. I like him for that: he will laugh last. Must be someone really extraordinary! How very nice to be the one to laugh last. He certainly will. What a wonderful being! I suppose I must call him a being. He's not a person exactly.

"But how wonderful of him to come back and alter all the world immediately! *Isn't* that extraordinary. I wonder if he'll have altered Marchbanks. Of course Marchbanks never *saw* him. But he heard him. Wouldn't that do as well, I wonder!—I *wonder*!"

She went off into a muse about Marchbanks. She and he were *such* friends. They had been friends like that for almost two years. Never lovers. Never that at all. But *friends*.

And after all, she had been in love with him: in her head. This seemed now so funny to her: that she had been, in her head, so much in love with him. After all, life was too absurd.

Because now she saw herself and him as such a funny pair. He so funnily taking life terribly seriously, especially his own life. And she so ridiculously *determined* to save him from himself. Oh, how absurd! *Determined* to save him from himself, and wildly in love with him in the effort. The determination to save him from himself.

Absurd! Absurd! Absurd! Since she had seen the man laughing among the holly bushes—*such* extraordinary, wonderful laughter—she had seen her own ridiculousness. Really, what fantastic silliness, saving a man from himself! Saving anybody. What fantastic silliness! How much more amusing and lively to let a man go to perdition in his own way. Perdition was more amusing than salvation, anyhow, and a much better place for most men to go to.

She had never been in love with any man, and only spuriously in love with Marchbanks. She saw it quite plainly now. After all, what nonsense it all was, this being-in-love business. Thank goodness she had never made the humiliating mistake.

No, the man among the holly bushes had made her see it all so plainly: the ridiculousness of being in love, the *infra dig* business of chasing a man or being chased by a man.

"Is love *really* so absurd and *infra dig*?" she said aloud to herself.

"Why, of course!" came a deep, laughing voice.

She started round, but nobody was to be seen.

"I expect it's that man again!" she said to herself. "It really *is* remarkable, you know. I consider it's a remarkable thing that I never really wanted a man, *any* man. And there I am over thirty. It *is* curious. Whether it's something wrong with me, or right with me, I can't say. I don't know till I've proved it. But I believe, if that man kept on laughing something would happen to me."

She smelt the curious smell of almond blossom in the room, and heard the distant laugh again.

"I do wonder why Marchbanks went with that woman last night—that Jewish-looking woman. Whatever could he want of her?—or she of him? So strange, as if they both had made up their minds to something! How extraordinarily puzzling life is! So messy, it all seems.

"Why does nobody ever laugh in life like that man? He *did* seem so wonderful. So scornful! And so proud! And so real! With those laughing, scornful, amazing eyes, just laughing and disappearing again. I can't imagine him chasing a Jewish-looking woman. Or chasing any woman, thank goodness. It's all *so* messy. My policeman would be messy if one would let him: like a dog. I do dislike dogs, really I do. And men do seem so doggy!—"

But even while she mused, she began to laugh again to herself with a long, low chuckle. How wonderful of that man to come and laugh like that and make the sky crack and shrivel like an old skin! Wasn't he wonderful! Wouldn't it be wonderful if he just touched her. Even touched her. She felt, if he touched her, she herself would emerge new and tender out of an old, hard skin. She was gazing abstractedly out of the window.

"There he comes, just now," she said abruptly. But she meant Marchbanks, not the laughing man.

There he came, his hands still shoved down in his overcoat pockets, his head still rather furtively ducked, in the bowler hat, and his legs still rather shambling. He came hurrying across the road, not looking up, deep in thought, no doubt. Thinking profoundly, with agonies of agitation, no doubt about his last night's experience. It made her laugh.

She, watching from the window above, burst into a long laugh, and the canaries went off their heads again.

He was in the hall below. His resonant voice was calling, rather imperiously;

"James! Are you coming down?"

"No," she called. "You come up."

He came up two at a time, as if his feet were a bit savage with the stairs for obstructing him.

In the doorway he stood staring at her with a vacant, sardonic look, his grey eyes moving with a queer light. And she looked back at him with a curious, rather haughty carelessness.

"Don't you want your breakfast?" she asked. It was his custom to come and take breakfast with her each morning.

"No," he answered loudly. "I went to a tea-shop."

"Don't shout," she said. "I can hear you quite well."

He looked at her with mockery and a touch of malice.

"I believe you always could," he said, still loudly.

"Well, anyway, I can now, so you needn't shout," she replied.

And again his grey eyes, with the queer, greyish phosphorescent gleam in them, lingered malignantly on her face.

"Don't look at me," she said calmly. "I know all about everything."

He burst into a pouf of malicious laughter.

"Who taught you—the policeman?" he cried.

"Oh, by the way, he must be downstairs! No, he was only incidental. So, I suppose, was the woman in the shawl. Did you stay all night?"

"Not entirely. I came away before dawn. What did you do?"

"Don't shout. I came home, long before dawn." And she seemed to hear the long, low laughter.

"Why, what's the matter?" he said curiously. "What have you been doing?"

"I don't quite know. Why?—are you going to call me to account?"

"Did you hear that laughing?"

"Oh yes. And many more things. And saw things, too."

"Have you seen the paper?"

"No. Don't shout, I can hear."

"There's been a great storm, blew out the windows and doors of the church outside here, and pretty well wrecked the place."

"I saw it. A leaf of the church Bible blew right in my face: from the Book of Job—" She gave a low laugh.

"But what else did you see?" he cried loudly.

"I saw *him*."

"Who?"

"Ah, that I can't say."

"But what was he like?"

"That I can't tell you. I don't really know."

"But you must know. Did your policeman see him, too?"

"No, I don't suppose he did. My policeman!" And she went off into a long ripple of laughter. "He is by no means mine. But I *must* go downstairs and see him."

"It's certainly made you very strange," Marchbanks said. "You've got no *soul*, you know."

"Oh, thank goodness for that!" she cried. "My policeman has one, I'm sure. *My policeman!*" And she went off again into a long peal of laughter, the canaries pealing shrill accompaniment.

"What's the matter with you?" he said.

"Having no soul. I never had one really. It was always fobbed off on me. Soul was the only thing there was between you and me. Thank goodness it's gone. Haven't you lost yours? The one that seemed to worry you, like a decayed tooth?"

"But what are you *talking* about?" he cried.

"I don't know," she said. "It's all so extraordinary. But look here, I *must* go down and see my policeman. He's downstairs in the sitting-room. You'd better come with me."

They went down together. The policeman, in his waistcoat and shirt-sleeves, was lying on the sofa, with a very long face.

"Look here!" said Miss James to him. "Is it true you're lame?"

"It is true. That's why I'm here. I can't walk," said the fair-haired young man as tears came to his eyes.

"But how did it happen? You weren't lame last night," she said.

"I don't know how it happened—but when I woke up and tried to stand up, I couldn't do it." The tears ran down his distressed face.

"How very extraordinary!" she said. "What can we do about it?"

"Which foot is it?" asked Marchbanks. "Let us have a look at it."

"I don't like to," said the poor devil.

"You'd better," said Miss James.

He slowly pulled off his stocking, and showed his white left foot curiously clubbed, like the weird paw of some animal. When he looked at it himself, he sobbed.

And as he sobbed, the girl heard again the low, exulting laughter. But she paid no heed to it, gazing curiously at the weeping young policeman.

"Does it hurt?" she asked.

"It does if I try to walk on it," wept the young man.

"I'll tell you what," she said. "We'll telephone for a doctor, and he can take you home in a taxi."

The young fellow shamefacedly wiped his eyes.

"But have you no idea how it happened?" asked Marchbanks anxiously.

"I haven't myself," said the young fellow.

At that moment the girl heard the low, eternal laugh right in her ear. She started, but could see nothing.

She started round again as Marchbanks gave a strange, yelping cry, like a shot animal. His white face was drawn distorted in a curious grin, that was chiefly agony, but partly wild recognition. He was staring with fixed eyes at something. And in the rolling agony of his eyes was the horrible grin of a man who realizes he has made a final, and this time fatal, fool of himself.

"Why," he yelped in a high voice, "I knew it was he!" And with a queer shuddering laugh he pitched forward on the carpet and lay writhing for a moment on the floor. Then he lay still, in a weird, distorted position, like a man struck by lightning.

Miss James stared with round, staring brown eyes.

"Is he dead?" she asked quickly.

The young poiceman was trembling so that he could hardly speak. She could hear his teeth chattering.

"Seems like it," he stammered.

There was a faint smell of almond blossom in the air.

MARGERY LAWRENCE
Robin's Rath

Margery Lawrence *(1889–1969) specialised in Gothic and romantic melodramas (*The Madonna of Seven Moons *was successfully filmed in 1944, starring Phyllis Calvert). She was also a strong believer in the occult and spiritualism, and many of her ghost stories and tales of reincarnation were based on accounts she heard at seances. The atmospheric 'Robin's Rath' appeared in her rare collection* Nights of the Round Table *(1926).*

The evening was chill with the cool dampness of February when we gathered for dinner, chatting, laughing, comparing notes as to the past month. There was a bowl of pearly snowdrops on the round table, delicately virginal, and Saunderson nodded towards them as he greeted Dan Vesey, the latest-comer, a shy pale fellow with lank black hair forever falling over his brow in a lovelock.

"Seasonable, eh, Dan? You're a February's child, aren't you? Thought so! Got anything in the shape of a story to fit this evening—something that'll tune in with February and rain and snowdrops?"

Dan Vesey nodded over his *potage Madeleine.*

"I think so—I hunted it up last night. I'll tell it you later—when we get to the usual coffee stage. But it's nothing like such a thrill as Hellier's—only just an ethereal, evanescent little story called 'Robin's Rath.' "

"So ye're goin' to buy Robin's Rath, young lady?"

Ellen Vandermyl raised her arched brows with a touch of hauteur at the old man's tone. Not the daughter of a hundred earls, but of one immensely wealthy pork-packer who could deny her nothing, even to the purchase of Ghyll Hall, she had, as have so many American women of bourgeois birth, the tiny feet and delicate complexion that is generally considered the heritage of the aristocrat alone. Now she tapped a smart brogued shoe with an equally smart cane as she answered old Giles' question, with a little note of asperity in her voice:

"Of course I am—I have—it goes with Ghyll Hall! Besides, when I get a path made it will make a perfect short cut to the golf-links."

There was a sudden stir and rustle among the group of villagers; with one accord they looked at old Giles—and there was a pointed little silence. Flushing with annoyance, Ellen glanced from one face to another. Her one wish was to get on well with the villagers of this tiny lovely village, Ghyllock, which seemed to live in the shelter of the old manor-house, Ghyll Hall, for centuries the seat of the Ruddocks, and now passing, like so many other many-memoried old houses, into the hands of the stranger. An only child, her father wax in her hands, the pretty spoilt American beauty had passed through Ghyllock once only, on a motor tour, and seeing the wonderful old house set in miles of green woods and meadows and fields, had given her father no peace till he offered to buy it for her—much as he would have endeavoured to buy the moon, had she wanted it! The grounds ran down to a narrow belt of woodland, thick with undergrowth, the tangling green luxuriance that had never known shears or pruning knife—Robin's Rath. Beyond lay the golf links, within easy walking distance of the Hall when the path mentioned should be cut—certainly it seemed a good idea, and there was some reason for Ellen's puzzled annoyance at the sudden silence that greeted her remark. Even the landlord of the picturesque inn, the "Goose with the Golden Eggs," lounging in the shadow of his own doorway to listen to the gossip under the great elm tree outside, put down his mug of beer and stared at her curiously. She spoke sharply, addressing old Giles, whose heavy white brows were drawn down over his intent old eyes in a heavy frown.

"What in the world's the matter? You all look as if I'd threatened to kill somebody!"

"Ye're cutting a path through the Rath?" Giles' voice was a little raised so that all might hear the enormity proposed. Ellen flushed angrily now, and spoke, settling her pointed chin more decidedly into her vivid blue woollen scarf.

"Certainly I am—it's the quickest way to the links. Is there any reason why I should not?"

Everyone was listening intently now, and Giles gave an odd laugh, still studying her under his shaggy brows.

"No, missy; no real reason. But ye shudna' try—ye shudna' try!"

"Why on earth?" Ellen was getting both thoroughly ruffled and a little alarmed now. The old man sent a swift glance round at the circle of interested faces.

"Robin's Rath's never bin touched, Missy. If ye'll tek an old man's advice ye'll leave it be—Robin's Rath's better as it is."

"Aye—aye, right enough." "Leave it be, Miss—better leave it be. . . ."

A confused chorus of voices from the watching group all gravely eyeing her, emphasised the old man's words, and with a quick angry shrug and laugh Ellen turned away, pushing the ends of the scarf into the front of her grey tweed jacket.

"Really, you are talking nonsense! I shall do what I choose with the place—sorry if it annoys you, but I really see no sense in what you say against the idea of cutting a path through a piece of wild land! Good day. . . ."

Her slim figure disappeared round the turn of the lane, and old Giles shrugged his shoulders as he took up his pipe again.

"No sense?—well, well! Happen she'll see sense before 'tes too late—happen she mayn't; then the Lord help her, for she's a pretty piece enough."

Ellen Vandermyl strode briskly along the narrow lane, still warm and flushed with annoyance at the recent little encounter. Her firm chin was set, and her dark eyes rather hard under their evenly marked brows. She was rather cross with herself also for becoming angry at what was, after all, a show of interest in her doings, which interest, up to the present, the villagers had been sadly devoid of, greatly to her vexation. She was quite determined to marry and settle down into an English country lady—the husband question could be settled later, though doubtless "Papa" would arrange that as easily as he had this, the purchase of the "seat," wonderful Ghyll Hall. Ellen had, beneath her greedy little modern tastes, a genuine sense of the beautiful and as she walked across the meadow-path homewards her eyes lighted with appreciation. The Hall faced her, far up the sloping side of the hill, backed by dark woods, and at the foot of the grounds, running into the lush water-meadow that she was crossing, the wide tangled woodland of Robin's Rath, a long narrow copse, cut the grounds of the Hall from the meadow like a dark ribbon of green wildness. Usually Ellen took the twisting path that led round the end of the Rath into the road that passed the Hall gates, but now just at the bend she stopped, and staring through the rough fence into the Rath, muttered something impatient to herself about the crass stupidity of the villagers. It would be so easy to cut a straight path through this—it couldn't be more than a hundred and fifty to two hundred yards across, and one walked straight into the meadow and thence to the links. Absurd, the Ruddocks never doing it—of course the undergrowth was woefully thick and obviously hadn't been touched for centuries, but a couple of good men with bill-hooks would soon do the job. Against a dark tree-trunk, only a few yards away, a man stood chewing a grass blade, hands in the pockets of his green corduroys, his eyes on her.

"Goodness!" It annoyed Ellen to be surprised, and she reflected with embarrassment that he must have been standing there all the time and overheard her irritable remarks about the villagers. He was only a keeper, probably, but it was none the less annoying to feel foolish, and Ellen's colour was considerably heightened when she spoke again. "Here! Who are you, and what are you doing on my land?"

The man removed the grass-blade and spoke, one hand still in his pocket, and a pair of odd, quick eyes, on her. His voice was rather brusque.

"Your land, hey, Miss?"

"Yes, mine." Her voice was brusquer, and the man laughed suddenly, with a lazy amusement.

"Yours?—sorry, Miss! I never knew. . . . Don't look cross at me, Missy. I'm only a keeper!" Again the tone of lazy amusement, and to her great vexation Ellen found her colour rising again beneath the casual gaze of the stranger's eyes. True, he called her "Miss," but somehow with a tone as if he found it rather amusing to do so. . . . Before she could speak again, suddenly with a quick lithe movement, he was at the fence, his long brown hands near to hers. He wore a green leather cap, very damaged and old, pulled over his eyes, and his eyes were light brown, almost yellow, and quick and bright as a bird's.

"Come in, Miss! You've never been into Robin's Rath yet, I'll go bail—not for all you're cutting a path-way through it!" Somehow, against her will, Ellen found herself scrambling over the fence and standing a little breathless and scratched, on the other side. The man in green was but little taller, and they faced each other, feet deep in thick tussocky grass. Ellen compressed her lips hard and clutched at her vanishing dignity; somehow it seemed childish and puerile under the man's dancing eyes, but she stuck to her pose doggedly.

"Er—no, I haven't had time to go through it—but if, as I suppose, you are one of Sir George Ruddock's keepers, perhaps you had better show me the best place to cut a path down to the meadow. . . . You are a keeper here, I suppose?"

The man in green was leading the way deep into the dusky heart of the Rath—standing aside, he held a branch away as he replied.

"Yes. . . . I'm a keeper here. Been here long enough, Missy. Longer than you'd think!"

"How long?" persisted the girl. The man's manner pricked her curiosity. He spoke the rough country dialect certainly, but still with an air of engaging nonchalance, as if he did it on purpose. . . . Was he a Ruddock? Come back in disguise to look after the lands of his fathers? Ellen's imagination, fed full on cinemas, French novels, and the yellow Press of her country, ranged excitedly among a thousand dramatic possibilities. . . . Turning to the man in green, changing her tactics, she found him looking down at her with a disconcerting little smile—she looked away, suddenly discomfited, and immediately exclaimed in astonished admiration:

"How lovely!" They faced a narrow little glade, thick with bluebells—the blue flood ran like spilt colour about the trunks of the trees as far as the eye could see; the dark tree-trunks and the shiver of pale young leaves above their heads were speckled and splashed with golden flecks and pools and spangles—for an enchanted moment Ellen stared, then turned to the man in green, leaning negligently up against a tree, his rough suit almost one with the mossy bark. He nodded, his eyes intent on hers.

"Yes. 'Tes good enough, eh? And right here, Missy, is where you were goin' to cut the path. 'Tis the narrowest part of Robin's Rath."

Ellen started. So this was it, was it? Another attempt on the part of these idiotic village people to influence her into leaving the Rath alone? Very cleverly done, she would admit—but what impertinence! Now just to show them she couldn't be dictated to she would insist on having the path cut, though a moment ago she had been on the verge of changing her mind. . . . Turning round, she laughed sharply, her chin in the air, and an acid remark on her tongue, but it died away unspoken as she met the strange keeper's odd light eyes. She felt somehow curiously embarrassed beneath the calm, quizzical gaze of this brown-faced fellow in the shabby green corduroys—biting her lips, she tossed her pretty spoilt head and caught back her dignity as lady-of-the-manor. Her tone as she spoke was delicately condescending.

"Oh, really! Thanks for pointing it out—I must get some men to come and start work on it immediately. Do you happen to know a couple of good woodmen?" She congratulated herself that this was neat, to ask him to recommend the despoilers of the green Rath that obviously meant so much to him. The man laughed, his curly head, now bare of any covering, tilted back against the brown bark of the tree.

"Good woodmen, hey? Who should know but I, who've spent day and night these—well, more years than you'd think, Missy—in the green Rath. . . . Oh yes—I could tell you of woodmen eno'—but it might be they wouldn't suit you; they're old . . . and set in their ways now. . . . No. No. They'd do a lot for me—but I wouldn't risk asking them to lay axe or bill-hook to Robin's Rath——"

"Who are you? What is your name?" Ellen asked suddenly, her puzzled eyes studying him.

"My name? Oh, my name is just Rob Woodson, Missy. But I've a lot of names. Happen if you ask the folk round here they'll call me the Man in Green . . ."

A wren flew whistling fussily across the glade, and the man held up a brown hand, his lips pursed to a tiny soothing note. To Ellen's great astonishment the wee brown bird lighted on his outstretched finger, chirruping agitatedly in his face. He nodded, laughed, and, flinging up his long arm, threw the bird into the air. Forgetting her annoyance, Ellen spoke delightedly.

"Oh, can you tame them, really? I wish you would tame some for me!"

Her vain little mind was already visualising a delicious picture of herself in white on the wide terrace of the Hall, surrounded by tiny fluttering creatures taking crumbs from her hand, unafraid, and in the background a circle of admiring guests. The man in green looked down at her and laughed amusedly.

"Teach you, eh? 'Twould take more than your little lifetime to learn what I know about birds, Miss. That little chap, now . . . he's in a rare taking, him and his missus, for fear you cut that path. His nest's in an elder bush right in the way, and she hasn't hatched her eggs yet."

"It's absurd to talk of birds in that way—as if they were human!" said Miss Vandermyl coldly, flushed and angry again now at the fresh introduction of the vexed question of the path. She moved away into the sun-patched bluebells, leaving a trail of crushed stalks and flattened blossoms behind her—turning a haughty head over her shoulder, she nodded a patronising good-bye to the strange keeper who stood knee-deep in the blue flood beneath the trees, watching her silently. She jumped as he answered her unspoken thought.

"A right to do what you like with your own land, eh, Missy? Why, that's fair. . . . But think a minute—what's the name of this green Rath, anyway? Robin's Rath—the Rath of Robin. Well, well, isn't that enough? Wait till Robin tells you what he thinks of that path of yours—cuttin' across his ground! Think it over, Missy . . . and come down and see the Rath again to-morrow. I'll be here—if you come to the Rath again to-morrow!" The light mocking voice died away behind her as Ellen Vandermyl hurried away—she flung a hasty glance over her shoulder as she scrambled out of the Rath into the wide cool stretch of turf that swept up to the Hall—the man in green had gone and only the sunlight twinkled through the leaves across the tree-trunk where he had been. . . .

Her aunt, Miss Eustasia Vandermyl, met her in the hall, and commented on the mess she had made of her smart tweed suit—torn in two or three places it was, and bits of leaf and twig stuck to it still. Ellen raised annoyed eyebrows and, slipping into another skirt, sat down to lunch, full of her adventure.

"Auntie—I had the most astonishing meeting this morning, coming up from the water-meadow through Robin's Rath." Molly the housemaid, a comely, strapping girl, daughter of old Giles, was handing her the potatoes at the moment of speaking, and Ellen went on:

"Do keep the dish still, Molly—what's the matter with you? Well, I came through the Rath—suppose that's why I've made such a mess of my tweed—the bushes can't have been cut for ages . . . there's not even a path. I shouldn't think anyone's ever even walked through till I did—absolutely wild it is. Lovely, of course, in a way . . ."

"Well," said Aunt Eustasia, with mild impatience, "is that all the adventure, or is there some more? Molly, the potatoes, please. Well?"

"Oh no! There's a lot more. I met a strange man there—a keeper he said he was. He said his name was Woodson—but he's not an ordinary keeper by any means."

Rosy Molly's pink cheeks had suddenly faded to white, and she stood with her hands knotted together in her apron as she listened, her round blue eyes on her unconscious mistress, eating her cutlet daintily as she went on:

"I can't help thinking he's one of the Ruddocks in disguise, or something of the sort—oh, yes, he speaks with a funny accent, but I feel it's put on somehow. Like all these crazy villagers, he seems set against this idea of mine of cutting a path through the Rath to the links."

"It's such a good idea, too," commented Eustasia, languidly. "What reason did he give against it?"

Ellen laughed with a trace of asperity, remembering her old vexation over the subject.

"Oh—no real reason at all! They none of them have. Only that it's never been done before—so English! As if that was a reason why it should never be done at all! I asked him to recommend two good woodmen—just out of sheer mischief, of course, as I knew he wouldn't—but he said those he knew were too old or something . . ."

"What did you say his name was?" Eustasia asked curiously.

"Woodson—Rob Woodson, he said," said Ellen, "but he said that the people around here knew him best as 'the Man in Green'."

Crash! Both ladies jumped and exclaimed as Molly's shaking red hands let fall the fruit dish she was just placing on the table—scolded, she had nothing to say but that "she couldn't help it"—"she was very sorry" . . . the door closed on her downcast figure, and Ellen laughed vexedly.

"What a fool! Well, Auntie, I'm going to lie down for a while, and then I shall make you doll me up for tea. Don't forget the Anselms and Lady Craven are coming. . . ."

The Anselms, Joe, Lylie and their mother were very charming, as was Lady Craven, and tea a complete success. Ellen looked charming in a vivid green frock, and accompanied Joe Anselm in several songs with great *éclat*—as an heiress, she was worth the county's cultivating, and certainly Ellen felt she stood on the threshold of her longed-for position in English society as she walked down the well-kept drive with her guests. Lady Craven's car drove away, but the others were walking—it was a lovely spring evening, and Joe Anselm good-looking and obviously rather intrigued with the pretty American. His mother, Lady Anselm, regarding possibilities with an amiably approving eye directed towards the paternal millions that would ultimately become Miss Vandermyl's, suggested that Ellen should walk back part of the way, at least, to the village. A wrap and hat hastily donned, Ellen joined them, and the merry little group descended the steep sloping lane to the village. Passing the end of Robin's Rath where it ran into the lane, Joe Anselm peered inside laughingly.

"Cut your famous path yet, Miss Vandermyl?"

"No," said Ellen, laughing. "I'm going to very soon, though!"

"Find any difficulty in getting woodmen?" asked Lylie Anselm, suddenly.

Ellen's brows wrinkled.

"Well—I haven't taken any very special pains to find any yet, but now you speak of it, I believe I shall find it difficult. The villagers don't seem to like the idea of my cutting a path at all!"

Lylie glanced at her brother oddly.

"Yes. I don't think you'll get any of the local men to touch Robin's Rath, Miss Vandermyl."

Ellen laughed vexedly—here again, even these aristocrats were casting cold water on her scheme! She answered with a touch of heightened colour.

"If they won't, I shall have some men over from Brayling or Little Witchet! But why in the world this extraordinary reluctance to have Robin's Rath touched? Even you—" Joe nodded, colouring a trifle.

"I wouldn't, Miss Vandermyl. Really I wouldn't—I'd leave the Rath as it is. . . ."

Ellen's temper, never too easy, suddenly snapped.

"This is *too* idiotic really! Why?"

Lylie came to the rescue of her brother.

"It's nothing, really, Miss Vandermyl. Only—a sort of story that the village people believe. We don't—but, anyway, one of the Ruddocks once tried to clear Robin's Rath and make it into a wild garden . . ."

Joe's glance held his sister's, and she stopped suddenly, to Ellen's great annoyance.

"Well? What happened?" Lylie was silent, but Joe answered, guardedly.

"They stopped. They never finished it. Something stopped them."

"Good Heavens—what?" Ellen's tone was frankly scornful, and the young man winced, but answered her unmoved.

"I don't know. . . . But nobody touches Robin's Rath—the villagers say—without some awful misfortune——"

"What rot!" In her relieved indignation Ellen was none too polite. "Really, Mr. Anselm, I thought you were more sensible! Anyway, it's safe enough to human beings, for I met one of Sir George Ruddock's old keepers there only this morning, and he was all right—said he spent all his time there!"

Joe's eyebrows were wrinkled, puzzled.

"Keeper—thought all the Ruddock's keepers left when—when the Hall was sold? What sort of a man is he?"

"Says his name is Woodson," said Ellen. "As to what he looks like—well, he's tall and brown-faced, dressed in green. . . ."

At that moment they stopped at the door of the village store, where Ellen was to say good-bye to them—Lady Anselm and her three dogs were a little behind, and the brother and sister stood silent, regarding Miss Vandermyl. There was a faint pause, and they looked at each other.

Lylie spoke softly, her voice oddly hushed.

"We know who you mean—now. No, we've never seen him. But you have—you've seen the Man in Green? Good-bye, Miss Vandermyl. . . ."

Oddly silent, the two strode away—round the bend of the road they looked at each other again, and Lylie's eyes were frightened.

"Joe—Oh, Joe! What can we do? She's seen him—and do you remember Andrew? Andrew persuaded Jim Ruddock to try and clear the Rath—and Andrew saw him. . . ."

Joe's freckled face twitched in painful memory of Andrew Stirling, his chum—first in all sports, bright and brave and handsome, and of that faint shadow of the Andrew they had known that had been found sprawling, half-dead, at the edge of the Rath one awful morning. With a jerk he brushed the memory away, and replied:

"We can't do anything, Lylie. We've done our best—and everybody's tried to warn her. But she's a wilful, spoilt little specimen, and I'm afraid it's useless. We can't—nobody can—you know it—say more than we have done. One can only warn her as best we can—and hope she'll take it. . . ."

Next morning was if anything, lovelier than before, and Ellen's little soul expanded beneath the life-giving sunlight as she wandered about the lovely old house and grounds, planning fresh alterations, improvements, everywhere. Her restless American mind, over-modern, unable to let anything alone, but must forever be tinkering with it, altering, experimenting, fairly purred in its pleasure at having this gorgeous piece of the old world to play with. The immense expanse of jade green turf that swept down from the Hall windows to the distant Rath, was to be cut up into flower beds and a pergola—two new tennis courts were to be laid down, thereby sacrificing an old walled garden that had stood for over three hundred years; a huge and wonderful oak that happened, unfortunately, to shade her bedroom windows too heavily was to go, and endless other alterations. . . .

"Good morning to you, Missy!" The man in green stood with his arms folded along the top of the rough fence that divided the Rath from the grounds.

"Oh—good morning!" Ellen was confused for a moment—why, she wondered, had she come wandering down to the Rath again, all unconsciously?

The man in green laughed suddenly, amusedly.

"You came because you said you would, of course! Now, now—no cross looks this wonderful morning! I know you never said so in words—why, come over again then, and we can talk in the Rath together, just we two."

Rob Woodson's voice was seductive, warm as the spring sunshine that flooded Miss Vandermyl's bare head where she stood, a few feet away from the fence, her eyes puzzled, half-dazed, half-frightened. She answered rather vaguely, her eyes on his merry, light brown orbs, twinkling at her beneath the pulled-down brim of his green cap.

"Why, I—of course, I was coming. I meant to come. . . ." The fence was high and the green tangled undergrowth of the Rath a few feet lower than the smooth-shaven lawn that met it. One doubtful hand on the fence, Ellen looked at the man in green questioningly. Pulling aside a slat or two, he made room for her feet to mount, then, as she balanced precariously on the top, stepped back and laughed, a full-throated gust of merriment that brought tears of vexation to the girl's eyes. At the sight the man in green stopped at once and came forward, his brown eyes suddenly tender behind their elfish laughter.

"That was too bad, little lady!" His voice was low and beautiful, and his arms were held out to her where she balanced on the top of the fence, level with his shoulders. "Let yourself go now—into my arms. . . ."

Obediently she sank forward into the arms held ready to receive her, and her head went down on his shoulder with a little tremulous sigh of happiness as his warm lips found hers. With the girl curled close in his arms, his head bent to hers, he turned swiftly into the heart of the Rath, and the green closed over them. . . .

Miss Eustasia Vandermyl kept lunch till almost two o'clock, and then, just as she was beginning to be seriously agitated, Ellen stepped into the dining-room through the open French window. Her eyes were wide and dazed, but her mouth was tremulously red, and she broke into a little running laugh of happiness at her aunt's grim face of disapproval. Coming forward, she kissed the old lady, to the latter's great astonishment—Ellen was never in the habit of kissing people, especially relations.

"Well! I'd begun to give you up, Ellen. And Mercy! what have you done to yourself?"

Eustasia's restless old hands were picking leaves, bits of moss and twigs from the girl's tumbled hair and skirt, but Ellen twitched away, and seizing an apple declared she was not hungry. Molly eyed her furtively with a sort of terrified interest as she served the older woman's meal, but Ellen's eyes were absent as she munched, and she never noticed. Lylie Anselm, striding down to the village later, met Molly on her afternoon out, and the two stopped. Molly had been in service with the Ruddocks, and known Lylie and her brother since babyhood. The village girl's usually rosy cheeks were pale again to-day, and she seized on Lylie with feverish urgency.

"Oh, Miss Lylie—I dunna how to say it—but I'm sa scared I cunna sleep o'nights. I mun tell you——"

"What is it?" Lylie said, though her own paling cheeks showed kinship with the fear that whitened the other's ruddiness.

They stood near the Rath, and Molly dropped her voice as she spoke.

"It's—it's the same coming as came to Muster Andrew — oh, Miss, I cunna bear it! Father he tried to warn her an' all—an' she wunna see, she wunna see! Messin' with the Rath an'all— d'ye mind how Muster Andrew wud say he met the Man in Green? . . ." The girl was nearly crying, and Lylie patted her arm soothingly.

"Don't worry, Molly—perhaps it'll be all right. Anyway, we've all tried to warn her—we can't do any more. If I were to tell her just the truth she would laugh—and besides, you know one can't. . . . Something stops it every time. . . ."

There was a crackling of elder bushes above them where the Rath ran up to a steep bank, and a wren flew out, chattering indignantly, almost as if he had been thrown out to startle the girls—with a scared little cry Molly took to her heels, and Lylie, her young lips compressed, strode on towards the village.

As she turned the bend in the path past the Rath that led into the water-meadow it seemed she heard a faint laugh somewhere deep in the green tangle of bramble and hawthorn and wild rose—Lylie's steps were no slower for that, for she was thinking of Andrew, as he used to be—and as he was—when the Rath had done with him.

The next two weeks were anxious ones for Miss Eustasia. Ellen, she thought, was suffering from some form of nerves—while she lost no interest in the house and grounds, and directed the workmen energetically in the alterations, she was given to sudden inexplicable absences from the house, sometimes in daytime, but more often now about dusk, and as the month was approaching its zenith, and the fat, honeycoloured Spring moon waxing larger each night, the evenings saw her less and less with her aunt. She came back from these expeditions faintly flushed, with eyes like stars, and an unwonted sweetness about her like a magic cloak—but for all that, distrait and absent, and with the vaguest possible explanations. All she would say was that she had been wandering in the Rath. At last her aunt grew suspicious of the mysterious Man in Green and one day interrogated Molly. The latter flushed and paled suddenly, and averred, with a furtive glance towards the Rath, sleeping in the warm pale afternoon sun, that the keeper was all right, she heard: was he well known? Well, yes—bin here a long time. Cunna tell how long—maybe years and years. Yes. Known him herself? Why no, ma'am—'twas a bit of a cold makin' her shiver like that—cunna help it, like. No. She'd heard tell of him often though—happen that was all ma'am wanted?

Satisfied, Miss Eustasia cast about for another reason, but found none, and at that moment Ellen stepped into the room from the garden, trailing a branch of bramble behind her, her dark hair starred with dew-wet convolvuli. She took no notice of her aunt, but stood with her face pressed against the cold pane, staring out into the slowly darkening garden towards the Rath.

Miss Eustasia spoke sharply.

"Really, Ellen! You might at least, when you *do* condescend to come in, take a little trouble to be pleasant! I get very little of your company these days."

Ellen smiled faintly and came over to her aunt, laying a slender arm scented with pines and bracken across the old lady's thin shoulders.

"Poor auntie! Never mind—I am very happy. Happier than I knew it was possible to be. What's worrying you, any way, dear?"

The old lady bit off a thread of silk viciously.

"Just this, my dear—you're not leading a healthy life, mooning about by yourself these days. What's happened to your golf that you were so keen on? Young Anselm came over yesterday to ask you to play, and you were away somewhere. . . ."

Ellen laughed. Now, as it always did sooner or later, the vaguely dreamy mood began to wear off, and the old Ellen, bright, poised, and self-sufficient, was speaking.

"That all? Dear me, I'll write him at once and suggest a day next week."

She moved to the writing-table and opened the blotter as she spoke. Eustasia finished off a flower of her embroidery emphatically as she began again.

"That reminds me—have you done anything about that path through the Rath? It's too silly for you to go a quarter of a mile round by the road when with a little trouble you could have that path cut."

Ellen's brow was wrinkled, almost as if she tried to catch a fleeting though half-forgotten thought.

"Oh yes. I'd somehow forgotten that. . . . I suppose it had better be done. It seems difficult to get men here though—perhaps I'd better leave it."

"Rubbish!" the old lady snapped. "Now you're writing, write to that firm at Little Witchet we passed in the car the other day, and tell them to send three or four men. To-day's Friday—say they had better come on Monday."

The room fell silent save for the faint scratching of Miss Vandermyl's pen on the paper—it was getting dark very rapidly, thought Miss Eustasia, and what a nuisance that straand of ivy tapping against the pane was—odd that she who was so sensitive to irritating noises had never noticed it before. Sitting back, Ellen sealed up both envelopes, and slipped them into her pocket. The tapping of the ivy seemed to have worried her too, for she opened the window and broke the trail off, impatiently flinging it into the garden. Stretching out her arms she yawned, and laughed.

"Well, that's done! Funny how I came to put off writing about that path these last two weeks—quite unlike my usual business-like ways. Papa always said I had the head of a business man—how he'd have laughed to see me wandering for hours about a damp wood!" Her laughter was frankly amused, and it was the old Ellen that glanced down into her aunt's eyes—cool, self-reliant, dominating. Miss Eustasia patted her hand.

"Glad to see you more like yourself again, dear. I admit that craze of yours for perpetually exploring the Rath worried me a little—what made you take to doing it, now?"

A faint puzzled crease crossed the girl's white forehead, and at that moment a belated wren fluttered against the rising wind past the window, cheeping feebly. Ellen passed her hand across her brow worriedly, then dropped it and laughed lightly.

"I really couldn't possibly say, dearest! I can't think now why I did it—just whim, I suppose. Now I'm going up to dress for dinner—come along."

It seemed to Miss Eustasia afterwards that never had Ellen been so bright and like her usual sparkling self as that last dinner-time; the idle, dreaming Ellen of the last two weeks seemed to have vanished like snow in spring, and thankfully Eustasia mentally composed another letter to Papa Vandermyl that should set his mind completely at rest concerning his wilful daughter, whose insistance on the purchase of the Hall had worried him considerably. They had coffee in the pretty drawing-room, and Ellen played . . . bright crisp rag-time music, sharply contrasted to her recent craze for Sibelius, Dvorak and Ravel. There was a small fire, for the storm had fulfilled its promise, and the bright rain spattered the long panes persistently, while a chilly little wind forced its way through the chinks of the curtains.

The evening passed peacefully, and at last Miss Eustasia, who had been nodding steadily before the fire for the last half-hour, rose and yawned, putting her eternal embroidery together.

"Well—you play delightfully, dear. But I think it's about time for bed, don't you? Are you coming?"

Ellen shook her head, her fingers still wandering absently over the keys.

"No. Not yet. Very soon, I think—good night, dear."

The door closed behind the old lady, and Ellen's hands fell from the keys. There was that tiresome ivy again tapping—it must be another piece. To-morrow she would have the whole thing cut away—it was maddening, this eternal tapping. Settling herself into a chair by the fire with a book she tried to read, but the tapping proved too distracting and at last, with an impatient exclamation, she got up and went to the window. Pulling aside the curtain, she gave a sudden gasp of terrified astonishment—pressed against the panes, his long-nailed fingers playing a tattoo on the glass, his light eyes gleaming luminous in the light, stood the Man in Green! Beckoning, he retreated, and vanished in the dark, wind-tossed trees—mechanically, with no thought of refusal, she fetched a cloak from the hall, and stepping out into the whirl of wind and rain, went steadily down the dark garden. The moon was full, but ragged clouds sailing across it obscured its light except for occasional glimpses—there was a faint growl of thunder in the distance, and the gusts of sharp wind flapped and buffeted her, flinging showers of heavy drops upon her uncovered hair from the overhanging trees. In the open the light rain stung her face like tiny needles; a sob rose in her throat as with wide, fixed bright eyes she pressed steadily on down the sloping lawns to the waiting Rath. Her mind was vaguely wandering down half-forgotten paths—she had been made one with the Rath, received into its arms—through Someone, but who she had forgotten. . . . The keeper—but, of course, she had always known he was no keeper . . . who was he? Never mind, it didn't matter, and she couldn't remember anything clearly. Only that there in the Rath she had known joy unspeakable, lain with her cheek pressed against the grass and bracken, played—so long ago it seemed!—with rabbit and wren and chaffinch, unfearing, friendly, with Someone's arm about her . . . drunk of its tiny stream, decked her hair with its flowers; the Rath had received her, and she had turned upon it and stabbed it to the heart. By a letter—a cruel letter, that even now lay in the pocket of the coat she wore. Now she was going to meet her just punishment. . . . With dark eyes wide and vague, she stumbled down the last steep grass slope and stopped, panting heavily, against the fence. Across the top the keeper leant, regarding her strangely from beneath his pulled-down cap, shiny with rain—she noticed dully that a spraying trail of ivy hung from his buttonhole, and idly wondered why; the brown hands of the man in green were clasped loosely together along the top of the fence, and with a sudden sick remembrance she thought again of the first time she had seen them thus. . . . The wind whistled and roared, rising to a gale around them, and in a lull she heard Rob Woodson speak.

"So you have come to the Rath again, little lady? To the Rath for the last time?" His tone was light, half-laughing, but a faint cold hint of menace rang through it, and his odd, luminous eyes regarded her curiously as she stood there, plucking unthinkingly at the moss on the fence, her dark curly hair whipped to a halo about her head, those beautiful eyes regarding him dully. Her mouth quivered suddenly, piteously, as she replied:

"Yes. I have come—for the last time. . . . What—what are you going to do with me?" Through the vaguely hypnotised look in her eyes crept a real gleam of fear, and she shivered involuntarily as he stretched out a long hand in invitation. Patting the place where the broken slats still spoke so vividly of that wonderful day two weeks ago—or was it two hundred years?—he smiled at her, shrinking in nameless terror on the other side.

"You have been made free of the Rath, fair Ellen! Why do you fear it?"

She raised tortured eyes to his, dumbly, and his smile broadened, eyes narrowing as he watched her terror-stricken face . . . grim fear held her in an icy grip, and feebly she fought with all that was left her of sanity to resist, but his eyes were merciless. Trembling, she mounted the fence, and as she balanced on the top, suddenly, swiftly, he held out his arms to her, his head flung back, laughing, a slant moonbeam gleaming on his light, cruel eyes, mocking, triumphant, inhuman.

"Come—let go and come to my arms, pretty maiden! Fall—fall, you who know what no other woman has known, and must die for the knowing—come to me!"

With a shouting rush and flurry of wind, with a beating of rain about her, the last shred of resistance fled from the girl as she fell forward, and dimly through the gathering mists she heard the voice of the Man in Green above her, through the wild howling of the gale that rocked the groaning trees—light, joyous, triumphant, as his lips closed on hers. . . .

"The Rath has received you, maiden, and the Rath rejects you, in this my last kiss on your human lips! For I—Rob Woodson—son of the woods, I am Robin, and this is my Rath! . . ."

A few months later the Hall was up for sale, and rebought by Sir George Ruddock, sorely repentant at ever having sold the house of his fathers; so the Ruddocks came back to Ghyll, and the pretty

American faded into a mere story, whispered to terrified ears on winter's evenings.

But far across the seas, in bustling New York, an anxious father goes from specialist to specialist with a lovely dark-eyed girl, once bright, alert, vivacious, now blank and dull, half-witted almost, with the springs of her vivid womanhood dried up and dead within her.

Now and then she gets restless and cries a little, on a wet spring night, and always she has ivy and green things of the wood in water in her room; but generally she goes through life smiling vaguely, gentle, silent and empty of soul as a doll. Indeed, as one great specialist said to another aside, too low for the agonised father to hear:

"She's as much mentality as a china doll now—no use to anyone, ever any more. Some shock must have killed the springs of vitality—but I wonder what it was?"

He may well wonder, since Ellen Vandermyl is the only one who knows, and she can only drift through life smiling at nothing, silent, with her womanhood dead within her since Robin Goodfellow kissed the soul away from her one stormy night, long ago, in a green glade in England.

J. SHERIDAN LE FANU
The Dream

Joseph Sheridan Le Fanu *(1814–73), great-nephew of the dramatist Richard Brinsley Sheridan, was unequalled in the Victorian era as a writer of mystery and supernatural tales. In the words of M.R. James, he 'stands absolutely in the first rank as a writer of ghost stories'. Among his many classics in the genre are 'The Familiar', 'Green Tea', and 'A Strange Event in the Life of Schalken the Painter'.*

'The Dream', from The Watcher and Other Weird Stories *(1894), originally appeared in the* Dublin University Magazine, *August 1838.*

Dreams! What age, or what country of the world, has not felt and acknowledged the mystery of their origin and end? I have thought not a little upon the subject, seeing it is one which has been often forced upon my attention, and sometimes strangely enough; and yet I have never arrived at anything which at all appeared a satisfactory conclusion. It does appear that a mental phenomenon so extraordinary cannot be wholly without its use. We know, indeed, that in the olden times it has been made the organ of communication between the Deity and His creatures; and when a dream produces upon a mind, to all appearance hopelessly reprobate and depraved, an effect so powerful and so lasting as to break down the inveterate habits, and to reform the life of an abandoned sinner, we see in the result, in the reformation of morals which appeared incorrigible, in the reclamation of a human soul which seemed to be irretrievably lost, something more than could be produced by a mere chimera of the slumbering fancy, something more than could arise from the capricious images of a terrified imagination. And while Reason rejects as absurd the superstition which will read a prophecy in every dream, she may, without violence to herself, recognize, even in the wildest and most incongruous of the wanderings of a slumbering intellect, the evidences and the fragments of a language which may be spoken, which *has* been spoken, to terrify, to warn and to command. We have reason to believe too, by the promptness of action which in the age of the prophets followed all intimations of this kind, and by the strength of conviction and strange permanence of the effects resulting from certain dreams in latter times—which effects we ourselves may have witnessed—that when this medium of communication has been employed by the Deity, the evidences of His presence have been unequivocal. My thoughts were directed to this subject in a manner to leave a lasting impression upon my mind, by the events which I shall now relate, the statement of which, however extraordinary, is nevertheless accurate.

About the year 17—, having been appointed to the living of C——h, I rented a small house in the town which bears the same name: one morning in the month of November, I was awakened before my usual time by my servant, who bustled into my bedroom for the purpose of announcing a sick call. As the Catholic Church holds her last rites to be totally indispensable to the safety of the departing sinner, no conscientious clergyman can afford a moment's unnecessary delay, and in little more than five minutes I stood ready, cloaked and booted for the road, in the small front parlour in which the messenger, who was to act as my guide, awaited my coming. I found a poor little girl crying piteously near the door, and after some slight difficulty I ascertained that her father was either dead or just dying.

"And what may be your father's name, my poor child?" said I. She held down her head as if ashamed. I repeated the question, and the wretched little creature burst into floods of tears still more bitter than she had shed before. At length, almost angered by conduct which appeared to me so unreasonable, I began to lose patience, and I said rather harshly,—

"If you will not tell me the name of the person to whom you would lead me, your silence can arise from no good motive, and I might be justified in refusing to go with you at all."

"Oh, don't say that—don't say that!" cried she. "Oh, sir, it was that I was afeard of when I would not tell you—I was afeard, when you heard his name, you would not come with me; but it is no use hidin' it now—it's Pat Connell, the carpenter, your honour."

She looked in my face with the most earnest anxiety, as if her very existence depended upon what she should read there. I relieved the child at once. The name, indeed, was most unpleasantly familiar to me; but, however fruitless my visits and advice might have been at another time, the present was too fearful an occasion to suffer my doubts of their utility, or my reluctance to re-attempting what appeared a hopeless task, to weigh even against the lightest chance that a consciousness of his imminent danger might produce in him a more docile and tractable disposition. Accordingly I told the child to lead the way, and followed her in silence. She hurried rapidly through the long narrow street which forms the great thoroughfare of the town. The darkness of the hour, rendered still deeper by the close approach of the old-fashioned houses, which lowered in tall obscurity on either side of the way; the damp, dreary chill which renders the advance of morning peculiarly cheerless, combined with the object of my walk—to visit the death-bed of a presumptuous sinner, to endeavour, almost against my own conviction, to infuse a hope into the heart of a dying reprobate—a drunkard but too probably perishing under the consequences of some mad fit of intoxication; all these circumstances served to enhance the gloom and solemnity of my feelings, as I silently followed my little guide, who with quick steps traversed the uneven pavement of the Main Street. After a walk of about five minutes, she turned off into a narrow lane, of that obscure and comfortless class which is to be found in almost all small old-fashioned towns, chill, without ventilation, reeking with all manner of offensive effluviæ, and lined by dingy, smoky, sickly and pent-up buildings, frequently not only in a wretched but in a dangerous condition.

"Your father has changed his abode since I last visited him, and, I am afraid, much for the worse," said I.

"Indeed he has, sir; but we must not complain," replied she. "We have to thank God that we have lodging and food, though it's poor enough, it is, your honour."

Poor child! thought I. How many an older head might learn wisdom from thee—how many a luxurious philosopher, who is skilled to preach but not to suffer, might not thy patient words put to the blush! The manner and language of my companion were alike above her years and station; and, indeed, in all cases in which the cares and sorrows of life have anticipated their usual date, and have fallen, as they sometimes do, with melancholy prematurity to the lot of childhood, I have observed the result to have proved uniformly the same. A young mind, to which joy and indulgence have been strangers, and to which suffering and self-denial have been familiarized from the first, acquires a solidity and an elevation which no other discipline could have bestowed, and which, in the present case, communicated a striking but mournful peculiarity to the manners, even to the voice, of the child. We paused before a narrow, crazy door, which she opened by means of a latch, and we forthwith began to ascend the steep and broken stairs which led to the sick man's room.

As we mounted flight after flight towards the garret-floor, I heard more and more distinctly the hurried talking of many voices. I could also distinguish the low sobbing of a female. On arriving upon the uppermost lobby, these sounds became fully audible.

"This way, your honour," said my little conductress; at the same time, pushing open a door of patched and half-rotten plank, she admitted me into the squalid chamber of death and misery. But one candle, held in the fingers of a scared and haggard-looking child, was burning in the room, and that so dim that all was twilight or darkness except within its immediate influence. The general obscurity, however, served to throw into prominent and startling relief the death-bed and its occupant. The light fell with horrible clearness upon the blue and swollen features of the drunkard. I did not think it possible that a human countenance could look so terrific. The lips were black and drawn apart; the teeth were firmly set; the eyes a little unclosed, and nothing but the whites appearing. Every feature was fixed and livid, and the whole face wore a ghastly and rigid expression of despairing terror such as I never saw equalled. His hands were crossed upon his breast, and firmly clenched; while, as if to add to the corpse-like effect of the whole, some white cloths, dipped in water, were wound about the forehead and temples.

As soon as I could remove my eyes from this horrible spectacle, I observed my friend Dr. D—, one of the most humane of a humane profession, standing by the bedside. He had been attempting, but unsuccessfully, to bleed the patient, and had now applied his finger to the pulse.

"Is there any hope?" I inquired in a whisper.

A shake of the head was the reply. There was a pause, while he continued to hold the wrist; but he waited in vain for the throb of life—it was not there: and when he let go the hand, it fell stiffly back into its former position upon the other.

"The man is dead," said the physician, as he turned from the bed where the terrible figure lay.

Dead! thought I, scarcely venturing to look upon the tremendous and revolting spectacle. Dead! without an hour for repentance, even a moment for reflection. Dead! without the rites which even the best should have. Was there a hope for him?

The glaring eyeball, the grinning mouth, the distorted brow—that unutterable look in which a painter would have sought to embody the fixed despair of the nethermost hell—These were my answer.

The poor wife sat at a little distance, crying as if her heart would break—the younger children clustered round the bed, looking with wondering curiosity upon the form of death, never seen before.

When the first tumult of uncontrollable sorrow had passed away, availing myself of the solemnity and impressiveness of the scene, I desired the heart-stricken family to accompany me in prayer, and all knelt down while I solemnly and fervently repeated some of those prayers which appeared most applicable to the occasion. I employed myself thus in a manner which I trusted was not unprofitable, at least to the living, for about ten minutes; and having accomplished my task, I was the first to arise.

I looked upon the poor, sobbing, helpless creatures who knelt so humbly around me, and my heart bled for them. With a natural transition I turned my eyes from them to the bed in which the body lay; and, great God! what was the revulsion, the horror which I experienced on seeing the corpse-like, terrific thing seated half upright before me. The white cloths which had been wound about the head had now partly slipped from their position, and were hanging in grotesque festoons about the face and shoulders, while the distorted eyes leered from amid them—

"A sight to dream of, not to tell."

I stood actually riveted to the spot. The figure nodded its head and lifted its arm, I thought, with a menacing gesture. A thousand confused and horrible thoughts at once rushed upon my mind. I had often read that the body of a presumptuous sinner, who, during life, had been the willing creature of every satanic impulse, had been known, after the human tenant had deserted it, to become the horrible sport of demoniac possession.

I was roused by the piercing scream of the mother, who now, for the first time, perceived the change which had taken place. She rushed towards the bed, but, stunned by the shock and overcome by the conflict of violent emotions, before she reached it she fell prostrate upon the floor.

I am perfectly convinced that had I not been startled from the torpidity of horror in which I was bound by some powerful and arousing stimulant, I should have gazed upon this unearthly apparition until I had fairly lost my senses. As it was, however, the spell was broken—superstition gave way to reason: the man whom all believed to have been actually dead was living!

Dr. D—was instantly standing by the bedside, and upon examination he found that a sudden and copious flow of blood had taken place from the wound which the lancet had left; and this, no doubt, had effected his sudden and almost preternatural restoration to an existence from which all thought he had been for ever removed. The man was still speechless, but he seemed to understand the physician when he forbade his repeating the painful and fruitless attempts which he made to articulate, and he at once resigned himself quietly into his hands.

I left the patient with leeches upon his temples, and bleeding freely, apparently with little of the drowsiness which accompanies apoplexy. Indeed, Dr. D—told me that he had never before witnessed a seizure which seemed to combine the symptoms of so many kinds, and yet which belonged to none of the recognized classes; it certainly was not apoplexy, catalepsy, nor *delirium tremens*, and yet it seemed, in some degree, to partake of the properties of all. It was strange, but stranger things are coming.

During two or three days Dr. D—would not allow his patient to converse in a manner which could excite or exhaust him, with anyone; he suffered him merely as briefly as possible to express his immediate wants. And it was not until the fourth day after my early visit, the particulars of which I have just detailed, that it was thought expedient that I should see him, and then only because it appeared that his extreme importunity and impatience to meet me were likely to retard his recovery more than the mere exhaustion attendant upon a short conversation could possibly do. Perhaps, too, my friend entertained some hope that if by holy confession his patient's bosom were eased of the perilous stuff which no doubt oppressed it, his recovery would be more assured and rapid. It was then, as I have said, upon the fourth day after my first professional call, that I found myself once more in the dreary chamber of want and sickness.

The man was in bed, and appeared low and restless. On my entering the room he raised himself in the bed, and muttered, twice or thrice—

"Thank God! Thank God!"

I signed to those of his family who stood by to leave the room, and took a chair beside the bed. So soon as we were alone, he said, rather doggedly—

"There's no use in telling me of the sinfulness of bad ways—I know it all. I know where they lead to—I have seen everything about it with my own eyesight, as plain as I see you." He rolled himself in the bed, as if to hide his face in the clothes; and then suddenly raising himself, he exclaimed with startling vehemence, "Look, sir! there is no use in mincing the matter: I'm blasted with the fires of hell; I have been in hell. What do you think of that? In hell—I'm lost for ever—I have not a chance. I am damned already—damned—damned!"

The end of this sentence he actually shouted. His vehemence was perfectly terrific; he threw himself back, and laughed, and sobbed hysterically. I poured some water into a tea-cup, and gave it to him. After he had swallowed it, I told him if he had anything to communicate, to do so as briefly as he could, and in a manner as little agitating to himself as possible; threatening at the same time, though I had no intention of doing so, to leave him at once in case he again gave way to such passionate excitement.

"It's only foolishness," he continued, "for me to try to thank you for coming to such a villain as myself at all. It's no use for me to wish good to you, or to bless you; for such as me has no blessings to give."

I told him that I had but done my duty, and urged him to proceed to the matter which weighed upon his mind. He then spoke nearly as follows:—

"I came in drunk on Friday night last, and got to my bed here; I don't remember how. Sometime in the night it seemed to me I wakened, and feeling unasy in myself, I got up out of the bed. I wanted the fresh air; but I would not make a noise to open the window, for fear I'd waken the crathurs. It was very dark and throublesome to find the door; but at last I did get it, and I groped my way out, and went down as asy as I could. I felt quite sober, and I counted the steps one after another, as I was going down, that I might not stumble at the bottom.

"When I came to the first landing-place—God be about us always!—the floor of it sunk under me, and I went down—down—down, till the senses almost left me. I do not know how long I was falling, but it seemed to me a great while. When I came rightly to myself at last, I was sitting near the top of a great table; and I could not see the end of it, if it had any, it was so far off. And there was men beyond reckoning sitting down all along by it, at each side, as far as I could see at all. I did not know at first was it in the open air; but there was a close smothering feel in it that was not natural. And there was a kind of light that my eyesight never saw before, red and unsteady; and I did not see for a long time where it was coming from, until I looked straight up, and then I seen that it came from great balls of blood-coloured fire that were rolling high overhead with a sort of rushing, trembling sound, and I perceived that they shone on the ribs of a great roof of rock that was arched overhead instead of the sky. When I seen this, scarce knowing what I did, I got up, and I said, 'I have no right to be here; I must go.' And the man that was sitting at my left hand only smiled, and said, 'Sit down again; you can *never* leave this place.' And his voice was weaker than any child's voice I ever heerd; and when he was done speaking he smiled again.

"Then I spoke out very loud and bold, and I said, 'In the name of God, let me out of this bad place.' And there was a great man that I did not see before, sitting at the end of the table that I was near; and he was taller than twelve men, and his face was very proud and terrible to look at. And he stood up and stretched out his hand before him; and when he stood up, all that was there, great and small, bowed down with a sighing sound; and a dread came on my heart, and he looked at me, and I could not speak. I felt I was his own, to do what he liked with, for I knew at once who he was; and he said, 'If you promise to return, you may depart for a season;' and the voice he spoke with was terrible and mournful, and the echoes of it went rolling and swelling down the endless cave, and mixing with the trembling of the fire overhead; so that when he sat down there was a sound after him, all through the place, like the roaring of a furnace. And I said, with all the strength I had, 'I promise to come back—in God's name let me go!'

"And with that I lost the sight and the hearing of all that was there, and when my senses came to me again, I was sitting in the bed with the blood all over me, and you and the rest praying around the room."

Here he paused, and wiped away the chill drops which hung upon his forehead.

I remained silent for some moments. The vision which he had just described struck my imagination not a little, for this was long before Vathek and the "Hall of Eblis" had delighted the world; and the description which he gave had, as I received it, all the attractions of novelty beside the impressiveness which always belongs to the narration of an *eye-witness*, whether in the body or in the spirit, of the scenes which he describes. There was something, too, in the stern horror with which the man related these things, and in the incongruity of his description with the vulgarly received notions of the great place of punishment, and of its presiding spirit, which struck my mind with awe, almost with fear. At length he said, with an expression of horrible, imploring earnestness, which I shall never forget—

"Well, sir, is there any hope; is there any chance at all? or is my soul pledged and promised away for ever? is it gone out of my power? must I go back to the place?"

In answering him, I had no easy task to perform; for however clear might be my internal conviction of the groundlessness of his fears, and however strong my scepticism respecting the reality of what he had described, I nevertheless felt that his impression to the contrary, and his humility and terror resulting from it, might be made available as no mean engines in the work of his conversion from profligacy, and of his restoration to decent habits and to religious feeling.

I therefore told him that he was to regard his dream rather in the light of a warning than in that of a prophecy; that our salvation depended not upon the word or deed of a moment, but upon the habits of a life; that, in fine, if he at once discarded his idle companions and evil habits, and firmly adhered to a sober, industrious, and religious course of life, the powers of darkness might claim his soul in vain, for that there were higher and firmer pledges than human tongue could utter, which promised salvation to him who should repent and lead a new life.

I left him much comforted, and with a promise to return upon the next day. I did so, and found him much more cheerful, and without any remains of the dogged sullenness which I suppose had arisen from his despair. His promises of amendment were given in that tone of deliberate earnestness which belongs to deep and solemn determination; and it was with no small delight that I observed, after repeated visits, that his good resolutions, so far from failing, did but gather strength by time; and when I saw that man shake off the idle and debauched companions whose society had for years formed alike his amusement and his ruin, and revive his long-discarded habits of industry and sobriety, I said within myself, There is something more in all this than the operation of an idle dream.

One day, some time after his perfect restoration to health, I was surprised, on ascending the stairs for the purpose of visiting this man, to find him busily employed in nailing down some planks upon the landing-place, through which, at the commencement of his mysterious vision, it seemed to him that he had sunk. I perceived at once that he was strengthening the floor with a view to securing himself against such a catastrophe, and could scarcely forbear a smile as I bid "God bless his work."

He perceived my thoughts, I suppose, for he immediately said: "I can never pass over that floor without trembling. I'd leave this house if I could, but I can't find another lodging in the town so cheap, and I'll not take a better till I've paid off all my debts, please God; but I could not be asy in my mind till I made it as safe as I could. You'll hardly believe me, your honour, that while I'm working, maybe a mile away, my heart is in a flutter the whole way back, with the bare thoughts of the two little steps I have to walk upon this bit of a floor. So it's no wonder, sir, I'd thry to make it sound and firm with any idle timber I have."

I applauded his resolution to pay off his debts, and the steadiness with which he perused his plans of conscientious economy, and passed on.

Many months elapsed, and still there appeared no alteration in his resolutions of amendment. He was a good workman, and with his better habits he recovered his former extensive and profitable employment. Everything seemed to promise comfort and respectability. I have little more to add, and that shall be told quickly. I had one evening met Pat Connell, as he returned from his work, and as usual, after a mutual, and on his side respectful salutation, I spoke a few words of encouragement and approval. I left him industrious, active, healthy—when next I saw him, not three days after, he was a corpse.

The circumstances which marked the event of his death were somewhat strange—I might say fearful. The unfortunate man had accidentally met an old friend just returned, after a long absence; and in a moment of excitement, forgetting everything in the warmth of his joy, he yielded to his urgent invitation to accompany him into a public-house, which lay close by the spot where the encounter had taken place. Connell, however, previously to entering the room, had announced his determination to take nothing more than the strictest temperance would warrant.

But oh! who can describe the inveterate tenacity with which a drunkard's habits cling to him through life? He may repent, he may reform, he may look with actual abhorrence upon his past profligacy; but amid all this reformation and compunction, who can tell the moment in which the base and ruinous propensity may not recur, triumphing over resolution, remorse, shame, everything, and prostrating its victim once more in all that is destructive and revolting in that fatal vice?

The wretched man left the place in a state of utter intoxication. He was brought home nearly insensible, and placed in his bed. The younger part of the family retired to rest much after their usual hour; but the poor wife remained up sitting by the fire, too much grieved and shocked at the occurrence of what she had so little expected, to settle to rest. Fatigue, however, at length overcame her, and she sank gradually into an uneasy slumber. She could not tell how long she had remained in this state; but when she awakened, and immediately on opening her eyes, she perceived by the faint red light of the smouldering turf embers, two persons, one of whom she recognized as her husband, noiselessly gliding out of the room.

"Pat, darling, where are you going?" said she.

There was no answer—the door closed after them; but in a moment she was startled and terrified by a loud and heavy crash, as if some ponderous body had been hurled down the stair.

Much alarmed, she started up, and going to the head of the staircase, she called repeatedly upon her husband, but in vain.

She returned to the room, and with the assistance of her daughter, whom I had occasion to mention before, she succeeded in finding and lighting a candle, with which she hurried again to the head of the staircase.

At the bottom lay what seemed to be a bundle of clothes, heaped together, motionless, lifeless—it was her husband. In going down the stairs, for what purpose can never now be known, he had fallen helplessly and violently to the bottom, and coming head foremost, the spine of the neck had been dislocated by the shock, and instant death must have ensued.

The body lay upon that landing-place to which his dream had referred.

It is scarcely worth endeavouring to clear up a single point in a narrative where all is mystery; yet I could not help suspecting that the second figure which had been seen in the room by Connell's wife on the night of his death might have been no other than his own shadow.

I suggested this solution of the difficulty; but she told me that the unknown person had been considerably in advance of her husband, and on reaching the door, had turned back as if to communicate something to his companion.

It was, then, a mystery.

Was the dream verified?—whither had the disembodied spirit sped? who can say? We know not. But I left the house of death that day in a state of horror which I could not describe. It seemed to me that I was scarce awake. I heard and saw everything as if under the spell of a nightmare. The coincidence was terrible.

R.H. MALDEN
The Sundial

Richard Henry Malden *(1879–1951) was Chaplain to King George V, Canon of Ripon Cathedral, and Dean of Wells. He wrote several theological books and a fine collection of supernatural tales,* Nine Ghosts *(1943), published as a tribute to M.R. James, his friend for over thirty years.*

The following story came into my hands by pure chance. I had wandered into a second-hand book-shop in the neighbourhood of the Charing Cross Road and was about to leave it empty-handed. On a shelf near the door my eye fell upon a copy of Hacket's *Scrinia Reserata* solidly bound in leather, which I thought well worth the few shillings which the proprietor was willing to accept for it. It is not an easy book to come by, and is of real value to anyone who wants to understand certain aspects of English Church History during the first half of the seventeenth century.

When I opened the book at home a thickish wad of paper fell out. It proved to consist of several sheets of foolscap covered with writing. I have reproduced the contents word for word.

From the look of the paper I judged that it had been there for at least thirty years. The author had not signed it, and there was nothing to indicate to whom the book had belonged. I think I could make a guess at the neighbourhood to which the story relates, and if I am right it should not be difficult to identify the house and discover the name of the tenant. But as he seems to have wished to remain anonymous he shall do so, as far as I am concerned.

The form of the story suggests that he intended to publish it; probably in some magazine. As far as I know it has not been printed before.

I belong to one of the numerous middle-class English families which for several generations have followed various professions, with credit, but without ever attaining any very special distinction.

In our case India could almost claim us as hereditary bondsmen. For more than a century most of our men had made their way there, and had served John Company or the Crown in various capacities. One of my uncles had risen to be Legal Member of the Viceroy's Council. So when my own time came, to India I went—in the Civil Service—and there I lived for five and twenty years.

My career was neither more nor less adventurous than the average. The routine of my work was occasionally broken by experiences which would sound incredible to an English reader, and therefore need not be set down here. Just before the time came for my retirement a legacy made me a good deal better off than I had had any reason to expect to be. So upon my return to England I found that it would be possible for me to adopt the life of a country gentleman, upon a modest scale, but with the prospect of finding sufficient occupation and amusement.

I was never married, and had been too long out of England to have any very strong ties remaining. I was free to establish myself where I pleased, and the advertisements in the *Field* and *Country Life* offered houses of every description in every part of the kingdom. After much correspondence, and some fruitless journeys, I came upon one which seemed to satisfy my requirements. It lay about sixty miles north of London upon a main line of railway. That was an important point, as I was a Fellow of both the Asiatic and Historical Societies, and had long looked forward to attending their meetings regularly. As a boy I had known the neighbourhood slightly and had liked it, though it is not generally considered beautiful. There were two packs of hounds within reach, which could be followed with such a stable as I should be able to afford.

The house was an old one. It had been a good deal larger, but part had been battered down during the Civil War, when it was besieged by the Parliamentary troops and never rebuilt. It belonged to one of the largest landowners in the county, whom I will call Lord Rye. It generally served as the dower-house of the family, but as there was at that moment no dowager Countess, and as Lord Rye himself was a young man, and both his sisters were married, it was not likely to be wanted for some time to come. It had been unoccupied for nearly two years. The last tenant, a retired doctor, had been found dead on the lawn at the bottom of the steps leading up to the garden door. His heart had been in a bad condition for some time past, so that his sudden death was not surprising; but the neighbouring village viewed the incident with some suspicion. One or two of the older people professed to remember traditions of "trouble" there in former years.

This had made it difficult to get a caretaker, and as Lord Rye was anxious to let again he was willing to take an almost nominal rent. In fact his whole attitude suggested that I was doing him a favour by becoming his tenant. About five hundred acres of shooting generally went with the house, and I was glad to find that I could have them very cheaply.

I moved in at midsummer, and each day made me more and more pleased with my new surroundings.

After my years in India the garden was a particular source of delight to me; but I will not describe it more minutely than is necessary to make what follows intelligible. Behind the house was a good-sized lawn, flanked by shrubbery. On the far side, parallel with the house, ran a splendid yew hedge, nearly fifteen feet high and very thick. It came up to the shrubbery at either end, but was pierced by two archways about thirty yards apart, giving access to the flower-garden beyond. Almost in the middle of the lawn was an old tree stump, or what looked like one, some three feet high. Though covered with ivy it was not picturesque, and I told Lord Rye that I should like to take it up. "Do by all means," he said, "I certainly should if I lived here. I believe poor Riley (the last tenant) intended to put a sundial there. I think it would look rather nice, don't you?"

This struck me as a good idea. I ordered a sundial from a well-known firm of heliological experts in Cockspur Street, and ordered the stump to be grubbed up as soon as it arrived.

One morning towards the end of September I woke unrefreshed after a night of troubled dreams. I could not recall them very distinctly, but I had seemed to be trying to lift a very heavy weight of some kind from the ground. But, before I could raise it, an overwhelming terror had taken hold of me—though I could not remember why—and I woke to find my forehead wet with perspiration. Each time I fell asleep again the dream repeated itself with mechanical regularity, though the details did not become any more distinct. So I was heartily glad it had become late enough to get up. The day was wet and chilly. I felt tired and unwell, and was, moreover, depressed by a vague sense of impending disaster. This was accentuated by a feeling that it lay within my power to avert the catastrophe, if only I could discover what it was.

In the afternoon the weather cleared, and I thought that a ride would do me good. I rode fairly for some distance, and it was past five o'clock before I had reached my own bounds'-ditch on my way home. At that particular place a small wood ran along the edge of my property for about a quarter of a mile. I was riding slowly down the outside, and was perhaps a hundred yards from the angle where I meant to turn it, when I noticed a man standing at the corner. The light was beginning to fail, and he was so close to the edge of the wood that at first I could not be sure whether it was a human figure, or only an oddly shaped tree-stump which I had never noticed before. But when I got a little nearer I saw that my first impression had been correct, and that it was a man. He semed to be dressed like an ordinary agricultural labourer. He was standing absolutely still and seemed to be looking very intently in my direction. But he was shading his eyes with his hand, so that I could not make out his face. Before I had got close enough to make him out more definitely he turned suddenly and vanished round the corner of the wood. His movements were rapid: but he somehow gave the impression of being deformed, though in what precise respect I could not tell. Naturally my suspicions were stirred, so I put my horse to a canter. But when we had reached the corner he shied violently, and I had some difficulty in getting him to pass it. When we had got round, the mysterious man was nowhere to be seen. In front and on the left hand lay a very large stubble field, without a vestige of cover of any kind. I could see that he was not crossing it, and unless he had flown he could not have reached the other side.

On the right hand lay the ditch bounding the wood. As is usual in that country it was both wide and deep, and had some two or three feet of mud and water at the bottom. If the man had gone that way he had some very pressing reason for wishing to avoid me: and I could detect no trace of his passage at any point.

So there was nothing to be done but go home, and tell the policeman next day to keep his eyes open for any suspicious strangers. However, no attempts were made upon any of my belongings, and when October came my pheasants did not seem to have been unlawfully diminished.

October that year was stormy, and one Saturday night about the middle of the month it blew a regular gale. I lay awake long listening to the wind, and to all the confused sounds which fill an old house in stormy weather. Twice I seemed to hear footsteps in the passage. Once I could have almost sworn my door was cautiously opened and closed again. When at last I dropped off I was disturbed by a repetition of my former dream. But this time the details were rather more distinct. Again I was trying to lift a heavy weight from the ground: but now I knew that there was something hidden under it. What the concealed object might be I could not tell, but as I worked to bring it to light a feeling began to creep over me that I did not want to see it. This soon deepened into horror at the bare idea of seeing it: though I had still no notion what manner of thing it might be. Yet I could not abandon my task. So presently I found myself in the position of working hard to accomplish what I would have given the world to have left undone. At this point I woke, to find myself shaking with fright, and repeating aloud the apparently meaningless sentence—"If you'll pull, I'll push."

I did not sleep for the rest of that night. Beside the noise of the storm the prospect of a repetition of that dream was quite enough to keep me awake. To add to my discomfort a verse from Ecclesiastes ran in my head with dismal persistence—"But if a man live many years and rejoice in them all, yet let him remember the days of darkness, for they shall be many." Days of darkness seemed to be coming upon me now, and my mind was filled with vague alarm.

The next day was fine, and after Church I thought I would see how my fruit trees had fared during the night. The kitchen-garden was enclosed by a high brick wall. On the side nearest the house there were two doors, which were always kept locked on Sunday. In the wall opposite was a trap-door, about three feet square, giving on to a rather untidy piece of ground, partly orchard and partly waste. When I had unlocked the door I saw standing by the opposite wall the figure which I had seen at the corner of the wood. His neck was abnormally long, and so malformed that his head lolled sideways on to his right shoulder in a disgusting and almost inhuman fashion. He was bent almost double; and I think he was misshapen in some other respect as well. But of that I could not be certain. He raised his hand with what seemed to be a threatening gesture, then turned, and slipped through the trap-door with remarkable quickness. I was after him immediately, but on reaching the opposite wall received a shock which stopped me like a physical blow. The trap-door was shut and bolted on the inside. I tried to persuade myself that a violent slam might make the bolts shoot, but I knew that that was really impossible. I had to choose between two explanations. Either my visitor was a complete hallucination, or else he possessed the unusual power of being able to bolt a door upon the side on which he himself was not. The latter was upon the whole the more comforting, and—in view of some of my Indian experiences—the more probable, supposition.

After a little hesitation I opened the trap and, as there was nothing to be seen, got through it and went up to the top of the orchard, where the kennels lay. But neither of my dogs would follow the scent. When brought to the spot where his feet must have touched the ground they whined and showed every symptom of alarm. When I let go of their collars they hurried home in a way which showed plainly what they thought of the matter.

This seemed to dispose of the idea of hallucination, and, as before, there was nothing else to be done but await developments as patiently as I could. For the next fortnight nothing remarkable took place. I had my usual health and as near an approach to my usual spirits as could reasonably be expected. I had visitors for part of the time, but no one to whom I should have cared to confide the story at this stage. I was not molested further by day, and my dreams, though varied, were not alarming.

On the morning of the 31st I received a letter announcing that my sundial had been despatched, and it duly arrived in the course of the afternoon. It was heavy, so by the time we had got it out of the railway van and on to the lawn it was too late to place it in position that day. The men departed to drink my health, and I turned towards the house. Just as I reached the door I paused. A sensation—familiar to all men who are much alone—had come over me, and I felt as if I were being watched from behind. Usually the feeling can be dispelled by turning round. I did so, but on this occasion the sense that I was not alone merely increased. Of course the lawn was deserted, but I stood looking across it for a few moments, telling myself that I must not let my nerves play me tricks. Then I saw a face detach itself slowly from the darkness of the hedge at one side of the left-hand arch. For a few seconds it hung, horribly poised, in the middle of the opening like a mask suspended by an invisible thread. Then the body to which it belonged slid into the clear space, and I saw my acquaintance of the wood and kitchen-garden, this time sharply outlined against a saffron sky. There could be no mistaking his bowed form and distorted neck, but now his appearance was made additionally abominable by his expression. The yellow sunset light seemed to stream all round him, and showed me features convulsed with fury. He gnashed his teeth and clawed the air with both hands. I have never seen such a picture of impotent rage.

It was more by instinct than by any deliberate courage that I ran straight across the lawn towards him. He was gone in a flash, and when I came through the archway where he had stood he was hurrying down the side of the hedge towards the other. He moved with an odd shuffling gait, and I made sure that I should soon overtake him. But to my surprise I found that I did not gain much. His limping shuffle took him over the ground as fast as I could cover it. In fact, when I reached the point from which I had started I thought I had actually lost a little. When we came round for the second time there was no doubt about it. This was humiliating, but I persevered, relying now on superior stamina. But during the third circuit it suddenly flashed upon me that our positions had become reversed. I was no longer the pursuer. He—it—whatever the creature was, was now chasing me, and the distance between us was diminishing rapidly.

I am not ashamed to admit that my nerve failed completely. I believe I screamed aloud. I ran on stumblingly, helplessly, as one runs in a dream, knowing now that the creature behind was gaining at every stride. How long the chase lasted I do not know, but presently I could hear his irregular footstep close behind me, and a horrible dank breath played about the back of my neck. We were on the side towards the house when I looked up and saw my butler standing at the garden door, with a note in his hand. The sight of his prosaic form seemed to break the spell which had kept me running blindly round and round the hedge. I was almost exhausted, but I tore across the lawn, and fell in a heap at the bottom of the steps.

Parker was an ex-sergeant of Marines, which amounts to saying that he was incapable of surprise and qualified to cope with any practical emergency which could arise. He picked me up, helped me into the house, gave me a tumbler of brandy diluted with soda-water, and fortified himself with another, without saying a word. How much he saw, or what he thought of it, I could never learn, for all subsequent approaches to the question were parried with the evasive skill which seems to be birthright of all those that go down to the sea in ships. But his general view of the situation is indicated by the fact that he sent for the Rector, not the doctor, and—as I learned afterwards—had a private conference with him before he left the house. Soon afterwards he joined the choir—or in his own phrase "assisted with the singing in the chancel"—and for many months the village church had no more regular or vocal attendant.

The Rector heard my story gravely, and was by no means disposed to make light of it. Something similar had come his way once before, when he had had the charge of a parish on the Northumbrian Border. He was confident, he said, that no harm could come to me that night, if I remained indoors, and departed to look up some of his authorities on such subjects.

That night was noisy with wind, so the insistent knocking which I seemed to hear during the small hours at the garden-door and ground-floor windows, which were secured with outside shutters, may have had no existence outside my imagination. I had asked Parker to occupy a dressing-room opening out of my bedroom for the night. He seemed very ready to do so, but I do not think that he slept very much either. Early next morning the Rector reappeared, saying that he thought he had got a clue, though it was impossible to say yet how much it might be worth. He had brought with him the first volume of the parish register, and showed me the following note on the inside of the cover:

"October 31st, 1578. On this day Jn. Croxton a Poore Man hanged himself from a Beame within his house. He was very stubborn Popish Recusant and ye manner of his Death was in accord with his whole Life. He was buried that evening at ye Cross Roades."

"It is unfortunate," continued the Rector, "that we have no sixteenth-century map of the parish. But there is a map of 1759 which marks a hamlet at the cross-roads just outside your gate. The hamlet doesn't exist now—you know that the population hereabouts is much less than it used to be—but it used to be called New Cross. I think that must mean that these particular cross-roads are comparatively recent. Now this house is known to have been built between 1596 and 1602. The straight way from Farley to Abbotsholme would lie nearly across its site. I think, therefore, that the Elizabethan Lord Rye diverted the old road when he laid out his grounds. That would also account for the loop which the present road makes"—here he traced its course with his finger on the map which he had brought.

"Now I strongly suspect that your visitor was Mr. Croxton, and that he is buried somewhere in your grounds. If we could find the place I think we could keep him quiet for the future. But I am afraid that there is nothing to guide us."

At this point Parker came in. "Beg your pardon, Sir, but Hardman is wishful to speak to you. About that there bollard on the quarter-deck, Sir—stump on the lawn, I should have said, Sir—what you told him to put over the side."

We went out, and found Hardman and the boy looking at a large hole in the lawn. By the side of it lay what we had taken for a tree stump. But it had never struck root there. It was a very solid wooden stake, some nine feet in length over all, with a sharp point. It had been driven some six feet into the ground, passing through a layer of rubble about three feet from the surface. At the bottom the hole widened, forming a large, and plainly artificial, cavity. The earth here looked as if it had been recently disturbed, but the condition of the stake showed that that was impossible. It was obvious to both of us that we had come upon Mr. Croxton's grave, at the original cross-roads, and that what had appeared to be natural stump was really the stake which had been driven through it to keep him there. We did not, of course, take the gardeners into our confidence, but told them to leave the place for the present as it might contain some interesting antiques—presumably Roman—which we would get out carefully with our own hands.

We soon enlarged the shaft sufficiently to explore the cavity at the bottom. We had naturally expected to find a skeleton, or something of the sort, there, but we were disappointed. We could not discover the slightest vestige of bones or body, or of any dust except that of natural soil. Once while we were working we were startled by a harsh sound like the cry of a nightjar, apparently very close at hand. But whatever it was passed away very quickly, as if the creature which had made it was on the wing, and it was not repeated.

By the Rector's advice we went to the churchyard and brought away sufficient consecrated earth to fill up the cavity. The shaft was filled up, and the sundial securely planted on top of it. The pious mottoes with which it was adorned, according to custom, assumed for the first time a practical significance.

"It not infrequently happens," said the Rector, "that those who for any reason have not received full Christian Burial are unable, or unwilling, to remain quiet in their graves, particularly if the interment has been at all carelessly carried out in the first instance. They seem to be particularly active on or about the anniversary of their death in any year. The range of their activities is varied, and it would be difficult to define the nature of the power which animates them, or the source from which it is derived. But I incline to think that it is less their own personality than some force inherent in the earth itself, of which they become the vehicle. With the exception of Vampires (who are altogether *sui generis* and virtually unknown in this country), they can seldom do much direct physical harm. They operate indirectly by terrifying, but are commonly compelled to stop there. But it is always necessary for them to have free access to their graves. If that is obstructed in any way their power seems to lapse. That is why I think that their vitality is in some way bred of the earth: and I am sure that you won't be troubled with any more visits now.

"Our friend was afraid that your sundial would interfere with his convenience, and I think he was trying to frighten you into leaving the house. Of course, if your heart had been weak he might have disposed of you as he did of your unfortunate predecessor. His projection of himself into your dreams was part of his general plan: I incline to think, however, that it was an error of judgement, as it might have put you on your guard. But I very much doubt whether he could have inflicted any physical injury on you if he had caught you yesterday afternoon."

"H'm," said I, "you might be right there. But I am very glad that I shall never know."

Next day Parker asked for leave to go to London. He returned with a large picture representing King Solomon issuing directions to a corvée of demons of repellent aspect whom he had (according to a well-known Jewish legend) compelled to labour at the building of the Temple. This he proceeded to affix with drawing-pins to the inside of the pantry door. He called my attention to it particularly, and said that he had got it from a Jew whom he had known in Malta, who had recently opened a branch establishment in the Whitechapel Road. I ventured to make some comment on the singularity of the subject, but Parker was, as usual, impenetrable. "Beggin' your pardon, Sir," he said, "there's some things what a civilian don't never 'ave no chance of learnin', not even if 'e 'ad the brains for it. I done my twenty-one years in the Service—*in puris naturalibus* all the time as the saying is—and" (pointing to the figure of the King) "you may lay to it that there man knew 'is business."

RICHARD MARSH
The Fifteenth Man

'Richard Marsh', *pseudonym of* Richard Bernard Heldmann *(1857–1915), was a prolific novelist whose greatest success was the horror novel* The Beetle *(1897) which outsold its contemporary rival, Bram Stoker's Dracula, for several years, and also adapted for both stage and screen. In addition to novels, he wrote hundreds of short stories, ranging from light romance to mystery, horror and detective fiction. "The Fifteenth Man" is taken from his collection* The Seen and the Unseen *(1900). Marsh died a few months after the birth of his grandson, Robert Aickman, whose story "The Unsettled Dust" introduces the present volume.*

It was not until we were actually in the field, and were about to begin to play, that I learnt that the Brixham men had come one short. It seemed that one of their men had been playing in a match the week before—in a hard frost, if you please! and, getting pitched on to his head, had broken his skull nearly into two clean halves. That is the worst of playing in a frost; you are nearly sure to come to grief. Not to ordinary grief, either, but a regular cracker. It was hard lines on the Brixham team. Some men always are getting themselves smashed to pieces just as a big match is due! The man's name was Joyce, Frank Joyce. He played half-back for Brixham, and for the county too—so you may be sure Lance didn't care to lose him. Still, they couldn't go and drag the man out of the hospital with a hole in his head big enough to put your fist into. They had tried to get a man to take his place, but at the last moment the substitute had failed to show.

"If we can't beat them—fifteen to their fourteen!—I think we'd better go in for challenging girls' schools. Last year they beat us, but this year, as we've one man to the good, perhaps we might manage to pull it off."

That's how Mason talked to us, as if *we* wanted them to win! Although they were only fourteen men, they could play. I don't think I ever saw a team who were stronger in their forwards. Lance, their captain, kicked off; Mason, our chief, returned. Then one of their men, getting the leather, tried a run. We downed him, a scrimmage was formed, then, before we knew it, they were rushing the ball across the field. When it did show, I was on it like a flash. I passed to Mason. But he was collared almost before he had a chance to start. There was another turn at scrimmaging, and lively work it was, especially for us who had the pleasure of looking on. So, when again I got a sight of it, I didn't lose much time. I had it up, and I was off. I didn't pass; I tried a run upon my own account. I thought that I was clear away. I had passed the forwards; I thought that I had passed the field, when, suddenly, someone sprang at me, out of the fog—it was a little thick, you know—caught me round the waist, lifted me off my feet, and dropped me on my back. That spoilt it! Before I had a chance of passing they were all on top of me. And again the ball was in the scrimmage.

When I returned to my place behind I looked to see who it was had collared me. The fellow, I told myself, was one of their half-backs. Yet, when I looked at their halves, I couldn't make up my mind which of them it was.

Try how we could—although we had the best of the play—we couldn't get across their line. Although I say it, we all put in some first-rate work. We never played better in our lives. We all had run after run, the passing was as accurate as if it had been mechanical, and yet we could not do the trick. Time after time, just as we were almost in, one of their men put a stop to our little game, and spoilt us. The funny part of the business was that, either owing to the fog, or to our stupidity, we could not make up our minds which of their men it was.

At last I spotted him. Mason had been held nearly on their goal line. I took it. I passed to Mason. I thought he was behind, when—he was collared and thrown.

"Joyce!" I cried. "Why, I thought that you weren't playing."

"What are you talking about?" asked one of their men. "Joyce isn't playing."

I stared.

"Not playing! Why, it was he who collared Mason."

"Stuff!"

I did not think the man was particularly civil. It was certainly an odd mistake which I had made. I was just behind Mason when he was collared, and I saw the face of the man who collared him.

I could have sworn it was Frank Joyce!

"Who was that who downed you just now?" I asked of Mason, directly I had the chance.

"Their half-back."

Their half-back! Their halves were Tom Wilson and Granger. How could I have mistaken either of them for Joyce?

A little later Giffard was puzzled.

"One of their fellows plays a thundering good game, but, do you know, I can't make out which one of them it is."

"Do you mean the fellow who keeps collaring."

"That's the man!"

The curious part of it was that I never saw the man except when he was collaring.

"The next time," said Giffard, when, for about the sixth time, he had been on the point of scoring, "if I don't get in, I'll know the reason why. I'll kill that man."

It was all very well to talk about our killing him. It looked very much more like his killing us. Mason passed the word that if there was anything like a chance we were to drop. The chance came immediately afterwards. They muffed somehow in trying to pass. Blaine got the leather. He started to run.

"Drop," yelled Mason.

In that fog, and from where Blaine was, dropping a goal was out of the question. He tried the next best thing—he tried to drop into touch. But the attempt was a failure. The kick was a bad one—the ball was as heavy as lead, so that there was not much kick in it—and as it was coming down one of their men, appearing right on the spot, caught it, dropped a drop which was a drop, sent the ball right over our heads, and as near as a toucher over the bar.

Just then the whistle sounded.

"Do you know," declared Ingall, as we were crossing over, "I believe they're playing fifteen men."

Mason scoffed.

"Do you think, without giving us notice, they would play fifteen when they told us they were only playing fourteen?"

"Hanged if I don't count them!" persisted Ingall.

He did, and we all did. We faced round and reckoned them up. There were only fourteen, unless one was slinking out of sight somewhere in the dim recesses of the fog, which seemed scarcely probable. Still Ingall seemed dissatisfied.

"They're playing four three-quarters," whispered Giffard, when the game restarted.

So they were—Wheeler, Pendleton, Marshall, and another. Who the fourth man was I couldn't make out. He was a big, strapping fellow, I could see that; but the play was so fast that more than that I couldn't see.

"Who is the fourth man?"

"Don't know; can't see his face. It's so confoundedly foggy!"

It was foggy; but still, of course, it was not foggy enough to render a man's features indistinguishable at the distance of only a few feet. All the same, somehow or other he managed to keep his face concealed from us. While Giffard and I had been whispering they had been packing in. The ball broke out our side. I had it. I tried to run. Instantly I saw that fourth three-quarter rush at me. As he came I saw his face. I was so amazed that I stopped dead. Putting his arms about me he held me as in a vice.

"Joyce!" I cried.

Before the word was out of my mouth half a dozen of their men had hold of the ball.

"Held! held!" they screamed.

"Down!" I gasped.

And it was down, with two or three of their men on top of me. They were packing the scrimmage before I had time to get fairly on my feet again.

"That was Joyce who collared me!" I exclaimed.

"Pack in! pack in!" shouted Mason from behind.

And they did pack in with a vengeance. Giffard had the ball. They were down on him; it was hammer and tongs. But through it all we stuck to the leather. They downed us, but not before we had passed it to a friend. Out of it came Giffard, sailing along as though he had not been swallowing mud in pailfuls. I thought he was clear–but no! He stopped short, and dropped the ball!—dropped it, as he stood there, from his two hands as though he were a baby! They asked no questions. They had it up; they were off with it, as though they meant to carry it home. They carried it, too, all the way—almost! It was in disagreeable propinquity to our goal by the time that it was held.

"Now then, Brixham, you've got it!"

That was what they cried.

"Steyning! Steyning! All together!"

That was what we answered. But though we did work all together, it was as much as we could manage.

"Where's Giffard?" bellowed Mason.

My impression was that he had remained like a sign-post rooted to the ground. I had seen him standing motionless after he had dropped the ball, and even as the Brixham men rushed past him. But just then he put in an appearance.

"I protest!" he cried.

"What about?" asked Mason.

"What do they mean by pretending they're not playing Frank Joyce when all the time they are?"

"Oh, confound Frank Joyce! Play up, do. You've done your best to give them the game already. Steady, Steyning, steady. Left, there, left. Centre, steady!"

We were steady. We were more than steady. Steadiness alone would not have saved us. We all played forward. At last, somehow, we got the ball back into something like the middle of the field. Giffard kept whispering to me all the time, even in the hottest of the rush.

"What lies, pretending that they're not playing Joyce!" Here he had a discussion with the ball, mostly on his knees. "Humbug about his being in the hospital!"

We had another chance. Out of the turmoil, Mason was flying off with a lead. It was the first clear start he had that day. When he has got that it is catch him who catch can! As he pelted off the fog, which kept coming and going, all at once grew thicker. He had passed all their men. Of ours, I was the nearest to him. It looked all the world to a china orange that we were going to score at last, when, to my disgust, he reeled, seemed to give a sort of spring, and then fell right over on to his back! I did not understand how he had managed to do it, but I supposed that he had slipped in the mud. Before I could get within passing distance the Brixham men were on us, and the ball was down.

"I thought you'd done it that time."

I said this to him as the scrimmage was being formed. He did not answer. He stood looking about him in a hazy sort of way, as though the further proceedings had no interest for him.

"What's the matter? Are you hurt?"

He turned to me.

"Where is he?" he asked.

"Where's who?"

I couldn't make him out. There was quite a curious look upon his face.

"Joyce!"

Somehow, as he said this, I felt a trifle queer. It was his face, or his tone, or something. "Didn't you see him throw me?"

I didn't know what he meant. But before I could say so we had another little rough and tumble—one go up and the other go down. A hubbub arose. There was Ingall shouting.

"I protest! I don't think this sort of thing's fair play."

"What sort of thing?"

"You said you weren't playing Joyce."

"*Said* we weren't! We aren't."

"Why, he just took the ball out of my hands! Joyce, where are you?"

"Yes, where is he?"

Then they laughed. Mason intervened.

"Excuse me, Lance; we've no objection to your playing Joyce, but why do you say you aren't?"

"I don't think you're well. I tell you that Frank Joyce is at this moment lying in Brixham hospital."

"He just now collared me."

I confess that when Mason said that I was a trifle staggered. I had distinctly seen that he had slipped and fallen. No one had been within a dozen yards of him at the time. Those Brixham men told him so—not too civilly.

"Do you fellows mean to say," he roared, "that Frank Joyce didn't just now pick me up and throw me?"

I struck in.

"I mean to say so. You slipped and fell. My dear fellow, no one was near you at the time."

He sprang round at me.

"Well, that beats anything!"

"At the same time," I added, "it's all nonsense to talk about Joyce being in Brixham hospital, because, since half-time at any rate, he's been playing three-quarter."

"Of course he has," cried Ingall. "Didn't I see him?"

"And didn't he collar me?" asked Giffard.

The Brixham men were silent. We looked at them, and they at us.

"You fellows are dreaming," said Lance. "It strikes me that you don't know Joyce when you see him."

"That's good," I cried, "considering that he and I were five years at school together."

"Suppose you point him out then?"

"Joyce!" I shouted. "You aren't ashamed to show your face, I hope?"

"Joyce!" they replied, in mockery. "You aren't bashful, Joyce?"

He was not there. Or we couldn't find him, at any rate. We scrutinised each member of the team; it was really absurd to suppose that I could mistake any of them for Joyce. There was not the slightest likeness.

Dryall appealed to the referee.

"Are you sure nobody's sneaked off the field?"

"Stuff!" he said. "I've been following the game all the time, and know every man who's playing, and Joyce hasn't been upon the ground."

"As for his playing three-quarter, Pendleton, Marshall, and I have been playing three-quarter all the afternoon, and I don't think that either of us is very much like Joyce."

This was Tom Wilson.

"You've been playing four three-quarters since we crossed over."

"Bosh!" said Wilson.

That was good, as though I hadn't seen the four with my own eyes.

"Play!" sang out the referee. "Don't waste any more time."

We were at it again. We might be mystified. There was something about the whole affair which was certainly mysterious to me. But we did not intend to be beaten.

"They're only playing three three-quarters now," said Giffard.

So they were. That was plain enough. I wondered if the fourth man had joined the forwards. But why should they conceal the fact that they had been playing four?

One of their men tried a drop. Mason caught it, ran, was collared, passed—wide to the left—and I was off. The whole crowd was in the centre of the field. I put on the steam. Lance came at me. I dodged, he missed. Pendleton was bearing down upon me from the right. I outpaced him. I got a lead. Only Rivers, their back, was between the Brixham goal and me. He slipped just as he made his effort. I was past. I was only a dozen yards to the goal. Nothing would stop me now. I was telling myself that the only thing left was the shouting, when, right in front of me, stood—Joyce! Where he came from I have not the least idea. Out of nothing, it seemed to me. He stood there, cool as a cucumber, waiting—as it appeared—until I came within his reach. His sudden appearance baulked me. I stumbled. The ball slipped from beneath my arm. I saw him smile. Forgetting all about the ball, I made a dash at him. The instant I did so he was gone!

I felt a trifle mixed. I heard behind me the roar of voices. I knew that I had lost my chance. But, at the moment, that was not the trouble. Where had Joyce come from? Where had he gone?

"Now then, Steyning! All together, and you'll do it!"

I heard Mason's voice ring out above the hubbub.

"Brixham, Brixham!" shouted Lance. "Play up!"

"Joyce or no Joyce," I told myself, "hang me if I won't do it yet!"

I got on side. Blaine had hold of the leather. They were on him like a cartload of bricks. He passed to Giffard.

"Don't run back!" I screamed.

They drove him back. He passed to me. They were on the ball as soon as I was. They sent me spinning. Somebody got hold of it. Just as he was off I made a grab at his leg. He went down on his face. The ball broke loose. I got on to my feet. They were indulging in what looked to me very much like hacking. We sent the leather through, and Lance was off! Their fellows backed him up in style. They kept us off until he had a start. He bore off to the right. Already he had shaken off our forwards. I saw Mason charge him. I saw that he sent Mason flying. I made for him. I caught him round the waist. He passed to Pendleton. Pendleton was downed. He lost the ball. Back it came to me, and I was off!

I was away before most of them knew what had become of the leather. Again there was only Rivers between the goal and me. He soon was out of the reckoning. The mud beat him. As he was making for me down he came upon his hands and knees. I had been running wide till then. When he came to grief I centred. Should I take the leather in, or drop?

"Drop!" shouted a voice behind.

That settled me. I was within easy range of the goal. I ought to manage the kick. I dropped—at least, I tried to. It was only a try, because, just as I had my toe against the ball, and was in the very act of kicking, Joyce stood right in front of me! He stood so close that, so to speak, he stood right on the ball. It fell dead, it didn't travel an inch. As I made my fruitless effort, and was still poised upon one leg, placing his hand against my chest, he pushed me over backwards. As I fell I saw him smile—just as I had seen him smile when he had baulked me just before.

I didn't feel like smiling. I felt still less like smiling when, as I yet lay sprawling, Rivers, pouncing on the ball, dropped it back into the centre of the field. He was still standing by me when I regained my feet. He volunteered an observation.

"Lucky for us you muffed that kick."

"Where's Joyce?" I asked.

"Where's who?"

"Joyce."

He stared at me.

"I don't know what you're driving at. I think you fellows must have got Joyce on the brain."

He returned to his place in the field. I returned to mine. I had an affectionate greeting from Giffard.

"That's the second chance you've thrown away. Whatever made you muff that kick?"

"Giffard," I asked, "do you think I'm going mad?"

"I should think you've gone."

I could not—it seems ridiculous, but I could not ask if he had seen Joyce. It was so evident that he had not. And yet, if I had seen him, he must have seen him too. As he suggested—I must have gone mad!

The play was getting pretty rough, the ground was getting pretty heavy. We had churned it into a regular quagmire. Sometimes we went above the ankle in liquid mud. As for the state that we were in!

One of theirs had the ball. Half a dozen of ours had hold of him.

"Held! held!" they yelled.

"It's not held," he gasped.

They had him down, and sat on him. Then he owned that it was held.

"Let it through," cried Mason, when the leather was in scrimmage.

Before our forwards had a chance they rushed it through. We picked it up; we carried it back. They rushed it through again. The tide of battle swayed, now to this side, now to that. Still we gained. Two or three short runs bore the ball within punting distance of their goal. We more than retained the advantage. Yard by yard we drove them back. It was a match against time. We looked like winning if there was only time enough. At last it seemed as though matters had approached something very like a settlement. Pendleton had the ball. Our men were on to him. To avoid being held he punted. But he was charged before he really had a chance. The punt was muddled. It was a catch for Mason.

He made his mark—within twenty yards of their goal! There is no better drop-kick in England than Alec Mason. If from a free kick at that distance he couldn't top their bar, we might as well go home to bed.

Mason took his time. He judged the distance with his eye. Then, paying no attention to the Brixham forward, who had stood up to his mark, he dropped a good six feet on his own side of it. There was an instant's silence. Then they raised a yell; for as the ball left Mason's foot one of their men sprang at him, and, leaping upwards, caught the ball in the air. It was wonderfully done! Quick as lighting, before we had recovered from our surprise, he had dropped the ball back into the centre of the field.

"Now then, Brixham," bellowed Lance.

And they came rushing on. They came on too! We were so disconcerted by Mason's total failure that they got the drop on us. They reached the leather before our back had time to return. It was all we could do to get upon the scene of action quickly enough to prevent their having the scrimmage all to themselves. Mason's collapse had put life into them as much as, for the moment, it had taken it out of us. They carried the ball through the scrimmage as though our forwards were not there.

"Now then, Steyning, you're not going to let them beat us!"

As Mason held his peace I took his place as fugleman.

But we could not stand against them—we could not—in scrimmage or out of it. All at once they seemed to be possessed. In an instant their back play improved a hundred per cent. One of their men, in particular, played like Old Nick himself. In the excitement—and they were an exciting sixty seconds—I could not make out which one of them it was; but he made things lively. He as good as played us single-handed; he was always on the ball; he seemed to lend their forwards irresistible impetus when it was in the scrimmage. And when it was out of it, wasn't he just upon the spot. He was ubiquitous—here, there, and everywhere. And at last he was off. Exactly how it happened is more than I can say, but I saw that he had the ball. I saw him dash away with it. I made for him. He brushed me aside as though I were a fly. I was about to start in hot pursuit when someone caught me by the arm. I turned—in a trifle of a rage. There was Mason at my side.

"Never mind that fellow. Listen to me." These were funny words to come from the captain of one's team at the very crisis of the game. I both listened and looked. Something in the expression of his face quite startled me. "Do you know who it was who spoilt my kick? It was either Joyce or—Joyce's ghost."

Before I was able to ask him what it was he meant there arose a hullaballoo of shouting. I turned just in time to see the fellow, who had run away with the leather, drop it, as sweetly as you please, just over our goal. They had won! And at that moment the whistle sounded—they had done it just on time!

The man who had done the trick turned round and faced us. He was wearing a worsted cap, such as brewers wear. Taking it off, he waved it over his head. As he did so there was not a man upon the field who did not see him clearly, who did not know who he was. He was Frank Joyce! He stood there for a moment before us all, and then was gone.

"Lance," shouted the referee, "here's a telegram for you."

Lance was standing close to Mason and to me. A telegraph boy came pelting up. Lance took the yellow envelope which the boy held out to him. He opened it.

"Why! what!" Through the mud upon his face he went white, up to the roots of his hair. He turned to us with startled eyes. "Joyce died in Brixham Hospital nearly an hour ago. The hospital people have telegraphed to say so."

JOHN METCALFE
Brenner's Boy

John Metcalfe *(1891–1965) wrote some of the most ingenious fantasy, macabre and supernatural stories ever written. His stories were collected together as* The Smoking Leg *(1925),* Judas *(1931), and* The Feasting Dead *(1954). 'Brenner's Boy' was originally printed as a separate volume in 1932.*

Warrant Officer Winter, in his middle sixties, remained a hard-headed man. Retired in 1904, he now, in 1912, was a member of the Royal Fleet Reserve and lived with his wife in a small whitewashed cottage on the Hampshire coast "Pompey" was not so far off—about seven miles—and over his nightly tot of lion's blood in the Calcutta Tavern he would survey, with conscientious censoriousness, the callow antics of occasional too-exuberant ratings off the *Excellent*—liberty men whose cap ribbons proclaimed them as having come "ashore" not from a ship at all but from the moaning, cordite-reeking Naval Gunnery School upon Whale Island.

Nowadays, it was his conviction, ratings were pampered. Owing, in part, to the ameliorated conditions achieved by Miss Agnes E. Weston, the bluejacket lived soft. The old spirit of natural enmity between the Wardroom and the lower deck was gone. He hummed, under his breath, a ditty, of which a line or two was missing in his memory:

Poll put her arms akimbo;
At the Admiral's house looked she.
To thoughts that were in limbo
She then to vent gave free.
"Oh you've got a roaring fire I'll bet
And in it your toes are jammed"
 (tum tiddy um tiddy um tum tum)
"Port Admiral, you be damned!"

Port Admirals for aught he knew might, as extreme cases, still be properly detested, especially by starving dollymops, so possibly the ballad, in the context of his scorn, was not entirely appropriate. But, in a rough way, it applied. He mused sourly, twirling the stem of his half-empty glass of rum. In *his* day almost any Admiral was hated *ipso facto* —Yes, old Brenner too.

2

Either he, Winter the hard-headed, had not proved quite insensible to flattery in that encounter, or else he must admit that Brenner wasn't quite so bad. A dry old stick, however, at the best. His mufti hung awkardly from clothes-horse shoulders; his voice, even in greeting, had an excoriating rasp. He seemed all knees and knuckles.

Winter, desperately reminiscent for the sake of sanity, strove to give the affair in retrospect a minute documentation. He could be sure of the date anyhow. The Navy had been out of white cap-covers for nearly three weeks. It was the twentieth of October, a snell and gloomy afternoon with a faint driving sting of rain. He was taking the 1–15 to Havant, where an uncle who had a little property to leave had just expired. The funeral was next day and Winter was stopping at Havant for the night.

On his way to Portsmouth he had looked in at the Calcutta. This had delayed him, and when at length he reached the station he had less than half a minute to find room in a crowded train. A football team, accompanied by supporters, was tumultuously en route for Brighton. Winter had finally flung himself into the first-class compartment which fatally happened to contain Rear Admiral Brenner, C.B., M.V.O.

Also there was the boy—stamping on Winter's boots, squirming and doubling, grimacing with brown minnow-eyes and a mouth stuffed with toffee—which before long exploded stickily on his father's waistcoat in a burst of raucous laughter. Old Brenner, that supposed martinette, could do nothing with the imp apparently. "Be quiet, Tinker . . . .. Do you hear? Sit still, Sir!" Owing to these distractions the Admiral's recognition of the W.O. was frosty. "Isn't your name Winter? On *Sutlej* I think, in '98."

"Yes, Sir". Winter's gaze was respectfully wooden. That old swine Brenner! He felt, momentarily, a mean glow of cynical gratification at Brenner's remembering him. Well, if—suddenly his mind grew blank in a kind of horror. "*On Sutlej I think, in* '98 . . . ." It was the boy, chanting, mimicking his father. A grey curtain of shame dropped between the two men. The Admiral's face paled. Hell seemed to be let loose. Winter averted his eyes.

So it went on. There were only the three of them in the compartment, and at Cosham, where tickets were examined, Brenner insisted on paying Winter's excess fare. Conversation was disjointed, thanks to Hell. Apart from the boy, Tinker, and with due regard to their differing ranks, retired Admiral and retired Warrant could doubtless have exchanged the remarks of two profound realists, neither one of them estimable or imagining himself to be so, yet each convinced that the remaining world was still less estimable. Each, had young Hell allowed him, might have felt for the other a grudging, semi-hostile admiration. . . . .

But the boy confused and impaired all this. He swaggered and spat twice—three times, upon the floor, then, crouching, peered out from between his father's legs like something in a den. His ears were patently unclean. Once, as they were nearing Fratton, Winter had to close his nostrils against an evil smell. Old Brenner sat rigid, raging. The *exposé* of his impotence turned Winter rather sick. Already he felt a potential blackmailer. At Havant he got out clumsily, half tripped by Tinker's toes, uttered a sheepishly constrained "Good afternoon, Sir".

What bothered him enormously afterwards was the difficulty he experienced in reconstructing the encounter. *Had* old Brenner really suggested anything about the boy—about his stopping with him, Winter, for a week or two? It seemed extravagantly unlikely. Yet it was true that they had swapped addresses, which was improbable enough. Brenner, however, had coldly promised to look into that entanglement about his Reserve grading and promotion. And possibly, in irony, he *might* have said something about a visit. "Winter'll give you plenty of rope-pie when you're with him!" For an instant the imp had sobered, leaned against Winter's knee. The minnow eyes grew soft and lush, repugnantly girlish. Winter, embarrassed, had shrunk away a little. From the coach behind them came a hoarse burst of singing. The footballers. "Bill Bailey" and "Let's all go down the Strand!" And outside it was grey, rain on the windows. The whole thing didn't seem real . . . .

"Rope-pie, indeed! Yes, some o' that'd do the little sod no harm!" Winter had laughed to himself later in bitter awkwardness. He had no child of his own. He had married a woman who had proved barren. Winter would sit in the Calcutta Tavern thinking hard thoughts about her, twirling his rum. And now he could not remember properly what old Brenner had really said. But he *must* remember. It was terribly important. His brain was splitting. Oh, my head, my poor head, my *head* . . . .

3

All that he had to go on for some time was a letter, which he had subsequently mislaid. He turned his cottage upside down in vain. The thing was lost.

The letter came at ten a.m. Winter's dowdy, wistful wife, Chrissie, brought it out to him as he was digging in the back garden. He read it, frowning. "It's from old Brenner. He's looking into that Reserve business he says . . . ." Winter had told Chrissie, curtly, about his meeting Brenner in the train a fortnight ago and had even mentioned Brenner's odious child, but now he did not show her the letter. He had a disquieting notion that there was something very wrong with it. He continued his digging and Chrissie returned indoors.

It was a grey November day, cold but dampish, and very still. Whale Island was booming away as usual, and Winter anticipated, with annoyance, that the heavy guns would presently bring the rain down. He felt surly, and that morning, aware of rheumatic twinges, had put on his red flannel body-belt. Even his cottage, frigidly spick and span, with its neatly furled ex-service look of something eternally standing at attention, got on his nerves. He was fed up with Chrissie. Not only had she given him no child but she was a liar as well. She had told him that her sister and brother-in-law, the Pinks, were definitely not coming again for another fortnight, and now it suddenly appeared that they *were* coming—to-morrow afternoon. His Sunday would be ruined.

Moreover, there was this letter.

Fishing it from his pocket as he strolled off after tea toward the Calcutta Tavern, he considered it uneasily. The body of the missive was satisfactory—a laconic intimation that affairs at the Reserve were being straightened out—and the address was the Cadogan Square address which the Admiral had already given him—but, underneath the crabbed signature, were written in an unformed, scrawling hand the words "on suttledge I think in ninety ate".

Whilst he was playing Crown and Anchor and other gambling games with a bunch of ex-Marines Winter became increasingly disturbed and out of sorts. The reek of smoke in the crowded room behind the saloon bar, the excited shouts of "House!" or "Clickety-click!", made his head ache. Evidently that little bastard had scribbled on the old fellow's letter, and Brenner hadn't spotted it. He must be amazingly careless. And the added words were actually a quotation. Brenner had used them himself and that damned kid had mimicked him. Extremely odd . . . .

The ex-W.O., in general a securely unimaginative individual, grew more and more perplexed. For some days after his meeting with Brenner he hadn't thought much about the matter, beyond recalling it occasionally with faint ironical distaste. But latterly, instead of letting it lapse in a normal manner, he had fallen to wondering about it, examining it uneasily. Now, with the arrival of the letter, he was obsessed with the feeling that the whole episode had been, in some vague way he couldn't put his finger on, "irregular". He racked his brains.

"On *Sutlej* I think, in '98." What had happened on *Sutlej* in '98? Brenner, certainly, was very much aboard, only he hadn't been an Admiral then of course. He had been a mere Commander, a justly unpopular and peppery old devil, dishing out plenteous 10 A. to defaulters, whilst Winter himself had been a C.P.O. On the whole they had rather disliked each other, but there had been no trouble. Winter had left with "Excellent" on his flimsy. It seemed natural enough that the old sod should remember him, and even exert himself about the Reserve business in a friendly way if he felt like it, now that they were both more or less civilians. Unusual, possibly, but yet entirely in order . . . .

Winter set off on his tramp homewards, still morosely brooding. Despite himself, he had been flattered by the Admiral's recognition, but, with a tight sneer, he had quashed the feeling. In any case, the spectacle of that old sea-dog's disgraceful incapacity to deal with a ten year's brat had quickly scandalised him. "Old sea-dog" hell! Winter had been degraded by his involvement, even as a mere onlooker, in something pitiable and faintly ludicrous.

Gaining the foot of the acclivity at the top of which his cottage was situated, he continued to cogitate. He wished he could remember what he and old Faceache had said to each other in the train a bit more clearly. It struck him for a moment as curious that he had forgotten everything but the barest scraps of their conversation, and that even these recollected fragments appeared vague and somehow not quite "right", improbable. For instance, he *fancied* now that the Admiral had made some remark about young Tinker's boarding with him for a while—in joke of course. And when the boy had sidled up against his knee Brenner had said, in obvious sarcasm, " . . . . seems to have taken quite a shine to you . . . ." Winter, laboriously plodding up the cliff, gave a dry, mirthless chuckle. "Perhaps the old fool thought that I could manage him a trifle better than he could himself. Wouldn't be difficult. If I had . . . ."

Suddenly his meditations were interrupted. From behind him at this instant came a burst of laughter. Winter, with a startled oath, swung round. It was dark, of course, but he could make out a low, curvetting figure pursuing him up the path. Winter drew out an electric torch, flashed it upon the approaching form, and stared, incredulous. His heart dropped in a quick dismay. Could this be possible? He peered more closely.

Yes, he was not mistaken. It was him all right, that boy—just as if Winter's thoughts had brought him here. It was Tinker, Tinker Brenner, carrying a small suitcase in one hand and waving to him with the other.

"What the . . . . what do . . . . what do you want?" Winter had halted, and Tinker was now beside him, laughing still, and—actually—circling round him, stabbing an extended thumb into his, Winter's, buttocks. The ex-W.O. circled too, to avoid him. "Hi—stop it, you . . . . Hold off there . . .!" In an unreasoned access of alarm he noticed that the boy had no proper boots; he was wearing patent-leather slippers—dancing pumps or something. And again, despite his astonishment, there came popping up into his mind, like a phrase of complete nonsense which had yet gathered a peculiarly unpleasant flavour, the question—*What* had happened upon *Sutlej*—in '98?

4

Anyhow, it was exactly twenty two minutes past nine in the evening of the third of November. Winter was destined to cling obstinately to this solid fact, feeling that the possession of a precise date helped him a little in a position which, on the face of it, was fantastic. He and the prancing Tinker had entered the cottage and Tinker was now swilling tea and bolting cold boiled bacon. He had already smashed one cup and stained the tablecloth. In response to feverish enquiries he had merely said: "*He* told me. *He* said I was going to stay with you". Chrissie and Winter, having lost all appetite for supper, stood staring at him from just outside the door-frame. Tinker paid them no attention whatsoever. Presently they retired by mute agreement to the kitchen and discussed the situation in hushed tones.

Chrissie, after the first shock, seemed less put out than Winter. The woman was such a fool that his fierce whispers of bewilderment failed to disturb her mulishly complacent brain. "He can't stay here. What are we to *do* with the little bastard? Just says '*He*' said he was to come. '*He*'—that means the old man, Brenner. But the kid hasn't got a letter—nothing. I don't believe it. Only saw him for a few minutes in the train. He's run away . . . . But why should he come *here*? Fancy his getting the address an' coming *here* . . . . Only saw him a few minutes, I tell you—in that train . . . ."

They crept back to the living-room to find it empty. "Where's he gorn?" said Winter. "You better go an' look." He waited, whilst Chrissie reconnoitred. Presently she returned on tiptoe, her eyes round. "'E's asleep! 'E's gorn to sleep—on our bed. Shall I wake 'im?"

Winter nodded, still annoyed with Chrissie. Her face had a wondering, furtive expression he didn't care about.

5

Brenner's boy spent, as nearly as circumstances permitted Winter to calculate, between fifty and fifty-seven hours at the cottage. During this time he was observed at close range by at least three other individuals. These people—Chrissie and the two Pinks—could all, if necessary, have been called on to corroborate the fact of his presence there and to give some description of his clothing, manners and general personal appearance.

He wore a grey tweed knickerbocker suit and heather-mixture "golf" stockings badly in need of darning. His face was thin, usually dirty, and adorned with large ears, like Brenner's own. Since his suitcase contained no night-apparel, Chrissie lent him for his slumbers an old flannel shirt of her husband's, which in the morning was found to be seriously defiled. On the first evening he had, as stated, simply thrown himself down on the Winter's' bed and gone to sleep there, but, after some discussion, it was decided to make him undress like a Christian. Chrissie prepared him an impromptu bed in the parlour and Winter, finally losing his temper at the boy's stubbornness, carried him out of their bedroom and dumped him, squirming, on the sofa.

What was to be done about it? Winter, after a disturbed Sunday breakfast, concocted and posted a letter to the Admiral. He had had half a mind to wire from Portsmouth, but, at the last moment, hesitated to appear too astonished and incredulous. There was, he kept strangely telling himself, just an off-chance that the child really might have come down with old Brenner's sanction. Yet that seemed quite absurd. Tinker had arrived unannounced; he had come in dancing slippers and without a nightdress; there had been, of course, no previous talk about "terms". And, in any case, Winter would rather have done without the boy and money both.

That was what he thought, savagely, on the first morning. Coming home from posting the letter, he found his *News of the World* turned into paper darts which littered the small living-room from end to end. The Pinks—Lydia and Harry—were on the scene, and Tinker had grabbed at Mrs. Pink's bead necklace and broken the thread. Chrissie was apologising and picking up the scattered beads . . . .

Without going into details it is enough to say that Tinker, as long as he stayed at the cottage, was a trial, a rare "handful". This is putting it mildly. Even from the start he was, of course, and in a curious way, much worse than that. Winter, before the boy disappeared at last, had struck him twice. Once upon the seat of his knickerbockers with a slipper and once with the flat of the hand on his face. The second time seemed to Winter the more serious. Rather oddly, he could not remember afterwards what especial piece of mischief had made him so angry. Probably Master Brenner had been setting up his usual terrible row, singing (if one could call it singing) in a cracked, caterwauling drone. It must have been that. The ex-Warrant thought he could recall his own words anyhow: "Oh, put a sock in it! Oh, for Christ's sake, pipe down . . . .!" He had been very riled.

What he did remember, quite plainly, was that, after the blow, Tinker had made no fuss. He had only seemed sobered and a little startled. Winter himself had looked uneasily at the mark, first white then red, which his palm had left on Tinker's cheek. Going into the hall, he met Chrissie, who had heard the slap. She was frightened again, and Winter felt a furious indignation with her, changing, to his surprise, into a kind of dull unhappiness. A lump even rose in his throat and his eyes grew moist. He and his wife just stared at each other without a word.

This was not everything. Besides the general anomaly of the situation were a good many things which struck the harrassed Warrant as peculiar. Most of all, the kid's dislike of going out of doors and his determined unwillingness to speak, or explain anything, about himself. On that first evening of his arrival Winter had done nothing but ask him questions, but he could get no proper answers. The brat would sing and swagger, shout for food when he was hungry, and, sometimes, mimic Winter and poor Chrissie in the rudest way, but into ordinary conversation he stubbornly refused to be beguiled. Coaxing and threats had no effect. His behaviour was so remote and standoffish toward other people it was really something like a cat's.

Harry Pink, whose new kodak had had to be snatched away from Tinker a little earlier in the afternoon and who was still very angry at the narrowness of its escape, whispered to Winter at the doorstep upon taking leave. He moved his head seriously up and down as he spoke, under his breath.

"Some cough-drop, that, you've got! If I was you I'd pack 'im 'ome, George, right away, I would . . . . .!"

Lydia nodded too. "So *rude*! And—and 'e's *queer*. I wouldn' keep 'im, George, I wouldn' reelly. Must be some mistake. 'E's—well, 'e's *funny*, sort of, kind of funny. Sort of gives one the creeps . . . .!"

6

Sunday had passed. Over the week-end, with its blank postal day, the Warrant had had to resign himself to marking time, but now that Monday morning, chill and overcast, was here and there was still no letter from the Admiral he found it difficult not to feel worried. Usually a phlegmatic and somewhat indurated individual, his mind sardonically schooled in the hard, 'wangling' guile of Gunroom politics, Winter was by no means the type to be easily fazed or rattled by any ordinary dilemma, yet, by degrees, the growing mystery of this affair began to tell on him. It certainly was very strange! he would repeat—not, after all, knowing quite what he really meant when he said that.

Whilst he remained anxious not to annoy old Brenner just as the promotion business was being settled, he nevertheless saw clearly that the present state of things could not continue. It was, of course, only the vague, intermittent haunting of his memory by the Admiral's remarks in the train which had prevented him from wiring to Cadogan Square at once. As it was, he decided to wait one more day and then, if he got no answer to his Sunday's letter, to send the Admiral a telegram. And, in regard to Tinker's boarding with them, even for a single week, he would, if necessary, have to write as tactfully as he could, explaining that they hadn't the accommodation.

In the first place, Winter doubted whether any compensation he was likely to receive would leave him a clear profit, and, in the second, the boy's society affected him in morbid and unpleasant ways. If it had simply been a question of Tinker's unsavoury habits and the depredations he occasioned, Winter, for adequate remuneration, might have borne with him and tried, eventually, to lick him into shape, supposing that was what old Brenner really wanted him to do.

He had lost his temper with the brat and struck him twice yesterday, and, possibly as a result, the kid seemed quieter today, much less unruly. But, beyond this, was something rather more disturbing, something which left him gravelled for an explanation. The child, he put it to himself, was 'queer', unlike a normal boy. He had been here now, how long? Almost forty-one hours—and he had hung about indoors all day, still making himself an awful nuisance certainly, and yet hardly saying a word to a soul. Chrissie had even feared he might be sickening for something. It would be a nice picnic if he came down on them with 'flu, for instance! At dinner he had eaten less than usual and after the meal sat idly flicking over the leaves of a copy of *Chips* and of other 'comics' which he had brought with him in his suitcase. As the afternoon wore on, Winter, who had had to abandon a long-projected visit to an old shipmate in Southsea, found himself looking at the boy in growing dissatisfaction. He had a feeling—preposterous of course yet difficult to shake off—that Tinker was not—how to put it?—not quite, not entirely, 'right'. He now remembered, too, though with contempt, a remark of Lydia's which Chrissie had retailed to him. Mrs. Pink, it seemed, when she had caught sight of Tinker through the doorway, had, in the first flush of amazement, made a curious mistake as to his sex. She had imagined, for a moment, that he was a girl! Winter had a low opinion of Lydia, but, all the same her foolish error vaguely disconcerted him. Somehow, it tended to re-enforce his own conviction that the child was, in some peculiar way, abnormal, and unnatural, not quite really 'there'. Yet by the number of cups and other articles of crockery that he had broken he must be reckoned very actual indeed!

After tea Winter followed Chrissie out into the kitchen. "That kid's the bleeding limit! If he was *mine* I'd show him! If *I* had a kid . . . .!" He saw Chrissie's moon face pucker. She was trying not to cry, regarding him covertly with that humble, apologetic glance which invariably exasperated him. He turned with an exclamation of disgust. No, he would never have a kid. It was her fault. He went back softly, his mind weighted with some suspicion that defied analysis, to peep in awkwardly on Brenner's boy.

Slowly the hours passed. It was dark outside. Dusk had fallen early and a damp moon arisen with a weeping wind. Tinker, sitting in the firelight, was still engrossed with *Chips*. He made no reply when Winter addressed him gruffly. "If I was you I wouldn't strain me eyes . . . . d'yer hear me?" Winter, after a pause, lit the gas, noisily pulled down the blinds. "You're going home tomorrer anyway . . . ." Tinker stirred at last, looked up. "Yes . . . . all right". Merely that. Winter stared at him a few moments in perplexity, then averted his eyes. What the hell was wrong with everything—wrong with himself? He 'came over' all queer when he looked at that boy. Wretched, indeed. He was overcome by an intense gloom, a strange, indefinable depression which had no adequate reason. He, Warrant Officer Winter, had got the pip and no mistake. His insides, he imagined, felt like the insides of a dog baying the moon or howling at music—listening to whatever tune it was the old cow died of . . . .

7

That night, after lying awake for several hours, he had a dream. It was still the previous evening and he had stolen into the parlour to look at Tinker. The kid, in the firelight fastened his brown eyes upon him in a smile. But the smile was unbearable. Winter couldn't stand it. It made him remember a tune, the tune and presently some of the words of a song he hated. The tune the old cow died of. It was on *Sutlej*, "in '98". That elderly, grizzled two-and-a-half-ringer, Merrow, was singing it, bawling it from the quarter-deck:

> Oh the clang of the wooden shoon
> Oh the dance and the merry tue-oon . . . .

Winter, with the song in his brain, stood staring in jaw-dropped misery at Tinker. And now Chrissie was beside him, staring too. “Oh, George”, he heard her say, in accents of intense, melancholy reproach, “Oh, George—'e's *fond* of you, 'e is, *fond* of you . . . .” All at once he felt her hand clutch his arm in horror. “Look! Look at 'is 'ead! ‘E's going bald!” The hair thinned as he gazed. It was Brenner and yet not Brenner. A black object like a large cockade with a zig-zag edge came up slowly between the boy's collar and his neck. Chrissie was screaming.

The Warrant awoke, bathed in sweat, his eyes streaming with tears, to find himself in bed, his wife beside him. Well, he would send a wire off at any rate, possibly take the boy up to old Brenner as he'd told him. After a while he dropped off to sleep again. His slumbers this time were so heavy that he did not wake till Chrissie roused him.

She was half dressed, shaking his shoulder, looking at him alarmedly. “Wake up, George! 'E's gorn! 'E's gorn, I say!”

It was true. There was no sign of Tinker. He must have left in the night, taking his suitcase with him.

Winter swore. He felt cold and cramped inside, and frightened. “If we can't find him I'll go up to London. Have to. It's serious, this. I'll have to see old Brenner”.

8

In the train to London Winter reproached himself many times for his gross stupidity. He could not now understand how he had failed to realise from the start that Tinker's descent upon them was unauthorised, that the whole business was extremely ‘fishy’. He ought to have wired to the Admiral immediately, and he was at a loss to comprehend the way in which he had delayed to do so. But it seemed that, in this predicament, his usual commonsense had been conspicuously lacking. The entire episode was like a dream in which even his own actions had been vague and indistinct. He had to pinch himself to believe that any of it had really happened.

However, he was certainly here, in this train, and on his way to Brenner's. There was no doubt about that. He had waited for the morning post before leaving his cottage, but there had still been no letter—only a small package, addressed to him in Harry Pink's familiar hand-writing, which he had thrust into his jacket pocket unopened. None of the few neighbours whom he had thought it worth while to question had seen anything of the decamping Tinker. At Portsmouth he had sent off a telegram to

Cadogan Square. It was now eleven thirty, and he would arrive at Victoria a little after one.

As the train rushed and roared through Havant Winter wondered what he was going to say to Brenner. Perhaps he ought to have notified the police. Supposing the kid had not turned up there yet, had not gone home at all . . . .! That would be a pretty state of things! Tinker's pockets had been found to contain a purse with some money, nearly a pound, so he would have enough to get home on—but there was no telling. Yes, it might have been wiser to have informed the police and waited instead of dashing off precipitately to see Brenner. And the old man would undoubtedly hold him, Winter, responsible for everything. Possibly, if the boy *had* got home all right, he would have complained to his father about the way Winter had struck him—and Brenner might be furious.

Outside, the day was misty. Thick banks of vapour were forming, blotting out wide patches of the landscape. Winter's head was throbbing. He hoped devoutly that there wouldn't be a fog in London to delay him. He was on tenterhooks to get the matter settled, had a sick feeling of suspense and apprehension. Not only was he mortified by what he now regarded as his own unaccountable negligence and culpable lack of 'savvy', ordinary 'nous', in the affair, and anxious as to what might be its upshot in a practical and worldly sense, but he was still bewildered, haunted by a curious, nagging doubt. The whole business bristled with improbabilities and contradictions. More and more, also, as he pondered it, he found himself relapsing into that state of deep and unexplained despondency which had enfolded him throughout the previous day. What the devil *was* wrong with him? And why, in particular, hadn't Brenner wired or written to him, answered that letter he had sent on Sunday?

Putting his hand into his pocket, he drew out Harry's package, which, as he was setting off for Portsmouth, he had snatched in a hurry from the postman and not troubled to take in to Chrissie. It was a stout brown envelope containing photographic prints, enclosed in a letter. Winter did no more than glance at the letter, but, in a sudden interest, he began to look over the snapshots, one by one. Mr. Pink, as he recalled, had been eager to try out his new camera, and had 'taken' the little party several times.

The Warrant, looking at the snapshots, knitted his brows together in a frown. He thumbed them over, at first in dim perplexity, and then, more rapidly, in something like dismay.

One, two, three, four, five, six—yes, they were all there . . . . A nervous oath escaped him. "Well, I'll be—!" He was trembling, beset by an actual physical chill. A man, smoking Woodbines in the opposite corner, turned his head in surprise, and Winter met his gaze blankly. The fog was thicker, and inside the compartment the incandescent gas shed a sickly radiance. Winter, with an effort, collected himself and thrust the photos back into his pocket. But he was shaking still. He glanced at his watch. With a feeling of cold aghastness he realised that his suspense must continue for another hour at least.

9

The house, when at length he did arrive there, cast a further chill upon his spirits. It was a large, severe residence, faced with stone, and ordinarily the Warrant would have felt scornful at the bare idea of his intruding into such a place. But his nervousness now was of a different kind. The fog had made it difficult to find his way. It was past two o'clock already. He rang the bell and waited, shifting impatiently from foot to foot.

Presently the door was opened by a man, a 'flunkey' Winter mechanically presumed. The fellow's face stared out in a hostile manner as if he were shocked. Winter began at once: "Can I see Admiral Brenner? My name's Winter. I've—"

He got no further for the man cut him short. "See Admiral Brenner? No, certainly you can't. Certainly not!" The low, prim voice had a tone of outraged rebuke. From behind the man, from the large, gloomy house, something passed out to Winter like a melancholy breath. The door was closing.

"But I must see him. It's important. If—" Winter, quivering with a strange desperation, had put a foot inside the door. The man, mouthing a horrified exclamation, tried to push him back, unavailingly. Within the house a crowing, raucous voice arose: "What's that? Who's there? What's happening?"

It was the Admiral. The lackey, extinguished by scandal, stood rigid. Brenner and Winter confronted each other.

"You . . . . *You* . . . . What do . . . ." Some emotion, evidently painful, choked the old man's words. His face was suffused. Winter, looking at him, had a dumb presentiment of horror. Yes, this *was* Brenner—knuckles, knees, and parchment mottled cheeks. He hadn't been mistaken as to *that* at anyrate. Yet he was afraid, wrapped still in an uncanny speculation. He was terribly afraid of he didn't quite know what—not quite, but almost.

Admiral Brenner slowly gained control of himself. He motioned the footman to depart.

"Come in here." He opened a door into a room on the left of the hall. Winter, entering after him, experienced an added chill, aware of something that he hadn't noticed from the foggy road outside. The room, until the Admiral switched on the electric light, was dark. The blinds were drawn.

Winter, fumbling his hat, began hurriedly. "I wrote to you on Sunday, Sir, and I sent you a telegram this morning. I hope that, er, that Master Brenner's got back safe, and—"

"You're mad!" The Admiral's voice rang with suppressed fury. His face was working; his eyes held tears, of grief or rage or both. He looked almost as if he were going to have a stroke. "You're crazy! Your letter—yes, I got your letter, and the wire . . . . How—how *dare* you . . . . How . . . . but you *must* be mad!"

Ex-Warrant Officer Winter, that usually hard-headed man, felt his mind growing blank, his legs enfeebled. His wits, apparently, had deserted him. It was only his evil genius, a morbid desire to get things straightened out and regularised, which impelled him to go on. He spoke woodenly from a glum trance in a sort of confused remonstrance, as if out of a moody rumination.

"But, Sir, I don't quite understand. You see, I wired to you that—that the boy'd given us the slip, gone off, and—"

He stopped. Old Brenner was struggling hard to say something, couldn't quite manage it. A white intermittent fleck which he rapidly and repeatedly licked away appeared at the corner of his mouth. Winter waited. At length the Admiral spoke.

"Get out! Get out of here! I—I won't have it! You're—you're mad I say . . . . My—my little boy, he's—He was here all the time. I don't know what you mean. He's never left this house. He was—very ill. You're crazy . . . . He—he died last night . . . ."

Winter moved to the door. For a moment he retained a stubborn determination to hear more, but his courage failed him. There was nothing to be made of this—nothing at all. He went out into the hall, opened the front door and closed it softly after him. The fog seemed to have cleared just a little. He put on his hat and stumbled down the steps.

10

And now, seven hours later, he was back again at the Calcutta Tavern, sipping his rum, utterly giving things up, unable to make head or tail of things at all. The Admiral, he was momentarily inclined to think, was very mad indeed. Obviously that must be so, for didn't Winter distinctly remember missing that kid only this very morning, setting off in such a God-damned twitter for London to get the matter straight? And it was only yesterday that he had *seen* the boy, with his own eyes. A man had to believe his own eyes or where the hell was he? Others had seen him too. The idea of a collective hallucination (though this phrase was not actually available to Winter) must be considered too absurd.

But at other moments his faith weakened. There were those snapshots of Harry Pink's in which Tinker should have appeared but didn't. It was perplexing. Perplexity and uncertainty were playing the very devil with him. Suddenly he put his hands up to his forehead. "Oh, my head, my poor head, my *head* . . . .!"

One or two fellows in the bar were looking at him curiously. Winter felt disconcerted. Had he let out anything about Chrissie yet? She was the one who had said, in his dream, that Tinker was fond of him. It was all her fault, when you really came down to brass tacks, because she hadn't given him a kid.

He had been sitting in rather a collapsed posture, in a corner, but now he straightened himself and spoke gruffly to a man he recognised. "You know my wife, eh?—Chrissie? Well, I've—just done her in. Strangled her, see?—like that!" He made a grotesque motion with thick fingers, sturdy thumbs.

The man looked at him oddly, laughed in an embarrassed way. Nobody else paid him any attention. The door opened, letting in a breath of colder air. Winter looked out through it vacantly. His eyes were hurting and he had a sharp pain in his temples. "Oh, my head, my poor head, my *head* . . . .!" he moaned. Between his locked fingers, as long as the door remained open, he could catch a glimpse of misty moonlight. For a moment he could smell the foggy night.

EDITH NESBIT
Uncle Abraham's Romance

Edith Nesbit *(1858–1924) is best remembered for her children's classics, notably* The Railway Children *(1906), successfully dramatised for both television and cinema. Early in her career she contributed some excellent ghost stories to* Argosy, Illustrated London News, *and other magazines, and the best of these were collected in* Grim Tales *(1893), including 'Man-Size in Marble', 'John Charrington's Wedding', and 'Uncle Abraham's Romance'.*

"No, my dear," my Uncle Abraham answered me, "no—nothing romantic ever happened to me—unless—but no; that wasn't romantic either—"

I was. To me, I being eighteen, romance was the world. My Uncle Abraham was old and lame. I followed the gaze of his faded eyes, and my own rested on a miniature that hung at his elbow-chair's right hand, a portrait of a woman, whose loveliness even the miniature-painter's art had been powerless to disguise—a woman with large eyes that shone, and face of that alluring oval which one hardly sees nowadays.

I rose to look at it. I had looked at it a hundred times. Often enough in my baby days I had asked, "Who's that, uncle?" and always the answer was the same: "A lady who died long ago, my dear."

As I looked again at the picture, I asked, "Was she like this?"

"Who?"

"Your—your romance!"

Uncle Abraham looked hard at me. "Yes," he said at last. "Very—very like."

I sat down on the floor by him. "Won't you tell me about her?"

"There's nothing to tell," he said. "I think it was fancy mostly, and folly; but it's the realest thing in my life, my dear."

A long pause. I kept silent. You should always give people time, especially old people.

"I remember," he said in the dreamy tone always promising so well to the ear that loves a story—"I remember, when I was a young man, I was very lonely indeed. I never had a sweetheart. I was always lame, my dear, from quite a boy; and the girls used to laugh at me."

Silence again. Presently he went on—

"And so I got into the way of mooning off by myself in lonely places, and one of my favourite walks was up through our churchyard, which was set on a hill in the middle of the marsh country. I liked that because I never met anyone there. It's all over, years ago. I was a silly lad; but I couldn't bear of a summer evening to hear a rustle and a whisper from the other side of the hedge, or maybe a kiss, as I went by.

"Well, I used to go and sit all by myself in the churchyard, which was always sweet with the thyme and quite light (on account of it's being so high) long after the marshes were dark. I used to watch the bats flitting about in the red light, and wonder why God didn't make everyone's legs straight and strong, and wicked follies like that. But by the time the light was gone I had always worked it off, so to speak, and could go home quietly, and say my prayers without bitterness.

"Well, one hot night in August, when I had watched the sunset fade and the crescent moon grow golden, I was just stepping over the low stone wall of the churchyard when I heard a rustle behind me. I turned round, expecting it to be a rabbit or a bird. It was a woman."

He looked at the portrait. So did I.

"Yes," he said, "that was her very face. I was a bit scared and said something—I don't know what—she laughed and said, did I think she was a ghost? and I answered back; and I stayed talking to her over the churchyard wall till 'twas quite dark, and the glow-worms were out in the wet grass all along the way home.

"Next night, I saw her again; and the next, and the next. Always at twilight time; and if I passed any lovers leaning on the stiles in the marshes it was nothing to me now."

Again my uncle paused. "It was very long ago," he said shyly, "and I'm an old man; but I know what youth means, and happiness, though I was always lame, and the girls used to laugh at me. I don't know how long it went on—you don't measure time in dreams—but at last your grandfather said I looked as if I had one foot in the grave, and he would be sending me to stay with our kin at Bath, and take the waters. I had to go. I could not tell my father why I would rather die than go."

"What was her name, Uncle?" I asked.

"She never would tell me her name, and why should she? I had names enough in my heart to call her by. Marriage? My dear, even then I knew marriage was not for me. But I met her night after night, always in our churchyard where the yew-trees were, and the old crooked gravestones so thick in the grass. It was there we always met and always parted. The last time was the night before I went away. She was very sad, and dearer than life itself. And she said—

" 'If you come back before the new moon, I shall meet you here just as usual. But if the new moon shines on this grave and you are not here—you will never see me again any more'."

She laid her hand on the tomb against which we had been leaning. It was an old, lichened, weather-worn stone, and its inscription was just

'SUSANNAH KINGSNORTH,
Ob. 1723.'

" ' I shall be here,' I said.

" ' I mean it," she said, very seriously and slowly, 'it is no fancy. You will be here when the new moon shines?'

"I promised, and after a while we parted.

"I had been with my kinsfolk at Bath for nearly a month. I was to go home on the next day when, turning over a case in the parlour, I came upon that miniature. I could not speak for a minute. At last I said, with dry tongue, and heart beating to the tune of heaven and hell:

" 'Who is this?'

" 'That?' said my aunt. 'Oh! She was betrothed to one of our family years ago, but she died before the wedding. They say she was a bit of witch. A handsome one, wasn't she?'

"I looked again at the face, the lips, the eyes of my dear lovely love, whom I was to meet to-morrow night when the new moon shone on that tomb in our churchyard.

" 'Did you say she was dead?' I asked, and I hardly knew my own voice.

" 'Years and years ago! Her name's on the back, and the date—'

"I took the portrait out from its case—I remember just the colour of its faded, red-velvet bed, and read on the back—'Susannah Kingsnorth, *Ob*. 1723.'

"That was in 1823." My uncle stopped short.

"What happened?" I asked breathlessly.

"I believe I had a fit," my uncle answered slowly; "at any rate, I was very ill."

"And you missed the new moon on the grave?"

"I missed the new moon on the grave."

"And you never saw her again?"

"I never saw her again—"

"But, uncle, do you really believe? Can the dead—was she—did you—"

My uncle took out his pipe and filled it.

"It's a long time ago," he said, "a many, many years. Old man's tales, my dear! Old man's tales. Don't you take any notice of them."

He lighted the pipe, and puffed silently a moment or two before he said: "But I know what youth means, and love and happiness, though I was always lame, and the girls used to laugh at me."

FITZ-JAMES O'BRIEN
What Was It?

Fitz-James O'Brien *(1826?–1862), Irish-born son of a lawyer, emigrated in 1852 to America, where he became the leading American writer of horror stories in the years immediately following the death of Edgar Allan Poe.* 'What Was It?' *(1859), a classic of supernatural fiction, undoubtedly influenced many later stories in the genre including Crawford's "The Upper Berth" and Bierce's "The Damned Thing".*

It is, I confess, with considerable diffidence that I approach the strange narrative which I am about to relate. The events which I purpose detailing are of so extraordinary a character that I am quite prepared to meet with an unusual amount of incredulity and scorn. I accept all such beforehand. I have, I trust, the literary courage to face unbelief. I have, after mature consideration, resolved to narrate, in as simple and straightforward a manner as I can compass, some facts that passed under my observation, in the month of July last, and which, in the annals of the mysteries of physical science, are wholly unparalleled.

I live at No.—Twenty-sixth Street, in New York. The house is in some respects a curious one. It has enjoyed for the last two years the reputation of being haunted. It is a large and stately residence, surrounded by what was once a garden, but which is now only a green enclosure used for bleaching clothes. The dry basin of what has been a fountain, and a few fruit-trees ragged and unpruned, indicate that this spot in past days was a pleasant, shady retreat, filled with fruits and flowers and the sweet murmur of waters.

The house is very spacious. A hall of noble size leads to a large spiral staircase winding through its centre, while the various apartments are of imposing dimensions. It was built some fifteen or twenty years since by Mr. A——, the well-known New York merchant, who five years ago threw the commercial world into convulsions by a stupendous bank fraud. Mr. A——, as every one knows, escaped to Europe, and died not long after, of a broken heart. Almost immediately after the news of his decease reached this country and was verified, the report spread in Twenty-sixth Street that No.—was haunted. Legal measures had dispossessed the widow of its former owner, and it was inhabited merely by a caretaker and his wife, placed there by the house-agent into whose hands it had passed for purposes of renting or sale. These people declared that they were troubled with unnatural noises. Doors were opened without any visible agency. The remnants of furniture scattered through the various rooms were, during the night, piled one upon the other by unknown hands. Invisible feet passed up and down the stairs in broad daylight, accompanied by the rustle of unseen silk dresses, and the gliding of viewless hands along the massive balusters. The caretaker and his wife declared they would live there no longer. The house-agent laughed, dismissed them, and put others in their place. The noises and supernatural manifestations continued. The neighborhood caught up the story, and the house remained untenanted for three years. Several persons negotiated for it; but, somehow, always before the bargain was closed they heard the unpleasant rumors and declined to treat any further.

It was in this state that my landlady, who at that time kept a boarding-house in Bleecker Street, and who wished to move further up town, conceived the bold idea of renting No.—Twenty-sixth Street. Happening to have in her house rather a plucky and philosophical set of boarders, she laid her scheme before us, stating candidly everything she had heard respecting the ghostly qualities of the establishment to which she wished to remove us. With the exception of two timid persons—a sea-captain and a returned Californian, who immediately gave notice that they would leave—all of Mrs. Moffat's guests declared that they would accompany her in her chivalric incursion into the abode of spirits.

Our removal was effected in the month of May, and we were charmed with our new residence. The portion of Twenty-sixth Street where our house is situated, between Seventh and Eighth Avenues, is one of the pleasantest localities in New York. The gardens back of the houses, running down nearly to the Hudson, form, in the summer time, a perfect avenue of verdure. The air is pure and invigorating, sweeping, as it does, straight across the river from the Weehawken heights, and even the ragged garden which surrounded the house, although displaying on washing days rather too much clothes-line, still gave us a piece of greensward to look at, and a cool retreat in the summer evenings, where we smoked our cigars in the dusk, and watched the fire-flies flashing their dark-lanterns in the long grass.

Of course we had no sooner established ourselves at No.—than we began to expect the ghosts. We absolutely awaited their advent with eagerness. Our dinner conversation was supernatural. One of the boarders, who had purchased Mrs. Crowe's "Night Side of Nature" for his own private delectation, was regarded as a public enemy by the entire household for not having bought twenty copies. The man led a life of supreme wretchedness while he was reading this volume. A system of espionage was established, of which he was the victim. If he incautiously laid the book down for an instant and left the room, it was immediately seized and read aloud in secret places to a select few. I found myself a person of immense importance, it having leaked out that I was tolerably well versed in the history of supernaturalism, and had once written a story the foundation of which was a ghost. If a table or a wainscot panel happened to warp when we were assembled in the large drawing-room, there was an instant silence, and every one was prepared for an immediate clanking of chains and a spectral form.

After a month of psychological excitement, it was with the utmost dissatisfaction that we were forced to acknowledge that nothing in the remotest degree approaching the supernatural had manifested itself. Once the black butler asseverated that his candle had been blown out by some invisible agency while he was undressing himself for the night; but as I had more than once discovered this colored gentleman in a condition when one candle must have appeared to him like two, I thought it possible that, by going a step further in his potations, he might have reversed this phenomenon, and seen no candle at all where he ought to have beheld one.

Things were in this state when an incident took place so awful and inexplicable in its character that my reason fairly reels at the bare memory of the occurrence. It was the tenth of July. After dinner was over I repaired, with my friend Dr. Hammond, to the garden to smoke my evening pipe. Independent of certain mental sympathies which existed between the Doctor and myself, we were linked together by a vice. We both smoked opium. We knew each other's secret, and respected it. We enjoyed together that wonderful expansion of thought, that marvellous intensifying of the perceptive faculties, that boundless feeling of existence when we seem to have points of contact with the whole universe—in short, that unimaginable spiritual bliss, which I would not surrender for a throne, and which I hope you, reader, will never—never taste.

Those hours of opium happiness which the Doctor and I spent together in secret were regulated with a scientific accuracy. We did not blindly smoke the drug of paradise, and leave our dreams to chance. While smoking, we carefully steered our conversation through the brightest and calmest channels of thought. We talked of the East, and endeavoured to recall the magical panorama of its glowing scenery. We criticised the most sensuous poets—those who painted life ruddy with health, brimming with passion, happy in the possession of youth and strength and beauty. If we talked of Shakespeare's "Tempest," we lingered over Ariel, and avoided Caliban. Like the Guebers, we turned our faces to the east, and saw only the sunny side of the world.

This skilful coloring of our train of thought produced in our subsequent visions a corresponding tone. The splendors of Arabian fairy-land dyed our dreams. We paced that narrow strip of grass with the tread and port of kings. The song of the *rana arborea,* while he clung to the bark of the ragged plum-tree, sounded like the strains of divine musicians. Houses, walls, and streets melted like rain-clouds, and vistas of unimaginable glory stretched away before us. It was a rapturous companionship. We enjoyed the vast delight more perfectly because, even in our most ecstatic moments, we were conscious of each other's presence. Our pleasures, while individual, were still twin, vibrating and moving in musical accord.

On the evening in question, the tenth of July, the Doctor and myself drifted into an unusually metaphysical mood. We lit our large meerschaums, filled with fine Turkish tobacco, in the core of which burned a little black nut of opium, that, like the nut in the fairy tale, held within its narrow limits wonders beyond the reach of kings; we paced to and fro, conversing. A strange perversity dominated the currents of our thought. They would *not* flow through the sun-lit channels into which we strove to divert them. For some unaccountable reason, they constantly diverged into dark and lonesome beds, where a continual gloom brooded. It was in vain that, after our old fashion, we flung ourselves on the shores of the East, and talked of its gay bazaars, of the splendors of the time of Haroun, of harems and golden palaces. Black afreets continually arose from the depths of our talk, and expanded, like the one the fisherman released from the copper vessel, until they blotted everything bright from our vision. Insensibly, we yielded to the occult force that swayed us, and indulged in gloomy speculation. We had talked some time upon the proneness of the human mind to mysticism, and the almost universal love of the terrible, when Hammond suddenly said to me, "What do you consider to be the greatest element of terror?"

The question puzzled me. That many things were terrible, I knew. Stumbling over a corpse in the dark; beholding, as I once did, a woman floating down a deep and rapid river, with wildly lifted arms, and awful, upturned face, uttering, as she drifted, shrieks that rent one's heart, while we, the spectators, stood frozen at a window which overhung the river at a height of sixty feet, unable to make the slightest effort to save her, but dumbly watching her last supreme agony and her disappearance. A shattered wreck, with no life visible, encountered floating listlessly on the ocean, is a terrible object, for it suggests a huge terror, the proportions of which are veiled. But it now struck me, for the first time, that there must be one great and ruling embodiment of fear—a King of Terrors, to which all others must succumb. What might it be? To what train of circumstances would it owe its existence?

"I confess, Hammond," I replied to my friend, "I never considered the subject before. That there must be one Something more terrible than any other thing, I feel. I cannot attempt, however, even the most vague definition."

"I am somewhat like you, Harry," he answered. "I feel my capacity to experience a terror greater than anything yet conceived by the human mind;—something combining in fearful and unnatural amalgamation hitherto supposed incompatible elements. The calling of the voices in Brockden Brown's novel of 'Wieland' is awful; so is the picture of the Dweller of the Threshold, in Bulwer's 'Zanoni'; but," he added, shaking his head gloomily, "there is something more horrible still than these."

"Look here, Hammond," I rejoined, "let us drop this kind of talk, for heaven's sake! We shall suffer for it, depend on it."

"I don't know what's the matter with me to-night," he replied, "but my brain is running upon all sorts of weird and awful thoughts. I feel as if I could write a story like Hoffman, to-night, if I were only master of a literary style."

"Well, if we are going to be Hoffmanesque in our talk, I'm off to bed. Opium and nightmares should never be brought together. How sultry it is! Good-night, Hammond."

"Good-night, Harry. Pleasant dreams to you."

"To you, gloomy wretch, afreets, ghouls, and enchanters."

We parted, and each sought his respective chamber. I undressed quickly and got into bed, taking with me, according to my usual custom, a book, over which I generally read myself to sleep. I opened the volume as soon as I had laid my head upon the pillow, and instantly flung it to the other side of the room. It was Goudon's "History of Monsters"—a curious French work, which I had lately imported from Paris, but which, in the state of mind I had then reached, was anything but an agreeable companion. I resolved to go to sleep at once; so, turning down my gas until nothing but a little blue point of light glimmered on the top of the tube, I composed myself to rest.

The room was in total darkness. The atom of gas that still remained alight did not illuminate a distance of three inches round the burner. I desperately drew my arm across my eyes, as if to shut out even the darkness, and tried to think of nothing. It was in vain. The confounded themes touched on by Hammond in the garden kept obtruding themselves on my brain. I battled against them. I erected ramparts of would-be blankness of intellect to keep them out. They still crowded upon me. While I was lying still as a corpse, hoping that by a perfect physical inaction I should hasten mental repose, an awful incident occurred. A Something dropped, as it seemed, from the ceiling, plumb upon my chest, and the next instant I felt two bony hands encircling my throat, endeavouring to choke me.

I am no coward, and am possessed of considerable physical strength. The suddenness of the attack, instead of stunning me, strung every nerve to its highest tension. My body acted from instinct, before my brain had time to realize the terrors of my position. In an instant I wound two muscular arms around the creature, and squeezed it, with all the strength of despair, against my chest. In a few seconds the bony hands that had fastened on my throat loosened their hold, and I was free to breathe once more. Then commenced a struggle of awful intensity. Immersed in the most profound darkness, totally ignorant of the nature of the Thing by which I was so suddenly attacked, finding my grasp slipping every moment, by reason, it seemed to me, of the entire nakedness of my assailant, bitten with sharp teeth in the shoulder, neck, and chest, having every moment to protect my throat against a pair of sinewy, agile hands, which my utmost efforts could not confine—these were a combination of circumstances to combat which required all the strength, skill, and courage that I possessed.

At last, after a silent, deadly, exhausting struggle, I got my assailant under by a series of incredible efforts of strength. Once pinned, with my knee on what I made out to be its chest, I knew that I was victor. I rested for a moment to breathe. I heard the creature beneath me panting in the darkness, and felt the violent throbbing of a heart. It was apparently as exhausted as I was; that was one comfort. At this moment I remembered that I usually placed under my pillow, before going to bed, a large yellow silk pocket-handkerchief. I felt for it instantly; it was there. In a few seconds more I had, after a fashion, pinioned the creature's arms.

I now felt tolerably secure. There was nothing more to be done but to turn on the gas, and having first seen what my midnight assailant was like, arouse the household. I will confess to being actuated by a certain pride in not giving the alarm before; I wished to make the capture alone and unaided.

Never losing my hold for an instant, I slipped from the bed to the floor, dragging my captive with me. I had but a few steps to make to reach the gas-burner; these I made with the greatest caution, holding the creature in a grip like a vice. At last I got within arm's-length of the tiny speck of blue light which told me where the gas-burner lay. Quick as lightning I released my grasp with one hand and let on the full flood of light. Then I turned to look at my captive.

I cannot even attempt to give any definition of my sensations the instant after I turned on the gas. I suppose I must have shrieked with terror, for in less than a minute afterward my room was crowded with the inmates of the house. I shudder now as I think of that awful moment. *I saw nothing!* Yes; I had one arm firmly clasped round a breathing, panting, corporeal shape, my other hand gripped with all its strength a throat as warm, and apparently fleshly, as my own; and yet, with this living substance in my grasp, with its body pressed against my own, and all in the bright glare of a large jet of gas, I absolutely beheld nothing! Not even an outline—a vapour!

I do not, even at this hour, realize the situation in which I found myself. I cannot recall the astounding incident thoroughly. Imagination in vain tries to compass the awful paradox.

It breathed. I felt its warm breath upon my cheek. It struggled fiercely. It had hands. They clutched me. Its skin was smooth, like my own. There it lay, pressed close up against me, solid as stone—and yet utterly invisible!

I wonder that I did not faint or go mad on the instant. Some wonderful instinct must have sustained me; for, absolutely, in place of loosening my hold on the terrible Enigma, I seemed to gain an additional strength in my moment of horror, and tightened my grasp with such wonderful force that I left the creature shivering with agony.

Just then Hammond entered my room at the head of the household. As soon as he beheld my face—which, I suppose, must have been an awful sight to look at—he hastened forward, crying, "Great heaven, Harry! what has happened?"

"Hammond! Hammond!" I cried, "come here. O, this is awful! I have been attacked in bed by something or other, which I have hold of; but I can't see it—I can't see it!"

Hammond, doubtless struck by the unfeigned horror expressed in my countenance, made one or two steps forward with an anxious yet puzzled expression. A very audible titter burst from the remainder of my visitors. This suppressed laughter made me furious. To laugh at a human being in my position! It was the worst species of cruelty. *Now*, I can understand why the appearance of a man struggling violently, as it would seem, with an airy nothing, and calling for assistance against a vision, should have appeared ludicrous. *Then*, so great was my rage against the mocking crowd that had I the power I would have stricken them dead where they stood.

"Hammond! Hammond!" I cried again, despairingly, "for God's sake come to me. I can hold the—the thing but a short while longer. It is overpowering me. Help me! Help me!"

"Harry," whispered Hammond, approaching me, "you have been smoking too much opium."

"I swear to you, Hammond, that this is no vision," I answered, in the same low tone. "Don't you see how it shakes my whole frame with its struggles? If you don't believe me, convince yourself. Feel it—touch it."

Hammond advanced and laid his hand in the spot I indicated. A wild cry of horror burst from him. He had felt it!

In a moment he had discovered somewhere in my room a long piece of cord, and was the next instant winding it and knotting it about the body of the unseen being that I clasped in my arms.

"Harry," he said, in a hoarse, agitated voice, for, though he preserved his presence of mind, he was deeply moved, "Harry, it's all safe now. You may let go, old fellow, if you're tired. The Thing can't move."

I was utterly exhausted, and I gladly loosed my hold.

Hammond stood holding the ends of the cord that bound the Invisible, twisted round his hand, while before him, self-supporting as it were, he beheld a rope laced and inter-laced, and stretching tightly around a vacant space. I never saw a man look so thoroughly stricken with awe. Nevertheless his face expressed all the courage and determination which I knew him to possess. His lips, although white, were set firmly, and one could perceive at a glance that, although stricken with fear, he was not daunted.

The confusion that ensued among the guests of the house who were witnesses of this extraordinary scene between Hammond and myself—who beheld the pantomime of binding this struggling Something—who beheld me almost sinking from physical exhaustion when my task of jailer was over—the confusion and terror that took possession of the bystanders, when they saw all this, was beyond description. The weaker ones fled from the apartment. The few who remained clustered near the door and could not be induced to approach Hammond and his Charge. Still incredulity broke out through their terror. They had not the courage to satisfy themselves, and yet they doubted. It was in vain that I begged of some of the men to come near and convince themselves by touch of the existence in that room of a living being which was invisible. They were incredulous, but did not dare to undeceive themselves. How could a solid, living, breathing body be invisible, they asked. My reply was this. I gave a sign to Hammond, and both of us—conquering our fearful repugnance to touch the invisible creature—lifted it from the ground, manacled as it was, and took it to my bed. Its weight was about that of a boy of fourteen.

"Now, my friends," I said, as Hammond and myself held the creature suspended over the bed, "I can give you self-evident proof that here is a solid, ponderable body, which, nevertheless, you cannot see. Be good enough to watch the surface of the bed attentively."

I was astonished at my own courage in treating this strange event so calmly; but I had recovered from my first terror, and felt a sort of scientific pride in the affair, which dominated every other feeling.

The eyes of the bystanders were immediately fixed on my bed. At a given signal Hammond and I let the creature fall. There was the dull sound of a heavy body alighting on a soft mass. The timbers of the bed creaked. A deep impression marked itself distinctly on the pillow, and on the bed itself. The crowd who witnessed this gave a low cry, and rushed from the room. Hammond and I were left alone with our Mystery.

We remained silent for some time, listening to the low, irregular breathing of the creature on the bed, and watching the rustle of the bed-clothes as it impotently struggled to free itself from confinement. Then Hammond spoke.

"Harry, this is awful."

"Ay, awful."

"But not unaccountable."

"Not unaccountable! What do you mean? Such a thing has never occurred since the birth of the world. I know not what to think, Hammond. God grant that I am not mad, and that this is not an insane fantasy!"

"Let us reason a little, Harry. Here is a solid body which we touch, but which we cannot see. The fact is so unusual that it strikes us with terror. Is there no parallel, though, for such a phenomenon? Take a piece of pure glass. It is tangible and transparent. A certain chemical coarseness is all that prevents its being so entirely transparent as to be totally invisible. It is not *theoretically impossible*, mind you, to make a glass which shall not reflect a single ray of light—a glass so pure and homogeneous in its atoms that the rays from the sun will pass through it as they do through the air, refracted but not reflected. We do not see the air, and yet we feel it."

"That's all very well, Hammond, but these are inanimate substances. Glass does not breathe, air does not breathe. *This* thing has a heart that palpitates—a will that moves it—lungs that play, and inspire and respire."

"You forget the phenomena of which we have so often heard of late," answered the Doctor, gravely. "At the meetings called 'spirit circles,' invisible hands have been thrust into the hands of those persons round the table—warm, fleshly hands that seemed to pulsate with mortal life."

"What? Do you think, then, that this thing is—"

"I don't know what it is," was the solemn reply; "but please the gods I will, with your assistance, thoroughly investigate it."

We watched together, smoking many pipes, all night long, by the bedside of the unearthly being that tossed and panted until it was apparently wearied out. Then we learned by the low, regular breathing that it slept.

The next morning the house was all astir. The boarders congregated on the landing outside my room, and Hammond and myself were lions. We had to answer a thousand questions as to the state of our extraordinary prisoner, for as yet not one person in the house except ourselves could be induced to set foot in the apartment.

The creature was awake. This was evidenced by the convulsive manner in which the bed-clothes were moved in its efforts to escape.

There was something truly terrible in beholding, as it were, those second-hand indications of the terrible writhings and agonized struggles for liberty which themselves were invisible.

Hammond and myself had racked our brains during the long night to discover some means by which we might realize the shape and general appearance of the Enigma. As well as we could make out by passing our hands over the creature's form, its outlines and lineaments were human. There was a mouth; a round, smooth head without hair; a nose, which, however, was little elevated above the cheeks; and its hands and feet felt like those of a boy. At first we thought of placing the being on a smooth surface and tracing its outline with chalk, as shoemakers trace the outline of the foot. This plan was given up as being of no value. Such an outline would give not the slightest idea of its conformation.

A happy thought struck me. We would take a cast of it in plaster of Paris. This would give us the solid figure, and satisfy all our wishes. But how to do it? The movements of the creature would disturb the setting of the plastic covering, and distort the mould. Another thought. Why not give it chloroform? It had respiratory organs—that was evident by its breathing. Once reduced to a state of insensibility, we could do with it what we would. Doctor X——was sent for; and after the worthy physician had recovered from the first shock of amazement, he proceeded to administer the chloroform. In three minutes afterward we were enabled to remove the fetters from the creature's body, and a modeller was busily engaged in covering the invisible form with the moist clay. In five minutes more we had a mould, and before evening a rough facsimile of the Mystery. It was shaped like a man—distorted, uncouth, and horrible, but still a man. It was small, not over four feet and some inches in height, and its limbs revealed a muscular development that was unparalleled. Its face surpassed in hideousness anything I had ever seen. Gustave Doré, or Callot, or Tony Johannot, never conceived anything so horrible. There is a face in one of the latter's illustrations to *Un Voyage où il vous plaira*, which somewhat approaches the countenance of this creature, but does not equal it. It was the physiognomy of what I should fancy a ghoul might be. It looked as if it was capable of feeding on human flesh.

Having satisfied our curiosity, and bound everyone in the house to secrecy, it became a question what was to be done with our Enigma? It was impossible that we should keep such a horror in our house; it was equally impossible that such an awful being should be let loose upon the world. I confess that I would have gladly voted for the creature's destruction. But who would shoulder the responsibility? Who would undertake the execution of this horrible semblance of a human being? Day after day this question was deliberated gravely. The boarders all left the house. Mrs. Moffat was in despair, and threatened Hammond and myself with all sorts of legal penalties if we did not remove the Horror. Our answer was, "We will go if you like, but we decline taking this creature with us. Remove it yourself if you please. It appeared in your house. On you the responsibility rests." To this there was, of course, no answer. Mrs. Moffat could not obtain for love or money a person who would even approach the Mystery.

The most singular part of the affair was that we were entirely ignorant of what the creature habitually fed on. Everything in the way of nutriment that we could think of was placed before it, but was never touched. It was awful to stand by, day after day, and see the clothes toss, and hear the hard breathing, and know that it was starving.

Ten, twelve days, a fortnight passed, and it still lived. The pulsations of the heart, however, were daily growing fainter, and had now nearly ceased. It was evident that the creature was dying for want of sustenance. While this terrible life-struggle was going on, I felt miserable. I could not sleep. Horrible as the creature was, it was pitiful to think of the pangs it was suffering.

At last it died. Hammond and I found it cold and stiff one morning in the bed. The heart had ceased to beat, the lungs to inspire. We hastened to bury it in the garden. It was a strange funeral, the dropping of that viewless corpse into the damp hole. The cast of its form I gave to Doctor X——, who keeps it in his museum in Tenth Street.

As I am on the eve of a long journey from which I may not return, I have drawn up this narrative of an event the most singular that has ever come to my knowledge.

VINCENT O'SULLIVAN
The Next Room

Vincent O'Sullivan *(1868–1940), a leading figure in* fin de siècle *society and a friend of Oscar Wilde (recorded in his book* Aspects of Wilde, *1936), is represented by no less than three stories in* The Supernatural Omnibus, *edited by Montague Summers in 1931. During the First World War, O'Sullivan returned to his birthplace, New York (where 'The Next Room' is situated), before settling in Paris. This story first appeared in the* Dublin Magazine *(October–December 1928).*

July 14. – I moved into the house this afternoon.

Now that I am settled, let me set down exactly the events which have brought me here. This diary-keeping habit of mine is an immense aid, I find, to clear thinking. And it is more necessary for me than for most men to keep my thoughts absolutely clear – to think and observe *precisely*, without any intermixture of drama or romance or sentiment.

A few days ago, then, it being Sunday, I was strolling along a street in one of the older parts of the Brooklyn district of New York. It was growing towards evening, the end of a day that had been terribly oppressive. Now and then lightning flickered over the sky. How still some of those streets in Brooklyn are! – for all the world as still and plaintive as the streets of a small New England town. Trees border the street; a footfall sounds afar off. Yet not a quarter of a mile away is a street of roaring traffic, and only a few blocks down nearer the river a noisy tenement district of Italians.

There was nobody, I think, in the street. Many of the people in this quarter are well-to-do, and close their houses in the summer. No doubt a fear of the storm had kept the usual Sunday promenaders indoors, or they were elsewhere – down at the sea-beaches or in the park. My footsteps sounded. Far off a bell for evening prayer tolled heavily.

Now as I came down the street I noticed a horse-drawn cab of the kind called a coupé standing in front of a house. Why should this have struck me as strange? Of course horse-drawn cabs are becoming rather an unusual sight in any district of New York, except for pleasure; and people do not take a closed cab on a very hot evening for pleasure. But it was not that. It was the cab taken in relation to the house.

It was a low wooden house, which had been left over from the first settlement of Brooklyn. On one side of it was a row of comparatively modern stone houses. On the other side was a vacant lot closed from the street by a high fence. The house itself looked shabby and dismal. The boards needed painting. Dingy green shutters were closed on all the windows, and tied together with pieces of rag to keep them from blowing open. It looked like a house that had been given over to negroes or other poor folk till it could be pulled down.

I stood on the opposite side of the way looking at it. The street-door was standing about a quarter open. The cab driver had got off his box and was sitting on the steps bare-headed and in his shirt-sleeves. He had a rather long beard, and otherwise did not look much like a coachman. I could not have been standing there more than half-a-minute before some words which I did not catch were spoken to the driver from within the house, and the door closed with a bang. The man got up and stationed himself at his horse's head, eyeing me with mistrust and defiance.

"Go a few blocks down," he called out offensively, "and you'll have the boats and the river to look at. What do you want here anyhow?"

There was nothing for it but to walk away. As I strolled along I turned to have another look at the house. Two of the upper floor windows looked upon the empty lot. They were shuttered like the others, but through the chinks of the shutters I could see a crimson light in the back room – not the white light of gas or electricity – a crimson light. It was now quite dusk, and the light was plain.

I came to where the street ended, and I had to turn right or left. Half-an-hour later I came back through the street. The cab was gone; the house was in darkness. There was an atmosphere about it such as we sometimes, though very exceptionally, perceive, without being able to analyse it, around certain men – I have never observed it in women – an atmosphere of isolation, of loneliness and fatality, of being under a curse. Some secret lodged inside the shell and discomposed the features, as a dread secret in the heart sometimes ravages the human face.

During the next two days I could think of little else. What was the cab doing before such a house? Cabs are expensive in New York, and the house looked as if the kind of people it might shelter in the normal course of life would not be in the habit of taking cabs. Why was the door partly open, and then shut as soon as those inside saw they were being watched? And what was the meaning of the crimson light?

On Wednesday I could not resist an impulse to see the house again. A board had been put on it saying it was to let, and the address of an agent was given. At once I was seized by a desire to live in the house. I was sure it had a mystery; perhaps I might fathom it. Besides, I have not been at all comfortable in the New York boarding-house which has been my abode since I arrived here from my engineering works in Mexico. The people were hostile and suspicious. I have never spoken at any length to any of them. I could tell by their looks and their veiled remarks that they thought I had been guilty of some atrocity. If you are different from the rest of the flock, they bite you. What a joy, I thought, to live in this little house away from faces and voices so unfriendly and exterior!

Yesterday I went to see the agent. The rent is exceptionally low. It seems they are only waiting to find a purchaser of the land before they tear down the old house. I took the house for three months, and paid in advance. I tried to find out something about the owner of the house and why he desired to let it but the agent was evasive.

"He has only just vacated the house – last Saturday in fact."

"Saturday?"

"Yes. He brought us the keys." He added: "You will find the house sufficiently furnished. I don't say it is well furnished, but all that is necessary is there."

And here I am. I have arranged with a coloured woman to come in a few times a week to set things in order. She comes early in the morning and stays about half an hour. What food I want I can prepare myself, or go to some restaurant near at hand. What a relief to be free from the chatter of the boarding-house table!

July 17. – I am very happy here. There is nothing at all strange about the house – or only one thing. The house is very poorly furnished with dilapidated furniture. The carpets are colourless and threadbare. The only sight of the former tenants is a pile of medical journals and some surgical bandages in the room at the back downstairs, and a pair of woman's stockings, left over the back of a chair in the front bedroom upstairs which I occupy. There is a telephone apparatus downstairs, but the wire has been cut. The strange thing – it *is* a little odd – is that the back room next to my bedroom is locked. There is not a key in the house which will open the door. I thought of notifying the agent; then I decided to let it be. After all, I cannot use the room.

July 26. – It has been terribly hot these last days, a thick-crushing heat under a sky tinged ruddy. Hardly any sunlight. I have been a few times in the street. Just below a dead cat lay for hours rotting under swarms of flies.

There is certainly something unusual about this house. When night falls, and I am sitting in the back room downstairs, I feel – I *know* that there is something alive in the house besides myself. Last night I placed W. J. Loudon's *Treatise on Rigid Dynamics* closed on the table, and went out of the room. When I returned the book was open and a leaf torn across. How did that happen? It may have been a lack of attention on my part. Perhaps I did it myself inadvertently? That is most likely. And yet I cannot escape the impression that it was done by somebody who is in the house and wants to attract my attention. There is no corner where anybody could possibly be concealed except the locked room. I could almost take my oath that I have heard footsteps up above and on the stairs – light footsteps and not sequential. This very night at twenty minutes past eleven a door upstairs banged. I hurried upstairs. My bedroom door stood open as usual. I tried the door of the next room. It was locked.

Several of the houses near by are empty. There are people living in the house two doors above. As I came in the other evening they were sitting on the steps taking the air. Their dog got between my legs, and by accident I trod on its paw. The dog yelped, and a woman on the steps violently accused me of kicking her dog. I noticed the singular hostility of the whole lot. As I entered my door, they were saying objectionable things about me. Is it possible that they know or suspect something against the former tenants, and identify me with them? In any case, a vague idea of calling on my neighbours with a view to finding out something about the history of the house and its owner had now been extinguished.

July 28. – I am persuaded that there must be somebody or something living in the locked room. Last night about one o'clock occurred a great thunderstorm. While it was at its height I, being in my bedroom, heard low cries on the other side of the wall. I rapped on the wall two or three times. Then the cries ceased; but it seemed to me that I could hear light footsteps in the next room.

I lay awake the best part of the night. About four o'clock I thought that I heard a cry again, and knocked on the wall; but there was no response.

This morning I made my way into the vacant lot which, as I have said, lies on the left side of the house. It is a dank, ugly place, into which cans, bottles, and other refuse have been cast. I found the shutters of the back room closed, just as they were the night I saw the crimson light behind them; but by standing in a far corner of the lot one can get a glimpse of the window-pane. I thought I saw a woman's face. It is difficult to say; perhaps my tired eyes played me a trick. Perhaps the sounds I heard last night are but imagination. Yet I was not used to be imaginative. And I can sketch the woman's face I saw. Here it is.

[*A sketch is inserted at this place*.]

But if a woman is really in the room, why does she not make some sign? She knows I am in the house: why does she not cry aloud for help? All I have heard up to this are moans so low and incoherent that I can scarcely be sure now that I did hear them. And how can she get food? If she gets any, it must be passed up to her window from the lot. But I have never heard a sound at the window. Is it possible that she is here voluntarily – that she is staying locked in a room, for some purpose of her own, or concerted with others?

July 29. – I heard the sounds again last night. There were the same low cries; and then the knocks came in reply to mine for a little, but soon ceased. This morning I asked the coloured woman, whom I have hardly set eyes on since I have been here, whether she could find a key for the locked door. But she said she knew nothing about the house: she had never been inside it till I came to live here.

I could easily break down the door with an axe, but the noise would be heard in this quiet street and draw the attention of the ill-natured neighbours, who would doubtless send the police to annoy me. Since the affair of the anarchist shells four years ago, I don't want any more of that kind of attention. Still, if the sounds continue, I must end by breaking in the door. I try the handle at least twenty times a day. It is a strong door and a strong lock.

July 30. – The terrible silence which replaces your thoughts, which is more terrible than anything *active*. The expectancy of what is going to happen. The imminent thing, unconditioned and appalling, perhaps atrocious. Whisperings.

July 31. – Last night, or rather this morning about two o'clock, I was lying awake in the darkness, with my ears strained to catch any sound in the next room. All day I had remained in my bedroom, sitting close up to the wall, or standing close to the locked door, lest I should miss the least movement. At one time I went out into the lot, and through the gap in the shutters I saw distinctly a head and shoulders. I could see no more than the back of the head, with a glimpse of the neck and shoulders, but enough to make out that it was a figure of utter desolation. It was as if she was standing with her face bent forward into her hands, in grief and hopelessness. For all the time I was there the figure never stirred, and I cannot say how this movelessness awed me.

But I heard no sound from the room all day or all night till two o'clock – 2.14 to be precise – this morning.

I had just struck a match to look at my watch, and the match was still in my hand when I heard the street door being opened and then closed. It was done without haste, but very softly. Then somebody began to creep up the stairs, slowly, with infinite precautions. I could hear each stair creak, and then a long pause before another step was taken.

During this time I thought of nothing but the plain fact. Somebody had entered the house: he was coming upstairs to enter my room or the next room. To open the door and shout would be to ask for death. In New York a man who breaks into a house by night has made up his mind to kill if necessary.

That was all I could think of at the moment. Meanwhile the steps arrived at the landing, and I heard the door of the next room being unlocked.

With the utmost care, calculating each movement, arranging beforehand where I was going to put my foot and my hand, I got out of bed and placed myself full length on the floor beside the wall. I was like a man who has just got a blow on the head. Whatever worry or torments may be harassing him, he can think of nothing else but the blow. I thought: he will certainly come in and kill me. In a little while I shall be lying here stabbed. If I open the window and cry out, he will stab me and then escape. I am in a trap. Why did I take the damned house?

It may have been only a few minutes, but it seemed to me like an hour that I lay waiting for the man to come in.

Then voices on the other side of the wall reached my ears. Perhaps they had been talking all the time, and that I had now grown calmer and recovered my powers of attention. I could not distinguish the words. The woman's voice seemed to plead. The man's was emphatic and intense. He was evidently trying to persuade her to some action. As I listened, I forgot my fears of being robbed and murdered. I took sides with the woman. At the first cry of distress I would rush to the next room and take my chance. Something bound me to her – the fact that we were living in the same house together, as likely as not, and that I had seen her weary face.

What happened to me I cannot say. The man must have been with her a considerable time, and yet it seemed not long till I heard him open the door. I heard him going downstairs. I had the impulse to open my door and look at him. But no sooner had I thought that than I decided it would be better to wait till he came again, when I should be prepared. I heard the street door closed quietly.

I might have seen him by opening the shutters and looking out, but my first thought was about the woman. Had he left her alive? I knocked hard at the wall. There was no answering knock. Then I went out on the landing and rapped on the door of the next room, and called.

Nothing.

I turned the handle, but the door was locked as usual. Dawn was just breaking in the sky.

August 1. – I stayed in the house all day yesterday. In the afternoon I went into the lot, and once more I thought I saw her near the window in the attitude of affliction I have described; but I am not sure. Last night I lay awake listening intently, but the man did not come. In the dead of night I heard her crying.

August 2. – This afternoon, about three o'clock, the door-bell rang, and I opened it to a florid, well-looking, middle-aged woman, almost fashionably dressed, who asked for Mrs. Purves. I said that Purves was the name of the owner of the house, but the house had been let to me. She seemed completely taken aback, and, as it were, stupefied at this news, and hurried away. No sooner was she in the street than she looked back with dismay at the house and began to weep.

Last night the cries came again. I hammered on the wall, and several times the wall was rapped in answer. I went to the door and called out: "Will you not speak to me? Do you want anything?

Shall I break down the door?" Distinctly I heard a low voice say, "No." So I passed the night.

August 3. – I have been to see the agent. I complained that there was a room shut off from the rest of the house.

"Oh, yes," he said. "I ought to have mentioned it before you signed the lease. The owner stipulated that one room was to be reserved. It is not an unusual clause in letting houses of any size. As you told me that you were going to live in the house by yourself, I supposed that with the rest of the house at your disposal you would have no objection."

"I should not," I said, "in an ordinary case." I hesitated, for I did not wish to tell him everything – I wished to find out how much he knew. "I don't want to use the room, but it seems to me that some very curious sounds come from there."

I could see that his face changed. He looked defiant and cunning, trying to spy out just where I was. He began to shuffle some papers on his desk, pretending he was busy.

"You look as if you need sleep. Perhaps this hot weather in the city does not agree with you. Why not pack your bag and go down to one of the near beaches for a few days? Long Beach – there's a fine sea there. Fine place to rest up."

I smiled at him compassionately. Poor fool! Did he think to deceive me with his clumsy fencing? I could see that he knew something that he did not want to tell. Go away indeed, and leave her alone for all the devilish machinations to do their worst on her!

I bought a revolver on my way back to the house, and it is by my hand as I write this.

11 *o'clock in the evening*. – I have not slept for a long time, and it is as much as I can do to keep my eyes open. But I dare not go to sleep, lest while I sleep the man should come in. I am firmly resolved, whether she wishes it or not, to face him, and if possible to get her out of his hands. She must be starving unless food is passed up to her through the window, at night or while I am out.

1 *o'clock in the morning*. – To keep myself awake, I have been writing an account of these happenings to a friend in Massachusetts. I shall have his reply in two or three days, and be guided by his opinion as to whether I should force the door or not.

I have just been to the door and called out to her: "Shall I bring you some food?" She replied with the same moaning "No" as before. "Speak to me, for God's sake!" I said. I heard her crying.

3.25 *a.m.* – Have I been asleep? I was awakened by a loud cry. *He* is with her. He is torturing her in some way.

I am writing this deliberately. It may be the last entry I shall ever make. I am calm. I have put the time in the margin. In ten minutes, if he does not come out, I will blow off the lock of the door with my revolver.

The ten minutes are up.

NOW.

[*Note by Vincent O'Sullivan*]

My poor friend, George Manders, was by profession a mining engineer. He returned about a year and a half ago from Mexico, where he had been working for some time. When he was found dead in the old wooden house he had rented in Brooklyn, I was sent for, because there was a letter on his table addressed to me.

Early in the morning of August 4, his body was discovered by the coloured woman who did the house work, lying face downward on the floor of the back room upstairs. He had shot through the lock of the door. A revolver with only one chamber emptied was found near him. He did not bear the mark of any wound.

The room looked like a commonplace bedroom without special character. I was told that the owner of the house, a Dr. Purves, desired to keep it shut because his wife had died in it only a few weeks before.

ROGER PATER
The Footstep of the Aventine

'Roger Pater' (Gilbert Roger Hudlestone, *1874–1936) was a Benedictine priest who wrote several religious volumes. His most popular book,* Mystic Voices *(1923), records a series of ghostly tales experienced by a clairaudient squire-priest Philip Rivers Pater. These "supernatural intuitions" have been favourably compared to R. H. Benson's stories in Paul the Minstrel.*

Like many another English Catholic gentleman, the squire is a conscientious reader of the *Tablet*, going through it week by week from the first page to the last, on the day that the paper arrives. One evening after dinner he was engaged in his weekly task, and Father Bertrand and myself were playing a quiet game of chess, when all at once the silence was broken by a sudden exclamation.

"Oh dear," he cried, "another old friend gone!" adding as he turned towards us, "It is Count Rudolf von Arenberg, Grand Master of the Knights of Malta; the 'Roman Letter' says he was found dead in his bed, on Monday of last week."

"Count Rudolf von Arenberg," repeated Father Bertrand thoughtfully, "I don't seem to recollect his name at all. Have you ever mentioned him to me, Philip? I thought I knew all your old friends, at any rate by name."

"Really, I can't say," replied the squire, "but it is possible I may not have done so. I knew him fairly intimately a good many years ago, and was once his guest for a considerable time, but for some time past I have heard nothing of him. Still, I remember him very well, for a curious incident occurred while I was staying with him, which made the visit stand out vividly in my memory."

"Would it be too much to ask what the incident was, sir?" I asked; for I had learned by now that such a phrase often indicated one of the old priest's experiences.

"I will tell you the story with pleasure," he replied, "but won't you finish your game first?"

"It is finished," said Father Bertrand with a smile. "My young friend is only one move off being checkmated—that's why he wants the story;" and he swept the pieces back into the box as I acknowledged my defeat. Then we moved up to the fire where the squire was sitting, and he began.

"For five or six years after my ordination I never went back to Rome, but after that I usually spent a month or two there every spring for quite a number of years. As a rule, I used to stay at the Austrian College, the Rector of which was a great friend of mine, as we had been fellow students at the *Accademia* years before. It was he who introduced me to Count Rudolf von Arenberg, who was a relation of his and had become Grand Master of the Knights of Malta several years before I first met him. You must remember their house on the Aventine, Bertrand, almost next door to your own Dominican church of Santa Sabina. It is the place where people go to see the famous view of St Peter's. You look through a little hole in the garden door, and there is the great dome right before you, framed by the two walls of clipped box trees that line the sides of the path.

"Nowadays, of course, the Knights of Malta are very few in number and almost all of them are Austrians for their only remaining houses are in Austria. The Grand Master, however, has to be in Rome for most of the year so Count Rudolf used to live up on the Aventine almost alone, and, as we soon became intimate, he begged me to make use of the large garden they have there whenever I cared to do so.

"One afternoon when I was there—I fancy it must have been the second or third year after we had first met—he asked me if I would come and stay with him on the Aventine for some weeks and act as his chaplain. It appeared that the official chaplain had been called home to Austria on business and was not likely to return for a month or more.

" 'Your only duty,' he explained, 'will be to say Mass in the chapel every day. You will have the chaplain's suite of rooms all to yourself, and as for meals, you can have them served in your own apartment or with myself, as you prefer. And I assure you,' he added, 'it will be not only a great convenience to me, but a joy as well if you can accommodate yourself to my proposal, and I am sure you will not regret your kindness in coming to my assistance.'

"That year, as it happened, I was not staying at the Austrian College, but in a hotel, which was not very pleasant; so I gladly availed myself of the offer he had made so gracefully, and next afternoon took possession of the chaplain's rooms. Count Rudolf was out when I arrived but Baldassare, the old, white-haired steward, who had been in the employ of the Knights for nearly forty years, received me with true Italian courtesy.

"The Roman house of the Knights stands on a corner of the Aventine hill, one side of which falls away abruptly towards the Tiber, the steep slope being cut back into terraces and laid out as a formal garden. Behind the house, the face of the hill turns almost at right angles with the terraced garden, and in those days the whole of the enclosure was laid out as a vineyard. This part is now the site of the huge international college of San Anselmo, which Leo XIII built a few years ago for students of the Benedictine Order, but at the time of which I am speaking it was still unbuilt on. At the far end, fully three hundred yards from the house, stands a great bastion, part of the fortification begun by Pope Paul IV but never completed, which was meant to command the Porta San Paolo, only a gunshot off.

"It was about an hour before sunset when I arrived, and after unpacking my belongings and settling into my new abode, I took my breviary and said my office in the vineyard, walking up and down the path that ran along the face of the hill and ended at the great bastion. As I finished, the sun was setting, so I turned back to the house and found my host walking on the upper terrace.

"He greeted me very kindly; we arranged about the hour for Mass and settled that I would take my meals with him and not alone, an arrangement which he said he would much prefer; then a bell rang in the little campanile and we adjourned to get ready for dinner. Not unnaturally, the conversation during the meal turned upon the history of the Knights of Malta and their establishment on the Aventine. The Grand Master was a mine of knowledge on the subject, and when the meal was over he took me upstairs to the Archivium, and showed me the splendid collection of documents relating to the history of the Order, kindly giving me permission to examine them as much as I wished during my stay on the Aventine.

"It was nearly midnight when I left my host and retired to my bedroom. Here I undressed and, after putting out the light, kneeled for a while in prayer by the open window. This window faced towards the vineyard, and as I rose from my knees I heard the sound of footsteps, pacing quietly along the path leading to the bastion. It was too dark to see anything, but I felt a momentary surprise, as the Romans always insist that the night air is unhealthy. Almost at once, however, it occurred to me that Count Rudolf was an Austrian and slightly contemptuous of Italian ideas, so I felt no doubt that it was he himself, taking a little stroll before going to bed.

"Next morning I spent three or four hours in the Archivium, and after lunch went for a long walk in the Campagna. The result was that I felt very tired after dinner, so I excused myself to the Grand Master, said my office, and was in bed about ten o'clock. That spring the weather was exceptionally warm, and though I went to sleep very quickly, I woke up after a time feeling hot and restless. I could not get to sleep again, so after a while I got out of bed and walked to the window to get some fresh air. To my surprise, I heard the same faint footfall which I had heard the night before, pacing along the path that led to the bastion. Whoever it was, he was nearing the house, for as I listened the sound grew steadily clearer and eventually the steps came right up to my window; but there was no moon and I could distinguish nothing.

" 'Evidently the Grand Master is a bad sleeper,' I said to myself; 'I must have been in bed a couple of hours at least, and here he is still walking in the vineyard.' I felt curious to know the time, but did not want him to think that I was watching, so I waited until the sound was far away again before striking a light. When I judged that he was almost at the farthest distance from the house, I lit a match and looked at my watch. It was twenty minutes to three! You can imagine my surprise; but, after all, it was no business of mine, so I got into bed again and was soon asleep.

"Next morning, when we met at breakfast, I looked curiously at Count Rudolf. He seemed perfectly fresh, and I could hardly believe he had been in bed for less than four hours. I did not like to ask him point blank why he had stayed up half the night, so I said casually:

" 'I hope you did not sit up late again last night, searching in the Archivium on my account.'

" 'Not at all,' said he, to my amazement. 'I was tired last night, though I had not your excuse, since I had not walked three leagues in the Campagna, but I went to bed soon after you did, and must have slept fully eight hours without waking.'

"It was on the tip of my tongue to tell him that I had heard someone in the vineyard on both the previous nights, but it struck me that it would be wiser to speak first to Baldassare. You have both lived in Italy, so you know the amazing way Italians have of being up at all hours of the night and sleeping during the day to make up for it. Possibly, I thought, it may have been Baldassare himself, or some watchman looking after the vineyard. Yes, I would speak to the steward before saying anything to the Grand Master.

"That morning Count Rudolf had to go into Rome on business, which left me to my own devices, and I was soon in conversation with the old steward. I told him how I had heard footsteps, but had failed to distinguish anyone in the darkness, and asked if he knew who could be patrolling the vineyard at night. The old man, listened intently to what I had to say, and waited without a word until I had finished.

" 'Don Filippo,' he said at length, 'you are a priest and you understand many things. I can tell you nothing about the footsteps except this, that when I first came here, forty years ago, the *capellano*, Don Angelo, warned me that such footsteps were often heard, and told me I need have no fear if I chanced to hear them also. I asked him what it was, but he would tell me no more; though I always think he could have told me, had he wished to.'

" 'And have you ever heard the footsteps yourself?' I asked him.

" 'I used to do so sometimes,' he answered, 'but for many years now I have slept in the little room above the porter's lodge, and the window there looks out eastward, so I have heard nothing.'

" 'And has nothing ever been seen?' I asked him.

" 'Nothing, Signor, so far as I know; but I think Don Angelo may have seen something for how else would he know who it is that walks?'

" 'Did you ever go into the vineyard at night to watch?' I asked.

" '*Madre di Dio*, I should think not,' said the old man, and he crossed himself at the suggestion. 'The Aventine has not a good reputation, Don Filippo. You know what kind of things used to take place here of old. No one wanders about the Aventine at midnight if he can help it.'

"It was clear that I should get nothing more out of Baldassare, so I thanked him and went back to my sitting-room. Here there were a number of portraits depicting past members of the Order, and I noticed for the first time that one of them bore the inscription *Don Angelo de Angelis, Capellano*, 1825–1866. I felt sure that this must be the Don Angelo of whom Baldassare had spoken, and I determined to ask Count Rudolf about him. That evening, therefore, at dinner, I contrived to turn the conversation on to the subject of the portraits in the house, and so to those in the chaplain's rooms, and the Grand Master told me about a number of them.

" 'But how stupid of me!' he broke out suddenly, 'I wonder I did not think of it sooner. Do you know that you have a compatriot among the chaplains whose pictures hang in your sitting-room?'

" 'Indeed,' I answered in surprise, 'and who is that?'

" 'To tell the truth,' he replied, 'I cannot for the life of me remember his surname, but he was Don Giovanni something. His portrait hangs next to that of old Don Angelo, who was the last chaplain here before my friend for whom you are so kindly supplying. Don Angelo was our chaplain for fully forty years, and he insisted on having his portrait hung next to that of the English chaplain, Don Giovanni. Indeed, I remember now that he had got together some materials for writing a life of him.'

" 'But how interesting!' I exclaimed. 'I suppose Don Angelo knew him personally. Was he the chaplain immediately before Don Angelo himself?'

" 'Oh dear no,' replied Count Rudolf, 'he died more than two hundred years ago, for he was chaplain in the time of Urban VIII. I really don't know why Don Angelo was so interested in him; but his collections for the biography must be in the Archivium upstairs—you shall go through them yourself, if you care to.'

"Of course I accepted the offer eagerly, and after dinner we went upstairs to find the papers. To my disappointment, the Grand Master was quite uncertain where they were kept, and in spite of a long search we failed to find them.

" 'I have seen the *dossier* myself, so it must be here,' he said, 'but it is some years ago, and I really do not remember where they are.'

"For a couple of hours we searched through cupboard after cupboard and my hopes were sinking very low, when all at once Count Rudolf gave a sharp exclamation.

" 'Why now, how foolish of me!' he exclaimed. 'I don't believe they are in this room at all. I feel almost sure that they are in your own apartment, in that little cupboard between the bookcases.'

"I did not remember any such cupboard, and said so, but the Grand Master was quite positive.

" 'Oh yes,' he said, 'there is such a cupboard, but you might easily overlook it. It is simply a narrow upright space in the angle of the wall where the two bookcases meet. The door looks like a solid pilaster, set across the angle. Let us go down and look there, at any rate.'

"To my sitting-room we went, then, and the theory proved correct. There was a tall narrow cupboard in the angle of the wall and of course I had never suspected that the carved wooden pilaster was really a door. Count Rudolf opened it with the key that fitted all the cases in the Archivium, and to my delight it contained a package of papers, endorsed *Vita di Don Giovanni Fenton, il solo capellano Inglese dei Cavalieri di San Giovanni sul' Aventino.** It was getting late now, so the Grand Master begged me to excuse him and left me, saying:

" 'Do not tire yourself by sitting up half the night reading Don Angelo's collection of notes. You can study the papers at leisure in the morning.'

"When he had gone I arranged the shade of my lamp so that the light fell on the two portraits of Don Giovanni and Don Angelo, and then seated myself before them in one of the big old-fashioned chairs. I must have stayed there, looking dreamily at the two portraits, for a considerable time when all at once an idea came into my mind. It struck me that I had never heard of Don Angelo until that morning, and that now I had learned two curious facts about him. The first one Baldassare had told me, viz., how interested he had been in the mysterious footsteps, and how apparently he, and he alone, knew who it was that walked. The second point Count Rudolf had supplied; I mean his deep and unexplained interest in the long-dead Don Giovanni, the only Englishman who had ever been chaplain at the Aventine house before myself, and how he had collected materials to write his life.

"Were these two interests connected? I asked myself; and if so, was it the Englishman, Don John Fenton, whose footstep was heard so often in the vineyard though no one had ever seen him?

"It was midnight now, and, moved by a sudden impulse, I walked through into the bedroom, opened the window wide, and listened. Sure enough, far away down the path to the bastion, I heard the faint sound of footsteps pacing slowly towards the house. I waited in silence as the sound grew closer, and finally

*Life of Don John Fenton, the only English chaplain of the Knights of St John upon the Aventine hill.

seemed to be just beneath the window. Then, silently, I leaned well out of the casement and said quietly in English:

" 'If you are Don John, the former English chaplain, tell me what it is you wish; I, too, am English and a priest.'

"The footsteps, till then quite regular, now ceased abruptly and there was perfect silence for a minute or so. Then I repeated my words and paused again for an answer. This time, from beneath the window, there came the faintest sound—I hardly know how to describe it, but it was like a stifled gasp, the kind of sound a man will sometimes make just before he dies, when he is trying to speak and cannot. After a pause I repeated what I had said a third time, very slowly and distinctly, and once more waited breathlessly for an answer.

"This time there was no doubt about the reply. Very faint it was, the merest whisper in fact, like someone speaking along the wall of a long gallery but the words were unmistakable.

" 'Burn, burn, burn,' it said; and then there was silence again.

" 'Burn what?' I asked quickly; but no answer came.

" 'What is it you wish me to burn?' I said. Still there was silence.

" 'Can you not tell me what it is I am to burn?' I asked a third time, and waited. The faintest possible murmur—like a smothered sigh—sounded for a moment only, and then absolute silence, not a footfall even. I remained at the window for quite another half-hour but heard nothing more; so, with a feeling of deep disappointment, I went to bed and eventually to sleep.

"Next morning, after breakfast, I set to work on the packet of papers which we had found the night before. I had decided that I would read straight through them first of all, and afterwards copy such as proved to be of interest. Most of the papers were written in the same hand as that on the outside of the packet, which, I had no doubt, was Don Angelo's, and they were evidently copies of documents in the archives and extracts from various sources. Besides these, however, there was a small package carefully fastened up, with a piece of paper folded round the whole and sealed in several places.

"On close examination I found that the wax looked recent and held strongly, while the paper of the wrapper was clearly ancient. I did not want to tear it, in case there might be writing on the inside, so I brought a candle to the marble-topped table by the window at which I was working, lit it, and held the blade of my knife in the flame until it was quite hot. I then passed it under the flap, cut through the seals without injuring the paper, and the wrapper was open.

"Sure enough, the inside of the sheet was written upon, the words being in Latin and written in the hand which I had decided was that of Don Angelo, though the paper of the cover was evidently far older. I cannot tell you the exact words after all these years, but the gist of them was that the writer had found the enclosed papers among some others in the archives, had removed them and sealed them up, since they appeared to be private and of a confidential nature.

"I felt some doubt whether I ought to go through the contents of the package without first asking the Grand Master's permission, but a glance at the uppermost paper dispelled my scruples, for I saw that it began, 'Jhon, my deare sonne,' and was, in fact, a letter written to the long-dead chaplain by his own mother. There were ten or a dozen such letters, all beginning the same way, and I quickly read them through, for they were quite short. I gathered that they had been written early in the seventeenth century, during the penal times, and that Don John was then in England. I guessed, too, that he was even then a priest, though there was nothing to reveal the fact except a reference to 'summe of youre custumers here,' which reminded me that I had seen a similar phrase used to describe Catholics in other documents of the persecution times, when it was important not to reveal to outsiders the religion of those referred to.

"After the letters, and apparently of about the same date, came a little notebook, formed by sewing together some half-dozen small sheets of paper. This contained, first, a list of addresses, some twenty or so in number, and I recognized several of them as the names of houses in the northern counties of England, which had belonged to well-known Catholic families, such as Gilling, Sizergh, and Hutton Hall. After most of the names were a few notes, such as a pedlar might have made; '4 yardes Bawdekinne' was one, I recollect, and another read '10 ditto for Ladye P. (blakke).' I felt pretty sure from this that Don John had carried on his ministrations in the disguise of a pedlar, and that the addresses were those of houses where he was sure of a safe refuge.

"The entries about silks and 'bawdekinne' were a difficulty, however, since some of them represented quite large amounts of material, and I could hardly suppose that the trade in stuffs was anything more than a blind. At the end of all I found a note in different ink, which suggested an explanation to me. It ran,

'Alle the sayd obligacions have nowe bene satisfyed,' from which I concluded that the entries of '10 yardes,' etc., were really notes of Masses he had undertaken; the '10 ditto for Ladye P.' being marked 'blakke' because Lady P. was dead, and the ten Masses were to be Requiems for her soul. This curious list and the letters I decided to copy, but before doing so I set to work to decipher the one paper still remaining out of the sealed packet.

"This document was in Latin, very difficult to read and full of abbreviations, the persons referred to being indicated by numbers instead of by their names. It took me well over an hour to make out the whole, but the time was well spent, for the document was evidently the most important of them all. It proved, in fact, to be nothing less than a long, written confession, made apparently by a priest, who had abjured the Catholic Faith through fear, and had accepted a benefice in the Established Church. It appeared that his anxiety for reconciliation was known, or at least suspected, by the authorities, who were watching him very closely in the hope of catching any priests with whom he might hold communication in his efforts to escape from the terrible predicament in which he found himself. The paper was not signed, and I gathered that it had been delivered to Don John by some third party, as it ended with an appeal to the reader to find some means of helping the poor wretch who had written it. I had just reached the end of this terrible narration, and was still lost in wonder and pity at the tragedy it contained, when a knock came at the door and Baldassare entered.

" 'The Grand Master sends his compliments, Signor,' he said, 'and will be grateful if you can come to him for a minute. There are some legal papers which he has to sign, and he begs you will be so kind as to witness the signature of them.'

"Of course I said I would come at once, and rising, followed the old steward out of the room. I did not expect to be away for more than a minute or two, so I left the papers and everything just as they were on the table by the window where I had been working. As it happened, I stayed with Count Rudolf quite a quarter of an hour; for, after the documents were witnessed, he asked what I had found in Don Angelo's *dossier*, and my description of the papers interested him greatly.

" 'It is really a wonderful find,' he said when I had finished, 'and I congratulate you on it most heartily. After luncheon you must show me the originals. I will not keep you now, for these papers must go off this morning, but later on I shall love to see your treasure.'

"Accordingly I left him to finish his business and went back to my own apartment. As I opened the door, I noticed a strong smell of burning paper, and a glance at the table revealed the cause. The candle I had so foolishly left alight by the window must have been softened by the heat of the sun's rays and had fallen over on to the marble-topped table, where it had set fire to the pile of papers I had left there. I ran across the room and saw with dismay that the whole collection was now no more than a heap of blackened ashes, mixed with a shapeless mass of dirty, congealed wax. My vexation was intense, the knowledge that the accident was due solely to my own carelessness did not lessen it, and on the impulse of the moment I cried out aloud.

" 'Ah! Don Giovanni, you have got your wish. The papers *are* burned, although I never meant to burn them.'

"To my amazement, from below the window there came the faintest possible whisper:

" '*Deo gratias*.'

"Instantly I thrust my head out of the casement and looked down. Of course there was no one there. That night, too, I sat up till well past midnight, listening for the sound of footsteps. But I heard nothing, nor did they ever come again through all the weeks I spent upon the Aventine.'

EDGAR ALLAN POE
William Wilson

Edgar Allan Poe *(1809–49), America's outstanding writer of horror literature, inspired and influenced countless later writers with his pathological and macabre stories and poems. The outstanding doppelgänger story, 'William Wilson' (first published in* Burton's Gentleman's Magazine, *October 1839) is semi-autobiographical, based on his own early years, including attendance at Manor House School in Stoke Newington, London.*

What say of it? what say of CONSCIENCE *grim,*
That spectre in my path?

CHAMBERLAYNE's *Pharronida.*

Let me call myself, for the present, William Wilson. The fair page now lying before me need not be sullied with my real appellation. This has been already too much an object for the scorn, for the horror, for the detestation of my race. To the uttermost regions of the globe have not the indignant winds bruited its unparalleled infamy? Oh, outcast of all outcasts most abandoned!—to the earth art thou not for ever dead? to its honours, to its flowers, to its golden aspirations?—and a cloud, dense, dismal, and limitless, does it not hang eternally between thy hopes and heaven?

I would not, if I could, here or to-day, embody a record of my later years of unspeakable misery and unpardonable crime. This epoch—these later years—took unto themselves a sudden elevation in turpitude, whose origin alone it is my present purpose to assign. Men usually grow base by degrees. From me in an instant all virtue dropped bodily as a mantle. From comparatively trivial wickedness I passed, with the stride of a giant, into more than the enormities of an Elah-Gabalus. What chance—what one event brought this evil thing to pass, bear with me while I relate. Death approaches, and the shadow which foreruns him has thrown a softening influence over my spirit. I long, in passing through the dim valley, for the sympathy, I had nearly said for the pity, of my fellow-men. I would fain have them believe that I have been in some measure the slave of circumstances beyond human control. I would wish them to seek out for me, in the details I am about to give, some little oasis of *fatality* amid a wilderness of error. I would have them allow, what they cannot refrain from allowing, that although temptation may have erewhile existed as great, man was never *thus*, at least, tempted before, certainly never *thus* fell. And is it therefore that he has never thus suffered? Have I not indeed been living in a dream? And am I not now dying a victim to the horror and the mystery of the wildest of all sublunary visions?

I am the descendant of a race whose imaginative and easily excitable temperament has at all times rendered them remarkable; and in my earliest infancy I gave evidence of having fully inherited the family character. As I advanced in years it was more strongly developed, becoming for many reasons a cause of serious disquietude to my friends, and of positive injury to myself. I grew self-willed, addicted to the wildest caprices, and a prey to the most ungovernable passions. Weak-minded, and beset with constitutional infirmities akin to my own, my parents could do but little to check the evil propensities which distinguished me. Some feeble and ill-directed efforts resulted in complete failure on their part, and of course in total triumph on mine. Thenceforward my voice was a household law, and at an age when few children have abandoned their leading-strings, I was left to the guidance of my own will, and became in all but name the master of my own actions.

My earliest recollections of a school-life are connected with a large rambling Elizabethan house, in a misty-looking village of England, where were a vast number of gigantic and gnarled trees, and where all the houses were excessively ancient. In truth, it was a dream-like and spirit-soothing place, that venerable old town. At this moment, in fancy, I feel the refreshing chilliness of its deeply-shadowed avenues, inhale the fragrance of its thousand shrubberies, and thrill anew with indefinable delight at the deep hollow note of the church-bell, breaking each hour with sullen and sudden roar upon the stillness of the dusky atmosphere in which the fretted Gothic steeple lay imbedded and asleep.

It gives me perhaps as much of pleasure as I can now in any manner experience to dwell upon minute recollections of the school and its concerns. Steeped in misery as I am—misery, alas! only too real—I shall be pardoned for seeking relief, however slight and temporary, in the weakness of a few rambling details. These, moreover, utterly trivial, and even ridiculous in themselves, assume to my fancy adventitious importance, as connected with a period and a locality when and where I recognise the first ambiguous monitions of the destiny which afterwards so fully overshadowed me. Let me then remember.

The house, I have said, was old and irregular. The grounds were extensive, and a high and solid brick wall, topped with a bed of mortar and broken glass, encompassed the whole. This prison-like rampart formed the limit of our domain: beyond it we saw but thrice a week, once every Saturday afternoon, when, attended by two ushers, we were permitted to take brief walks in a body through some of the neighbouring fields; and twice during Sunday, when we were paraded in the same formal manner to the morning and evening service in the one church of the village. Of this church the principal of our school was pastor. With how deep a spirit of wonder and perplexity was I wont to regard him from our remote pew in the gallery, as with step solemn and slow he ascended the pulpit! This reverend man, with countenance so demurely benign, with robes so glossy and so clerically flowing, with wig so minutely powdered, so rigid and so vast—could this be he who, of late, with sour visage, and in snuffy habiliments, administered, ferule in hand, the Draconian laws of the academy? O gigantic paradox, too utterly monstrous for solution!

At an angle of the ponderous wall frowned a more ponderous gate. It was riveted and studded with iron bolts, and surmounted with jagged iron spikes. What impressions of deep awe did it inspire! It was never opened save for the three periodical egressions and ingressions already mentioned; then in every creak of its mighty hinges we found a plenitude of mystery, a world of matter for solemn remark, or for more solemn meditation.

The extensive enclosure was irregular in form, having many capacious recesses. Of these, three or four of the largest constituted the play-ground. It was level, and covered with fine hard gravel. I well remember it had no trees, nor benches, nor anything similar within it. Of course it was in the rear of the house. In front lay a small parterre, planted with box and other shrubs, but through this sacred division we passed only upon rare occasions indeed, such as a first advent to school or final departure thence, or perhaps when a parent or friend having called for us, we joyfully took our way home for the Christmas or Midsummer holidays.

But the house!—how quaint an old building was this! to me how veritably a palace of enchantment! There was really no end to its windings, to its incomprehensible subdivisions. It was difficult, at any given time, to say with certainty upon which of its two stories one happened to be. From each room to every other there were sure to be found three or four steps either in ascent or descent. Then the lateral branches were innumerable, inconceivable, and so returning in upon themselves that our most exact ideas in regard to the whole mansion were not very far different from those with which we pondered upon infinity. During the five years of my residence here, I was never able to ascertain with precision in what remote locality lay the little sleeping apartment assigned to myself and some eighteen or twenty other scholars.

The school-room was the largest in the house—I could not help thinking, in the world. It was very long, narrow, and dismally low, with pointed Gothic windows and a ceiling of oak. In a remote and terror-inspiring angle was a square enclosure of eight or ten feet, comprising the *sanctum*, "during hours", of our principal, the Reverend Dr. Bransby. It was a solid structure, with massy door, sooner than open which, in the absence of the "dominie", we would all have willingly perished by the *peine forte et dure*. In other angles were two other similar boxes, far less reverenced, indeed, but still greatly matters of awe. One of these was the pulpit of the "classical" usher, one of the "English and mathematical". Interspersed about the room, crossing and recrossing in endless irregularity, were innumerable benches and desks, black, ancient, and time-worn, piled desperately with much-bethumbed books, and so beseamed with initial letters, names at full length, grotesque figures, and other multiplied efforts of the knife, as to have entirely lost what little of original form might have been their portion in days long departed. A huge bucket with water stood at one extremity of the room, and a clock of stupendous dimensions at the other.

Encompassed by the massy walls of this venerable academy, I passed, yet not in tedium or disgust, the years of the third lustrum of my life. The teeming brain of childhood requires no external world of incident to occupy or amuse it; and the apparently dismal monotony of a school was replete with more intense excitement than my riper youth has derived from luxury, or my full manhood from crime. Yet I must believe that my first mental development had in it much of the uncommon—even much of the *outré*. Upon mankind at large the events of very early existence rarely leave in mature age any definite impression. All is grey shadow— a weak and irregular remembrance—an indistinct regathering of feeble pleasures and phantasmagoric pains. With me this is not so. In childhood I must have felt with the energy of a man what I now find stamped upon memory in lines as vivid, as deep, and as durable as the *exergues* of the Carthaginian medals.

Yet in fact—in the fact of the world's view—how little was there to remember! The morning's awakening, the nightly summons to bed; the connings, the recitations; the periodical half-holidays, and perambulations; the play-ground, with its broils, its pastimes, its intrigues;—these, by a mental sorcery long forgotten, were made to involve a wilderness of sensation, a world of rich incident, and universe of varied emotion, of excitement the most passionate and spirit-stirring. *"Oh, le bon temps, que ce siècle de fer!"*

In truth, the ardour, the enthusiasm, and the imperiousness of my disposition, soon rendered me a marked character among my schoolmates, and by slow, but natural gradations, gave me an ascendancy over all not greatly older than myself—over all with a single exception. This exception was found in the person of a scholar, who, although no relation, bore the same Christian and surname as myself, a circumstance, in fact, little remarkable; for notwithstanding a noble descent, mine was one of those every-day appellations which seem, by prescriptive right, to have been, time out of mind, the common property of the mob. In this narrative I have therefore designated myself as William Wilson—a fictitious title not very dissimilar to the real. My namesake alone, of those who in school phraseology constituted "our set", presumed to compete with me in the studies of the class—in the sports and broils of the play-ground—to refuse implicit belief in my assertions, and submission to my will—indeed, to interfere with my arbitrary dictation in any respect whatsoever. If there is on earth a supreme and unqualified despotism, it is the despotism of a master-mind in boyhood over the less energetic spirits of its companions.

Wilson's rebellion was to me a source of the greatest embarrassment: the more so as, in spite of the bravado with which in public I made a point of treating him and his pretensions, I secretly felt that I feared him, and could not help thinking the equality which he maintained so easily with myself a proof of his true superiority, since not to be overcome cost me a perpetual struggle. Yet this superiority—even this equality—was in truth acknowledged by no one but myself; our associates, by some unaccountable blindness, seemed not even to suspect it. Indeed, his competition, his resistance, and especially his impertinent and dogged interference with my purposes, were not more pointed than private. He appeared to be destitute alike of the ambition which urged, and of the passionate energy of mind which enabled me to excel. In his rivalry he might have been supposed actuated solely by a whimsical desire to thwart, astonish, or mortify myself; although there were times when I could not help observing, with a feeling made up of wonder, abasement, and pique, that he mingled with his injuries, his insults, or his contradictions, a certain most inappropriate, and assuredly most unwelcome *affectionateness* of manner. I could only conceive this singular behaviour to arise from a consummate self-conceit assuming the vulgar airs of patronage and protection.

Perhaps it was this latter trait in Wilson's conduct, conjoined with our identity of name, and the mere accident of our having entered the school upon the same day, which set afloat the notion that we were brothers among the senior classes in the academy. These do not usually inquire with much strictness into the affairs of their juniors. I have before said, or should have said, that Wilson was not, in the most remote degree, connected with my family. But assuredly if we *had* been brothers we must have been twins; for, after leaving Dr. Bransby's, I casually learned that my namesake was born on the nineteenth of January 1809—and this a somewhat remarkable coincidence, for the day is precisely that of my own nativity.

It may seem strange that in spite of the continual anxiety occasioned me by the rivalry of Wilson, and his intolerable spirit of contradiction. I could not bring myself to hate him altogether. We had, to be sure, nearly every day a quarrel, in which, yielding me publicly the palm of victory, he in some manner contrived to make me feel that it was he who had deserved it, yet a sense of pride on my part and a veritable dignity on his own, kept us always upon what are called "speaking terms", while there were many points of strong congeniality in our tempers, operating to awake in me a sentiment which our position alone, perhaps, prevented from ripening into friendship. It is difficult indeed to define or even to describe my real feelings towards him. They formed a motley and heterogeneous admixture; some petulant animosity, which was not yet hatred, some esteem, more respect, much fear, with a world of uneasy curiosity. To the moralist it will be unnecessary to say in addition that Wilson and myself were the most inseparable of companions.

It was no doubt the anomalous state of affairs existing between us which turned all my attacks upon him (and they were many, either open or covert) into the channel of banter or practical joke (giving pain while assuming the aspect of mere fun), rather than into a more serious and determined hostility. But my endeavours on this head were by no means uniformly successful, even when my plans were the most wittily concocted; for my namesake had much about him, in character, of that unassuming and quiet austerity which, while enjoying the poignancy of its own jokes, has no heel of Achilles in itself, and absolutely refuses to be laughed at. I could find, indeed, but one vulnerable point, and that, lying in a personal peculiarity, arising perhaps from constitutional disease, would have been spared by any antagonist less at his wits' end than myself; my rival had a weakness in the faucial or guttural organs which precluded him from raising his voice at any time *above a very low whisper*. Of this defect I did not fail to take what poor advantage lay in my power.

Wilson's retaliations in kind were many; and there was one form of his practical wit that disturbed me beyond measure. How his sagacity first discovered at all that so petty a thing would vex me is a question I never could solve, but having discovered, he habitually practised the annoyance. I had always felt aversion to my uncourtly patronymic and its very common, if not plebeian praenomen. The words were venom in my ears; and when, upon the day of my arrival, a second William Wilson came also to the academy, I felt angry with him for bearing the name, and doubly disgusted with the name because a stranger bore it, who would be the cause of its twofold repetition, who would be constantly in my presence, and whose concerns, in the ordinary routine of the school business, must inevitably, on account of the detestable coincidence, be often confounded with my own.

The feeling of vexation thus engendered grew stronger with every circumstance tending to show resemblance, moral or physical, between my rival and myself. I had not then discovered the remarkable fact that we were of the same age; but I saw that we were of the same height, and I perceived that we were even singularly alike in general contour of person and outline of feature. I was galled, too, by the rumour touching a relationship, which had grown current in the upper forms. In a word, nothing could more seriously disturb me (although I scrupulously concealed such disturbance), than any allusion to a similarity of mind, person, or condition existing between us. But, in truth, I had no reason to believe that (with the exception of the matter of relationship, and in the case of Wilson himself) this similarity had ever been made a subject of comment, or even observed at all by our schoolfellows. That *he* observed it in all its bearings, and as fixedly as I, was apparent; but that he could discover in such circumstances so fruitful a field of annoyance can only be attributed, as I said before, to his more than ordinary penetration.

His cue, which was to perfect an imitation of myself, lay both in words and in actions, and most admirably did he play his part. My dress it was an easy matter to copy; my gait and general manner were without difficulty appropriated; in spite of his constitutional defect, even my voice did not escape him. My louder tones were of course unattempted, but then the key, it was identical; *and his singular whisper, it grew the very echo of my own.*

How greatly this most exquisite portraiture harassed me (for it could not justly be termed a caricature), I will not now venture to describe. I had but one consolation—in the fact that the imitation, apparently, was noticed by myself alone, and that I had to endure only the knowing and strangely sarcastic smiles of my namesake himself. Satisfied with having produced in my bosom the intended effect, he seemed to chuckle in secret over the sting he had inflicted, and was characteristically disregardful of the public applause which the success of his witty endeavours might have so easily elicited. That the school, indeed, did not feel his design, perceive its accomplishment, and participate in his sneer, was for many anxious months a riddle I could not resolve. Perhaps the *gradation* of his copy rendered it not so readily perceptible, or more possibly I owed my security to the masterly air of the copyist, who, disdaining the letter (which in a painting is all the obtuse can see), gave but the full spirit of his original for my individual contemplation and chagrin.

I have already more than once spoken of the disgusting air of patronage which he assumed toward me, and of his frequent officious interference with my will. This interference often took the ungracious character of advice; advice not openly given, but hinted or insinuated. I received it with a repugnance which gained strength as I grew in years. Yet, at this distant day, let me do him the simple justice to acknowledge that I can recall no occasion when the suggestions of my rival were on the side of those errors of follies so usual to his immature age and seeming inexperience; that his moral sense, at least, if not his general talents and worldly wisdom, was far keener than my own; and that I might to-day have been a better, and thus a happier man, had I less frequently rejected the counsels embodied in those meaning whispers which I then but too cordially hated and too bitterly despised.

As it was, I at length grew restive in the extreme under his distasteful supervision, and daily resented more and more openly what I considered his intolerable arrogance. I have said that, in the first years of our connection as schoolmates, my feelings in regard to him might have been easily ripened into friendship; but, in the latter months of my residence at the academy, although the intrusion of his ordinary manner had, beyond doubt, in some measure abated, my sentiments, in nearly similar proportion, partook very much of positive hatred. Upon one occasion he saw this, I think, and afterwards avoided, or made a show of avoiding me.

It was about the same period, if I remember aright, that, in an altercation of violence with him, in which he was more than usually thrown off his guard, and spoke and acted with an openness of demeanour rather foreign to his nature, I discovered, or fancied I discovered, in his accent, his air, and general appearance a something which first startled, and then deeply interested me, by bringing to mind dim visions of my earliest infancy, wild, confused, and thronging memories of a time when memory herself was yet unborn. I cannot better describe the sensation which oppressed me than by saying that I could with difficulty shake off the belief of my having been acquainted with the being who stood before me at some epoch very long ago, some point of the past even infinitely remote. The delusion, however, faded rapidly as it came, and I mention it at all but to define the day of the last conversation I there held with my singular namesake.

The huge old house, with its countless subdivisions, had several large chambers communicating with each other, where slept the greater number of the students. There were, however (as must necessarily happen in a building so awkwardly planned), many little nooks or recesses, the odds and ends of the structure, and these the economic ingenuity of Dr. Bransby had also fitted up as dormitories, although, being the merest closets, they were capable of accommodating but a single individual. One of these small apartments was occupied by Wilson.

One night, about the close of my fifth year at the school, and immediately after the altercation just mentioned, finding every one wrapped in sleep, I arose from bed, and, lamp in hand, stole through a wilderness of narrow passages from my own bedroom to that of my rival. I had long been plotting one of those ill-natured pieces of practical wit at his expense in which I had hitherto been so uniformly unsuccessful. It was my intention now to put my scheme in operation, and I resolved to make him feel the whole extent of the malice with which I was imbued. Having reached his closet I noiselessly entered, leaving the lamp, with a shade over it, on the outside. I advanced a step and listened to the sound of his tranquil breathing. Assured of his being asleep, I returned, took the light, and with it again approached the bed. Close curtains were around it, which, in the prosecution of my plan, I slowly and quietly withdrew, when the bright rays fell vividly upon the sleeper, and my eyes, at the same moment, upon his countenance. I looked, and numbness, an iciness of feeling, instantly pervaded my frame. My breast heaved, my knees tottered, my whole spirit became possessed with an objectless yet intolerable horror. Gasping for breath, I lowered the lamp in still nearer proximity to the face. Were these—*these* the lineaments of William Wilson? I saw, indeed, that they were his, but I shook as if with a fit of the ague in fancying they were not. What *was* there about them to confound me in this manner? I gazed, while my brain reeled with a multitude of incoherent thoughts. Not thus he appeared, assuredly not *thus*, in the vivacity of his waking hours. The same name, the same contour of person, the same day of arrival at the academy; and then his dogged and meaningless imitation of my gait, my voice, my habits, and my manner! Was it, in truth, within the bounds of human possibility that *what I now saw* was the result merely of the habitual practice of this sarcastic imitation? Awe-stricken, and with a creeping shudder, I extinguished the lamp, passed silently from the chamber, and left at once the halls of that old academy, never to enter them again.

After a lapse of some months, spent at home in mere idleness, I found myself a student at Eton. The brief interval had been sufficient to enfeeble my remembrance of the events at Dr. Bransby's, or at least to effect a material change in the nature of the feelings with which I remembered them. The truth, the tragedy, of the drama was no more. I could now find room to doubt the evidence of my senses, and seldom called up the subject at all but with wonder at the extent of human credulity, and a smile at the vivid force of the imagination which I hereditarily possessed. Neither was this species of scepticism likely to be diminished by the character of the life I led at Eton. The vortex of thoughtless folly into which I there so immediately and so recklessly plunged, washed away all but the froth of my past hours, engulfed at once every solid or serious impression, and left to memory only the veriest levities of a former existence.

I do not wish, however, to trace the course of my miserable profligacy here—a profligacy which set at defiance the laws, while it eluded the vigilance of the institution. Three years of folly, passed without profit, had but given me rooted habits of vice, and added, in a somewhat unusual degree, to my bodily stature, when, after a week of soulless dissipation, I invited a small party of the most dissolute students to a secret carousal in my chambers. We met at a late hour of the night, for our debaucheries were to be faithfully protracted until morning. The wind flowed freely, and there were not wanting other and perhaps more dangerous seductions, so that the grey dawn had already faintly appeared in the east, while our delirious extravagance was at its height. Madly flushed with cards and intoxication, I was in the act of insisting upon a toast of more than wonted profanity when my attention was suddenly diverted by the violent, although partial, unclosing of the door of the apartment, and by the eager voice of a servant from without. He said that some person, apparently in great haste, demanded to speak with me in the hall.

Wildly excited with wine, the unexpected interruption rather delighted than surprised me. I staggered forward at once, and a few steps brought me to the vestibule of the building. In this low and small room there hung no lamp, and now no light at all was admitted, save that of the exceedingly feeble dawn which made its way through the semi-circular window. As I put my foot over the threshold I became aware of the figure of a youth about my own height, and habited in a white kerseymere morning frock, cut in the novel fashion of the one I myself wore at the moment. This the faint light enabled me to perceive, but the features of his face I could not distinguish. Upon my entering he strode hurriedly up to me, and, seizing me by the arm with a gesture of petulant impatience, whispered the words "William Wilson!" in my ear.

I grew perfectly sober in an instant.

There was that in the manner of the stranger, and in the tremulous shake of his uplifted finger, as he held it between my eyes and the light, which filled me with unqualified amazement; but it was not this which had so violently moved me. It was the pregnancy of solemn admonition in the singular, low, hissing utterance, and, above all, it was the character, the tone, *the key*, of those few simple, and familiar, yet *whispered* syllables, which came with a thousand thronging memories of by-gone days, and struck upon my soul with the shock of a galvanic battery. Ere I could recover the use of my senses he was gone.

Although this event failed not of a vivid effect upon my disordered imagination, yet was it evanescent as vivid. For some weeks, indeed, I busied myself in earnest inquiry, or was wrapped in a cloud of morbid speculation. I did not pretend to disguise from my perception the identity of the singular individual who thus perseveringly interfered with my affairs, and harassed me with his insinuated counsel. But who and what was this Wilson?—and whence came he?—and what were his purposes? Upon neither of these points could I be satisfied—merely ascertaining, in regard to him, that a sudden accident in his family had caused his removal from Dr. Bransby's academy on the afternoon of the day in which I myself had eloped. But in a brief period I ceased to think upon the subject, my attention being all absorbed in a contemplated departure for Oxford. Thither I soon went, the uncalculating vanity of my parents furnishing me with an outfit and annual establishment, which would enable me to indulge at will in the luxury already so dear to my heart—to vie in profuseness of expenditure with the haughtiest heirs of the wealthiest earldoms in Great Britain.

Excited by such appliances to vice, my constitutional temperament broke forth with redoubled ardour, and I spurned even the common restraints of decency in the mad infatuation of my revels. But it were absurd to pause in the detail of my extravagance. Let it suffice, that among spendthrifts I out-Heroded Herod, and that, giving name to a multitude of novel follies, I added no brief appendix to the long catalogue of vices then usual in the most dissolute university of Europe.

It could hardly be credited, however, that I had, even here, so utterly fallen from the gentlemanly estate as to seek acquaintance with the vilest arts of the gambler by profession, and, having become an adept in his despicable science, to practise it habitually as a means of increasing my already enormous income at the expense of the weak-minded among my fellow-collegians. Such, nevertheless, was the fact: and the very enormity of this offence against all manly and honourable sentiment proved beyond doubt, the main, if not the sole reason of the impunity with which it was committed. Who, indeed, among my most abandoned associates would not rather have disputed the clearest evidence of his senses than have suspected of such courses the gay, the frank, the generous William Wilson—the noblest and most liberal commoner at Oxford—him whose follies (said his parasites) were but the follies of youth and unbridled fancy—whose errors but inimitable whim—whose darkest vice but a careless and dashing extravagance?

I had been now two years successfully busied in this way when there came to the university a young *parvenu* nobleman, Glendinning—rich, said report, as Herodes Atticus—his riches, too, as easily acquired. I soon found him of weak intellect and, of course, marked him as a fitting subject for my skill. I frequently engaged him in play, and contrived with the gambler's usual art to let him win considerable sums, the more effectually to entangle him in my snares. At length, my schemes being ripe, I met him (with the full intention that this meeting should be final and decisive) at the chambers of a fellow-commoner (Mr. Preston), equally intimate with both, but who, to do him justice, entertained not even a remote suspicion of my design. To give to this a better colouring, I had contrived to have assembled a party of some eight or ten, and was solicitously careful that the introduction of cards should appear accidental and originate in the proposal of my contemplated dupe himself. To be brief upon a vile topic, none of the low finesse was omitted, so customary upon similar occasions, that it is a just matter for wonder how any are still found so besotted as to fall its victim.

We had protracted our sitting far into the night, and I had at length effected the manoeuvre of getting Glendinning as my sole antagonist. The game, too, was my favourite *écarté*. The rest of the company interested in the extent of our play, had abandoned their own cards, and were standing around us as spectators. The *parvenu*, who had been induced by my artifices in the early part of the evening to drink deeply, now shuffled, dealt, or played, with a wild nervousness of manner for which his intoxication, I thought, might partially, but could not altogether account. In a very short period he had become my debtor to a large amount, when, having taken a long draught of port, he did precisely what I had been coolly anticipating—he proposed to double our already extravagant stakes. With a well-feigned show of reluctance, and not until after my repeated refusal had seduced him into some angry words which gave a colour of *pique* to my compliance, did I finally comply. The result, of course, did but prove how entirely the prey was in my toils: in less than an hour he had quadrupled his debt. For some time his countenance had been losing the florid tinge lent it by the wine, but now, to my astonishment, I perceived that it had grown to a pallor truly fearful. I say to my astonishment. Glendinning had been represented to my eager inquiries as immeasurably wealthy; and the sums which he had as yet lost, although in themselves vast, could not, I supposed, very seriously annoy, much less so violently affect him. That he was overcome by the wine just swallowed was the idea which most readily presented itself; and, rather with a view to the preservation of my own character in the eyes of my associates, than from any less interested motive, I was about to insist, peremptorily, upon a discontinuance of the play, when some expressions at my elbow from among the company, and an ejaculation evincing utter despair on the part of Glendinning, gave me to understand that I had effected his total ruin under circumstances which, rendering him an object for the pity of all, should have protected him from the ill offices even of a fiend.

What now might have been my conduct it is difficult to say. The pitiable condition of my dupe had thrown an air of embarrassed gloom over all, and for some moments a profound silence was maintained, during which I could not help feeling my cheeks tingle with the many burning glances of scorn or reproach cast upon me by the less abandoned of the party. I will even own that an intolerable weight of anxiety was for a brief instant lifted from my bosom by the sudden and extraordinary interruption which ensued. The wide heavy folding-doors of the apartment were all at once thrown open to their full extent, with a vigorous and rushing impetuosity that extinguished, as if by magic, every candle in the room. Their light, in dying, enabled us just to perceive that a stranger had entered, about my own height, and closely muffled in a cloak. The darkness, however, was now total, and we could only *feel* that he was standing in our midst. Before any one of us could recover from the extreme astonishment into which this rudeness had thrown all, we heard the voice of the intruder.

"Gentlemen," he said, in a low, distinct, and never-to-be-forgotten *whisper* which thrilled to the very marrow of my bones.

"Gentlemen, I make no apology for this behaviour, because, in thus behaving, I am but fulfilling my duty. You are, beyond doubt, uninformed of the true character of the person who has to-night won at *écarté* a large sum of money from Lord Glendinning. I will therefore put you upon an expeditious and decisive plan of obtaining this very necessary information. Please to examine at your leisure the inner linings of the cuff of his left sleeve, and the several little packages which may be found in the somewhat capacious pockets of his embroidered morning wrapper."

While he spoke, so profound was the stillness that one might have heard a pin drop upon the floor. In ceasing, he departed at once, and as abruptly as he had entered. Can I—shall I describe my sensations? Must I say that I felt all the horrors of the damned? Most assuredly I had little time for reflection. Many hands roughly seized me upon the spot, and lights were immediately re-procured. A search ensued. In the lining of my sleeve were found all the court cards essential in *écarté*, and in the pockets of my wrapper a number of packs, facsimiles of those used at our sittings, with the single exception that mine were of the species called, technically, *arrondées*; the honours being slightly convex at the ends, the lower cards slightly convex at the sides. In this disposition, the dupe who cuts, as customary, at the length of the pack, will invariably find that he cuts his antagonist an honour; while the gambler, cutting at the breadth, will, as certainly, cut nothing for his victim which may count in the records of the game.

Any burst of indignation upon this discovery would have affected me less than the silent contempt, or the sarcastic composure, with which it was received.

"Mr. Wilson," said our host, stooping to remove from beneath his feet an exceedingly luxurious cloak of rare furs, "Mr. Wilson, this is your property." (The weather was cold; and, upon quitting my own room, I had thrown a cloak over my dressing wrapper, putting it off upon reaching the scene of play.) "I presume it is supererogatory to seek here (eyeing the folds of the garment with a bitter smile) for any further evidence of your skill. Indeed, we have had enough. You will see the necessity, I hope, of quitting Oxford—at all events, of quitting instantly my chambers."

Abased, humbled to the dust as I then was, it is probable that I should have resented this galling language by immediate personal violence, had not my whole attention been at the moment arrested by a fact of the most startling character. The cloak which I had worn was of a rare description of fur; how rare, how extravagantly costly, I shall not venture to say. Its fashion, too, was of my own fantastic invention, for I was fastidious to an absurd degree of coxcombry in matters of this frivolous nature. When, therefore, Mr. Preston reached me that which he had picked up upon the floor, and near the folding doors of the apartment, it was with an astonishment nearly bordering upon terror, that I perceived my own already hanging on my arm (where I had no doubt unwittingly placed it), and that the one presented me was but its exact counterpart in every, in even the minutest possible particular. The singular being who had so disastrously exposed me had been muffled, I remembered, in a cloak, and none had been worn at all by any of the members of our party with the exception of myself. Retaining some presence of mind, I took the one offered me by Preston, placed it unnoticed over my own, left the apartment with a resolute scowl of defiance, and next morning, ere dawn of day, commenced a hurried journey from Oxford to the continent in a perfect agony of horror and of shame.

I fled in vain. My evil destiny pursued me as if in exultation, and proved indeed that the exercise of its mysterious dominion had as yet only begun. Scarcely had I set foot in Paris ere I had fresh evidence of the detestable interest taken by this Wilson in my concerns. Years flew while I experienced no relief. Villain!—at Rome, with how untimely, yet with how spectral an officiousness, stepped he in between me and my ambition! At Vienna, too—at Berlin—and at Moscow! Where, in truth, had I *not* bitter cause to curse him within my heart? From his inscrutable tyranny did I at length flee, panic-stricken, as from a pestilence; and to the very ends of the earth *I fled in vain.*

And again, and again, in secret communion with my own spirit, would I demand the questions "Who is he?—whence came he?—and what are his objects?" But no answer was there found. And then I scrutinised, with a minute scrutiny, the forms, and the methods, and the leading traits of his impertinent supervision. But even here there was very little upon which to base a conjecture. It was noticeable, indeed, that in no one of the multiplied instances in which he had of late crossed my path had he so crossed it except to frustrate those schemes, or to disturb those actions, which, if fully carried out, might have resulted in bitter mischief. Poor justification this, in truth, for an authority so imperiously assumed! Poor indemnity for natural rights of self-agency so pertinaciously, so insultingly denied!

I had also been forced to notice that my tormentor for a very long period of time (while scrupulously and with miraculous dexterity maintaining his whim of an identity of apparel with myself) had so contrived it, in the execution of his varied interference with my will, that I saw not at any moment the features of his face. Be Wilson what he might, *this*, at least was but the veriest of affectation or of folly. Could he, for an instant, have supposed that, in my admonisher at Eton—in the destroyer of my honour at Oxford—in him who thwarted my ambition at Rome, my revenge at Paris, my passionate love at Naples, or what he falsely termed my avarice in Egypt—that in this, my arch-enemy and evil genius, I could fail to recognise the William Wilson of my school-boy days—the namesake, the companion, the rival—the hated and dreaded rival at Dr. Bransby's? Impossible!— But let me hasten to the last eventful scene of the drama.

Thus far I had succumbed supinely to this imperious domination. The sentiment of deep awe with which I habitually regarded the elevated character, the majestic wisdom, the apparent omnipresence and omnipotence of Wilson, added to a feeling of even terror, with which certain other traits in his nature and assumptions inspired me, had operated hitherto to impress me with an idea of my own utter weakness and helplessness, and to suggest an implicit, although bitterly reluctant submission to his arbitrary will. But, of late days, I had given myself up entirely to wine, and its maddening influence upon my hereditary temper rendered me more and more impatient of control. I began to murmur—to hesitate—to resist. And was it only fancy which induced me to believe that, with the increase of my own firmness, that of my tormentor underwent a proportional diminution? Be this as it may, I now began to feel the inspiration of a burning hope, at length nurtured in my secret thoughts a stern and desperate resolution that I would submit no longer to be enslaved.

It was at Rome, during the Carnival of 18—, that I attended a masquerade in the palazzo of the Neapolitan Duke Di Broglio. I had indulged more freely than usual in the excesses of the wine-table, and now the suffocating atmosphere of the crowded rooms irritated me beyond endurance. The difficulty, too, of forcing my way through the mazes of the company contributed not a little to the ruffling of my temper; for I was anxiously seeking (let me not say with what unworthy motive) the young, the gay, the beautiful wife of the aged and doting Di Broglio. With a too unscrupulous confidence she had previously communicated to me the secret of the costume in which she would be habited, and now, having caught a glimpse of her person, I was hurrying to make my way into her presence. At this moment I felt a light hand placed upon my shoulder, and that ever-remembered, low, damnable *whisper* within my ear.

In an absolute frenzy of wrath, I turned at once upon him who had thus interrupted me, and seized him violently by the collar. He was attired, as I had expected, in a costume altogether similar to my own; wearing a Spanish cloak of blue velvet, be-girt about the waist with a crimson belt sustaining a rapier. A mask of black silk entirely coverd his face.

"Scoundrel!" I said, in a voice husky with rage, while every syllable I uttered seemed as new fuel to my fury; "scoundrel! impostor! accursed villain! you shall not—you *shall not* dog me unto death! Follow me, or I stab you where you stand!"—and I broke my way from the ballroom into a small ante-chamber adjoining, dragging him unresistingly with me as I went.

Upon entering, I thrust him furiously from me. He staggered against the wall, while I closed the door with an oath, and commanded him to draw. He hesitated but for an instant; then, with a slight sigh, drew in silence, and put himself upon his defence.

The contest was brief indeed. I was frantic with every species of wild excitement, and felt within my single arm the energy and power of a multitude. In a few seconds I forced him by sheer strength against the wainscoting, and thus, getting him at mercy, plunged my sword, with brute ferocity, repeatedly through and through his bosom.

At that instant some person tried the latch of the door. I hastened to prevent an intrusion, and then immediately returned to my dying antagonist. But what human language can adequately portray *that* astonishment, *that* horror which possessed me at the spectacle then presented to view? The brief moment in which I averted my eyes had been sufficient to produce apparently a material change in the arrangements at the upper or farther end of the room. A large mirror—so at first it seemed to me in my confusion—now stood where none had been perceptible before; and, as I stepped up to it in extremity of terror, mine own image, but with features all pale and dabbled in blood, advanced to meet me with a feeble and tottering gait.

Thus it appeared, I say, but was not. It was my antagonist—it was Wilson who then stood before me in the agonies of his dissolution. His mask and cloak lay where he had thrown them upon the floor. Not a thread in all his raiment—not a line in all the marked and singular lineaments of his face which was not, even in the most absolute identity, *mine own*!

It was Wilson; but he spoke no longer in a whisper, and I could have fancied that I myself was speaking while he said:

"*You have conquered and I yield. Yet, henceforward art thou also dead—dead to the World, to Heaven, and to Hope! In me didst thou exist—and, in my death, see by this image, which is thine own, how utterly thou hast murdered thyself.*"

FORREST REID
Courage

Forrest Reid *(1876–1947), the Irish author, wrote several much-admired novels (*Uncle Stephen, The Bracknels, Apostate, The Retreat*), as well as critical studies of W.B. Yeats and Walter de la Mare, and an invaluable book on the* Illustrators of the Sixties. *Several of his best tales evoked a lyrical world in which hints of the supernatural are contrasted with the realities of everyday life. A favourite theme was boyhood and the longing for an ideal dream playmate. "Courage" originally appeared in his book* A Garden by the Sea: stories and sketches *(1918).*

When the children came to stay with their grandfather, young Michael Aherne, walking with the others from the station to the rectory, noticed the high grey wall that lined one side of the long, sleepy lane, and wondered what lay beyond it. Far above his head, over the tops of the mossy stones, trees stretched green arms that beckoned to him, and threw black shadows on the white, dusty road. His four brothers and sisters, stepping demurely beside tall, rustling Aunt Caroline, left him lagging behind, and, when a white bird fluttered out for a moment into the sunlight, they did not even see it. Michael called to them, and eight eyes turned straightway to the trees, but were too late. So he trotted on and took fat, tired Barbara's place by Aunt Caroline.

"Does anybody live there?" he asked; but Aunt Caroline shook her head. The house, whose chimneys he presently caught a glimpse of through the trees, had been empty for years and years; the people to whom it belonged lived somewhere else.

Michael learned more than this from Rebecca, the cook, who told him that the house was empty because it was haunted. Long ago a lady lived there, but she had been very wicked and very unhappy, poor thing, and even now could find no rest in her grave. . . .

It was on an afternoon when he was all alone that Michael set out to explore the stream running past the foot of the rectory garden. He would follow it, he thought, wherever it led him; follow it just as his father, far away in wild places, had followed mighty rivers into the heart of the forest. The long, sweet, green grass brushed against his legs, and a white cow, with a buttercup hanging from the corner of her mouth, gazed at him in mild amazement as he flew past. He kept to the meadow side, and on the opposite bank the leaning trees made little magic caves tapestried with green. Black flies darted restlessly about, and every now and again he heard strange splashes—splashes of birds, of fish: the splash of a rat; and once the heavy, floundering splash of the cow herself, plunging into the water up to her knees. He watched her tramp through the sword-shaped leaves of a bed of irises, while the rich black mud oozed up between patches of bright green weed. A score of birds màde a quaint chorus of trills and peeps, chuckles and whistles; a wren, like a tiny winged mouse, flitted about the ivy-covered bole of a hollow elm. Then Michael came unexpectedly to the end of his journey, for an iron gate was swung here right across the stream, and on either side of it, as far as he could see, stretched a high grey wall.

He paused. The gate was padlocked, and its spiked bars were so narrow that to climb it would not be easy. Suddenly a white bird rose out of the burning green and gold of the trees, and for a moment, in the sunlight, it was the whitest thing in the world. Then it flew back again into the mysterious shadow, and Michael stood breathless.

He knew now where he was, knew that this wall must be a continuation of the wall in the lane. The stooping trees leaned down as if to catch him in their arms. He looked at the padlock on the gate and saw that it was half eaten by rust. He took off his shoes and stockings. Stringing them about his neck, he waded through the water and with a stone struck the padlock once, twice—twice only, for at the second blow the lock dropped into the stream, with a dull splash. Michael tugged at the rusty bolt, and in a moment or two the gate was open. On the other side he clambered up the bank to put on his shoes, and it was then that, as he glanced behind him, he saw the gate swing slowly back in silence.

That was all, yet it somehow startled him, and he had a fantastic impression that he had not been meant to see it. "Of course it must have moved of its own weight," he told himself, but it gave him an uneasy feeling as of some one following stealthily on his footsteps, and he remembered Rebecca's story.

Before him was a dark, moss-grown path, like the narrow aisle of a huge cathedral whose pillars were the over-arching trees. It seemed to lead on and on through an endless green stillness, and he stood dreaming on the outermost fringe, wondering, doubting, not very eager to explore further.

He walked on, and the noise of the stream died away behind him, like the last warning murmur of the friendly world outside. Suddenly, turning at an abrupt angle, he came upon the house. It lay beyond what had once been a lawn, and the grass, coarse and matted, grew right up to the doorsteps, which were green, with gaping apertures between the stones. Ugly, livid stains, lines of dark moss and lichen, crept over the red bricks; and the shutters and blinds looked as if they had been closed for ever. Then Michael's heart gave a jump, for at that moment an uneasy puff of wind stirred one of the lower shutters, which flapped back with a dismal rattle.

He stood there while he might have counted a hundred, on the verge of flight, poised between curiosity and fear. At length curiosity, the spirit of adventure, triumphed, and he advanced to a closer inspection. With his nose pressed to the pane, he gazed into a large dark room, across which lay a band of sunlight, thin as a stretched ribbon. He gave the window a tentative push, and, to his surprise, it yielded. Had there been another visitor here? he wondered. For he saw that the latch was not broken, must have been drawn back from within, or forced, very skilfully, in some way that had left no mark upon the woodwork. He made these reflections and then, screwing up his courage, stepped across the sill.

Once inside, he had a curious sense of relief. He could somehow *feel* that the house was empty, that not even the ghost of a ghost lingered there. With this certainty, everything dropped consolingly, yet half disappointingly, back into the commonplace, and he became conscious that outside it was broad daylight, and that ghost stories were nothing more than a kind of fairy tale. He opened the other shutters, letting the rich afternoon light pour in. Though the house had been empty for so long, it smelt sweet and fresh, and not a speck of dust was visible anywhere. He drew his fingers over the top of one of the little tables, but so clean was it that it might have been polished that morning. He touched the faded silks and curtains, and sniffed at faintly-smelling china jars.

Over the wide carved chimney-piece hung a picture of a lady, very young and beautiful. She was sitting in a chair, and beside her stood a tall, delicate boy of Michael's own age. One of the boy's hands rested on the lady's shoulder, and the other held a gilt-clasped book. Michael, gazing at them, easily saw that they were mother and son. The lady seemed to him infinitely lovely, and presently she made him think of his own mother, and with that he began to feel homesick, and all kinds of memories returned to him. They were dim and shadowy, and, as he stood there dreaming, it seemed to him that somehow his mother was bound up with this other lady—he could not tell how—and at last he turned away, wishing that he had not looked at the picture. He drew from his pocket the letter he had received that morning. His mother was better; she would soon be quite well again. Yesterday she had been out driving for more than an hour, she told him, and to-day she felt a little tired, which was why her letter must be rather short. . . . And he remembered, remembered through a sense of menacing trouble only half realised during those days of uneasy waiting in the silent rooms at home; only half realised even at the actual moment of good-bye—remembered that last glimpse of her face, smiling, smiling so beautifully and bravely. . . .

He went out into the hall and unbarred and flung wide the front door, before ascending to the upper storeys. He found many curious things, but, above all, in one large room, he discovered a whole store of toys—soldiers, puzzles, books, a bow and arrows, a musical box with a little silver key lying beside it. He wound it up, and a gay, sweet melody tinkled out into the silence, thin and fragile, losing itself in the empty vastness of that still house, like the flicker of a taper in a cave.

He opened a door leading into a second room, a bedroom, and, sitting down in the window-seat, began to turn the pages of an old illuminated volume he found there, full of strange pictures of saints and martyrs, all glowing in gold and bright colours, yet somehow sinister, disquieting. It was with a start that, as he looked up, he noticed how dark it had become indoors. The pattern had faded out of the chintz bed curtains, and he could no longer see clearly into the further corners of the room. It was from these corners that the darkness seemed to be stealing out, like a thin smoke, spreading slowly over everything. Then a strange fancy came to him, and it seemed to him that he had lived in this house for years and years, and that all his other life was but a dream. It was so dark now that the bed curtains were like pale shadows, and outside, over the trees, the moon was growing brighter. He must go home. . . .

He sat motionless, trying to realise what had happened, listening, listening, for it was as if the secret, hidden heart of the house had begun very faintly to beat. Faintly at first, a mere stirring of the vacant atmosphere, yet, as the minutes passed, it gathered strength, and with this consciousness of awakening life a fear came also. He listened in the darkness, and though he could hear nothing, he had a vivid sense that he was no longer alone. Whatever had dwelt here before had come back, was perhaps even now creeping up the stairs. A sickening, stupefying dread paralysed him. It had not come for him, he told himself—whatever it was. It wanted to avoid him, and perhaps he could get downstairs without meeting it. Then it flashed across his mind, radiantly, savingly, that if he had not seen it by now it was only because it *was* avoiding him. He sprang to his feet and opened the door—not the door leading to the other room, but one giving on the landing.

Outside, the great well of the staircase was like a yawning pit of blackness. His heart thumped as he stood clutching at the wall. With shut eyes, lest he should see something he had no desire to see, he took two steps forward and gripped the balusters. Then, with eyes still tightly shut, he ran quickly down—quickly, recklessly, as if fire was burning his heels.

Down in the hall, the open door showed as a dim silver-grey square, and he ran to it, but the instant he passed the threshold his panic left him. A fear remained, but it was no longer blind and brutal. It was as if a voice had spoken to him, and, as he stood there, a sense that everything swayed in a balance, that everything depended upon what he did next, swept over him. He looked up at the dark, dreadful staircase. Nothing had pursued him, and he knew now that nothing *would* pursue him. Whatever was there was not there for that purpose, and if he were to see it he must go in search of it. But if he left it? If he left it now, he knew that he should leave something else as well. In forsaking one he should forsake both; in losing one he should lose both. Another spirit at this moment was close to him, and it was the spirit of his mother, who, invisible, seemed to hold his hand and keep him there upon the step. But why—why? He could only tell that she *wanted* him to stay: but of that he was certain. If he were a coward she would know. It would be impossible to hide it from her. She might forgive him—she would forgive him—but it could never be the same again. He steadied himself against the side of the porch. The cold moonlight washed through the dim hall, and turned to a glimmering greyness the lowest flight of stairs. With sobbing breath and wide eyes he retraced his steps, but at the foot of the stairs he stopped once more. The greyness ended at the first landing; beyond that, an impenetrable blackness led to those awful upper storeys. He put his foot on the lowest stair, and slowly, step by step, he mounted, clutching the balusters. He did not pause on the landing, but walked on into the darkness, which seemed to close about his slight figure like the heavy wings of a monstrous tomb.

On the uppermost landing of all, the open doors allowed a faint light to penetrate. He entered the room of the toys and stood beside the table. The beating of the blood in his ears almost deafened him. "If only it would come now!" he prayed, for he felt that he could not tolerate the strain of waiting. But nothing came; there was neither sight nor sound. At length he made his final effort, and crossing to the door, which was now closed, turned the handle. For a moment the room seemed empty, and he was conscious of a sudden, an immense relief. Then, close by the window-seat, in the dim twilight, he perceived something. He stood still, while a deathly coldness descended upon him. At first hardly more than a shadow, a thickening of the darkness, what he gazed upon made no movement, and so long as it remained thus, with head mercifully lowered, he felt that he could bear it. But the suspense tortured him, and presently a faint moan of anguish rose from his dry lips. With that, the grey, marred face, the face he dreaded to see, was slowly lifted. He tried to close his eyes, but could not. He felt himself sinking to the ground, and clutched at the doorpost for support. Then suddenly he seemed to know that it, too, this—this thing—was afraid, and that what it feared was his fear. He saw the torment, the doubt and despair, that glowed in the smoky dimness of those hollowed, dreadful eyes. How changed was this lady from the bright, beautiful lady of the picture! He felt a pity for her, and as his compassion grew his fear diminished. He watched her move slowly towards him—nearer, nearer—only now there was something else that mingled with his dread, battling with it, overcoming it; and when at last she held out her arms to him, held them wide in a supreme, soundless appeal, he knew that it had conquered. He came forward and lifted his face to hers. At the same instant she bent down over him and seemed to draw him to her. An icy coldness, as of a dense mist, enfolded him, and he felt and saw no more. . . .

When he opened his eyes the moon was shining upon him, and he knew at once that he was alone. He knew, moreover, that he was now free to go. But the house no longer held any terror for him, and, as he scrambled to his feet, he felt a strange happiness that was very quiet, and a little like that he used to feel when, after he had gone up to bed, he lay growing sleepier and sleepier, while he listened to his mother singing. He must go home, but he would not go for a minute or two yet. He moved his hand, and it struck against a box of matches lying on a table. He had not known they were there, but now he lighted the tall candles on the chimney-piece, and as he did so he became more vividly aware of what he had felt dimly ever since he had opened his eyes. Some subtle atmospheric change had come about, though in what it consisted he could not at once tell. It was like a hush in the air, the strange hush which comes with the falling of snow. But how could there be snow in August? and, moreover, this was within the house, not outside. He lifted one of the candlesticks and saw that a delicate powder of dust had gathered upon it. He looked down at his own clothes—they, too, were covered with that same thin powder. Then he knew what was happening. The dust of years had begun to fall again; silently, slowly, like a soft and continuous caress, laying everything in the house to sleep.

Dawn was breaking when, with a candle in either hand, he descended the broad, whitening staircase. As he passed out into the garden he saw lanterns approaching, and knew they had come to look for him. They were very kind, very gentle with him, and it was not till the next day that he learned of the telegram which had come in his absence.

MRS. J.H. RIDDELL
The Last of Squire Ennismore

Mrs. J.H. Riddell *(née Charlotte Cowan, 1832–1906) was a very popular Victorian novelist who wrote some of the best ghost stories of the period. Six were collected as* Weird Stories *(1882), and several more appeared in various other collections and magazines.*

"Did I see it myself? No, sir; I did not see it; and my father before me did not see it; nor his father before him, and he was Phil Regan, just the same as myself. But it is true, for all that; just as true as that you are looking at the very place where the whole thing happened. My great-grandfather (and he did not die till he was ninety-eight) used to tell, many and many's the time, how he met the stranger, night after night, walking lonesome-like about the sands where most of the wreckage came ashore."

"And the old house, then, stood behind that belt of Scotch firs?"

"Yes; and a fine house it was, too. Hearing so much talk about it when a boy, my father said, made him often feel as if he knew every room in the building, though it had all fallen to ruin before he was born. None of the family ever lived in it after the squire went away. Nobody else could be got to stop in the place. There used to be awful noises, as if something was being pitched from the top of the great staircase down into the hall; and then there would be a sound as if a hundred people were clinking glasses and talking all together at once. And then it seemed as if barrels were rolling in the cellars; and there would be screeches, and howls, and laughing, fit to make your blood run cold. They say there is gold hid away in the cellars; but no one has ever ventured to find it. The very children won't come here to play; and when the men are ploughing the field behind, nothing will make them stay in it, once the day begins to change. When the night is coming on, and the tide creeps in on the sand, more than one thinks he has seen mighty queer things on the shore."

"But what is it really they think they see? When I asked my

landlord to tell me the story from beginning to end, he said he could not remember it; and, at any rate, the whole rigmarole was nonsense, put together to please strangers."

"And what is he but a stranger himself? And how should he know the doings of real quality like the Ennismores? For they were gentry, every one of them—good old stock; and as for wickedness, you might have searched Ireland through and not found their match. It is a sure thing, though, that if Riley can't tell you the story, I can; for, as I said, my own people were in it, of a manner of speaking. So, if your honour will rest yourself off your feet, on that bit of a bank, I'll set down my creel and give you the whole pedigree of how Squire Ennismore went away from Ardwinsagh.

"It was a lovely day, in the early part of June; and, as the Englishman cast himself on a low ridge of sand, he looked over Ardwinsagh Bay with a feeling of ineffable content. To his left lay the Purple Headland; to his right, a long range of breakers, that went straight out into the Atlantic till they were lost from sight; in front lay the Bay of Ardwinsagh, with its bluish-green water sparkling in the summer sunlight, and here and there breaking over some sunken rock, against which the waves spent themselves in foam.

"You see how the current's set, Sir? That is what makes it dangerous for them as doesn't know the coast, to bathe here at any time, or walk when the tide is flowing. Look how the sea is creeping in now, like a race-horse at the finish. It leaves that tongue of sand bars to the last, and then, before you could look round, it has you up to the middle. That is why I made bold to speak to you; for it is not alone on the account of Squire Ennismore the bay has a bad name. But it is about him and the old house you want to hear. The last mortal being that tried to live in it, my great-grandfather said, was a creature, by name Molly Leary; and she had neither kith nor kin, and begged for her bite and sup, sheltering herself at night in a turf cabin she had built at the back of a ditch. You may be sure she thought herself a made woman when the agent said, 'Yes: she might try if she could stop in the house; there was peat and bog-wood,' he told her, 'and half-a-crown a week for the winter, and a golden guinea once Easter came,' when the house was to be put in order for the family; and his wife gave Molly some warm clothes and a blanket or two; and she was well set up.

"You may be sure she didn't choose the worst room to sleep in;

and for a while all went quiet, till one night she was wakened by feeling the bedstead lifted by the four corners and shaken like a carpet. It was a heavy four-post bedstead, with a solid top: and her life seemed to go out of her with the fear. If it had been a ship in a storm off the Headland, it couldn't have pitched worse and then, all of a sudden, it was dropped with such a bang as nearly drove the heart into her mouth.

"But that, she said, was nothing to the screaming and laughing, and hustling and rushing that filled the house. If a hundred people had been running hard along the passages and tumbling downstairs, they could not have made greater noise.

"Molly never was able to tell how she got clear of the place; but a man coming late home from Ballycloyne Fair found the creature crouched under the old thorn there, with very little on her—saving your honour's presence. She had a bad fever, and talked about strange things, and never was the same woman after."

"But what was the beginning of all this? When did the house first get the name of being haunted?"

"After the old Squire went away: that was what I purposed telling you. He did not come here to live regularly till he had got well on in years. He was near seventy at the time I am talking about; but he held himself as upright as ever, and rode as hard as the youngest; and could have drunk a whole roomful under the table, and walked up to bed as unconcerned as you please at the dead of the night.

"He was a terrible man. You couldn't lay your tongue to a wickedness he had not been in the forefront of—drinking, duelling, gambling,—all manner of sins had been meat and drink to him since he was a boy almost. But at last he did something in London so bad, so beyond the beyonds, that he thought he had best come home and live among people who did not know so much about his goings on as the English. It was said that he wanted to try and stay in this world for ever; and that he had got some secret drops that kept him well and hearty. There was something wonderful queer about him, anyhow.

"He could hold foot with the youngest; and he was strong, and had a fine fresh colour in his face; and his eyes were like a hawk's; and there was not a break in his voice—and him near upon threescore and ten!

"At last and at long last it came to be the March before he was seventy—the worst March ever known in all these parts—such blowing, sleeting, snowing, had not been experienced in the memory of man; when one blusterous night some foreign vessel went to bits on the Purple Headland. They say it was an awful sound to hear the death-cry that went up high above the noise of the wind; and it was as bad a sight to see the shore there strewed with corpses of all sorts and sizes, from the little cabin-boy to the grizzled seaman.

"They never knew who they were or where they came from, but some of the men had crosses, and beads, and such like, so the priest said they belonged to him, and they were all buried deeply and decently in the chapel graveyard.

"There was not much wreckage of value drifted on shore. Most of what is lost about the Head stays there; but one thing did come into the bay—a puncheon of brandy.

"The Squire claimed it; it was his right to have all that came on his land, and he owned this sea-shore from the Head to the breakers—every foot—so, in course, he had the brandy; and there was sore illwill because he gave his men nothing, not even a glass of whiskey.

"Well, to make a long story short, that was the most wonderful liquor anybody ever tasted. The gentry came from far and near to take share, and it was cards and dice, and drinking and story-telling night after night—week in, week out. Even on Sundays, God forgive them! The officers would drive over from Ballycloyne, and sit emptying tumbler after tumbler till Monday morning came, for it made beautiful punch.

"But all at once people quit coming—a word went round that the liquor was not all it ought to be. Nobody could say what ailed it, but it got about that in some way men found it did not suit them.

"For one thing, they were losing money very fast.

"They could not make head against the Squire's luck, and a hint was dropped the puncheon ought to have been towed out to sea, and sunk in fifty fathoms of water.

"It was getting to the end of April, and fine, warm weather for the time of year, when first one and then another, and then another still, began to take notice of a stranger who walked the shore alone at night. He was a dark man, the same colour as the drowned crew lying in the chapel graveyard, and had rings in his ears, and wore a strange kind of hat, and cut wonderful antics as he walked, and had an ambling sort of gait, curious to look at. Many tried to talk to him, but he only shook his head;

so, as nobody could make out where he came from or what he wanted, they made sure he was the spirit of some poor wretch who was tossing about the Head, longing for a snug corner in holy ground.

"The priest went and tried to get some sense out of him.

" 'Is it Christian burial you're wanting?' asked his reverence; but the creature only shook his head.

" 'Is it word sent to the wives and daughters you've left orphans and widows, you'd like?' But no; it wasn't that.

" 'Is it for sin committed you're doomed to walk this way? Would masses comfort ye? There's a heathen,' said his reverence; 'Did you ever hear tell of a Christian that shook his head when masses were mentioned?'

" 'Perhaps he doesn't understand English, Father,' says one of the officers who was there; 'Try him with Latin.'

"No sooner said than done. The priest started off with such a string of aves and paters that the stranger fairly took to his heels and ran.

" 'He is an evil spirit,' explained the priest, when he stopped, tired out, 'and I have exorcised him.'

" 'But next night my gentleman was back again, as unconcerned as ever.

" 'And he'll just have to stay,' said his reverence, 'for I've got lumbago in the small of my back, and pains in all my joints—never to speak of a hoarseness with standing there shouting; and I don't believe he understood a sentence I said.'

"Well, this went on for a while, and people got that frightened of the man, or appearance of a man, they would not go near the sand; till in the end, Squire Ennismore, who had always scoffed at the talk, took it into his head he would go down one night, and see into the rights of the matter. He, maybe, was feeling lonesome, because, as I told your honour before, people had left off coming to the house, and there was nobody for him to drink with.

"Out he goes, then, bold as brass; and there were a few followed him. The man came forward at sight of the Squire and took off his hat with a foreign flourish. Not to be behind in civility, the Squire lifted his.

" 'I have come, sir,' he said, speaking very loud, to try to make him understand, 'to know if you are looking for anything, and whether I can assist you to find it.'

"The man looked at the Squire as if he had taken the greatest liking to him, and took off his hat again.

" 'Is it the vessel that was wrecked you are distressed about?'

"There came no answer, only a mournful shake of the head.

" 'Well, *I* haven't your ship, you know; it went all to bits months ago; and, as for the sailors, they are snug and sound enough in consecrated ground.'

"The man stood and looked at the Squire with a queer sort of smile on his face.

" 'What *do* you want?' asked Mr. Ennismore in a bit of a passion. 'If anything belonging to you went down with the vessel, it's about the Head you ought to be looking for it, not here—unless, indeed, its after the brandy you're fretting!'

"Now, the Squire had tried him in English and French, and was now speaking a language you'd have thought nobody could understand; but, faith, it seemed natural as kissing to the stranger.

" 'Oh! That's where you are from, is it?' said the Squire. 'Why couldn't you have told me so at once? I can't give you the brandy, because it mostly is drunk; but come along, and you shall have as stiff a glass of punch as ever crossed your lips.' And without more to-do off they went, as sociable as you please, jabbering together in some outlandish tongue that made moderate folks' jaws ache to hear it.

"That was the first night they conversed together, but it wasn't the last. The stranger must have been the height of good company, for the Squire never tired of him. Every evening, regularly, he came up to the house, always dressed the same, always smiling and polite, and then the Squire called for brandy and hot water, and they drank and played cards till cock-crow, talking and laughing into the small hours.

"This went on for weeks and weeks, nobody knowing where the man came from, or where he went; only two things the old housekeeper did know—that the puncheon was nearly empty, and that the Squire's flesh was wasting off him; and she felt so uneasy she went to the priest, but he could give her no manner of comfort.

"She got so concerned at last that she felt bound to listen at the dining-room door; but they always talked in that foreign gibberish, and whether it was blessing or cursing they were at she couldn't tell.

"Well, the upshot of it came one night in July—on the eve of the Squire's birthday—there wasn't a drop of spirit left in the puncheon—no, not as much as would drown a fly. They had drunk the whole lot clean up—and the old woman stood trembling, expecting every minute to hear the bell ring for more brandy, for where was she to get more if they wanted any?

"All at once the Squire and the stranger came out into the hall. It was a full moon, and light as day.

" 'I'll go home with you to-night by way of a change,' says the Squire.

" 'Will you so?' asked the other.

" 'That I will,' answered the Squire.

" 'It is your own choice, you know.'

" 'Yes; it is my own choice; let us go.'

"So they went. And the housekeeper ran up to the window on the great staircase and watched the way they took. Her niece lived there as housemaid, and she came and watched, too; and, after a while, the butler as well. They all turned their faces this way, and looked after their master walking beside the strange man along these very sands. Well, they saw them walk on, and on, and on, and on, till the water took them to their knees, and then to their waists, and then to their arm-pits, and then to their throats and their heads; but long before that the women and the butler were running out on the shore as fast as they could, shouting for help."

"Well?" said the Englishman.

"Living or dead, Squire Ennismore never came back again. Next morning, when the tides ebbed again, one walking over the sand saw the print of a cloven foot—that he tracked to the water's edge. Then everybody knew where the Squire had gone, and with whom."

"And no more search was made?"

"Where would have been the use searching?"

"Not much, I suppose. It's a strange story, anyhow."

"But true, your honour—every word of it."

"Oh! I have no doubt of that," was the satisfactory reply.

L.T.C.ROLT

The Garside Fell Disaster

Lionel Thomas Caswall Rolt *(1910–74) was a leading authority on engineering, railways, canals, and industrial archaeology, all subjects used to great effect in his memorable collection of ghost stories* Sleep No More *(1948).*

"Yes, I'm an old railwayman I am, and proud of it. You see, I come of a railway family, as you might say, for I reckon there've been Boothroyds on the railway—in the signal cabin or on the footplate mostly—ever since old Geordie Stevenson was about. We haven't always served the same company. There were four of us. My two elder brothers followed my father on the North-Western, but I joined the Grand Trunk, and Bert, our youngest, he went east to Grantham. He hadn't been long there before he was firing on one of Patrick Stirling's eight-foot singles, the prettiest little locos as ever was or ever will be I reckon. He finished up driver on Ivatt's "Atlantics" while Harry and Fred were working "Jumbos" and "Precursors" out of Crewe. I could have had the footplate job myself easy enough if I'd a mind; took it in with my mother's milk I did, if you follow my meaning. But (and sometimes I'm not sure as I don't regret it) I married early on, and the old woman persuaded me to go for a more settled job, so it was the signal box for me. A driver's wife's a widow most o' the week, see, unless he happens to click for a regular local turn.

"The first job I had on my own was at Garside on the Carlisle line south of Highbeck Junction, and it was here that this business as I was speaking of happened; a proper bad do it was, and the rummest thing as ever I had happen in all my time.

"Now you could travel the railways from one end to t'other, Scotland and all, but I doubt you'd find a more lonesome spot than Garside, or one so mortal cold in winter. I don't know if you've ever travelled that road, but all I know is it must have cost a mint of money. You see, the Grand Trunk wanted their own road to Scotland, but the East Coast lot had taken the easiest pick, and the North-Western had the next best run through Preston and over Shap, so there was nothing else for them but to carry their road over the mountains. It took a bit of doing, I can tell you, and I know, for when I was up there, there was plenty of folks about who remembered the railway coming. They told me what a game it was what with the snow and the wind, and the clay that was like rock in summer and a treacle pudding in winter.

"Garside Box takes its name from Garside Fell same as the tunnel. There's no station there, for there isn't a house in sight, let alone a village, and my cottage was down at Frithdale about half an hour's walk away. It was what we call a section box, just a small box, the signals, and two 'lie-by' roads, one on the up and one on the down side, where goods trains could stand to let the fast trains through if need be. Maybe you know how the block system works; how you can only admit one train on to a section at a time. Well, it would have been an eight-mile section, heavily graded at that, from Highbeck to Ennerthwaite, the next station south, and it might have taken a heavy goods anything up to half an hour to clear it. That's why they made two sections of it by building Garside box just midway between the two. It was over a thousand feet up, not far short of the summit of the line; in fact, looking south from my box I could see that summit, top of the long bank up from Ennerthwaite. Just north of the box was the mouth of the tunnel, a mile and a half of it, under Garside Fell. If ever you should come to walk over those mountains you couldn't miss the ventilation shafts of the tunnel. It looks kind of queer to see those great stone towers a-smoking and steaming away up there in the heather miles and miles from anywhere with not a soul for company and all so quiet. Not that they smoke now as much as they did, but I'll be coming to that presently.

"Well, as I've said before, you could travel the length and breadth of England before you'd find a lonelier place than Garside. Job Micklewright, who was ganger on the section, would generally give me a look up when he went by, and if I switched a goods into the 'lie-by', more often than not the fireman or the guard would pass the time of day, give me any news from down the line, and maybe make a can of tea on my stove. But otherwise I wouldn't see a soul from the time I came on till I got my relief. Of course there was the trains, but then you couldn't call them company, not properly speaking. Hundreds and hundreds of folks must have passed me by every day, and yet there I was all on my own with only a few old sheep for company, and the birds crying up on the moor. Funny that, when you come to think of it, isn't it? Mind you, I'm not saying it wasn't grand to be up there on a fine day in summer. You could keep your town life then. It made you feel as it was good to be alive what with the sun a-shining and the heather all out, grasshoppers ticking away and the air fairly humming with bees. Yes, you got to notice little things like that, and as for the smell of that moor in summer, why, I reckon I can smell it now. It was a different tale in winter though. Cold? It fair makes me shiver to think on it. I've known the wind set in the north-east for months on end, what we call a lazy wind—blows through you, see, too tired to go round. Sometimes it blew that strong it was all you could do to stand against it. More than once I had the glass of my windows blown in, and there were times when I thought the whole cabin was going what with the roaring and rattling and shaking of it. Just you imagine climbing a signal ladder to fix a lamp in that sort of weather; it wasn't easy to keep those lamps in, I can tell you. Then there was the snow; you don't know what snow is down here in the south. The company was well off for ploughs and we'd no lack of good engines even in those days, but it used to beat them. Why, I've known it snow for two days and a night, blowing half a gale all the while, and at the end of it there's been a drift of snow twenty feet deep in the cutting up by the tunnel.

"But in spite of all the wind and the snow and the rain (Lord, how it could rain!) it was the mists as I hated most. That may sound funny to you, but then no signalman can a-bear mist and fog, it kind of blinds you, and that makes you uneasy. It's for the signalman to judge whether he shall call out the fogmen, and that's a big responsibility. It may come up sudden after sundown in autumn, you calls your fogmen, and by the time they come on it's all cleared off and they want to know what the hell you're playing at. So another time you put off calling them, but it don't clear, and before you know where you are you've got trains over-running signals. We had no fogmen at Garside, there was little occasion for them, but we kept a box of detonators in the cabin. All the same, I didn't like fog no more for that. They're queer things are those mountain mists. Sometimes all day I'd see one hanging on the moor, perhaps only a hundred yards away, but never seeming to come no nearer. And then all on a sudden down it would come so thick that in a minute, no more, I couldn't see my home signals. But there was another sort of fog at Garside that I liked even less, and that was the sort that came out from the tunnel. Ah! now that strikes you as funny, doesn't it? Maybe you're thinking that with such a lonesome job I took to fancying things. Oh, I know, I know, if you're a nervy chap it's easy to see things in the mist as have no right to be there, or to hear queer noises when really it's only the wind shouting around or humming in the wires. But I wasn't that sort, and what's more I wasn't the only one who found out that there was something as wasn't quite right about Garside. No, you can take it from me that what I'm telling you is gospel, as true as I'm sitting in this bar a-talking to you.

"No doubt you've often looked at the mouth of a railway tunnel and noticed how the smoke comes a-curling out even though there may be not a sight or sound of any traffic. Well, the first thing I noticed about Garside tunnel was that, for all its ventilation shafts, it was the smokiest hole I'd ever seen. Not that this struck me as queer, at least not at first. I remember, though, soon after I came there I was walking up from Frithdale one Monday morning for the early turn and saw that number two shaft way up on the fell was smoking like a factory chimney. That did seem a bit strange, for there was precious little traffic through on a Sunday in those days; in fact, Garside box was locked out and they worked the full eight-mile section. Still, I didn't give much thought to it until one night about three weeks later. It was almost dark, but not so dark that I couldn't just see the tunnel mouth and the whitish-looking smoke sort of oozing out of it. Now, both sections were clear, mind; the last train through had been an up Class A goods and I'd had the 'out of section' from Highbeck south box a good half-hour before. But, believe it or not, that smoke grew more and more as I watched it. At first I thought it must be a trick of the wind blowing through the tunnel, though the air seemed still enough for once in a way. But it went on coming out thicker and thicker until I couldn't see the tunnel itself at all, and it came up the cutting toward my box for all the world like a wall of fog. One minute there was a clear sky overhead, the next minute—gone—and the smell of it was fit to choke you. Railway tunnels are smelly holes at the best of times, but that smell was different somehow, and worse than anything I've ever struck. It was so thick round my box that I was thinking of looking out my fog signals, when a bit of a breeze must have got up, for all on a sudden it was gone as quick as it came. The moon was up, and there was the old tunnel plain in the moonlight, just smoking away innocent like as though nothing had happened. Fair made me rub my eyes. 'Alf,'

I says to myself, 'you've been dreaming,' but all the while I knew I hadn't.

"At first I thought I'd best keep it to myself, but the same thing happened two or three times in the next month or so until one day, casual like, I mentioned it to Perce Shaw who was my relief. He'd had it happen, too, it seemed, but like me he hadn't felt like mentioning it to anyone. 'Well,' I says to him, 'it's my opinion there's something queer going on, something that's neither right nor natural. But if there's one man who should know more than what we do it's Job Micklewright. After all,' I says, 'he walks through the blinking tunnel.'

"Job didn't need much prompting to start him off. The very next morning it was, if I remember rightly. The old tunnel was smoking away as usual when out he comes. He climbs straight up into my box, blows out his light, and sits down by my stove a-warming himself, for the weather was sharp. 'Cold morning,' I says. 'Ah,' he says, rubbing his hands. 'Strikes cold, it does, after being in there.' 'Why?' I asks. 'Is it that warm inside there then, Job? It certainly looks pretty thick. Reckon you must have a job to see your way along.' Job said nothing for a while, only looked at me a bit old-fashioned, and went on rubbing his hands. Then he says, quiet like, 'I reckon you won't be seeing much more of me, Alf.' That surprised me. 'Why?' I asks. 'Because I've put in for a shift,' he says. 'I've had enough of this beat.' 'How's that, Job?' I says. 'Don't you fancy that old tunnel?' He looked up sharp at that. 'What makes you talk that road?' he asks. 'Have you noticed something, too, then?' I nodded my head, and told him what I'd seen, which was little enough really when you come to weigh it up. But Job went all serious over it. 'Alf,' he says, 'I've been a good chapel man all my life, I never touch a drop of liquor, you know that, and you know as I wouldn't tell you the word of a lie. Well, then, I'm telling you, Alf,' he says, 'as that tunnel's no fit place for a God-fearing man. What you've seen's the least of it. I know no more than you what it may be, but there's something in there that I don't want no more truck with, something I fear worse than the day of judgment. It's bad, and it's getting worse. That's why I'm going to flit. At first I noticed nothing funny except it was a bit on the smoky side and never seemed to clear proper. Then I found it got terrible stuffy and hot in there, especially between two and three shafts. Very dry it is in there, not a wet patch anywhere, and one day when I dodged into a manhole to let a train by, I found the bricks was warm. "That's a rum do," I says to myself. Since then the smoke or the fog or whatever it may be has been getting thicker, and maybe it's my fancy or maybe it's not, but it strikes me that there's queer things moving about in it, things I couldn't lay name to even if I could see them proper. And as for the heat, it's proper stifling. Why I could take you in now and you'd find as you couldn't bear your hand on the bricks round about the place I know of. This last couple or three days has been the worst of all, for I've seen lights a-moving and darting about in the smoke, mostly round about the shaft openings, only little ones mind, but kind of flickering like flames, only they don't make no sound, and the heat in there fit to smother you. I've kept it to myself till now, haven't even told the missis, for I thought if I let on, folks would think I was off my head. What it all means, Alf, only the Lord himself knows, all I know is I've had enough."

"Now I must say, in spite of what I'd seen, I took old Job's yarn with a pinch of salt myself until a couple of nights after, and then I saw something that made me feel that maybe he was right after all. It had just gone dark, and I was walking back home down to Frithdale, when, chancing to look round, I saw there was a light up on the Fell. It was just a kind of a dull glow shining on smoke, like as if the moor was afire somewhere just out of sight over the ridge. But it wasn't the time of year for heather burning—the moor was like a wet sponge—and when I looked again I saw without much doubt that it was coming from the tunnel shafts. Mind you, I wouldn't have cared to stake my oath on it at the time. It was only faint, like, but I didn't like the look of it at all.

"That was the night of February the first, 1897, I can tell you that because it was exactly a fortnight to the night of the Garside disaster, and that's a date I shall never forget as long as I live. I can remember it all as though it were yesterday. It was a terrible rough night, raining heavens hard, and the wind that strong over the moor you could hardly stand against it. I was on the early turn that week, so the missis and I had gone to bed about ten. The next thing I knew was her a-shaking and shaking at my shoulder and calling, 'Alf, Alf, wake up, there's summat up.' What with the wind roaring and rattling round, it was a job to hear yourself think. 'What's up?' I asks, fuddled like. 'Look out of the window,' she cries out, 'there's a fire up on the Fell; summat's up I tell you.' Next minute I was pulling on my clothes, for there wasn't any doubt about it this time. Out there in the dark the tunnel shafts were flaming away like ruddy beacons. Just you try to imagine a couple of those old-fashioned iron furnaces flaring out on the top of a mountain at the back of beyond, and you'll maybe understand why the sight put the fear of God into us.

"I set off up to Garside Box just as fast as I could go, and most of the menfolk out of the village after me, for many of them had been wakened by the noise of the storm, and those who hadn't soon got the word. I had a hurricane-lamp with me, but I could hardly see the box for the smoke that was blowing down the cutting from the tunnel. Inside I found Perce Shaw in a terrible taking. His hair was all singed, his face was as white as that wall, and 'My God!', or 'You can't do nothing', was all he'd say, over and over again. I got through to Ennerthwaite and Highbeck South and found that they'd already had the 'section blocked' from Perce. Then I set detonators on the down line, just in case, and went off up to the tunnel. But I couldn't do no good. What with the heat and the smoke I was suffocating before I'd got a hundred yards inside. By the time I'd got back to the box I found that Job Micklewright and some of the others had come up, and that they'd managed to quiet Perce enough to tell us what had happened.

"At half-past midnight, it seems, he took an up goods from Highbeck South Box and a few minutes later got the 'entering section'. Ten minutes after that he accepted the down night 'Mountaineer' from Ennerthwaite. (That was one of our crack trains in those days—night sleeper with mails, first stop Carlisle.) Now it's a bank of one in seventy most of the way up from Highbeck, so it might take a heavy goods quarter of an hour to clear the section, but when the fifteen minutes was up and still no sign of her, Perce began to wonder a bit—Thought she must be steaming bad. Then he caught the sound of the 'Mountaineer' beating it up the bank from Ennerthwaite well up to her time, for the wind was set that road, but he didn't see no cause then to hold her up, Highbeck having accepted her. But just as he heard her top the bank and start gathering speed, a great column of smoke came driving down the cutting and he knew that there was something wrong, for there was no question of it being anything but smoke this time. Whatever was up in the tunnel it was too late to hold up the 'Mountaineer'; he put his home 'on', but she'd already passed the distant and he doubted whether her driver saw it in the smoke. The smoke must have warned him, though, for he thought he heard him shut off and put on the vacuum just as he went into the tunnel. But he was travelling very fast, and he must have been too late. He hoped that the noise he heard, distant like, was only the wind, but running as she was she should have cleared Highbeck South Box in under four minutes, so when the time went by and no 'out of section' came through (what he must of felt waiting there for that little bell to ring twice and once!) he sent out the 'section blocked', both roads, and went up off the line to see what he could do.

"What exactly happened in that tunnel we never shall know. We couldn't get in for twenty-four hours on account of the heat, and then we found both trains burnt out, and not a mortal soul alive. At the inquiry they reckoned a spark from the goods loco must have set her train afire while she was pulling up the bank through the tunnel. The engine of the 'Mountaineer' was derailed. They thought her driver, seeing he couldn't pull up his train in time, had taken the only chance and put on speed hoping to get his train by, but that burning wreckage had fouled his road. Perce got no blame, but then we only told them what we *knew* and not what we *thought*. Perce and I and especially Job Micklewright might have said a lot more than we did, but it wouldn't have done no good, and it might have done us a lot of harm. The three of us got moved from Garside after that—mighty glad we were to go, too—and I've never heard anything queer about the place since.

"Mind you, we talked about it a lot between ourselves. Perce and I reckoned the whole thing was a sort of warning of what was going to happen. But Job, who was a local chap born and bred, he thought different. He said that way back in the old days they had another name for Garside Fell. Holy Mountain they called it, though to my way of thinking 'unholy' would have been nearer the mark. When he was a little 'un, it seems the old folks down in Frithdale and round about used to tell queer tales about it. Anyway, Job had some funny idea in his head that there was something in that old mountain that should never have been disturbed, and he reckoned the fire kind of put things right again. Sort of a sacrifice, if you follow my meaning. I can't say I hold with such notions myself, but that's my tale of what the papers called the Garside Fell Disaster, and you can make of it what you like."

DAVID G. ROWLANDS
The Tears of Saint Agathé

David G. Rowlands *(b. 1941), a biochemist by profession, has had many excellent and original ghost stories published in anthologies and magazines over the past twenty years, and has been a regular contributor to* Ghosts & Scholars *(annually since 1979) and the* Holly Bough, *a Christmas magazine published by the* Cork Examiner. *Father O'Connor, a Catholic priest with a keen interest in the supernatural, is featured in many of his best ghost stories including the one reprinted here, from* Saints and Relics *(Haunted Library, 1983).*

Dedicated to the late Dennis Allenden who loved the French minor railways and the Vivarais in particular.

As a dilatory student of cinematic art I had made a note to watch the much-vaunted Truffaut film *Anne & Muriel* if it were shown on TV. I had stuck it out for half-an-hour and was about to give up in despair, when Fr O'Connor looked in. To my surprise he pointed at the screen. The scene showed a steam engine pulling a load of timber past a train stopped at a station.

"Reseau du Vivarais!" he exclaimed.

The scene changed, and mindful of my visitor's prejudices, I switched off the rest of the film.

"What on earth are you interested in French railways for?" I asked.

He chuckled. "It's a long story. I'll tell you some other time", and we fell to discussing other matters.

In the event, it was many months before either of us remembered the untold story . . . but I give it now, in the good Father's own words.

I had met Fr Petitpierre in Rome when we were both acting as amanuenses to our respective Diocesans at a Bishop's junketing, and from him I had heard all about his home – a grey, flower-bedecked town in the Eastern Massif Centrale, among the hills of Ardeche and Haut Loire. We had got on well together, my Irish brogue confusing his recognition of my "English" just as my ear found difficulty with his Auvergnat French. We exchanged invitations to visit one another and, as events fell out, it was my turn to comply first.

I reached the Velay Plateau by the SNCF's branchline from that Industrial Gomorrah, St Etienne, and was decanted alone on to the station at Dunieres. There I had to change to the narrow-gauge, the Chemins de Fer Departementaux Reseau du Vivarais to give it full titular honours. Adjoining the platform (which was hardly one brick high) were some spindly narrow tracks; rusty and half buried in grass. There was a wooden hut, which I took to be the station building, and nothing to be seen but a steam locomotive oozing thick brown smoke and shunting some wagons. Our SNCF train had been five minutes late by my pocket *Horaires*; could I have missed the connection?

This was aggressively confirmed by the Chef du Gare of the narrow-gauge. "The Vivarais waits not on the SNCF," he pronounced. "The Autorail has left this five minutes."

Here was a fine situation! I was about to try and explain my predicament in execrable French when a phone jangled inside the hut. The Chef sped away and could be heard in voluble discourse. He returned full of desolation. That had been my friend Monsieur le Curé from St Agathé, to check that I was on the Autorail. Seized with an idea the Chef rushed back to the phone and I heard him shouting into the instrument. Clearly it was not good to offend M. le Curé!

He returned importantly. "They will hold the Autorail at Tence," he said, and was off across the tracks, shouting to the driver of the shunting engine. After much gesticulation, pointing at me and down the line, the situation became *mouvementé*. A coach of faded green paint, lettered grandly "CFD" in large yellow letters, was found and a string of empty timber bolsters hastily attached. More verbal fireworks over the phone (there were no signals it seemed!) and I was escorted over the lines and ushered into the coach by *Le Conducteur,* who was brushing the crumbs of his *repas* from waistcoat and moustache. With a roar from the whistle we were shooed away from the station by the Chef, and I settled back as we plunged into a tunnel.

We emerged to light and the full heat of the Auvergnat sun, as we climbed upward to the river's source, passing through halts marked only by white dusty road crossings and through more important stations with square brick buildings washed in pastel shades typical of French minor railways.

As we drew into Tence, little men appeared gesticulating enthusiastically as our Mallet locomotive subsided steamily alongside a bright and aggressive red and cream railcar which was throbbing and popping to itself in Gallic tones. With much ceremony I was ushered aboard the Autorail, but not before I had blessed the train crew at their request.

Suddenly – and I mean suddenly! – we were off. We growled and puttered ever upwards, through wooded slopes with the river deeper and deeper below, round sharp curves and across elegant bridges to St Chambon. Then we were over the watershed and passing snow fences, for we were three thousand feet up at summit of the Velay hills.

And so into Ardeche. A short, rushing descent which left my stomach about a mile back up the line, brought us – *allegro* with klaxons – into the little station of St Agathé.

The air was fresh and thin, exhilarating when out of the sun, and full of the tang of woodsmoke. Fr Pierre was on the platform to meet me. We embraced, and I was treated to some ceremony over greeting the Chef du Gare and his staff . . . one of whom presented me with a posy of mountain flowers. It was but a short step into the station *buvette.* Here my request for a glass of water caused some consternation, but once I had satisfied my parched mouth, I was able to reassure them by giving full attention to the *vin rosé* which accompanied our *petit dejeuner.* Once served, we had the place to ourselves and I was struck by the deference accorded to my companion.

I commented on this and he smiled.

"Ah, well, you see I am *Le Chaperon* of St Agathé."

"What on earth does that mean?" I asked. "I had meant to ask you about St Agathé and her origins. I don't recall her."

"You surprise me," he replied drily. "Do you not read your copy of *The Word*? There was an article on us, three issues ago."

I laughed and confessed, "I am a little behind with my reading."

"Well, there it was. I opposed the publicity, but 'They' decided the story of our *petit* Agathé was a good topic for the 'comic' which – as you know – goes out not only to our clergy, but to all sorts and conditions: layfolk, newspapers . . . Well, I expect trouble here . . . we shall have to guard the shrine."

"But no-one steals relics these days," I expostulated. "I almost wish they would, it might indicate a return to some piety. There are no marauding monks to fear in the Ardeche."

"Pah!" he snapped his fingers. "It isn't the relics they want, *enfant,* but the settings. Nowadays these hills are full of tourists."

"There wasn't a soul on the train," I protested, looking uphill from our café to the sleeping town, baking in the afternoon sun.

"They come by coach, *imbecile*, and they take anything that is not nailed down . . . and a lot that is," he finished wryly.

I had to bite my lip and stifle a smile, for Fr Petitpierre's words evoked a vision of the little town stripped bare of everything – like the raid of Abu Hassan (Bluto) and his thieves in the Popeye cartoon of *Ali Baba*. (Galloping through the town, they even took the gateman's false teeth.) But my companion was rising from the table.

"Come, I will show you the shrine and on the way I will tell you the story of St Agathé. But first, we have a bicycle for you."

We left the *buvette* and crossed the rails to the workshops. "A bicycle?" I said. "With all these hills?"

"You may walk beside it," he said patiently, "But a bicycle is a mark of your status here. My people will expect you to have a bicycle."

"I'd prefer a donkey," I said ungraciously . . . but we were by then the object of much deference from the workshop staff, who had produced the machine.

Hitching up my cassock, I mounted reluctantly, conscious of a respectful silence, and pedalled an impressive course around the obstacles in the yard . . . only to deposit myself in a heap in the hot dust, sending the ubiquitous chickens scuttling and clucking in fright. The infernal machine had that most diabolical of European devices: a back-pedal brake!

As we plodded uphill with the bicycles, I learned the history of St Agathé. She was a twelve-year-old Gallic-Roman Christian martyred for her persistent piety and miracles during the persecutions by the Emperor Maximilian in the third century. She was desired by the Devil, and on steadfastly refusing his wiles, he touched her on the cheek, leaving a mole-like mark which spread. (Probably a rodent ulcer, I thought sceptically.) The local people loved the little girl, and after her cruel death kept her bones and other humble relics at a shrine within their village at Gaen. There she remained for many, many years, her shrine visited by the pious seeking blessing and young mothers bringing their children that their lives might be influenced by the child saint.

So things remained until the early ninth century and the time of Charlemagne. His son, Louis the Pious, gave funds for establishing a monastry nearby, but it did not prosper because of the lack of saintly relics. A brother was sent to serve at the shrine of *petit* Agathé, gained local confidence and was made guardian of the relics. Then one night he fled with the bones and a miraculous cloth. This cloth was a ragged piece of material – allegedly rent from her shift – which periodically, and mysteriously, became wet as if with her tears. The villagers' entreaties for the return of their treasures were ignored by the hard-hearted Prior of the Monastery, which was thereafter known as St Agathé's, and the relics were hidden in a place known only to the senior brothers, but probably beneath the altar of their chapel. They were not to benefit from their theft however, for a dire sickness broke out among the brethren – an affliction of the lungs – and all perished, their faces turning black. The brief span of Louis' piety was over; he lost interest in the monastery and the brethren were not replaced. The monastic buildings were put to secular use, so avoided the Suppressions, and grew into the town of St Agathé, the chapel becoming the church of the saint. Her bones were never found, though the village priest of Gaen spent many years searching the precinct, and it was assumed that they were safely buried under the altar. The miraculous cloth was recovered however: the monks had made a box for it, which was kept on a dais in their refectory. Probably they had touched the box and muttered a quick prayer for blessing daily, as they filed in and out at meal-times. The box was reinstated at the shrine by the village priest and there it remained. Over the years the gifts of faithful pilgrims, coming to seek the little saint's blessing, paid for the ornamentation and enrichment of the box . . . and it became encrusted with jewels and gold work, though quite hidden beneath a pile of monstrances, crucifixes and other gifts – the tawdriness of which fortunately concealed the treasures below.

We made a detour across the hillside to visit the shrine and to pray. It was a roughly-hewn tunnel, unadorned by any masonry, which opened into an inner chamber. A single oil-lamp burning fitfully before a *prie-Dieu* threw a flickering light on to the vast heap of trinkets at the rear. The miraculous cloth (said Fr Pierre) was still at the bottom of the heap.

"Does it still perform its wonder of becoming wet with the girl's tears?" I asked.

"We do not know for sure," he admitted, tapping his nose. "As *Le Chaperon* I avow belief in the phenomenon, and as long as it satisfies my people, I am content. I have no wish to investigate . . . my devotion is to protect the relic, not to examine it and probe its mysteries."

"Hmm," I said sceptically. "It all smacks of superstition to me, and I don't know what your Bishop would say."

"Peace, *gringalet,* he is content. My people are superstitious and I have no wish to upset their allegiance to St Agathé; you must be content with that."

We reached the old town some time later, and I took a draught from the spring that emerged from beneath the old monastic church. There was a bronze cup affixed beside a pipe-spout, and an early inscription had recently been re-cut in the nearby stonework to the effect that this water was the gift of St Agathé to pilgrims. I thanked her, and we entered the cool interior of the church.

It was a fascinating place. Most of the window lights were of rather milky plain glass which gave a strange light as if the opacity of ages was filtering out components of the spectrum, but there was one small window of beautiful 12th century stained glass, which I was delighted to see had been glazed over with modern glass to protect it. I commended my companion's interest. There were few traces of the original 9th century foundation, but the 12th and 13th century stonework was everywhere, and richly carved too – the local stone being soft to the chisel.

Fr Pierre showed me a remarkable panel beneath the altar cloth, a stone relief depicting the wicked vigour of the Prince of Terrors and his gibbering miscegenetic cohorts. His skeletal limbs protruded from a monkish habit, and a grinning skull lurked within the cowl, no whit abashed by the tiny figure in a ragged shift confronting the salacious revels. It was a marvellous piece of workmanship, wonderfully preserved, though I was staggered that the authorities had let it remain. I will not particularise further on what aspect of his satanic majesty most shocked me, but if you have seen the hill carving at Cerne Abbas you will know what I mean. I judged it 13th century at the very latest, but Fr Pierre was emphatic in placing it much earlier. I promised myself a return to the church on the morrow when I could spend many hours exploring its structural treasures.

The priest's house was also part of the old foundation, but completely rebuilt in the 19th century due to a fire. I was made comfortable in an upper room with scrubbed floorboards, over which a few woollen mats had been scattered, and a bed of simple linen on a fragrant mattress filled with lavender straws. We had a meal of bread and cheese and the local *Rosé*, and were early to bed, with the prospect of an early call to Prime celebration in the church.

It was only just light when Fr Pierre awoke me to wash quickly in the bowl he placed beside the bed. He led the way into the church via an enclosed passageway, and I served his Mass.

We were breakfasting on figs and what is nowadays unpalatably called muesli, when he was summoned by an anxious and breathless youngster. I caught the words *grandmere* and *se mourier*. As he hunted swiftly for his bag with communion vessels, he said to me:

"Could you possibly cycle down to the shrine and refill the oil lamp for me? It is one of my charges to ensure that it burns always."

The prospect of an early-morning ride across the hills was appealing so I readily agreed. He indicated a tin amphora of colza oil and departed to his duty.

The sun was rising to dispel a patchy mist that hung over the hillside as I set out. It was very cold, and I shuddered to think what an Auvergnat winter might be like. After a few minutes of pedalling along the chalky pathways, however, I was warmer. It was not so easy to proceed on the stone chips as I had envisaged, and I was glad to see the opening of the cave come into sight. As I rounded a hillock and began the steep descent to the cave, I could have sworn I saw the figure of a child run inside the entrance, but decided it must have been the denuded bush on the scree that waved in a breeze now whipping round the hillside. While thinking on this, I became aware that my bicycle was gathering speed rapidly and reached to apply the non-existent hand-brake. I also back-pedalled automatically, and instantly the bike was out from under me, skidding away on the loose stone chips – that infernal back-pedal brake! My head struck a rocky outcrop with a jar that seemed to tingle all down my spine . . .

Strangely I was quite conscious and as I shook my head to clear my whirling senses, I was aware that a child was kneeling beside me, dressed in rough, home-spun garb. She was as brown as a nut – so brown as to be almost 'coloured' – and her cheek nearest me was disfigured with a long, suppurating sore. Without a word, she scrambled to her feet and pulled me upright. Clearly she wanted me to go into the cave.

The hole seemed much larger than I remembered and very dark – like the interior of the 'flea pit' picture palace that was a rare treat of my youth. My small guide was scarcely in the mould of usherettes though. The cinema illusion was heightened by a tableau which I perceived ahead of us . . . I say 'us', but my companion had gone to take her place in the tableau, which was no longer static. She was facing me, a small, proud figure shaking her head defiantly at the monk who had his back to me, and loomed over her. I heard no words, but judging from the spreading gestures of his sleeves he was appealing for, or offering, something. I moved round the cave to see what he was at, and I'm sorry to this day that I did so, for I would never have conceived that a skull could leer so, or that a form so revoltingly bony could be so uncompromisingly – well – masculine. The only effect on the lassie, however, was to make her laugh: inspiration indeed for ridicule annihilates obscenity. The fiend snarled in rage and extended a sinewy limb to touch her on the cheek, whereupon her laughter vanished and she clutched her face in anguish. Just as I braced myself to intervene, the scene froze – like a sudden still frame in a motion picture – and resolved into the carved altar panel of the church on the hill whither I had clearly been translated.

Little Agathé – for I could not doubt who she was – ran back and pulled me up to the panel. She put a small, brown, splay-toed foot against the Devil and all his works, and pushed. The stone panel pivoted centrally and to my astonishment, my young friend slipped into the orifice and vanished, just as the stone swung back into place again.

As I stood there gawping, I became aware of a company of monks filling the chancel and of their sacristan presenting a new reliquary to the altar. He led the way out and I followed on the heels of the brethren, round a cloistered walk to the refectory, where they each kissed the open reliquary as they filed in past the sacristan. Bringing up the rear, I looked into the box and saw some dried scraps of what might be twisted wax and a drab piece of crumpled brown cloth or parchment. Could this indeed be the miraculous fabric? Familiar as I was with relicta, I bent to make a closer inspection and, as I did so, fell forward – through the box and the ghostly sacristan's arm – while a nauseous smell of death and decay engulfed me . . . to become the fragrant scent of lavender.

I found myself in bed at the priest's house, head bandaged with cold cloths and my temples throbbing madly. His anxious face was looking down at me. After that I remember nothing until, it transpired, a day later when I awoke again, with a bad headache and stiff limbs. The village woman at the bedside called Fr Petitpierre who rose from a chair.

"My dear Dermot," he said stretching, and seizing my hand which was painfully skinned. "You have given us a bad fright. You have been unconscious for two days past."

You may imagine I had plenty of food for thought. The doctor who had been summoned from Tence kept me in bed for several days more. I had been discovered – or at least my bicycle and spilled colza oil had – by a shepherd, Grosjean. After falling I had obviously dragged myself into the cave and collapsed across the pile of holy trinkets in the corner.

When a telegram about my mishap had been despatched to my Bishop in England, I waited the chance to talk to Fr Pierre. I chose breakfast time as the most prosaic, and recounted my 'vision' – for want of a better word. He was not as incredulous as I had feared . . . in fact we went into the church then and there, and stood looking at the altar panel. It was no less disquieting than before, and I shuddered slightly as my companion put a sandalled foot against his rampant majesty, and pushed. There was a scraping and grinding of stone upon stone and the panel pivoted on some hidden counterpoise. He crossed himself in amazement, "Holy Mother!", and groped inside, his face looking grotesquely up at me alongside the altar wall; a study in surprise and trepidation.

"There's something there," he puffed.

With true restraint he withdrew his arm and went to fetch a lamp and a winding sheet. It was just as well, for as he manipulated the object – a wormy wooden box – on to the sheet and carefully withdrew it, the casket crumbled in a heap of dusty debris and brown powder. It was indeed a moment of wonder! Little Agathé's remains had been found after more than a thousand years.

We secured the precious dust in a glass bottle and debated what had best be done. Our decision involved poor Fr Pierre in a long train journey to Tournon, for an interview with the Cardinal-Bishop's secretary, and then with His Eminence in person. It was well that I had grown up with Irish peasantry and the concept of *festina lente*, for it took a long time for His Eminence to make the necessary journey out to St Agathé – much delay and hullabaloo (Talk about the Mills of God!) – but it gave me time to write a full account to my own master, who replied – resignedly – that I was a comfort to those in trouble . . . and that if they weren't in trouble when I arrived, then they would be soon after.

The little town and its dignitaries reeled under the arrival of this Prince of the Church, but after a long session – a *very* long session because of the communication problem – at which I told my story and suffered the rigorous cross-questioning of both himself and his secretary, His Eminence decided that the remains we had discovered could be pronounced genuine, subject to dating by the Papal Laboratories. The day of the discovery was thereafter pronounced a Festival. He was adamant, however, that there was no case for investigating the jewelled box at the shrine itself, so I reserved my qualms on that score until my return to England.

Back at my duties in the Midlands, I talked long and to good effect with my Diocesan. How far up the hierarchy – or Paparchy – he had to go I have no idea, but it certainly took a very long time: about two years to be precise. At my suggestion, the Papal Commission which investigated the Gaen shrine included that talented anthropologist Sister Monica Verona among its complement. (She who had scandalised her Mother Superior by wanting to read *Nature* instead of her devotional book.) She undertook the opening of the reliquary in a 'glove box' and with all due precaution. After prolonged and clinical examination of the detrited contents, she pronounced them "incredibly old and possibly former human viscera".

Father O'Connor paused at my excited gestures.

"Father," I cried, "are you telling me that jewelled box at Gaen contained Little Agathé's innards, preserved for over fifteen hundred years? That takes some believing! Come now, it couldn't be true, surely?"

"You must believe what you wish," he replied quietly. "We have no proof one way or the other."

"But Father," I went on, "you've forgotten the cloth and the 'tears' of Agathé! What of them?"

He shook his head. "There are two theories, in fact. One – accepted by Fr Petitpierre and his superiors – that this miraculous relic has still to be found. It is a theory that suits everyone except Sister Monica and myself. The second is Sister Monica's. Namely that the alleged cloth was, in fact, pancreatic tissue infected with a microfloral pathogen of the *Aspergillus* type. Sporulation would account for the occasional wetting of the 'cloth' as the spores liquified. But what makes it highly probable from my viewpoint is that such spores are today known to cause a virulent lethal infection of the lungs called Aspergillosis."

"Well?" I asked. "How does that validate the theory?"

He smiled. "You have forgotten the unscrupulous monks of Louis' monastery. They kissed the open box daily, remember? And they all perished of a lung sickness."

"But why just those monks?" I asked. "Why not – for example – the priest who rediscovered the box? You can't tell me he didn't look inside!"

"A difficulty I grant you, and I am aware of the tenuous nature of this explanation, but I understand that it could simply be a matter of timing: it is only the *inhaled* spores at a *certain stage* of their development that are lethal, and one could bath in the liquid without harm."

We brooded in silence awhile, before he added, "There was one question I didn't feel equal to broaching with Sister Monica – that sore on the poor child's face. I'd still like to think it was a rodent skin ulcer, but after my venereal vision – as my Bishop was wont to call it – I can't be sure. All I do know is that the thought of that child's courage and piety have lightened the hearts of the faithful for centuries, and I have a particular devotion to her. Fr Petitpierre allocated me a small portion of her dust, as a reward for finding her, and it is among my most precious possessions."

"SAKI"
The Soul of Laploshka

"Saki" (Hector Hugh Munro, *1870–1916) ranks as one of the most skilful, humorous and cynical masters of the short story, with a special talent for weaving the comic with the supernatural. 'The Soul of Laploshka' is taken from his second collection,* Reginald in Russia *(1910).*

Laploshka was one of the meanest men I have ever met, and quite one of the most entertaining. He said horrid things about other people in such a charming way that one forgave him for the equally horrid things he said about oneself behind one's back. Hating anything in the way of ill-natured gossip ourselves, we are always grateful to those who do it for us and do it well. And Laploshka did it really well.

Naturally Laploshka had a large circle of acquaintances, and as he exercised some care in their selection it followed that an appreciable proportion were men whose bank balances enabled them to acquiesce indulgently in his rather one-sided views on hospitality. Thus, although possessed of only moderate means, he was able to live comfortably within his income, and still more comfortably within those of various tolerantly disposed associates.

But towards the poor or to those of the same limited resources as himself his attitude was one of watchful anxiety; he seemed to be haunted by a besetting fear lest some fraction of a shilling or franc, or whatever the prevailing coinage might be, should be diverted from his pocket or service into that of a hard-up companion. A two-franc cigar would be cheerfully offered to a wealthy patron, on the principle of doing evil that good may come, but I have known him indulge in agonies of perjury rather than admit the incriminating possession of a copper coin when change was needed to tip a waiter. The coin would have been duly returned at the earliest opportunity—he would have taken means to ensure against forgetfulness on the part of the borrower—but accidents might happen, and even the temporary estrangement from his penny or sou was a calamity to be avoided.

The knowledge of this amiable weakness offered a perpetual temptation to play upon Laploshka's fears of involuntary generosity. To offer him a lift in a cab and pretend not to have enough money to pay the fare, to fluster him with a request for sixpence when his hand was full of silver just received in change, these were a few of the petty torments that ingenuity prompted as occasion afforded. To do justice to Laploshka's resourcefulness it must be admitted that he always emerged somehow or other from the most embarrassing dilemma without in any way compromising his reputation for saying "No". But the gods send opportunities at some time to most men, and mine came one evening when Laploshka and I were supping together in a cheap boulevard restaurant. (Except when he was the bidden guest of some one with an irreproachable income, Laploshka was wont to curb his appetite for high living; on such fortunate occasions he let it go on an easy snaffle.) At the conclusion of the meal a somewhat urgent message called me away, and without heeding my companion's agitated protest, I called back cruelly, "Pay my share; I'll settle with you tomorrow." Early on the morrow Laploshka hunted me down by instinct as I walked along a side street that I hardly ever frequented. He had the air of a man who had not slept.

"You owe me two francs from last night," was his breathless greeting.

I spoke evasively of the situation in Portugal, where more trouble seemed brewing. But Laploshka listened with the abstraction of the deaf adder, and quickly returned to the subject of the two francs.

"I'm afraid I must owe it to you," I said lightly and brutally. "I haven't a sou in the world," and I added mendaciously, "I'm going away for six months or perhaps longer."

Laploshka said nothing, but his eyes bulged a little and his cheeks took on the mottled hues of an ethnographical map of the Balkan Peninsula. That same day, at sundown, he died. "Failure of the heart's action" was the doctor's verdict; but I, who knew better, knew that he had died of grief.

There arose the problem of what to do with his two francs. To have killed Laploshka was one thing; to have kept his beloved money would have argued a callousness of feeling of which I am not capable. The ordinary solution, of giving it to the poor, would by no means fit the present situation, for nothing would have distressed the dead man more than such a misuse of his property. On the other hand, the bestowal of two francs on the rich was an operation which called for some tact. An easy way out of the difficulty seemed, however, to present itself the following Sunday, as I was wedged into the cosmopolitan crowd which filled the side-aisle of one of the most popular Paris churches. A collecting-bag, for "the poor of Monsieur le Curé," was buffeting its tortuous way across the seemingly impenetrable human sea, and a German in front of me, who evidently did not wish his appreciation of the magnificent music to be marred by a suggestion of payment, made audible criticisms to his companion on the claims of the said charity.

"They do not want money," he said; "they have too much money. They have no poor. They are all pampered."

If that were really the case my way seemed clear. I dropped Laploshka's two francs into the bag with a murmured blessing on the rich of Monsieur le Curé.

Some three weeks later chance had taken me to Vienna, and I sat one evening regaling myself in a humble but excellent little Gasthaus up in the Währinger quarter. The appointments were primitive, but the Schnitzel, the beer, and the cheese could not have been improved on. Good cheer brought good custom, and with the exception of one small table near the door every place was occupied. Half-way through my meal I happened to glance in the direction of that empty seat, and saw that it was no longer empty. Poring over the bill of fare with the absorbed scrutiny of one who seeks the cheapest among the cheap was Laploshka. Once he looked across at me, with a comprehensive glance at my repast, as though to say, "It is my two francs you are eating," and then looked swiftly away. Evidently the poor of Monsieur le Curé had been genuine poor. The Schnitzel turned to leather in my mouth, the beer seemed tepid; I left the Emmenthaler untasted. My one idea was to get away from the room, away from the table where *that* was seated; and as I fled I felt Laploshka's reproachful eyes watching the amount that I gave to the piccolo—out of his two francs. I lunched next day at an expensive restaurant which I felt sure that the living Laploshka would never have entered on his own account, and I hoped that the dead Laploshka would observe the same barriers. I was not mistaken, but as I came out I found him miserably studying the bill of fare stuck up on the portals. Then he slowly made his way over to a milk-hall. For the first time in my experience I missed the charm and gaiety of Vienna life.

After that, in Paris or London or wherever I happened to be, I continued to see a good deal of Laploshka. If I had a seat in a box at a theatre I was always conscious of his eyes furtively watching me from the dim recesses of the gallery. As I turned into my club on a rainy afternoon I would see him taking inadequate shelter in a doorway opposite. Even if I indulged in the modest luxury of a penny chair in the Park he generally confronted me from one of the free benches, never staring at me, but always elaborately conscious of my presence. My friends began to comment on my changed looks, and advised me to leave off heaps of things. I should have liked to have left off Laploshka.

On a certain Sunday—it was probably Easter, for the crush was worse than ever—I was again wedged into the crowd listening to the music in the fashionable Paris church, and again the collection-bag was buffeting its way across the human sea. An English lady behind me was making ineffectual efforts to convey a coin into the still distant bag, so I took the money at her request and helped it forward to its destination. It was a two-franc piece. A swift inspiration came to me, and I merely dropped my own sou into the bag and slid the silver coin into my pocket. I had withdrawn Laploshka's two francs from the poor, who should never have had that legacy. As I backed away from the crowd I heard a woman's voice say, "I don't believe he put my money in the bag. There are swarms of people in Paris like that!" But my mind was lighter than it had been for a long time.

The delicate mission of bestowing the retrieved sum on the deserving rich still confronted me. Again I trusted to the inspiration of accident, and again fortune favoured me. A shower drove me, two days later, into one of the historic churches on the left bank of the Seine, and there I found, peering at the old wood-carvings, the Baron R., one of the wealthiest and most shabbily dressed men in Paris. It was now or never. Putting a strong American inflection into the French which I usually talked with an unmistakable British accent, I catechized the Baron as to the date of the church's building, its dimensions, and other details which an American tourist would be certain to want to know. Having acquired such information as the Baron was able to impart on short notice, I solemnly placed the two-franc piece in his hand, with the hearty assurance that it was "pour vous," and turned to go. The Baron was slightly taken aback, but accepted the situation with a good grace. Walking over to a small box fixed in the wall, he dropped Laploshka's two francs into the slot. Over the box was the inscription, "Pour les pauvres de M. le Curé."

That evening, at the crowded corner by the Café de la Paix, I caught a fleeting glimpse of Laploshka. He smiled, slightly raised his hat, and vanished. I never saw him again. After all, the money had been *given* to the deserving rich, and the soul of Laploshka was at peace.